Tom Clancy

Ever since the phenomenal international success of *The Hunt for Red October*, his controversial, ground-breaking first novel, Tom Clancy has been one of the world's fastest-selling authors. His bestselling novels, many of them featuring Jack Ryan, include *Red Storm Rising*, *Patriot Games*, *The Cardinal of the Kremlin*, *Clear and Present Danger*, *Without Remorse*, *Debt of Honour* and *Executive Orders*. He is also the author of the non-fiction books *Submarine*, *Armoured Warfare*, *Fighter Wing* and *Marine*. He lives in Maryland, USA.

The Sum of All Fears is the fourth of Tom Clancy's novels to have been made into a major film, following the highly successful *The Hunt for Red October*, *Patriot Games* and *Clear and Present Danger*.

THE SUM OF ALL FEARS

'I was quite entranced by Clancy's skill in recounting the extraordinarily complex series of events that bring great nations to the point of total war. Clancy is a brilliant describer of events. I read his lucid exposition with delight.'

PATRICK O'BRIAN, *Washington Post*

'Leaves newspaper headlines in the dust . . . a tour de force.'   *New York Times*

'Clancy knows how to build a thriller . . . stirring and vivid.'   *Boston Globe*

'Truly chilling . . . harrowing.'   *Chicago Tribune*

TOM CLANCY

THE SUM
OF ALL FEARS

HarperCollins*Publishers*

HarperCollins*Publishers*
77–85 Fulham Palace Road,
Hammersmith, London W6 8JB

www.**fire**and**water**.com

Film tie-in edition 2002
1 3 5 7 9 8 6 4 2

Previously published in paperback by
HarperCollins 1993, and by Fontana 1992

First published in Great Britain by
HarperCollins*Publishers* 1991

First published in the USA by
G.P. Putnam's Sons 1991

Copyright © Jack Ryan Enterprises Ltd 1991

The Author asserts the moral right to
be identified as the author of this work

ISBN 0 00 714733 3

Set in Trump Mediaeval

Printed and bound in Great Britain by
Clays Ltd, St Ives plc

ACKNOWLEDGEMENTS

As is always the case, there are people to thank.

Russ, for his excruciatingly patient education
in physics (the mistakes are mine, not his);

Barry, for his insights;

Steve, for the mindset;

Ralph, for his analysis;

John, for the law;

Fred, for the access;

Gerry, for his friendship;

Quite a few others who entertained my endless
questions and ideas – even the dumb ones;

And all the men of good will who hope, as I do,
that the corner may finally be turned,
and were willing to talk about it.

For Mike and Peggy Rodgers,
a sailor and his lady – and all the men and women
of the U.S. Armed Forces, because the noblest
of ideas have always been protected
by warriors

Why, you may take the most gallant sailor, the most intrepid airman or the most audacious soldier, put them at a table together – what do you get! The sum of their fears.

WINSTON CHURCHILL

[T]he two contenders met, with all their troops, on the field of Camlan to negotiate. Both sides were fully armed and desperately suspicious that the other side was going to try some ruse or stratagem. The negotiations were going along smoothly until one of the knights was stung by an asp and drew his sword to kill the reptile. The others saw the sword being drawn and immediately fell upon each other. A tremendous slaughter ensued. The chronicle ... is quite specific about the point that the slaughter was excessive chiefly because the battle took place without preparations and premeditation.

HERMAN KAHN, On Thermonuclear War

PROLOGUE

Broken Arrow

'Like a wolf on the fold.' In recounting the Syrian attack on the Israeli-held Golan Heights at 1400 local time on Saturday, October 6th, 1973, most commentators automatically recalled Lord Byron's famous line. There is also little doubt that that is precisely what the more literarily inclined Syrian commanders had in mind when they placed the final touches on the operations plans that would hurl more tanks and guns at the Israelis than any of Hitler's vaunted panzer generals had ever dreamed of having.

However, the sheep found by the Syrian Army that grim October day were more like bighorn rams in autumn rut than the more docile kind found in pastoral verse. Outnumbered by roughly nine to one, the two Israeli brigades on the Golan were crack units. The 7th Brigade held the northern Golan and scarcely budged, its defensive network a delicate balance of rigidity and flexibility. Individual strongpoints held stubbornly, channeling the Syrian penetrations into rocky defiles, where they could be pinched off and smashed by roving bands of Israeli armor which lay in wait behind the Purple Line. By the time reinforcements began arriving on the second day, the situation was still in hand – but barely. By the end of the fourth day, the Syrian tank army that had fallen upon the 7th lay a smoking ruin before it.

The Barak ('Thunderbolt') Brigade held the southern heights and was less fortunate. Here the terrain was less well-suited to the defense, and here also the Syrians appear to have been more ably led. Within hours the

Barak had been broken into several fragments. Though each piece would later prove to be as dangerous as a nest of vipers, the Syrian spearheads were quick to exploit the gaps and race towards their strategic objective, the Sea of Galilee. The situation that developed over the next thirty-six hours would prove to be the gravest test of Israeli arms since 1948.

Reinforcements began arriving on the second day. These had to be thrown into the battle area piecemeal – plugging holes, blocking roads, even rallying units that had broken under the desperate strain of combat and, for the first time in Israeli history, fled the field before the advancing Arabs. Only on the third day were the Israelis able to assemble their armored fist, first enveloping, then smashing the three deep Syrian penetrations. The changeover to offensive operations followed without pause. The Syrians were hurled back towards their own capital by a wrathful counterattack, and surrendered a field littered with burned-out tanks and shattered men. At the end of this day the troopers of the Barak and the 7th heard over their unit radio nets a message from Israeli Defense Forces High Command.

You have saved the people of Israel.

And so they had. Yet outside Israel, except for schools in which men learn the profession of arms, this epic battle is strangely unremembered. As in the Six Day War of 1967, the more freewheeling operations in the Sinai were the ones that attracted the excitement and admiration of the world: bridging the Suez, the Battle of the 'Chinese' Farm, the encirclement of the Egyptian 3rd Army – this despite the fearful implications of the Golan fighting, which was far closer to home. Still, the survivors of those two brigades knew what they had done, and their officers could revel in the knowledge that among professional soldiers who know the measure of skill and courage that such a stand entails, their Battle for the Heights would be remembered with Thermopylae, Bastogne and Gloucester Hill.

Each war knows many ironies, however, and the October War was no exception. As is true of most

2

glorious defensive stands, this one was largely unnecessary. The Israelis had misread intelligence reports which, had they been acted on as little as twelve hours earlier, would have enabled them to execute pre-set plans and pour reserves onto the Heights hours before the onslaught commenced. Had they done so, there would have been no heroic stand. There would have been no need for their tankers and infantrymen to die in numbers so great that it would be weeks before the true casualty figures were released to a proud, but grievously wounded nation. Had the information been acted upon, the Syrians would have been massacred before the Purple Line for all their lavish collection of tanks and guns, and there is little glory in massacres. This failure of intelligence has never been adequately explained. Did the fabled Mossad fail so utterly to discern the Arabs' plans? Or did Israeli political leaders fail to recognize the warnings they received? These questions received immediate attention in the world press, of course, most particularly in regard to Egypt's assault-crossing of the Suez, which breached the vaunted Bar-Lev Line.

Equally serious but less well appreciated was a more fundamental error made years earlier by the usually prescient Israeli general staff. For all its firepower, the Israeli Army was not heavily outfitted with tube artillery, particularly by Soviet standards. Instead of heavy concentrations of mobile field guns, the Israelis chose to depend heavily on large numbers of short-range mortars, and attack aircraft. This left Israeli gunners on the Heights outnumbered twelve to one, subject to crushing counter-battery fire, and unable to provide adequate support to the beleaguered defenders. That error cost many lives.

As is the case with most grave mistakes, this one was made by intelligent men, for the very best of reasons. The same attack-fighter that struck the Golan could rain steel and death on the Suez as little as an hour later. The IAF was the first modern air force to pay systematic attention to 'turn-around time.' Its ground crewmen were trained to act much like a racing car's pit crew, and their speed and skill effectively doubled each plane's striking power, making the IAF a profoundly flexible and weighted instrument, and making a Phantom or a Skyhawk appear to be more valuable than a dozen mobile field guns.

What the Israeli planning officers had failed to take fully into account was the fact that the Soviets were the ones arming the Arabs, and, in doing so, would inculcate their clients with their own tactical philosophies. Intended to deal with NATO air power always deemed better than their own, Soviet surface-to-air missile (SAM) designers had always been among the world's best. *Russian* planners saw the coming October War as a splendid chance to test their newest tactical weapons and doctrine. They did not spurn it. The Soviets gave their Arab clients a SAM network such as the North Vietnamese or Warsaw Pact forces of the time dared not dream about, a nearly solid phalanx of interlocking missile batteries and radar systems deployed in depth, along with new mobile SAMs that could advance with the armored spearheads, extending the 'bubble' of counter-air protection under which ground action could continue without interference. The officers and men who were to operate those systems had been painstakingly trained, many within the Soviet Union with the full benefit of everything the Soviets and Vietnamese had learned of American tactics and technology, which the Israelis were correctly expected to imitate. Of all the Arab soldiers in the October War, only these men would achieve their pre-war objectives. For two days they effectively neutralized the IAF. Had ground operations gone according to plan, that would have been enough.

And it is here that the story has its proper beginning. The situation on the Golan Heights was immediately evaluated as serious. The scarce and confused information coming in from the two stunned brigade staffs led the Israeli High Command to believe that tactical control of the action had been lost. It seemed that their greatest nightmare had finally occurred: they had been caught fatally unready; their northern kibbutzim were vulnerable; their civilians, their *children* lay in the path of a Syrian armored force that by all rights could roll down from the Heights with the barest warning. The initial reaction of the staff operations officers was something close to panic.

But panic is something that good operations officers also plan for. In the case of a nation whose enemies' avowed objective was nothing short of physical annihilation, there was no defensive measure that could be called extreme. As early as 1968, the Israelis, like their American and NATO counterparts, had based their ultimate plan on the nuclear option. At 03.55 hours, local time, on October 7th, just fourteen hours after the actual fighting began, the alert orders for OPERATION JOSHUA were telexed to the IAF base outside Beersheba.

Israel did not have many nuclear weapons at the time – and denies having any to this date. Not that many would be needed, if it came to that. At Beersheba, in one of the countless underground bomb-storage bunkers, were twelve quite ordinary-looking objects, indistinguishable from the many other items designed to be attached to tactical aircraft, except for the silver-red striped labels on their sides. No fins were attached, and there was nothing unusual in the streamlined shape of the burnished-brown aluminum skin, with barely visible seams and a few shackle points. There was a reason for that. To an unschooled or cursory observer, they might easily have been mistaken for fuel tanks or napalm canisters, and such objects hardly merit a second look. But each was a plutonium fission bomb with a nominal yield of 60 kilotons, quite enough to carve the heart out of a large city, or to kill thousands of troops in the field, or, with the addition of cobalt jackets – stored separately, but readily attachable to the external skin – to poison a landscape to all kinds of life for years to come.

On this morning, activity at Beersheba was frantic. Reserve personnel were still streaming into the base from the previous day's devotions and family-visiting all over the small country. Those men on duty had been so for too long a time for the tricky job of arming aircraft with lethal ordnance. Even the newly-arriving men had had precious little sleep. One team of ordnancemen, for security reasons not told the nature of their task, was arming a flight of A-4 Skyhawk strike-fighters with nuclear weapons under the eyes of two officers, known as 'watchers,' for that was their job, to keep visual track of everything that had to do with nuclear weapons. The bombs were wheeled under the center-line hardpoint of each of the four aircraft, lifted carefully by the hoisting arm, then shackled into place. The least exhausted of the groundcrew might have noticed that the arming devices and tail fins had not yet been attached to the bombs. If so they doubtless concluded that the officer assigned to that task was running late – as was nearly everything this cold and fateful morning. The nose of each weapon was filled with electronics gear. The actual exploder mechanism and capsule of nuclear material – collectively known as the 'physics package' – were already in the bombs, of course. The Israeli weapons, unlike American ones, were not designed to be carried by alert aircraft during the time of peace, and they lacked the elaborate safeguards installed in American weapons by the technicians at the Pantex assembly plant, outside Amarillo, Texas. The fusing systems comprised two packages, one for attachment to the nose, and one integral with the tail fins. These were stored separately from the bombs themselves. All in all, the weapons were very unsophisticated by American or Soviet standards, in the same sense that a pistol is far less sophisticated than a machine-gun, but, at close range, equally lethal.

Once the nose and fin packages were installed and activated, the only remaining activation procedure was the installation of a special arming panel within the cockpit of each fighter, and the attachment of the power plug from the aircraft to the bomb. At that point the bomb would be 'released to local control,' placed in the hands of a young, aggressive pilot, whose job was then to loft it in a maneuver called The Idiot's Loop which tossed the bomb on a ballistic path that would – probably

— allow him and his aircraft to escape without harm when the bomb detonated.

Depending on the exigencies of the moment and the authorization of the 'watchers,' Beersheba's senior ordnance officer had the option to attach the arming packages. Fortunately, this officer was not at all excited about the idea of having half-live 'nukes' sitting about on a flight line that some lucky Arab might attack at any moment. A religious man, for all the dangers that faced his country on that cold dawn, he breathed a silent prayer of thanks when cooler heads prevailed in Tel Aviv, and gave the order to stand JOSHUA down. The senior pilots who would have flown the strike mission returned to their squadron ready-rooms and forgot what they had been briefed to do. The senior ordnance officer immediately ordered the bombs removed, and returned to their place of safe-keeping.

The bone-tired groundcrew began removing the weapons, just as the other teams arrived on their own carts for the task of rearming the Skyhawks with Zuni rocket clusters. The strike order had been put up: *The Golan.* Hit the Syrian armored columns advancing on the Barak's sector of Purple Line from Kafr Shams. The ordnancemen jostled under the aircraft, two teams each trying to do their jobs, one team trying to remove bombs that they didn't know to be bombs at all, while the other hung Zunis on the wings.

There were more than four strike aircraft cycling through Beersheba, of course. The dawn's first mission over the Suez was just returning — what was left of it. The RF-4C Phantom reconnaissance aircraft had been lost, and its F-4E fighter escort limped in trailing fuel from perforated wing tanks and with one of its two engines disabled. The pilot had already radioed his warning in: there was some new kind of surface-to-air missile, maybe that new SA-6; its radar-tracking systems had not registered on the Phantom's threat-receiver; the recce bird had had no warning at all, and only luck had enabled him to evade the four targeted on his aircraft. That fact was flashed to IAF high command even before the

7

aircraft touched down gingerly on the runway. The plane was directed to taxi down to the far end of the ramp, close to where the Skyhawks stood. The Phantom's pilot followed the jeep to the waiting fire-fighting vehicles, but just as it stopped, the left main tire blew out. The damaged strut collapsed as well and 45,000 pounds of fighter dropped to the pavement like dishes from a collapsed table. Leaking fuel ignited, and a small but deadly fire enveloped the aircraft. An instant later, 20mm ammunition from the fighter's gun pod started cooking off, and one of the two crewmen was screaming within the mass of flames. Firefighters moved in with water-fog. The two 'watcher' officers were the closest, and raced towards the flames to drag the pilot clear. All three were peppered by fragments from the exploding ammunition, while a fireman coolly made his way through the flames to the second crewman and carried him out, singed but alive. Other firemen collected the watchers and the pilot, and loaded their bleeding bodies into an ambulance.

The nearby fire distracted the ordnancemen under the Skyhawks. One bomb, the one on aircraft number three, dropped a moment too soon, crushing the team supervisor's legs on the hoist. In the shrieking confusion of the moment, the team lost track of what was being done. The injured man was rushed to the base hospital while the three dismounted nuclear weapons were carted back to the storage bunker – in the chaos of an airbase on the first full day of a shooting war, the empty cradle of one of the carts somehow went unnoticed. The aircraft line chiefs arrived a moment later to begin abbreviated pre-flight checks as the jeep arrived from the ready shack. Four pilots jumped off it, each with a helmet in one hand and a tactical map in the other, each furiously eager to lash out at his country's enemies.

'What the hell's that?' snapped eighteen-year-old Lieutenant Mordecai Zadin. Called Motti by his friends, he had the gangling awkwardness of his age.

'Fuel tank, looks like,' replied the line chief. He was

a reservist who owned a garage in Haifa, a kindly, competent man of fifty years.

'Shit,' the pilot replied, almost quivering with excitement. 'I don't need extra fuel to go to the Golan and back!'

'I can take it off, but I'll need a few minutes.' Motti considered that for a moment. A *sabra* from a northern kibbutz, a pilot for barely five months, he saw the rest of his comrades strapping into their aircraft. Syrians were attacking towards the home of his parents, and he had a sudden horror of being left behind on his first combat mission.

'Fuck it! You can strip it off when I get back.' Zadin went up the ladder like a shot. The chief followed, strapping the pilot in place, and checking the instruments over the pilot's shoulder.

'She's ready, Motti! Be careful.'

'Have some tea for me when I get back.' The youngster grinned with all the ferocity such a child could manage. The line chief slapped him on the helmet.

'You just bring my airplane back to me, *menchkin. Mazeltov.*'

The chief dropped down to the concrete, and removed the ladder. He next gave the aircraft a last visual scan for anything amiss, as Motti got his engine turning. Zadin worked the flight controls and eased the throttle to full idle, checking fuel and engine-temperature gauges. Everything was where it should be. He looked over to the flight leader and waved his readiness. Motti pulled down the manual canopy, took a last look at the line chief, and fired off his farewell salute.

At eighteen, Zadin was not a particularly young pilot by IAF standards. Selected for his quick boy's reactions and aggressiveness, he'd been identified as a likely prospect four years earlier, and had fought hard for his place in the world's finest air force. Motti loved to fly, had wanted to fly ever since, as a toddler, he'd seen a Bf-109 training aircraft that an ironic fate had given Israel to start its air force. And he loved his Skyhawk. It was a pilot's aircraft. Not an electronicized monster like the

Phantom, the A-4 was a small, responsive bird of prey that leaped at the twitch of his hand on the stick. Now he would fly combat. He was totally unafraid. It never occurred to him to fear for his life – like any teenager he was certain of his own immortality, and combat flyers are selected for their lack of human frailty. Yet he marked the day. Never had he seen so fine a dawn. He felt supernaturally alert, aware of everything: the rich wake-up coffee; the dusty smell of the morning air at Beersheba; now the manly scents of oil and leather in the cockpit; the idle static on his radio circuits; and the tingle of his hands on the control stick. He had never known such a day and it never occurred to Motti Zadin that fate would not give him another.

The four-plane formation taxied in perfect order to the end of runway zero-one. It seemed a good omen, taking off due north, towards an enemy only fifteen minutes away. On command of his flight leader – himself a mere twenty-one – all four pilots pushed their throttles to the stops, tripped their brakes, and dashed forward into the cool, calm, morning air. In seconds, all were airborne and climbing to five thousand feet, careful to avoid the civilian air traffic of Ben Gurion International Airport, which in the mad scheme of life in the Middle East was still fully active.

The captain gave his usual series of terse commands, just like a training flight: tuck it in, check engine, ordnance, electrical systems. Heads up for MiGs and friendlies. Make sure your IFF is squawking green. The fifteen minutes it took to fly from Beersheba to the Golan passed rapidly. Zadin's eyes strained to see the volcanic escarpment for which his older brother had died while taking it from the Syrians only six years before. The Syrians would not get it back, Motti told himself.

'Flight: turn right to heading zero-four-three. Targets are tank columns four kilometers east of the line. Heads up. Watch for SAMs and ground fire.'

'Lead, Four: I have tanks on the ground at one,' Zadin reported coolly. 'Look like our Centurions.'

'Good eye, Four,' the captain replied. 'They're friendly.'

'I got a beeper, *I got launch warning*!' someone called. Eyes scanned the air for danger.

'*SHIT!*' called an excited voice. 'SAMs low at twelve coming up!'

'I see them. Flight, left and right, break NOW!' the captain commanded.

The four Skyhawks scattered by elements. There were a dozen SA-2 missiles several kilometers off, like flying telephone poles, coming towards them at Mach-3. The SAMs split left and right too, but clumsily, and two exploded in a mid-air collision. Motti rolled right and hauled his stick into his belly, diving for the ground and cursing the extra wing weight. Good, the missiles were not able to track them down. He pulled level a bare hundred feet above the rocks, still heading towards the Syrians at four hundred knots, shaking the sky as he roared over the cheering, beleaguered troopers of the Barak.

The mission was a washout as a coherent strike, Motti already knew. It didn't matter. He'd get some Syrian tanks. He didn't have to know exactly whose, so long as they were Syrian. He saw another A-4 and formed up just as it began its firing run. He looked forward and saw them, the dome shapes of Syrian T-62s. Zadin toggled his arming switches without looking. The reflector gunsight appeared in front of his eyes.

'Uh-oh, more SAMs, coming in on the deck.' It was the captain's voice, still cool. Motti's heart skipped a beat: a swarm of missiles, smaller ones – are these the SA-6s they told us about? he wondered quickly – was tracing over the rocks towards him. He checked his ESM gear; it had not sensed the attacking missiles. There was no warning beyond what his eyes told him. Instinctively, Motti clawed for altitude in which to maneuver. Four missiles followed him up. Three kilometers away. He snap-rolled right, then spiraled down and left again. That fooled three of them, but the fourth followed him down.

An instant later it exploded, a bare thirty meters from his aircraft.

The Skyhawk felt as though it had been kicked aside ten meters or more. Motti struggled with the controls, getting back level just over the rocks. A quick look chilled him. Whole sections of his port wing were shredded. Warning beepers in his headset and flight instruments reported multiple disaster: hydraulics zeroing out, radio out, generator out. But he still had manual flight controls, and his weapons could fire from back-up battery power. At that instant he saw his tormentors: a battery of SA-6 missiles, four launcher vehicles, a Straight Flush radar van, and a heavy truck full of reloads, all four kilometers away. His hawk's eyes could even see the Syrians struggling with the missiles, loading one onto a launcher rail.

They saw him, too, and then began a duel no less epic for its brevity.

Motti eased as far down as he dared with his buffeting controls and carefully centered the target in his reflector sight. He had forty-eight Zuni rockets. They fired in salvos of four. At two kilometers he opened fire into the target area. The Syrian missileers somehow managed to launch another SAM. There should have been no escape, but the SA-6 had a radar-proximity fuse, and the passing Zunis triggered it, exploding the SAM harmlessly half a kilometer away. Motti grinned savagely beneath his mask, as he fired rockets and now twenty-millimeter cannon fire into the mass of men and vehicles.

The third salvo hit, then four more, as Zadin kicked rudder to drop his rockets all over the target area. The missile battery was transformed into an inferno of diesel fuel, missile propellant, and exploding warheads. A huge fireball loomed in his path, and Motti tore through it with a feral shout of glee, his enemies obliterated, his comrades avenged.

Zadin had but a moment of triumph. Great sheets of the aluminum which made up his aircraft's left wing were being ripped away by the four-hundred-knot slipstream. The A-4 began shuddering wildly. When Motti turned left for home, the wing collapsed entirely. The Skyhawk disintegrated in mid-air. It took only a few seconds before the teenaged warrior was smashed on the basaltic rocks of the Golan Heights, neither the first nor the last to die there. No other of his flight of four survived.

Of the SAM battery, almost nothing was left. All six vehicles had been blasted to fragments. Of the ninety men who had manned them, the largest piece recovered was the headless torso of the battery commander. Both he and Zadin had served their countries well, but as is too often the case, conduct which in another time or place might have inspired the heroic verse of a Virgil or a Tennyson went unseen and unknown. Three days later, Zadin's mother received the news by telegram, learning again that all Israel shared her grief, as if such a thing were possible for a woman who had lost two sons.

But the lingering footnote to this bit of unreported history was that the unarmed bomb broke loose from the disintegrating fighter and proceeded yet further eastward, falling far from the fighter-bomber's wreckage to bury itself meters from the home of a Druse farmer. It was not until three days later that the Israelis discovered that their bomb was missing, and not until the day after the October War ended that they were able to reconstruct the details of its loss. This left the Israelis with a problem insoluble even to their imaginations. The bomb was somewhere behind Syrian lines – but where? Which of the four aircraft had carried it? Where had it gone down? They could hardly ask the Syrians to search for it. And could they tell the Americans, from whom the 'special nuclear material' had been adroitly and deniably obtained?

And so the bomb lay unknown, except to the Druse farmer who simply covered it over with two meters of dirt and continued to farm his rocky patch.

CHAPTER 1

The Longest Journey . . .

Arnold van Damm sprawled back in his executive swivel chair with all the elegance of a rag doll tossed into a corner. Jack had never seen him wear a coat except in the presence of the President, and not always then. At formal affairs that required black tie, Ryan wondered if Arnie needed a Secret Service agent standing by with a gun. The tie was loose in the unbuttoned collar, and he wondered if it had ever been tightly knotted. The sleeves on Arnie's L. L. Bean blue-striped shirt were rolled up, and grimy at the elbows because he usually read documents with his forearms planted on the chronically cluttered desk. But not when speaking to someone. For important conversations, the man leaned back, resting his feet on a desk drawer. Barely fifty, van Damm had thinning gray hair and a face as lined and care-worn as an old map, but his pale blue eyes were always alert, and his mind keenly aware of everything that went on within or beyond his sight. It was a quality that went along with being the President's Chief of Staff.

He poured his Diet Coke into an oversized coffee mug that featured an emblem of the White House on one side and 'Arnie' engraved on the other, and regarded the Deputy Director of Central Intelligence with a mixture of wariness and affection. 'Thirsty?'

'I can handle a real Coke if you have one down there,' Jack observed with a grin. Van Damm's left hand dropped below sight, and a red aluminum can appeared on a ballistic path that would have terminated in Ryan's lap had he not caught it. Opening the can under the circumstances was a tricky exercise, but Jack ostentatiously aimed the can at van Damm when he popped the top. Like the man or not, Ryan told himself, he had style. He was unaffected by his job, except when he had to be. This was not such a time. Arnold van Damm only acted important for outsiders. Insiders didn't need an act.

'The Boss wants to know what the hell is going on over there,' the Chief of Staff opened.

'So do I.' Charles Alden, the President's National Security Advisor, entered the room. 'Sorry I'm late, Arnie.'

'So do we, gentlemen,' Jack replied. 'That hasn't changed in a couple of years. You want the best stuff we've got?'

'Sure,' Alden said.

'Next time you fly to Moscow, look out for a large white rabbit with waistcoat and pocket watch. If he offers you a trip down a rabbit hole, take it and let me know what you find down there,' Ryan said with mock gravity. 'Look, I'm not one of those right-wing idiots who moans for a return to the Cold War, but then, at least, the Russians were predictable. The poor bastards are starting to act like we do now. They're unpredictable as hell. The funny part is, now I can understand what a pain in the ass we always were to the KGB. The political dynamic over there is changing on a daily basis. Narmonov is the sharpest political in-fighter in the world, but every time he goes to work, it's another crisis.'

'What sort of cat is he?' van Damm asked. 'You've met the man.' Alden had met Narmonov, but van Damm had not.

'Only once,' Ryan cautioned.

Alden settled down in an armchair. 'Look, Jack, we've seen your file. So has the Boss. Hell, I've almost got him to respect you. Two Intelligence Stars, the submarine business, and, Jesus, the thing with Gerasimov. I've heard of still waters running deep, fella, but never this deep. No wonder Al Trent thinks you're so damned smart.' The Intelligence Star was CIA's highest decoration for performance in the field. Jack actually had three. But the citation for the third was locked away in a very safe place, and was something so secret that even the new President didn't and would never know. 'So prove it. Talk to us.'

'He's one of those rare ones. He thrives on chaos. I've met docs like that. There are some, a rare few, who keep working in emergency rooms, doing trauma and stuff like that, after everybody else burns out. Some people just groove to pressure and stress, Arnie. He's one of them. I don't think he really likes it, but he's good at it. He must have the physical constitution of a horse –'

'Most politicians do,' van Damm observed.

'Lucky them. Anyway, does Narmonov really know where he's going? I think the answer is both yes and no. He has some sort of idea where he's moving his country to, but how he gets there, and exactly where he's going to be when he arrives, that he doesn't know. That's the kind of balls the man has.'

'So, you like the guy.' It was not a question.

'He could have snuffed my life out as easy as popping open this can of Coke, and he didn't. Yeah,' Ryan admitted with a smile, 'that does compel me to like him a little. You'd have to be a fool not to admire the man. Even if we were still enemies, he'd still command respect.'

'So we're not enemies?' Alden asked with a wry grin.

'How can we be?' Jack asked in feigned surprise. 'The President says that's a thing of the past.'

The Chief of Staff grunted. 'Politicians talk a lot. That's what they're paid for. Will Narmonov make it?'

Ryan looked out the window in disgust, mainly at his own ability to answer the question. 'Look at it this way: Andrey Il'ych has got to be the most adroit political operator they've ever had. But he's doing a high-wire act. Sure, he's the best around, but remember when Karl Wallenda was the best high-wire guy around? He ended up as a red smear on the sidewalk because he had one bad day in a business where you only get one goof. Andrey Il'ych is in the same kind of racket. Will he make it? People have been asking that for eight years! We think so – I think so – but . . . but, hell this is virgin ground,

Arnie. We've never been here before. Neither has he. Even a goddamned weather forecaster has a data-base to help him out. The two best Russian historians we have are Jake Kantrowitz at Princeton and Derek Andrews at Berkeley, and they're a hundred-eighty degrees apart at the moment. We just had them both into Langley two weeks ago. Personally, I lean towards Jake's assessment, but our senior Russian analyst thinks Andrews is right. You pays your money and you takes your choice. That's the best we got. You want pontification, check the news-papers.'

Van Damm grunted and went on. 'Next hot spot?'

'The nationalities question is the big killer,' Jack said. 'You don't need me to tell you that. How will the Soviet Union break up – what republics will leave – when and how, peacefully or violently? Narmonov is dealing with that on a daily basis. That problem is here to stay.'

'That's what I've been saying for about a year. How long to let things shake out?' Alden wanted to know.

'Hey, I'm the guy who said East Germany would take at least a year to change over – I was the most optimistic guy in town at the time, and I was wrong by eleven months. Anything I or anyone else tells you is a wild-ass guess.'

'Other trouble spots?' van Damm asked next.

'There's always the Middle East –' Ryan saw the man's eyes light up.

'We want to move on that soon.'

'Then I wish you luck. We've been working on that since Nixon and Kissinger back during the '73 semi-finals. It's chilled out quite a bit, but the fundamental problems are still there, and sooner or later, it's going to be thawed. I suppose the good news is that Narmonov doesn't want any part of it. He may have to support his old friends, and selling them weapons is a big money-maker for him, but if things blow up, he won't push like they did in the old days. We learned that with Iraq. He might continue to pump weapons in – I think he won't, but it's a close call – but he will do nothing more than that to support an Arab attack on Israel. He won't move his ships, and he won't alert troops. I doubt he's willing even to back them if they rattle their sabers a little. Andrey Il'ych says those weapons are for defense, and I think he means it, despite the word we're getting from the Israelis.'

'That's solid?' Alden asked. 'State says different.'

'State's wrong,' Ryan replied flatly.

'So does your boss,' van Damm pointed out.

'In that case, sir, I must respectfully disagree with the DCI's assessment.'

Alden nodded. 'Now I know why Trent likes you. You don't talk like a bureaucrat. How have you lasted so long, saying what you really think?'

'Maybe I'm the token.' Ryan laughed, then turned serious. 'Think about it. With all the ethnic crap he's dealing with, taking an active role bears as many dangers as advantages. No, he sells weapons for hard currency and only when the coast is clear. That's business, and that's as far as it goes.'

'So, if we can find a way to settle things down . . . ?' Alden mused.

'He might even help. At worst, he'll stand by the sidelines and bitch that he's not in the game. But tell me, how do you plan to settle things down?'

'Put a little pressure on Israel,' van Damm replied simply.

'That's dumb for two reasons. It's wrong to pressure Israel until their security concerns are alleviated, and their security concerns will not be alleviated until some of the fundamental issues are settled first.'

'Like . . . ?'

'Like what is this conflict all about.' *The one thing that everyone overlooks.*

'It's religious, but the damned fools believe in the same things!' van Damm growled. 'Hell, I read the Koran last month, and it's the same as what I learned in Sunday school.'

'That's true,' Ryan agreed, 'but so what? Catholics and Protestants both believe that Christ is the son of God, but that hasn't stopped Northern Ireland from blowing

up. Safest place in the world to be Jewish. The friggin'
Christians are so busy killing one another off that they
don't have time to be anti-semitic. Look, Arnie, however
slight the religious differences in either place may appear
to us, to *them* they appear big enough to kill over. That's
as big as they need to be, pal.'

'True, I guess,' the Chief of Staff agreed reluctantly.
He thought for a moment. 'Jerusalem, you mean?'

'Bingo.' Ryan finished off his Coke and crushed the
can before flipping it into van Damm's trash can for two.
'The city is sacred to three religions – think of them as
three tribes – but it physically belongs to only one of
them. That one is at war with one of the others. The
volatile nature of the region militates towards putting
some armed troops in the place, but whose? Remember,
some Islamic crazies shot up Mecca not that long ago.
Now, if you put an Arab security force in Jerusalem, you
create a security threat to Israel. If things stay as they
are, with only an Israeli force, you offend the Arabs. Oh,
and forget the UN. Israel won't like it because the Jews
haven't made out all that well in the place. The Arabs
won't like it because there's too many Christians. And
we won't like it because the UN doesn't like us all that
much. The only available international body is distrusted by everyone. Impasse.'

'The President really wants to move on this,' the Chief
of Staff pointed out. *We have to do something to make
it look like we're DOING SOMETHING.*

'Well, next time he sees the Pope, maybe he can ask
for high-level intercession.' Jack's irreverent grin froze
momentarily. Van Damm thought he was cautioning
himself against speaking badly of the President, whom
he disliked. But then Ryan's face went blank. Arnie
didn't know Jack well enough to recognize the look.
'Wait a minute . . .'

The Chief of Staff chuckled. It wouldn't hurt for the
President to see the Pope. It always looked good with
the voters, and after that the President would have a
well-covered dinner with B'nai B'rith to show that he
liked all religions. In fact, as van Damm knew, the Presi-

dent only went to church for show now that his children were grown. That was one amusing aspect of life. The Soviet Union was turning back to religion in its search for societal values, but the American political left had turned away long ago and had no inclination to turn back, lest it should find the same values that the Russians were searching for. Van Damm had started off as a left-wing believer, but twenty-five years of hands-on experience in government had cured him of that. Now he distrusted ideologues of both wings with equal fervor. He was the sort to look for solutions whose only attraction was that they might actually work. His reverie on politics took him away from the discussion of the moment.

'You thinking about something, Jack?' Alden asked.

'You know, we're all "people of the book," aren't we?' Ryan asked, seeing the outline of a new thought in the fog.

'So?'

'And the Vatican is a real country, with real diplomatic status, but no armed forces ... they're Swiss ... and Switzerland is neutral, not even a member of the UN. The Arabs do their banking and carousing there ... gee, I wonder if he'd go for it ... ?' Ryan's face went blank again, and van Damm saw Jack's eye center as the lightbulb flashed on. It was always exciting to watch an idea being born, but less so when you didn't know what it was.

'Go for what? *Who* go for *what*?' the Chief of Staff asked with some annoyance. Alden just waited.

Ryan told them.

'I mean, a large part of this whole mess is over the Holy Places, isn't it? I could talk to some of my people at Langley. We have a really good –'

Van Damm leaned back in his chair. 'What sort of contacts do you have? You mean talking to the Nuncio?'

Ryan shook his head. 'The Nuncio is a good old guy, Cardinal Giancatti, but he's just here for show. You've been here long enough to know that, Arnie. You want to talk to folks who know stuff, you go to Father Riley at Georgetown. He taught me when I got my doctorate at G-Town. We're pretty tight. He's got a pipeline into The General.'

'Who's that?'

'The Father General of the Society of Jesus. The head Jesuit, Spanish guy, his name is Francisco Alcalde. He and Father Tim taught together at St John Bellarmine University in Rome. They're both historians, and Father Tim's his unofficial rep over here. You've never met Father Tim?'

'No. Is he worth it?'

'Oh, yeah. One of the best teachers I ever had. Knows D.C. inside and out. Good contacts back at the home office.' Ryan grinned, but the joke was lost on van Damm.

'Can you set up a quiet lunch?' Alden asked. 'Not here, someplace else.'

'The Cosmos Club up in Georgetown. Father Tim belongs. The University Club is closer, but –'

'Right. Can he keep a secret?'

'A *Jesuit* keep a secret?' Ryan laughed. 'You're not Catholic, are you?'

'How soon could you set it up?'

'Tomorrow or day after all right?'

'What about his loyalty?' van Damm asked out of a clear sky.

'Father Tim is an American citizen and he's not a security risk. But he's also a priest, and he has taken vows to what he naturally considers an authority higher than the Constitution. You can trust the man to honor all his obligations, but don't forget what all those obligations are,' Ryan cautioned. 'You can't order him around, either.'

'Set up the lunch. Sounds like I ought to meet the guy in any case. Tell him it's a get-acquainted thing,' Alden said. 'Make it soon. I'm free for lunch tomorrow and next day.'

'Yes, sir.' Ryan stood.

*

The Cosmos Club in Washington is located at the corner of Massachusetts and Florida Avenues. The former manor house of Sumner Welles, Ryan thought it looked naked without about four hundred acres of rolling ground, a stable of thoroughbred horses, and perhaps a resident fox that the owner would hunt, but not too hard. These were surroundings the place had never possessed, and Ryan wondered why it had been built in this place in this style, so obviously at odds with the realities of Washington, but built by a man who had understood the workings of the city so consummately well. Chartered as a club of the intelligentsia – membership was based on 'achievement' rather than money – it was known in Washington as a place of erudite conversation, and the worst food in a town of undistinguished restaurants. Ryan led Alden into a small private room upstairs.

Father Timothy Riley, S.J., was waiting for them, a briar pipe clamped in his teeth as he paged through the morning's *Post*. A glass sat at his right hand, a skim of sherry at the bottom of it. Father Tim was wearing a rumpled shirt and a jacket that needed pressing, not the formal priest's uniform that he saved for important meetings and had been hand-tailored by one of the nicer shops on Wisconsin Avenue. But the white Roman collar was stiff and bright, and Jack had the sudden thought that despite all his years of Catholic education he didn't know what the things were made of. Starched cotton? Celluloid like the detachable collars of his grandfather's age? In either case, its evident rigidity must have been a reminder to its wearer of his place in this world, and the next.

'Hello, Jack!'

'Hi, Father. This is Charles Alden, Father Tim Riley.' Handshakes were exchanged, and places at the table selected. A waiter came in and took drink orders, closing the door as he left.

'How's the new job, Jack?' Riley asked.

'The horizons keep broadening,' Ryan admitted. He left it at that. The priest would already know the problems Jack was having at Langley.

'We've had this idea about the Middle East, and Jack

23

suggested that you'd be a good man to discuss it with,' Alden said, getting everyone back to business. He had to stop when the waiter returned with drinks and menus. His discourse on the idea took several minutes.

'That's interesting,' Riley said, when it was all on the table.

'What's your read on the concept?' the National Security Advisor wanted to know.

'Interesting . . .' The priest was quiet for a moment.

'Will the Pope . . . ?' Ryan stopped Alden with a wave of the hand. Riley was not a man to be hurried when he was thinking. He was, after all, an historian, and they didn't have the urgency of medical doctors.

'It certainly is elegant,' Riley observed after thirty seconds. 'The Greeks will be a major problem, though.'

'The Greeks? How so?' Ryan asked in surprise.

'The really contentious people right now are the Greek Orthodox. We and they are at each other's throats half the time over the most trivial administrative issues. You know, the rabbis and the imams are actually more cordial at the moment than the Christian priests are. That's the funny thing about religious people, it's hard to predict how they'll react. Anyway, the problems between the Greeks and Romans are mainly administrative – who gets custody over which site, that sort of thing. There was a big go-round over Bethlehem last year, who got to do the midnight mass in the Church of the Nativity. It is awfully disappointing, isn't it?'

'You're saying it won't work because two Catholic churches can't – '

'I said there could be a problem, Dr Alden. I did not say that it wouldn't work.' Riley lapsed back into silence for a moment. 'You'll have to adjust the troika . . . but given the nature of the operation, I think we can get the right kind of cooperation. Co-opting the Greek Orthodox is something you'll have to do in any case. They and the Muslims get along very well, you know.'

'How so?' Alden asked.

'Back when Mohammed was chased out of Medina by the pre-Muslim pagans, he was granted asylum at the

Monastery of St Catherine in the Sinai – it's a Greek Orthodox shrine. They took care of him when he needed a friend. Mohammed was an honorable man; that monastery has enjoyed the protection of the Muslims ever since. Over a thousand years, and that place has never been troubled despite all the nasty things that have happened in the area. There is much to admire about Islam, you know. We in the West often overlook that because of the crazies who call themselves Muslims – as though we don't have the same problem in Christianity. There is much nobility there, and they have a tradition of scholarship that commands respect. Except that nobody over here knows much about it,' Riley concluded.

'Any other conceptual problems?' Jack asked.

Father Tim laughed: 'The Council of Vienna! How did you forget that, Jack?'

'What?' Alden sputtered in annoyance.

'1815. Everybody knows that! After the final settlement of the Napoleonic Wars, the Swiss had to promise never to export mercenaries. I'm sure we can finesse that. Excuse me, Dr Alden. The Pope's guard detachment is composed of Swiss mercenaries. So was the French king's once – they all got killed defending King Louis and Marie Antoinette. Same thing nearly happened to the Pope's troops once, but they held the enemy off long enough for a small detachment to evacuate the Holy Father to a secure location, Castel Gandolfo, as I recall. Mercenaries used to be the main Swiss export, and they were feared wherever they went. The Swiss Guards of the Vatican are mostly for show now, of course, but once upon a time the need for them was quite real. In any case, Swiss mercenaries had such a ferocious reputation that a footnote of the Council of Vienna, which settled the Napoleonic Wars, compelled the Swiss to promise not to allow their people to fight anywhere but at home and the Vatican. But, as I just said, that is a trivial problem. The Swiss would be delighted to be seen helping solve this problem. It could only increase their prestige in a region where there is a lot of money.'

'Sure,' Jack observed. 'Especially if we provide their

equipment. M-1 tanks, Bradley fighting vehicles, cellular communications . . .'

'Come on, Jack,' Riley said.

'No, Father, the nature of the mission will demand some heavy weapons, for psychological impact if nothing else. You have to demonstrate that you're serious. Once you do that, then the rest of the force can wear the Michaelangelo jumpsuits and carry their halberds and smile into the cameras – but you still need a Smith & Wesson to beat four aces, especially over there.'

Riley conceded the point. 'I like the elegance of the concept, gentlemen. It appeals to the noble. Everyone involved claims to believe in God by one name or another. By appealing to them in His name . . . hmm, that's the key, isn't it? The City of God. When do you need an answer?'

'It's not all that high-priority,' Alden answered. Riley got the message. It was a matter of official White House interest, but was not something to be fast-tracked. Neither was it something to be buried on the bottom of someone's desk pile. It was, rather, a back-channel inquiry to be handled expeditiously and very quietly.

'Well, it has to go through the bureaucracy. The Vatican has the world's oldest continuously-operating bureaucracy in the world, remember.'

'That's why we're talking to you,' Ryan pointed out. 'The General can cut through all the crap.'

'That's no way to talk about the princes of the church, Jack!' Riley nearly exploded with laughter.

'I'm a Catholic, remember? I understand.'

'I'll drop them a line,' Riley promised. *Today*, his eyes said.

'Quietly,' Alden emphasized.

'Quietly,' Riley agreed.

Ten minutes later, Father Timothy Riley was back in his car for the short drive back to his office at Georgetown. Already his mind was at work. Ryan had guessed right about Father Tim's connections and their importance. Riley was composing his message in Attic Greek, the language of philosophers never spoken by more than fifty thousand people, but the language in which he'd studied Plato and Aristotle at Woodstock Seminary in Maryland all those years before.

Once in his office, he instructed his secretary to hold all calls, closed the door, and activated his personal computer. First he inserted a disk that allowed the use of Greek characters. Riley was not a skilled typist – having both a secretary and a computer rapidly erodes that skill – and it took him an hour to produce the document he needed. It was printed up as a double-spaced nine-page letter. Riley next opened a desk drawer and dialed in his code for a small but secure office safe that was concealed in what appeared to be a file drawer. Here, as Ryan had long suspected, was a cipher book, laboriously hand-printed by a young priest on the Father General's personal staff. Riley had to laugh. It just wasn't the sort of thing one associated with the priesthood. In 1944, when Admiral Chester Nimitz had suggested to John Cardinal Spellman, Catholic Vicar General for the U.S. military, that perhaps the Marianas Islands needed a new bishop, the Cardinal had produced his cipher book, and used the communications network of the U.S. Navy to have a new bishop appointed. As with any other organization, the Catholic Church occasionally needed a secure communications link, and the Vatican cipher service had been around for centuries. In this case, the cipher key for this day was a lengthy passage from Aristotle's discourse on Being *qua* Being, with seven words removed, and four grotesquely misspelled. A commercial encryption program handled the rest. Then he had to print out a new copy and set it aside. His computer was again switched off, erasing all record of the communique. Riley next faxed the letter to the Vatican, and shredded all the hard copies. The entire exercise took three laborious hours, and when he informed his secretary that he was ready to get back to business, he knew that he'd have to work far into the night. Unlike an ordinary businessman, Riley didn't swear.

*

'I don't like this,' Leary said quietly behind his binoculars.

'Neither do I,' Paulson agreed. His view of the scene through the ten-power telescopic sight was less panoramic and far more focused. Nothing about the situation was pleasing. The subject was one the FBI had been chasing for more than ten years. Implicated in the deaths of two special agents of the Bureau and a United States Marshal, John Russell (a/k/a Matt Murphy, a/k/a Richard Burton, a/k/a Red Bear) had disappeared into the warm embrace of something called The Warrior Society of the Sioux Nation. There was little of the warrior about John Russell. Born in Minnesota far from the Sioux reservation, he'd been a petty felon whose one major conviction had landed him in prison. It was there that he had discovered his ethnicity and begun thinking like his perverted image of a Native American – which to Paulson's way of thinking had more of Mikhail Bakunin in it than of Cochise or Toohoolhoolzote. Joining another prison-born group called the American Indian Movement, Russell had been involved in a half-dozen nihilistic acts, ending with the deaths of three federal officers, then vanished. But sooner or later they all screwed up, and today was John Russell's turn. Taking its chance to raise money by running drugs into Canada, the Warrior Society had made its mistake, and allowed its plans to be overheard by a federal informant.

They were in the ghostly remains of a farming town six miles from the Canadian border. The FBI Hostage Rescue Team, as usual without any hostages to rescue, was acting its role as the Bureau's premier S W A T team. The ten men deployed on the mission under squad supervisor Dennis Black were under the administrative control of the Special Agent in Charge of the local field office. That was where the Bureau's customary professionalism had come to a screeching halt. The local S-A-C had set up an elaborate ambush plan that had started badly and nearly ended in disaster, with three agents already in hospitals from the auto wrecks and two more with serious gunshot wounds. In return, one subject was known dead, and maybe another was wounded, but no one was sure at the moment. The rest – three or four, they were not sure of that either – were holed up in what had once been a motel. What they knew for sure was that either the motel had a still-working phone or, more likely, the subjects had a cellular 'brick' and had called the media. What was happening now was of such magnificent confusion as to earn the admiration of Phineas T. Barnum. The local S-A-C was trying to salvage what remained of his professional reputation by using the media to his advantage. What he hadn't figured out yet was that handling network teams dispatched from as far away as Denver and Chicago wasn't quite the same thing as dealing with the local reporters fresh from journalism school. It was very hard to call the shots with the pros.

'Bill Shaw is going to have this guy's balls for brunch tomorrow,' Leary observed quietly.

'That does us a whole lot of good,' Paulson replied. A snort. 'Besides, what balls?'

'What you got?' Black asked over the secure radio circuit.

'Movement, but no ID,' Leary replied. 'Bad light. These guys may be dumb, but they're not crazy.'

'The subjects have asked for a TV reporter to come in with a camera, and the S-A-C has agreed.'

'Dennis, have you –' Paulson nearly came off the scope at that.

'Yes, I have,' Black replied. 'He says he's in command.' The Bureau's negotiator, a psychiatrist with hard-won expertise in these affairs, was still two hours away, and the S-A-C wanted something for the evening news. Black wanted to throttle the man, but he couldn't, of course.

'Can't arrest the guy for incompetence,' Leary said, his hand over the microphone. *Well, the only thing these bastards don't have is a hostage. So, why not give 'em one? That'll give the negotiator something to do.*

'Talk to me, Dennis,' Paulson said next.

'Rules of Engagement are in force, on my authority,' Supervisory Special Agent Black said. 'The reporter is a female, twenty-eight, blonde and blue, about five-six. Cameraman is a black guy, dark complexion, six-three. I told him where to walk. He's got brains, and he's playing ball.'

'Roger that, Dennis.'

'How long you been on the gun, Paulson?' Black asked next. The book said that a sniper could not stay fully alert on the gun for more than thirty minutes, at which point the observer and sniper exchanged positions. Dennis Black figured that someone had to play by the book.

'About fifteen minutes, Dennis. I'm okay . . . okay, I got the newsies.'

They were very close, a mere hundred fifteen yards from the front door of the block building. The light was not good. The sun would set in another ninety minutes. It had been a blustery day. A hot south-westerly wind was ripping across the prairie. Dust stung the eyes. Worse, the wind was hitting over forty knots and was directly across his line of sight. That sort of wind could screw up his aim by as much as four inches.

'Team is standing by,' Black advised. 'We just got Compromise Authority.'

'Well, at least he isn't a total asshole,' Leary replied over the radio. He was too angry to care if the S-A-C heard that or not. More likely, the dumbass had just choked again.

Both sniper and observer wore ghillie suits. It had taken them two hours to get into position, but they were effectively invisible, their shaggy camouflage blending them in with the scrubby trees and prairie grass here. Leary watched the newsies approach. The girl was pretty, he thought, though her hair and makeup had to be suffering from the dry, harsh wind. The man on the camera looked like he could have played guard for the Vikings, maybe tough and fast enough to clear the way for that sensational new halfback, Tony Wills. Leary shook it off.

'The cameraman has a vest on. Girl doesn't.' *You*

stupid bitch, Leary thought. *I know Dennis told you what these bastards were all about.*

'Dennis said he was smart.' Paulson trained the rifle on the building. 'Movement at the door!'

'Let's everyone try to be smart,' Leary murmured.

'Subject One in sight,' Paulson announced. 'Russell's coming out. Sniper One is on target.'

'Got him,' three voices replied at once.

John Russell was an enormous man. Six-five, over two-hundred-fifty pounds of what had once been athletic but was now a frame running to fat and dissolution. He wore jeans, but was bare-chested with a headband securing his long black hair in place. His chest bore tattoos, some professionally done, but more of the prison spit-and-pencil variety. He was the sort of man police preferred to meet with gun in hand. He moved with the lazy arrogance that announced his willingness to depart from the rules.

'Subject One is carrying a large, blue-steel revolver,' Leary told the rest of the team. *Looks like an N-Frame Smith . . .* 'I, uh – Dennis, there's something odd about him . . .'

'What is it?' Black asked immediately.

'Mike's right,' Paulson said next, examining the face through his scope. There was a wildness to his eyes. 'He's on something, Dennis, he's doped up. Call those newsies back!' But it was too late for that.

Paulson kept the sight on Russell's head. Russell wasn't a person now. He was a subject, a target. The team was now acting under the Compromise Authority rule. At least the S-A-C had done that right. It meant that if something went badly wrong, the HRT was free to take whatever action its leader deemed appropriate. Further, Paulson's special Sniper Rules of Engagement were explicit. If the subject appeared to threaten any agent or civilian with deadly force, then his right index finger would apply four pounds, three ounces of pressure to the precision-set trigger of the rifle in his grasp.

'Let's everybody be real cool, for Christ's sake,' the sniper breathed. His Unertl telescopic sight had cross-hairs and stadia marks. Automatically Paulson reestimated the range, then settled down while his brain tried to keep track of the gusting wind. The sight reticle was locked on Russell's head, right on the ear, which made a fine point of aim.

It was horridly comical to watch. The reporter smiling, moving the microphone back and forth. The burly cameraman aiming his minicam with its powerful single light running off the battery pack around the black man's waist. Russell was speaking forcefully, but neither Leary nor Paulson could hear a word he was saying against the wind. The look on his face was angry from the beginning, and did not improve. Soon his left hand balled into a fist, and his fingers started flexing around the grips of the revolver in his right. The wind buffeted the silk blouse close around the reporter's braless chest. Leary remembered that Russell had a reputation as a sexual athlete, supposedly on the brutal side. But there was a strange vacancy to his face. His expression went from emotionless to passionate in what had to be a chemically-induced whipsaw state that only added to the stress of being trapped by FBI agents. He calmed suddenly, but it wasn't a normal calm.

That asshole S-A-C, Leary swore at himself. *We ought to just back off and wait them out. The situation is stabilized. They're not going anywhere. We could negotiate by phone and just wait them out. . . .*

'Trouble!'

Russell's free hand grabbed the reporter's upper right arm. She tried to draw back, but possessed only a fraction of the strength required to do so. The cameraman moved. One hand came off the Sony. He was a big, strong man, and might have pulled it off, but his move only provoked Russell. The subject's gun hand moved.

'On target on target on target!' Paulson said urgently. *Stop, you asshole, STOP NOW!* He couldn't let the gun come up very far. His brain was racing, evaluating the situation. A large-frame Smith & Wesson, maybe a .44. It made big, bloody wounds. Maybe the subject was just punctuating his words, but Paulson didn't know or care what those words were. He was probably telling the black guy on the camera to stop; the gun seemed to be pointing more that way than at the girl, but the gun was still coming up and —

The crack of the rifle stopped time like a photograph. Paulson's finger had moved, seemingly of its own accord, but training had simply taken over. The rifle surged back in recoil, and the sniper's hand was already moving to work the bolt and load another round. The wind had chosen a bad moment to gust, throwing Paulson's aim off ever so slightly to the right. Instead of drilling through the center of Russell's head, the bullet struck well forward of the ear. On hitting bone, it fragmented. The subject's face was ripped explosively from the skull. Nose, eyes, and forehead vanished into a wet red mist. Only the mouth remained, and that was open and screaming, as blood vented from Russell's head as though from a clogged showerhead. Dying, but not dead, Russell jerked one round off at the cameraman before falling forward against the reporter. Then the cameraman was down, and the reporter was just standing there, not having had enough time even to be shocked by the blood and tissue on her clothing and face. Russell's hands clawed briefly at a face no longer there, then went still. Paulson's radio headset screamed 'GO GO GO!' but he scarcely took note of it. He drove the second round into the chamber, and spotted a face in a window of the building. He recognized it from photographs. It was a subject, a bad guy. And there was a weapon there, looked like an old Winchester lever-action. It started moving. Paulson's second shot was better than the first, straight into the forehead of Subject Two, someone named William Ames.

Time started again. The HRT members raced in, dressed in their black Nomex coveralls and body armor. Two dragged the reporter away. Two more did the same with the cameraman, whose Sony was clasped securely to his chest. Another tossed an explosive flash-bang grenade through the broken window while Dennis Black and the remaining three team members dove through the open door. There were no other shots. Fifteen seconds later, the radio crackled again.

'This is Team Leader. Building search complete. Two subjects down and dead. Subject Two is William Ames. Subject Three is Ernest Thorn, looks like he's been dead for a while from two in the chest. Subjects' weapons are neutralized. Site is secure. Repeat, site secure.'

'Jesus!' It was Leary's first shooting involvement after ten years in the Bureau. Paulson got up to his knees, after clearing his weapon, folded the rifle's bipod legs, then trotted towards the building. The local S-A-C beat him there, service automatic in hand, standing over the prone body of John Russell. It was just as well that the front of Russell's head was hidden. Every drop of blood he'd once had was now on the cracked cement sidewalk.

'Nice job!' the S-A-C told everyone. That was his last mistake in a day replete with them.

'You ignorant, shit-faced asshole!' Paulson pushed him against the painted block walls. 'These people are dead because of you!' Leary jumped between them, pushing Paulson away from the surprised senior agent. Dennis Black appeared next, his face blank.

'Clean up your mess,' he said, leading his men away before something else happened. 'How's that newsie?'

The cameraman was lying on his back, the Sony at his eyes. The reporter was on her knees, vomiting. She had good cause. An agent had already wiped her face, but her expensive blouse was a red obscenity that would occupy her nightmares for weeks to come.

'You okay?' Dennis asked. 'Turn that goddamned thing off!'

He set the camera down, switching off the light. The cameraman shook his head and felt at a spot just below the ribs. 'Thanks for the advice, brother. Gotta send a letter to the people that make this vest. I really – ' And his voice stopped. Finally the realization of what had happened took hold, and the shock started. 'Oh God, oh, sweet merciful Jesus!'

Paulson walked to the Chevy Carryall and locked his rifle in the rigid guncase. Leary and one other agent stayed with him, telling him that he had done exactly the right thing. They'd do that until Paulson got over his stress period. It wasn't the sniper's first kill, but while they had all been different incidents, they were all the same, all things to be regretted. The aftermath to a real shooting does not include a commercial.

The reporter suffered the normal post-traumatic hysteria. She ripped off her blood-soaked blouse, forgetting that there was nothing under it. An agent wrapped a blanket around her and helped to steady her down. More news crews were converging on the scene, most heading towards the building. Dennis Black got his people together to clear their weapons and help with the two civilians. The reporter recovered in a few minutes. She asked if it had really been necessary, then learned that her cameraman had taken a shot that had been stopped by the Second Chance vest the Bureau had recommended to both of them, but which she had rejected. She next entered the elation phase, just as happy as she could be that she could still breathe. Soon the shock would return, but she was a bright journalist, despite her youth and inexperience, and had already learned something important. Next time, she'd listen when someone gave her good advice; the nightmares would merely punctuate the importance of the lesson. Within thirty minutes, she was standing up without assistance, wearing her back-up outfit, giving a level if brittle account of what had happened. But it was the tape footage that would impress the people at Black Rock, headquarters of CBS. The cameraman would get a personal letter from the head of the News Division. The footage had everything: drama, death, a courageous (and attractive) reporter, and would run as the lead piece for the evening news broadcast for this otherwise slow news day, to be repeated by all the network morning shows the next day. In each case the anchor would solemnly warn people that what they were about to see might disturb the sensitive – just to make sure that everyone understood that something especially juicy was about to screen. Since everyone had more than one chance to view the event, quite a few had their tape

35

machines turning the second time around. One of them was the head of the Warrior Society. His name was Marvin Russell.

It had started innocently enough. His stomach was unsettled when he awoke. The morning jogs became a little more tiresome. He didn't feel quite himself. *You're over thirty*, he told himself. *You're not a boy anymore.* Besides, he'd always been vigorous. Maybe it was just a cold, a virus, the lingering effects of bad water, some stomach bug. He'd just work his way out of it. He added weight to his pack, took to carrying a loaded magazine in his rifle. He'd gotten lazy, that's all. That was easily remedied. He was nothing if not a determined man.

For a month or so, it worked. Sure, he was even more tired, but that was to be expected with the extra five kilos of weight he carried. He welcomed the additional fatigue as evidence of his warrior's virtue, went back to simpler foods, forced himself to adopt better sleep habits. It helped. The muscle aches were no different from the time he'd entered this demanding life, and he slept the dreamless sleep of the just. What had been tough became tougher still as his focused mind gave its orders to a recalcitrant body. Could he not defeat some invisible microbe? Had he not bested far larger and more formidable organisms? The thought was less a challenge than a petty amusement. As with most determined men, his competition was entirely within himself, the body resisting what the mind commanded.

But it never quite went away. Though his body became leaner and harder, the aches and the nausea persisted. He became annoyed with it, and the annoyance first surfaced in jokes. When his senior colleagues took note of his discomfort, he called it morning sickness, evoking gales of rough laughter. He bore the discomfort for another month, then found that it was necessary to lighten his load to maintain his place in front with the leaders. For the first time in his life, faint doubts appeared like wispy clouds in the clear sky of his determined self-image. It was no longer an amusement.

He stuck with it for still another month, never slacking in his routine except for the additional hour of sleep that he imposed on his otherwise tireless regimen. Despite this, his condition worsened – well, not exactly worsened, but did not improve a bit. Maybe it was merely the increasing years, he finally admitted to himself. He was, after all, only a man, however hard he worked to perfect his form. There was no disgrace in that, determined though he might have been to prevent it.

Finally, he started grumbling about it. His comrades were understanding. All of them were younger than he, many having served their leader for five years or more. They revered him for his toughness, and if the toughness showed a few hairline cracks, what did it mean except that he was human after all, and all the more admirable because of it? One or two suggested home remedies, but finally a close friend and comrade told him that he was foolish indeed not to see one of the local doctors – his sister's husband was a good one, a graduate of British medical schools. Determined as he was to avoid this abnegation of his person, it was time to take what he knew to be good advice.

The doctor was as good as advertised. Sitting behind his desk in a starched white laboratory coat, he took a complete medical history, then performed a preliminary examination. There was nothing overtly wrong. He talked about stress – something his patient needed no lectures about – and pointed out that over the years stress claimed an increasingly heavy forfeit on those who bore it. He talked about good eating habits, how exercise could be overdone, how rest was important. He decided that the problem was a combination of various small things, including what was probably a small but annoying intestinal disorder, and prescribed a drug to ameliorate it. The doctor concluded his lecture with a soliloquy about patients who were too proud to do what was good for them, and how foolish they were. The patient nodded approvingly, according the physician deserved respect. He'd given not dissimilar lectures to his own subordinates, and was as determined as always to do things in exactly the right way.

The medication worked for a week or so. His stomach almost returned to normal. Certainly it improved, but he noted with annoyance that it wasn't quite the same as before. Or was it? It was, he admitted to himself, hard to remember such trivial things as how one felt on awakening. The mind, after all, concerned itself with the great ideas, like mission and purpose, and left the body to attend its own needs and leave the mind alone. The mind wasn't supposed to be bothered. The mind gave orders and expected them to be followed. It didn't need distractions like this. How could purpose exist with distractions? He'd determined his life's purpose long years before.

But it simply would not go away, and finally he had to return to the physician. A more careful examination was undertaken. He allowed his body to be poked and prodded, to have his blood drawn by a needle instead of the more violent instruments for which he had prepared himself. Maybe it was something almost serious, the physician told him, a low-order systemic infection, for example. There were drugs to treat that. Malaria, once pandemic to the region for example, had similar but more serious debilitating effects, as did any number of maladies which had once been serious but were now easily defeated by the forces available to modern medicine. The tests would show what was wrong, and the doctor was determined to fix it. He knew of his patient's purpose in life, and shared it from a safer and more distant perspective.

He returned to the doctor's office two days later. Immediately, he knew that something was wrong. He'd seen the same look often enough on the face of his intelligence officer. Something unexpected. Something to interfere with plans. The doctor began speaking slowly, searching for words, trying to find a way to make the message easier, but the patient would have none of that. He had chosen to live a dangerous life, and demanded the information as directly as he would have given it.

The physician nodded respectfully, and replied in kind. The man took the news dispassionately. He was accustomed to disappointments of many kinds. He knew what lay at the end of every life, and had many times helped to deliver it to others. So. Now it lay in his path also, to be avoided if possible but there nonetheless, perhaps near, perhaps not. He asked what could be done, and the news was less bad than he had expected. The doctor did not insult him with words of comfort, but read his patient's mind and explained the facts of the matter. There were things to be done. They might succeed. They might not. Time would tell. His physical strength would help a great deal, as would his iron determination. A proper state of mind, the physician told him, was highly important. The patient almost smiled at that, but stopped himself. Better to show the courage of a stoic than the hope of a fool. And what was death, after all? Had he not lived a life dedicated to justice? To the will of God? Had he not sacrificed his life to a great and worthy purpose?

But that was the rub. He was not a man who planned on failure. He had selected a goal for his life, and years before determined to reach it, regardless of cost to himself or others. On that altar he had sacrificed everything he might have been, the dreams of his dead parents, the education which they had hoped he would use for the betterment of himself and others, a normal, comfortable life with a woman who might bear him sons – all of that he had rejected in favor of a path of toil, danger, and utter determination to reach that single, shining goal.

And now? Was it all for nothing? Was his life to end without meaning? Would he never see the day for which he had lived? Was God that cruel? All these thoughts paraded through his consciousness while his face remained neutral, his eyes guarded as always. No. He would not let that be. God could not have deserted him. He would see the day – or at least see it grow closer. His life would have meaning after all. It had not been all for nothing, nor would what future he might yet have be for nothing. On that, too, he was determined.

Ismael Qati would follow his doctor's orders, do what must be done to extend his time, and perhaps defeat this internal enemy, as insidious and contemptible as those outside. In the meantime, he would redouble his efforts, push himself to the limits of physical endurance, ask his God for guidance, look for a sign of His will. As he had fought his other enemies, so would he fight this one, with courage and total dedication. He'd never known mercy in his life, after all, and he would not start showing it now. If he had to face death, the deaths of others paled even further than usual. But he would not lash out blindly. He would do what he had to do. He would carry on as before, waiting for the chance that his faith told him must lie somewhere beyond his sight, between himself and the end of his path. His determination had always been directed by intelligence. It was that which explained his effectiveness.

CHAPTER 2

Labyrinths

The letter from Georgetown arrived in a Roman office, scarce minutes after transmission, where, as with any bureaucracy, the night clerk (what intelligence agencies call a Watch Officer) simply dropped it on the proper desk and went back to his studies for an exam on the metaphysical discourse of Aquinas. A young Jesuit priest named Hermann Schörner, private secretary to Francisco Alcalde, Father General of the Society of Jesus, arrived the next morning promptly at seven and began sorting the overnight mail. The fax from America was third from the top, and stopped the young cleric in his tracks. Cipher traffic was a routine part of his job, but was not all that common. The code prefix at the top of the communication indicated the originator and the priority. Father Schörner hurried through the rest of the mail and went immediately to work.

The procedure was an exact inversion of what Father Riley had done, except that Schörner's typing skills were excellent. He used an optical scanner to transcribe the text into a personal computer and punched up the decryption program. Irregularities on the facsimile copy caused some garbles, but that was easily fixed, and the clear-text copy – still in Attic Greek, of course – slid out of the ink-jet printer. It had required merely twenty minutes, as opposed to Riley's three laborious hours. The young priest prepared morning coffee for himself and his boss, then read the letter with his second cup of the day. How extraordinary, Schörner reflected.

Reverend Francisco Alcalde was an elderly but uncommonly vigorous man. At sixty-six, he still played a fair game of tennis, and was known to ski with the Holy Father. A gaunt, wiry six-four, his thick mane of gray hair was brush-cut over deep-set owlish eyes. Alcalde was a man with solid intellectual credentials. The master of eleven languages, had he not been a priest he might have become the foremost medieval historian in Europe. But he was, before all things, a priest whose administrative duties chafed against his desire for both teaching and pastoral ministry. In a few years, he would leave his post as Father General of Roman Catholicism's largest and most powerful order, and find himself again as a university instructor, illuminating young minds, and leaving campus to celebrate mass in a small working-class parish where he could concern himself with ordinary human needs. That, he thought, would be the final blessing of a life cluttered with so many of them. Not a perfect man, he frequently wrestled with the pride that attended his intellect, trying and not always succeeding to cultivate the humility necessary to his vocation. Well, he sighed, perfection was a goal never to be reached, and he smiled at the humor of it.

'*Guten Morgen, Hermann!*' he said, sweeping through the door.

'*Buon giorno,*' the German priest replied, then lapsed into Greek. 'Something interesting this morning.'

The busy eyebrows twitched at the message, and he jerked his head towards the inner office. Schörner followed with the coffee.

'The tennis court is reserved for four o'clock,' Schörner said, as he poured his boss's cup.

'So you can humiliate me yet again?' It was occasionally joked that Schörner could turn professional, contributing his winnings to the Society, whose members were required to take a vow of poverty. 'So, what is the message?'

'From Timothy Riley in Washington.' Schörner handed it over.

Alcalde donned his reading glasses and read slowly. He left his coffee untouched and, on finishing the message, read through it again. Scholarship was his life, and Alcalde rarely spoke about something without reflection.

'Remarkable. I've heard of this Ryan fellow before ... isn't he in intelligence?'

'Deputy Director of the American CIA. We educated him. Boston College and Georgetown. He's principally a bureaucrat, but he's been involved in several operations in the field. We don't know all of the details, but it would appear that none were improper. We have a small dossier on him. Father Riley speaks very highly of Dr Ryan.'

'So I see.' Alcalde pondered that for a moment. He and Riley had been friends for thirty years. 'He thinks this proposal may be genuine. And you, Hermann?'

'Potentially, it is a gift from God.' The comment was delivered without irony.

'Indeed. But an urgent one. What of the American President?'

'I would guess that he has not yet been briefed, but soon will be. As to his character?' Schörner shrugged. 'He could be a better man.'

'Who of us could not?' Alcalde said, staring at the wall. 'Yes, Father.'

'How is my calendar for today?' Schörner ran over the list from memory. 'Very well ... call Cardinal D'Antonio and tell him that I have something of importance. Fiddle the schedule as best you can. This is something that calls for immediate attention. Call Timothy, thank him for his message, and tell him that I am working on it.'

Ryan awoke reluctantly at five-thirty. The sun was an orange-pink glow that back-lit the trees, ten miles away on Maryland's eastern shore. His first considered course of action was to draw the shades. Cathy didn't have to go into Hopkins today, though it took him half the walk to the bathroom to remember why. His next action was to take two extra-strength Tylenol. He'd had too much to drink the previous night, and that, he reminded himself, was three days in a row. But what was the alternative? Sleep came increasingly hard to him, despite work hours that grew longer and fatigue that –

'Damn,' he said, squinting at himself in the mirror. He looked terrible. He padded his way into the kitchen for coffee. Everything was better after coffee. His stomach contracted itself into a tight, resentful ball on seeing the wine bottles still sitting on the countertop. A bottle and a half, he reminded himself. Not two. He hadn't drunk two full bottles. One had already been opened. It wasn't that bad. Ryan flipped the switch for the coffee machine and headed for the garage. There he climbed into the station wagon and drove to the gate to get his paper. Not all that long ago he'd walked out to get it, but, hell, he told himself, he wasn't dressed. That was the reason. The car radio was set to an all-news station, and he got his first exposure to what the world was doing. The ball scores. The Orioles had lost again. Damn, and he was supposed to take little Jack to a game. He'd promised after the last little-league game he'd missed. And when, he asked himself, are you going to do that, next April? Damn.

Well, the whole season, practically, was ahead. School wasn't even out yet. He'd get to it. Sure. Ryan tossed the morning *Post* on the car seat and drove back to the house. The coffee was ready. First good news of the day. Ryan poured himself a mug and decided against breakfast. Again. That was bad, a part of his mind warned him. His stomach was in bad enough shape already, and two mugs of straight dripped coffee would not help. He forced his mind into the paper to stifle that voice.

It is not often appreciated how much intelligence services depend on the news media for their information. Part of it was functional. They were in much the same business, and the intelligence services didn't have the brain market cornered. More to the point, Ryan reflected, the newsies didn't pay people for information. Their confidential sources were driven either by conscience or anger to leak whatever information they let out, and that made for the best sort of information; any intelligence officer could tell you that. Nothing like anger or principle to get a person to leak all sorts of juicy

44

stuff. Finally, though the media was replete with lazy people, quite a few smart ones were drawn by the better money that went with news-gathering. Ryan had learned which by-lines to read slowly and carefully. And he noted the datelines, as well. As Deputy Director of the Central Intelligence Agency, he knew which department heads were strong and which were weak. The *Post* gave him better information, for example, than the German desk. The Middle East was still quiet. The Iraq business was finally settling out. The new arrangement over there was taking shape, at long last. *Now, if we could just do something about the Israeli side* . . . It would be nice, he thought, to set that whole area to rest. And Ryan believed it possible. The East–West confrontation which had predated his birth was now a thing of history, and who would have believed that? Ryan refilled his mug without looking, something that even a hangover allowed him to do. And all in just a brief span of years – less time, in fact, than he had spent in the Agency. Damn. Who would have believed it?

Now, that was so amazing that Ryan wondered how long people would be writing books about it. Generations, at least. The next week, a KGB representative was coming into Langley to seek advice on parliamentary oversight. Ryan had counseled against letting him in – and the trip was being handled with the utmost secrecy – because the Agency still had Russians working for it, and the knowledge that KGB and CIA had instituted official contacts on anything would terrify them (equally true, Ryan admitted to himself, of Americans still in the employ of KGB . . . probably). It was an old friend coming over, Sergey Golovko. Friend, Ryan snorted, turning to the sports page. The problem with the morning paper was that it never had the results of last night's game . . .

Jack's return to the bathroom was more civilized. He was awake now, though his stomach was even less happy with the world. Two antacid tablets helped that. And the Tylenol were working. He'd reenforce that with two more at work. By six-fifteen, he was washed, shaved, and dressed. He kissed his still-sleeping wife on the way out

– was rewarded by a vague *hmmm* – and opened the front door in time to see the car pulling up the driveway. It troubled Ryan vaguely that his driver had to awaken far earlier than he to get here on time. It bothered him a little more who his driver was.

'Morning, Doc,' John Clark said with a gruff smile. Ryan slid into the front seat. There was more leg room, and he thought it would insult the man to sit in back.

'Hi, John,' Jack replied.

Tied it on again last night, eh, Doc? Clark thought. *Damned fool. For someone as smart as you are, how can you be so dumb? Not getting the jogging in either, are you?* he wondered, on seeing how tight the DDCI's belt looked. Well, he'd just have to learn, as Clark had learned, that late nights and too much booze were for dumb kids. John Clark had turned into a paragon of healthy virtue before reaching Ryan's age. He figured that it had saved his life at least once.

'Quiet night,' Clark said next, heading out the driveway.

'That's nice.' Ryan picked up the dispatch box and dialed in the code. He waited until the light flashed green before opening it. Clark was right, there wasn't much to be looked at. By the time they were halfway to Washington, he'd read everything and made a few notes.

'Going to see Carol and the kids tonight?' Clark asked as they passed over Maryland Route 3.

'Yeah, it is tonight, isn't it?'

'Yep.'

It was a regular once-a-week routine. Carol Zimmer was the Laotian widow of Air Force sergeant Buck Zimmer, and Ryan had promised to take care of the family after Buck's death. Few people knew of it – fewer people knew of the mission on which Buck had died – but it gave Ryan great satisfaction. Carol now owned a 7-Eleven between Washington and Annapolis. It gave her family a steady and respectable income when added to her husband's pension, and, with the educational trust fund that Ryan had established, guaranteed that each of the eight would have a college degree when the time came – as it had already come for the eldest son. It would be a long haul to finish that up. The youngest was still in diapers.

'Those punks ever come back?' Jack asked.

Clark just turned and grinned. For several months after Carol took the business over, some local toughs had taken to hanging out at the store. They had objected to a Laotian woman and her mixed-race kids owning a business in the semi-rural area. Finally she had mentioned it to Clark. John had given them one warning, which they had been too dense to heed. Perhaps they'd mistaken him for an off-duty police officer, someone not to be taken too seriously. John and his Spanish-speaking friend had set things right, and after the gang leader had gotten out of the hospital, the punks had never come near the place. The local cops had been very understanding, and business had taken an immediate twenty-percent increase. *I wonder if that guy's knee ever came all the way back!* Clark wondered with a wistful smile. *Maybe now he'll take up an honest trade . . .*

'How are the kids doing?'

'You know, it's kinda hard to get used to the idea of having one in college, Doc. A little tough on Sandy, too . . . Doc?'

'Yeah, John?'

'Pardon my saying so, but you look a little rocky. You want to back it off a little.'

'That's what Cathy says.' It occurred to Jack to tell Clark to mind his own business, but you didn't say that sort of thing to a man like Clark, and besides, he was a friend. And besides that, he was correct.

'Docs are usually right,' John pointed out.

'I know. It's just a little – a little stressful at the office. Got some stuff happening, and –'

'Exercise beats the hell out of booze, man. You're one of the smartest guys I know. Act smart. End of advice.' Clark shrugged, and returned his attention to the morning traffic.

'You know, John, if you had decided to become a doc,

47

you would have been very effective,' Jack replied with a chuckle.

'How so?'

'With a bedside manner like yours, people would be afraid not to do what you said.'

'I am the most even-tempered man I know,' Clark protested.

'Right, noone's ever lived long enough for you to get really mad. They're dead by the time you're mildly annoyed.'

And that was why Clark was Ryan's driver. Jack had engineered his transfer out of the Directorate of Operations to become a Security and Protective Officer. DCI Cabot had eliminated fully twenty percent of the field force, and people with paramilitary experience had been first on the block. Clark's expertise was too valuable to lose, and Ryan had bent two rules and outright evaded a third to accomplish this much, aided and abetted by Nancy Cummings and a friend in the Admin Directorate. Besides, Jack felt very safe around this man, and he was able to train the new kids in the SPO unit. He was even a superb driver, and as usual, he got Ryan into the basement garage right on time.

The Agency Buick slid into its spot, and Ryan got out, fiddling with his keys. The one for the executive elevator was on the end, and two minutes later, he arrived at the seventh floor, walking from the corridor to his office. The DDCI's office adjoins the long, narrow suite accorded the DCI, who was not at work yet. A small, surprisingly modest place for the number-two man in the country's premier intelligence service, it overlooked the visitor-parking lot, beyond which was the thick stand of pines that separated the Agency compound from the George Washington Parkway and the Potomac River valley beyond. Ryan had kept Nancy Cummings from his previous and brief stint as Deputy Director (Intelligence). Clark took his seat in that office, going over dispatches that pertained to his duties, in preparation for the morning SPO conference – they concerned themselves with which terrorist group was making noise at the moment. No serious attempt had ever been made on a senior Agency executive, but history was not their institutional concern. The future was, and even CIA didn't have a particularly bright record for predicting that.

Ryan found his desk neatly piled with material too sensitive for the car's dispatch case, and prepped himself for the morning department-head meeting, which he co-chaired with the DCI. There was a drip-coffee machine in his office. Next to it was a clean but never-used mug that had once belonged to the man who'd brought him into the Agency, Vice Admiral James Greer. Nancy took care of that, and Ryan never began a day at Langley without thinking of his dead boss. So. He rubbed his hands across his face and eyes, and went to work. What new and interesting things did the world hold in store this day?

The logger, like most of his trade, was a big, powerful man. Six-four, and two hundred twenty pounds of former all-state defensive end, he'd joined the Marines instead of going to college – could have, he thought, could have taken the scholarship to Oklahoma or Pitt, but he'd decided against it. And he knew that he would never have wanted to leave Oregon for good. A college degree would have meant that. Maybe play pro ball, and then – turn into a 'suit'? No. Since childhood he'd loved the outdoor life. He made a good living, raised his family in a friendly small town, lived a rough, healthy life, and was the best damned man in the company for dropping a tree straight and soft. He drew the special ones.

He yanked the string on the big, two-man chainsaw. On a silent command, his helper took his end off the ground as the logger did the same. The tree had already been notched with a double-headed axe. They worked the saw in slowly and carefully. The logger kept one eye on the chainsaw while the other watched the tree. There was an art to doing this just right. It was a point of honor with him that he didn't waste an inch of wood he didn't have to. Not like the guys down at the mill, though they'd told him that the mill wouldn't touch this baby. They pulled the saw after completing the first cut, and started the second without pausing for breath. This time it took four minutes. The logger was tensely alert now. He felt a puff of wind on his face and paused to make sure it was blowing the way he wanted. A tree, no matter how large, was a plaything for a stiff wind – especially when nearly cut in half . . .

It was swaying at the top now . . . almost time. He backed the saw off and waved to his helper. *Watch my eyes, watch my hands!* The kid nodded seriously. About another foot would do it, the logger knew. They completed it very slowly. It abused the chain, but this was the dangerous part. Safety guys were monitoring the wind, and . . . now!

The logger brought the saw out and dropped it. The helper took the cue and backed off ten yards as his boss did the same. Both watched the base of the tree. If it kicked, that would tell them of the danger.

But it didn't. As always, it seemed so agonizingly slow. This was the part the Sierra Club liked to film, and the logger understood why. So slow, so agonizing, like the tree knew it was dying, and was trying not to, and losing, and the groan of the wood was a moan of despair. Well, yes, he thought, it did seem like that, but it was only a goddamned tree. The cut widened as he watched and the tree fell. The top was moving very fast now, but the danger was at the bottom, and that's what he continued to watch. As the trunk passed through the forty-five-degree mark, the wood parted completely. The body of the tree kicked then, moving over the stump about four feet, like the death rattle of a man. Then the noise. The immense swish of the top branches ripping through the air. He wondered quickly how fast the top was moving. Speed of sound, maybe? No, not that fast . . . and then – WHUMP! the tree actually bounced, but softly, when it hit the wet ground. Then it lay still. It was lumber now. That was always a little sad. It had been a pretty tree.

The Japanese official came over next, the logger was surprised to see. He touched the tree and murmured something that must have been a prayer. That amazed him, it seemed like something an Indian would do – interesting, the logger thought. He didn't know that Shinto was an animistic religion with many similarities to those of Native Americans. Talking to the spirit of the tree? Hmph. Next he came to the logger.

'You have great skill,' the little Japanese said with an exquisitely polite bow.

'Thank you, sir.' The logger nodded his head. It was the first Japanese he'd ever met. Seemed like a nice enough guy. And saying a prayer to the tree . . . that had class, the logger thought on reflection.

'A great pity to kill something so magnificent.'

'Yeah, I guess it is. Is it true that you will put this in a church, like?'

'Oh, yes. We no longer have trees like this, and we need four huge beams. Twenty meters each. This one tree will do all of them, I hope,' the man said, looking back at the fallen giant. 'They must all come from a single tree. It is the tradition of the temple, you see.'

'Ought to,' the logger judged. 'How old's the temple?'

'One thousand two hundred years. The old beams – they were damaged in the earthquake two years ago, and must be replaced very soon. With luck, these should last as long. I hope they will. It is a fine tree.'

Under the supervision of the Japanese official, the fallen tree was cut into manageable segments – they weren't all that manageable. Quite a bit of special equipment had to be assembled to get this monster out, and Georgia-Pacific was charging a huge amount of money for the job. But that was not a problem. The Japanese, having selected the tree, paid without blinking. The representative even apologized for the fact that he didn't want the GP mill to work the tree. It was a religious thing, he explained slowly and clearly, and no insult to the American workers was intended. The senior GP executive nodded. That was okay with him. It was their tree now. They'd let it season for a little while before loading it on an American-flag timber carrier for the trip across the Pacific, where the log would be worked with skill and due religious ceremony – by hand, the GP man was amazed to hear – for its new and special purpose. That it would never reach Japan was something that none of them knew.

The term trouble-shooter was particularly awkward for a law-enforcement official, Murray thought. Of course, as he leaned back in the leather chair, he could feel the 10mm Smith & Wesson automatic clipped to his waistband. He ought to have left it in his desk drawer, but he liked the feel of the beast. A revolver man for most of his career, he'd quickly come to love the compact power of the Smith. And Bill understood. For the first time in recent memory, the Director of the Federal Bureau of Investigation was a career cop who'd started his career on the street, busting bad guys. In fact, Murray and Shaw had started off in the same field division. Bill was slightly more skilled at the administrative side, but no one mistook him for a headquarters weenie. Shaw had first gotten high-level attention by staring down two armed bank robbers before the cavalry'd had time to arrive. He'd never fired his weapon in anger, of course – only a tiny percentage of FBI agents ever did – but he'd convinced those two hoods that he could drop both of them. There was steel under the gentlemanly velvet, and one hell of a brain. Which was why Dan Murray, a deputy assistant director, didn't mind working as Shaw's personal problem-solver.

'What the hell do we do with this guy?' Shaw asked, with quiet disgust.

Murray had just finished his report on the Warrior Case. Dan sipped at his coffee and shrugged.

'Bill, the man is a genius with corruption cases – best we've ever had. He just doesn't know dick about the muscle end of the business. He got out of his depth with this one. Luckily enough, no permanent damage was done.' And Murray was right. The newsies had treated the Bureau surprisingly well for saving the life of their reporter. What was truly amazing was the fact that the newsies had never quite understood that the reporter had

had no place in that particular arena. As a result, they were grateful to the local SAC for letting the news team on the scene, and grateful to the Hostage Rescue Team for saving both of them when things had taken a dangerous turn. It wasn't the first time the Bureau had reaped a PR bonanza from a near-catastrophe. The FBI was more jealous of its public relations than any government agency, and Shaw's problem was simply that to fire SAC Walt Hoskins would look bad. Murray pressed on. 'He's learned his lesson. Walt isn't stupid, Bill.'

'And bagging the governor last year was some coup, wasn't it?' Shaw grimaced. Hoskins *was* a genius at political corruption cases. A state governor was now contemplating life in a federal prison because of him. That was how Hoskins had become a Special-Agent-in-Charge in the first place. 'You have something in mind, Dan?'

'ASAC Denver,' Murray replied with a mischievous twinkle. 'It's elegant. He goes from a little field office to head of corruption cases in a major field division. It's a promotion that takes him out of command and puts him back in what he's best at – and if the rumbles we're getting out of Denver are right, he'll have lots of work to do. Like maybe a senator and a congresswoman – maybe more. The preliminary indications on the water project look big. I mean *real* big, Bill: like twenty million bucks changing hands.'

Shaw whistled respectfully at that. 'All that for one senator and one congresscritter?'

'Like I said, maybe more. The latest thing is some environmental types being paid off – in government and out. Who do we have better at unraveling a ball of yarn that big? Walt's got a nose for this sort of thing. The man can't draw his gun without losing a few toes, but he's one hell of a bird-dog.' Murray closed the folder in his hands. 'Anyway, you wanted me to look around and make a recommendation. Send him to Denver, or retire him. Mike Delaney is willing to rotate back this way – his kid's going to start at GW this fall, and Mike wants to teach down at the Academy. That gives you the opening. It's all very neat and tidy, but it's your call, Director.'

'Thank you, Mr Murray,' Director Shaw said gravely. Then his face broke into a grin. 'Remember when all we had to worry about was chasing bank bandits? I *hate* this admin crap!'

'Maybe we shouldn't have caught so many,' Dan agreed. 'We'd still be working riverside Philly and having a beer with the troops at night. Why do people toast success? It just screws up your life.'

'We're both talking like old farts.'

'We both are old farts, Bill,' Murray pointed out. 'But at least I don't travel around with a protective detail.'

'You son of a bitch!' Shaw gagged, and dribbled coffee down his necktie. 'Oh, Christ, Dan!' he gasped, laughing. 'Look what you made me do.'

'Bad sign when a guy can't hold his coffee, Director.'

'Out! Get the orders cut before I bust you back to the street.'

'Oh, no, please, not that, anything but that!' Murray stopped laughing and turned semi-serious for a moment. 'What's Kenny doing now?'

'Just got his assignment to his submarine, USS *Maine*. Bonnie's doing fine with the baby due in December. Dan?'

'Yeah, Bill?'

'Nice call on Hoskins. I needed an easy out on that. Thanks.'

'No problem, Bill. Walt will jump at it. I wish they were all this easy.'

'You following up on the Warrior Society?'

'Freddy Warder's working on it. We just might roll those bastards up in a few months.'

And both knew that would be nice. There were not many domestic terrorist groups left. Reducing their number by one more by the end of the year would be another major coup.

It was dawn in the Dakota badlands. Marvin Russell knelt on the hide of a bison, facing the sunrise. He wore jeans, but was bare-chested and barefoot. He was not a tall man, but there was no mistaking the power in him.

During his first and only stint in prison – for burglary – he'd learned about pumping iron. It had begun merely as a hobby to work off surplus energy, had grown with the understanding that physical strength was the only form of self-defense that a man in the penitentiary could depend upon, and then blossomed into the attribute he'd come to associate with a warrior of the Sioux Nation. His five feet, eight inches of height supported fully two hundred pounds of lean, hard muscle. His upper arms were the size of some men's upper legs. He had the waist of a ballerina and the shoulders of an NFL linebacker. He was also slightly mad, but Marvin Russell did not know that.

Life had not given him or his brother much of a chance. Their father had been an alcoholic who had worked occasionally and not well as an auto mechanic to provide money that he had transferred regularly and immediately to the nearest package store. Marvin's memories of childhood were bitter ones: shame for his father's nearly perpetual state of inebriation, and shame greater still for what his mother did while her husband was passed-out drunk in the living room. Food came from the government dole, after the family had returned from Minnesota to the reservation. Schooling came from teachers who despaired of accomplishing anything. His neighborhood had been a scattered collection of government-built plain block houses that stood like specters in perpetual clouds of blowing prairie dust. Neither Russell boy had ever owned a baseball glove. Neither had known a Christmas as much other than a week or two when school was closed. Both had grown in a vacuum of neglect and learned to fend for themselves at an early age.

At first this had been a good thing, for self-reliance was the way of their people, but all children need direction, and direction was something the Russell parents had been unable to provide. The boys had learned to shoot and hunt before they learned to read. Often the dinner had been something brought home with .22-caliber holes in it. Almost as often, they had cooked the meals. Though not the only poor and neglected youth of their settlement, they had without doubt been at the bottom, and while some of the local kids had overcome their backgrounds, the leap from poverty to adequacy had been far too broad for them. From the time they had begun to drive – well before the legal age – they'd taken their father's dilapidated pickup a hundred miles or more on clear cool nights to distant towns where they might obtain some of the things their parents had been unable to provide. Surprisingly, the first time they'd been caught – by another Sioux holding a shotgun – they'd taken their whipping manfully and been sent home with bruises and a lecture. They'd learned from that. From that moment on, they'd only robbed whites.

In due course, they'd been caught at that, also, red-handed inside a country store, by a tribal police officer. It was their misfortune that any crime committed on federal property was a federal case, and further that the new district court judge was a man with more compassion than perception. A hard lesson at that point might – or might not – have changed their path, but instead they'd gotten an administrative dismissal and counseling. A very serious young lady with a degree from the University of Wisconsin had explained to them over months that they could never have a beneficial self-image if they lived by stealing the goods of others. They would have more personal pride if they found something worthwhile to do. Emerging from that session wondering how the Sioux Nation had ever allowed itself to be over-run by white idiots, they learned to plan their crimes more carefully.

But not carefully enough, since the counselor could not have offered them the graduate-school expertise that the Russell boys might have received in a proper prison. And so they were caught, again, a year later, but this time off the reservation, and this time they found themselves dispatched to a year and a half of hard time because they'd been burglarizing a gun shop.

Prison had been the most frightening experience of their lives. Accustomed to land as open and vast as the western sky, they'd spent over a year of their lives in a cage smaller than the federal government deemed appropriate for a badger in a zoo, and surrounded by people far worse than their most inflated ideas of their own toughness. Their first night on the blocks, they'd learned from screams that rape was not a crime inflicted exclusively on women. Needing protection, they had almost immediately been swept into the protective arms of their fellow Native American prisoners of the American Indian Movement.

They had never given much thought to their ancestry. Subliminally, they might have sensed that their peer group did not display the qualities they had seen on those occasions when the family TV had worked, and probably felt some vague shame that they had always been different. They'd learned to snicker at Western movies, of course, whose 'Indian' actors were most often whites or Mexicans, mouthing words that reflected the thoughts of Hollywood scriptwriters who had about as much knowledge of the West as they had of Antarctica, but even there the messages had left a negative image of what they were and from what roots they had come. The American Indian Movement had changed all that. Everything was the White Man's fault. Espousing ideas that were a mix of trendy East Coast anthropology, a dash of Jean Jacques Rousseau, more than a little John Ford Western (what else, after all, was the American cultural record?), and a great deal of misunderstood history, the Russell brothers came to understand that their ancestors were of noble stock, ideal hunter-warriors who had lived in harmony with nature and the gods. The fact that the Native Americans had lived in as peaceful a state as the Europeans – the word 'Sioux' in Indian dialect means 'snake', and was not an appellation assigned with affection – and that they had only begun roaming the Great Plains in the last decade of the 18th Century were somehow left out, along with the vicious intertribal wars. Times had once been far better. They had been masters of their land, following the buffalo, hunting, living a healthy and satisfying life under the stars, and, occasionally, fighting short, heroic contests among themselves – rather like medieval jousts. Even the torture of captives was explained as an opportunity for warriors to display their stoic courage to their admiring if sadistic murderers.

Every man craves nobility of spirit, and it wasn't Marvin Russell's fault that the first such opportunity came from convicted felons. He and his brother learned about the gods of earth and sky, beliefs in which had been cruelly suppressed by false, white beliefs. They learned about the brotherhood of the plains, about how the whites had stolen what was rightfully theirs, had killed the buffalo which had been their livelihood, had divided, compressed, massacred, and finally imprisoned their people, leaving them little beyond alcoholism and despair. As with all successful lies, the cachet to this one was a large measure of truth.

Marvin Russell greeted the first orange limb of the sun, chanting something that might or might not have been authentic – no one really knew anymore, least of all him. But prison had not been an entirely negative experience. He'd arrived with a third-grade reading level, and left with high-school equivalency. Marvin Russell had not ever been a dullard, and it was not his fault either that he'd been betrayed by a public school system that had consigned him to failure before birth. He read books regularly, everything he could get on the history of his people. Not quite everything. He was highly selective in the editorial slant of the books he picked up. Anything in the least unfavourable to his people, of course, reflected the prejudice of whites. The Sioux had not been drunks before the whites arrived, had not lived in squalid little villages, had certainly not abused their children. That was all the invention of the white man.

But how to change things? he asked the sun. The glowing ball of gas was red with yet more blowing dust from this hot, dry summer, and the image that came to Marvin was of his brother's face. The stop-motion freeze-frame of the TV news. The local station had done things with the tape that the network had not. Every frame of the incident had been examined separately. The bullet striking John's face, two frames of his brother's face detaching itself from the head. Then the ghastly aftermath of the bullet's passage. The gunshot – damn that nigger and his vest! – and the hands coming up like something in a Roger Corman movie. He'd watched it five times, and each pixel of each image was so firmly fixed in his memory that he knew he'd never be able to forget it.

Just one more dead Indian. 'Yes, I saw some good Indians,' General William Tecumseh – a Native American name! – Sherman had said once. 'They were dead.' John Russell was dead, killed like so many without the chance for honorable combat, shot down like the animal a Native American was to whites. But more brutally than most. Marvin was sure the shot had been arranged with care. Cameras rolling. That wimp pussy reporter with her high-fashion clothes. She'd needed a lesson in what was what, and those FBI assassins had decided to give it to her. Just like the cavalry of old at Sand Creek and Wounded Knee and a hundred other nameless, forgotten battlefields.

And so Marvin Russell faced the sun, one of the gods of his people, and searched for answers. The answer wasn't here, the sun told him. His comrades were not reliable. John had died learning that. Trying to raise money with drugs! Using drugs! As though the whiskey the white man had used to destroy his people wasn't bad enough. The other 'warriors' were creatures of their white-made environment. They didn't know that they'd already been destroyed by it. They called themselves Sioux warriors, but they were drunkards, petty criminals who had labored and failed to succeed even in that undemanding field. In a rare flash of honesty – how could one be dishonest before one of his gods? – Marvin admitted to himself that they were less than he. As his brother had been. Stupid to join their foolish quest for drug money. And ineffective. What had they ever accomplished? They'd killed an FBI agent and a United States Marshal, but that was long in the past. Since then? Since then they had merely talked about their one shining moment.

But what sort of moment had it been? What had they accomplished? Nothing. The reservation was still there. The liquor was still there. The hopelessness was still there. Had anyone even noticed who they were and what they did? No. All they had accomplished was to anger the forces that continued to oppress them. So now the Warrior Society was hunted, even on its own reservation, living not like warriors at all, but like hunted animals. But they were supposed to be the hunters, the sun told him, not the prey.

Marvin was stirred by the thought. *He* was supposed to be the hunter. The whites were supposed to fear *him*. It had once been so, but was no more. He was supposed to be the wolf in the fold, but the white sheep had grown so strong that they didn't know there was such a thing as a wolf, and they hid behind formidable dogs who were not content to stay with the flocks, but hunted the wolves themselves until they and not the sheep were frightened, driven, nervous creatures, prisoners on their own range.

So, he had to leave his range.

He had to find his brother wolves. He had to find wolves for whom the hunt was still real.

CHAPTER 3

. . . a Single Sit

This was the day. His day. Captain Benjamin Zadin had enjoyed rapid career growth in the Israeli National Police. The youngest captain on the force, he was the last of three sons, the father of two sons of his own, David and Mordecai, and until very recently had been on the brink of suicide. The death of his beloved mother and the departure of his beautiful but adulterous wife had come within a single week, and that had only been two months before. Despite having done everything he'd ever planned on doing, he'd suddenly been faced with a life that seemed empty and pointless. His rank and pay, the respect of his subordinates, his demonstrated intelligence and clear-headedness in times of crisis and tension, his military record on dangerous and difficult border-patrol duty, they were all as nothing compared to an empty house of perverse memories.

Though Israel is regarded most often as 'the Jewish state,' that name disguises the fact that only a fraction of the country's population is actively religious. Benny Zadin had never been so, despite the entreaties of his mother. Rather he'd enjoyed the swinging life-style of a modern hedonist, and not seen the inside of a *shul* since his Bar Mitzvah. He spoke and read Hebrew because he had to – it was the national language – but the rules of his heritage were to him a curious anachronism, a backward aspect of life in what was otherwise the most modern of countries. His wife had only accentuated that. One might measure the religious fervor of Israel, he'd often joked, by the swimming suits on its many beaches. His wife's background was Norwegian. A tall, skinny

61

blonde, Elin Zadin looked about as Jewish as Eva Braun – that was their joke on the matter – and still enjoyed showing off her figure with the skimpiest of bikinis, and sometimes only half of that. Their marriage had been passionate and fiery. He'd known that she'd always had a wandering eye, of course, and had occasionally dallied himself, but her abrupt departure to another had surprised him – more than that, the manner of it had left him too stunned to weep or beg, had merely left him alone in a home that also contained several loaded weapons whose use, he knew, might easily have ended his pain. Only his sons had stopped that. He could not betray them as he'd been betrayed, he was too much of a man for that. But the pain had been – still was – very real.

Israel is too small a country for secrets. It was immediately noticed that Elin had taken up with another man, and the word had quickly made its way to Benny's station, where men could see from the hollow look around the eyes that their commander's spirit had been crushed. Some wondered how and when he would bounce back, but after a week the question had changed to whether he would do so at all. At that point, one of Zadin's squad sergeants had taken matters in hand. Appearing at his captain's front door on a Thursday evening, he'd brought with him Rabbi Israel Kohn. On that evening, Benjamin Zadin had rediscovered God. More than that, he told himself, surveying the Street of the Chain in Old Jerusalem, he knew again what it was to be a Jew. What had happened to him was God's punishment, no more, no less. Punishment for ignoring the words of his mother, punishment for his adultery, for the wild parties with his wife and others, for twenty years of evil thoughts and deeds while pretending to be a brave and upstanding commander of police and soldiers. But today he would change all that. Today he would break the law of man to expiate his sins against the Word of God.

It was early in the morning of what promised to be a blistering day, with a dry easterly wind blowing in from

Arabia. He had forty men arrayed behind him, all of them armed with a mixture of automatic rifles, gas guns, and other arms that fired 'rubber bullets,' more accurately called missiles, made of ductile plastic that could knock a grown man down, and if the marksman were very careful, stop a heart from blunt trauma. His police were needed to allow the law to be broken – which was not the idea that Captain Zadin's immediate superiors had in mind – and to stop the interference of others willing to break a higher law to keep him from his job. That was the argument Rabbi Kohn had used, after all. Whose law was it? It was a question of metaphysics, something far too complicated for a simple police officer. What was far simpler, as the Rabbi had explained, was the idea that the site of Solomon's Temple was the spiritual home of Judaism and the Jews. The site on Temple Mount had been chosen by God, and if men had disputed that fact, it was of little account. It was time for Jews to reclaim what God had given them. A group of ten conservative and Hasidic rabbis would today stake out the place where the new temple would be reconstructed in precise accordance with the Holy Scriptures. Captain Zadin had orders to prevent their march through the Chain Gate, to stop them from doing their work, but he would ignore those orders, and his men would do as he commanded, protecting them from the Arabs who might be waiting with much the same intentions as he was supposed to have.

He was surprised that the Arabs were there so early. No better than animals, really, the people who'd killed David and Motti. His parents had told all of their sons what it had been like to be a Jew in Palestine in the 1930s, the attacks, the terror, the envy, the open hatred, how the British had refused to protect those who had fought with them in North Africa – against those who had allied themselves with the Nazis. The Jews could depend on noone but themselves and their God, and keeping faith with their God meant reestablishing His Temple on the rock where Abraham had forged the covenant between his people and their Lord. The government either didn't understand that or was willing to play politics with the destiny of the only country in the world where Jews were truly safe. His duty as a Jew superseded that, even if he'd not known it until quite recently.

Rabbi Kohn showed up at the appointed time. Alongside him was Rabbi Eleazar Goldmark, a tattooed survivor of Auschwitz, where he had learned the importance of faith while in the face of death itself. Both men held a bundle of stakes and surveyors' string. They'd make their measurements, and from this day forward a relay of men would guard the site, eventually forcing the government of Israel to clear the site of Muslim obscenities. An upwell of popular support throughout the country, and a flood of money from Europe and America, would allow the project to be completed in five years – and then no one would ever be able to talk about taking this land away from those to whom God Himself had deeded it.

'Shit,' muttered someone behind Captain Zadin, but a turn and a look from his commander stifled whoever had blasphemed the moment of destiny.

Benny nodded to the two leading Rabbis, who marched off. The police followed their captain, fifty meters behind. Zadin prayed for the safety of Kohn and Goldmark, but knew that the danger they faced was fully accepted, as Abraham had accepted the death of his son as a condition of God's Law.

But the faith that had brought Zadin to this moment had blinded him to what should have been the obvious fact that Israel was indeed a country too small for secrets, and that fellow Jews who viewed Kohn and Goldmark as simply another version of Iran's fundamentalist ayatollas knew of what was happening, and that as a result the word had gotten out. TV crews were assembled in the square at the foot of the Wailing Wall. Some wore the hard hats of construction workers in anticipation of the rain of stones that surely was coming. Perhaps that was all the better, Captain Zadin thought as he followed the rabbis to the top of Temple Mount. The world should know what was happening. Unconsciously, he increased his pace to close on Kohn and Goldmark. Though they might accept the idea of martyrdom, his job was to protect them. His right hand went down to the holster at his hip and made sure the flap wasn't too tight. He might need that pistol soon.

The Arabs were there. It was a disappointment that there were so many, like fleas, like rats in a place they didn't belong. Just so long as they kept out of the way. They wouldn't, of course, and Zadin knew it. They were opposed to the Will of God. That was their misfortune.

Zadin's radio squawked, but he ignored it. It would just be his commander, asking him what the hell he was up to, and ordering him to desist. Not today. Kohn and Goldmark strode fearlessly to the Arabs blocking their path. Zadin nearly wept at their courage and their faith, wondering how the Lord would show his favor to them, hoping that they would be allowed to live. Behind him, about half his men were truly with him, which was possible because Benny had worked his watch bill to make it so. He knew without looking that they were not using their Lexan shields; instead, safety switches on their shoulder weapons were now being flicked to the OFF position. It was hard waiting for it, hard to anticipate the first cloud of stones that would be coming at any moment.

Dear God, please let them live, please protect them. Spare them as you spared Isaac.

Zadin was now less than fifty meters behind the two courageous rabbis, one Polish-born, a survivor of the infamous camps where his wife and child had died, where he had somehow kept his spirit and learned the importance of faith; the other American-born, a man who'd come to Israel, fought in her wars, and only then turned to God, as Benny himself had done so brief a span of days before.

The two were barely ten meters from the surly, dirty Arabs when it happened. The Arabs were the only ones who could see that their faces were serene, that they truly welcomed whatever the morning might hold for them, and only the Arabs saw the shock and the puzzlement on the face of the Pole, and the stunned pain on the American's at the realization of what fate had in mind.

On command, the leading row of Arabs, all of them teenagers with a lengthy history of confrontation, sat down. The hundred young men behind them did the same. Then the front row started clapping. And singing. Benny took a moment to comprehend it, though he was as fluent in Arabic as any Palestinian.

> We shall overcome
> We shall overcome
> We shall overcome some day

The TV crews were immediately behind the police. Several of them laughed in surprise at the savage irony of it. One of them was CNN correspondent Pete Franks who summed it up for everyone: '*Son of a BITCH!*' And in that moment Franks knew that the world had changed yet again. He'd been in Moscow for the first democratic meeting of the Supreme Soviet, in Managua the night the Sandinistas had lost their sure-thing election, and in Beijing to see the Goddess of Liberty destroyed. *And now this?* he thought. *The Arabs finally wised up. Holy shit.*

'I hope you have that tape rolling, Mickey.'

'Are they singing what I think they're singing?'

'Sure as hell sounds like it. Let's get closer.'

The leader of the Arabs was a twenty-year-old sociology student named Hashimi Moussa. His arm was permanently scarred from an Israeli club, and half his teeth were gone from a rubber bullet whose shooter had been especially angry on one particular day. No one questioned his courage. He'd had to prove that beyond doubt. He'd had to face death a dozen times before his position of leadership had been assured, but now he had it, and people listened to him, and he was able to activate an idea he'd cherished for five endless, patient years. It had taken three days to persuade them, then the fantastic good luck of a Jewish friend disgusted with the religious conservatives of his country who'd spoken a little too loudly about the plans of this day. Perhaps it was destiny, Hashimi thought, or the Will of Allah, or simply luck. Whatever it was, this was the moment he'd lived for since his fifteenth year, when he'd learned of Gandhi and King, and how they had defeated force with naked, passive courage. Persuading his people had meant stepping back from a warrior code that seemed part of their genes, but he'd done it. Now his beliefs would be put to the test.

All Benny Zadin saw was that his path was blocked. Rabbi Kohn said something to Rabbi Goldmark, but neither turned back to where the police were stopped, because to turn away was to admit defeat. Whether they were too shocked at what they saw or too angry, he would never learn. Captain Zadin turned to his men.

'Gas!' He'd planned this part in advance. The four men with gas guns were all religious men. They leveled their weapons and fired simultaneously into the crowd. The gas projectiles were dangerous and it was remarkable that no one was injured by them. In a few seconds, gray clouds of tear gas bloomed within the mass of sitting Arabs. But on command, each of them donned a mask to protect himself from it. This impeded their singing, but not their clapping or resolution, and it only enraged Captain Zadin further when the easterly wind blew the gas towards his men and away from the Arabs. Next, men with insulated gloves lifted the hot projectiles and threw them back towards the police. In a minute, they were able to remove their masks, and there was laughter in their singing now.

Next, Zadin ordered the rubber bullets launched. He had six men armed with these weapons, and from a range of fifty meters they could force any man to run for cover. The first volley was perfect, hitting six of the Arabs in the front line. Two cried out in pain. One collapsed, but not one man moved from his place except to succor the injured. The next volley was aimed at heads not chests, and Zadin had the satisfaction of seeing a face explode in a puff of red.

The leader – Zadin recognized the face from earlier

encounters – stood and gave a command the Israeli captain could not hear. But its significance became clear immediately. The singing became louder. Another volley of rubber bullets followed. One of his marksmen was very angry, the police commander saw. The Arab who'd taken one fully in the face now took another in the top of his head, and with it his body went limp in death. It should have warned Benny that he had already lost control of his men, but worse still was that he was losing control of himself.

Hashimi did not see the death of his comrade. The passion of the moment was overwhelming. The consternation on the faces of the two invading rabbis was manifest. He could not see the faces of the police behind their masks, but their actions, their movements, made their feelings clear. In a brilliant moment of clarity, he knew that he was winning, and he shouted again to his people to redouble their efforts. This they did in the face of fire and death.

Captain Benjamin Zadin stripped off his helmet and walked forcefully towards the Arabs, past the rabbis who had suddenly been struck with incomprehensible indecision. Would the Will of God be upset by the discordant singing of some dirty savages?

'Uh-oh,' Pete Franks observed, his eyes streaming from the gas that had blown over his face.

'I got it,' the cameraman said without bidding, zooming his lens in on the advancing Israeli police commander. 'Something is going to happen – this guy looks pissed, Pete!'

Oh, God, Franks thought. Himself a Jew, himself strangely at home in this barren but beloved land, he knew that history was occurring before his eyes yet again, was already composing his two or three minutes of verbal reporting that would overlay the tape his cameraman was recording for posterity, and was wondering if another Emmy might be in his future for doing his tough and dangerous job supremely well.

It happened quickly, much too quickly, as the captain strode directly to the Arab leader. Hashimi now knew that a friend was dead, his skull caved in by what was supposed to be a non-lethal weapon. He prayed silently for the soul of his comrade and hoped that Allah would understand the courage required to face death in this way. He would. Hashimi was sure of that. The Israeli approaching him was a face known to him. Zadin, the name was, a man who'd been there before often enough, just one more Israeli face most often hidden behind a Lexan mask and drawn gun, one more man unable to see Arabs as people, to whom a Muslim was the launcher for a rock or a Molotov cocktail. Well, today he'd learn different, Hashimi told himself. Today he'd see a man of courage and conviction.

Benny Zadin saw an animal, like a stubborn mule, like – what? He wasn't sure what he saw, but it wasn't a man, wasn't an Israeli. They'd changed tactics, that was all, and the tactics were womanly. They thought this would stand in the way of his purpose? Just as his wife had told him that she was leaving for the bed of a better man, that he could have the children, that his threats to beat her were empty words, that he couldn't do that, wasn't man enough to take charge of his own household. He saw that beautiful empty face and wondered why he hadn't taught her a lesson; she'd just stood there, not a meter away, staring at him, smiling – finally laughing at his inability to do what his manhood had commanded him to do, and, so, passive weakness had defeated strength.

But not this time.

'Move!' Zadin commanded in Arabic.

'No.'

'I will kill you.'

'You will not pass.'

'Benny!' a level-headed member of the police screamed. But it was too late for that. For Benjamin Zadin, the deaths of his brothers at Arab hands, the way his wife had left, and the way these people just sat in his way was too much. In one smooth motion, he drew his service automatic and shot Hashimi in the forehead. The Arab youth fell forward, and the singing and clapping

69

stopped. One of the other demonstrators started to move, but two others grabbed him, and held him fast. Others began praying for their two dead comrades. Zadin turned his gun hand to one of these, but though his finger pressed on the trigger, something stopped him a gram short of the release pressure. It was the look in the eyes, the courage there, something other than defiance. Resolution, perhaps . . . and pity, for the look on Zadin's face was anguish that transcended pain, and the horror of what he had done crashed through his consciousness. He had broken faith with himself. He had killed in cold blood. He had taken the life of someone who had threatened no man's life. He had murdered. Zadin turned to the rabbis, looking for something, he knew not what, and whatever he sought simply was not there. As he turned away, the singing began again. Sergeant Moshe Levin came forward and took the captain's weapon.

'Come on, Benny, let's get you away from this place.'

'What have I done?'

'It is done, Benny. Come with me.'

Levin started to lead his commander away, but he had to turn and look at the morning's handiwork. Hashimi's body was slumped over, a pool of blood coursing down between the cobblestones. The sergeant knew that he had to do or say something. It wasn't supposed to be like this. His mouth hung open, and his face swung from side to side. In that moment, Hashimi's disciples knew that their leader had won.

Ryan's phone rang at 2:03 Eastern Daylight Time. He managed to get it before the start of the second ring.

'Yeah?'

'This is Saunders at the Ops Center. Get your TV on. In four minutes, CNN is running something hot.'

'Tell me about it.' Ryan's hand fumbled for the remote controller and switched the bedroom TV on.

'You ain't gonna believe it, sir. We copied it off the CNN satellite feed, and Atlanta is fast-tracking it onto the network. I don't know how it got past Israeli censors. Anyway –'

'Okay, here it comes.' Ryan rubbed his eyes clear just in time. He had the TV sound muted to keep from disturbing his wife. The commentary was unnecessary in any case. 'Dear God in heaven . . .'

'That about covers it, sir,' the senior watch officer agreed.

'Send my driver out now. Call the Director, tell him to get in fast. Get hold of the duty officer at the White House Signals Office. He'll alert the people on his end. We need the DDI, and the desks for Israel, Jordan – hell, that whole area, all the desks. Make sure State's up to speed –'

'They have their own –'

'I know that. Call them anyway. Never assume anything in this business, okay?'

'Yes, sir. Anything else?'

'Yeah, send me about four hours' more sleep.' Ryan set the phone down.

'Jack . . . was that –' Cathy was sitting up. She'd just caught the replay.

'It sure was, babe.'

'What's it mean?'

'It means the Arabs just figured out how to destroy Israel.' *Unless we can save the place.*

Ninety minutes later, Ryan turned on the West Bend drip machine behind his desk before running over the notes from the night duty staff. It would be a day for coffee. He'd shaved in the car on the way in, and a look at the mirror showed that he'd not done a very good job of it. Jack waited until he had a full cup before marching into the Director's office. Charles Alden was there with Cabot.

'Good morning,' the National Security Advisor said.

'Yeah,' the Deputy Director replied in a husky voice. 'What do you suppose is good about it? The President know yet?'

'No, I didn't want to disturb him until we know something. I'll talk to him when he wakes up – sixish. Marcus, what do you think of your Israeli friends now?'

'Have we developed anything else, Jack?' Director Cabot asked his subordinate.

'The shooter is a police captain, according to the insignia. No name on him yet, no background. The Israelis have him in the jug somewhere and they're not saying anything. From the tape it looks like two definitely dead, probably a few more with minor injuries. Chief of Station has nothing he can report to us except that it really happened, and we have that on tape. Nobody seems to know where the TV crew is. We did not have any assets at the site when all this happened, so we're going exclusively from the news coverage.' *Again*, Ryan didn't add. The morning was bad enough. 'Temple Mount is shut down, guarded by their army now, nobody in or out, and they've closed access to the Wailing Wall also. That may be a first. Our embassy over there has not said anything, they're waiting for instructions from here. Same story for the others. No official reaction from Europe yet, but I expect that to change within the hour. They're at work already, and they got the same pictures from their Sky News service.'

'It's almost four,' Alden said, wearily checking his watch. 'In three hours people are going to have their breakfast upset – what a hell of a thing to see in the morning. Gentlemen, I think this one's going to be big. Ryan, you called it. I remember what you said last month.'

'Sooner or later, the Arabs had to wise up,' Jack said. Alden nodded agreement. It was gracious of him, Jack noted. He'd said the same thing in one of his books several years earlier.

'I think Israel can weather this, they always have –' Jack cut his Director off.

'No way, boss,' Ryan said. Someone had to straighten Cabot out. 'It's what Napoleon said about the moral and the physical. Israel depends absolutely on having the moral high-ground. Their whole cachet is that they are the only democracy in the region, that they are the guys in white hats. That concept died about three hours ago. Now they look like Bull – whoever it was – in Selma,

Alabama, except he used water hoses. The civil-rights community is going to go berserk.' Jack paused to sip at his coffee. 'It's a simple question of justice. When the Arabs were throwing rocks and cocktails, the police could say that they were using force in response to force. Not this time. Both the deaders were sitting down and not threatening anybody.'

'It's the isolated act of one deranged man!' Cabot announced angrily.

'Not so, sir. The one shot with a pistol was like you say, but the first victim was killed with two of those rubber bullets at a range of more than twenty yards – with *two* aimed shots from a single-shot weapon. That's cold, and it wasn't any accident.'

'Are we sure he's dead?' Alden asked.

'My wife's a doc, and he looked dead to her. The body spasmed and went limp, probably indicating death from massive head trauma. They can't say this guy tripped and fell onto the curb. This really changes things. If the Palestinians are smart, they'll double-down their bets. They'll stay with this tactic and wait for the world to respond. If they do that, they can't lose,' Jack concluded.

'I agree with Ryan,' Alden said. 'There'll be a UN resolution before dinner. We'll have to go along with it, and that just might show the Arabs that non-violence is a better weapon than rocks are. What will the Israelis say? How will they react?'

Alden knew what the answer was. This was to enlighten the DCI, so Ryan took the question. 'First they'll stonewall. They're probably kicking themselves for not intercepting the tape, but it's a little late for that. This was almost certainly an unplanned incident – I mean that the Israeli government is as surprised as we are – otherwise they would have grabbed the TV crew. That police captain is having his brain picked apart now. By lunchtime they'll say that he's crazy – hell, he probably is – and that this is an isolated act. How they do their damage control is predictable, but –'

'It's not going to work,' Alden interrupted. 'The President's going to have to have a statement out by nine.

We can't call this a "tragic incident." It's cold-blooded murder of an unarmed demonstrator by a state official.'

'Look, Charlie, this is just an isolated incident,' Director Cabot said again.

'Maybe so, but I've been predicting this for five years.' The National Security Advisor stood and walked to the windows. 'Marcus, the only thing that has held Israel together for the past thirty years has been the stupidity of the Arabs. Either they never recognized that Israeli legitimacy is based entirely on their moral position or they just didn't have the wit to care about it. Israel is now faced with an impossible ethical contradiction. If they really are a democracy that respects the rights of its citizens, they have to grant the Arabs broader rights. But that means playing hell with their political integrity, which depends on soothing their own extreme religious elements – and that crowd doesn't care a rat's ass about Arab rights, does it? But if they cave in to the religious zealots and stonewall, try to gloss over this thing, then they are not a democracy, and that imperils the political support from America without which they cannot survive economically or militarily. The same dilemma applies to us. Our support for Israel is based on their political legitimacy as a functioning liberal democracy, but that legitimacy just evaporated. A country whose police murder unarmed people has no legitimacy, Marcus. We can no more support an Israel that does things like this than we could have supported Somoza, Marcos, or any other tinpot dictator –'

'God damn it, Charlie! Israel isn't –'

'I know that, Marcus. They're not. They're really not. But the only way they can prove that is to change, to become true to what they have always claimed to be. If they stonewall on this, Marcus, they're doomed. They'll lean on their political lobby and find out it isn't there anymore. If it goes that far, then they embarrass our government even more than it already is, and we'll be faced with the possible necessity of overtly cutting them off. We can't do that either. We must find another alternative.' Alden turned back from the window. 'Ryan, that

74

idea of yours is now on the front burner. I'll handle the President and State. The only way we can get Israel out of this is to find some kind of a peace plan that works. Call your friend at Georgetown and tell him it's no longer a study. Call it Project PILGRIMAGE. By tomorrow morning I need a good sketch of what we want to do, and how we want to do it.'

'That's awful fast, sir,' Ryan observed.

'Then don't let me stop you, Jack. If we don't move quickly on this, God only knows what might happen. You know Scott Adler at State?'

'We've talked a few times.'

'He's Brent Talbot's best man. I suggest you get together with him after you check with your friends. He can cover your backside on the State Department flank. We can't trust that bureaucracy to do anything fast. Better pack some bags, boy, you're going to be busy. I want facts, positions, and a gold-plated evaluation just as fast as you can generate it, and I want it done black as a coal mine.' That last remark was aimed at Cabot. 'If this is going to work, we can't risk a single leak.'

'Yes, sir,' Ryan said. Cabot just nodded.

Jack had never been in the faculty residence at Georgetown. It struck him as odd, but he shoved that thought aside as breakfast was served. Their table overlooked a parking lot.

'You were right, Jack,' Riley observed. 'That was nothing to wake up to.'

'What's the word from Rome?'

'They like it,' the president of Georgetown University replied simply.

'How much?' Ryan asked.

'You're serious?'

'Alden told me two hours ago that this is now on the front burner.'

Riley accepted this news with a nod. 'Trying to save Israel, Jack?'

Ryan didn't know how much humor was in the question, and his physical state did not allow levity. 'Father, all I'm doing is following up on something – you know, orders?'

'I am familiar with the term. Your timing was pretty good on floating this thing.'

'Maybe so, but let's save the Nobel Prize for some other time, okay?'

'Finish your breakfast. We can still catch everybody over there before lunch, and you look pretty awful.'

'I feel pretty awful,' Ryan admitted.

'Everybody should stop drinking about forty,' Riley observed. 'After forty you really can't handle it anymore.'

'You didn't,' Jack noted.

'I'm a priest. I have to drink. What exactly are you looking for?'

'If we can get preliminary agreement from the major players, we want to get negotiations going ASAP, but this end of the equation has to be done very quietly. The President needs a quick evaluation of his options. That's what I'm doing.'

'Will Israel play?'

'If they don't, they're fucked – excuse me, but that's exactly where things are.'

'You're right, of course, but will they have the sense to recognize their position?'

'Father, all I do is gather and evaluate information. People keep asking me to tell fortunes, but I don't know how. What I do know is that what we saw on TV is going to ignite the biggest firestorm since Hiroshima, and we sure as hell have to try to do something before it burns up a whole region.'

'Eat. I have to think for a few minutes, and I do that best when I'm chewing on something.'

It was good advice, Ryan knew a few minutes later. The food soaked up the coffee acid in his stomach, and the energy from the food would help him get through the day. Inside an hour, he was on the move again, this time to the State Department. By lunch he was on his way home to pack, managing to nap for three hours along the way. He stopped back at Alden's White House office for a session that dragged far into the night. Alden had really taken charge there, and the skull session in his office covered a huge amount of ground. Before dawn Jack headed off to Andrews Air Force Base. He was able to call his wife from the VIP Lounge. Jack had hoped to take his son to a ball game over the weekend, but for him there wouldn't be a weekend. A final courier arrived from CIA, State, and the White House, delivering two hundred pages of data that he'd have to read on the way across the Atlantic.

CHAPTER 4

Promised Land

The U.S. Air Force's Ramstein air base is set in a German valley, a fact which Ryan found slightly unsettling. His idea of a proper airport was one on land that was flat as far as the eye could see. He knew that it didn't make much of a difference, but it was one of the niceties of air travel to which he'd become accustomed. The base supported a full wing of F-16 fighter-bombers, each of which was stored in its own bomb-proof shelter which in its turn was surrounded by trees – the German people have a mania for green things that would impress the most ambitious American environmentalists. It was one of those remarkable cases in which the wishes of the tree-huggers coincided exactly with military necessity. Spotting the aircraft shelters from the air was extremely difficult, and some of the shelters – French-built – had trees planted on top of them, making camouflage both aesthetically and militarily pleasing. The base also housed a few large executive aircraft, including a converted 707 with 'The United States of America' painted on it. Resembling a smaller version of the President's personal transport, it was known locally as 'Miss Piggy,' and was assigned to the use of the commander of USAF units in Europe. Ryan could not help but smile. Here were over seventy fighter aircraft tasked to the destruction of Soviet forces which were now drawing back from Germany, housed on an environmentally admirable facility, which was also home to a plane called Miss Piggy. The world was truly mad.

On the other hand, traveling Air Force guaranteed excellent hospitality and VIP treatment worthy of the name, in this case at an attractive edifice called the Cannon Hotel. The base commander, a full colonel, had met his VC-20B Gulfstream executive aircraft and whisked him off to his Distinguished Visitor's quarters where a slide-out drawer contained a nice collection of liquor bottles to help him to conquer jetlag with nine hours of drink-augmented sleep. That was just as well, because the available television service consisted of a single channel. By the time he awoke at about six in the morning, local, he was almost in sync with the time zones, stiff and hungry, having almost survived another bout with travel shock. He hoped.

Jack didn't feel like jogging. That was what he told himself. In fact he knew that he couldn't have jogged half a mile with a gun to his head. And so he walked briskly. He soon found himself being passed by early-morning exercise nuts, many of whom had to be fighter pilots, they were so young and lean. Morning mist hung in the trees that were planted nearly to the edge of the black-topped roads. It was much cooler than at home, with the still air disturbed every few minutes by the discordant roar of jet engines – 'the sound of freedom' – the audible symbol of military force that had guaranteed the peace of Europe for over forty years – now resented by the Germans, of course. Attitudes change as rapidly as the times. American power had achieved its goal and was becoming a thing of the past, at least as far as Germany was concerned. The inter-German border was gone. The fences and guard towers were down. The mines were gone. The plowed strip of dirt that had remained pristine for two generations to betray the foot-prints of defectors was now planted with grass and flowers. Locations in the east once examined in satellite photos or about which Western intelligence agencies had sought information at the cost of both money and blood were now walked over by camera-toting tourists, among whom were intelligence officers more shocked than bemused at the rapid changes that had come and gone like the sweep of a spring tide. *I knew that was right about this place*, some thought. Or, *How did we ever blow that one so badly?*

Ryan shook his head. It was more than amazing. The question of the two Germanys had been the centerpiece of East–West conflict since before his birth, had appeared to be the one unchanging thing in the world, the subject of enough white papers and Special National Intelligence Estimates and news stories to fill the entire Pentagon with pulp. All the effort, all the examination of minutiae, the petty disputes – gone. Soon to be forgotten. Even scholarly historians would never have the energy to look at all the data that had been thought important – crucial, vital, worthy of men's lives – and was now little more than a vast footnote to the end of the Second World War. This base had been one such item. Designed to house the aircraft whose task it was to clear the skies of Russian planes and crush a Soviet attack, it was now an expensive anachronism whose residential apartments would soon house German families. Ryan wondered what they'd do with the aircraft shelters like that one there . . . Wine cellars, maybe. The wine was pretty good.

'Halt!' Ryan stopped cold in his tracks and turned to see where the sound had come from. It was an Air Force security policeman – woman. Girl, actually, Ryan saw, though her M-16 rifle neither knew nor cared about plumbing fixtures.

'Did I do something wrong?'

'ID, please.' The young lady was quite attractive, and quite professional. She also had a backup in the trees. Ryan handed over his CIA credentials.

'I've never seen one of these, sir.'

'I came in last night on the VC-20. I'm staying over at the Inn, room 109. You can check with Colonel Parker's office.'

'We're on security alert, sir,' she said next, reaching for her radio.

'Just do your job, miss – excuse me, Sergeant Wilson. My plane doesn't leave till ten.' Jack leaned against a tree to stretch. It was too nice a morning to get excited about anything, even if there were two armed people who didn't know who the hell he was.

'Roger.' Sergeant Becky Wilson switched off her radio. 'The Colonel's looking for you, sir.'

'On the way back, I turn left at the Burger King?'

'That's right, sir.' She handed his ID back with a smile.

'Thanks, sarge. Sorry to bother you.'

'You want a ride back, sir? The colonel's waiting.'

'I'd rather walk. He can wait, he's early.' Ryan walked away from a buck-sergeant who now had to ponder the importance of a man who kept her base commander sitting on the front step of the Cannon. It took ten brisk minutes, but Ryan's directional sense had not left him, despite the unfamiliar surroundings and a six-hour time differential.

'Morning, sir!' Ryan said as he vaulted the wall into the parking lot.

'I set up a little breakfast with COMUSAFE staff. We'd like your views on what's happening in Europe.'

Jack laughed. 'Great! I'm interested in hearing yours.' Ryan walked off toward his room to dress. *What makes them think I know anything more than they do!* By the time his plane left, he'd learned four things he hadn't known. Soviet forces withdrawing from what had formerly been called East Germany were decidedly unhappy with the fact that there was no place for them to withdraw to. Elements of the former East German army were even less happy about their enforced retirement than Washington actually knew; they probably had allies among ex-members of the already de-established Stasi. Finally, though an even dozen members of the Red Army Faction had been apprehended in Eastern Germany, at least that many others had gotten the message and vanished before they, too, could be swept up by the *Bundes Kriminal Amt*, the German federal police. That explained the security alert at Ramstein, Ryan was told.

The VC-20B lifted off from the airfield just after ten in the morning, headed south. Those poor terrorists, he thought, devoting their lives and energy and intellect to something that was vanishing more swiftly than the

German countryside below him. Like children whose mother had died. No friends now. They'd hidden out in Czechoslovakia and the German Democratic Republic, blissfully unaware of the coming demise of both communist states. Where would they hide now? Russia? No chance. Poland? That was a laugh. The world had changed under them, and was about to change again, Ryan thought with a wistful smile. Some more of their friends were about to watch the world change. Maybe, he corrected himself. Maybe . . .

'Hello, Sergey Nikolayevich,' Ryan had said as the man had entered his office, a week before.

'Ivan Emmetovich,' the Russian had replied, holding out his hand. Ryan remembered the last time they'd been this close, on the runway of Moscow's Sheremetyevo Airport. Golovko had held a gun in his hand then. It had not been a good day for either, but as usual, it was funny the way things had worked out. Golovko, for having nearly, but not quite, prevented the greatest defection in Soviet history, was now First Deputy Chairman of the Committee for State Security. Had he succeeded, he would not have gone quite so far, but for being very good, if not quite good enough, he'd been noticed by his own President, and his career had taken a leap upward. His security officer had camped in Nancy's office with John Clark, as Ryan had led Golovko into his.

'I am not impressed.' Golovko looked around disapprovingly at the painted gypsum-board drywall. Ryan did have a single decent painting borrowed from a government warehouse, and, of course, the not-exactly-required photo of President Fowler over by the clothes tree on which Jack hung his coat.

'I do have a nicer view, Sergey Nikolayevich. Tell me, is the statue of Iron Feliks still in the middle of the square?'

'For the moment.' Golovko smiled. 'Your Director is out of town, I gather.'

'Yes, the President decided that he needed some advice.'

'On what?' Golovko asked with a crooked smile.

'Damned if I know,' Ryan answered with a laugh. *Lots of things*, he didn't say.

'Difficult, is it not? For both of us.' The new KGB Chairman was not a professional spook either – in fact, that was not unusual. More often than not, the director of that grim agency had been a Party man, but the Party was becoming a thing of history also, and Narmonov had selected a computer expert who was supposed to bring new ideas into the Soviet Union's chief spy agency. That would make it more efficient. Ryan knew that Golovko had an IBM PC behind his desk in Moscow now.

'Sergey, I always used to say that if the world made sense, I'd be out of a job. So, look what's happening. Want some coffee?'

'I would like that, Jack.' A moment later he expressed approval of the brew.

'Nancy sets it up for me every morning. So. What can I do for you?'

'I have often heard that question, but never in such surroundings as this.' There was a rumbling laugh from Ryan's guest. 'My God, Jack, do *you* ever wonder if this is all the result of some drug-induced dream?'

'Can't be. I cut myself shaving the other day, and I didn't wake up.'

Golovko muttered something in Russian that Jack didn't catch, though his translators would when they went over the tapes.

'I am the one who reports to our parliamentarians on our activities. Your Director was kind enough to respond favorably to our request for advice.'

Ryan couldn't resist that opening: 'No problem, Sergey Nikolayevich. You can screen all your information through me. I'd be delighted to tell you how to present it.' Golovko took it like a man.

'Thank you, but the Chairman might not understand.' With jokes aside, it was time for business.

'We want a *quid pro quo*.' The fencing began.

'And that is?'

'Information on the terrorists you guys used to support.'

'We cannot do that,' Golovko said flatly.

'Sure you can.'

Next Golovko waved the flag: 'An intelligence service cannot betray confidences and continue to function.'

'Really? Tell Castro that next time you see him,' Ryan suggested.

'You're getting better at this, Jack.'

'Thank you, Sergey. My government is most gratified indeed for your President's recent statement on terrorism. Hell, I like the guy personally. You know that. We're changing the world, man. Let's clean a few more messes up. You never approved of your government's support for those creeps.'

'What makes you believe that?' the First Deputy Chairman asked.

'Sergey, you're a professional intelligence officer. There's no way you can personally approve the actions of undisciplined criminals. I feel the same way, of course, but in my case it's personal.' Ryan leaned back with a hard look. He would always remember Sean Miller and the other members of the Ulster Liberation Army who'd made two earnest attempts to kill Jack Ryan and his family. Only three weeks earlier, after years exhausting every legal opportunity, after three writs to the Supreme Court, after demonstrations and appeals to the Governor of Maryland and the President of the United States for executive clemency, Miller and his colleagues had, one by one, walked into the gas chamber in Baltimore, and been carried out half an hour later, quite dead. *And may God have mercy on their souls,* Ryan thought. *If God has a strong enough stomach.* One chapter in his life was now closed for good.

'And the recent incident . . . ?'

'The Indians? That merely illustrates my case. Those "revolutionaries" were dealing drugs to make money. They're going to turn on you, the people you used to fund. In a few years, they're going to be more of a problem for you than they ever were for us.' That was entirely correct, of course, and both men knew it. The terrorist-drug connection was something the Soviets were starting to worry about. Free enterprise was starting most rapidly of all in Russia's criminal sector. That was as troubling to Ryan as to Golovko. 'What do you say?'

Golovko inclined his head to the side. 'I will discuss it with the Chairman. He will approve.'

'Remember what I said over in Moscow a couple of years back? Who needs diplomats to handle negotiations when you have real people to settle things?'

'I expected a quote from Kipling or something similarly poetic,' the Russian observed dryly. 'So, how do you deal with your Congress?'

Jack chuckled. 'Short version is, you tell them the truth.'

'I needed to fly eleven thousand kilometers to hear you say that?'

'You select a handful of people in your parliament you can trust to keep their mouths shut, and whom the rest of parliament trust to be completely honest – that's the hard part – and you brief them into everything they need to know. You have to set up ground rules –'

'Ground rules?'

'A baseball term, Sergey. It means the special rules that apply to a specific playing field.'

Golovko's eyes lit up. 'Ah, yes, that is a useful term.'

'Everyone has to agree on the rules, and you may never, ever break them.' Ryan paused. He was talking like a college lecturer again, and it wasn't fair to speak that way to a fellow professional.

Golovko frowned. That was the hard part, of course: never, ever breaking the rules. The intelligence business wasn't often that cut and dried. And conspiracy was part of the Russian soul.

'It's worked for us,' Ryan added.

Or has it? Ryan wondered. *Sergey knows if it has or not . . . well, he knows some things that I don't. He could tell me if we've had major leaks on The Hill since Peter Henderson . . . but at the same time he knows that we've penetrated so many of their operations despite their manic passion for the utmost secrecy.* Even the Soviets had admitted it publicly: the hemorrhage of defectors from KGB over the years had gutted scores of exquisitely-planned operations against America and the West. In the Soviet Union as in America, secrecy was designed to shield failure as well as success.

'What it comes down to is trust,' Ryan said after another moment. 'The people in your parliament are patriots. If they didn't love their country, why would they put up with all the bullshit aspects of public life? It's the same here.'

'Power,' Golovko responded at once.

'No, not the smart ones, not the ones you will be dealing with. Oh, there'll be a few idiots. We have them here. They are not an endangered species. But there are always those who're smart enough to know that the power that comes with government service is an illusion. The duty that comes along with it is always greater in magnitude. No, Sergey, for the most part you'll be dealing with people as smart and honest as you are.'

Golovko's head jerked at the compliment, one professional to another. He'd guessed right a few minutes earlier, Ryan was getting good at this. He started to think that he and Ryan were not really enemies any longer. Competitors, perhaps, but not enemies. There was more than professional respect between them now.

Ryan looked benignly at his visitor, smiling inwardly at having surprised him. And hoping that one of the people Golovko would select for oversight would be Oleg Kirolovich Kadishev, code-name SPINNAKER. Known in the media as one of the most brilliant Soviet parliamentarians in a bumptious legislative body struggling to build a new country, his reputation for intelligence and integrity belied the fact that he'd been on the CIA payroll for several years, the best of all the agents recruited by Mary Pat Foley. *The game goes on,* Ryan thought. The rules were different. The world was different. But the game went on. Probably always would, Jack thought, vaguely sorry it was true. But, hell, America even spied on Israel — it was called 'keeping an eye on things'; it was *never* called 'running an operation.' The oversight people in Congress would have leaked that in a minute. *Oh, Sergey, do you have a lot of new things to learn about!*

Lunch followed. Ryan took his guest to the executive dining room, where Golovko found the food somewhat better than KGB standards – something Ryan would not have believed. He also found that the top CIA executives wanted to meet him. The Directorate chiefs and their principal deputies all stood in line to shake his hand and be photographed. Finally there was a group photo before Golovko had taken the executive elevator back to his car. Then the people from Science and Technology, and security, had swept every inch of every corridor and room Golovko and his bodyguard had traveled. Finding nothing, they had swept again. And again. And once more, until it was decided that he had not availed himself of the opportunity to play his own games. One of the S&T people had lamented the fact that it just wasn't the same anymore.

Ryan smiled, remembering the remark. Things were happening so goddamned fast. He settled back into the chair and tightened his seatbelt. The VC-20 was approaching the Alps, and the air might be bumpy there.

'Want a paper, sir?' the attendant asked. It was a girl for a change, and a pretty one. Also married and pregnant. A pregnant staff sergeant. It made Ryan uneasy to be served by someone like that.

'What d'you have?'

'*International Trib.*'

'Great!' Ryan took the paper – and nearly gasped. There it was, right on the front page. Some bonehead had leaked one of the photos. Golovko, Ryan, the directors of S&T, Ops, Admin, Records, and Intelligence, plunging through their lunches. None of the American identities were secret, of course, but even so . . .

'Not a real good picture, sir,' the sergeant noted with a grin. Ryan was unable to be unhappy.

'When are you due, Sarge?'

'Five more months, sir.'

'Well, you'll be bringing your child into a much better world than the one either one of us was stuck with. Why don't you sit down and relax? I'm not liberated enough to be waited on by a pregnant lady.'

The *International Herald Tribune* is a joint venture of the *New York Times* and the *Washington Post*. The one sure way for Americans traveling in Europe to keep track of the ball scores and important comic strips, it had already broadened its distribution into what had been the Eastern Bloc, to serve American businessmen and tourists who were flooding the former communist nations. The locals also used it, both as a way to hone their English skills and to keep track of what was happening in America, more than ever a fascination to people learning how to emulate something they'd been raised to hate. In addition it was as fine an information source as had ever been available in those countries. Soon everyone was buying it, and the American management of the paper was expanding operations to broaden its readership still further.

One such regular reader was Günther Bock. He lived in Sofia, Bulgaria, having left Germany – the eastern part – rather hurriedly some months before, after a warning tip from a former friend in the Stasi. With his wife, Petra, Bock had been a unit leader in the Baader-Meinhof Gang, and after that had been crushed by the West German police, in the Red Army Faction. Two near arrests by the *Bundeskriminalamt* had frightened him across the Czech border, and thence on to the DDR, where he had settled into a quiet semi-retirement. With a new identity, new papers, a regular job – he never showed up, but the employment records were completely *in Ordnung* – he deemed himself safe. Neither he nor Petra had reckoned with the popular revolt that had overturned the government of the *Deutsche Demokratische Republik*, but they both decided that they could survive that change in anonymity. They'd never counted on a popular riot storming into Stasi headquarters, either. That event had resulted in the destruction of literally millions of documents. Many of the documents had not been destroyed, however. Many of the rioters had been agents of the *Bundesnachrichtendienst,* the West German intelligence agency, who'd been in the front ranks of the intruders, and known exactly which rooms to savage. Within days, people from the RAF had started disappearing. It had been hard to tell at first. The DDR telephone system was so decrepit that getting phone calls through had never been easy, and for obvious security reasons the former associates had not lived in the same areas, but when another married couple had failed to make a rendezvous for dinner, Günther and Petra had sensed trouble. Too late. While the husband made rapid plans to leave the country, five heavily armed GSG-9 commandos had kicked down the flimsy door of the Bock apartment in East Berlin. They'd found Petra nursing one of her twin daughters, but whatever sympathy they might have felt at so touching a scene had been mitigated by the fact that Petra Bock had murdered three West German citizens, one quite brutally. Petra was now in a maximum-security prison, serving a life sentence in a country where 'life' meant that you left prison in a casket or not at all. The twin daughters were the adopted children of a Munich police captain and his barren wife.

It was very odd, Günther thought, how much that stung him. After all, he was a revolutionary. He had plotted and killed for his cause. It was absurd that he would allow himself to be enraged by the imprisonment of his wife . . . and the loss of his children. But. But they had Petra's nose and eyes, and they'd smiled for him. They would not be taught to hate him, Günther knew. They'd never even be told who he and Petra had been. He'd dedicated himself to something larger and grander than mere corporeal existence. He and his colleagues had made a conscious and reasoned decision to build a better and more just world for the common man, and yet – and yet he and Petra had decided, also in a reasoned and conscious way, to bring into it children who would learn their parents' ways, to be the next generation of Bocks, to eat the fruits of their parents' heroic labor. Günther was enraged that this might not happen.

Worse still was his bewilderment. What *had* happened was quite impossible. *Unmöglich. Unglaublich.* The people, the common *Volk* of the DDR had risen up like revolutionaries themselves, forsaking their nearly perfect socialist state, opting instead to merge with the exploitative monstrosity crafted by the imperialist powers. They'd been seduced by Blaupunkt appliances and Mercedes automobiles, and – what? Günther Bock genuinely did not understand. Despite his inborn intelligence, the events did not connect into a comprehensible pattern. That the people of his country had examined 'scientific socialism' and decided it did not work and could never work – that was too great a leap of imagination for him to make. He'd committed too much of his life to Marxism ever to deny it. Without Marxism, after all, he was a criminal, a common murderer. Only his heroic revolutionary *ethos* elevated his activities above the acts of a thug. But his revolutionary *ethos* had been summarily rejected by his own chosen beneficiaries. That was simply impossible. *Unmöglich.*

It wasn't quite fair that so many impossible things piled one upon another. As he opened the paper he'd bought twenty minutes before at a kiosk seven blocks from his current residence, the photo on the front page caught his eye, as the paper's editor had fully intended.

CIA FETES KGB, the caption began.

'Was ist das denn für Quatsch!' Günther muttered.

'In yet another remarkable turn in a remarkable time, the Central Intelligence Agency hosted the First Deputy Chairman of the KGB in a conference concerning "issues of mutual concern" to the world's two largest intelligence empires . . .' the story read. 'Informed sources confirm that the newest area of East–West cooperation will include information-sharing on the increasingly close ties between international terrorists and the international drug trade. CIA and KGB will work together to . . .'

Bock set the paper down and stared out the window.

He knew what it was to be a hunted animal. All revolutionaries did. It was the path he had chosen, along with Petra, and all their friends. The task was a clear one. They would test their cunning and skill against their enemies. The forces of light against the forces of darkness. Of course, it was the forces of light that had to run and hide, but that was a side issue. Sooner or later, the situation would be reversed when the common people saw the truth and sided with the revolutionaries. Except for one little problem. The common people had chosen to go another way. And the terrorist world was rapidly running out of dark places in which the forces of light might hide.

He'd come to Bulgaria for two reasons. Of all the former East Bloc countries, Bulgaria was the most backward and because of it had managed the most orderly transition from communist rule. In fact, communists still ran the country, though under different names, and the country was still politically safe, or at least neutral. The Bulgarian intelligence apparat, once the source of designated killers for KGB whose hands had finally become too clean for such activity, was still peopled with reliable friends. *Reliable friends*, Günther thought. But the Bulgarians were still in the thrall of their Russian masters – associates, now – and if KGB were really cooperating with CIA . . . The number of safe places was being reduced by one more digit.

Günther Bock should have felt a chill at the increased personal danger. Instead his face flushed and pulsed with rage. As a revolutionary he'd often enough bragged that every hand in the world was turned against him – but whenever he'd said that, it had been with the inner realization that such was not and would never be the case. Now his boast was becoming reality. There were still places to run, still contacts he could trust. But how many? How soon before trusted associates would bend to the changes in the world? The Soviets had betrayed themselves and world socialism. The Germans. The Poles. The Czechs, the Hungarians, the Romanians. Who was next?

Couldn't they see? It was all a trap, some kind of incredible conspiracy of counter-revolutionary forces. A lie. They were casting away what could be – should be – was – the perfect social order of structured freedom from want, orderly efficiency, of fairness and equality. Of . . .

Could that all be a lie? Could it all have been a horrible mistake? Had he and Petra killed those cowering exploiters for nothing?

But it didn't matter, did it? Not to Günther Bock, not right now. He was soon to be hunted again. One more safe patch of ground was about to become a hunting preserve for his enemies. If the Bulgarians shared their papers with the Russians, if the Russians had a few men in the right office, with the right credentials and the right access, his address and new identity could already be on its way to Washington, and from there to BND headquarters, and in a week's time he might be sharing a cell close to Petra's.

Petra, with her light brown hair and laughing blue eyes. As brave a girl as any man could want. Seemingly cold to her victims, wonderfully warm to her comrades. So fine a mother she'd been to Erika and Ursel, so superior at that task as she'd been at every other she'd ever attempted. Betrayed by supposed friends, caged like an animal, robbed of her own offspring. His beloved Petra, comrade, lover, wife, believer. Robbed of her life. And now he was being driven farther from her. There had to be a way to change things back.

But first, he had to get away.

Bock set the paper down and tidied up the kitchen. When things were clean and neat, he packed a single bag and left the apartment. The elevator had quit again, and he walked down the four flights to the street. Once there he caught a tram. In ninety minutes he was at the airport. His passport was a diplomatic one. In fact he had six of them carefully concealed in the lining of his Russian-made suitcase, and, ever the careful man, three of them were the numerical duplicates of others held by real Bulgarian diplomats, unknown to the Foreign

Ministry office that kept the records. That guaranteed him free access to the most important ally of the international terrorist: air transport. Before time for lunch, his flight rotated off the tarmac, headed south.

Ryan's flight touched down at a military airport outside Rome just before noon, local time. By coincidence they rolled in right behind yet another VC-20B of the 89th Military Airlift Wing that had arrived only a few minutes earlier from Moscow. The black limousine on the apron was waiting for both aircraft.

Deputy Secretary of State Scott Adler greeted Ryan as he stepped off with an understated smile.

'Well?' Ryan asked through the airport sounds.

'It's a go.'

'Damn,' Ryan said as he took Adler's hand. 'How many more miracles can we expect this year?'

'How many do you want?' Adler was a professional diplomat who'd worked his way up the Russian side of the State Department. Fluent in their language, well-versed in their politics, past and present, he understood the Soviets as did few men in government – including Russians themselves. 'You know the hard part about this?'

'Getting used to hearing *da* instead of *nyet*, right?'

'Takes all the fun out of negotiations. Diplomacy can really be a bitch when both sides are reasonable.' Adler laughed as the car pulled off.

'Well, this ought to be a new experience for both of us,' Jack observed soberly. He turned to watch 'his' aircraft prepare for an immediate departure. He and Adler would be traveling together for the rest of the trip.

They sped towards central Rome with the usual heavy escort. The Red Brigade, so nearly exterminated a few years earlier, was back in business, and even if it hadn't been, the Italians were careful protecting foreign dignitaries. In the right-front seat was a serious-looking chap with a little Beretta squirt-gun. There were two lead cars, two chase cars, and enough cycles for a motocross race. The speedy progress down the ancient streets of Rome made Ryan wish he were back in an airplane. Every Italian driver, it seemed, had ambitions to ride in the Formula One circuit. Jack would have felt safer in a car with Clark, driving an unobtrusive vehicle on a random path, but in his current position his security arrangements were ceremonial in addition to being practical. There was one other consideration, of course . . .

'Nothing like a low profile,' Jack muttered to Adler.

'Don't sweat it. Every time I've come here it's been the same way. First time?'

'Yep. First time in Rome. I wonder how I've ever missed coming here – always wanted to, the history and all.'

'A lot of that,' Adler agreed. 'Think we might make a little more?'

Ryan turned to look at his colleague. Making history was a new thought to him. Not to mention a dangerous one. 'That's not my job, Scott.'

'If this does work, you know what'll happen.'

'Frankly, I never bothered thinking about that.'

'You ought to. No good deed ever goes unpunished.'

'You mean Secretary Talbot . . . ?'

'No, not him. Definitely not my boss.'

Ryan looked forward to see a truck scuttle out of the way of the motorcade. The Italian police officer riding on the extreme right of the motorcycle escort hadn't flinched a millimeter.

'I'm not in this for credit. I just had an idea, is all. Now I'm just the advance man.'

Adler shook his head slightly and kept his peace. *Jesus, how did you ever last this long in government service!*

The striped jumpsuits of the Swiss Guards had been designed by Michaelangelo. Like the red tunics of the British guardsmen, they were anachronisms from a bygone era when it had made sense for soldiers to wear brightly-coloured uniforms, and also, like the guardsmen uniforms, they were kept on more for their attractiveness to tourists than for any practical reason. The men and their weapons look so *quaint*. The Vatican guards carried halberds, evil-looking long-handled axes made

94

originally for infantrymen to unhorse armored knights –
as often as not by crippling the horse the enemy might
be riding; horses didn't fight back very well, and war is
ever a practical business. Once off his mount, an armored
knight was dispatched with little more effort than that
required to break up a lobster – and about as much
remorse. People thought medieval weapons romantic
somehow, Ryan told himself, but there was nothing
romantic about what they were designed to do. A
modern rifle might punch holes in some other fellow's
anatomy. These were made to dismember. Both methods
would kill, of course, but at least rifles made for neater
burial.

The Swiss guards had rifles, too, Swiss rifles made by
SIG. Not all of them wore Renaissance costumes, and
since the attempt on John Paul II, many of the guards
had received additional training, quietly and unobtrus-
ively, of course, since such training did not exactly fit
the image of the Vatican. Ryan wondered what Vatican
policy was on the use of deadly force, whether the chief
of the guards chafed at the rules imposed from on high
by people who certainly did not appreciate the nature of
the threat and the need for decisive protective action. But
they'd do their best within their constraints, grumbling
among themselves and voicing their opinions when the
time seemed right, just like everyone else in that
business.

A bishop met them, an Irishman named Shamus
O'Toole whose thick red hair clashed horribly with his
clothing. Ryan was first out of the car, and his first
thought was a question: was he supposed to kiss
O'Toole's ring or not? He didn't know. He hadn't met a
real bishop since his confirmation – and it had been a
long time since sixth grade in Baltimore. O'Toole deftly
solved that problem by grasping Ryan's hand in a bearish
grip.

'So many Irishmen in the world!' he said with a wide
grin.

'Somebody has to keep things straight, Excellency.'

'Indeed, indeed!' O'Toole greeted Adler next. Scott was

Jewish and had no intentions to kiss anyone's ring. 'Would you come with me, gentlemen?'

Bishop O'Toole led them into a building whose history might have justified three scholarly volumes, plus a picture book for its art and architecture. Jack barely noticed the two metal detectors they passed through on the third floor. Leonardo da Vinci might have done the job, so skillfully were they concealed in doorframes. Just like the White House. The Swiss guards didn't all wear uniforms. Some of the people prowling the halls in soft clothes were too young and too fit to be bureaucrats, but for all that the overall impression was a cross between visiting an old art museum and a cloister. The clerics wore cassocks, and the nuns – they were here in profusion also – were not wearing the semi-civilian attire adopted by their American counterparts. Ryan and Adler were parked briefly in a waiting room, more to appreciate the surroundings than to inconvenience them, Jack was sure. A Titian madonna adorned the opposite wall, and Ryan admired it while Bishop O'Toole announced the visitors.

'God, I wonder if he ever did a small painting?' Ryan muttered. Adler chuckled.

'He did know how to capture a face and a look and a moment, didn't he? Ready?'

'Yeah,' Ryan said. He felt oddly confident.

'Gentlemen!' O'Toole said from the open door. 'Will you come this way, please?' They walked through yet another anteroom. This one had two secretarial desks, both unoccupied, and another set of doors that looked fourteen feet tall.

The office of Giovanni Cardinal D'Antonio would have been used in America for balls or formal occasions of state. The ceiling was frescoed, the walls covered with blue silk, and the floor in ancient hardwood accented with rugs large enough for an average living room. The furniture was probably the most recent in manufacture, and that looked to be at least two hundred years old, brocaded fabric taut over the cushions and gold leaf on the curved wooden legs. A silver coffee service told Ryan where to sit.

The cardinal came towards them from his desk, smiling in the way that a king might have done a few centuries earlier to greet a favored minister. D'Antonio was a man of short stature, and clearly one who enjoyed good food. He must have been a good forty pounds overweight. The room air reported that he was a man who smoked, something he ought to have stopped, since he was rapidly approaching seventy years of age. The old, pudgy face had an earthy dignity to it. The son of a Sicilian fisherman, D'Antonio had mischievous brown eyes to suggest a roughness of character that fifty years of service to the church had not wholly erased. Ryan knew his background and could easily see him pulling in nets at his father's side, back a very long time ago. The earthiness was also a useful disguise for a diplomat, and that's what D'Antonio was by profession, whatever his vocation might have been. A linguist like many Vatican officials, he was a man who had spent thirty years practicing his trade, and the lack of military power that had crippled his efforts at making the world change had merely taught him craftiness. In intelligence parlance he was an agent of influence, welcome in many settings, always ready to listen or offer advice. Of course, he greeted Adler first.

'So good to see you again, Scott.'

'Eminence, a pleasure as always.' Adler took the offered hand and smiled his diplomat's smile.

'And you are Dr Ryan. We have heard so many things about you.'

'Thank you, Your Eminence.'

'Please, please.' D'Antonio waved both men to a sofa so beautiful that Ryan flinched at resting his weight on it. 'Coffee?'

'Yes, thank you,' Adler said for both of them. Bishop O'Toole did the pouring, then sat down to take notes. 'So good of you to allow us in at such short notice.'

'Nonsense.' Ryan watched in no small amazement as the cardinal reached inside his cassock and pulled out a

97

cigar holder. A tool that looked like silver, but was probably stainless steel, performed the appropriate surgery on the largish brown tube, then D'Antonio lit it with a gold lighter. There wasn't even an apology about the sins of the flesh. It was as though the cardinal had quietly flipped off the 'dignity' switch to put his guests at ease. More likely, Ryan thought, he merely worked better with a cigar in his hand. Bismarck had felt the same way.

'You are familiar with the rough outlines of our concept,' Adler opened.

'*Si*. I must say that I find it very interesting. You know, of course, that the Holy Father proposed something along similar lines some time ago.'

Ryan looked up at that. He hadn't.

'When the initiative first came out, I did a paper on its merits,' Adler said. 'The weak point was the inability to address security considerations, but in the aftermath of the Iraq situation, we have the opening. Also, you realize, of course, that our concept does not exactly –'

'Your concept is acceptable to us,' D'Antonio said with a regal wave of his cigar. 'How could it be otherwise?'

'That, Eminence, is precisely what we wanted to hear.' Adler picked up his coffee. 'You have no reservations?'

'You will find us highly flexible, so long as there is genuine good will among the active parties. If there is total equality among the participants, we can agree unconditionally to your proposal.' The old eyes sparkled. 'But can you guarantee equality of treatment?'

'I believe we can,' Adler said seriously.

'I think it should be possible, else we are all charlatans. What of the Soviets?'

'They will not interfere. In fact, we are hoping for open support. In any case, what with the distractions they already have –'

'Indeed. They will benefit from the diminution of the discord in the region, the stability on various markets, and general international good will.'

Amazing, Ryan thought. *Amazing how matter-of-factly people have absorbed the changes in the world.*

*As though they had been expected. They had not. Not
by anyone. If anyone had suggested their possibility ten
years earlier, he would have been institutionalized.*

'Quite so.' The Deputy Secretary of State set down his
cup. 'Now on the question of the announcement . . .'

Another wave of the cigar. 'Of course, you will want
the Holy Father to make it.'

'How very perceptive,' Adler observed.

'I am not yet completely senile,' the cardinal replied.
'And press leaks?'

'We would prefer none.'

'That is easily accomplished in this city, but in yours?
Who knows of this initiative?'

'Very few,' Ryan said, opening his mouth for the first
time since sitting down. 'So far, so good.'

'But on your next stop . . . ?' D'Antonio had not been
informed of their next stop, but it was the obvious
one.

'That might be a problem,' Ryan said cautiously.
'We'll see.'

'The Holy Father and I will both be praying for your
success.'

'Perhaps this time your prayers will be answered,'
Adler said.

Fifty minutes later, the VC-20B lifted off again. It
soared upward across the Italian coast, then turned
southwest to recross Italy on the way to its next destination.

'Jesus, that was fast,' Jack observed when the seatbelt
light went off. He kept his buckled, of course. Adler lit
a cigarette and blew smoke at the window on his side of
the cabin.

'Jack, this is one of those situations where you do it
fast or it doesn't get done.' He turned and smiled.
'They're rare, but they happen.'

The cabin attendant – this one was a male – came aft
and handed both men copies of a print-out that had just
arrived on the aircraft facsimile machine.

'What?' Ryan observed crossly. 'What gives?'

*

In Washington people do not always have time to read the papers, at least not all the papers. To assist those in government service to see what the press is saying about things is an in-house daily press-summary sheet called *The Early Bird*. Early editions of all major American papers are flown to D.C. on regular airline flights, and before dawn they are vetted for stories relating to all manner of government operations. Relevant material is clipped and photocopied, then distributed by the thousands to various offices whose staff members then repeat the process by highlighting individual stories for their superiors. This process is particularly difficult in the White House, whose staff members are by definition interested in everything.

Dr Elizabeth Elliot was Special Assistant to the President for National Security Affairs. The immediate subordinate to Dr Charles Alden, whose title was the same, but without the 'Special,' Liz, also referred to as 'E.E.,' was dressed in a fashionable linen suit. Current fashions dictated that women's 'power' clothing was not mannish but feminine, the idea being that since even the most obtuse of men would be able to tell the difference between themselves and women, there was little point in trying to conceal the truth. The truth was that Dr Elliot was not physically unattractive and enjoyed dressing to emphasize the fact. Tall at five feet eight inches, and with a slender figure that long work hours and mediocre food sustained, she did not like playing second-fiddle to Charlie Alden. And besides, Alden was a Yalie. She'd most recently been Professor of Political Science at Bennington, and resented the fact that Yale was considered more prestigious by whatever authorities made such judgments.

Current work schedules at the White House were easier than those of only a few years earlier, at least in the national-security shop. President Fowler did not feel the need for a first-thing-in-the-morning intelligence briefing. The world situation was far more pacific than any of his predecessors had known, and Fowler's main problems were of the domestic political variety. Commentary on that could readily be had from watching morning TV news shows, something Fowler did by watching two or more TV sets at the same time, something that had infuriated his wife and still bemused his staffers. That fact meant that Dr Alden didn't have to arrive until 8:00 or so to get his morning briefing, after which he would brief the President at 9:30. President Fowler didn't like dealing directly with the briefing officers from CIA. As a result, it was E.E. who had to arrive just after six so that *she* could screen dispatches and message traffic, confer with the CIA watch officers (she didn't like them either), and their counterparts from State and Defense. She also got to read over *The Early Bird*, and to highlight items of interest for her boss, the estimable Dr Charles Alden.

Like I'm a goddamned addle-brained simpering secretary, E.E. fumed.

Alden, she thought, was a logical contradiction. A liberal who talked tough, a skirt-chaser who supported women's rights, a kindly, considerate man who probably enjoyed using her like a goddamned functionary. That he was also a distinguished observer and an amazingly accurate forecaster of events, with an even dozen books – each of them thoughtful and perceptive – was beside the point. He was in *her* job. It had been promised to her while Fowler had still been a longshot candidate. The compromise that had placed Alden in his west-wing corner office and her in the basement was merely another of those acts that political figures use as excuses to violate their word without anything more than a perfunctory apology. The Vice President had demanded and gotten the concession at the convention; he'd also gotten what should have been her office on the main level for one of his own people, relegating her to this most prestigious of dungeons. In return for that, the Veep was a team player, and his tireless campaigning was widely regarded as having made the difference. The Vice President had delivered California, and without California, J. Robert Fowler would still be governor of Ohio. And so she had a twelve-by-fifteen office in the basement, playing secretary and/or administrative assistant to a goddamned Yalie who appeared once a month on the Sunday talk shows, and hobnobbed with chiefs of state with her as lady-in-goddamned-waiting.

Dr Elizabeth Elliot was in her normal early-morning mood, which was foul, as any White House regular could testify. She walked out of her office and into the White House Mess for a refill of her coffee cup. The strong drip coffee only made her mood the fouler, a thought that stopped her in her tracks and forced a self-directed smile she never bothered displaying for any of the security personnel who checked her pass every morning at the west ground-level entrance. They were just cops, after all, and cops were nothing to get excited about. Food was served by Navy stewards, and the only good thing about them was that they were largely minorities, many Filipinos in what she deemed a disgraceful carryover from America's colonial-exploitation period. The long-service secretaries and other support personnel were not political, hence mere bureaucrats of one description or another. The important people in this building were political. What little charm E.E. had was saved for them. The Secret Service agents observed her movements with about as much interest as they might have accorded the President's dog, if he'd had a dog, which he didn't. Both they and the professionals who ran the White House, despite the arrivals and departures of various self-inflated egos in human form, regarded her as just another of many politically-elevated individuals who would depart in due course while the pros stayed on, faithfully doing their duty in accordance with their oaths of office. The White House caste system was an old one, with each regarding all the others as less than itself.

Elliot returned to her desk, and set her coffee down to get a good stretch. The swivel chair was comfortable – the physical arrangements here were first-rate, far better than those at Bennington – but the endless weeks of early mornings and late nights had taken a physical toll in addition to that on her character. She told herself that she ought to return to working out. At least to walk.

Many staffers took part of lunch to pace up and down the mall. The more energetic even jogged. Some female staffers took to jogging with military officers detailed to the building, especially the single ones, doubtless drawn to the short haircuts and simplistic mentalities that attached to uniformed service. But E.E. didn't have time for that, and so she settled for a stretch before sitting down with a muttered curse. Department head at America's most important women's college, and here she was playing secretary to a goddamned Yalie. But bitching didn't ever fix things, and she went back to work.

She was halfway through the *Bird*, and flipped to a new page as she picked up her yellow highlighting pen. The articles were unevenly set. Almost all were just crooked enough on the redacted pages to annoy, and E.E. was a pathologically neat person. At the top of page eleven was a small piece from the *Hartford Courant*. ALDEN PATERNITY CASE read the headline. Her coffee mug stopped in mid-flight.

What!

> Suit papers will be filed this week in New Haven by Ms. Marsha Blum, alleging that her newly-born daughter was fathered by Professor Charles W. Alden, former Chairman of the Department of History at Yale, and currently National Security Advisor to President Fowler. Claiming a two-year relationship with Dr Alden, Ms. Blum, herself a doctoral candidate in Russian history, is suing Alden for lack of child support . . .

'That randy old goat,' Elliot whispered to herself.

And it was true. That thought came to her in a blazing moment of clarity. It had to be. Alden's amorous adventures were already the subject of humorous columns in the *Post*. Charlie chased skirts, slacks, any garment that had a woman inside it.

Marsha Blum . . . Jewish? Probably. The jerk was

banging one of his doctoral students. Knocked her up even. I wonder why she just didn't get an abortion and be done with it! I bet he dumped her, and she was so mad . . .

Oh, God, he's scheduled to fly to Saudi Arabia later today . . .

We can't let that happen . . .

The idiot. No warning. He didn't talk to anyone about it. He couldn't have. I would have heard. Secrets like that last about as long as they take to repeat in the lavatory. What if he hadn't even known himself? Could this Blum girl be that angry with Charlie? That resulted in a smirk. *Sure, she could.*

Elliot lifted her phone . . . and paused for a moment. You didn't just call the President in his bedroom. Not for just anything. Especially not when you stood to make a personal gain from what happened.

On the other hand . . .

What would the Vice President say? Alden was really his man. But the VP was pretty strait-laced. Hadn't he warned Charlie to keep a lower profile on his womanizing? Yes, three months ago. The ultimate political sin. He'd gotten caught. Not with his hand in the cookie jar either. That brought out a short bark of a laugh. *Stumpfing* one of his seminar girls! What an asshole! And this guy was telling the President how to conduct affairs of state. That almost unleashed a giggle.

Damage control.

The feminists would freak. They'd ignore the stupidity of the Blum girl for not taking care of her unwanted — was it? — pregnancy in the feminist way. After all, what was 'pro-choice' all about? She'd made her choice, period. To the feminist community it was simply a case of a male turd who had exploited a sister and was now employed by a supposedly pro-feminist President.

The anti-abortion crowd would also disapprove . . . even more violently. They'd recently done something intelligent, which struck Elizabeth Elliot as nothing short of miraculous. Two stoutly conservative senators were sponsoring legislation to compel 'illegitimate fathers' to support their irregular offspring. If abortion was to be outlawed, it had finally occurred to those Neanderthals that someone had to do something about the unwanted children. Moreover, that crowd was on another morality kick, and they were kicking the Fowler Administration for a number of reasons already. To the right-wing nuts, Alden would just be another irresponsible lecher, a white one – so much the better – and one in an administration they loathed.

E.E. considered all the angles for several minutes, forcing herself to be dispassionate, examining the options, thinking it through from Alden's angle. What could he do? Deny it was his? Well, a genetic testing would establish that, and that was guts-ball, something for which Alden probably didn't have the stomach. If he admitted it . . . well, clearly he couldn't marry the girl (the article said she was only twenty-four). Supporting the child would be an admission of paternity, a gross violation of academic integrity. After all, professors weren't supposed to bed their students. That it happened, as E.E. well knew, was beside the point. As with politics, the rule in academia was to avoid detection. What might be the subject of a hilarious anecdote over a faculty lunch table became infamy in the public press.

Charlie's gone, and what timing . . .

E.E. punched the number to the upstairs bedroom.

'The President, please. This is Dr Elliot calling.' A pause while the Secret Service agent asked if the President would take the call. *God, I hope I didn't catch him on the crapper!* But it was too late to worry about that.

The hand came off the mouthpiece at the other end of the circuit. Elliot heard the whirring sound of the President's shaver, then a gruff voice.

'What is it, Elizabeth?'

'Mr President, we have a little problem I think you need to see right away.'

'Right away?'

'Now, sir. It's potentially damaging. You'll want Arnie there also.'

'It's not the proposal that we're –'

'No, Mr President. Something else. I'm not kidding. It's potentially very serious.'

'Okay, come on up in five minutes. I presume you can wait for me to brush my teeth?' A little presidential humor.

'Five minutes, sir.'

The connection was broken. Elliot set the phone down slowly. Five minutes. She'd wanted more time than that. Quickly she took her makeup case from a desk drawer and hurried off to the nearest bathroom. A quick look in the mirror . . . no, first she had to take care of the morning coffee. Her stomach told her that an antacid tablet might be a good idea, too. She did that, then rechecked her hair and face. They'd do, she decided. Just some minor repairs to her cheek highlights . . .

Elizabeth Elliot, Ph.D., walked stiffly back to her office and took another thirty seconds to compose herself before lifting *The Early Bird* and leaving for the elevator. It was already at the basement level, the door open. It was manned by a Secret Service agent who smiled good morning at the arrogant bitch only because he was inveterately polite, even to people like E.E.

'Where to?'

Dr Elliot smiled most charmingly. 'Going up,' she told the surprised agent.

CHAPTER 5

Changes and Guards

Ryan stayed in VIP quarters at the U.S. Embassy, waiting
for the clock hands to move. He was taking Dr Alden's
place in Riyadh, but since he was visiting a prince, and
princes don't like their calendars rearranged any more
than the next man, he had to sit tight while the clock
simulated Alden's flight time across the world to where
Ryan was. After three hours he got tired of watching
satellite TV, and took a walk, accompanied by a discreet
security guard. Ordinarily, Ryan would have availed
himself of the man's services as a tour guide, but not
today. Now he wanted his brain in neutral. It was his
first time in Israel and he wanted his impressions to
be his own while his mind played over what he'd been
watching on TV.

It was hot here on the streets of Tel Aviv, and hotter
still where he was going, of course. The streets were
busy with people scurrying about shopping or pursuing
business. There was the expected number of police
about, but more discordant was the occasional civilian
toting an Uzi sub-machinegun, doubtless on his – or her
– way to or from a reserve meeting. It was the sort of
thing to shock an American anti-gun nut (or warm the
heart of a pro-gun nut). Ryan figured that the weapons
display probably knocked the hell out of purse-snatching
and street crime. Ordinary civil crime, he knew, was
pretty rare here. But terrorist bombings and other less
pleasant acts were not. And things were getting worse
instead of better. That wasn't new either.

The Holy Land, sacred to Christians, Muslims, and
Jews, he thought. Historically, it had the misfortune to

be at the crossroads between Europe and Africa on one hand – the Roman, Greek, and Egyptian empires – and Asia on the other – the Babylonians, Assyrians, and Persians – and one constant fact in military history was that a crossroads was always contested by somebody. The rise of Christianity, followed 700 years later by the rise of Islam, hadn't changed matters very much, though it had redefined the teams somewhat, and given wider religious significance to the crossroads already contested for three millennia. And that only made the wars all the more bitter.

It was easy to be cynical about it. The First Crusade, 1086, Ryan thought it was, had mainly been about extras. Knights and nobles were passionate people, and produced more offspring than their castles and associated cathedrals could support. The son of a noble could hardly take up farming, and those not eliminated by childhood disease had to go *somewhere*. And when Pope Urban II had sent out his message that the infidels had overrun the land of Christ, it became possible for men to launch a war of aggression to reclaim land of religious importance *and* to find themselves fiefdoms to rule, peasants to oppress, and trade routes to the Orient on which to sit and charge their tolls. Whichever objective might have been the more important probably differed from one heart to another, but they all had known of both. Jack wondered how many different kinds of feet had trodden on these streets, and how they had reconciled their personal-political-commercial objectives with their putatively holy cause. Doubtless the same had been true of Muslims, of course, since 300 years after Mohammed the venal had doubtless added their ranks to those of the devout, just as it had happened in Christianity. Stuck in the middle were the Jews, those not scattered by the Romans, or those who had found their way back. The Jews had probably been treated more brutally by the Christians back in the early second millennium, something else which had since changed, probably more than once.

Like a bone, an immortal bone fought over by endless packs of hungry dogs.

But the reason the bone was not ever destroyed, the reason the dogs kept coming back over the span of centuries was what the land represented. So much history. Scores of historical figures had been here, including the Son of God, as the Catholic part of Ryan believed. Beyond the significance of the very location, this narrow land bridge between continents and cultures, were thoughts and ideals and hopes that lived in the minds of men, somehow embodied in the sand and stones of a singularly unattractive place that only a scorpion could really love. Jack supposed that there were five great religions in the world, only three of which had really spread beyond their own point of origin. Those three had their home within a few miles of where he stood.

So, of course, this is where they fight wars.

The blasphemy was stunning. Monotheism had been born here, hadn't it? Starting with the Jews, and built upon by Christians and Muslims, here was the place where the idea had caught on. The Jewish people – Israelites seemed too strange a term – had defended their faith with stubborn ferocity for thousands of years, surviving everything the animists and pagans could throw at them, and then facing their sternest tests at the hands of religions grown on the ideas that they had defended. It hardly seemed fair – it wasn't fair at all, of course – but religious wars were the most barbaric of all. If one were fighting for God Himself, then one could do nearly anything. One's enemies in such a war were also fighting against God, a hateful and damnable thing. To dispute the authority of Authority itself – well, each soldier could see himself as God's own avenging sword. There could be no restraint. One's actions to chastise the enemy/sinner were sanctioned as thoroughly as anything could be. Rapine, plunder, slaughter, all the basest crimes of man would become something more than right – made into a duty, a Holy Cause, not sins at all. Not just being paid to do terrible things, not just sinning because sin felt good, but being told that you could literally get away with anything, because God really was on your side. They even took it to the grave. In England, knights who had served in the Crusades were buried under stone effigies whose legs were crossed instead of lying side by side – the mark of a holy crusader – so that all eternity could know that they'd served their time in God's name, wetting their swords in children's blood, raping anything that might have caught their lonely eyes, and stealing whatever wasn't set firmly in the ground. All sides. The Jews mainly as victims, but taking their part on the hilt end of the sword when they got the chance, because all men were alike in their virtues and vices.

The bastards must have loved it, Jack thought bleakly, watching a traffic cop settling a dispute at a busy corner. *There must have been some genuinely good men back then. What did they do? What did they think? I wonder what God thought?*

But Ryan wasn't a priest or a rabbi or an imam. Ryan was a senior intelligence officer, an instrument of his country, an observer and reporter of information. He continued looking around, and forgot about history for the moment.

The people were dressed for the oppressive heat, and the bustle of the streets made him think of Manhattan. So many of them had portable radios. He passed a sidewalk restaurant and saw no less than ten people listening to an hourly news broadcast. Jack had to smile at that. His kind of people. When driving his car, the radio was always tuned to an all-news D.C. station. The eyes he saw flickered about. The level of alertness was so pervasive that it took him a few moments to grasp it. Like the eyes of his own security guard. Looking for trouble. Well, that made sense. The incident on Temple Mount had not sparked a wave of violence, but such a wave was expected – it did not surprise Ryan that the people in his sight failed to recognize the greater threat to them that came from the absence of violence. Israel had a myopia of outlook that was not hard to comprehend. The Israelis, surrounded by countries that had every reason to see the

Jewish state immolated, had elevated paranoia to an art form, and national security to an obsession. One thousand nine hundred years after Masada and the diaspora, they'd returned to a land they'd consecrated, fleeing oppression and genocide . . . only to invite more of the same. The difference was that they now held the sword, and had well and truly learned its use. But that, too, was a dead end. Wars were supposed to end in peace, but none of their wars had really ended. They'd stopped, been interrupted, no more than that. For Israel, peace had been nothing more than an intermission, time to bury the dead and train the next class of fighters. The Jews had fled from near-extermination at Christian hands, betting their existence on their ability to defeat Muslim nations that had at once voiced their desire to finish what Hitler had started. And God probably thought exactly what He had thought during the Crusades. Unfortunately, parting seas and fixing the sun in the sky seemed to be things of the Old Testament. Men were supposed to settle things now. But men didn't always do what they were supposed to do. When Thomas More had written *Utopia*, the state in which men acted morally in all cases, he had given both the place and the book the same title. The meaning of 'Utopia' is 'Noplace.' Jack shook his head and turned a corner down another street of white-painted stucco buildings.

'Hello, Dr Ryan.'

The man was in his middle fifties, shorter than Jack, and more heavy-set. He had a full beard, neatly trimmed, but speckled with gray, and looked less like a Jew than a unit commander in Sennacherib's Assyrian army. A broadsword or mace would not have been out of place in his hand. Had he not been smiling, Ryan would have wanted John Clark at his side.

'Hello, Avi. Fancy meeting you here.'

General Abraham Ben Jakob was Ryan's counterpart in the Mossad, assistant director of the Israeli foreign-intelligence agency. A serious player in the intelligence trade, Avi had been a professional army officer until 1968, a paratrooper with extensive special-operations experience who'd been talent-scouted by Rafi Eitan and brought into the fold. His path had crossed Ryan's half a dozen times in the past few years, but always in Washington. Ryan had the utmost respect for Ben Jakob as a professional. He wasn't sure what Avi thought of him. General Ben Jakob was very effective at concealing his thoughts and feelings.

'What is the news from Washington, Jack?'

'All I know is what I saw on CNN at the embassy. Nothing official yet, and even if there were, you know the rules better than I do, Avi. Is there a good place to eat around here?'

That had already been planned, of course. Two minutes and a hundred yards later, they were in the back room of a quiet mom-and-pop place where both men's security guards could keep an eye on things. Ben Jakob ordered two Heinekens.

'Where you're going, they do not serve beer.'

'Tacky, Avi. Very tacky,' Ryan replied after his first sip.

'You are taking Alden's place in Riyadh, I understand.'

'How could the likes of me ever take Dr Alden's place anywhere?'

'You will be making your presentation about the same time Adler makes his. We are interested to hear it.'

'In that case you will not mind waiting, I guess.'

'No preview, not even one professional to another?'

'Especially not one professional to another.' Jack drank his beer right out of the bottle. The menu, he saw, was in Hebrew. 'Guess I'll have to let you order ... That damned fool!' *I've been left holding the bag before, but never one this big.*

'Alden.' It was not a question. 'He's *my* age. Good God, he should know that experienced women are both more reliable and more knowledgeable.' Even in affairs of the heart, his terminology was professional.

'He might even pay more attention to his wife.'

Ben Jakob grinned. 'I keep forgetting how Catholic you are.'

'That's not it, Avi. What lunatic wants more than *one* woman in his life?' Ryan asked deadpan.

'He's gone. That's the evaluation of our embassy.' *But what does that mean?*

'Maybe so. Nobody asked me for an opinion. I really respect the guy. He gives the President good advice. He listens to us, and when he disagrees with the Agency, he generally has a good reason for doing so. He caught *me* short on something six months back. The man is brilliant. But playing around like that . . . well, I guess we all have our faults. What a damn-fool reason to lose a job like that. Can't keep his pants zipped.' *And what timing,* Jack raged at himself.

'Such people cannot be in government service. They are too easy to compromise.'

'The Russians are getting away from honey traps . . . and the girl was Jewish, wasn't she? One of yours, Avi?'

'*Doctor* Ryan! Would *I* do such a thing?' If a bear could laugh, it would have sounded like Avi Ben Jakob's outburst.

'Can't be your operation. There was evidently no attempt at blackmail.' Jack nearly crossed the line with that one. The general's eyes narrowed.

'It was not our operation. You think us mad? Dr Elliot will replace Alden.'

Ryan looked up from his beer. He hadn't thought about that. *Oh, shit . . .*

'Both your friend and ours,' Avi pointed out.

'How many government ministers have you disagreed with in the last twenty years, Avi?'

'None, of course.'

Ryan snorted and finished off the bottle. 'What was that you said earlier, the part about one professional to another, remember?'

'We both do the same thing. Sometimes, when we are very lucky, they listen to us.'

'And some of the times they listen to us, we're the ones who're wrong . . .'

General Ben Jakob didn't alter his steady, relaxed gaze into Ryan's face when he heard that. It was yet another sign of Ryan's growing maturity. He genuinely liked Ryan as a man and as a professional, but personal likes and dislikes had little place in the intelligence trade. Something fundamental was happening. Scott Adler had been to Moscow. Both he and Ryan had visited Cardinal D'Antonio in the Vatican. As originally planned, Ryan was supposed to backstop Adler here with the Israeli Foreign Ministry, but Alden's astounding *faux pas* had changed that.

Even for an intelligence professional, Avi Ben Jakob was a singularly well-informed man. Ryan waffled on the question of whether or not Israel was America's most dependable ally in the Middle East. That was to be expected from an historian, Avi judged. Whatever Ryan thought, most Americans did regard Israel that way, and as a result, Israelis heard more from inside the American government than any other country – more even than the British, who had a formal relationship with the American intelligence community.

Those sources had informed Ben Jakob's intelligence officers that Ryan was behind what was going on. That seemed incredibly unlikely. Jack was very bright, almost as smart as Alden, for example, but Ryan had also defined his own role as a servant, not a master, an implementer of policy, not a maker of it. Besides, the American President did not like Ryan, and had not hidden the fact from his inner circle. Elizabeth Elliot was reported to hate him, Avi knew. Something that had happened before the election, an imagined slight, a harsh word. Well, government ministers were notoriously touchy. *Not like Ryan and me*, General Ben Jakob thought. Both he and Ryan had faced death more than once, and perhaps that was their bond. They didn't have to agree on everything. There was respect between them.

Moscow, Rome, Tel Aviv, Riyadh. What could he deduce from that?

Scott Adler was Secretary of State Talbot's picked man, a highly skilled professional diplomat. Talbot was also bright. President Fowler might not have been terribly impressive, but he had selected superior cabinet officers and personal advisers. Except for Elliot, Avi corrected himself. Talbot used Deputy Secretary Adler to do his important advance work. And when Talbot himself entered formal negotiations, Adler was always at his side.

The most amazing thing, of course, was that not one of the Mossad's informants had a clue what was going on. *Something important in the Middle East*, they said. *Not sure what . . . I heard that Jack Ryan at the Agency had something to do with it . . .* End of report.

It should have been infuriating, but Avi was used to that. Intelligence was a game where you never saw all the cards. Ben Jakob's brother was a pediatrician with similar problems. A sick child rarely told him what was wrong. Of course, his brother could always ask, or point, or probe . . .

'Jack, I must tell my superiors something,' General Ben Jakob said plaintively.

'Come on, General.' Jack turned and waved for another beer. 'Tell me, what the hell happened on the Mount?'

'The man was – deranged. In the hospital they have a suicide watch on him. His wife had just left him, he came under the influence of a religious fanatic, and . . .' Ben Jakob shrugged. 'It was terrible to see.'

'That's true, Avi. Do you have any idea the political fix you're in now?'

'Jack, we've been dealing with this problem for –'

'I thought so. Avi, you are one very bright spook, but you do not know what's happening this time. You really don't.'

'So tell me.'

'I didn't mean that, and you know it. What happened a couple days ago has changed things forever, General. You must know that.'

'Changed to what?'

'You're going to have to wait. I have my orders, too.'

'Does your country threaten us?'

'Threaten? That will never happen, Avi. How could it?' Ryan warned himself that he was talking too much. *This guy is good*, Jack reminded himself.

'But you cannot dictate policy to us.'

Jack bit off his reply. 'You're very clever, General, but I still have my orders. You have to wait. I'm sorry that your people in D.C. can't help you, but neither can I.'

Ben Jakob changed tack yet again. 'I'm even buying you a meal, and my country is not so rich as yours.'

Jack laughed at his tone. 'Good beer, too, and as you say, I can't do this where you say I'm going. If that's where I'm going . . .'

'Your air crew has already filed the flight plan. I checked.'

'So much for secrecy.' Jack accepted the new bottle with a smile for the waiter. 'Avi, let it rest for a while. Do you really think that we'd do anything to compromise your country's security?'

Yes! the General thought, but he couldn't say that, of course. Instead he said nothing. But Ryan wasn't buying, and used the silence to change the course of the discussion himself.

'I hear you're a grandfather now.'

'Yes, my daughter added to the gray in my beard. A daughter of her own, Leah.'

'You have my word: Leah will have a secure country to grow up in, Avi.'

'And who will see to that?' Ben Jakob asked.

'The same people who always have.' Ryan congratulated himself for the answer. The poor guy really was desperate for information, and he was sad that Avi had made it so obvious. *Well, even the best of us can be pushed into corners . . .*

Ben Jakob made a mental note to have the file on Ryan updated. The next time they met, he wanted to have better information. The General wasn't a man who enjoyed losing at anything.

Dr Charles Alden contemplated his office. He wasn't leaving quite yet, of course. It would harm the Fowler Administration. His resignation, signed and sitting on the green desk blotter, was for the end of the month. But that was just for show. As of today, his duties were at an end. He'd show up, read the briefing papers, scribble his notes, but Elizabeth Elliot would do the briefs now. The President had been regretful, but his usual cool self. *Sorry to lose you, Charlie, really sorry, especially now, but I'm afraid there's just no other way . . .* He'd managed to retain his dignity in the Oval Office despite the rage he'd felt. Even Arnie van Damm had been human enough to observe 'Oh, shit, Charlie!' Though enraged at the political damage to his boss, van Damm had at least mixed a little humanity and locker-room sympathy with his anger. But not Bob Fowler, champion of the poor and the helpless.

It was worse with Liz. That arrogant bitch, with her silence and her eloquent eyes. She'd get the credit for what he had done. She knew it, and was already basking in it.

The announcement would be made in the morning. It had already been leaked to the press. By whom was anyone's guess. Elliot, displaying her satisfaction? Arnie van Damm, in a rapid effort at damage control? One of a dozen others?

The transition from power to obscurity comes fast in Washington. The embarrassed look on the face of his secretary. The forced smiles of the other bureaucrats in the West Wing. But obscurity comes only after a blaze of publicity to announce the fact: like the flare of light from an exploding star, public death is preceded by dazzling fanfare. That was the media's job. The phone was ringing off the hook. There had been twenty of them waiting outside his house in the morning, cameras at the ready, sun-like lights blazing in his face. And knowing what it had to be even before the first question.

That foolish little bitch! With her cow-like eyes and cow-like udders and broad cow-like hips. How could he have been so stupid! Professor Charles Winston Alden sat in his expensive chair and stared at his expensive desk. His head was bursting with a headache that he attributed to stress and anger. And he was right. But he failed to allow for the fact that his blood-pressure was nearly double what it should have been, driven to new heights by the stress of the moment. He similarly failed to consider the fact that he had not taken his anti-hypertensive medication in the past week. A prototypical professor, he was always forgetting the little things while his methodical mind picked apart the most intricate of problems.

And so it came as a surprise. It started at an existing weakness in part of the Circle of William, the brain's own blood-beltway. Designed to get blood to any part of the brain, as a means of bypassing vessels that might become blocked with age, the vessel carried a huge amount of blood. Twenty years of high blood-pressure, and twenty years of his taking his medication only when he remembered that he had an upcoming doctor's appointment, and the added stress of seeing his career stop with a demeaning personal disgrace, culminated in a rupture of the vessel on the right side of his head. What had been a searing migraine headache became death itself. Alden's eyes opened wide, and his hands flew up to grasp his skull as though to hold it together. It was too late for that. The rip widened, allowing more blood to escape. This both deprived important parts of his brain of the oxygen needed to function and further boosted intra-cranial pressure to the point that other brain cells were squeezed to extinction.

Though paralyzed, Alden did not lose consciousness for quite some time, and his brilliant mind recorded the event with remarkable clarity. Already unable to move, he knew that death was coming for him. *So close*, he thought, his mind racing to outrun death. *Thirty-five years to get here. All those books. All those seminars. The bright young students. The lecture circuit. The talk shows. The campaigns. All to get here. I was so close to accomplishing something important. Oh, God! To die now, to die like this!* But he knew that death was here, that he had to accept it. He hoped that someone would forgive him. He hadn't been a bad man, had he? He'd tried so hard to make a difference, to make the world a better place, and now on the brink of something really important ... so much the better for everyone if this had happened while he was mounted on that foolish little cow . . . better still, he knew in one final moment, if his studies and his intellect had been his only pass –

Alden's disgrace and *de facto* firing determined the fact that his death would take long to discover. Instead of being buzzed by his secretary every few minutes, it took nearly an hour. Because she was intercepting all calls to him, none were forwarded. It would not have mattered in any case, though it would cause his secretary some guilt for weeks to come. Finally, when she was ready to leave for the day, she decided that she had to tell him so. She buzzed him over the intercom, and got no response. Frowning, she paused, then buzzed him again. Still nothing. Next she rose and walked to the door, knocking on it. Finally she opened it, and screamed loudly enough that the Secret Service agents outside the Oval Office in the opposite corner of the building heard her. The first to arrive was Helen D'Agustino, one of the President's personal bodyguards, who'd been walking the corridors to loosen up after sitting most of the day.

'Shit!' And that fast her service revolver was out. She'd never seen so much blood in her life, all coming out of Alden's right ear and puddling on his desk. She shouted an alert over her radio transmitter. It had to be a head shot. Her sharp eyes swept the room, tracking over the front sight of her Model 19 Smith & Wesson. *Windows intact.* She darted across the room. *Nobody here. So, what then?*

Next she felt with her left hand for Alden's pulse on the carotid artery. Of course there was none, but training dictated that she had to check. Outside the room, all exits to the White House were blocked, guns were drawn, and visitors froze in their tracks. Secret Service agents were conducting a thorough check of the entire building.

'Goddamn!' Pete Connor observed as he entered the room.

'Sweep is complete!' a voice told both of them through their ear-pieces. 'Building is clear. HAWK is secure.' 'Hawk' was the President's code-name with the Secret

Service. It displayed the agent's institutional sense of humor, both for its association with the President's name and its ironic dissonance with his politics.

'Ambulance is two minutes out!' the communications center added. They could get an ambulance faster than a helicopter.

'Stand easy, Daga,' Connor said. 'I think the man had a stroke.'

'Move!' This was a Navy chief medical corpsman. The Secret Service agents were trained in first aid, of course, but the White House always had a medical team standing by, and the corpsman was first on the scene. He carried the sort of duffel bag carried by corpsmen in the field, but didn't bother opening it. There was just too much blood on the desk, he saw instantly, and the top of the puddle was congealing. The corpsman decided not to disturb the body – it was a potential crime scene, and the Secret Service guys had briefed him on that set of rules – most of the blood had come out Dr Alden's right ear. There was a trickle from the left one also, and post-mortem lividity was already starting in what parts of the face he could see. Diagnoses didn't come much easier than that.

'He's dead, probably been close to an hour, guys. Cerebral hemorrhage. Stroke. Isn't this guy a hypertensive?'

'Yeah, I think so,' Special Agent D'Agustino said after a moment.

'You'll have to post him to be sure, but that's what he died of. Blow-out.'

A physician arrived next. He was a Navy captain, and confirmed his chief's observation.

'This is Connor, tell the ambulance to take it easy. PILGRIM is dead, looks like from natural causes. Repeat, PILGRIM is dead,' the principal agent said over his radio.

The post-mortem examination would check for many things, of course. Poison. Possible contamination of his food or water. But the White House environment was monitored on a continuous basis. D'Agustino and Connor shared a look. Yes, he had suffered from high blood pressure, and he sure as hell had had a bad day. Just about as bad as they get.

'How is he?' Heads turned. It was HAWK, the President himself, with a literal ring of agents around him, pressing through the door. And Dr Elliot behind him. D'Agustino made a mental note that they'd have to make up a new code-name for her. She wondered if HARPY might suffice. Daga didn't like the bitch. No one on the Presidential Security Detail did. But they weren't paid to like her, or for that matter, even to like the President.

'He's dead, Mr President,' the doctor said. 'It appears he suffered a massive stroke.'

The President took the news without a visible reaction. The Secret Service agents reminded themselves that he'd seen his wife through a multi-year battle against multiple sclerosis, finally losing her while still governor of Ohio. It must have drained the man, they thought, wanting it to be true. It must have stripped all of his emotions away. Certainly there were few emotions left in him. He made a clucking sound, and grimaced, and shook his head, and then he turned away.

Liz Elliot took his place, peering over the shoulder of an agent. Helen D'Agustino examined her face as Elliot pressed forward to get her look. Elliot liked to wear makeup, Daga knew, and she watched the new National Security Advisor pale beneath it. Certainly it was a horrible scene, D'Agustino knew. It looked as though a bucket of red paint had been spilled on the desk.

'Oh, God!' Dr Elliot whispered.

'Out of the way, please!' called a new voice. It was an agent with a stretcher. He pushed Liz Elliot roughly out of the way. Daga noticed that she was too shocked to be angry at that, that her face was still very white, her eyes unfocused. She might think she's a tough bitch, Special Agent D'Agustino thought, but she's not as tough as she thinks. The thought gave the agent satisfaction.

Little weak at the knees, eh Liz? Helen D'Agustino, one month out of the Secret Service Academy, had been out on a discreet surveillance when the subject — a counterfeiter – had 'made' her and for some reason she'd never understood come out with a large automatic pistol. He'd even fired a round in her direction. No more than that, though. She'd earned her nickname, Daga, by drawing her S&W and landing three right in the poor bastard's ten-ring at a range of thirty-seven feet, just like a cardboard target at the range. Just that easy, too. She'd never even dreamed about it. And so Daga was one of the guys, a member of the Service pistol team when they'd out-shot the Army's elite Delta Force commandos. Daga was tough. Clearly Liz Elliot was not, however arrogant she might be. *No guts, lady!* It did not occur to Special Agent Helen D'Agustino at that moment that Liz Elliot was HAWK's chief advisor for national security.

It had been a quiet meeting, the first such meeting that Günther Bock remembered. None of the blustering rhetoric so beloved of the revolutionary soldiers. His old comrade-in-arms, Ismael Qati, was normally a firebrand, eloquent in five languages, but Qati was subdued in every way, Bock saw. The ferocity of his smile was not there. The sweeping gestures that had always punctuated his words were more restrained, and Bock wondered if the man might not be feeling well.

'I grieved when I heard the news of your wife,' Qati said, turning to personal matters for a moment.

'Thank you, my friend.' Bock decided to put his best face on it: 'It is a small thing compared to what your people have endured. There are always setbacks.'

There were more than a few in this case, and both knew it. Their best weapon had always been solid intelligence information. But Bock's had dried up. The Red Army Faction had drawn for years on all sorts of information. Its own people within the West German government. Useful tidbits from the East German intelligence apparat, and all the Eastern Bloc clones of their common master, the KGB. Doubtless a good deal of their data had come from Moscow, routed through the smaller nations for political reasons that Bock had never questioned.

After all, World Socialism is itself a struggle with numerous tactical moves. *Used to be*, he corrected himself.

It was all gone now, the help upon which he'd been able to draw. The East Bloc intelligence services had turned on their revolutionary comrades like cur dogs. The Czechs and Hungarians had literally *sold* information on them to the West! The East Germans had given it away in the name of Greater German cooperation and brotherhood. East Germany – the German Democratic Republic – no longer existed. Now it was a mere appendage to capitalist Germany. And the Russians . . . Whatever indirect support they'd ever had from the Soviets was gone, possibly forever. With the demise of socialism in Europe, their sources within various government institutions had been rolled up, turned double-agent, or simply stopped delivering, having lost their faith in a socialist future. At a stroke, the best and most useful weapon of the European revolutionary fighters had disappeared.

Fortunately, it was different here, different for Qati. The Israelis were as foolish as they were vicious. The one constant thing in the world, both Bock and Qati knew, was the inability of the Jews to make any kind of meaningful political initiative. Formidable as they were at the business of war, they had always been hopelessly inept at the business of peace. Added to that was their ability to dictate policy to their own masters as though they didn't want peace at all. Bock was not a student of world history, but he doubted that there was any precedent for such behaviour as this. The ongoing revolt of both indigenous Israeli Arabs and Palestinian captives in the occupied territories was a bleeding sore on the soul of Israel. Once able to infiltrate Arab groups at will, Israeli police and domestic intelligence agencies were gradually being shut out as popular support for this rebellion became more and more fixed in the minds of their enemies. At least Qati had an ongoing operation to command. Bock envied him that, however bad the tactical situation might be. Another perverse advantage for Qati was the efficiency of his enemy. Israeli intelligence had waged its shadow war against the Arab freedom fighters for two generations now. Over that time the foolish ones had died by the guns of Mossad officers. Those still alive, like Qati, were the survivors, the strong, clever, dedicated products of a Darwinian selection process.

'How are you dealing with informers?' Bock asked.

'We found one last week,' Qati answered with a cruel smile. 'He identified his case officer before he died. Now we have him under surveillance.'

Bock nodded. Once the Israeli officer would merely have been assassinated, but Qati had learned. By watching him – very carefully and only intermittently – they might identify other infiltrators.

'And the Russians?' This question got a strong reaction.

'The pigs! They give us nothing of value. We are on our own. It has always been so.' Qati's face showed what had today been rare animation. It came, then went, and the Arab's face lapsed back into enveloping fatigue.

'You seem tired, my friend.'

'It has been a long day. For you also, I think.'

Bock allowed himself a yawn and a stretch. 'Until tomorrow?'

Qati rose with a nod, guiding his visitor to his room. Bock took his hand before retiring. They'd known each other for almost twenty years. Qati returned to the living room, and walked outside. His security people were in place and alert. Qati spoke with them briefly, as always, because loyalty resulted from attention to the needs of one's people. Then he, too, went to bed. He paused for evening prayers, of course. It troubled him vaguely that his friend Günther was an unbeliever. Brave, clever, dedicated though he was, he had no faith, and Qati did not understand how any man could carry on without that.

Carry on! Does he carry on at all! Qati asked himself as he lay down. His aching legs and arms at last knew rest, and though the pain in them didn't end, at least it changed. Bock was finished, wasn't he? Better for him if

124

Petra had died at the hands of GSG-9. They must have wanted to kill her, those German commandos, but the rumor was that they'd found her with a babe suckling on each breast, and you could not be a man and kill such a picture as that. Qati himself, for all his hatred for Israelis, could not do that. It would be an offense against God Himself. Petra, he thought, smiling in the dark. He'd taken her once, when Günther had been away. She'd been lonely, and he'd been hot-blooded from a successful operation in Lebanon, the killing of an Israeli advisor to the Christian militia, and so they'd shared their revolutionary fervor for two blazing hours.

Does Günther know? Did Petra tell him?

Perhaps she did. It wouldn't matter. Bock was not that sort of man, not like an Arab for whom it would have been a blood insult. Europeans were so casual about such things. It was a curiosity to Qati that they should be that way, but there were many curiosities in life. Bock was a true friend. Of that he was sure. The flame burned in Günther's soul as truly and brightly as it did in his own. It was sad that events in Europe had made life so hard on his friend. His woman caged. His children stolen. The very thought of it chilled Qati's blood. It was foolish of them to have brought children into the world. Qati had never married, and enjoyed the company of women rarely enough. In Lebanon ten years earlier, all those European girls, some in their teens even. He remembered with a quiet smile. Things no Arab girl would ever learn to do. So hot-blooded they'd been, wanting to show how dedicated they were. He knew that they had used him as surely as he'd used them. But Qati had been younger then, with a young man's passions.

Those passions were gone. He wondered if they would ever return. He hoped they would. He hoped mainly that he'd recover well enough that he'd have the energy for more than one thing. Treatment was going well, the doctor said. He was tolerating it much better than most. If he always felt tired, if the crippling bouts of nausea came from time to time, he mustn't be discouraged. That was normal – no, the normal way of things was not even so 'good' as this. There was real hope, the doctor assured him on every visit. It wasn't merely the things any doctor would say to encourage his patient, the doctor had told him last week. He was truly doing well. He had a good chance. The important thing, Qati knew, was that he had something still to live for. He had purpose. That, he was sure, was the thing keeping him alive.

'What's the score?'

'Just carry on,' Dr Cabot replied over the secure satellite link. 'Charlie had a massive stroke at his desk.' A pause. 'Maybe the best thing that could have happened to the poor bastard.'

'Liz Elliot taking over?'

'That's right.'

Ryan compressed his lips into a tight grimace, as though he'd just taken some particularly foul medicine. He checked his watch. Cabot had arisen early to make the call and give the instructions. He and his boss were not exactly friends, but the importance of this mission had overcome that. Maybe it would be the same with E.E., Ryan told himself.

'Okay, boss. I take off in ninety minutes, and we deliver our pitches simultaneously, as per the plan.'

'Good luck, Jack.'

'Thank you, Director.' Ryan punched the OFF button on the secure phone console. He walked out of the communications room and back to his room. His bag was already packed. All he had to do was knot his tie. The coat went over his shoulder. It was too hot here for that, and hotter still where he was going. He'd have to wear a coat there. It was expected, one of those curious rules of formal behavior that demanded the maximum discomfort to attain the proper degree of decorum. Ryan lifted his bag and left the room.

'Synchronize our watches?' Adler was waiting outside and chuckled.

'Hey, Scott, that isn't my idea!'

'It does make sense . . . kinda.'

'I suppose. Well, I got an airplane to catch.'

'Can't take off without you,' Adler pointed out.

'One advantage to government service, isn't it?' Ryan looked up and down the corridor. It was empty, though he wondered if the Israelis had managed to bug it. If so, the Muzak might interfere with their bugs. 'What do you think?'

'Even money.'

'That good?'

'Yeah,' Adler said with a grin. 'This is the one, Jack. It was a good idea you had.'

'Not just mine. I'll never get any credit for it anyway. Nobody'll ever know.'

'We'll know. Let's get to work.'

'Let me know how they react. Good luck, man.'

'I think *mazeltov* is the proper expression.' Adler took Ryan's hand. 'Good flight.'

The embassy limo took Ryan directly to the aircraft, whose engines were already turning. It had priority clearance to taxi, and was airborne in less than five minutes from the time he boarded. The VC-20B headed south, down the dagger-shape that was Israel, then east over the Gulf of Aqaba and into Saudi airspace.

As was his custom, Ryan stared out the window. His mind went over what he was supposed to do, but that had been rehearsed for over a week, and his brain could do that quietly while Ryan stared. The air was clear, the sky virtually cloudless as they flew over what was to all appearances a barren wasteland of sand and rock. What color there was came from stunted bushes too small to pick out individually, and had the general effect of an unshaven face. Jack knew that much of Israel looked exactly the same, as did the Sinai, where all those tank battles had been fought, and he found himself wondering why men chose to die for land like this. But they had, for almost as long as man had existed on the planet. Man's first organized wars had been fought here, and they hadn't stopped. At least not yet.

Riyadh, the capital of Saudi Arabia, is roughly in the center of the country, which is as large as all of America east of the Mississippi. The executive aircraft made a relatively fast descent, allowed by the modest amount of air traffic here, and the air was agreeably smooth as the pilot brought the aircraft low into the Riyadh International. In another few minutes, the Gulfstream taxied towards the cargo terminal, and the attendant opened the forward door.

After two hours' exposure to air conditioning, Jack felt as though he'd stepped into a blast furnace. The shade temperature was over 110, and there was no shade. Worse, the sun reflected off the pavement as though from a mirror, so intensely that Ryan's face stung from it. There to greet him was the deputy chief of mission at the embassy, and the usual security people. In a moment, he was sweating inside yet another embassy limo.

'Good flight?' the DCM asked.

'Not bad. Everything ready here?'

'Yes, sir.'

It was nice to be called 'sir,' Jack thought. 'Well, let's get on with it.'

'My instructions are to accompany you as far as the door.'

'That's right.'

'You might be interested to know that we haven't had any press inquiries. D.C. has kept this one pretty quiet.'

'That'll change in about five hours.'

Riyadh was a clean city, though quite different from Western metropolises. The contrast with Israeli towns was remarkable. Nearly everything was new. Only two hours away, but that was by air. This place had never been the crossroads Palestine had been. The ancient trading routes had given the brutal heat of Arabia a wide berth, and though the coastal fishing and trading towns had known prosperity for millennia, the nomadic people of the interior had lived a stark existence, held together only by their Islamic faith, which was in turn anchored by the holy cities of Mecca and Medina. Two things had changed that. The British in the First World War had used this area as a diversion against Ottoman Turkey, drawing their forces here and away from sites which might have been of greater utility to their allies in Germany and Austria-Hungary. Then in the 1930s, oil had been discovered. Oil in quantities so vast as to make Texas an apostrophe. With that, first the Arab world had changed, and then the whole world had soon followed.

From the first, the relationship between the Saudis and the West had been delicate. The Saudis were still a curious mixture of the primitive and the sophisticated. Some people on this peninsula were but a single generation from nomadic life that was little different from that of the wanderers of the Bronze Age. At the same time, there was an admirable tradition of Koranic scholarship, a code that was harsh but scrupulously fair, and remarkably similar to the Talmudic traditions of Judaism. In a brief span of time these people had become accustomed to wealth beyond count or meaning. Viewed as comic wastrels by the 'sophisticated' West, they were merely the newest entry in a long line of *nouveau riche* nations of which America had been a recent part. A *nouveau riche* himself, Ryan smiled at some of the buildings in sympathy. People with 'old' money – earned by bumptious ancestors whose rough manners had long since been conveniently forgotten – were always uncomfortable around those who had made, not inherited, their comforts. As it was with individuals, so it was with nations. The Saudis and their Arab brethren were still learning how to be a nation, much less a rich and influential one, but the process was an exciting one for them and their friends. They'd had some easy lessons, and some very hard ones, most recently with their neighbors of the north. For the most part they had learned well, and now Ryan hoped that the next step would be as easily made. A nation achieves greatness by helping others to make peace, not by demonstrating prowess at war or commerce. To learn that, it had taken America from the time of Washington to the time of Theodore Roosevelt, whose Nobel Peace Prize adorned the room in the White House that still bore his name. *It took us almost a hundred twenty years*, Jack thought, as the car turned and slowed. *Teddy got the Prize for arbitrating some little piss-ant border dispute, and we're asking these folks to help us settle the most dangerous flash-point in the civilized world after merely fifty years of effective nationhood. What reason do we have to look down on these people?*

There is a choreography to occasions of state as delicate and as adamant as any ballet. The car – it used to be a carriage – arrives. The door is opened by a functionary – who used to be called a footman. The Official waits in dignified solitude while the Visitor alights from the car. The Visitor nods to the footman if he's polite, and Ryan was. Another, more senior, functionary first greets the Visitor, then conducts him to the Official. On both sides of the entryway are the official guards, who were in this case uniformed, armed soldiers. Photographers had been left out, for obvious reasons. Such affairs would be more comfortable in temperatures under a hundred degrees, but at least here there was shade from a canopy, as Ryan was conducted to his Official.

'Welcome to my country, Dr Ryan.' Prince Ali bin Sheik extended a firm hand to Jack.

'Thank you, Your Highness.'

'Would you follow me?'

'Gladly, sir.' *Before I melt.*

Ali led Jack and the DCM inside, where they parted ways. The building was a palace – Riyadh had quite a few palaces, since there were so many royal princes – but Ryan thought 'working palace' might have been a more accurate term. It was smaller than the British counterparts Ryan had visited, and cleaner, Jack saw, somewhat to his surprise. Probably because of the cleaner and dryer air of the region, which contrasted to the damp, sooty atmosphere of London. It was also air-conditioned. The inside temperature could not have been far above eighty-five, which somehow seemed comfortable to Ryan. The Prince was dressed in flowing robes with a headdress held atop his head by a pair of circular – whats? Ryan wondered. He ought to have gotten briefed on that, Jack thought too late. Alden was supposed to have done this anyway. Charlie knew this area far better than he did, and – but Charlie Alden was dead, and Jack was carrying the ball.

Ali bin Sheik was referred to at State and CIA as a Prince-Without-Portfolio. Taller, thinner, and younger than Ryan, he advised the King of Saudi Arabia on foreign affairs and intelligence matters. Probably the Saudi intelligence service – British-trained – reported to him, but that was not as clear as it should have been, doubtless another legacy of the Brits, who took their secrecy far more seriously than Americans. Though the file on Ali was a thick one, it mainly dealt with his background. Educated at Cambridge, he'd become an Army officer, and continued his professional studies at Leavenworth and Carlyle Barracks in the United States. At Carlyle he'd been the youngest man in his class, a colonel at 27 – to be a royal prince was career-enhancing – and finished third in a group whose top ten graduates had each gone on to command a division or equivalent post. The Army General who'd briefed Ryan on Ali remembered his classmate fondly as a young man of no mean intellectual gifts and superb command potential. Ali had played a major role in persuading the King to accept American aid during the Iraqi war. He was regarded as a serious player quick to make decisions and quicker still to express displeasure at having his time wasted, despite his courtly manners.

The Prince's office was easily identified by the two officers at the double doors. A third man opened them, bowing to both as they passed.

'I've heard much about you,' Ali said casually.

'All good, I trust,' Ryan replied, trying to be at ease.

Ali turned with an impish smile. 'We have some mutual friends in Britain, Sir John. Do you keep current with your small-arms skills?'

'I really don't have the time, sir.'

Ali waved Jack to a chair. 'For some things, one should make time.'

Both sat, and things became formal. A servant appeared with a silver tray, and poured coffee for both men before withdrawing.

'I sincerely regret the news on Dr Alden. For so fine a man to be brought down so foolishly ... May God have mercy on his soul. At the same time, I have looked forward to meeting you for some time, Dr Ryan.'

Jack sipped at his coffee. It was thick, bitter, and hideously strong.

'Thank you, Your Highness. Thank you also for agreeing to see me in the place of a more senior official.'

'The most effective efforts at diplomacy often begin informally. So, how may I be of service?' Ali smiled and leaned back in his chair. The fingers of his left hand toyed with his beard. His eyes were as dark as flint, and though they seemed to gaze casually at his visitor, the atmosphere in the room was now businesslike. And that, Ryan saw, was fast enough.

'My country wishes to explore a means of – that is, the rough outline of a plan with which to alleviate tensions in this area.'

'With Israel, of course. Adler, I presume, is delivering the same proposal to the Israelis at this moment?'

'Correct, Your Highness.'

'That is dramatic,' the Prince observed with an amused smile. 'Do go on.'

Jack began his pitch: 'Sir, our foremost consideration in this matter must be the physical security of the State of Israel. Before either of us was born, America and other countries stood by and did very little to prevent the extermination of six million Jews. The guilt attending that infamy lies heavy on my country.'

Ali nodded gravely before speaking. 'I have never understood that. Perhaps you might have done better, but the strategic decisions made during the war by Roosevelt and Churchill were made in good faith. The issue with the shipload of Jews that nobody wanted prior to the outbreak of war, of course, is another issue entirely. I find it very strange indeed that your country did not grant asylum to those poor people. Fundamentally, however, no one saw what was coming, not the Jews, not the Gentiles, and by the time it became clear what was happening, Hitler had physical control of

Europe, and no direct intervention on your part was possible. Your leaders decided at that time that the best way to end the slaughter was to win the war as expeditiously as possible. That was logical. They might have made a political issue of the ongoing *Endlösung*, I believe the term was, but they decided that it would be ineffective from a practical point of view. That, in retrospect, was probably incorrect, but the decision was not made in malice.' Ali paused to let his history lesson sink in for a moment. 'In any case, we understand and conditionally accept the reasons behind your national goal to preserve the State of Israel. Our acceptance, as I am sure you will understand, is conditional upon your recognition of other people's rights. This part of the world is not composed of Jews and savages.'

'And that, sir, is the basis of our proposal,' Ryan replied. 'If we can find a formula that recognizes those other rights, will you accept a plan in which America is the guarantor of Israeli security?' Jack didn't have time to hold his breath for the reply.

'Of course. Have we not made that clear? Who else but America can guarantee the peace? If you must put troops in Israel to make them feel secure, if you must execute a treaty to formalize your guarantee, those are things we can accept, *but* what of Arab rights?'

'What is your view of how we should address those rights?' Jack asked.

Prince Ali was stunned by the question. Was not Ryan's mission to present the American plan? He almost lapsed into anger, but Ali was too clever for that. It wasn't a trap he saw. It was a fundamental change in American policy.

'Dr Ryan, you asked that question for a reason, but it was a rhetorical question nonetheless. I believe the answer to that question is yours to make.'

The answer took three minutes.

Ali shook his head sadly. 'That, Dr Ryan, is something we would probably find acceptable, but the Israelis will never agree to it even though we might – more precisely, they would reject it for the very reason that we would accept it. They should agree to it, of course, but they will not.'

'Is it acceptable to your government, sir?'

'I must, of course, present it to others, but I think our response would be favorable.'

'Any objections at all?'

The Prince paused to finish his coffee. He stared over Ryan's head towards something on the far wall. 'We could offer several modifications, none of them really substantive to the central thesis of your scheme. Actually, I think the negotiations on those minor issues would be easily and quickly accomplished, since they are not matters of consequence to the other interested parties.'

'And who would be your choice for the Muslim representative?'

Ali leaned forward. 'That is simple. Anyone could tell you. The Imam of the Al-Aqusa Mosque is a distinguished scholar and linguist. His name is Ahmed bin Yussif. Ahmed is consulted by scholars throughout Islam for his opinions on matters of theology. Sunni, Shi'a, all defer to him on selected issues. He is even a Palestinian by birth.'

'That easy?' Ryan closed his eyes and let out a breath. He'd guessed right on that one. Yussif was not exactly a political moderate, and had called for the expulsion of Israel from the West Bank. But he had also denounced terrorism *per se* on theological grounds. He wasn't quite perfect, but if the Muslims could live with him, he was perfect enough.

'You are very confident, Dr Ryan.' Ali shook his head. 'Too confident. I grant you that your plan is fairer than anything I or my government expected, but it will never happen.' Ali paused again and fixed Ryan with his eyes. 'Now I must ask myself if this was ever a serious proposal, or merely something to give the appearance of fairness.'

'Your Highness, President Fowler addresses the United Nations General Assembly next Thursday. He will present this very plan then, live and in color. I am authorized to extend your government an invitation to the Vatican to negotiate the treaty formally.'

The Prince was sufficiently surprised by that that he lapsed into an Americanism: 'Do you really think you can bring this off?'

'Your Highness, we're going to give it one hell of a try.'

Ali rose and walked to his desk. There he lifted a phone, pushed a button and spoke rapidly and, to Ryan, incomprehensibly. Jack had a sudden, giddy moment of whimsy. The Arabic language, as with the Hebrew, went from right to left instead of left to right, and Ryan wondered how one's brain dealt with that.

Son of a BITCH, Jack thought to himself. *This just might work!*

Ali replaced the phone and turned to his visitor. 'I think it is time for us to see His Majesty.'

'That fast?'

'One advantage to our form of government is that when one government minister wishes access to another, it is merely a matter of calling a cousin or an uncle. We are a family business. I trust that your President is a man of his word.'

'The UN speech is already written. I've seen it. He expects to take heat from the Israeli lobby at home. He's ready for that.'

'I've seen them in action, Dr Ryan. Even when we were fighting for our lives alongside American soldiers, they denied us weapons we needed for our own security. Do you think that will change?'

'Soviet communism is at an end. The Warsaw Pact is at an end. So many things that shaped the world I grew up in are gone, and gone forever. It's time to get rid of the rest of the turmoil in the world. You ask if we can do it – why not? Sir, the only constant factor in human existence is change.' Jack knew that he was being outrageously confident, and wondered how Scott Adler was doing in Jerusalem. Adler wasn't a screamer, but he knew how to lay down the word. That hadn't been done with the Israelis for a long enough time that Jack didn't know when it had last been – or ever – been tried. But the President *was* committed to this. If the Israelis tried to stop it, they might just find out how lonely the world was.

'You forgot God, Dr Ryan.'

Jack smiled. 'No, Your Highness. That's the point, isn't it?'

Prince Ali wanted to smile, but didn't. It wasn't time yet. He pointed to the door. 'Our car is waiting.'

At the New Cumberland Army Depot in Pennsylvania, the storage facility for standards and flags dating back to Revolutionary times, a Brigadier General and a professional antiquarian laid flat on a table the dusty regimental colors once carried by the 10th United States Cavalry. The General wondered if some of the grit on the standard was left over from Colonel John Grierson's campaign against the Apaches. This standard would go to the regiment. It wouldn't see much use. Maybe once a year it would be taken out, but from this pattern a new one would be made. That this was happening at all was a curiosity. In an age of cutbacks, a new unit was forming. Not that the General objected. The 10th had a distinguished history, but had never gotten its fair shake from Hollywood, for example, which had made but a single movie about the Black regiments. For the 10th was one of four Black units – the 9th and 10th Cavalry, the 24th and 25th Infantry – each of which had played its part in settling the West. This regimental standard dated back to 1866. Its centrepiece was a buffalo, since the Indians who'd fought the troopers of the 10th thought their hair similar to the rough coat of an American bison. Black soldiers had been there at the defeat of Geronimo, and saved Teddy Roosevelt's ass on the charge up San Juan Hill, the General knew. It was about time that they got a little official recognition and if the President had ordered it for political reasons, so what? The 10th had an honorable history, politics notwithstanding.

'Take a week,' the civilian said. 'I'll do this one personally. God, I wonder what Grierson would have thought of the TO & E for the Buffalos today!'

'It is substantial,' the General allowed. He'd commanded the 11th Armored Cavalry Regiment a few years earlier. The Black Horse Cav was still in Germany, though he wondered how much longer that would last. But the historian was right. With 129 tanks, 228 armored personnel carriers, 24 self-propelled guns, 83 helicopters, and 5,000 troopers, a modern Armored Cavalry Regiment was in fact a reinforced brigade, fast-moving and very hard-hitting.

'Where are they going to be based?'

'The regiment will form up at Fort Stewart. After that, I'm not sure. Maybe it'll be the round-out for 18th Airborne Corps.'

'Paint them brown, then?'

'Probably. The regiment knows about deserts, doesn't it?' The General felt the standard. Yeah, there was still grit in the fabric, from Texas, and New Mexico, and Arizona. He wondered if the troopers who had followed this standard knew that their outfit was being born anew. Maybe so.

CHAPTER 6

Maneuvers

The Navy's change-of-command ceremony, little changed since the time of John Paul Jones, concluded on schedule at 11:24. It had been held two weeks earlier than expected, so that the departing skipper could more quickly assume the Pentagon duty that he would just as happily have avoided. Captain Jim Rosselli had brought USS *Maine* through the final eighteen months of her construction at General Dynamics' Electric Boat Division at Groton, Connecticut, through the launching and final outfitting, through builder's trials and acceptance trials, through commissioning, through shakedown and post-shakedown availability, through a day of practice missile shoots out of Port Canaveral, and through the Panama Canal for her trip to the missile-submarine base at Bangor, Washington. His last job had been to take the boat – *Maine* was huge, but in U.S. Navy parlance still a 'boat' – on her first deterrence patrol into the Gulf of Alaska. That was over now, and, four days after returning his boat to port, he ended his association with the boat by turning her over to his relief, Captain Harry Ricks. It was slightly more complicated than that, of course. Missile submarines since the first, USS *George Washington* – long since converted to razor blades and other useful consumer items – had two complete crews, called 'Blue' and 'Gold.' The idea was simply that the missile boats could spend more time at sea if the crews switched off duty. Though expensive, it worked very effectively. The 'Ohio' class of fleet ballistic missile submarines was averaging over two-thirds of their time at sea, with continuing 70-day patrols divided by 25-day refit periods.

Rosselli had, therefore, really given Ricks half of the command of the massive submarine, and full command of the 'Gold' crew, which was now vacating the ship for the 'Blue' crew, which would conduct the next patrol.

The ceremony concluded, Rosselli retired one last time to his stateroom. As the 'plankowner' commanding officer, certain special souvenirs were his for the asking. A piece of teak decking material drilled for cribbage pegs was part of the tradition. That the skipper had never played cribbage in his life, after a single failed attempt, was beside the point. These traditions were not quite as old as Captain John Paul Jones, but were just as firm. His ball-cap, with 'C.O.' and 'PLANKOWNER' emblazoned in gold on the back, would form part of his permanent collection, as would a ship's plaque, a photo signed by the entire crew, and various gifts from Electric Boat.

'God, I've wanted one of these!' Ricks said.

'They are pretty nice, Captain,' Rosselli replied with a wistful smile. It really wasn't fair. Only the best of officers got to do what he'd done, of course. He'd had command of a fast-attack, USS *Honolulu*, whose reputation as a hot and lucky boat he had continued for his two-and-a-half-year tour as CO. Then he'd been given the Gold crew of USS *Tecumseh*, where he'd excelled yet again. This third – and most unusual – command tour had been necessarily abbreviated. His job had been to oversee the shipwrights at Groton, then get the boat 'dialed in' for her first real team of COs. He'd only had the boat underway for – what? A hundred days, something like that. Just enough to get to know the girl.

'You're not making it any easier on yourself, Rosey,' said the squadron commander, Captain (now a Rear Admiral Selectee) Bart Mancuso.

Rosselli tried to put humor in his voice. 'Hey, Bart, one wop to another, show some pity, eh?'

'I hear ya', *paisan*. It isn't supposed to be easy.'

Rosselli turned to Ricks. 'Best crew I ever had. The XO is going to be one hell of a skipper when the time comes. The boat is fuckin' perfect. Everything works. The refit's a waste of time. The only thing on the gripe sheet that matters is the wiring in the wardroom pantry. Some yard electrician crossed a few cables, and the breakers aren't labeled right. Regs say we have to reset the wiring instead of relabelling the breakers. And that's it. *Nothing* else.'

'Power plant?'

'Four-point-oh, people and equipment. You've seen the results of the ORSE, right?'

'Um-hum.' Ricks nodded. The ship had scored almost perfectly on the Operational Reactor Safeguards Examination, which was the Holy Grail of the nuclear community.

'Sonar?'

'The equipment is the best in the fleet – we got the new upgrade before it became standard. I worked a deal with the guys at SubGru Two right before we commissioned. One of your old guys, Bart. Dr Ron Jones. He's with Sonosystems, even rode for a week with us. The ray-path analyzer is like magic. Torpedo department needs a little work, but not much. I figure they can knock another thirty seconds off their average time. A young chief – matter of fact that department's pretty young across the board. Hasn't quite settled in yet, but they're not much slower than the guys I had on *Tecumseh*, and if I'd had a little more time I could have gotten them completely worked up.'

'No sweat,' Ricks observed comfortably. 'Hell, Jim, I have to have something to do. How many contacts did you have on the patrol?'

'One Akula-class, the *Admiral Lunin*. Picked her up three times, never closer than sixty thousand yards. If he got a sniff of us – hell, he didn't. Never turned towards us. We held him for sixteen hours once. Had really good water, and, well –' Rosselli smiled '– I decided to trail him for a while, way the hell away, of course.'

'Once a fast-attack, always a fast-attack,' Ricks said with a grin. He was a life-long boomer driver, and the idea did not appeal to him, but what the hell, it wasn't a time to criticize.

'Nice profile you did on him,' Mancuso put in, to show

that he wasn't the least offended by Rosselli's action. 'Pretty good boat, isn't it?'

'The Akula? Too good. But not good enough,' Rosselli said. 'I wouldn't start worrying until *we* find a way to track these mothers. I tried when I had *Honolulu*, against Richie Seitz on *Alabama*. He greased my ass for me. Only time that ever happened. I figure God could find an Ohio, but He'll have to have a good day.'

Rosselli wasn't kidding. The Ohio-class of missile submarines were more than just quiet. Their level of radiated noise was actually lower than the background noise level of the ocean, like a whisper at a rock concert. To hear them you had to get incredibly close, but to prevent that from happening, the Ohios had the best sonar systems yet devised. The Navy had done everything right with this class. The original contract had specified a maximum speed of 26–7 knots. The first Ohio had made 28.5. On builder's trials *Maine* had made 29.1, due to a new and very slick super-polymer paint. The seven-bladed propeller enabled almost twenty knots without a hint of noisy cavitation, and the reactor plant operated in almost all regimes on natural convection circulation, obviating the need for potentially noisy feed-pumps. The Navy's mania for noise-control had reached its pinnacle in this class of submarine. Even the blades of the galley mixer were coated with vinyl to prevent metal-to-metal clatter. What Rolls-Royce was to cars, Ohio was to submarines.

Rosselli turned. 'Well, she's yours now, Harry.'

'You couldn't have set her up much better, Jim. Come on, the O-Club's open, and I'll buy you a beer.'

'Yeah,' the former commanding officer observed with a husky voice. On the way out, members of the crew lined up to shake his hand one last time. By the time Rosselli got to the ladder, there were tears in his eyes. On the walk down the brow, they were running down his cheeks. Mancuso understood. It had been the same for him. A good CO developed a genuine love for his boat and his men, and for Rosselli it was worse still. He'd had his extra shots at command, more than even he had gotten, and that made the last one all the harder to leave. Like Mancuso, all Rosselli could look forward to now was a staff job, commanding a desk, nevermore to hold that god-like post of commanding officer of a ship of war. He'd be able to ride the boats, of course, to rate skippers, check ideas and tactics, but henceforth he'd be a tolerated visitor, never really welcome aboard. Most uncomfortable of all, he'd have to avoid revisiting his former command, lest the crew compare his command style to that of their new CO, possibly undermining the new man's command authority. It was, Mancuso reflected, like it must have been for immigrants, as it had been for his own ancestors, looking back one last time at Italy, knowing that they would never return to it, that their lives were irrevocably changed.

The three men climbed into Mancuso's staff car for the ride to the reception at the Officers Club. Rosselli set his souvenirs on the floor and extracted a handkerchief to wipe his eyes. *It isn't fair, just isn't fair. To leave command of a ship like this one to be a goddamned telephone operator at the NMCC. Joint service billet, my ass!* Rosselli blew his nose and contemplated the shore duty that the remainder of his active career held.

Mancuso looked away in quiet respect.

Ricks just shook his head. No need to get all that emotional about it. He was already making mental notes. The Torpedo Department wasn't up to speed yet, eh? Well, he'd do something about *that!* And the XO was supposed to be super-hot. Hmph. What skipper ever failed to praise his XO? If this guy thought he was ready for command, that meant an XO who might be a little *too* ready, and might not be totally supportive, might be feeling his oats. Ricks had had one of those already. Such XOs often needed some subtle reminders of who was boss. Ricks knew how to do that. The good news, the most important news, of course, was about the power plant. Ricks was a product of the Nuclear Navy's obsession with the nuclear power plant. It was something the Squadron Commander, Mancuso, was overly casual about, Ricks judged. The same was probably true of Rosselli. So, they'd passed their ORSE – so what? On *his* boats, the engineering crew had to be ready for an ORSE every goddamned day. One problem with those Ohios was that the systems worked so well people took things casually. That would be doubly true after maxing their ORSE. Complacency was the harbinger of disaster. And these fast-attack guys and their dumb mentality! *Tracking* an Akula, for God's sake! Even from sixty-K yards, what did this lunatic think he was doing?

Ricks' motto was that of the boomer community: WE HID WITH PRIDE (the less polite version was CHICKEN OF THE SEA). If they can't find you, they can't hurt you. Boomers weren't supposed to go around looking for trouble. Their job was to run from it. Missile submarines weren't actually combatant ships at all. That Mancuso didn't reprimand Rosselli on the spot was amazing to Ricks.

He had to consider that, however. Mancuso hadn't reprimanded Rosselli. He'd commended him.

Mancuso was his squadron commander, and did have those two Distinguished Service Medals. It wasn't exactly fair that Ricks was a boomer type stuck working for a fast-attack puke, but there it was. A charger himself, he was clearly a man who wanted aggressive skippers. And Mancuso was the guy who'd be doing his fitness reports. That was the central truth in the equation, wasn't it? Ricks was an ambitious man. He wanted command of a squadron, followed by a nice Pentagon tour, then he'd get his star as a Rear Admiral (Lower Half), then command of a Submarine Group – the one at Pearl would be nice; he liked Hawaii – after which he'd be very well-suited for yet another Pentagon tour. Ricks was a man who'd mapped out his career path while still a lieutenant. So long as he did everything exactly by The Book, more exactly than anyone else, he'd stick to that path.

He hadn't quite planned on working for a fast-attack type, though. He'd have to adapt. Well, he knew how to do that. If that Akula showed up on his next patrol, he'd do what Rosselli had done – but better, of course. He had to. Mancuso would expect it, and Ricks knew that he was in direct competition with thirteen other SSBN COs. To get that squadron command, he had to be the best of fourteen. To be the best, he had to do things that would impress the squadron commander. Okay, so to keep his career path as straight as it had been for twenty years, he had to do a few new and different things. Ricks would have preferred not to, but career came first, didn't it? He knew that he was destined to have an Admiral's flag in the corner of his Pentagon office someday – someday soon. He'd make the adjustment. With an Admiral's flag came a staff, and a driver, and his own parking place in the acres of Pentagon blacktop, and further career-enhancing jobs that might, if he were very lucky, culminate in the E-Ring office of the CNO – better yet, Director of Naval Reactors, which was technically junior to the CNO, but carried with it eight full years in place. He knew himself better suited for that job, which was the one that set policy for the entire nuclear community. DNR wrote The Book. Everything he had to do was set forth in The Book. As the Bible was the path to salvation for Christian and Jew, The Book was the path of flag rank. Ricks knew The Book. Ricks was a brilliant engineer.

J. Robert Fowler was human after all, Ryan told himself. The conference was held upstairs, on the bedroom level of the White House, because the air conditioning in the West Wing was down for repairs, and the sun blasting through the windows of the Oval Office made that room uninhabitable. Instead they were using an upstairs sitting room, the one often delegated for the buffet line at those 'informal' White House dinners that the President liked to have for 'intimate' groups of fifty or so. The antique chairs were grouped around a largish dinner table in a room whose walls were decorated with a mural melange of historical scenes. Moreover, it was a shirtsleeve environment. Fowler was a man uncomfortable with the trappings of his office. Once a federal prosecutor, an attorney who had not once defended a criminal before entering politics with both feet and never looking back, he'd grown up in an informal working environment and seemed to prefer a tie loose in his collar and sleeves rolled up to the elbow. It seemed so very odd to Ryan, who knew the President also to be priggish and stiff in his relationship with subordinates. Odder still, the President had walked into the room carrying the sports page from the *Baltimore Sun*, which he preferred to the local papers' sports coverage. President Fowler was a rabid football fan. The first NFL pre-season games were already history, and he was handicapping the teams for the coming season. The DDCI shrugged, leaving his coat on. There was as much complexity in this man as any other, Jack knew, and complexities were not predictable.

The President had discreetly cleared his calendar for this afternoon conference. Sitting at the head of the table, and directly under an air-conditioning vent, Fowler actually smiled a little as his guests took their places. At his left was G. Dennis Bunker, Secretary of Defense. Former CEO of Aerospace, Inc., Bunker was a former USAF fighter pilot who'd flown 100 missions in the early days of Vietnam, then left the service to found a company he'd ultimately built into a multi-billion-dollar empire that sprawled across southern California. He'd sold that and all his other commercial holdings to take this job, keeping only one enterprise under his control – the San Diego Chargers. That retention had been the subject of considerable joshing during his confirmation hearings, and there was light-hearted speculation that Fowler liked Bunker mainly for his SecDef's love of football. Bunker was a rarity in the Fowler administration, as close to a hawk as anyone here, a knowledgeable player in the defense area whose lectures to men in uniform were listened to. Though he'd left the Air Force as a captain, he'd left with three Distinguished Flying Crosses earned driving his F-105 fighter-bomber 'downtown' into the environs of Hanoi. Dennis Bunker had seen the elephant. He could talk tactics with captains and strategy with generals. Both the uniforms and the politicians respected the SecDef, and that was rare.

Next to Bunker was Brent Talbot, Secretary of State.

A former professor of political science at Northwestern University, Talbot was a long-time friend and ally of the President. Seventy years old, with regal white hair over a pale, intelligent face, Talbot was less an academic than an old-fashioned gentleman, albeit one with a killer instinct. After years of sitting on PFIAB – the President's Foreign Intelligence Advisory Board – and countless other commissions, he was in a place where he could make his impact felt. The archetypical outside-insider, he'd finally picked a winning horse in Fowler. He was also a man with genuine vision. The changes in the East–West relationship signalled to the SecState a historic opportunity to change the face of the world, and he wanted his name on the changes.

On the President's right was his Chief of Staff, Arnold van Damm. This was, after all, a political assembly, and political advice was of paramount import. Next to van Damm was Elizabeth Elliot, the new National Security Advisor. She looked rather severe today, Ryan noted, dressed in an expensive suit with a wispy cravat knotted around her pretty, thin neck. Beside her was Marcus Cabot, Director of Central Intelligence, and Ryan's immediate boss.

The second-rank people were farther away from the seat of power, of course. Ryan and Adler were at the far end of the table, both to separate them from the President and to allow their fuller visibility to the senior members of the conference when they began speaking.

'This your year, Dennis?' the President asked the SecDef.

'You bet it is!' Bunker said. 'I've waited long enough, but with those two new linebackers, this year we're going to Denver.'

'Then you'll meet the Vikings there,' Talbot observed. 'Dennis, you had the first draft pick, why didn't you take Tony Wills?'

'I have three good running backs. I needed linebackers, and that kid from Alabama is the best I've ever seen.'

'You'll regret it,' the Secretary of State pronounced. Tony Wills had been drafted from Northwestern. An academic All-American, Rhodes Scholar, winner of the Heisman Trophy, and the kid who had almost single-handedly resurrected Northwestern as a football school, Wills had been Talbot's prize student. By all accounts an exceptional young man, people were already talking about his future in politics. Ryan thought that premature, even in America's changing political landscape. 'He'll kick your butt, third game of the season. And then again in the Superbowl, if your team makes it that far, which I doubt, Dennis.'

'We'll see,' Bunker snorted.

The President laughed as he arranged his papers. Liz Elliot tried and failed to hide her disapproval, Jack noted from twenty feet away. Her papers were already arranged, her pen in its place to make notes, and her face impatient at the locker-room talk at her end of the table. Well, she had the job she'd angled for, even if it had taken a death – Ryan had heard the details by now – to get it for her.

'I think we'll call the meeting to order,' President Fowler said. Noise in the room stopped cold. 'Mr Adler, could you fill us in on what happened on your trip?'

'Thank you, Mr President. I would say that most of the pieces are in place. The Vatican agrees to the terms of our proposal unconditionally, and is ready to host the negotiations at any time.'

'How did Israel react?' Liz Elliot asked, to show that she was on top of things.

'Could have been better,' Adler said neutrally. 'They'll come, but I expect serious resistance.'

'How serious?'

'Anything they can do to avoid being nailed down, they'll do. They are very uncomfortable with this idea.'

'This was hardly unexpected, Mr President,' Talbot added.

'What about the Saudis?' Fowler asked Ryan.

'Sir, my read is that they'll play. Prince Ali was very optimistic. We spent an hour with the King, and his reaction was cautious but positive. Their concern is that the Israelis won't do it, no matter what pressure we put on them, and they are worried about being left hanging. Setting that aside for the moment, Mr President, the Saudis appear quite willing to accept the plan as drafted, and to accept their participatory role in its implementation. They offered some modifications, which I outlined in my briefing sheet. As you can see none of them are substantively troublesome. In fact, two of them look like genuine enhancements.'

'The Soviets?'

'Scott handled that,' Secretary Talbot replied. 'They have signed off on the idea, but their read also is that Israel will not cooperate. President Narmonov cabled us day before yesterday that the plan is wholly compatible with his government's policy. They are willing to underwrite the plan to the extent that they will restrict arms sales to the other nations in the region to cover defensive needs only.'

'Really?' Ryan blurted.

'That does clobber one of your predictions, doesn't it?' DCI Cabot noted with a chuckle.

'How so?' the President asked.

'Mr President, arms sales to that area are a major cash cow for the Sovs. For them to reduce those sales will cost them billions in hard-currency earnings that they really need.' Ryan leaned back and whistled. 'That is surprising.'

'They also want to have a few people at the negotiations. That seems fair enough. The arms-sales aspect of the treaty – if we get that far – will be set up as a side-bar codicil between America and the Soviets.' Liz Elliot smiled at Ryan. She'd predicted that development.

'In return, the Soviets want some help on farm commodities, and a few trade credits,' Talbot added. 'It's cheap at the price. Soviet cooperation in this affair is hugely important to us, and the prestige associated with the treaty is important for them. It's a very equitable deal for the both of us. Besides, we have all that wheat lying around and doing nothing.'

'So, the only stumbling block is Israel?' Fowler asked the table. He was answered with nods. 'How serious?'

'Jack,' Cabot said, turning to his deputy, 'how did Avi Ben Jakob react to things?'

'We had dinner the day before I flew to Saudi Arabia. He looked very unhappy. Exactly what he knew I do not know. I didn't give him very much to warn his government with, and –'

'What does "not very much" mean, Ryan?' Elliot snapped down the table.

'Nothing,' Ryan answered. 'I told him to wait and see. Intelligence people don't like that. I would speculate that he knew something was up, but not what.'

'The looks I got at the table over there were pretty surprised,' Adler said to back Ryan up. 'They expected something, but what I gave them wasn't it.'

The Secretary of State leaned forward. 'Mr President, Israel has lived for two generations under the fiction that they and they alone are responsible for their national security. It's become almost a religious belief over there – and despite the fact that we give them vast amounts of arms and other grants every year, it is their government policy to live as though that idea were true. Their institutional fear is that once they mortgage their national security to the good will of others, they become vulnerable to the discontinuance of that good will.'

'You get tired of hearing that,' Liz Elliot observed coldly.

Maybe you wouldn't if six million of your relatives got themselves turned into air pollution, Ryan thought to himself. *How the hell can we not be sensitive to memories of the Holocaust?*

'I think we can take it as given that a bilateral defense treaty between the United States and Israel will sail through the Senate,' Arnie van Damm said, speaking for the first time.

'How quickly can we deploy the necessary units to Israeli territory?' Fowler wanted to know.

'It would take roughly five weeks from the time you push the button, sir,' the SecDef replied. 'The 10th Armored Cavalry Regiment is forming up right now. That's essentially a heavy brigade force, and it'll defeat

– make that "destroy" – any armored division the Arabs could throw at it. To that we'll add a Marine unit for show, and with the home-port deal at Haifa, we'll almost always have a carrier battle-group in the Eastern Med. Toss in the F-16 wing from Sicily, and you've got a sizable force. The military will like it, too. It gives them a big play area to train in. We'll use our base in the Negev the same way we use the National Training Center in Fort Irwin. The best way to keep that unit tight and ready is to train the hell out of it. It'll be expensive to run it that way, of course, but –'

'But we'll pay that price,' Fowler said, cutting Bunker off gently. 'It's more than worth the expenditure, and we won't have any problems on The Hill keeping that funded, will we, Arnie?'

'Any congressman who bitches about this will have his career cut short,' the Chief of Staff said confidently.

'So, it's just a matter of eliminating Israeli opposition?' Fowler went on.

'Correct, Mr President,' Talbot replied for the assembly.

'What's the best way to do that?' This Presidential question was rhetorical. That answer was already delineated. The current Israeli government, like all which had preceded it for a decade, was a shaky coalition of disparate interests. The right kind of shove from Washington would bring it down. 'What about the rest of the world?'

'The NATO countries will not be a problem. The rest of the UN will go along grudgingly,' Elliot said, before Talbot could speak. 'So long as the Saudis play ball on this, the Islamic world will fall into line. If Israel resists, they'll be as alone as they have ever been.'

'I don't like putting too much pressure on them,' Ryan said.

'Dr Ryan, that's not within your purview,' Elliot said gently. A few heads moved slightly, and a few eyes narrowed, but no one rose to Jack's defense.

'That is true, Dr Elliot,' Ryan said, after the awkward silence. 'It is also true that too much pressure might have an effect opposite from what the President intends. Then there is a moral dimension that needs to be considered.'

'Dr Ryan, this is all about the moral dimension,' the President said. 'The moral dimension is simply put: there has been enough war there, and it is time to put an end to it. Our plan is a means of doing that.'

Our plan, Ryan heard him say. Van Damm's eyes flickered for a moment, then went still. Jack realized that he was as alone here in this room as the President intended Israel to be. He looked down at his notes and kept his mouth shut. *Moral dimension, my ass!* Jack thought angrily. *This is about setting footprints in the sands of time, and about the political advantages of being seen as The Great Peacemaker.* But it wasn't a time for cynicism, and though the plan was no longer Ryan's, it was a worthy one.

'If we have to squeeze them, how do we go about it?' President Fowler asked lightly. 'Nothing harsh, just to send a quiet and intelligible message.'

'There's a major shipment of aircraft spares ready to go next week. They're replacing the radar systems on all their F-15 fighters,' Secretary of Defense Bunker said. 'There are other things, too, but that radar system is very important to them. It's brand-new. We're just installing it ourselves. The same is true for the F-16's new missile system. Their air force is their crown jewel. If we are forced to withhold that shipment for technical reasons, they'll get the signal loud and clear.'

'Can it be done quietly?' Elliot asked.

'We can let them know that if they make noise, it won't help,' van Damm said. 'If the speech goes over well at the UN, as it should, we might be able to obviate their congressional lobby.'

'It might be preferable to sweeten the deal by allowing them to get more arms instead of crippling systems they already have.' That was Ryan's last toss. Elliot slammed the door on the DDCI.

'We can't afford that.'

The Chief of Staff agreed: 'We can't possibly squeeze any more defense dollars out of the budget, even for Israel. The money just isn't there.'

'I'd prefer to let them know ahead of time – if we really intend to squeeze them,' the Secretary of State said.

Liz Elliot shook her head. 'No. If they need to get the message, let them get it the hard way. They like to play tough. They ought to understand.'

'Very well.' The President made a last note on his pad. 'We hold until the speech next week. I change the speech to include an invitation to enter formal negotiations in Rome starting two weeks from yesterday. We let Israel know that they either play ball or face the consequences, and that we're not kidding this time. We send that message as Secretary Bunker suggested, and do that by surprise. Anything else?'

'Leaks?' van Damm said quietly.

'What about Israel?' Elliot asked Scott Adler.

'I told them that this was highly sensitive, but . . .'

'Brent, get on the phone to their Foreign Minister, and tell them that if they start making noise prior to the speech, there will be major consequences.'

'Yes, Mr President.'

'And as far as this group is concerned, there will be no leaks.' That Presidential command was aimed at the far end of the table. 'Adjourned.'

Ryan took his papers and walked outside. Marcus Cabot joined him in the hall after a moment.

'You should know when to keep your mouth shut, Jack.'

'Look, Director, if we press them too hard –'

'We'll get what we want.'

'I think it's wrong, and I think it's dumb. We'll get what we want. Okay, so it takes a few extra months, we'll still get it. We don't have to threaten them.'

'The President wants it done that way.' Cabot ended the discussion by walking off.

'Yes, sir,' Jack responded to thin air.

The rest of the people filed out. Talbot gave Ryan a wink and a nod. The rest, except for Adler, avoided eye contact. Adler came over after a whisper from his boss.

'Nice try, Jack. You almost got yourself fired a few minutes ago.'

That surprised Ryan. Wasn't he supposed to say what he thought? 'Look, Scott, if I'm not allowed to –'

'You're not allowed to cross the President, not this one. You do not have the rank to make adverse advice stick. Brent was ready to make that point, but you got in the way – and you lost, and you didn't leave him any room to maneuver. So, next time keep it zipped, okay?'

'Thanks for your support,' Jack answered with an edge on his voice.

'You blew it, Jack. You said the right thing the wrong way. Learn from that, will you?' Adler paused. 'The boss also says "well done" for your work in Riyadh. If you'd just learn when to shut up, he says, you'd be a lot more effective.'

'Okay, thanks.' Adler was right, of course. Ryan knew it.

'Where you headed?'

'Home. I don't have anything left to do today at the office.'

'Come along with us. Brent wants to talk to you. We'll have a light dinner at my shop.' Adler led Jack to the elevator.

'Well?' the President asked, still back in the room.

'I'd say it looks awfully good,' van Damm said. 'Especially if we can bring this one in before the elections.'

'Be nice to hold a few extra seats,' Fowler agreed. The first two years of his administration had not been easy. Budget problems, added to an economy that couldn't seem to decide what it wanted to do, had crippled his programs and saddled his tough managerial style with more question marks than exclamation points. The congressional elections in November would be the first real public response to their new President, and early poll numbers looked exceedingly iffy. It was the general way of things that the President's party lost seats in off-year elections, but this President could not afford to lose many. 'Shame we have to pressure the Israelis, but . . .'

'Politically it'll be worth it – if we can bring the treaty off.'

'We can,' Elliot said, leaning against the doorframe. 'If we make the time-line, we can have the treaties out of the Senate by October 16th.'

'You are one ambitious lady, Liz,' Arnie noted. 'Well, I have work to do. If you will excuse me, Mr President?'

'See you tomorrow, Arnie.'

Fowler walked over to the windows facing Pennsylvania Avenue. The blistering heat of early August rose in shimmers from the streets and sidewalks. Across the street in Lafayette Park, there remained two anti-nuclear-weapons signs. That garnered a smirk and a snort from Fowler. Didn't those dumb hippies know that nukes were a thing of the past? He turned.

'Join me for dinner, Elizabeth?'

Dr Elliot smiled at her boss. 'Love to, Bob.'

The one good thing about his brother's involvement with drugs was that he had left nearly a hundred thousand dollars cash behind in a battered suitcase. Marvin Russell had taken that and driven to Minneapolis, where he'd bought presentable clothes, a decent set of luggage, and a ticket. One of the many things he'd learned in prison was the proper methodology for obtaining an alternate identity. He had three of them, complete with passports, that no cop knew anything about. He'd also learned about keeping a low profile. His clothes were presentable, but not flashy. He purchased a stand-by ticket on a flight he expected to be underbooked, saving himself another few hundred dollars. That $91,545.00 had to last him a long time, and life got expensive where he was heading. Life also got very cheap, he knew, but not in terms of money. A warrior could face that, he decided early on.

After a layover in Frankfurt, he traveled on in a southerly direction. No fool, Russell had once participated in an international conference of sorts – he'd sacrificed a total identity-set for that trip, four years previously. At the conference he'd made a few contacts. Most importantly of all, he'd learned of contact procedures. The international terrorist community was a careful one. It had to be, with all the forces arrayed against it, and Russell did not know his luck – of the three contact numbers he remembered, one had long since been compromised and two Red Brigade members rolled quietly up with it. He used one of the others, and that number still worked. The contact had led him to a dinner meeting in Athens where he'd been checked and cleared for further travel. Russell hurried back to his hotel – the local food did not agree with him – and sat down to wait for the phone to ring. To say he was nervous was an understatement. For all Marvin's caution, he knew that he was vulnerable. With not even a pocket-knife to defend himself – travelling with weapons was far too dangerous – he was an easy mark for any cop who carried a gun. What if this contact line had been burned? If it had, he'd be arrested here, or summoned into a carefully-prepared ambush from which he'd be lucky to escape alive. European cops weren't as mindful of constitutional rights as the Americans – but that thought died a rapid and quiet death. How kindly had the FBI treated his brother?

Damn! One more Sioux warrior shot down like a dog. Not even time to sing his Death Song. They'd pay for that. But only if he lived long enough, Marvin Russell corrected himself.

He sat by the window, the lights behind him extinguished, watching the traffic, watching for approaching police, waiting for the phone to ring. How would he make them pay? Russell asked himself. He didn't know, and really didn't care. Just so there was something he could do. The money belt was tight around his waist. One drawback of his physical condition was that there wasn't much slack in his waistline to take up. But he couldn't risk losing his money – without it, where the hell would he be? Keeping track of money was a pain in the ass, wasn't it? Marks in Germany. Drachmas or douche-bags or something else here. Fortunately, you got your airline tickets with bucks. He traveled American-flag carriers mainly for that reason, certainly not because he liked the sight of the Stars and Stripes on the tail fins of the aircraft. The phone rang. Russell lifted it.

'Yes?'

'Tomorrow, nine-thirty, be in front of the hotel, ready to travel. Understood?'

'Nine-thirty. Yes.' The phone clicked off before he could say more.

'Okay,' Russell said to himself. He rose and moved towards the bed. The door was double-locked and chained, and he had a chair propped under the knob. Marvin pondered that. If he were being set up, they'd bag him like a duck in autumn right in front of the hotel, or maybe they'd take him away by car and spring the trap away from civilians . . . that was more likely, he judged. But certainly they wouldn't go to all the trouble of setting up a rendezvous and then kick in the door here. Probably not. Hard to predict what cops would do, wasn't it? So he slept in his jeans and shirt, the money belt securely wrapped around his waist. After all, he still had thieves to worry about . . .

The sun rose about as early here as it did at home. Russell awoke with the first pink-orange glow. On checking in he'd requested an east-facing room. He said his prayers to the sun and prepared himself for travel. He had breakfast sent up – it cost a few extra drachmas, but what the hell? – and packed what few things he'd removed from his suitcase. By nine he was thoroughly ready and thoroughly nervous. If it was going to happen, it would happen in thirty minutes. He could easily be dead before lunch, dead in a foreign land, distant from the spirits of his people. Would they even send his body back to the Dakotas? Probably not. He'd just vanish from the face of the earth. The actions he ascribed to policemen were the same ones he would himself have taken, but what would be good tactics for a warrior were something else to cops, weren't they? Russell paced the room, looking out the window at the cars and street vendors. Any one of those people selling trinkets or Cokes to the tourists could so easily be a police officer. No, more than one, more like ten. Cops didn't like fair fights, did they? They shot from ambush and attacked in gangs.

9:15. The numbers on the digital clock marched forward with a combination of sloth and alacrity that depended entirely on how often Russell turned to check them. It was time. He lifted his bags and left the room without a backward glance. It was a short walk to the elevator, which arrived quickly enough that it piqued Russell's paranoia yet again. A minute later, he was in the lobby. A bellman offered to take his bags, but he declined the offer and made his way to the desk. The only thing left on his bill was breakfast, which he settled with his remaining local currency. He had a few minutes left over, and walked to the newsstand for a copy of anything that was in English. What was happening in the world? It was an odd moment of curiosity for Marvin, whose world was a constricted one of threats and responses and evasions. What was the world? he asked himself. It was what he could see at the time, little more than that, a bubble of space defined by what his senses reported to him. At home he could see distant horizons and a huge enveloping dome of sky. Here, reality was circumscribed by walls, and stretched a mere hundred feet from one horizon to another. He had a sudden attack of anxiety, knowing what it was to be a hunted animal, and struggled to fight it off. He checked his watch: 9:28. Time.

Russell walked outside to the cab stand, wondering what came next. He set his two bags down, looking about as casually as he could manage in the knowledge that guns might even now be aimed at his head. Would he die as John had died? A bullet in the head, no warning at all, not even the dignity an animal might have? That was no way to die, and the thought of it sickened him. Russell balled his hands into tight, powerful fists to control the trembling as a car approached. The driver was looking at him. This was it. He lifted his bags and walked to it.

'Mr Drake?' It was the name under which Russell was currently traveling. The driver wasn't the one he'd met for dinner. Russell knew at once that he was dealing with pros, who compartmented everything. That was a good sign.

'That's me,' Russell answered with a smile/grimace.

The driver got out and opened the trunk. Russell

heaved the bags in, then walked to the passenger door and got in the front seat. If this were a trap, he could throttle the driver before he died. At least he'd accomplish that much.

Fifty meters away, Sergeant Spiridon Papanicolaou of the Hellenic National Police sat in an old Opel liveried as a taxi. Sitting there with an extravagant black mustache and munching on a breakfast roll, he looked like anything but a cop. He had a small automatic in the glove box, but like most European cops, he was not skilled in its use. The Nikon camera sitting in a clip holder under his seat was his only real weapon. His job was surveillance, actually working at the behest of the Ministry of Public Order. His memory for faces was photographic – the camera was for people lacking the talent of which he was justifiably proud. His method of operation was one that required great patience, but Papanicolaou had plenty of that. Whenever his superiors got wind of a possible terrorist operation in the Athens area, he prowled hotels and airports and docks. He wasn't the only such officer, but he was the best. He had a nose for it as his father had had a nose for where the fish were running. And he hated terrorists. In fact, he hated all variety of criminals, but terrorists were the worst of the lot, and he chafed at his government's off-again/on-again interest in running the murderous bastards out of his ancient and noble country. Currently the interest was on-again. A week earlier there had been a possible sighting report of someone from the PFLP near the Parthenon. Four men from his squad were at the airport. A few others were checking the cruise docks, but Papanicolaou liked to check the hotels. They had to stay somewhere. Never the best – they were too flashy. Never the worst – these bastards liked a modest degree of comfort. The middle sort, the comfortable family places on the secondary streets, with lots of college-age travelers whose rapid shuffling in and out made for difficulty in spotting one particular face. But Papanicolaou had his father's eyes. He could recognize a face from half a second's exposure at seventy meters.

And the driver of that blue Fiat was a 'face.' He couldn't remember if it had a name attached to it, but he remembered seeing the face somewhere. The 'Unknown' file, probably, one of the hundreds of photographs in the files that came in from Interpol and the military-intelligence people whose lust for the blood of terrorists was even more frustrated by their government's policy. This was the country of Leonidas and Xenophon, Odysseus and Achilles. Greece – Hellas to the sergeant – was the home of epic warriors and the very birthplace of freedom and democracy, not a place for foreign scum to kill with impunity . . .

Who's the other one? Papanicolaou wondered. *Dresses like an American . . . odd features, though.* He raised the camera in one smooth motion, zoomed the lens to full magnification and got off three rapid frames before putting it back down. The Fiat was moving . . . well, he'd see where it was going. The sergeant switched off his on-call light and headed out of the cab rank.

Russell settled back in the seat. He didn't bother with the seatbelt. If he had to escape the car, he didn't want to be bothered. The driver was a good one, maneuvering in and out of traffic, which was lively here. He didn't say a word. That was fine with Russell, too. The American moved his head to the side, and scanned forward, looking for a trap. His eyes flickered around the inside of the car. No obvious places to hide a weapon. No visible microphones or radio equipment. That didn't mean anything, but he looked anyway. Finally he pretended to relax and cocked his head in a direction from which he could look ahead and also behind by eyeing the right-side mirror. His hunter's instincts were taut and alert this morning. There was potential danger everywhere.

The driver took what seemed to be an aimless path. It was hard for Russell to be sure, of course. The streets of this city had predated chariots, much less automobiles, and later concessions made to wheeled vehicles had fallen short of making Athens a Los Angeles. Though the autos on the street were tiny ones, traffic seemed to be a constant, moving, anarchic log-jam. He wanted to know where they were going, but there was no sense in asking. He would be unable to distinguish between a truthful answer and a lie – and even if he got a straight answer, it probably would not have meant anything to him. He was for better or worse committed to this course of action, Russell knew. It didn't make him feel any more comfortable, but to deny the truth of it was to lie to himself, and Russell was not that sort. The best he could do was to stay alert. That he did.

The airport, Papanicolaou thought. That was certainly convenient. In addition to his squad-mates, there were at least twenty other officers there, armed with pistols and sub-machineguns. That should be easy. Just move a few of the plain-clothes people in close while two heavily-armed people in uniform strolled by, and take them down – he liked that American euphemism – quickly and cleanly. Off into a side room to see if they were what he thought, and if not – well, then his captain would fuss over them. Sorry, he'd say, but you fit a description we got from – whomever he might conveniently blame; maybe the French or Italians – and one cannot be too careful with international air travel. They would automatically upgrade whatever tickets the two people had to first-class ones. It almost always worked.

On the other hand, if that face was what Papanicolaou thought it was, well, then he'd have gotten his third terrorist of the year. Maybe even the fourth. Just because the other one dressed like an American didn't mean he had to be one. Four in just eight months – no, only seven months, the sergeant corrected himself. Not bad for one somewhat eccentric cop who liked to work alone. Papanicolaou allowed his car to close in slightly. He didn't want to lose these fish in traffic.

Russell counted a bunch of cabs. They had to cater to tourists mainly, or other people who didn't care to drive in the local traffic . . . *that's odd*. It took him a moment to figure why. Oh, sure, he thought, its dome light wasn't on. Only the driver. Most of the others had passengers, but even those without had their dome lights on. It must have been the on-duty light, he judged. But that one's was out. Russell's driver had it easy, taking the next right turn to head down towards what appeared to be something akin to a real highway. Most of the cabs failed to take the turn. Though Russell didn't know it, they were heading either towards museums or shopping areas. But the one with the light out followed them around the corner, fifty yards back.

'We're being followed,' Marvin announced quietly. 'You have a friend watching our back?'

'No.' The driver's eyes immediately went up to the mirror. 'Which one do you think it is?'

'I don't "think," sport. It's the taxi fifty yards back, right side, dirty-white, without the dome-light on, I don't know the make of the car. He's made two turns with us. You should pay better attention,' Russell added, wondering if this was the trap he feared. He figured he could kill the driver easily enough. A little guy with a skinny neck that he could wring as easily as he killed a mourning dove, yeah, it wouldn't be hard.

'Thank you. Yes, I should . . .' the driver replied, after identifying the cab. *And who might you be . . . ! We'll see.* He made another random turn. It followed.

'You are correct, my friend,' the driver said thoughtfully. 'How did you know?'

'I pay attention to things.'

'So I see . . . this changes our plans somewhat.' The driver's mind was racing. Unlike Russell, he knew that he hadn't been set up. Though he had been unable to establish his guest's bonafides, no intelligence or police officer would have given him that warning. Well, probably not, he corrected himself. But there was one way to check that. He was also angry at the Greeks. One of his comrades had disappeared off the streets of Piraeus in April, to turn up in Britain a few days later. That friend was now in Parkhurst Prison on the Isle of Wight. They'd once been able to operate in relative impunity in Greece, most often using the country as a safe transit point. He knew that doing actual operations here had been a mistake – just having the country as a sallyport had been quite valuable enough, an advantage not to be squandered – but that didn't mitigate his anger at the Greek police.

'It may be necessary to do something about this.'

Russell's eyes went back to the driver. 'I don't have a weapon.'

'I do. I would prefer not to use it. How strong are you?'

By way of answering, Russell reached out his left hand and squeezed the driver's right knee.

'You have made your point,' the driver said with a level voice. 'If you cripple me, I cannot drive.' *Now, how do we do this . . . !* 'Have you killed before?'

'Yes,' Russell lied. He hadn't ever personally killed a man, but he'd killed enough other things. 'I can do that.'

The driver nodded and increased speed on his way out of town. He had to find . . .

Papanicolaou frowned. They were not heading to the airport. Too bad. Good thing he hadn't called it in. Well. He allowed himself to lay back, shielding himself with other vehicles. The paint job on the Fiat made it easy to spot, and as traffic thinned out, he could take it a little more casually. Maybe they were going to a safe house. If so, he'd have to be very careful, but also if so, he'd have a valuable piece of information. Identifying a safe house was about the best thing he could accomplish. Then the muscle boys could move in, or the intelligence squad could stake it out, identifying more and more faces, then assaulting the place in such a way as to arrest three or even more of the bastards. There could be a decoration and promotion at the end of this surveillance. Again he thought of making a radio call, but – but what did he really know? He was letting his excitement get away with him, wasn't he? He had a probable identification on a face without a name. Might his eyes have deceived him? Might the face be something other than what he thought? A common criminal, perhaps?

Spiridon Papanicolaou grumbled a curse at fate and luck, his trained eyes locked on the car. They were entering an old part of Athens, with narrow streets. Not a fashionable area, it was a working-class neighborhood with narrow streets, mainly empty. Those with jobs were at them. Housewives were at the local shops. Children played in parks. Quite a few people were taking their holidays on the islands, and the streets were emptier than one might have expected. The Fiat slowed suddenly and turned right into one of many anonymous sidestreets.

'Ready?'

'Yes.'

The car stopped briefly. Russell had already removed his jacket and tie, still wondering if this could be the final act of the trap, but he didn't really care anymore. What would happen would happen. He flexed his hands as he walked back up the street.

Sergeant Spiridon Papanicolaou increased speed to approach the corner. If they were heading into this rabbit warren of narrow lanes, he could not maintain visual contact without getting closer. Well, if they identified him, he'd call for help. Police work was unpredictable, after all. As he approached the corner, he saw a man standing on the side street, looking at a paper. Not either of the men he was shadowing. This one wasn't wearing a jacket, though his face was turned away, and the way he was standing there was like something in a movie. The sergeant smiled wryly at that – but the smile stopped at once.

As soon as Papanicolaou was fully onto the sidestreet, he saw the Fiat, no more than twenty meters away, and backing up rapidly towards him. The police officer stood on the brakes to stop his taxi, and started to think about reversing himself when an arm reached across his face. His hands came off the wheel to grab it, but the powerful hand gripped his chin, and another seized the back of his neck. His instinct to turn and see what was happening was answered by the way one hand wrenched his head to the left, and he saw the face of the American – but then he felt his vertebrae strain for a brief instant and snap with an audible sound that announced his death to Papanicolaou as surely and irrevocably as a bullet. Then he knew. The man did have odd features, like something else from a movie, like something . . .

Russell jumped out of the way and waved. The Fiat

pulled forward again, then went into reverse and slammed hard into the taxi. The driver's head lolled forward atop its broken neck. Probably the man was dead already, Russell knew, but that wasn't a matter of concern. Yes, it was. He felt for a pulse, then made sure the neck was well and truly snapped – he worked it around to make sure the spine was severed, too – before moving to the Fiat. Russell smiled to himself as he got in. *Gee, that wasn't so hard . . .*

'He's dead. Let's get the hell out of here!'

'Are you sure?'

'I broke his neck like a toothpick. Yeah, he's dead, man. It was easy. Little pencil-neck of a guy.'

'Like me, you mean?' The driver turned and grinned. He'd have to dump the car, of course, but the joy of their escape and the satisfaction of the killing was sufficient to the moment. And he had found a comrade, a worthy one. 'Your name is?'

'Marvin.'

'I am Ibrahim.'

The President's speech was a triumph. The man did know how to deliver a good performance, Ryan told himself as the applause rippled across the General Assembly auditorium in New York. His gracious, if rather cold, smile thanked the assembled representatives of a hundred sixty or so countries. The cameras panned to the Israeli delegation, whose clapping was rather more perfunctory than that of the Arab states – there evidently hadn't been time to brief them. The Soviets outdid themselves, joining those who stood. Jack lifted the remote control and switched off the set before the ABC commentator could summarize what the President had said. Ryan had a draft of the speech on his desk, and had made notes of his own. Moments earlier, the invitations had been telexed by the Vatican to all of the concerned foreign ministries. All would come to Rome in ten days. The draft treaty was ready for them. Quiet, rapid moves by a handful of ambassadors and deputy-assistant-secretaries of state had informed other governments of what was in the offing, and uniform approval had come back. The Israelis knew about that. The proper back-channel leaks had been allowed to percolate in the desired direction. If they stonewalled – well, Bunker had put a hold on that shipment of aircraft parts, and the Israelis had been too shocked to react yet. More accurately, they'd been told not to react if they ever wanted to see the new radar systems. There were already rumbles from the Israeli lobby, which had its own sources throughout the US government, and was making discreet calls to key members of Congress. But Fowler had briefed the congressional leadership two days earlier, and the initial read on the Fowler Plan was highly favorable. The chairman and ranking member of the Senate Foreign Relations Committee had promised passage of both draft treaties in under a week. It was going to happen, Jack thought to himself. It might really work. Certainly it wouldn't hurt anything. All the good will America had generated in its own adventure in the Persian Gulf was on the line. The Arabs would see this as a fundamental change in US policy – which it was – America was slapping Israel down. Israel would see it the same way, but that wasn't really true. The peace would be guaranteed the only way that was possible, by American military and political power. The demise of East–West confrontation had made it possible for America, acting in accord with the other major powers, to dictate a just peace. *What we think a just peace is,* Ryan corrected himself. *God, I hope this works out.*

It was too late for that, of course. It had, after all, been his idea. The Fowler Plan. They had to break the cycle, to find a way out of the trap. America was the only country trusted by both sides, a fact won with American blood on the one hand, and vast amounts of money on the other. America had to guarantee the peace, and the peace had to be founded on something looking recognizably like justice to all concerned. The equation was both simple and complex. The principles could be expressed in a single short paragraph. The details of execution would take a small book. The monetary cost – well, the enabling legislation would sail through Congress despite the size of it. Saudi Arabia was actually underwriting a quarter of the cost, a concession won only four days earlier by Secretary Talbot. In return, the Saudis would be buying yet another installment of high-tech arms, which had been handled by Dennis Bunker. Those two had really handled their end superbly, Ryan knew. Whatever the President's faults, his two most important cabinet members – two close friends – were the best such team he'd ever seen in government service. And they'd served their President and their country well in the past week.

'This is going to work,' Jack said quietly to himself in the privacy of his office. 'Maybe, maybe, maybe.' He checked his watch. He'd have a read on that in about three hours.

Qati faced his television with a frown. *Was it possible?* History said no, but –

But the Saudis had broken off their supply of money, seduced by the help America had given them against Iraq. And his organization had bet on the wrong horse in that one. Already his people were feeling the financial pinch, though they'd been careful to invest what funds they had received over the previous generation. Their Swiss and other European bankers had ensured a steady flow of money, and the pinch was more psychological than real, but to the Arab mind the psychological *was* real, just as it was to any politically astute mind.

The key to it, Qati knew, was whether or not the Americans would put real pressure on the Zionists. They'd never done so. They'd allowed the Israelis to attack an American warship and kill American sailors – and forgiven them before the bleeding had stopped, before the last victim had died. When American military forces had to fight for every dollar of funds from their own Congress, that same spineless body of political whores fell over itself giving arms to the Jews. America had never pressured Israel in any meaningful way. That was the key to his existence, wasn't it? So long as there was no peace in the Middle East, he had a mission: the destruction of the Jewish State. Without that –

But the problems in the Middle East predated his birth. They might go away, but only when –

But it was a time for truth, Qati told himself, stretching tired and sore limbs. What prospects for destroying Israel did he have? Not from without. So long as America supported the Jews, and so long as the Arab states failed to unite . . .

And the Russians? The cursed Russians had stood like begging dogs at the end of Fowler's speech.

It *was* possible. The thought was no less threatening to Qati than the first diagnosis of his cancer. He leaned back in his chair and closed his eyes. What if the Americans did pressure the Jews? What if the Russians did support his absurd new plan? What if the Israelis gave in to the pressure? What if the Palestinians found the concessions demanded of Israel to their taste? It could work. The Zionist state might continue to exist. The Palestinians might find contentment in their new land. A *modus vivendi* might evolve into being.

It would mean that his life had been to no purpose. It would mean that all the things he had worked for, all the sacrifice and self-denial had gone for nothing. His freedom-fighters had fought and died for a generation . . . for a cause that might be forever lost.

Betrayed by his fellow Arabs, whose money and political support had sustained his men.

Betrayed by the Russians, whose support and arms had sustained his movement from its birth.

Betrayed by the Americans – the most perversely of all. By taking away their enemy.

Betrayed by Israel – by making something akin to a fair peace. It wasn't fair at all, of course. So long as a single Zionist lived on Arab lands, there would be no fairness.

Might he be betrayed by the Palestinians also? What if they came to accept this? Where would his dedicated fighters come from?

Betrayed by everyone!

167

No, God could not let that be. God was merciful, and gave his light to the faithful.

No, this could not really happen. It wasn't possible. Too many things had to fall into place for this hellish vision to become real. Had not there been so many peace plans for this region? So many visions. And where had they led? Even the Carter–Sadat–Begin talks in America, where the Americans had browbeaten their putative allies into serious concessions, had choked and died when Israel had utterly failed to consider an equitable settlement for the Palestinians. No, Qati was sure of that. Perhaps he could not depend on the Russians. Perhaps he could not depend on the Saudis. Certainly he could not depend on the Americans. But he could depend on Israel. The Jews were far too stupid, far too arrogant, far too short-sighted to see that their best hope for long-term security could only lie in an equitable peace. The irony struck him very hard, hard enough to garner a smile. It had to be God's plan, that his movement would be safeguarded by his bitterest enemies. Their obstinacy, their stiff Jewish necks would never bow to this. And if that was what was required for the war to continue, then the fact of it, and the irony of it, could only be a sign from God Himself that the cause guiding Qati and his men was indeed the Holy Cause they believed it to be.

'Never! Never will I bow to this infamy!' the Defense Minister shouted. It was a dramatic performance, even for him. He'd pounded the table hard enough to upset his water glass, and the puddle from it threatened to seep over the edge and into his lap. He studiously ignored it as his fierce blue eyes swept around the cabinet room.

'And what if Fowler is serious with his threats?'

'We'll break his career!' Defense said. 'We can do that. We've jerked American politicians into line before!'

'More than we've been able to do here,' the Foreign Minister observed *sotto voce* to his neighbor at the table.

'What was that?'

'I said it might not be possible in this case, Rafi.' David Askenazi took a sip from his glass before going on. 'Our ambassador in Washington tells me that his people on The Hill find real support for Fowler's plan. The Saudi ambassador threw a major party last weekend for the congressional leadership. He performed well, our sources tell us. Right, Avi?'

'Correct, Minister,' General Ben Jakob answered. His boss was out of the country at the moment, and he spoke for the Mossad. 'The Saudis and the rest of the "moderate" Gulf states are willing to end their declared state of war, to institute ministerial relations with us preparatory for full recognition at an unspecified later date, and to underwrite part of the American costs for stationing their troops and planes here – plus, I might add, picking up the entire cost of the peace-keeping force *and* the economic rehabilitation of our Palestinian friends.'

'How do we say "no" to that?' the Foreign Minister inquired dryly. 'Are you surprised at the support in the American Congress?'

'It's all a trick!' Defense insisted.

'If so, it's a damnably clever one,' Ben Jakob said.

'You believe this twaddle, Avi? *You?*' Ben Jakob had been Rafi Mandel's best battalion commander in the Sinai, so many years before.

'I don't know, Rafi.' The deputy director of the Mossad had never been more cognizant of his position as a deputy, and speaking in the name of his boss did not come easily.

'Your evaluation?' the Prime Minister asked gently. Someone at the table, he decided, had to be calm.

'The Americans are entirely sincere,' Avi replied. 'Their willingness to provide a physical guarantee – the mutual-defense treaty, and the stationing of troops – is genuine. From a strictly military point of – '

'I speak for the defense of Israel!' Mandel snarled.

Ben Jakob turned to stare his former commander down. 'Rafi, you have always outranked me, but I've killed my share of enemies, and you know it well.' Avi paused for a moment to let that rest on the table. When he went on, his voice was quiet and measured and dispassionate as he allowed his reason to overcome emotions no less strong than Mandel's. 'The American military units represent a serious commitment. We're talking about a twenty-five percent increase in the striking power of our air force, and that tank unit is more powerful than our strongest brigade. Moreover, I do not see how that commitment can ever be withdrawn. For that to happen – our friends in America will never let it happen.'

'We've been abandoned before!' Mandel pointed out coldly. 'Our only defense is ourselves.'

'Rafi,' the Foreign Minister said. 'My friend, where has that led us? You and I have fought together, too, and not merely in this room. Is there to be no end to it?'

'Better no treaty than a bad treaty!'

'I agree,' the Prime Minister said. 'But how bad will this treaty be?'

'We have all read the draft. I will propose some modest changes, but, my friends, I think it is time,' the Foreign Minister said. 'My advice to you is that we accept the Fowler Plan, with certain conditions.' The Foreign Minister outlined them.

'Will the Americans grant those, Avi?'

'They'll complain about the cost, but our friends in their Congress will go along, whether President Fowler approves them or not. They will recognize our historic concessions, and they will wish to make us feel secure within our borders.'

'Then I will resign!' Rafi Mandel shouted.

'No, Rafi, you will not,' the Prime Minister said, growing a little tired of his histrionics. 'If you resign, you cast yourself out. You want this seat someday, and you will never have it if you leave the cabinet now.'

Mandel flushed crimson at that rebuke.

The Prime Minister looked around the room. 'So, what is the opinion of the government?'

Forty minutes later, Jack's phone rang. He lifted it, noting that it was his most secure line, the direct one that bypassed Nancy Cummings.

'Ryan.' He listened for a minute and made some notes. 'Thanks.'

Next the DDCI rose and walked into Nancy's office, then turned left through the door into Marcus Cabot's more capacious room. Cabot was lying on the couch in the far corner. Like Judge Arthur Moore, his predecessor, Cabot liked to smoke the occasional cigar. His shoes were off, and he was reading over a file with striped tape on the borders. Just one more secret file in a building full of them. The folder dropped, and Cabot, looking like a pink, chubby volcano, eyed Ryan as he approached.

'What is it, Jack?'

'Just got a call from our friend in Israel. They're coming to Rome, and the cabinet voted to accept the treaty terms, with a few modifications.'

'What are they?' Ryan handed over his notes. Cabot scanned them. 'You and Talbot were right.'

'Yeah, and I should have let him play the card instead of me.'

'Good call, you predicted all but one.' Cabot rose and slipped into his black loafers before walking to his desk. Here he lifted a phone. 'Tell the President I'll meet him at the White House when he gets back from New York. I want Talbot and Bunker there also. Tell him it's a go.' He set the phone back in the cradle. He grinned around the cigar in his teeth, trying to look like George Patton, who hadn't smoked to the best of Ryan's knowledge. 'How about that?'

'How long you figure to finalize it?'

'With the advance work you and Adler did, plus the finishing work from Talbot and Bunker . . . ? Hmm. Give it two weeks. Won't go as fast as it did with Carter at Camp David, because too many professional diplomats are involved, but in fourteen days the President takes his seven-four-seven to Rome to sign the documents.'

'You want me to go down with you to the White House?'

'No, I'll handle it.'

'Okay.' That wasn't unexpected. Ryan left the room the same way he'd come in.

CHAPTER 7

The City of God

The cameras were in place. Air Force C-5B Galaxy transports had loaded the newest state-of-the-art ground-station vans at Andrews Air Force Base and flown them to Leonardo da Vinci Airport. This was less for the signing ceremony – if they got that far, commentators worried – than what wags called the pre-game show. The fully digital improved-definition equipment just coming on line, the producers felt, would better depict the art collections that litter Vatican walls as trees line national parks. Local carpenters and specialists from New York and Atlanta had worked around the clock to build the special booths from which the network anchors would broadcast. All three network morning news shows were originating from the Vatican. CNN was also there in force, as were NHK, BBC, and nearly every other television network in the world, all fighting for space in the grand piazza that sprawls before the church begun in 1503 by Bramante, carried on by Raphael, Michelangelo, and Bernini. A brief but violent windstorm had carried spray from the central fountain into the *Deutsche Welle* anchor booth and shorted out a hundred thousand marks' worth of equipment. Vatican officials had finally protested that there would be no room for the people to witness the event – for which they prayed – but by then it had been far too late. Someone remembered that in Roman times this had been the site of the Circus Maximus, and it was generally agreed that this was the grandest circus of recent years. Except that the Roman 'circus' was mainly for chariot races.

The TV people enjoyed their stay in Rome. The crews

for *Today* and *Good Morning America* were able, for once, to rise indecently late instead of before the paperboy, to begin their broadcasts after lunch – !!! – and finish in time for afternoon shopping, followed by dinner at one of Rome's many fine restaurants. Their research people scoured reference books for historical remote locations like the Colosseum – correctly called the Flavian Amphitheater, one careful back-room type discovered – where people waxed rhapsodic on the Roman substitute for NFL football: combat, to the death, man against man, man against beast, beast against Christian, and various other permutations thereof. But it was the Forum that was the symbolic focus for their time in Rome. Here were the ruins of Rome's civic center, where Cicero and Scipio had walked and talked and met with supporters and opponents, the place to which visitors had come for centuries. Eternal Rome, mother of a vast empire, playing yet another role on the world stage. In its center was the Vatican, just a handful of acres, really, but a sovereign country nonetheless. 'How many divisions has the Pope?' a TV anchorman quoted Stalin, then rambled into a discourse on how the Church and its values had outlasted Marxism-Leninism to the extent that the Soviet Union had decided to open diplomatic relations with the Holy See, and had its own evening news, *Vremya*, originating from a booth less than fifty yards from his own.

Additional attention was given to the two other religions present in the negotiations. At the arrival ceremony, the Pope had recalled an incident from the earliest days of Islam: a commission of Roman Catholic bishops had traveled to Arabia, essentially on an intelligence-gathering mission to see what Mohammed was up to. After a cordial first meeting, the senior Bishop had asked where he and his companions might celebrate Mass. Mohammed had immediately offered the use of the mosque in which they stood. After all, the Prophet had observed, is this not a house consecrated to God? The Holy Father extended the same courtesy to the Israelis. In both cases there was some measure of discomfort to the more conservative churchmen present, but the Holy Father had swept that aside with a speech characteristically delivered in three languages.

'In the name of the God Whom we all know by different names, but Who is nevertheless the same God of all men, we offer our city to the service of men of good will. We share so many beliefs. We believe in a God of mercy and love. We believe in the spiritual nature of man. We believe in the paramount value of faith, and in the manifestation of that faith in charity and brotherhood. To our brothers from distant lands, we give you greetings and we offer our prayers that your faith will find a way to the justice and the peace of God to which all of our faiths direct us.'

'Wow,' a morning-show anchor observed off-mike. 'I'm beginning to think this circus is serious.'

But coverage didn't stop there, of course. In the interest of fairness, balance, controversy, a proper understanding of events, and selling commercials, the TV coverage included the head of a Jewish paramilitary group who vociferously recalled Ferdinand and Isabella's expulsion of the Jews from Iberia, the czar's Black Hundreds, and, naturally, Hitler's Holocaust – which he emphasized further because of German reunification – and concluded that Jews were fools to trust anyone at all except the weapons in their own strong hands. From Qum, the Ayatolla Daryaei, the religious leader of Iran and long an enemy of everything Americans did, railed against all unbelievers, consigning each and every one to his personal version of hell, but translation made understanding difficult for American viewers, and his grandiloquent ranting was cut short. A self-styled 'Charismatic Christian' from the American South got the most air time. After first denouncing Roman Catholicism as the quintessential Anti-Christ, he repeated his renowned claim that God didn't even *hear* the prayers of the Jews, much less the infidel Muslims, whom he called Mohammedans as an unnecessary further insult.

But somehow those demagogues were ignored – more correctly, their views were. The TV networks received thousands of angry calls that such bigots were given air time at all. This delighted the TV executives, of course. It meant that people would return to the same show seeking further outrage. The American bigot immediately noticed a dip in his contribution envelopes. B'nai B'rith raced to condemn the off-the-reservation rabbi. The leader of the League of Islamic Nations, himself a distinguished cleric, denounced the radical imam as a heretic against the words of the Prophet, whom he quoted at length to make his point. The TV networks provided all of the countervailing commentary also, thus showing balance enough to pacify some viewers and enrage others.

Within a day, one newspaper column noted that the thousands of correspondents attending the conference had taken to calling it the Peace Bowl, in recognition of the circular configuration of the Piazza San Pietro. The more observant realized that this was evidence of the strain on reporters with a story to cover but nothing to report. Security at the conference was hermetically tight. Those participants who came and went were carried about by military aircraft via military air bases. Reporters and cameramen with their long lenses were kept as far from the action as possible, and for the most part travel was accomplished in darkness. The Swiss Guards of the Vatican, outfitted though they were in Renaissance jumpsuits, let not a mouse pass by their lines, and perversely when something significant did happen – the Swiss Defense Minister discreetly entered a remote doorway – no one noticed.

Polling information in numerous countries showed uniform hope that this would be the one. A world tired of discord and riding a euphoric wave of relief at recent changes in East–West relations somehow sensed that it was. Commentators warned that there had been no harder issue in recent history, but people the world over prayed in a hundred languages and a million churches for an end to this last and most dangerous dispute on the planet. To their credit, the TV networks reported that, too.

Professional diplomats, some of them the most certified of cynics who hadn't seen the inside of a church since childhood, felt the weight of such pressure as they had never known. Sketchy reports from Vatican custodial staffers spoke of solitary midnight walks down the nave of Saint Peter's, strolls along outside balconies on clear, starlit nights, long talks of some participants with the Holy Father. But nothing else. The highly-paid TV anchors stared at one another in awkward silences. Print journalists struggled and stole any good idea they could find just so that they could produce some copy. Not since Carter's marathon stint at Camp David had such weighty negotiations proceeded with so little reportage.

And the world held its breath.

The old man wore a red fez trimmed with white. Not many continued the characteristic manner of dress, but this one kept to the way of his ancestors. Life was hard for the Druse, and the one solace he had lay in the religion he'd observed for all of his sixty-six years.

The Druse are members of a Middle Eastern religious sect combining aspects of Islam, Christianity, and Judaism, founded by Al-hakim bi'amrillahi, Caliph of Egypt in the 11th Century, who had deemed himself the incarnation of God Himself. Living for the most part in Lebanon, Syria, and Israel, they occupy a precarious niche in the societies of all three nations. Unlike Muslim Israelis, they are allowed to serve in the armed forces of the Jewish state, a fact that does not engender trust for the Syrian Druse in the government that rules over them. While some Druse have risen to command in the Syrian army, it was well-remembered that one such officer, a colonel commanding a regiment, had been executed after the 1973 war for being forced off a strategic crossroads. Though in strictly military terms he'd fought bravely and well, and had been lucky to extract what remained of his command in good order, the loss of that crossroads had cost the Syrian army a pair of tank brigades, and as a result the colonel had been summarily executed ... for being unlucky, and probably for being a Druse.

The old farmer didn't know all of the details behind that story, but knew enough. The Syrian Muslims had killed another Druse then, and more since. He accordingly trusted no one from the Syrian army or government. But that did not mean that he had the least affection for Israel, either. In 1975, a long-barrelled Israeli 175mm gun had scoured his area, searching for a Syrian ammunition depot, and the fragments from one stray round had mortally wounded his wife of forty years, adding loneliness to his surfeit of misery. What for Israel was a historical constant was for this simple farmer an immediate and deadly fact of life. Fate had decided that he should live between two armies, both of which regarded his physical existence as an annoying inconvenience. He was not a man who had ever asked much of life. He had a small holding of land which he farmed, a few sheep and goats, a simple house built of stones he'd carried from his rocky fields. All he wanted to do was live. It was not, he'd once thought, all that much to ask, but sixty-six turbulent years had proven him wrong and wrong again. He'd prayed for mercy from his God, and for justice, and for just a few comforts – he'd always known that wealth would never be his – so that his lot and that of his wife would be just a little easier. But that had never happened. Of the five children his wife had borne him, only one had survived into his teens, and that son had been conscripted into the Syrian army in time for the 1973 war. His son had more luck than the entire family had known: when his BTR-60 personnel carrier had taken a hit from an Israeli tank, he'd been thrown out the top, losing only an eye and a hand in the process. Alive, but half-blinded, he'd married and given his father grandchildren as he lived a modestly successful life as a merchant and money-lender. Not much of a blessing, in contrast to what else had happened in his life, it seemed to the farmer the only joy he'd known.

The farmer grew his vegetables and grazed his few head of stock on his rocky patch close to the Syrian—

Lebanese border. He didn't persevere, didn't really endure, and even survival was an overstatement of his existence. Life for the farmer was nothing more than a habit he could not break, an endless succession of increasingly weary days. When each spring his ewes produced new lambs, he prayed quietly that he'd not live to see them slaughtered – but he also resented the fact that these meek and foolish animals might outlast himself.

Another dawn. The farmer neither had nor needed an alarm clock. When the sky brightened, the bells of his sheep and goats started to clatter. His eyes opened, and he again became conscious of the pain in his limbs. He stretched in his bed, then rose slowly. In a few minutes he'd washed and scraped the gray stubble from his face, eaten his stale bread and strong, sweet coffee, and begun one more day of labor. The farmer did his gardening in the morning, before the heat of the day really took hold. He had a sizable garden, because selling off its surplus in the local market provided cash for the few things that he counted as luxuries. Even that was a struggle. The work punished his arthritic limbs, and keeping his animals away from the tender shoots was one more curse in his life, but the sheep and goats could also be sold for cash, and without that money he would long since have starved. The truth of the matter was that he ate adequately from the sweat of his wrinkled brow, and had he not been so lonely, he could have eaten more. As it was, solitude had made him parsimonious. Even his gardening tools were old. He trudged out to the field, the sun still low in the sky, to destroy the weeds that every day sprang up anew among his vegetables. If only someone could train a goat, he thought, echoing words of his father and grandfather. A goat that would eat the weeds but not the plants, that would be something. But a goat was no more intelligent than a clod of dirt, except when it came to doing mischief. The three-hour effort of lifting the mattock and tearing up the weeds began in the same corner of the garden, and he worked his way up one row and down the next with a steady pace that belied his age and infirmity.

CLUNK.

What was that? The farmer stood up straight and wiped some sweat away. Halfway through the morning labor, beginning to look forward to the rest that came with attending to the sheep . . . Not a stone. He used his tool to pull the dirt away from – oh, that.

People often wonder at the process. Farmers the world over have joked of it since farming first began, the way that farm fields produce rocks. Stone fences along New England lanes attest to the superficially mysterious process. Water does it. Water falling as rain seeps into the soil. In the winter the water freezes into ice, which expands as it becomes a solid. As it expands, it pushes up rather than down, because pushing up is easier. That action moves rocks in the soil to the surface, and so fields grow rocks, something especially true in the Golan region of Syria, whose soil is a geologically recent construct of volcanism, and whose winters, surprisingly to many, can grow cold and frosty.

But this one was not a rock.

It was metallic, a sandy brown color, he saw, pulling the dirt away. Oh, yes, that day. The same day his son had been –

What do I do about this damned thing! the farmer asked himself. It was, of course, a bomb. He wasn't so foolish that he didn't know that much. How it had gotten here was a mystery, of course. He'd never seen any aircraft, Syrian or Israeli, drop bombs anywhere close to his farm, but that didn't matter. He could scarcely deny that it was here. To the farmer it might as well have been a rock, just a big, brown rock, too big to dig out and carry off to the edge of the field, big enough to interrupt two rows of carrots. He didn't fear the thing. It had not gone off, after all, and that meant that it was broken. Proper bombs fell off airplanes and exploded when they hit the ground. This one had just dug its small crater, which he'd filled back up the next day, unmindful at the time of the injuries to his son.

Why couldn't it have just stayed two meters down, where it belonged! he asked himself. But that had never been the pattern of his life, had it? No, anything that could do him harm had found him, hadn't it? The farmer wondered why God had been so cruel to him. Had he not said all his prayers, followed all of the strict rules of the Druse? What had he ever asked for? Whose sins was he expiating?

Well. There was no sense asking such questions at this late date. For the moment, he had work to do. He continued his weeding, standing on the exposed tip of the bomb to get a few, and worked his way down the row. His son would visit in a day or two, allowing the old man to see and beam at his grandchildren, the one unqualified joy of his life. He'd ask his son's advice. His son had been a soldier, and understood such things.

It was the sort of week that any government employee hated. Something important was happening in a different time zone. There was a six-hour differential, and it seemed very strange to Jack that he was being afflicted with jet-lag without having traveled anywhere.

'So, how's it going over there?' Clark asked from the driver's seat.

'Damned well.' Jack flipped through the documents. 'The Saudis and Israelis actually agreed on something yesterday. They both wanted to change something, and both actually proposed the same change.' Jack chuckled at that. It had to be accidental, and if they'd known, both sides would have changed their positions.

'That must have embarrassed the hell out of some-body!' Clark laughed aloud, thinking the same as his boss. It was still dark, and the one good thing about the early days was that the roads were empty. 'You really liked the Saudis, didn't you?'

'Ever been over there?'

'Aside from the war, you mean? Lots of times, Jack. I staged into Iran from there back in '79 and '80, spent a lot of time with the Saudis, learned the language.'

'What did you think of the place?' Jack asked.

'I liked it there. Got to know one guy pretty well, a major in their army – spook really, like me. Not much field experience, but a lot of book-learning. He was smart enough to know that he had a lot to learn, and he listened when I told him stuff. Got invited to his house a coupla-three times. He had two sons, nice little kids. One's flying fighters now. Funny how they treat their women, though. Sandy'd never go for it.' Clark paused as he changed lanes to pass a truck. 'Professionally speaking, they were cooperative as hell. Anyway, what I saw I sort of liked. They're different from us, but so what? World ain't full of Americans.'

'What about the Israelis?' Jack asked as he closed the document case.

'I've worked with them once or twice – well, more than that, Doc, mainly in Lebanon. Their intelligence guys are real pros, cocky, arrogant bastards, but the ones I met had a lot to be cocky about. Fortress mentality, like – us-and-them mentality, y'know? Also understandable.' Clark turned. 'That's the big hang-up, isn't it?'

'What do you mean?'

'Weaning them away from that. It can't be easy.'

'It isn't. I wish they'd wake up to the way the world is now,' Ryan growled.

'Doc, you have to understand. They all think like front-line grunts. What do you expect? Hell, man, their whole country is like a free-fire zone for the other side. They have the same way of thinking that us line-animals had in 'Nam. There are two kinds of people – your people, and everybody else.' John Clark shook his head. 'You know how many times I've tried to explain that to kids at The Farm? Basic survival mentality. The Israelis think that way 'cause they can't think any other way. The Nazis killed millions of Jews and we didn't do dick about it – well, okay, maybe we couldn't have done anything 'cause of the way things were at the time. Then again, I wonder if Hitler was all that hard a target if we woulda ever got serious about doing his ass.

'Anyway, I agree with you that they have to look beyond all that, but you gotta remember that we're asking one hell of a lot.'

'Maybe you should have been along when I met with Avi,' Jack observed with a yawn.

'General Ben Jakob? Supposed to be one tough, serious son of a bitch. His troops respect the man. That says a lot. Sorry I wasn't there, boss, but that two weeks of fishing was just about what I needed.' Even line-animals got vacations.

'I hear you, Mr Clark.'

'Hey, I gotta go down to Quantico this afternoon to re-qualify on pistol. If you don't mind me saying so, you look like you could use a little stress-relief, man. Why not come on down? I'll get a nice little Beretta for you to play with.'

Jack thought about that. It sounded nice. In fact, it sounded great. But. But he had too much work to do.

'No time, John.'

'Aye aye, sir. You're not getting your exercise, you're drinking too goddamned much, and you look like shit, Dr Ryan. That is my professional opinion.'

About what Cathy told me last night, but Clark doesn't know just how bad it is. Jack stared out the window at the lights of houses whose government-worker occupants were just waking up.

'You're right. I have to do something about it, but today I just don't have the time.'

'How about tomorrow at lunch we take a little run?'

'Lunch with the directorate chiefs,' Jack evaded.

Clark shut up and concentrated on his driving. When would the poor, dumb bastard learn? Smart guy as he was, he was letting the job eat him up.

The President awoke to find an unkempt mountain of blonde hair on his chest, and a thin, feminine arm flung across him. There were worse ways to awaken. He asked himself why he'd waited so long. She'd been clearly available to him for – God, for years. In her forties, but lithe and pretty, as much as any man could want, and the President was a man with a man's needs. His wife, Marian, had lingered for years, bravely fighting the MS that had ultimately stolen her life, but only after crushing what had once been a lively, charming, intelligent, bubbling personality, the light of his life, Fowler remembered. What personality he'd once had had largely been her creation, and it had died its own lingering death. A defense mechanism, he knew. All those endless months. He'd had to be strong for her, to provide for her the stoic reserve of energy without which she would have died so much sooner. But doing that had made an automaton of Bob Fowler. There was only so much personality, so much strength, so much courage a man contained, and as Marian's life had drained away, so had his humanity ebbed with it. And perhaps more than that, Fowler admitted to himself.

The perverse thing was that it had made him a better politician. His best years as governor and his presidential campaign had displayed the calm, dispassionate, intellectual reason that the voters had wanted, much to the surprise of pundits and mavens or whatever you called the commentators who thought they knew so much but never tried to find out themselves. It had also helped that his predecessor had run an unaccountably dumb campaign, but Fowler figured he would have won anyway.

The victory, almost two Novembers ago, had left him the first President since – Cleveland, wasn't it? – without a wife. And also without much of a personality. The Technocrat President, the editorial writers called him. That he was by profession a lawyer didn't seem to matter to the news media. Once they had a simple label that all could agree on, they made it truth whether it was accurate or not. The Ice Man.

If only Marian could have lived to see this. She'd known he wasn't made of ice. There were those who remembered what Bob Fowler had once been like, a passionate trial lawyer, advocate of civil rights, the scourge of organized crime. The man who cleaned up Cleveland. Not for very long, of course, for all such victories, like those in politics, were transitory. He remembered the birth of each of his children, the pride of fatherhood, the love of his wife for him and their two children, the quiet dinners in candle-lit restaurants. He remembered meeting Marian at a high-school football game, and she'd loved the spectacle as much as he ever had. Thirty years of marriage which had begun while both were still in college, the last three of which had been an ongoing nightmare as the disease that had manifested itself in her late thirties had in her late forties taken a dramatic and downward turn and, finally, a death too long in coming but too soon in arriving, by which time he'd been too exhausted even to shed tears. And then the years of aloneness.

Well, perhaps that was over.

Thank God for the Secret Service, Fowler thought. In the governor's mansion in Columbus it would quickly have gotten out. But not here. Outside his door was a pair of armed agents, and down the hall that Army warrant officer with the leather briefcase called the Football, an appellation which did not please the President, but there were things even he could not change. His National Security Advisor could, in any case, share his bed, and the White House staffers kept the secret. That, he thought, was rather remarkable.

Fowler looked down at his lover. Elizabeth was undeniably pretty. Her skin was pale because her work habits denied her sunlight, but he preferred women with pale, fair skin. The covers were askew because of the previous night's gyrations, and he could examine her back; the skin was so smooth and soft. He felt her relaxed breath on his chest, and the way her left arm wrapped around him. He ran a hand down her back and was rewarded by a *hmmmmm* and a slight increase in pressure from the sleeping hug she gave him.

There was a discreet knock at the door. The President pulled the covers up and coughed. After a five-count, the door opened, and an agent came in with a coffee tray with some document print-outs before withdrawing. Fowler knew he couldn't trust one of the ordinary staff *that* far, but the Secret Service really was the American version of the Praetorian Guard. The agent never betrayed his emotions, except for a good-morning nod at

The Boss, as the agents referred to him. The devotion they gave him was almost slavish. Though well-educated men and women, they really did have a simple outlook on things, and Fowler knew that there was room in the world for such people. Someone, often someone quite skilled, had to carry out the decisions and orders of his or her superiors. The gun-toting agents were sworn to protect him, even to interpose their bodies between the President and any danger – the maneuver was called 'catching the bullet' – and it amazed Fowler that such bright people could train themselves to do something so selflessly dumb. But it was to his benefit. As was their discretion. Well, the joke was that such good help was hard to come by. It was true: you had to be President to have that kind of servant.

Fowler reached for his coffee and poured a cup one-handed. He drank it black. After his first sip he used a remote-control to switch on a TV set. It was tuned to CNN, and the lead story – it was two in the afternoon there – was Rome, of course.

'Mmmmm.' Elizabeth moved her head, and her hair swept across him. She always awoke slower than he. Fowler ran a finger down her spine, earning himself a last cuddle before her eyes opened. Her head came up with a violent start.

'*Bob!*'

'Yes?'

'Somebody's been here!' She pointed to the tray with the cups, and knew that Fowler hadn't fetched it himself.

'Coffee?'

'*BOB!*'

'Look, Elizabeth, the people outside the door know that you're here. What do you think we are hiding, and from whom are we hiding it? Hell, they probably have microphones in here.' He'd never said that before. He didn't know for sure, and had studiously refrained from inquiring, but it was a logical thing to expect. The institutional paranoia of the Secret Service denied the agents the ability to trust Elizabeth or anyone else, except the President. Therefore, if she tried to kill him, they needed to know, so that the agents outside the door could burst in with their guns and save HAWK from his lover. There probably were microphones. Cameras, too? No, probably not cameras, but surely there had to be microphones. Fowler actually found that thought somewhat stimulating, a fact that editorial writers would never have believed. Not The Ice Man.

'My God!' Liz Elliot had never thought of that. She hoisted herself up, and her breasts dangled deliciously before his eyes. But Fowler was not that sort of morning person. Mornings were for work.

'I am the President, Elizabeth,' Fowler pointed out as she disengaged herself. The idea of cameras occurred to her, too, and she quickly rearranged the bedclothes. Fowler smiled at the foolishness of it. 'Coffee?' he asked again.

Elizabeth Elliot almost giggled. Here she was, in the President's bed, naked as a jaybird, with armed guards outside the door. But Bob had *let someone in the room!* The man was incredible. Had he even covered her up? She could ask, but decided not to, fearing that he might display his twisted sense of humor, which was at its best when it was slightly cruel. And yet. Had she ever had so good a lover as he? The first time – it must have been years, but he was so patient, so . . . respectful. So easy to manage. Elliot smiled her secret smile to herself. He could be directed to do exactly what she wanted, when she wanted it, and do it consummately well, for he loved to give pleasure to a woman. Why? she wondered. Perhaps he wanted to be remembered. He was a politician, after all, and what they all craved was a few lines in history books. Well, he'd have those, one way or another. Every President did, even Grant and Harding were remembered, and with what was happening . . . Even here he craved being remembered, and so he did what the woman wanted, if the woman had the wit to ask.

'Turn the sound up,' Liz said. Fowler complied at once, she was gratified to see. So eager to please, even in this. So, why the hell had he let some servant in with the coffee! There was no understanding this man. He was already reading over the faxes from Rome.

'My dear, this is going to work. I hope your bags are packed, Elizabeth.'

'Oh?'

'The Saudis and the Israelis actually agreed on the big one last night . . . according to Brent – God, this is amazing! He had separate solo sessions with both sides, and both of them suggested the same thing . . . and to keep them from knowing it, he simply cycled back and forth as he said it would probably be acceptable . . . then confirmed it on another round trip! Ha!' Fowler slapped the back of his hand on the page. 'Brent is really delivering for us. And that Ryan guy, too. He's a pretentious pain in the ass, but that idea of his –'

'Come on, Bob! It wasn't even original. Ryan just repeated some things other people have been saying for years. It was new to Arnie, but Arnie's interests stop at the White House fence. Giving credit to Ryan for this is like saying he managed a nice sunset for you.'

'Maybe,' the President allowed. He thought there was more to the DDCI's concept-proposal than that, but it wasn't worth upsetting Elizabeth about. 'Ryan did do a nice job with the Saudis, remember?'

'He'd be a lot more effective if he'd just keep his mouth shut. Fine, he gave the Saudis a good brief. That's not exactly a great moment in American foreign policy, is it? Giving briefs is his job. Brent and Dennis are the guys who really pulled it together, not Ryan.'

'I suppose not. You're right, I guess. Brent and Dennis are the ones who got the final commitments to the conference . . . Brent says three more days, maybe four.' The President handed the faxes over. It was time for him to rise and prepare for a day's work, but before he did he ran a hand over a particular curve in the sheet, just to let her know that . . .

'Stop that!' Liz giggled to make it sound playful. He did as told, of course. To ease the blow, she leaned over for a kiss, which was delivered, bad breath and all, just as requested.

*

'What gives?' a truck driver asked at the lumber terminal. Four enormous trailers sat in a line, away from the stacks of felled trees being prepared for shipment to Japan. 'They were here last time, too.'

'Going to Japan,' the dispatcher observed, going over the trucker's manifest.

'So what here ain't?'

'Something special. They're paying to have those logs kept that way, renting the trailers and everything. I hear the logs are being made into beams for a church or temple or something. Look close — they're chained together. Tied with a silk rope, too, but chains to make sure they stay together. Something about the tradition of the temple or something. Going to be a bitch of a rigging job to load them on the ship that way.'

'Renting the trailers just to keep the logs in a special place? Chaining them together. Jeez! They got more money'n brains, don't they?'

'What do we care?' the dispatcher asked, tired of answering the same question every time a driver came through his office.

And they were sitting there. The idea, the dispatcher thought, was to let the logs season some. But whoever had thought that one up hadn't been thinking very clearly. This was the wettest summer on record in an area known for its precipitation, and the logs, which had been heavy with moisture when their parent tree had been felled, were merely soaking up more rain as it fell down across the yard. The stubs of branches trimmed off in the field hadn't helped much either. The rain just soaked into the exposed capillaries and proceeded into the trunk. The logs were probably heavier now than when they had been cut. Maybe they should throw a tarp over them, the dispatcher thought, but then they'd just be trapping the moisture in, and besides, the orders were to let them sit on the trailers. It was raining now. The yard was turning into a damned swamp, the mud churned by every passing truck and loading machine. Well, the Japanese probably had their own plans for seasoning and working the logs. Their orders precluded doing any real seasoning here, and it was their money. Even when they were loaded on the ship, they were supposed to be carried topside, the last items loaded on the MV *George McReady* for shipment across the Pacific. Sure as hell they'd get wet that way, too. If they got much wetter, the dispatcher thought, someone would have to be careful with them. If they got dropped into the river, they would scarcely float.

The farmer knew that his grandchildren were embarrassed by his backwardness. They resisted his hugs and kisses, probably complained a little before their father brought them out here, but he didn't mind. Children today lacked the respect of his generation. Perhaps that was a price for their greater opportunities. The cycle of the ages was breaking. His life had been little different from ten generations of ancestors, but his son was doing better despite his injuries, and his children would do better still. The boys were proud of their father. If their schoolmates commented adversely on their Druse religion, the boys could point out that their father had fought and bled against the hated Israelis, had even killed a few of the Zionists. The Syrian government was not totally ungrateful to its wounded veterans. The farmer's son had his own modest business, and government officials did not harass him, as they might otherwise have done. He'd married late, which was unusual for the area. His wife was pretty enough, and respectful – she treated the farmer well, possibly in gratitude for the fact that he had never shown an interest in moving into her small household. The farmer showed great pride in his grandchildren, strong, healthy boys, headstrong and rebellious as boys should be. The farmer's son was similarly proud, and was prospering. He and his father walked outside after the noon meal. The son looked at the garden that he'd once weeded, and felt pangs of guilt that his father was still working there every day. But hadn't he offered to take his father in? Hadn't he offered to give his father a little money? All such offers had been rejected. His father didn't have much, but he did have his stubborn pride.

'The garden looks very healthy this year.'

'The rain has been good,' the farmer agreed. 'There are many new lambs. It has not been a bad year. And you?'

'My best year. Father, I wish you did not have to work so hard.'

'Ah!' A wave of the hand. 'What other life have I known? This is my place.'

The courage of the man, the son thought. And the old man did have courage. He endured. Despite everything. He had not been able to give his son much, but he had passed along his stoic courage. When he'd found himself lying stunned on the Golan Heights, twenty meters from the smoking wreckage of the personnel carrier, he could have just lain down to die, the son knew, his eye put out, and his left hand a bloody mess that doctors would later have to remove. He could have just lain there on the ground and died, but he'd known that giving up was not something his father would have done. And so he'd risen and walked six kilometers to a battalion aid station, arriving there still carrying his rifle and accepting treatment only after making his report. He had a decoration for that, and his battalion commander had made life a little easier for him, giving him some money to start his little shop, making sure that local officials knew that he was to be treated with respect. The colonel had given him the money, but his father had given him the courage. If only he would now accept a little help.

'My son, I need your advice.'

That was something new. 'Certainly, father.'

'Come I will show you.' He led his son into the garden, where the carrots were. With his foot, he scraped dirt off the –

'Stop!' the son nearly screamed. He took his father by the arm and pulled him back. 'My God, how long has that been there?'

'Since the day you were hurt,' the farmer answered.

The son's right hand went to his eye patch, and for one horrid moment the terror of the day came back to him. The blinding flash, flying through the air, his dead comrades screaming as they burned to death. The Israelis had done that. One of their cannons had killed his mother, and now – this?

What was it? He commanded his father to stay put and walked back to see. He moved very carefully, as though he were traversing a minefield. His assignment in the army had been with the combat engineers; though his unit had been committed to battle with the infantry, their job was supposed to have been laying a minefield. It was big, it looked like a thousand-kilo bomb. It had to be Israeli; he knew that from the color. He turned to look at his father.

'This has been here since then?'

'Yes. It made its own hole, and I filled it in. The frost must have brought it up. Is there danger? It is broken, no?'

'Father, these things never truly die. It is very dangerous. Big as it is, if it goes off it could destroy the house and you in it!'

The farmer gestured contempt for the thing. 'If it wanted to explode, it would have done so when it fell.'

'That is not true! You will listen to me on this. You will not come close to this cursed thing!'

'And what of my garden?' the farmer asked simply.

'I will find a way to have this removed. Then you can garden.' The son considered that. It would be a problem. Not a small problem, either. The Syrian army did not have a pool of skilled people to disarm unexploded bombs. Their method was to detonate them in place, which was eminently sensible, but his father would not long survive the destruction of his house. His wife would not easily tolerate having him in their own home, and he could not help his father rebuild, not with only one hand. The bomb had to be removed, but who would do that?

'You must promise me that you will not enter the garden!' the son announced sternly.

'As you say,' the farmer replied. He had no intention

of following his son's orders. 'When can you have it removed?'

'I don't know. I need a few days to see what I can do.'

The farmer nodded. Perhaps he'd follow his son's instructions after all, at least about not approaching this dead bomb. It had to be dead, of course, despite what his son had said. The farmer knew that much of fate. If the bomb had wanted to kill him, it would have happened by now. What other misfortune had avoided him?

The newsies finally got something to sink their teeth into the next day. Dimitrios Stavarkos, Patriarch of Constantinople, arrived by car – he refused to fly in helicopters – in broad daylight.

'A nun with a beard?' a cameraman asked over his hot mike as he zoomed in. The Swiss Guards at the door rendered honors, and Bishop O'Toole conducted the new visitor inside and out of view.

'Greek,' the anchorman observed at once. 'Greek Orthodox, must be a bishop or something. What's he doing here?' the anchor mused.

'What do we know about the Greek Orthodox Church?' his producer asked.

'They don't work for the Pope. They allow their priests to marry. The Israelis threw one of them in prison once for giving arms to the Arabs, I think,' someone else observed over the line.

'So, the Greeks get along with the Arabs, but not the Pope? What about the Israelis?'

'Don't know,' the producer admitted. 'Might be a good idea to find out.'

'So, now there are four religious groups involved.'

'Is the Vatican really involved, or did they just offer this place as neutral ground?' the anchor asked. Like most anchormen, he was at his best when reading copy from a teleprompter.

'When has this happened before? If you want "neutral," you go to Geneva,' the cameraman observed. He liked Geneva.

'What gives?' one of the researchers entered the booth. The producer filled her in.

'Where's that damned consultant?' the anchor growled.

'Can you run the tape back?' the researcher asked. The control-room crew did that, and she freeze-framed the monitor.

'Dimitrios Stavarkos. He's the Patriarch of Constantinople – Istanbul to you, Rick. He's the head of all the Orthodox churches, kind of like the Pope. The Greek, Russian, and Bulgarian Orthodox Churches have their own heads, but they all defer to the Patriarch. Something like that.'

'They allow their priests to marry, don't they?'

'Their priests, yes . . . but as I recall if you become a bishop or higher, you have to be celibate –'

'Bummer,' Rick observed.

'Stavarkos led the battle with the Catholics over the Church of the Nativity last year – won it, too, as I recall. He really pissed a few Catholic bishops off. What the hell is *he* doing here?'

'You're supposed to tell us that, Angie!' the anchor noted crossly.

'Hold your water, Rick.' Angie Miriles was tired of dealing with the air-headed prima donna. She sipped at her coffee for a minute or two, and made her announcement. 'I think I have this figured out.'

'You mind filling us in?'

'Welcome!' Cardinal D'Antonio kissed Stavarkos on both cheeks. He found the man's beard distasteful, but that could not be helped. The Cardinal led the Patriarch into the conference room. There were sixteen people grouped around a table, and at the foot of it was an empty chair. Stavarkos took it.

'Thank you for joining us,' said Secretary Talbot.

'One does not reject an invitation of this sort,' the Patriarch replied.

'You've read the briefing material?' That had been delivered by messenger.

'It is very ambitious,' Stavarkos allowed cautiously.

'Can you accept your role in the agreement?'

This was going awfully fast, the Patriarch thought. But – 'Yes,' he answered simply. 'I require plenipotentiary authority over all Christian shrines in the Holy Land. If that is agreed to, then I will gladly join your agreement.'

D'Antonio managed to keep his face impassive. He controlled his breathing and prayed rapidly for divine intervention. He'd never quite be able to decide whether he got it or not.

'It is very late in the day for such a sweeping demand.' Heads turned. The speaker was Dmitriy Popov, First Deputy Foreign Minister of the Soviet Union. 'It is also inconsiderate to seek unilateral advantage when everyone here has conceded so much. Would you stand in the way of the accord on that basis alone?'

Stavarkos was not accustomed to such direct rebukes.

'The question of Christian shrines is not of direct significance to the agreement, Your Eminence,' Secretary Talbot observed. 'We find your conditional willingness to participate disappointing.'

'Perhaps I misunderstood the briefing material,' Stavarkos allowed, covering his flanks. 'Could you perhaps clarify what my status would be?'

'No way,' the anchor snorted.

'Why not?' Angela Miriles replied. 'What else makes sense?'

'It's just too much.'

'It is a lot,' Miriles agreed, 'but what else fits?'

'I'll believe it when I see it.'

'You might not see it. Stavarkos doesn't much like the Roman Catholic Church. That battle they had last Christmas was a nasty one.'

'How come we didn't report it, then?'

'Because we were too damned busy talking about the downturn in Christmas sales figures,' *you asshole*, she didn't add.

'A separate commission, then?' Stavarkos didn't like that.

'The Metropolitan wishes to send his own representative,' Popov said. Dmitriy Popov still believed in Marx rather than God, but the Russian Orthodox Church was *Russian*, and Russian participation in the agreement had to be real, however minor this point might appear. 'I must say that I find this matter curious. Do we hold up the agreement on the issue of which Christian church is the most influential? Our purpose here is to defuse a potential flashpoint for war between Jews and Muslims, and the Christians stand in the way?' Popov asked the ceiling – a little theatrically, D'Antonio thought.

'This side issue is best left to a separate committee of Christian clerics,' Cardinal D'Antonio finally allowed himself to say. 'I pledge you my word before God that sectarian squabbles are at an end!'

I've heard that before, Stavarkos reminded himself – and yet. And yet, how could he allow himself to be so petty? He reminded himself also of what the scriptures taught, and that he believed in every word of it. *I am making a fool of myself, and doing it before the Romans and the Russians!* An additional consideration was that the Turks merely tolerated his presence in Istanbul – Constantinople! – and this gave him the chance to earn immense prestige for his churches and his office.

'Please forgive me. I have allowed some regrettable incidents to color my better judgment. Yes, I will support this agreement, and I will trust my brethren to keep their word.'

Brent Talbot leaned back in his chair and whispered his own prayer of thanks. Praying wasn't a habit with the Secretary of State, but here, in these surroundings, how could one avoid it?

'In that case, I believe we have an agreement.' Talbot looked around the table, and one after another, the heads nodded, some with enthusiasm, some with resignation. But they all nodded. They had reached an agreement.

'Mr Adler, when will the documents be ready for initialing?' D'Antonio asked.

'Two hours, Your Eminence.'

'Your Highness,' Talbot said as he rose to his feet, 'Your Eminences, Ministers, we have done it.'

Strangely, they scarcely realized what they had done. The process had lasted for quite some time, and as with all such negotiations, the process had become reality, and the objective had become something separate from it. Now suddenly they were at the place they all intended to reach, and the wonder of the fact gave to them a sense of unreality that, for all their collective expertise at formulating and reaching foreign-policy goals, overcame their perceptions. Each of the participants stood, as Talbot did, and the movement, the stretch of legs, altered their perceptions somewhat. One by one, they understood what they had done. More importantly, they understood that they had actually done it. The impossible had just happened.

David Askenazi walked around the table to Prince Ali, who had handled his country's part in the negotiations, and extended his hand. That wasn't good enough. The Prince gave the Minister a brotherly embrace.

'Before God, there will be peace between us, David.'

'After all these years, Ali,' replied the former Israeli tanker. As a lieutenant, Askenazi had fought in the Suez in 1956, again as a captain in 1967, and his reserve battalion had reinforced the Golan in 1973. Both men were surprised by the applause that broke out. The Israeli burst into tears, embarrassing himself beyond belief.

'Do not be ashamed. Your personal courage is well known, Minister,' Ali said graciously. 'It is fitting that a soldier should make the peace, David.'

'So many deaths. All those fine young boys who – on both sides, Ali. All those boys.'

'But no more.'

'Dmitriy, your help was extraordinary,' Talbot told his Russian counterpart, at the other end of the table.

'Remarkable what can happen when we cooperate, is it not?'

What occurred to Talbot had come already to Askenazi: 'Two whole generations pissed away, Dmitriy. All that wasted time.'

'We cannot recover lost time,' Popov replied. 'We can have the wit not to lose any more.' The Russian smiled crookedly. 'For moments like this, there should be vodka.'

Talbot jerked his head towards Prince Ali. 'We don't all drink.'

'How can they live without vodka?' Popov chuckled.

'One of the mysteries of life, Dmitriy. We both have cables to send.'

'Indeed we do, my friend.'

To the fury of the correspondents in Rome, the first to break the story was a *Washington Post* reporter in Washington. It was inevitable. She had a source, an Air Force sergeant who did electronic maintenance on the VC-25A, the President's new military version of the Boeing 747. The sergeant had been prepped by the reporter. Everyone knew that the President was heading to Rome. It was just a question of when. As soon as the sergeant learned that she'd be heading out, she'd ostensibly called home to check that her good uniform was back from the cleaners. That she had called the wrong number was an honest mistake. It was just that the reporter had the same gag message on her answering machine. That was the story she'd use if she ever got caught, but she didn't in this case, and didn't ever expect to be.

An hour later, at the routine morning meeting between the President's press secretary and the White House correspondents, the *Post* reporter announced an 'unconfirmed report' that Fowler was going to Rome – and did this mean that the treaty negotiations had reached an impasse or success? The press secretary was caught short by that. He'd just learned ten minutes before that he'd be flying to Rome, and as usual was sworn to total secrecy – an admonition that carried about as much weight as sunlight on a cloudy day. He allowed himself to be surprised by the question, though, and that surprised the man who had fully expected to engineer the leak – but only *after* lunch at the afternoon briefing. His 'no comment' hadn't carried enough conviction, and the White House correspondents smelled the blood in the water. They all had edited copies of the President's appointments schedule, and sure enough, there were names to check with.

The President's aides were already making calls to cancel appointments and appearances. Even the President cannot allow important people to be inconvenienced without warning, and while those might keep secrets, not all of their assistants and secretaries can. It was a classic case of the phenomenon upon which a free press depends. People who know things cannot keep them inside. Especially secret things. Within an hour, confirmation was obtained from four widely-separated sources: President Fowler had cancelled several days' worth of appointments. The President was going somewhere, and it wasn't Peoria. That was enough for all the TV networks to run bulletins timed to erase segments of various game shows with hastily-written statements, which immediately cut to commercials, denying millions of people the knowledge of what the word or phrase was, but informing them of the best way to get their clothes clean despite deep grass stains.

It was late afternoon in Rome, a sultry, humid summer day, when the pool headquarters was told that three, only three, cameras – and no correspondents – would be permitted into the building whose outside had been subjected to weeks of careful scrutiny. In the 'green room' trailers near each of the anchor booths, the network anchors on duty had makeup applied and hustled to their chairs, putting their earpieces in and waiting for word from their directors.

The picture that appeared simultaneously on the booth monitors and TV sets all over the world showed the conference room. In it was a large table all of whose seats were filled. At its head was the Pope, and before him was a folder of folio size, made of red calfskin – the reporters would never know of the momentary panic that had erupted when someone realized that he *didn't* know what kind of leather it was, and had to check with the supplier; fortunately, no one objected to the skin of a calf.

It had been agreed that no statement would be made here. Preliminary statements would be made in the capitals of each of the participants, and the really flowery speeches were being drafted for the formal signing ceremonies. A Vatican spokesman delivered a written release to all of the TV correspondents. It said in essence that a draft treaty concerning a final settlement of the Middle East dispute had been negotiated, and that the draft was ready for initialing by representatives of the interested nations. The formal treaty documents would be signed by the chiefs of state and/or foreign ministers in several days. The text of the treaty was not available for release, nor were its provisions. This did not exactly thrill the correspondents – mainly because they realized that the treaty details would be broken from the foreign ministries in the respective capitals of the concerned nations, to other reporters.

The red folder was passed from place to place. The order of the initialers, the Vatican statement pointed out, had been determined by lot, and it turned out that the Israeli Foreign Minister went first, followed by the Soviet, the Swiss, the American, the Saudi, and the Vatican representatives. Each used a fountain pen, and a curved blotter was applied to each set of initials by the priest who moved the document from place to place. It wasn't much of a ceremony, and it was swiftly accomplished. Handshakes came next, followed by a lengthy bit of mutual applause. And that was it.

'By God,' Jack said, watching the TV picture change. He looked down to the fax of the treaty outline, and it was not very different from his original concept. The Saudis had made changes, as had the Israelis, the Soviets, the Swiss, and, of course, the State Department, but the original idea was his – except insofar as he himself had borrowed ideas from a multitude of others. There were few genuinely original ideas. What he'd really done had been to organize them, and pick an historically correct moment to make his comment. That was all. For all that it was the proudest moment of his life. It was a shame that there was no one to congratulate him.

In the White House, President Fowler's best speech-writer was already working on the first draft of his speech. The American President would have primacy of place at the ceremony because it had been his idea, after all, his speech before the UN that had brought them all together in Rome. The Pope would speak – hell, they would all speak, the speechwriter thought, and for her that was a problem, since each speech had to be original and un-repetitive. She realized that she'd probably still be working on it while hopping the Atlantic on the -25A, pecking busily away on her laptop. But that, she knew, was what they paid her for, and Air Force One had a laser-jet printer.

Upstairs in the Oval Office the President was looking over his hastily revised schedule. A committee of new Eagle Scouts would have to be disappointed, as would the new Wisconsin Cheese Queen, or whatever the young lady's title was, and a multitude of business people whose importance in their own small ponds quite literally paled when they entered the side door into the President's workshop. His appointments secretary was getting the word out. Some people whose visits were genuinely important were being shoe-horned into every spare minute of the next thirty-six hours. That would make the President's next day and a half as hectic as it ever got, but that, too, was part of the job.

'Well?' Fowler looked up to see Elizabeth Elliot grinning at him through the open door to the secretary's ante-room.

Well, this is what you wanted, isn't it? Your presidency will forever be remembered as the one in which the Middle East problems were settled once and for all. If – Liz admitted to herself in a rare moment of objective clarity – *it all works out, which is not a given in such disputes as this.*

'We have done a service to the whole world, Elizabeth.' By 'we' he actually meant 'I,' Elliot knew, but that was fair enough. It was Bob Fowler who'd endured the months of campaigning on top of his executive duties in Columbus, the endless speeches, kissing babies and kissing ass, stroking legions of reporters whose faces changed far more rapidly than their brutally repetitive questions. It was an endurance race to get into this one small room, this seat of executive power. It was a process that somehow did not break the men – pity it was still only men, Liz thought – who made it safely here. But the prize for all the effort, all the endless toil, was that the person who occupied it got to take the credit. It was a simple historical convention that people assumed the President was the one who directed things, who made the decisions. Because of that, the President was the one who got the kudos and the barbs. The President was responsible for what went well and for what went badly. Mostly that concerned domestic affairs, the blips in the unemployment figures, interest rates, inflation (whole-sale and retail), and the all-powerful Leading Economic Indicators, but on rare occasions, something really important happened, something that changed the world. Reagan, Elliot admitted to herself, would be remembered by history as the guy who'd happened to be around when the Russians decided to cash in their chips on Marxism, and Bush was the man who'd collected that particular political pot. Nixon was the man who'd opened the door to China, and Carter the one who had come so tanta-lizingly close to doing what Fowler would now be remembered for. The American voters might select their political leaders for pocketbook issues, but history was made of more important stuff. What earned a man a few paragraphs in a general-history text and focused volumes of scholarly study were the fundamental changes in the shape of the political world. That was what really counted. Historians remembered the ones who shaped political events – Bismarck, not Edison – treating technical changes in society as though they were driven by political factors, and not the reverse, which, she judged, might have been equally likely. But historiography had its own rules and conventions that had little to do with reality, because reality was too large a thing to grasp, even for academics working years after events. Politicians played within those rules, and that suited them because following those rules meant that when something memorable happened, the historians would remember them.

'Service to the world?' Elliot responded after a lengthy pause. 'Service to the world. I like the sound of that. They called Wilson the man who kept us out of war. You will be remembered as the one who put an end to war.'

Fowler and Elliot both knew that scant months after being reelected on that platform, Wilson had led America into his first truly foreign war, the war to end all wars, optimists had called it, well before holocaust and nuclear nightmares. But this time, both thought, it was more than mere optimism, and Wilson's transcendent vision of what the world could be was finally within the grasp of the political figures who made the world into the shape of their own choosing.

The man was a Druse, an unbeliever, but for all that he was respected. He bore the scars of his own battle with the Zionists. He'd gone into battle, and been decorated for his courage. He'd lost his mother to their inhuman weapons. And he'd supported the movement whenever asked. Qati was a man who had never lost touch with the fundamentals. As a boy he'd read the *Little Red Book* of Chairman Mao. That Mao was, of course, an infidel of the worst sort – he'd refused even to acknowledge the idea of a God and persecuted those who worshipped – was beside the point. The revolutionary was a fish who swam in a peasant sea, and maintaining the good will of those peasants – or in this case, a shopkeeper – was the foundation of whatever success he might enjoy. This Druse had contributed what money he could, had once sheltered a wounded freedom fighter in his home. Such debts were not forgotten. Qati rose from his desk to greet the man with a warm handshake and the perfunctory kisses.

'Welcome, my friend.'

'Thank you for seeing me, Commander.' The shop-keeper seemed very nervous, and Qati wondered what the problem was.

'Please, take a chair. Abdullah,' he called, 'would you bring coffee for our guest?'

'You are too kind.'

'Nonsense. You are our comrade. Your friendship has not wavered in – how many years?'

The shopkeeper shrugged, smiling inwardly that this investment was about to pay off. He was frightened of Qati and his people – that was why he had never crossed them. He also kept Syrian authorities informed of what he'd done for them, because he was wary of those people, too. Mere survival in that part of the world was an art form, and a game of chance.

'I come to you for advice,' he said, after his first sip of coffee.

'Certainly.' Qati leaned forward in his chair. 'I am honored to be of help. What is the problem, my friend?'

'It is my father.'

'How old is he now?' Qati asked. The farmer had occasionally given his men gifts also, most often a lamb. Just a peasant, and an infidel peasant at that, but he was one who shared his enemy with Qati and his men.

'Sixty-six – you know his garden?'

'Yes, I was there some years ago, soon after your mother was killed by the Zionists,' Qati reminded him.

'In his garden there is an Israeli bomb.'

'Bomb? You mean a shell.'

'No, Commander, a bomb. What you can see of it is half a meter across.'

'I see – and if the Syrians learn of it . . .'

'Yes, as you know, they explode such things in place. My father's house would be destroyed.' The visitor held up his left forearm. 'I cannot be of much help rebuilding

203

it, and my father is too old to do it himself. I come here to ask how one might go about removing the damned thing.'

'You have come to the right place. Do you know how long it has been there?'

'My father says that it fell the very day this happened to me.' The shopkeeper gestured with his ruined arm again.

'Then surely Allah smiled on your family that day.'

Some smile, the shopkeeper thought, nodding.

'You have been our most faithful friend. Of course we can help you. I have a man highly skilled in the business of disarming and removing Israeli bombs – and then he takes the guts from them and makes bombs for our use.' Qati stopped and held up an admonishing finger. 'You must never repeat that.'

The visitor jerked somewhat in his chair. 'For my part, Commander, you may kill all of them you wish, and if you can do it from a bomb the pigs dropped into my father's garden, I will pray for your safety and success.'

'Please excuse me, my friend. No insult was intended. I must say such things, as you can understand.' Qati's message was fully understood.

'I will never betray you,' the shopkeeper announced forcefully.

'I know this.' Now it was time to keep faith with the peasant sea. 'Tomorrow I will send my man to your father's home. *Insh'Alláh*,' he said, God willing.

'I am in your debt, Commander.' *Sometime between now and the new year*, he hoped.

CHAPTER 8

The Pandora Process

The converted Boeing 747 rotated off the Andrews runway just before sunset. President Fowler had had a bad day and a half of briefings and unbreakable appointments. He would have two more even worse; even presidents are subject to the vagaries of ordinary human existence, and in this case, the eight-hour flight to Rome was coupled with a six-hour time change. The jet-lag would be a killer. Fowler was a seasoned enough traveler to know that. To attenuate the worst of it, he'd fiddled with his sleep pattern yesterday and today so that he'd be sufficiently tired to sleep most of the way across, and the VC-25A had lavish accommodations to make the flight as comfortable as Boeing and the United States Air Force could arrange. An easy-riding aircraft, the -25A had its Presidential accommodations in the very tip of the nose. The bed – actually a convertible sofa – was of decent size and the mattress had been selected for his personal taste. The aircraft was also large enough that a proper separation between the press and the administration people was possible – nearly two hundred feet, in fact; the press was in a closed-off section in the tail – and while his press secretary was dealing with the reporters aft, Fowler was discreetly joined by his National Security Advisor. Pete Connor and Helen D'Agustino shared a look that an outsider might take to be blank, but which spoke volumes within the close fraternity of the Secret Service. The Air Force Security Policeman assigned to the door just stared at the aft bulkhead, trying not to smile.

*

'So, Ibrahim, what of our visitor?' Qati asked.

'He is strong, fearless, and quite cunning, but I don't know what possible use we have for him,' Ibrahim Ghosn replied. He related the story of the Greek policeman.

'Broke his neck?' At least the man was not a plant . . . that is, if the policeman had really died, and this was not an elaborate ruse of the Americans, Greeks, Israelis, or God only knew who.

'Like a twig.'

'His contacts in America?'

'They are few. He is hunted by their national police. His group, he says, killed three of them, and his brother was recently ambushed and murdered by them.'

'He is ambitious in his choice of enemies. His education?'

'Poor in formal terms, but he is clever.'

'Skills?'

'Few that are of use to us.'

'He *is* an American,' Qati pointed out. 'How many of those have we had?'

Ghosn nodded. 'That is true, Commander.'

'The chance that he could be an infiltrator?'

'I would say slim, but we must be careful.'

'In any case, I have something I need you to do.' Qati explained about the bomb.

'Another one?' Ghosn was an expert at this task, but he was not exactly excited about being stuck with it. 'I know the farm – that foolish old man. I know, I know, his son fought against the Israelis, and you like the cripple.'

'That cripple saved the life of a comrade. Fazi would have bled to death had he not received shelter in that little shop. He didn't have to do that. That was at a time when the Syrians were angry with us.'

'All right. I have nothing to do for the rest of the day. I need a truck and a few men.'

'This new friend is strong, you say. Take him with you.'

'As you say, Commander.'

'And be careful!'

'*Insh'Allah.*' Ghosn was almost a graduate of the American University of Beirut – almost because one of his teachers had been kidnapped, and two others had used that as an excuse to leave the country. That had denied Ghosn the last nine credit hours needed for a degree in engineering. Not that he really needed it. He'd been at the top of his class, and learned well enough from the textbooks without having to listen to the explanations of instructors. He'd spent quite a bit of time in labs of his own making. Ghosn had never been a front-line soldier of the movement. Though he knew how to use small arms, his skills with explosives and electronic devices were too valuable to be risked. He was also youthful in appearance, handsome, and quite fair-skinned, as a result of which he traveled a lot. An advance-man of sorts, he often surveyed sites for future operations, using his engineer's eye and memory to sketch maps, determine equipment needs, and provide technical support for the actual operations people, who treated him with far more respect than an outsider might have expected. Of his courage there was no doubt. He'd proven his bravery more than once, defusing unexploded bombs and shells that the Israelis had left in Lebanon, then reworking the explosives recovered into bombs of his own. Ibrahim Ghosn would have been a welcome addition to any one of a dozen professional organizations anywhere in the world. A gifted, if largely self-taught engineer, he was also a Palestinian whose family had evacuated Israel at the time of the country's founding, confidently expecting to return as soon as the Arab armies of the time erased the invaders quickly and easily. But that happy circumstance had not come about, and his childhood memories were of crowded, insanitary camps where antipathy for Israel had been a creed as important as Islam. It could not have been otherwise. Disregarded by the Israelis as people who had voluntarily left their country, largely ignored by other Arab nations who might have made their lot easier but had not, Ghosn and those like him were mere pawns in a great game whose players had never agreed upon the rules. Hatred of Israel and its friends came as naturally as breathing, and finding ways to end the lives of such people was his task in life. It had never occurred to him to wonder why.

Ghosn got the keys for a Czech-built GAZ-66 truck. It wasn't as reliable as a Mercedes, but a lot easier to obtain – in this case it had been funnelled to his organization through the Syrians years before. On the back was a home-built A-frame. Ghosn loaded the American in the cab with himself and the driver. Two other men rode on the loadbed as the truck pulled out of the camp.

Marvin Russell examined the terrain with the interest of a hunter in a new territory. The heat was oppressive, but really no worse than the Badlands during a bad summer wind, and the vegetation – or lack of it – wasn't all that different from the reservation of his youth. What appeared to others as bleak was just another dusty place to an American raised in one. Except here they didn't have the towering thunderstorms – and the tornados they spawned – of the American Plains. The hills were also higher than the rolling Badlands. Russell had never seen mountains before. Here he saw them, high and dry and hot enough to make a climber gasp. Most climbers, Marvin Russell thought. He could hack it. He was in shape, better shape than these Arabs.

The Arabs, on the other hand, seemed to be believers in guns. So many guns, mostly Russian AK-47s at first, but soon he was seeing heavy anti-aircraft guns, and the odd battery of surface-to-air missiles, tanks, and self-propelled field guns belonging to the Syrian army. Ghosn noted his guest's interest, and started explaining things.

'These are here to keep the Israelis out,' he said, casting his explanation in accordance with his own beliefs. 'Your country arms the Israelis, and the Russians arm us.' He didn't add that this was becoming increasingly tenuous.

'Ibrahim, have you been attacked?'

'Many times, Marvin. They send their aircraft. They send commando teams. They have killed thousands of my people. They drove us from our land, you see. We are forced to live in camps that –'

'Yeah, man. They're called reservations where I come from.' That was something Ghosn didn't know about. 'They came to our land, the land of our ancestors, killed off the buffalo, sent in their army, and massacred us. Mainly they attacked camps of women and children. We tried to fight back. We killed a whole regiment under General Custer at a place called the Little Big Horn – that's the name of a river – under a leader named Crazy Horse. But they didn't stop coming. Just too many of them, too many soldiers, too many guns, and they took the best of our land, and left us shit, man. They make us live like beggars. No, that's not right. Like animals, like we're not people, even, 'cause we were in a place they wanted to have, and they just moved us out, like sweepin' away the garbage.'

'I didn't know about that,' Ghosn said, amazed that his were not the only people to be treated that way by the Americans and their Israeli vassals. 'When did it happen?'

'Hundred years ago. Actually started around 1865. We fought, man, we did the best we could, but we didn't have much of a chance. We didn't have friends, see? Didn't have friends like you got. Nobody gave us guns and tanks. So they killed off the bravest. Mainly they trapped the leaders and murdered them – Crazy Horse and Sitting Bull died like that. Then they squeezed us and starved us until we had to surrender. Left us dusty, shitty places to live, sent us enough food to keep us alive, but not enough to be strong. When some of us try to fight back, try to be men – well, I told you what they did to my brother. Shot him from ambush like he was an animal. Did it on television, even, so's people would know what happened when an Indian got too big for his britches.'

The man *was* a comrade, Ghosn realized. This was no infiltrator, and his story was no different from the story of a Palestinian. Amazing.

'So, why did you come here, Marvin?'

'I had to leave before they got me, man. I ain't proud of it, but what else could I do – you want me to wait till they could ambush me?' Russell shrugged. 'I figured I'd come someplace, find people like me, maybe learn a few things, learn how I could go back, maybe, teach my people how to fight back some.' Russell shook his head. 'Hell, maybe it's all hopeless, but I ain't gonna give in – you understand that?'

'Yes, my friend, I understand. It has been so with my people since before I was born. But you, too, must understand: it is not hopeless. So long as you stand up and fight back, there is always hope. That is why they hunt you – because they fear you!'

'Hope you're right, man.' Russell stared out the open window, and the dust stung his eyes, 7,000 miles from home. 'So, what are we doing?'

'When you fought the Americans, how did your warriors get weapons?'

'Mainly we took what they left behind.'

'So it is with us, Marvin.'

Fowler woke up about halfway across the Atlantic. Well, that was a first, he told himself. He'd never managed to do it in an airplane before. He wondered if any US President had, or done it on the way to see the Pope, or with his National Security Advisor. He looked out the windows. It was bright this far north – the aircraft was close to Greenland – and he wondered for a moment if it were morning or still night. That was almost a metaphysical question on an airplane, of course, which changed the time far faster than a watch could.

Also metaphysical was his mission. This would be remembered. Fowler knew his history. This was something unique. It had never happened before. Perhaps it was the beginning of the process, perhaps the end of it, but what he was up to was simply expressed. He would put an end to war. J. Robert Fowler's name would be associated with this treaty. It was the initiative of his Presidential administration. His speech at the UN had called the nations of the world to the Vatican. His subordinates had run the negotiations. His name would be the first on the treaty documents. His armed forces would guarantee the peace. He had truly earned his place in history. That was immortality, the kind that all men wanted but few earned. Was it any wonder that he was excited? he asked himself with dispassionate reflectivity.

A president's greatest fear was gone now. He'd asked himself that question from the first moment, the first fleeting self-directed thought, while still a prosecutor chasing after the *capo* of the Cleveland family of La Cosa Nostra – *if you're the President, what if you have to push the button?* Could he have done it? Could he have decided that the security of his country required the deaths of thousands – millions – of other human beings? Probably not, he judged. He was too good a man for that. His job was to protect people, to show them the way, to lead them along a beneficial path. They might not always understand that he was right and they wrong, that his vision was the correct one, the logical one. Fowler knew himself to be cold and aloof on such matters, but he was always right. Of that he was certain. He had to be certain, of himself and his motivations. Were he ever wrong, he knew, his conviction would be mere arrogance, and he'd faced that charge often enough. The one thing he was unsure about was his ability to face a nuclear war.

But that was no longer an issue, was it? Though he'd never admit it publicly, Reagan and Bush had ended that chance, forcing the Soviets to face their own contradictions, and facing them, to change their ways. And it had all happened in peace, because men really were more logical than beasts. There would continue to be hot spots, but so long as he did his job right they would not get out of hand – and the trip he was making now would end the most dangerous problem remaining in the world, the one with which no recent administration could cope. What Nixon and Kissinger had failed to do, what had defied the valiant efforts of Carter, the half-hearted attempts of Reagan, and the well-meaning gambits of Bush and his own predecessor, what all had failed to do,

Bob Fowler would accomplish. It was a thought in which to bask. Not only would he find his place in the history books, but he would also make the rest of his presidency that much easier to manage. This would also put the seal on his second term, a forty-five state majority, solid control of Congress, and the remainder of his sweeping social programs. With historic accomplishments like this one came international prestige and immense domestic clout. It was power of the best kind, earned in the best way, and the sort that he could put to the best possible use. With a stroke of a pen – actually several pens, for that was the custom – Fowler became great, a giant among the good, and a good man among the powerful. Not once in a generation did a single man have such a moment as this. Maybe not once in a century. And no one could take it away.

The aircraft was traveling at 43,000 feet, moving at a ground speed of 633 knots. The placement of his cabin allowed him to look forward, as a President should look, and down at a world whose affairs he was managing so well. The ride was silky smooth, and Bob Fowler was going to make history. He looked over to Elizabeth, lying on her back, her right hand up around her head, and the covers down at her waist, exposing her lovely chest to his eyes. While most of the rest of the passengers fidgeted in their seats, trying to get some sleep, he looked. Fowler didn't want to sleep right now. The President had never felt more like a man, a great man to be sure, but at this moment, just a man. His hand slid across her breasts. Elizabeth's eyes opened wide and she smiled, as though in her dreams she had read his thoughts.

Just like home, Russell thought to himself. The house was made of stones instead of block, and the roof was flat instead of peaked, but the dust was the same, and the pathetic little garden was the same. And the man might as easily have been a Sioux, the tiredness in his eyes, the bent back, the old, gnarled hands of one defeated by others.

'This must be the place,' he said, as the truck slowed.

'The old man's son fought the Israelis and was badly wounded. Both have been friends to us.'

'You have to look out for your friends,' Marvin agreed. The truck stopped, and Russell had to hop out to allow Ghosn to step down.

'Come along, I will introduce you.'

It was all surprisingly formal to the American. He didn't understand a word, of course, but he didn't have to. The respect of his friend Ghosn for the old one was good to see. After a few more remarks, the farmer looked at Russell and bowed his head, which embarrassed the American. Marvin took his hand gently and shook it in the manner of his people, muttering something that Ghosn translated. Then the farmer led them into his garden.

'Damn,' Russell observed when he saw it.

'American Mark 84 2,000 pound bomb, it would appear . . .' Ghosn said off-handedly, then knew he was wrong . . . the nose wasn't quite right . . . of course, the nose was crushed and distorted . . . but oddly so . . . He thanked the farmer and waved him back to the truck. 'First we must uncover it. Carefully, very carefully.'

'I can handle that,' Russell said. He went back to the truck, and selected a folding shovel of a military design.

'We have people –' The American cut Ghosn off.

'Let me do it. I'll be careful.'

'Do not touch it. Use the shovel to dig around it, but use your hands to remove the soil from the bomb itself. Marvin, I warn you, this is very dangerous.'

'Better step back, then.' Russell turned and grinned. He had to show this man that he was courageous. Killing the cop had been easy, no challenge at all. This was different.

'And leave my comrade in danger?' Ghosn asked rhetorically. He knew that this was the intelligent thing to do, what he would have done had his own people done the digging, because his skills were too valuable to be risked stupidly, but he could not show weakness in front of the American, could he? Besides, he could watch and see if the man was as courageous as he seemed.

Ghosn was not disappointed. Russell stripped to the waist and got on his knees to dig around the periphery of the bomb. He was even careful of the garden, far more so than Ghosn's men would have been. It took an hour until he'd dug a shallow pit around the device, piling up the soil in four neat mounds. Already Ghosn knew that there was something odd here. It was not a Mark 84. It had roughly the same size, but the shape was wrong, and the bombcase was ... just wasn't right. The Mark 84 had a sturdy case made of cast steel, so that when the explosive filler detonated, the case would be transformed into a million razor-sharp fragments, the better to tear men to bits. But not this one. In two visible places the case was broken, and it wasn't quite thick enough for that kind of bomb. So what the hell was it?

Russell moved in closer and used his hands to pull the dirt off the surface of the bomb itself. He was careful and thorough. The American worked up a good sweat but didn't slacken his efforts even once. The muscles in his arms rippled, and Ghosn admired him for that. The man had a physical power like none he had ever seen. Even Israeli paratroopers didn't look so formidable. He'd excavated two or three tons of dirt, yet he barely showed the effort, his movements as steady and powerful as a machine.

'Stop for a minute,' Ghosn said. 'I must get my tools.'

'Okay,' Russell replied, sitting back and staring at the bomb.

Ghosn returned with a rucksack and a canteen, which he handed to the American.

'Thanks, man. It is a little warm here.' Russell drank half a liter of water. 'Now what?'

Ghosn took a paint brush from the sack and began sweeping the last of the dirt from the weapon. 'You should leave now,' he warned.

'That's okay, Ibrahim. I'll stay if you don't mind.'

'This is the dangerous part.'

'You stayed by me, man,' Russell pointed out.

'As you wish. I am now looking for the fuse.'

'Not in front?' Russell pointed to the nose of the bomb.

'Not there. There is usually one at the front – it appears to be missing, that's just a screw-on cap – one in the middle, and one at the back.'

'How come it don't have no fins on it?' Russell asked. 'Don't bombs have fins on 'em, you know, like an arrow?'

'The fins were probably stripped off when it hit the ground. That's often how we find such bombs, because the fins come off and lie on the surface.'

'Want me to uncover the back of the thing, then?'

'Very, very carefully, Marvin. Please.'

'Okay, man.' Russell moved around his friend and resumed pulling the dirt off the back end of the bombcase. Ghosn, he noted, was one cool son of a bitch. Marvin was as scared as he had ever been, this close to a shitload of explosives, but he could not and damned well would not show anything that looked like fear to this guy. Ibrahim might be a little pencil-necked geek, but the dude had real balls, dicking with a bomb like this. He noted that Ghosn was sweeping the dirt off like he was using the brush on a girl's tits, and made his own efforts just as cautious. Ten minutes later, he had uncovered the back.

'Ibrahim?'

'Yes, Marvin?' Ghosn said without looking.

'There ain't nothing here. The back's just a hole, man.'

Ghosn lifted the brush from the case and turned to look. That was odd. But he had other things to do. 'Thank you. You can stop now. I still have not found a fuse.'

Russell backed off, sat on a mound of dirt, and proceeded to empty the rest of the canteen. On reflection he walked over to the truck. The three men there along with the farmer were just standing – the farmer watching in the open, the others observing more circumspectly behind the stone walls of the house. Russell tossed one man the empty canteen, and had a full one returned the same way. He gave a thumbs-up sign to all of them and walked back to the bomb.

'Back off for a minute and have a drink,' Marvin said on his return.

'Good idea,' Ghosn agreed, setting his brush down next to the bomb.

'Find anything?'

'A plug connection, nothing else.' That was odd, too, Ghosn thought, pulling the top off the canteen. There were no stenciled markings, just a silver-and-red label block near the nose. Color-codes were common on bombs, but he'd never seen that one before. So, what was this damned thing? Maybe an FAE or some kind of sub-munition canister? Something old and obsolete that he'd never seen before. It had come down in 1973, after all. Maybe something that had long since gone out of service. That was very bad news. If it were something he'd never seen before, it might have a fusing system that he didn't know. His manual for dealing with such things was Russian in origin, though printed in Arabic. Ghosn had long since committed it to memory, but there was no description for anything like this. And that was truly frightening. Ghosn took a long pull from the canteen and then poured a little across his face.

'Take it easy, man,' Russell said, noticing the man's tension.

'This job is never easy, my friend, and it is always very frightening.'

'You look pretty cool, Ibrahim.' It wasn't a lie. While brushing the dirt off, he looked like a doctor, almost, doing something real hard, Russell thought, but doing it. The little fucker had balls, Marvin told himself again.

Ghosn turned and grinned. 'That is all a lie. I am quite terrified. I truly hate doing this.'

'You got a big pair, boy, and that's no shit.'

'Thank you. Now I must return while I still can. You really should leave, you know.'

Russell spat into the dirt. 'Fuck it.'

'That would be very difficult.' Ghosn grinned. 'And if you got a reaction from "her", you might not like it.'

'I guess when these suckers come, the earth really does move!'

Ghosn knew enough of American idiom that he fell backwards and laughed uproariously. 'Please, Marvin, do not say such things when I am working!' *I like this man!* Ghosn told himself. *We are too humorless a lot. I like this American!* He had to wait another few minutes before he calmed down enough to resume his work.

Another hour's brushing showed nothing. There were seams in the bombcase, even some sort of hatch . . . he'd never seen that before. But no fuse point. If there were one, it had to be underneath. Russell moved away some more dirt, allowing Ghosn to continue his search, but again, nothing. He decided to examine the back.

'There's a flashlight in my sack . . .'

'Got it.' Russell handed the light over.

Ghosn lay down on the dirt and contorted himself to look into the hole. It was dark, of course, and he switched on the light . . . He saw electrical wiring, and something else, some sort of metal framework – lattice-work would be more accurate. He judged he could see perhaps eighty centimeters . . . and if this were a real bomb, there would not be so much empty space. So. So. Ghosn tossed the light to the American.

'We have just wasted five hours,' he announced.

'Huh?'

'I don't know what this thing is, but it is not a bomb.' He sat up and had a brief attack of the shakes, but it didn't last long.

'What is it then?'

'Some kind of electronic sensing device, perhaps, a warning system. Maybe a camera pod – the lens assembly must be underneath. That doesn't matter. What is important is that it is no bomb.'

'So, now what?'

'We move it, take it back with us. It might be valuable. Perhaps something we can sell to the Russians or the Syrians.'

'So the old guy was worried about nothing?'

'Correct.' Ghosn rose and the two men walked back to the truck. 'It is safe now,' he told the farmer. Might as well tell him what he wanted to know, and why

217

confuse him with the facts of the matter? The farmer kissed Ghosn's dirty hands, and those of the American, which further embarrassed Russell.

The driver pulled the truck around, and backed into the garden, careful to do as little damage to the rows of vegetables as possible. Russell watched as two men filled a half-dozen sandbags and hoisted them into the truck. Next they put a sling around the bomb, and began to crank it up with a winch. The bomb – or whatever it was – was heavier than expected, and Russell took over the hand winch, displaying his strength yet again as he cranked it up alone. The Arabs swung the A-frame forward, then he lowered the bomb into the nest made of sandbags. A few ropes secured it in place, and that was that.

The farmer would not let them leave. He brought out tea and bread, insisting on feeding the men before they left, and Ghosn accepted the man's hospitality with appropriate humility. Four lambs were added to the truck's load before they left.

'That was a good thing you did, man,' Russell observed as they pulled off.

'Perhaps,' Ghosn said tiredly. Stress was so much more tiring than actual labor, though the American seemed to handle both quite well. Two hours later, they were back in the Bekaa Valley. The bomb – Ghosn didn't know what else to call it – was dropped unceremoniously in front of his workshop, and the party of five went to feast on fresh lamb. To Ghosn's surprise, the American had never had lamb before, and so was properly introduced to the traditional Arab delicacy.

'Got something interesting, Bill,' Murray announced, as he came into the Director's office.

'What's that, Danny?' Shaw looked up from his appointments schedule.

'A cop got himself killed over in Athens, and they think it was an American who did it.' Murray filled Shaw in on the technical details.

'Broke his neck barehanded?' Bill asked.

'That's right. The cop was a skinny little guy,' Murray said, 'but . . .'

'Jesus. Okay, let's see.' Murray handed the photo over. 'We know this guy, Dan? It's not the best picture in the world.'

'Al Denton thinks it might be Marvin Russell. He's playing computer games on the original slide. There were no prints or other forensic stuff. The car was registered to a third party who disappeared, probably never existed in the first place. The driver of the other vehicle is an unknown. Anyway, it fits Russell's description, short and powerful, and the cheekbones and coloration make him look like an Indian. Clothing is definitely American. So's the suitcase.'

'So you think he skipped the country after we got his brother . . . smart move,' Shaw judged. 'He was supposed to be the bright one, wasn't he?'

'Smart enough to get teamed up with an Arab.'

'Think so?' Shaw examined the other face. 'Could be Greek, or anything Mediterranean. Skin's a little fair for an Arab, but it's a pretty ordinary face, and you said it's an unknown. Gut call, Dan?'

'Yep.' Murray nodded. 'I checked the file. A confidential informant told us a few years ago that Marvin made a trip east a few years back and made contacts with the PFLP. Athens is a convenient place to renew the association. Neutral ground.'

'Also a good place to make connections for a drug deal,' Shaw suggested. 'What current info do we have on Brother Marvin?'

'Not much. Our best CI out there is back in the joint – had a brawl with a couple of reservation cops and came off second-best.'

Shaw grunted. The problem with Confidential Informants, of course, was that most of them were criminals who did illegal things and regularly ended up in jail. That both established their bonafides and made them temporarily useless. Such were the rules of the game. 'Okay,' the FBI Director said. 'You want to do something. What is it?'

'With a little nudge, we can spring the CI on good-time rules and get him back into the Warrior Society. If this is a terrorist connection, we'd better start running some leads down. Ditto if it's for drugs. Interpol has already come up blank on the driver. No record of his face for either terrorist or drug connections. The Greeks have come to a blank wall. Information on the car didn't lead them anywhere. They have a dead sergeant, and all they got to go on is two faces with no names attached. Sending the photo to us was their last shot. They figured him for an American . . .'

'Hotel?' the Director asked, ever the investigator.

'Yeah, they identified that – that is, they know it's one of two places side by side. There were ten people with American passports who checked out that day, but they're both little places with lots of in-and-out, and they came up with nothing useful for identification purposes. The hotel staff is forgetful. That kind of a place. Who's to say that our friend even stayed there? The Greeks want us to do follow-up on the names from the hotel register,' Murray concluded.

Bill Shaw handed the photo back. 'That's simple enough. Run with it.'

'Already being done.'

'Assuming we know that these two had anything to do with the killing. Well, you gotta go with your best guess. Okay: let the US Attorney know that our CI has paid his debt to society. It's about time we ran those "warriors" down once and for all.' Shaw had won his spurs on counter-terrorism, and that class of criminal was still his first hate.

'Yeah, I'll play up the drug connection on that. We ought to have him sprung in two weeks or so.'

'Fair enough, Dan.'

'When's the President get into Rome?' Murray asked.

'Pretty soon. Really something, isn't it?'

'Bet your ass, man. Kenny'd better find himself another line of work soon. Peace is breaking out.'

Shaw grinned. 'Who woulda thunk it? We can always

get him a badge and a gun so's he can earn an honest living.'

Presidential security was completed with a discreetly located flight of four Navy Tomcat fighters that had followed the VC-25A at a distance of five miles while a radar-surveillance aircraft made sure that nothing was approaching Air Force One. Normal commercial traffic was set aside, and the environs of the military airfield being used for the arrival had not so much been combed as strained. Already waiting on the pavement was the President's armored limousine, which had been flown in a few hours earlier by an Air Force C-141B, and enough Italian soldiers and police to discourage a regiment of terrorists. President Fowler emerged from his private washroom shaved and scrubbed pink, his tie exquisitely knotted, and smiling as brightly as Pete and Daga had ever seen. *As well he might*, Connor thought. The agent did not moralize as deeply as D'Agustino did. The President was a man, and as most presidents were, a lonely man – doubly so with the loss of his wife. Elliot might be an arrogant bitch, but she was undeniably attractive, and if that's what it took to allay the stress and pressure of the job, then that's what it took. The President had to relax, else the job would burn him up – as it had burned others up – and that was bad for the country. So long as HAWK didn't break any major laws, Connor and D'Agustino would protect both his privacy and his pleasure. Pete understood. Daga merely wished that he had better taste. E.E. had left the quarters a little earlier, and was dressed in something especially nice. She joined the President in the dining area just before landing for coffee and donuts. There was no denying that she was attractive, especially this morning. Maybe, Special Agent Helen D'Agustino thought, she was a good lay. Certainly she and the President were the best-rested people on the flight. The media pukes – the Secret Service has an institutional dislike for reporters – had squirmed and fidgeted in their seats throughout the flight, and looked rumpled, despite their upbeat expressions. The most harried of all was the President's speechwriter, who'd worked through the night without pause, except for coffee and head-calls, and finally delivered the speech to Arnie van Damm a bare twenty minutes before touchdown. Fowler had run through it over breakfast and loved it.

'Callie, this is just wonderful!' The President beamed at the weary staff member, who had the literary elegance of a poet. Fowler amazed everyone in sight by giving the young lady – she was still on the sunny side of thirty – a hug that left tears in Callie Weston's eyes. 'Get yourself some rest, and enjoy Rome.'

'A pleasure, Mr President.'

The aircraft came to a stop at the appointed place. The mobile stairs came immediately into place. A section of red carpet was rolled in place to lead from the stairs to the longer carpet that led in turn to the podium. The President and Prime Minister of Italy moved to their appointed places, along with the US Ambassador, and the usual hangers-on, including some exhausted protocol officers who'd had to plan this ceremony literally on the fly. The door of the aircraft was opened by an Air Force sergeant. Secret Service agents looked outside suspiciously for any sign of trouble, and caught glances from other agents of the advance team. When the President appeared, the Italian Air Force band played its arrival fanfare, different from the traditional American 'Ruffles and Flourishes.'

The President made his way down the steps alone, walking from reality to immortality, he reflected. Reporters noticed that his stride was bouncy and relaxed, and envied him the comfortable quarters where he could sleep in regal solitude. Sleep was the only sure cure for jetlag, and clearly the President had enjoyed a restful flight. The Brooks Brothers suit was newly-pressed – Air Force One has all manner of amenities – his shoes positively sparkled, and his grooming was perfection itself. Fowler made his way to the US Ambassador and his wife, who conducted him to the Italian president. The band struck up 'The Star-Spangled Banner.' Next came the traditional review of the assembled troops, and a brief arrival speech that only hinted at the eloquence that would soon follow. In all, it took twenty minutes before Fowler got into his car, along with the ambassador, Dr Elliot, and his personal bodyguards.

'First one of those I've ever enjoyed,' was Fowler's evaluation of the ceremony. There was general agreement that the Italians had handled it with elegance.

'Elizabeth, I want you to stay close. There are a few aspects to the agreement that we need to go over. I need to see Brent, too. How's he doing?' Fowler asked the ambassador.

'Tired but pretty happy with himself,' Ambassador Coates replied. 'The last negotiation session lasted over twenty hours.'

'What's the local press saying?' E. E. asked.

'They're euphoric. They all are. This is a great day for the whole world.' *It's happening on my turf, and I'll be there to see it!* Jed Coates said to himself. *Not often you get to see history made.*

'Well, that was nice.'

The National Military Command Center – NMCC – is located in the D-Ring of the Pentagon near the River Entrance. One of the few such installations in government which actually looks like its Hollywood renditions, it is an arena roughly the size and proportions of a basketball court and two stories in height. NMCC is in essence the central telephone switchboard for the United States military. It is not the only one – the nearest alternate is at Fort Ritchie in the Maryland hills – since it is far too easy to destroy, but it is the most conveniently located of its type. It's a regular stop for VIPs who want to see the sexier parts of the Pentagon, much to the annoyance of the staff for whom it's merely the place where they work.

Adjoining the NMCC is a smaller room in which one can see a set of IBM PC/AT personal computers – old ones with 5.25-inch floppy drives – that constitute the Hot Line, the direct communications link between the

American and Soviet presidents. The NMCC 'node' for the link was not the only one, but it was the primary down-link. That fact was not widely known in America, but it had been purposefully made known to the Soviets. Some form of direct communications between the two countries would be necessary even during an on-going nuclear war, and letting the Soviets know that the only readily usable down-link was here might serve, some 'experts' had judged three decades earlier, as a life-insurance policy for the area.

That, Captain James Rosselli, USN, thought, was just so much theoretician-generated horseshit. That no one had ever seriously questioned it was another example of all the horseshit that lay and stank within Washington in general and the Pentagon in particular. With all the nonsense that took place within the confines of Inter-state 495, the Washington Beltway, it was just one more bit of data accepted as gospel, despite the fact that it didn't make a whole lot of sense. To 'Rosey' Rosselli, Washington, D.C. was about 300 square miles sur-rounded by reality. He wondered if the laws of physics even applied inside the Beltway. He'd long since given up on the laws of logic.

Joint duty, Rosey grunted to himself. The most recent effort of Congress to reform the military – something it was singularly unable to do for itself, he groused – had prescribed that uniformed officers who aspired to flag rank – and which of them didn't? – had to spend some of their time in close association with peers from the other uniformed services. Rosselli had never been told how hanging around with a field-artilleryman might make him a better submarine driver, but then no one else had evidently wondered about that. It was simply accepted as an article of faith that cross-pollination was good for something, and so the best and brightest officers were taken away from their professional specialties and dropped into things which they knew not the first thing about. Not that they'd ever learn how to do their new jobs, of course, but they might learn just enough to be dangerous, plus losing currency in what they were supposed to do. That was Congress's idea of military reform.

'Coffee, Cap'n?' an Army corporal asked.

'Better make it decaf,' Roscy replied. *If my disposition gets any worse, I might start hurting people.*

Work here was career-enhancing. Rosselli knew that, and he also knew that being here was partly his fault. He'd majored in sub and minored in spook throughout his career. He'd already had a tour at the Navy's intelligence headquarters at Suitland, Maryland, near Andrews Air Force Base. At least this was a better commute – he'd gotten official housing at Bolling Air Force Base, and the trip to the Pentagon was a relatively simple hop across I-295/395 to his reserved parking place, another perk that came with duty in the NMCC, and one worth shedding blood for.

Once duty here had been relatively exciting. He remembered when the Soviets had splashed the Korean Airlines 747 and other incidents, and it must have been wonderfully chaotic during the Iraq war – that is, when the senior watch officer wasn't answering endless calls of 'what's happening?' to anyone who'd managed to get the direct-line number. But now?

Now, as he had just watched on his desk TV, the President was about to defuse the world's biggest remaining diplomatic bomb, and soon Rosselli's work would mostly involve taking calls about collisions at sea, or crashed airplanes, or some dumbass soldier who'd gotten himself run over by a tank. Such things were serious, but not matters of great professional interest. So here he was. His paperwork was finished. That was something Jim Rosselli was good at – he'd learned how to shuffle papers in the Navy, and here he had a superb staff to help him with it – and the rest of the day was mainly involved with sitting and waiting for something to happen. The problem was that Rosselli was a do-er, not a wait-er, and who wanted a disaster to happen anyway?

'Gonna be a quiet day.' This was Rosselli's XO, an Air Force F-15 pilot, Lieutenant Colonel Richard Barnes.

'I think you're right, Rocky.' *Just what I wanted to hear!* Rosselli checked his watch. It was a twelve-hour

225

shift, with five hours left to go. 'Hell, it's getting to be a pretty quiet world.'

'Ain't it the truth.' Barnes turned back to the display screen. *Well, I got my two MiGs over the Persian Gulf. At least it hasn't been a complete waste of time.*

Rosselli stood and decided to walk around. The duty watch officers thought this was to look at what they were doing, to make sure they were doing something. One senior civilian ostentatiously continued doing the *Post* crossword. It was his 'lunch' break and he preferred eating here to the mostly empty cafeterias. Here he could watch TV. Rosselli next wandered over to the left into the Hot Line room, and he was lucky for a change. A message was announced by the dinging of a little bell. The actual message received looked like random garbage, but the encryption machine changed that into cleartext Russian which a Marine translated:

> 'So you think you know the real meaning of
>   fear?
> Yeah, you think you do know, but I doubt it.
> When you sit in a shelter with bombs falling
>   all over,
> And the houses around you are burning like
>   torches,
> I agree that you experience horror and fright.
> For such moments are dreadful, for as long as
>   they last,
> But the all-clear sounds – then it's okay –
> You take a deep breath, the stress has passed
>   by,
> But real fear is a stone deep down in your chest.
> You hear me! A stone. That's what it is, no
>   more.

'Ilya Selvinskiy,' the Marine lieutenant said.

'Hmph?'

'Ilya Selvinskiy, Russian poet, did some famous work during the Second World War. I know this one, *Sprakh,* the title is "Fear." It's very good.' The young officer

grinned. 'My opposite number is pretty literate. So . . .'
TRANSMISSION RECEIVED. THE REST OF THE POEM
IS EVEN BETTER, ALEKSEY, the lieutenant typed,
STAND BY FOR REPLY.

'What do you send back?' Rosselli asked.

'Today . . . maybe a little Emily Dickinson. She was a
morbid bitch, always talking about death and stuff. No,
better yet – Edgar Allan Poe. They really like him over
there. Hmmm, which one . . . ?' The lieutenant opened
a desk drawer and pulled out a volume.

'Don't you do it in advance?' Rosselli asked.

The Marine grinned up at his boss. 'No, sir, that's
cheating. We used to do it that way, but we changed
things about two years ago, when things lightened up.
Now it's sort of a game. He picks a poem, and I have to
respond with a corresponding passage from an American
poet. It helps pass the time, Cap'n. Good for language
skills on both sides. Translating poetry is a bitch – good
exercise.' The Soviet side transmitted its messages in
Russian, and the Americans in English, necessitating
skilled translators at both ends.

'Much real business on the line?'

'Captain, I've never seen much more than test messages. Oh, when we have the Sec-State flying over, sometimes we check weather data. We even chatted a little
about hockey when their national team came over to
play with the NHL guys last August, but mainly it's
duller than dirt, and that's why we trade poetry passages.
Weren't for that, we'd all go nuts. Shame we can't talk
like on CB or something, but the rules are the rules.'

'Guess so. They say anything about the treaty stuff in
Rome?'

'Not a word. We don't do that, sir.'

'I see.' Rosselli watched the lieutenant pick a stanza
from 'Annabel Lee.' He was surprised. Rosey had expected something from 'The Raven.' Nevermore . . .

The arrival day was one of rest and ceremony – and
mystery. The treaty terms had still not been leaked, and
news agencies, knowing that something 'historic' had

happened, were frantic to discover exactly what it was. To no avail. The chiefs of state of Israel, Saudi Arabia, Switzerland, the Soviet Union, the United States of America, and their host, Italy, arrayed themselves around a massive 15th Century table, punctuated with their chief diplomats and representatives of the Vatican and the Greek Orthodox church. In deference to the Saudis, toasts were offered in water or orange juice, which was the only discordant note of the evening. Soviet President Andrey Il'ych Narmonov was particularly effusive. His country's participation in the treaty was a matter of great importance, and the inclusion of the Russian Orthodox Church on the Commission for Christian Shrines would have major political import in Moscow. The dinner lasted three hours, after which the guests departed in view of the cameras on the far side of the avenue, and once more the newsies were thunderstruck by the fellowship. A jovial Fowler and Narmonov traveled together to the former's hotel and availed themselves for only the second time of the opportunity to discuss matters of bilateral interest.

'You have fallen behind in your deactivation of your missile forces,' Fowler observed after pleasantries were dispensed with. He eased the blow by handing over a glass of wine.

'Thank you, Mr President. As we told your people last week, our disposal facility has proven inadequate. We can't dismantle the damned things fast enough, and our nature-lovers in parliament are objecting to our method of neutralizing the propellant stocks.'

Fowler smiled in sympathy. 'I know the problem, Mr President.' The environmental movement had taken off in the Soviet Union the previous spring, with the Russian parliament passing a new set of laws modeled on – but much tougher than – American statutes. The amazing part was that the central Soviet government were abiding by the laws, but Fowler couldn't say that. The environmental nightmare inflicted on that country by more than seventy years of Marxism would take a generation of tough laws to fix. 'Will this affect the dead-line for fulfilling the treaty requirements?'

'You have my word, Robert,' Narmonov said sol-emnly. 'The missiles will be destroyed by 1st March even if I must blow them up myself.'

'That is good enough for me, Andrey.'

The reduction treaty, a carryover from the previous administration, mandated a 50 percent reduction in intercontinental launchers by the coming spring. All of America's Minuteman-II missiles had been tagged for destruction, and the US side of the treaty obligations was fully on track. As had been done under the Intermediate Nuclear Forces Treaty, the surplus missiles were dis-mantled to their component stages, which were either crushed or otherwise destroyed before witnesses. The news had covered the first few destructions, then grown tired of it. The missile silos, also under inspection, were stripped of their electronic equipment and, in the case of American structures, fifteen had already been declared surplus and sold – in four cases, farmers had purchased them and converted them to real silos. A Japanese con-glomerate that had large holdings in North Dakota had further purchased a command bunker and made it into a wine cellar for the hunting lodge its executives used each fall.

American inspectors on the Soviet side reported that the Russians were trying mightily, but that the plant built for dismantlement of the Russian missiles had been poorly designed, as a result of which the Soviets were 30 percent behind schedule. Fully a hundred missiles were sitting on trailers outside the plant, the silos they'd left already destroyed by explosives. Though the Soviets had in each case removed and burned the guidance package in front of American inspectors, there were lingering intelligence evaluations that it was all a sham – the erec-tor trailers, some argued, could elevate and fire the missiles. Suspicion of the Soviets was too hard a habit to break for some in the US intelligence community, as was doubtless true of the Russians as well, Fowler thought.

'This treaty is a major step forward, Robert,' Narmonov said, after a sip from his wine glass – now that they were alone they could relax like gentlemen, the Russian thought with a sly grin. 'You and your people are to be congratulated.'

'Your help was crucial to its success, Andrey,' Fowler replied graciously. It was a lie, but a politic one which both men understood. In fact it was not a lie, but neither man knew that.

'One less trouble spot for us to worry about. How blind we were!'

'That is true, my friend, but it is behind us. How are your people dealing with Germany?'

'The army is not happy, as you might imagine –'

'Neither is mine.' Fowler interrupted gently with his pronouncement. 'Soldiers are like dogs. Useful, of course, but they must know who the master is. Like dogs, they can be forgetful, and must be reminded from time to time.'

Narmonov nodded thoughtfully as the translation came across. It was amazing how arrogant this man was. Just what his intelligence briefings had told him, the Soviet president noted. And patronizing, too. Well, the American had the luxury of a firm political system, Andrey Il'ych told himself. It allowed Fowler to be so sure of himself while he, Narmonov, had to struggle every day with a system not yet set in stone. Or even wood, the Russian thought bleakly. What a luxury indeed to be able to look on soldiers as dogs to be cowed. Didn't he know that dogs had teeth? So strange the Americans were. Throughout Communist rule in the Soviet Union, they had fretted about the political muscle of the Red Army – when in fact it had had none at all after Stalin's elimination of Tukhachevskiy. But now they discounted all such stories while the dissolution of the iron hand of Marxism-Leninism was allowing soldiers to think in ways that would have ended in execution only a few years earlier. Well, this was no time to disabuse the American of his illusions, was it?

'Tell me, Robert, this treaty idea – where exactly did

it come from?' Narmonov asked. He knew the truth and wanted to see Fowler's abilities as a liar.

'Many places, as with all such ideas,' the President replied lightly. 'The moving force was Charles Alden – poor bastard. When the Israelis had that terrible incident, he activated his plan immediately and – well, it worked, didn't it?'

The Russian nodded again, and made his mental notes. Fowler lied with skill, evading the substance of the question to give a truthful but evasive answer. Khrushchev was right, as he'd already known. Politicians all the world over are not terribly different. It was something to remember about Fowler. He didn't like sharing credit, and was not above lying in the face of a peer, even over something so small as this. Narmonov was vaguely disappointed. Not that he'd expected anything else, but Fowler could have shown grace and humanity. He'd stood to lose nothing by it, after all. Instead he was as petty as any local Party *apparatchik*. *Tell me, Robert,* Narmonov asked behind a poker face that would have stood him well in Las Vegas, *what sort of man are you!*

'It is late, my friend,' Narmonov observed. 'Tomorrow afternoon, then?'

Fowler stood. 'Tomorrow afternoon, Andrey.'

Bob Fowler escorted the Russian to the door and saw him off, then returned to his suite of rooms. Once there he pulled the hand-written check-list out of his pocket to make sure he'd asked all the questions.

'Well?'

'Well, the missile problem, he says, is exactly what our inspectors said it is. That ought to satisfy the guys at DIA.' A grimace; it wouldn't. 'I think he's worried about his military.'

Dr Elliot sat down. 'Anything else?'

The President poured her a glass of wine, then sat beside his National Security Advisor. 'The normal pleasantries. He's a very busy, very worried man. Well, we knew that, didn't we?'

Liz swirled the wine around the glass and sniffed at it.

She didn't like Italian wines, but this one wasn't bad. 'I've been thinking, Robert . . .'

'Yes, Elizabeth?'

'What happened to Charlie . . . we need to do something. It isn't fair that he should have disappeared like that. He's the guy who put this treaty on track, isn't he?'

'Well, yes,' Fowler agreed, sipping at his own replenished glass. 'You're right, Elizabeth. It really was his effort.'

'I think we should let that out – quietly, of course. At the very least –'

'Yes, he should be remembered for something other than a pregnant grad student. That's very gracious of you, Elizabeth.' Fowler tapped his glass against hers. 'You handle the media people. You're releasing the treaty details tomorrow before lunch?'

'That's right, about nine, I think.'

'Then after you're finished, take a few of the journalists aside and give it to them on background. Maybe Charlie will rest a little easier.'

'No problem, Mr President,' Liz agreed. Exorcizing that particular demon came easily enough, didn't it? Was there anything she could not talk him into?

'Big day tomorrow.'

'The biggest, Bob, the biggest.' Elliot leaned back and loosened the scarf from her throat. 'I never thought I'd ever have a moment like this.'

'I did,' Fowler observed with a twinkle in his eye. There came a momentary pang of conscience. He'd expected to have it with someone else, but that was fate, wasn't it? Fate. The world was so strange. But he had no control over that, did he? And fate had decreed that he would be here at the moment in question, with Elizabeth. It wasn't his doing, was it? Therefore, he decided, there was no guilt, was there? How could there be guilt? He was making the world into a better, safer, more peaceful place. How could guilt attach to that?

Elliot closed her eyes as the President's hand caressed her offered neck. Never in her wildest dreams had she expected a moment like this.

The entire floor of the hotel was reserved for the President's party, and the two floors under it. Italian and American guards stood at all the entrances, and at various places in the buildings along the street. But the corridor outside the President's suite of rooms was the exclusive domain of the Presidential Protective Detail. Connor and D'Agustino made their own final check before retiring for the evening. A full squad of ten agents were in view, and another ten were behind various closed doors. Three of the visible agents had FAG-bags, black satchels across their chests. Officially called fast-action-gun bags, each contained an Uzi sub-machinegun, which could be extracted and fired in about a second and a half. Anyone who got this far would find a warm reception.

'I see HAWK and HARPY are discussing affairs of state,' Daga observed quietly.

'Helen, I didn't think you were so much a prude,' Pete Connor replied with a sly grin.

'None of my business, but in the old days people outside the door had to be eunuchs or something.'

'Keep talking like that and Santa will drop coal in your stocking.'

'I'd settle for that new automatic the FBI adopted,' Daga said with a chuckle. 'They're like teenagers. It's unseemly.'

'Daga . . .'

'I know, he's The Boss, and he's a big boy, and we have to look the other way. Relax, Pete, you think I'm going to blab to a reporter?' She opened the door to the fire stairs and saw three agents, two of whom had their FAG-bags at the ready.

'And I was about to offer you a drink, too . . .' Connor said deadpan. It was a joke. He and Daga were non-drinkers while on duty, and they were nearly always on duty. It wasn't that he had never thought about getting into her pants. He was divorced, as was she, but it would never have worked, and that was that. She knew it, too, and grinned at him.

'I could use one – the stuff they have here is what I was raised on. What a crummy job this is!' A final look down the corridor. 'Everybody's in place, Pete. I think we can call it a night.'

'You really like the tcn-millimeter?'

'Fired one last week up at Greenbelt. Got a possible with my first string. It doesn't get much better than that, lover.'

Connor stopped dead in his tracks and laughed. 'Christ, Daga!'

'People might notice?' D'Agustino batted her eyes at him. 'See what I mean, Pete?'

'God, who ever heard of a Guinea puritan?'

Helen D'Agustino elbowed the senior agent in the ribs and made her way to the elevator. Pete was right. She was turning into a damned prude, and she'd never ever been like that. A passionate woman whose single attempt at marriage had collapsed because one household wasn't large enough for two assertive egos – at least not two Italian ones – she knew she was allowing her prejudices to color her judgment. That was not a healthy thing, even over something both trivial and divorced from her job. What HAWK did on his own time was his business, but the look in his eyes . . . He was infatuated with the bitch. Daga wondered if any president had allowed that to happen. Probably, she admitted. They were only men, after all, and all men sometimes thought from the testicles instead of the brain. That the President should become a lackey of such a shallow woman as this – that was what offended her. But that, she admitted to herself, was both odd and inconsistent. After all, women didn't come much more liberated than she was. So why, she asked herself, was it bothering her? It had been too long a day for that. She needed sleep, and knew that she'd only get five or six hours before she was on duty again. *Damn these overseas trips . . .*

'So what is it?' Qati asked, just after dawn. He'd been away the previous day, meeting some other guerrila leaders, and also for a trip to the doctor, Ghosn knew, though he could not ask about that.

234

'Not sure,' the engineer replied. 'I'd guess a jamming pod, something like that.'

'That's useful,' the commander said at once. Despite the rapprochement, or whatever the key phrase was, between East and West, business was still business. The Russians still had a military, and that military still had weapons. Countermeasures against those weapons were items of interest. Israeli equipment was particularly prized, since the Americans copied it. Even old equipment showed how the Israeli engineers thought through problems, and could provide useful clues to newer systems.

'Yes, we should be able to sell it to our Russian friends.'

'How did the American work out?' Qati asked next.

'Quite well. I do like him, Ismael. I understand him better now.' The engineer explained why. Qati nodded.

'What should we do with him, then?'

Ghosn shrugged. 'Weapons training, perhaps? Let's see if he fits in with the men.'

'Very well. I'll send him out this morning to see how well he knows combat skills. And you, how soon will you pick the thing apart?'

'I planned to do it today.'

'Excellent. Do not let me stop you.'

'How are you feeling, Commander?'

Qati frowned. He felt terrible, but he was telling himself that part of that was the possibility of some sort of treaty with the Israelis. Could it be real? Could it be possible? History said no, but there had been so many changes ... Some sort of agreement between the Zionists and the Saudis ... well, after the Iraq business, what could he expect? The Americans had played their role, and now they were presenting some kind of bill. Disappointing, but hardly unexpected, and whatever the Americans were up to would divert attention away from the latest Israeli atrocity. That people calling themselves Arabs had been so womanly as to meekly accept fire and death ... Qati shook his head. You didn't fight that way. So, the Americans would do something or other to neutralize the political impact of the Israeli massacre, and the Saudis were playing along like the lapdogs they were. Whatever was in the offing, it could hardly affect the Palestinian struggle. He should soon be feeling better, Qati told himself.

'It is of no account. Let me know when you've determined exactly what it is.'

Ghosn took his dismissal and left. He was worried about his commander. The man was ill – he knew that much from his brother-in-law, but exactly how sick he didn't know. In any case, he had work to do.

The workshop was a disreputable-looking structure of plain wood walls and a roof of corrugated steel. Had it looked more sturdy, some Israeli F-16 pilot might have destroyed it years before.

The bomb – he still thought of it by that name – lay on the dirt floor. An A-frame like that used for auto or truck service stood over it, with a chain for moving the bomb if necessary, but yesterday two men had set it up in accordance with his instructions. Ghosn turned on the lights – he liked a brightly-lit work-area – and contemplated the . . . bomb.

Why do I keep calling it that? he asked himself. Ghosn shook his head. The obvious place to begin was the access door. It would not be easy. Impact with the ground had telescoped the bombcase, doubtless damaging the internal hinges . . . but he had all the time he wanted.

Ghosn selected a screwdriver from his tool box and went to work.

President Fowler slept late. He was still fatigued from the flight, and . . . he almost laughed at himself in the mirror. Good Lord, three times in less than 24 hours . . . wasn't it? He tried to do the arithmetic in his head, but the effort defeated him before his morning coffee. In any case, three times in relatively short succession. He hadn't done *that* in quite a long time! But he'd also gotten his rest. His body was composed and relaxed after the morning shower, and the razor plowed through the cream on his face, revealing a man with younger, leaner features that matched the twinkle in his eyes. Three minutes later, he selected a striped tie to go with the white shirt and gray suit. Not somber, but serious was the prescription for the day. He'd let the churchmen dazzle the cameras with their red silk. His speech would be all the more impressive if delivered by a well turned-out businessman/politician, which was his political image, despite the fact that he'd never in his life run a private business of any sort. A serious man, Bob Fowler – with a common touch to be sure, but a serious man whom one could trust to do The Right Thing.

Well, I will sure as hell prove that today, the President of the United States told himself in yet another mirror as he checked his tie. His head turned at the knock on the door. 'Come in.'

'Good morning, Mr President,' said Special Agent Connor.

'How are you today, Pete?' Fowler asked, turning back to the mirror . . . the knot wasn't quite right, and he started afresh.

'Fine, thank you, sir. It's a mighty nice day outside.'

'You people never get enough rest. Never get to see the sights, either. That's my fault, isn't it?' *There*, Fowler thought, *that's perfect*.

'It's okay, Mr President. We're all volunteers. What do you want for breakfast, sir?'

'Good morning, Mr President!' Dr Elliot came in behind Connor. 'This is the day!'

Bob Fowler turned with a smile. 'It sure as hell is! Join me for breakfast, Elizabeth?'

'Love to. I have the morning brief – it's a nice short one for a change.'

'Pete, breakfast for two . . . a big one. I'm hungry.'

'Just coffee for me,' Liz said to the servant. Connor caught the tone of her voice, but did not react beyond nodding before he left. 'Bob, you look wonderful.'

'So do you, Elizabeth.' And so she did, in her most expensive suit, which was also serious-looking, but just feminine enough. She took her seat and did the briefing.

'CIA says the Japanese are up to something,' she said as she concluded.

'What?'

'They caught a whiff, Ryan says, of something in the next round of trade negotiations. The Prime Minister is quoted as saying something unkind.'

'What exactly?'

' "This is the last time we'll be cut out of our proper role on the world stage, and I'll make them pay for this," ' Dr Elliot quoted. 'Ryan thinks it's important.'

'What do you think?'

'I think Ryan's being paranoid again. He's been cut out of this end of the treaty works, and he's trying to remind us how important he is. Marcus agrees with my assessment, but forwarded the report out of a fit of objectivity,' Liz concluded with heavy irony.

'Cabot is something of a disappointment, isn't he?' Fowler observed as he looked over the briefing notes.

'He doesn't seem very effective at telling his people who the boss is. He's being captured by the bureaucracy over there, especially Ryan.'

'You really don't like him, do you?' the President noted.

'He's arrogant. He's –'

'Elizabeth, he has a very impressive record. I don't much care for him either as a person, but as an intelligence officer he has done a lot of things very, very well.'

'He's a throwback. He's James Bond, or thinks he is. Fine,' Elliot admitted, 'he's done some important things, but that sort of thing is history. We need someone now with a broader view.'

'Congress won't go for it,' the President said, as breakfast was wheeled in. The food had been scanned for radioactives, checked for electronic devices, and sniffed for explosives – which, the President thought, put one hell of a strain on the dogs, who probably liked sausage as well as he did. 'We'll serve ourselves, thanks,' the President dismissed the Navy steward before going on. 'They love him there, Congress loves the guy.' He didn't have to add the fact that Ryan, as Deputy Director of Central

Intelligence, was not merely a Presidential appointee. He'd also been through a confirmation hearing in the US Senate. Such people were not easily dismissed. There had to be a reason.

'I never have figured that out. Especially Trent. Of all the people to sign off on Ryan, why him?'

'Ask him,' Fowler suggested, as he buttered his pancakes.

'I have. He danced around the issue like the prima ballerina at the New York Ballet.' The President laughed uproariously at that.

'Christ, woman, don't ever let *anybody* hear you say that!'

'Robert, we both support the estimable Mr Trent's choice of sexual preference, but he is a prissy son of a bitch and we both know it.'

'True,' Fowler had to agree. 'So, what are you telling me, Elizabeth?'

'It's time for Cabot to put Ryan in his place.'

'How much of this is envy for Ryan's part in the treaty, Elizabeth?'

Elliot's eyes flared, but the President was looking at his plate. She took a deep breath before speaking, and tried to decide if it were a goad or not. Probably not, but the President wasn't the sort to be impressed by emotions in matters like this. 'Bob, we've been through that. Ryan connected a few ideas that other people had already come up with. He's an intelligence officer, for God's sake! All they do is *report* what other people do.'

'He's done more than that.' Fowler saw where this was going, but it was fun to play games with her.

'Fine, he's killed people! Is that what's special about him? James goddamned Bond! You even let them execute the ones who –'

'Elizabeth, those terrorists also killed seven Secret Service agents. My life depends on those people, and it would have been damned ungracious and just plain idiotic of me to commute the sentences of people who had killed their colleagues.' The President almost frowned at that – *So much for strongly-held principle, eh, Bob?*

a voice asked him – but managed to control himself.

'And now you can't do it at all, or people will say that you failed to do it once out of personal self-interest. You allowed yourself to be trapped and out-maneuvered,' she pointed out. She had been goaded after all, Liz decided, and answered in kind, but Fowler wasn't buying.

'Elizabeth, I may be the only former prosecutor in America who doesn't believe in capital punishment, but . . . we do live in a democracy, and the people support the idea.' He looked up from his meal. 'Those people were terrorists. I can't say I'm happy that I allowed them to be executed, but if anyone deserved it, they did. The time wasn't right to make a statement on that issue. Maybe in my second term. We have to wait for the right case. Politics is the art of the possible. That means one thing at a time, Elizabeth. You know that as well as I do.'

'If you don't do something, you'll wake up and find that Ryan is running CIA for you. He's able, I admit, but he's something from the past. He's the wrong person for the times we live in.'

God, you're an envious woman, Fowler thought. *But we all have our weaknesses.* It was time to stop playing with her, though. It wouldn't do to offend her too deeply.

'What do you have in mind?'

'We can ease him out.'

'I'll think about it – Elizabeth, let's not spoil the day with a discussion like this one, okay? How do you plan to break the news of the treaty terms?'

Elliot leaned back and sipped at her coffee. She reproached herself for moving too soon and too passionately on this. She disliked Ryan greatly, but Bob was right. It wasn't the time, wasn't the place. She had all the time in the world to make her play, and she knew that she had to do it with skill.

'A copy of the treaty, I think.'

'Can they read that fast?' Fowler laughed. The media was full of such illiterates.

'You should see the speculation. The lead *Times* piece was faxed in this morning. They're frantic. They'll eat it up. Besides, I ginned up some Cliff Notes for them.'

'However you want to do it,' the President said, as he finished off his sausage. He checked his watch. Timing was everything. There was a six-hour time difference between Rome and Washington. That meant the treaty could not be signed until two in the afternoon at the earliest, so as to catch the morning news shows. But the American people had to be prepped for the news, and that meant that the TV crews had to have the details of the treaty by three, Eastern Daylight Time, in order to absorb everything fully. Liz would break the news at nine, twenty minutes from now, he noted. 'And you'll be playing up Charlie's part in it?'

'Right. It's only fair that he should get most of the credit.'

And so much for Ryan's part in the process, Bob Fowler noted without comment. *Well, Charlie was the guy who really got it moving, wasn't he?* Fowler felt vaguely sorry for Ryan. Though he also thought the DDCI something from the past, he'd learned all that the man had done, and was impressed. Arnie van Damm thought a lot of Ryan, also, and Arnie was the best judge of character in the administration. But Elizabeth was his National Security Advisor, and he could not have her and the DDCI at each other's throats, could he? No, he couldn't. It was that simple.

'Dazzle them, Elizabeth.'

'Won't be hard.' She smiled at him and left.

The task proved much harder than he'd expected. Ghosn thought about asking for help, but decided against it. Part of his aura in the organization was that he worked alone with these things, except for the donkey work for which he would occasionally require a few strong backs.

The bomb/device/pod turned out to be of sturdier construction than he'd expected. Under the strong work lights, he took the time to wash it off with water, and found a number of unexplained items. There were screw-in points which were plugged shut with slot-bolts. On removing one, he found yet another electrical lead.

More surprising, the bombcase was thicker than he'd expected. He'd dismantled an Israeli jamming pod before, but though it had mostly been of aluminum construction, there had been several places where the case had been of fiberglass or plastic, which was transparent to electronic radiation.

He'd started on the access hatch, but found it nearly impossible to pry open and tried to find something easier. But there wasn't anything easier. Now he returned to the hatch, frustrated that several hours of work had led nowhere.

Ghosn sat back and lit a cigarette. *What are you?* he asked the object.

It was so much like a bomb, he realized. The heavy case – why hadn't he realized that it was so damned heavy, too heavy for a jamming pod ... but it couldn't be a bomb, could it? No fuses, no detonator, what he had seen of the inside was electrical wiring and connectors. It *had to be* some kind of electronic device. He stubbed the cigarette out in the dirt and walked over to his work bench.

Ghosn had a wide variety of tools, one of which was a gasoline-powered rotary saw, useful for cutting steel. It was really a two-man tool, but he decided to use it alone, and to use it on the hatch, which had to be less sturdy than the case itself. He set the cutting depth to nine millimeters and started the tool, manhandling it onto the hatch. The sound of the saw was dreadful, more so as the diamond-edge of the blade bit into the steel, but the weight of the saw was sufficient to keep it from jerking off the bomb, and he slowly worked it down along the edge of the access hatch. It took twenty minutes for him to make the first cut. He stopped the saw and set it aside, then probed the cut with a bit of thin wire.

Finally! he told himself. He was through. He'd guessed right. The rest of the bombcase seemed to be ... four centimeters or so, but the hatch was only a quarter of that. Ghosn was too happy to have accomplished *something* to ask himself why a jamming pod needed a full centimeter of hardened steel around it. Before starting again, he donned ear protection. His ears were ringing from the abuse of the first cut, and he didn't want a headache to make the job worse than it already was.

The 'Special Report' graphics appeared on all the TV networks within seconds of one another. The network anchors who'd risen early – by the standards of their stint in Rome, that is – to receive their brief from Dr Elliot raced to their booths literally breathless, and handed over their notes to their respective producers and researchers.

'I knew it,' Angela Miriles said. 'Rick, I *told* you!'

'Angie, I owe you lunch, dinner, and maybe breakfast in any restaurant you can name.'

'I'll hold you to that,' the chief researcher chuckled. The bastard could afford it.

'How do we do this?' the producer asked.

'I'm going to wing it. Give me two minutes, and we're flying.'

'Shit,' Angie observed quietly to herself. Rick didn't like winging it. He did, however, like scooping the print reporters, and the timing of the event made that a gimme. *Take that*, New York Times! He sat still only long enough for makeup, then faced the cameras as the network's expert – some expert! Miriles thought to herself – joined Rick in the anchor booth.

'Five!' the assistant director said. 'Four, three, two, one!' His hand jerked at the anchor.

'It's real,' Rick announced. 'In four hours, the President of the United States, along with the President of the Soviet Union, the King of Saudi Arabia, and the Prime Ministers of Israel and Switzerland, plus the chiefs of two major religious groups will sign a treaty that offers the hope for a complete settlement of the disputed areas of the Middle East. The details of the treaty are stunning.' He went on for three uninterrupted minutes, speaking rapidly, as though to race with his counterparts on the other networks.

'There has been nothing like this in living memory,

243

yet another miracle – no, yet another milestone on the road to world peace. Dick?' The anchor turned to his expert commentator, a former ambassador to Israel.

'Rick, I've been reading this for half an hour now, and I still don't believe it. Maybe this is a miracle. We sure picked the right place for it. The concessions made by the Israeli government are stunning, but so are the guarantees that America is making to secure the peace. The secrecy of the negotiations is even more impressive. Had these details broken as recently as two days ago, the whole thing might have come apart before our eyes, but here and now, Rick, here and now, I believe it. It's real. You said it right. It's real. It's really happening, and in a few hours we'll see the world change once more.

'This would never have happened but for the unprecedented cooperation of the Soviet Union, and clearly we owe a vast debt of thanks to the embattled Soviet president, Andrey Narmonov.'

'What do you make of the concessions made by all the religious groups?'

'Just incredible. Rick, there have been religious wars in this region for virtually all of recorded history. But we should put in here that the architect of the treaty was the late Dr Charles Alden. A senior administration official was generous in praise to the man who died only weeks ago, and died in disgrace. What a cruel irony it is that the man who really identified the base problem in the region as the artificial incompatibility of the religions, all of which began in this one troubled region, that man is not here to see his vision become reality. Alden was apparently the driving force behind this agreement, and one can only hope that history will remember that, despite the timing and circumstances of his death, it was Dr Charles Alden of Yale who helped to make this miracle happen.' The former ambassador was also a Yalie, and a classmate of Charlie Alden.

'What of the others?' the anchor asked.

'Rick, when something of this magnitude happens – and it's darned rare when it does – there are always a lot of people who play their individual roles, and all of those roles are important. The Vatican Treaty was also the work of Secretary Brent Talbot, ably supported by Undersecretary Scott Adler, who is, by the way, a brilliant diplomatic technician and Talbot's right-hand man. At the same time, it was President Fowler who approved this initiative, who used muscle when that was needed, and who took Charlie's vision forward after his death. No president has ever had the political courage and dazzling vision to stake his political reputation on so wild a gambit. Had we failed on this, one can scarcely imagine the political fallout, but Fowler pulled it off. This is a great day for American diplomacy, a great day for East–West understanding, and perhaps the greatest moment for world peace in all of human history.'

'I couldn't have said it better, Dick. What about the Senate, which has to approve the Vatican Treaty, and also the US–Israeli Bilateral Defense Treaty?'

The commentator grinned and shook his head in overt amusement. 'This will go through the United States Senate so fast that the President might smear the printer's ink on the bill. The only thing that can slow this up is the rhetoric you'll hear in the committee room and on the Senate floor.'

'But the cost of stationing American troops – '

'Rick, we have a military for the purpose of preserving the peace. That's their job, and to do that job in this place, America will pay whatever it costs. This isn't a sacrifice for the American tax-payer. It's a privilege, an historic honor to place the seal of American strength on the peace of the world. Rick, this is what America is all about. Of course we'll do it.'

'And that's it for now,' Rick said, turning back to Camera One. 'We'll be back in two and a half hours for live coverage of the signing of the Vatican Treaty. We now return you to New York. This is Rick Cousins reporting to you from the Vatican.'

'Son of a bitch!' Ryan breathed. This time, unfortunately, the TV had awakened his wife, who was watching the events on the tube with interest.

'Jack, how much did you –' Cathy stood and went off to make the morning coffee. 'I mean, you went over there, and you –'

'Honey, I was involved. I can't say how much.' Jack knew he ought to have been angry at how credit for the first proposal had been assigned to Alden, but Charlie had been a good guy, even if he had displayed his share of human weaknesses, and Alden had pushed it along when it had needed a push. Besides, he told himself, history will find out a little, as it usually did. The real players knew. He knew. He was used to being in the background, to doing things that others didn't and couldn't know about. He turned to his wife and smiled.

And Cathy knew. She'd heard him speculating aloud a few months earlier. Jack didn't know that he murmured to himself when he shaved, and thought he didn't wake her up when he arose so early, but she'd never yet failed to see him off, even if she didn't open her eyes. Cathy liked the way he kissed her, thinking her asleep, and didn't want to spoil it. He was having trouble enough. Jack was hers, and the goodness of the man was no mystery to his wife.

It's not fair, the other Dr Ryan told herself. *It was Jack's idea, at least part of it was*. How many other things didn't she know? It was a question Caroline Muller Ryan, M.D., F.A.C.S., rarely asked herself. But she could not pretend that Jack's nightmares weren't real. He had trouble sleeping, was drinking too much, and what sleep he had was littered with things she could never ask about. Part of that frightened her. What had her husband done? What guilt was he carrying?

Guilt! Cathy asked herself. Why had she asked herself that?

Ghosn pried the hatch off after three hours. He'd had to change a blade on the cutting tool, but the delay had mainly resulted from the fact that he ought to have asked for an extra hand but been too proud to do so. In any case it was done, and a prybar finished the job. The engineer took a work-light and looked into the thing. He found yet another mystery.

The inside of the device was a metal lattice-frame – titanium perhaps? he wondered – which held in place a cylindrical mass ... secured with heavy bolts. Ghosn used his work-light to look around the cylinder and saw more wires, all connected to the cylinder. He caught the edge of a largish electronic device ... some sort of radar transceiver, he thought. Aha! So it was some sort of ... but why, then ... ? Suddenly he knew that he was missing something ... something big. But what? The markings on the cylinder were in Hebrew, and he didn't know that other Semitic language well, and he didn't understand the significance of these markings. The frame which held it, he saw, was partially designed as a shock-absorber ... and it had worked admirably. The framing was grossly distorted, but the cylinder it held seemed largely intact. Damaged to be sure, but it had not split ... Whatever was inside the cylinder was supposed to be protected against shock. That made it delicate, and THAT meant it was some sort of delicate electronic device. So he came back to the idea that it was a jamming pod. Ghosn was too focused to realize that his mind had closed out other options; that his engineer's brain was so fixed on the task at hand that he was ignoring possibilities and the signals that presented them. Whatever it was, however, he had to get it out first. He next selected a wrench and went to work on the bolts securing the cylinder in place.

Fowler sat in a 16th-century chair, watching the protocol officers flutter around like pheasants unable to decide whether to walk or fly. People commonly thought that affairs like this one were run smoothly by professional stage-managers who planned everything in advance. Fowler knew better. Sure, things were smooth enough when there had been time enough – a few months – to work out all the details. But this affair had been set up with days, not months, of preparation, and the dozen or so protocol officers had scarcely decided who was the boss among themselves. Curiously, it was the Russian and the Swiss officers who were the calmest, and before the American president's eyes, it was they who huddled and worked out a quick alliance, then presented their plan – whatever it was – to the others, which they then put into play. Just like a good football squad, the President smiled to himself. The Vatican representative was too old for a job like this. The guy – a bishop, Fowler thought, maybe a monsignor – was over sixty and suffering from an anxiety attack that might just kill him. Finally the Russian took him aside for two quick minutes, nods were exchanged and a handshake, then people started moving as though they had a common purpose. Fowler decided that he'd have to find out the Russian's name. He looked like a real pro. More importantly, it was hugely entertaining to watch, and it relaxed the President at a moment when he needed the relaxation.

Finally – only five minutes late, and that was a miracle, Fowler thought with a suppressed grin – the various heads of state rose from their chairs, summoned like the members of a wedding party by the nervous mother-in-law-to-be, and told where to stand in line. More perfunctory handshakes were exchanged, along with a few jokes that suffered from the absence of translators. The Saudi king looked cross at the delays. As well he might, Fowler thought. The King probably had other things on his mind. Already there were death threats directed at him. But there was no fear on the man's face, Bob Fowler saw. He might be a humorless man, but he had the bearing and courage – and the class, the President admitted to himself – that went with his title. It had been he who'd first committed to the talks after two hours with Ryan. That was too bad, wasn't it? Ryan had filled in for Charlie Alden, taking his assignment to himself at that. He'd allowed himself to forget just how frantic the initial maneuvers had been. Scott Adler in Moscow, Rome, and Jerusalem, and Jack Ryan in Rome and Riyadh. They'd done very well, and neither would ever get much credit. Such were the rules of history,

President Fowler concluded. If they'd wanted credit, they ought to have tried for his job.

Two liveried Swiss Guards opened the immense bronze doors, revealing the corpulent form of Giovanni Cardinal D'Antonio. The sun-bright TV lights surrounded him with a man-made halo that nearly elicited a laugh from the President of the United States of America. The procession into the room began.

Whoever had built this thing, Ghosn thought, knew a thing or two about designing for brute force. It was odd, he thought. Israeli equipment always had a delicacy to it – no, wrong term. The Israelis were clever, efficient, elegant engineers. They made things as strong as they had to be, no more, no less. Even their *ad-hoc* gear showed foresight and meticulous workmanship. But this one . . . this one was over-engineered to a fare-thee-well. It had been hurriedly designed and assembled. It was almost crude, in fact. He was grateful for that. It made disassembly easier. No one had thought to include a self-destruct device that he'd have to figure out first – the Zionists were getting devilishly clever at that! One such sub-system had nearly killed Ghosn only five months earlier, but there was none here. The bolts holding the cylinder in place were jammed, but still straight, and that meant it was just a matter of having a big enough wrench. He squirted penetrating oil onto each, and after waiting for fifteen minutes and two cigarettes, he attached the wrench to the first. The initial turns came hard, but soon the bolt allowed itself to be withdrawn. Five more to go.

It would be a long afternoon. The speeches came first. The Pope began, since he was the host, and his rhetoric was surprisingly muted, drawing quiet lessons from Scripture, again focusing on the similarities among the three religions present. Earphones gave each of the chiefs of state and religious figures simultaneous translations, which were quite unnecessary, as each of them had a written copy of the various speeches, and the men around the table struggled not to yawn, for speeches were only speeches, after all, and politicians have trouble listening to the words of others, even other chiefs of state. Fowler had the most trouble. He'd be going last. He surreptitiously checked his watch, keeping his face blank as he pondered the ninety minutes left to go.

It took another forty minutes, but finally all the bolts came out. Big, heavy, non-corrosive ones. This thing had been built to last, Ghosn thought, but that merely worked to his benefit. Now, to get the cylinder out. He took another careful look for possible anti-tamper devices – caution was the only defense in a job like his – and felt around the inside of the pod. The only thing connected was the radar transceiver, though there were three other plug connections, they were all vacant. In his fatigue, it did not strike Ghosn as odd that all three were facing him, easily accessible. The cylinder was jammed in place by the telescoped framing, but with the bolts removed, it was just a matter of applying enough force to drag it clear.

Andrey Il'ych Narmonov spoke briefly. His statement, Fowler thought, was simple and most dignified, showing remarkable modesty that was sure to elicit comment from the commentators.

Ghosn set an additional block and tackle on the A-frame. The cylinder, conveniently enough, had a hoist eye built into it. Thankfully the Israelis didn't like to waste energy any more than he did. The remainder of the pod was less heavy than he expected, but in a minute he had the cylinder hoisted to the point at which its friction in its nesting frame was lifting the whole pod. That couldn't last. Ghosn sprayed more penetrating oil on the internal frame, and waited for gravity to assert itself . . . but after a minute his patience wore thin, and he found a gap large enough for a prybar and started levering the frame away from the cylinder walls one fraction of a millimeter at a time. Inside of four minutes, there was a brief shriek of protesting metal, and the pod fell free. Then it was just a matter of pulling on the chain and hoisting the cylinder free.

The cylinder was painted green, and had its own access hatch, which was not entirely surprising. Ghosn identified the type of wrench he needed and began work on the four bolts holding it in place. These bolts were tight, but yielded quickly to his pressure. Ghosn was going faster now, and the excitement that always came near the end of the job took hold, despite the good sense that told him to relax.

Finally, it was Fowler's turn.

The President of the United States walked to the lectern, a brown-leather folder in his hands. His shirt was starched stiff as plywood, and it was already chafing his neck, but he didn't care. This was the moment for which he had prepared his entire life. He looked straight into the camera, his face set in an expression serious but not grave, elated but not yet joyous, proud but not arrogant. He nodded to his peers.

'Holy Father, Your Majesty, Mr President,' Fowler began, 'Messrs Prime Minister, and to all the people of our troubled but hopeful world:

'We have met in this ancient city, a city that has known war and peace for three thousand years and more, a city from which sprang one of the world's great civilizations, and is today home to a religious faith greater still. We have all come from afar, from deserts and from mountains, from sweeping European plains and from yet another city by a wide river, but unlike many foreigners who have visited this ancient city, we have all come in peace. We come with a single purpose – to bring an end to war and suffering, to bring the blessings of peace to one more troubled part of a world now emerging from a history bathed in blood but lit by the ideals that set us apart from the animals as a creation in the image of God.' He looked down only to turn pages. Fowler knew how to give a speech. He'd had lots of practice over the previous thirty years, and he delivered this one as confidently as he'd addressed a hundred juries, measuring his words and his cadences, adding emotional content that belied his Ice Man image, using his voice like a musical instrument, something physical that was subordinate to and part of his intense personal will.

'This city, this Vatican state, is consecrated to the service of God and man, and today it has fulfilled that purpose better than at any time. For today, my fellow citizens of the world, today we have achieved another part of the dream that all men and women share wherever they may live. With the help of your prayers, through a vision given us so many centuries ago, we have come to see that peace is a better thing than war, a goal worthy of efforts even more mighty, demanding courage far greater than is required for the shedding of human blood. To turn away from war, to turn towards peace, is the measure of our strength.

'Today it is my honor, and a privilege that all of us share, to announce to the world a treaty to put a final end to the discord that has sadly defiled an area holy to us all. With this agreement, there will be a final solution based on justice, and faith, and the word of the God Whom we all know by different names, but Who knows each of us.

'This treaty recognizes the rights of all men and women in the region to security, and freedom of religion, to freedom of speech, to the basic dignity enshrined in the knowledge that all of us are God's creation, that each of us is unique, but that we are all equal in His sight . . .'

The final hatch came open. Ghosn closed his eyes and whispered a fatigued prayer of thanks. He'd been at this for hours, skipping his noon meal. He set the hatch down, placing the bolts on the concave surface so that they wouldn't be lost. Ever the engineer, Ghosn was neat and tidy in everything he did. Inside the hatch was a plastic seal, still tight, he noted with admiration. That was a moisture and weather seal. And *that* definitely made it a sophisticated electronic device. Ghosn touched it gently. It wasn't pressurized. He used a small knife to cut the plastic, and peeled it carefully aside. He looked for the first time into the cylinder, and it was as though a hand of ice suddenly gripped his heart. He was looking at a distorted sphere of yellow-gray . . . like dirty bread dough.

It was a bomb.

At least a self-destruct device. A very powerful one, fifty kilos of high-explosive . . .

Ghosn backed off; a sudden urge to urinate gripped his loins. The engineer fumbled for a smoke and lit it on the third attempt. How had he missed . . . what? What had he missed? Nothing. He'd been as careful as he always was. The Israelis hadn't killed him yet. Their design engineers were clever, but so was he.

Patience, he told himself. He commenced a new examination of the cylinder's exterior. There was the wire, still attached, from the radar device, and three additional plug points, all of them empty.

What do I know of this thing?

Radar transceiver, heavy case, access hatch . . . explosive sphere wired with . . .

Ghosn leaned forward again to examine the object. At regular and symmetrical intervals in the sphere were detonators . . . the wires from them were . . .

It isn't possible. No. It cannot be that!

Ghosn removed the detonators one by one, detaching the wires from each, and setting them down on a blanket, slowly and carefully, for detonators were the most twitchy things man made. The high explosive, on the other hand, was so safe to use that you could pinch off a piece and set it on fire to boil water. He used the knife to pry loose the surprisingly hard blocks.

'There is an ancient legend of Pandora, a woman of mythology given a box. Though told not to open it, she foolishly did so, admitting strife and war and death into our world. Pandora despaired at her deeds until she found, remaining alone in the bottom of the nearly empty box, the spirit of hope. We have seen all too much of war and strife, but now we have finally made use of hope. It has been a long road, a bloody road, a road marked with despair, but it has always been an upward road, because hope is humanity's collective vision of what can, should, and *must* be, and hope has led us to this point.

'That ancient legend may have its origin in paganism, but its truth is manifest today. On this day we put war and strife and unnecessary death back into the box. We close the box on conflict, leaving in our possession hope, Pandora's last and most important gift to all humanity. This day is the fulfillment of the dream of all mankind.

'On this day, we have accepted from the hands of God the gift of peace.

'Thank you.' The President smiled warmly at the cameras and made his way to his chair amid the more-than-polite applause of his peers. It was time to sign the treaty. The moment was here, and after being the last speaker, Fowler would be the first to sign. The moment came quickly, and J. Robert Fowler became a man of history.

He was not going slowly now. He pulled the blocks away, knowing as he did so that he was being reckless and wasteful, but now he knew – thought he knew – what he had in his hands.

And there it was, a ball of metal, a shining nickel-plated sphere, not corroded or damaged by its years in the Druse's garden, protected by the plastic seal of the Israeli engineers. It was not a large object, not much larger than a ball that a child might play with. Ghosn knew what he would do next. He reached his hand all the way into the sundered mass of explosives, extending his fingers to the gleaming nickel surface.

Ghosn's fingertips brushed the ball of metal. It was warm to the touch.

'Allahu akhbar!'

CHAPTER 9

Resolve

'This is interesting.'

'It's a rather unique opportunity,' Ryan agreed.

'How reliable – how trustworthy?' Cabot asked.

Ryan smiled at his boss. 'Sir, that's always the question. You have to remember how the game works. You're never sure of anything – that is, what certainty you have generally takes years to acquire. This game only has a few rules, and nobody ever knows what the score is. In any case, this is a lot more than a defection.' His name was Oleg Yurievich Lyalin – Cabot didn't know that yet – and he was a KGB 'Illegal' who operated without the shield of diplomatic immunity and whose cover was that of a representative of a Soviet industrial concern. Lyalin ran a string of agents with the code-name of THISTLE, and he was running it in Japan. 'This guy is a real field-spook. He's got a better net going than the KGB *Rezident* in Tokyo, and his best source is right in the Japanese cabinet.'

'And?'

'And he's offering us the use of his network.'

'Is this as important as I'm starting to think it is . . . ?' The DCI asked his deputy.

'Boss, we rarely get a chance like this. We've never really run ops in Japan. We lack a sufficient number of Japanese-speaking people – even here on the inside to translate their documents – and our priorities have always been elsewhere. So just establishing the necessary infrastructure to conduct ops there would take years. But the Russians have been working in Japan since before the Bolsheviks took over. The reason is historical:

the Japanese and the Russkies have fought wars for a long time, and they've always regarded Japan as a strategic rival – as a result of which they placed great emphasis on operations there even before Japanese technology became so important to them. What he is doing is essentially giving us the Russian business at a bargain price, the inventory, the accounts receivables, the physical plant, everything. It doesn't get much better than this.'

'But what he's asking . . .'

'The money? So what? That's not a thousandth of a percent of what it's worth to our country,' Jack pointed out.

'It's a million dollars a month!' Cabot protested. *Tax free!* the Director of Central Intelligence did not add.

Ryan managed not to laugh. 'So, the bastard's greedy, okay? Our trade deficit with Japan is how much at last count?' Jack inquired with a raised eyebrow. 'He's offering us whatever we want for as long as we want it. All we have to do is arrange to pick him up and fly him and his family over whenever it becomes necessary. He doesn't want to retire to Moscow. He's forty-five, and that's the age when they get antsy. He has to rotate home in ten years – to what? He's lived in Japan almost continuously for thirteen years. He likes affluence. He likes cars, and VCRs, and not standing in line for potatoes. He likes us. About the only people he doesn't like is the Japanese – he doesn't like them at all. He figures he's not even betraying his country, 'cause he's not giving us anything he isn't feeding them, and part of the deal is that he does nothing against Mother Russia. Fine, I can live with that.' Ryan chuckled for a moment. 'It's capitalism. The man is starting an elite news service, and it's information we can really use.'

'He's charging enough.'

'Sir, it's worth it. The information he can give us will be worth billions in our trade negotiations, and billions in federal taxes as a result. Director, I used to be in the investment business, that's how I made my money. Investment opportunities like this come along about once every ten years. The Directorate of Operations wants to run with it. I agree. We'd have to be crazy to say "no" to this guy. His introductory package – well, you've had a chance to read it, right?'

The introductory package was the minutes of the last Japanese cabinet meeting, every word, grunt, and hiss. It was highly valuable for psychological analysis if nothing else. The nature of the exchange in the cabinet meetings could tell American analysts all sorts of things about how their government thought and reached decisions. That was data often inferred, but never confirmed.

'It was most enlightening, especially what they said about the President. I didn't forward that. No sense getting him annoyed at a time like this. Okay – the operation is approved, Jack. How do we run things like this?'

'The code-name we've selected is MUSHASHI. That's the name of a famous samurai dueling master, by the way. The operation will be called NIITAKA. We'll use Japanese names for the obvious reason –' Jack decided to explain; though Cabot was bright, he was new to the intelligence trade '– in the event of compromise or a leak from our side, we want it to appear that our source is Japanese, not Russian. Those names stay in this building. For outsiders who get let into this, we use a different code-name. That one will be computer-generated, and it'll change on a monthly basis.'

'And the real name of the agent?'

'Director, it's your choice. You have the right to know it. I deliberately have not told you to this point because I wanted you to see the whole picture first. Historically it's evenly split, some directors want to know, and about the same number do not. It's a principle of intelligence operations that the fewer the number of people who know things, the less likely that there will be any sort of leak. Admiral Greer used to say the First Law of Intelligence Operations is that the likelihood of an operation's being burned was proportional to the *square* of the people in on the details. Your call, sir.'

Cabot nodded thoughtfully. He decided to temporize. 'You liked Greer, didn't you?'

'Like a father, sir. After I lost Dad in the plane crash,

well, the Admiral sort of adopted me.' *More like I adopted him*, Ryan thought. 'On MUSHASHI, you'll probably want to think it through.'

'And if the White House asks to know the details?' Cabot asked next.

'Director, despite what MUSHASHI thinks, his employers will regard what he is doing as high treason, and that's a capital crime over there. Narmonov is a good guy and all that, but the Soviets have executed forty people that we know of for espionage. That included TOP HAT, JOURNEYMAN, and a guy named Tolkachev, all of whom were highly productive agents for us. We tried to do a trade in all three cases, but they were popped before negotiations had a chance to get underway. The appeals process in the Soviet Union is still somewhat abbreviated,' Ryan explained. 'The simple fact, sir, is that if this guy gets burned, he will probably be shot right in the head. That's why we take agent-identity so seriously. If we screw up, people die, *glasnost* notwithstanding. Most presidents understand that. One more thing.'

'Yes?'

'He's told us something else. He wants all his reports to be handled physically, not by cable. If we don't agree, he doesn't do business. Okay, technically that's no problem. We've done that before with agents of this caliber. The nature of his information is such that immediacy is not required. There's daily air service to and from Japan via United, Northwest, and even All Nippon Airways straight into Dulles International Airport.'

'But . . .' Cabot's face twisted into a grimace.

'Yeah.' Jack nodded. 'He doesn't trust our communications security. That scares me.'

'You don't think . . . ?'

'I don't know. We've had very limited success penetrating Soviet ciphers for the past few years. NSA assumes that they have the same problems with ours. Such assumptions are dangerous. We've had indications before that our signals are not fully secure, but this one comes from a very senior guy. I think we have to take this seriously.'

'Just how scary could this be?'

'Terrifying,' Jack answered flatly. 'Director, for obvious reasons we have numerous communications systems. We have MERCURY right downstairs to handle all of our stuff. The rest of the government mainly uses stuff from NSA; Walker and Pelton compromised their systems a long time ago. Now, General Olson over at Fort Meade says they've fixed all that, but for expense reasons they have not fully adopted the TAPDANCE onetime systems that they've been playing with. We can warn NSA again – I think they'll ignore this warning also, but we have to do it – and on our end, I think it's time to act. For starters, sir, we need to think about a reexamination of MERCURY.' That was the CIA's own communications nexus, located a few floors below the Director's office, and using its own encrypting systems.

'Expensive,' Cabot noted seriously. 'With our budget problems . . .'

'Not half as expensive as a systematic compromise of our message traffic is. Director, there is *nothing* as vital as secure communications links. Without that, it doesn't matter what else we have. Now, we've developed our own one-time system. All we need is authorization of funds to make it go.'

'Tell me about it. I haven't been briefed in.'

'Essentially, it's our own version of the TAPDANCE. It's a one-time pad with transpositions stored on laserdisk CD ROM. The transpositions are generated from atmospheric radio noise, then superencrypted with noise from later in the day – atmospheric noise is pretty random, and by using two separate sets of the noise, and using a computer-generated random algorithm to mix the two, well, the mathematicians say that's as random as it gets. The transpositions are generated by computer and fed onto laser-disks in realtime. We use a different disk for every day of the year. Each disk is unique, two copies only, one to the station, one in MERCURY – no backups. The laser-disk reader we use at both ends looks normal, but has a beefed-up laser, and as it reads the transposition codes from the disk, it also burns them right off the plastic. When the disk is used up, or the day ends – and the day will end first, since we're talking billions of characters per disk – the disk is destroyed by baking it in a microwave oven. That takes two minutes. It ought to be secure as hell. It can only be compromised at three stages: first, when the disks are manufactured; second, from disk-storage here; third, from disk-storage in each station. Compromise of one station does not compromise anyone else. We can't make the disks tamper-proof – we've tried, and it would both cost too much and make them overly vulnerable to accidental damage. The down-side of this is that it'll require us to hire and clear about twenty new communications technicians. The system is relatively cumbersome to use, hence the increased number of communicators. The main expense component is here. The field troops we've talked to actually prefer the new system because it's user-friendly.'

'How much to set it up?'

'Fifty million dollars. We have to increase the size of MERCURY, and set up the manufacturing facility. We have the space, but the machinery is expensive. From the time we get the money, we could have it up and running in maybe as little as three months.'

'I see your point. It's probably worth doing, but getting the money . . . ?'

'With your permission, sir, I could talk to Mr Trent about it.'

'Hmmm.' Cabot stared down at his desk. 'Okay, feel him out very gently. I'll bring this up with the President when he gets back. I'll trust you on MUSHASHI. You and who else know his real name?'

'The DO, Chief of Station Tokyo, and his case officer.' The Director of Operations was Harry Wren, and if he were not quite Cabot's man, he was the man Cabot had picked for the job. Wren was on his way to Europe at the moment. A year ago Jack had thought the choice a mistake, but Wren was doing well. He'd also picked a superb deputy, actually a pair of them: the famous Ed and Mary Pat Foley, one of whom – Ryan could never decide which – would have been his choice for DO. Ed was the organization man, and Mary Pat was the cowboy side of the best husband–wife team the Agency had ever fielded. Making Mary Pat a senior executive would have been a worldwide first, and probably worth a few votes in Congress. She was pregnant again with her third, but that wasn't expected to slow Supergirl down. The Agency had its own day-care center, complete to cipher locks on the doors, a heavily-armed response team of security officers, and the best play equipment Jack had ever seen.

'Sounds good, Jack. I'm sorry I faxed the President as soon as I did. I ought to have waited.'

'No problem, sir. The information was thoroughly laundered.'

'Let me know what Trent thinks about the funding.'

'Yes, sir.' Jack left for his office. He was getting good at this, the DDCI told himself. Cabot wasn't all that hard to manage.

Ghosn took his time to think. This was not a time for excitement, not a time for precipitous action. He sat down in the corner of his shop and chain-smoked his cigarettes for several hours, all the time staring at the gleaming metal ball that lay on the dirt floor. *How radioactive is it?* one part of his brain wondered almost continuously, but it was a little late for that. If that heavy sphere were giving off hard gammas, he was already dead, another part of his brain had already decided. This was a time to think and evaluate. It required a supreme act of will for him to sit still, but he managed it.

For the first time in many years he was ashamed of his education. He had expertise both in electrical and mechanical engineering, but he'd hardly bothered cracking a book about their nuclear equivalent. *What possible use could such a thing have for him?* he asked himself on the rare occasions that he'd considered acquiring knowledge in that area. *Obviously none.* As a result of that, he'd limited himself to broadening and deepening his knowledge in areas of direct interest: mechanical and electronic fusing systems, electronic counter-measure gear, the physical characteristics of explosives, the capabilities of explosive-sensing systems. He was a real expert on this last category of study. He read everything he could find on the instrumentation used in detecting explosives at airports and other areas of interest.

Number One, Ghosn told himself on lighting cigarette number 54 of the day, *every book I can find on nuclear materials, their physical and chemical properties: bomb technology, bomb physics: radiological signatures ... the Israelis must know the bomb is missing – since 1973!* he thought in amazement. *Then why ... ! Of course. The Golan Heights are volcanic in origin. The underlying rock and the soil in which those poor farmers tried to raise their vegetables were largely basaltic, and basalt had a relatively high background-radiation count ... the bomb was buried two or three meters in rocky soil, and whatever emissions it gave off were lost in background count ...*

I'm safe! Ghosn realized.

Of course! If the weapon were that 'hot', it would have been better shielded! Praise be to Allah for that!

Can I ... can I! That was the question, wasn't it?

Why not!

'Why not?' Ghosn said aloud. 'Why not. I have all the necessary pieces, damaged, but ...'

Ghosn stubbed the cigarette out in the dirt next to all the others and rose. His body was racked by coughing – he knew that cigarettes were killing him ... more dangerous than that ... but they were good for thinking.

The engineer lifted the sphere. What to do with it? For the moment, he set it in the corner and covered it with a tool box. Then he walked out of the building towards his jeep. The drive to headquarters took fifteen minutes.

'I need to see the Commander,' Ghosn told the chief guard.

'He just retired for the evening,' the guard said. The entire detail was becoming protective of their commander.

'He'll see me.' Ghosn walked right past him and into the building.

Qati's quarters were on the second floor. Ghosn went up the steps, past another guard and pulled open the bedroom door. He heard retching from the adjoining bathroom.

'Who the devil is it?' a cross voice asked. 'I told you that I didn't want to be disturbed!'

'It's Ghosn. We need to talk.'

'Can't it wait?' Qati appeared from the lighted doorway. His face was ashen. It came out as a question, not an order, and that told Ibrahim more than he'd ever known of his Commander's condition. Perhaps this would make him feel better.

'My friend, I need to show you something. I need to show it to you tonight.' Ghosn strained to keep his voice level and unexcited.

'Is it that important?' Almost a moan.

'Yes.'

'Tell me about it.'

Ghosn just shook his head, tapping his ear as he did so. 'It's something interesting. That Israeli bomb has some new fusing systems. It nearly killed me. We need to warn our colleagues about it.'

'Bomb? I thought –' Qati stopped himself. His face cleared for a moment and the Commander's expression formed a question. 'Tonight, you say?'

'I'll drive you over myself.'

Qati's strength of character prevailed. 'Very well. Let me get my clothes on.'

Ghosn waited downstairs. 'The Commander and I have to go see about something.'

'Mohammed!' the chief guard called, but Ghosn cut him off.

'I'll take the Commander myself. There is no security problem in my shop.'

'But –'

'But you worry like an old woman! If the Israelis were that clever, you'd already be dead, and the Commander with you!' It was too dark to see the expression on the

263

guard's face, but Ghosn could feel the rage that radiated towards him from the man, an experienced front-line fighter.

'We'll see what the Commander says!'

'What's the problem now?' Qati emerged from the door, tucking his shirt in.

'I'll drive you myself, Commander. We don't need a security force for this.'

'As you say, Ibrahim.' Qati walked to the jeep and got in. Ghosn drove off past some astonished security guards.

'What exactly is this all about?'

'It's a bomb after all, not an electronics pod,' the engineer replied.

'So? We've retrieved scores of the cursed things! What is this all about?'

'It is easier to show you.' The engineer drove rapidly, watching the road. 'If you think I have wasted your time – when we are done, feel free to end my life.'

Qati's head turned at that. The thought had already occurred to him, but he was too good a leader for that. Ghosn might not be the material of a fighter, but he was an expert at what he did. His service to the organization was as valuable as any man's. The Commander endured the rest of the ride in silence, wishing the medicines he was taking allowed him to eat – no, to retain what he ate.

Fifteen minutes later, Ghosn parked his jeep fifty meters from the shop, and led his Commander to the building by an indirect route. By this time Qati was thoroughly confused and more than a little angry. When the lights went on, he saw the bombcase.

'So, what about it?'

'Come here.' Ghosn led him to the corner. The engineer bent down and lifted the tool box. 'Behold!'

'What is it?' It looked like a small cannonball, a sphere of metal. Ghosn was enjoying this. Qati was angry, but that would soon change.

'It's plutonium.'

The commander's head snapped around as though driven by a steel spring. 'What? What do –'

Ghosn held up his hand. He spoke softly, but positively. 'What I am sure of, Commander, is that this is the explosive portion of an atomic bomb. An Israeli atomic bomb.'

'Impossible!' the Commander whispered.

'Touch it,' Ghosn suggested.

The Commander bent down and touched a finger to it. 'It's warm, why?'

'From the decay of alpha particles. A form of radiation that is not harmful – here it is not, in any case. That is plutonium, the explosive element of an atomic bomb. It can be nothing else.'

'You're sure?'

'Positive, absolutely positive. It can only be what I say it is.' Ghosn walked over to the bombcase. 'These –' he held up some tiny electronic parts ' – they look like glass spiders, no? They are called kryton switches, they perform their function with total precision, and that kind of precision is necessary for only one application found inside a bombcase. These explosive blocks, the intact ones, note that some are hexagons, some are pentagons? That is necessary to make a perfect explosive sphere. A shaped charge, like that for an RPG, but the focus is inward. These explosive blocks are designed to crush that sphere to the size of a walnut.'

'But it's metal! What you say is not possible.'

'Commander, I do not know as much as I should of these matters, but I do know a little. When the explosives go off, they compress that metal sphere as though it were made of rubber. It is possible – you know what an RPG does to the metal on a tank, no? There is enough explosive here for a hundred RPG projectiles. They will crush the metal as I say. When it is compressed, the proximity of the atoms begins a nuclear chain-reaction. Think, Commander:

'The bomb fell into the old man's garden on the first day of the October War. The Israelis were frightened by the force of the Syrian attack, and they were immensely surprised by the effectiveness of the Russian rockets. The aircraft was shot down, and the bomb was lost. The exact circumstances don't matter. What matters, Ismael, is that we have the parts of a nuclear bomb.' Ghosn pulled out another cigarette and lit it.

'Can you . . .'

'Possibly,' the engineer said. Qati's face was suddenly cleared of the pain he'd known for over a month.

'Truly Allah is beneficent.'

'Truly He is. Commander, we need to think about this, very carefully, very thoroughly. And security . . .'

Qati nodded. 'Oh, yes. You did well to bring me here alone. For this matter we can trust no one . . . no one at all . . .' Qati let his voice trail off, then turned to his man. 'What do you need to do?'

'My first need is for information – books, Commander. And do you know where I must go to get them?'

'Russia?'

Ghosn shook his head. 'Israel, Commander. Where else?'

Representative Alan Trent met with Ryan in a House hearing room. It was the one used for closed-door hearings, and was swept daily for bugs.

'How's life treating you, Jack?' the congressman asked.

'No special complaints, Al. The President had a good day.'

'Indeed he did – the whole world did. The country owes you a debt of thanks, Dr Ryan.'

Jack's smile dripped with irony. 'Let's not allow anybody to learn that, okay?'

Trent shrugged. 'Rules of the game. You should be used to it by now. So. What brings you down on such short notice?'

'We have a new operation going. It's called Niitaka.' The DDCI explained on for several minutes. At a later date he would have to hand over some documentation. All that was required now was notification of the operation and its purpose.

'A million dollars a month. That's *all* he wants?' Trent laughed aloud.

'The Director was appalled,' Jack reported.

'I've always liked Marcus, but he's a tight-fisted son of a bitch. We've got two certified Japan-bashers on the oversight committee, Jack. It's going to be hard to rein them in with this stuff.'

'Three, counting you, Al.'

Trent looked very hurt. 'Me, a Japan-basher? Just because there used to be two TV factories in my district, and a major auto-parts supplier has laid off half its people? Why the hell should I be the least bit angry about that? Let me see the cabinet minutes,' the congressman commanded.

Ryan opened his case. 'You can't copy them, you can't quote from them. Look, Al, this is a long-term op and – '

'Jack, I didn't just get into town from the chicken ranch, did I? You've turned into a humorless SOB. What's the problem?'

'Long hours,' Jack explained, as he handed the papers over. Al Trent was a speed reader, and flicked through the pages with indecent speed. His face went into neutral, and he turned back into what he was before all things, a cold, calculating politician. He was well to the left side of the spectrum, but, unlike most of his ilk, Trent let his ideology stop at the water's edge. He also saved his passion for the House floor and his bed at home. Elsewhere he was icily analytical.

'Fowler will go ballistic when he sees this. They are the most arrogant people. You've sat in on cabinet meetings. Ever hear stuff like this?' Trent asked.

'Only on political matters. I was surprised by the tone of the language, too, but it might just be a cultural thing, remember.'

The congressman looked up briefly. 'True. Beneath the patina of good manners, they can be wild and crazy folks, kind of like the Brits, but this is like Animal House . . . Christ, Jack, this is explosive. Who recruited him?'

'The usual mating dance. He shows up at various receptions, and Chief of Station Tokyo caught a whiff, let it simmer for a few weeks, then made his move. The Russian handed over the packet and his contractual demands.'

'Why Operation NIITAKA, by the way? I've heard that before somewhere, haven't I?'

'I picked it myself. When the Japanese strike force was heading for Pearl Harbor, the mission-execute signal was "Climb Mount Niitaka." Remember, you're the only guy here who knows that word. We're going onto a monthly-change identification cycle on this. This is hot enough that we're giving him the whole treatment.'

'Right,' Trent agreed. 'What if this guy's an agent provocateur?'

'We've wondered about that. It's possible, but unlikely. For KGB to do that — well, it kinda breaks the rules as they are understood now, doesn't it?'

'Wait!' Trent read over the last page again. 'What the hell's this about communications?'

'What it is is scary.' Ryan explained what he wanted to do.

'Fifty million? You sure?'

'That's the one-time start-up costs. Then there's the new communicators. Total annual costs after start-up are about fifteen million.'

'Pretty reasonable, actually.' Trent shook his head. 'NSA is quoting a much higher price to switch over to their system.'

'They have a bigger infrastructure to worry about. That number I gave you ought to be solid. MERCURY is pretty small.'

'How soon do you want it?' Trent knew that Ryan quoted hard budget numbers. It came from his business experience, Al knew, which was pretty thin in government service.

'Last week would be nice, sir.'

Trent nodded. 'I'll see what I can do. You want it "black," of course?'

'Like a cloudy midnight,' Ryan answered.

'God damn it!' Trent swore. 'I've *told* Olson about

this. His technical weenies do their rain-dance and he buys it every time. What if –'

'Yeah, what if all our communications are compromised.' Jack did not make it a question. 'Thank God for *glasnost*, eh?'

'Does Marcus understand the implications?'

'I explained it to him this morning. He understands. Al, Cabot may not have all the experience you or I would like, but he's a fast learner. I've had worse bosses.'

'You're too loyal. Must be a lingering symptom of your time in the Marines,' Trent observed. 'You'd be a good director.'

'Never happen.'

'True. Now that Liz Elliot is National Security Advisor, you'll have to cover your ass. You know that.'

'Yep.'

'What in hell did you do to piss her off? Not that it's all that hard to do.'

'It was back right after the convention,' Ryan explained. 'I was up in Chicago to brief Fowler. She caught me tired from a couple of long trips and she yanked my chain pretty hard. I yanked back.'

'Learn to be nice to her,' Trent suggested.

'Admiral Greer said that.'

Trent handed the papers back to Ryan. 'It is difficult, isn't it?'

'Sure is.'

'Learn anyway. Best advice I can give you.' *Probably a total waste of time, of course.*

'Yes, sir.'

'Good timing on the request, by the way. The rest of the committee will be impressed as hell with the new operation. The Japan-bashers will put the word out to their friends on Appropriations that the Agency is really doing something useful. We'll have the money to you in two weeks if we're lucky. What the hell, fifty million bucks – chicken feed. Thanks for coming down.'

Ryan locked his case and stood. 'Always a pleasure.'

Trent shook his hand. 'You're a good man, Ryan. What a damned shame you're straight.'

Jack laughed. 'We all have our handicaps, Al.'

Ryan returned to Langley to put the Niitaka documents back in secure storage, and that ended his work for the day. He and Clark took the elevator down to the garage, and left the building an hour early, something they did every two weeks or so. Forty minutes later, they pulled into the parking lot of a 7-Eleven between Washington and Annapolis.

'Hello, Doc Ryan!' Carol Zimmer said from behind the register. One of her sons relieved her there, and she led Jack into the back room. John Clark checked out the store. He wasn't worried about Ryan's security, but he had some lingering worries about the way some local toughs felt about the Zimmer enterprise. He and Chavez had taken care of that one gang leader, having done so in front of three of his minions, one of whom had tried to interfere. Chavez had shown mercy to that lad, who hadn't required an overnight stay at the local hospital. That, Clark judged, was a sign of Ding's growing maturity.

'How is business?' Jack asked in the back room.

'We up twenty-six 'rcent from this time las' year.'

Carol Zimmer had been born in Laos less than forty years before, rescued from a hilltop fortress by an Air Force special-operations helicopter just as the North Vietnamese Army had overrun that last outpost of American power in Northern Laos. She'd been sixteen at the time, the last living child of a Hmong chieftain who'd served American interests and his own – he'd been a willing agent – courageously and well, and to the death. She'd married Air Force sergeant Buck Zimmer, who'd died in yet another helicopter after yet another betrayal, and then Ryan had stepped in. He hadn't lost his business sense despite his years of government service. He'd selected a good site for the store, and as fate had it, they hadn't needed his educational trust fund for the first of the kids now in college. With a kind word from Ryan to Father Tim Riley, the lad had a full scholarship at

Georgetown and was already dean's-listed in pre-med. Like most Asians, Carol had a reverence for learning that bordered on religious fanaticism, and which she passed on to all of her kids. She also ran her store with the mechanistic precision a Prussian sergeant expected of an infantry squad. Cathy Ryan could have performed a surgical procedure on the register counter. It was that clean. Jack smiled at the thought. Maybe Laurence Alvin Zimmer, Jr. would do just that.

Ryan looked over the books. His CPA certificate had lapsed, but he could still read a balance sheet.

'You eat dinnah with us?'

'Carol, I can't. I have to get home. My son has a little-league game tonight. Everything's okay? No problems – not even those punks?'

'They not come back. Mistah Clark scare them away fo' good!'

'If they ever come back, I want you to call me right away,' Jack said seriously.

'Okay, okay. I learn lesson,' she promised him.

'Fine. You take care.' Ryan stood.

'Doc Ryan?'

'Yes?'

'Air Force say Buck die in accident. I never ask any-body, but I ask you: Accident, no accident?'

'Carol, Buck lost his life doing his job, saving lives. I was there. So was Mr Clark.'

'The ones make Buck die . . . ?'

'You have nothing to fear from them,' Ryan said evenly. 'Nothing at all.' Jack saw the recognition in her eyes. Though Carol had modest language skills, she'd caught what he'd meant by his answer.

'Thank you, Doc Ryan. I never ask again, but I must know.'

'It's okay.' He was surprised she'd waited so long.

The bulkhead-mounted speaker rattled. 'Conn, sonar. I have a routine noise level bearing zero-four-seven, desig-nate contact Sierra-5. No further information at this time. Will advise.'

'Very well.' Captain Ricks turned to the plotting table. 'Tracking party, begin your TMA.' The Captain looked around the room. Instruments showed a speed of seven knots, a depth of four hundred feet, and a course of three-zero-three. The contact was broad on his starboard beam.

The ensign commanding the tracking party immediately consulted the Hewlett-Packard mini-computer located in the starboard-after corner of the attack center. 'Okay,' he announced, 'I have a trace angle ... little shaky ... computing now.' That took the machine all of two seconds. 'Okay, I have a range gate ... it's a convergence zone, range between three-five and four-five thousand yards if he's in CZ-1, five-five and six-one thousand yards for CZ-2.'

'It's almost too easy,' the XO observed to the skipper.

'You're right, X, disable the computer,' Ricks ordered.

Lieutenant Commander Wally Claggett, Executive Officer, 'Gold,' USS *Maine* walked back to the machine and switched it off. 'We have a casualty to the HP computer ... looks like it'll take hours to fix,' he announced. 'Pity.'

'Thanks a lot,' Ensign Ken Shaw observed quietly to the quartermaster hunched next to him at the chart table.

'Be cool, Mr Shaw,' the petty officer whispered back. 'We'll take care o'ya. Don't need that thing now anyway, sir.'

'Let's keep it quiet in the attack center!' Captain Ricks observed.

The submarine's course took her northwest. The sonar operators fed information to the attack center as she did so. Ten minutes later, the tracking party made its decision.

'Captain,' Ensign Shaw announced. 'Estimate contact Sierra-5 is in the first CZ, range looks like three-nine thousand yards, course is generally southerly, speed between eight and ten knots.'

'You can do better than that!' the CO announced sharply.

'Conn, sonar, Sierra-5 looks like Akula-class Soviet fast-attack, preliminary target ident is Akula number six, the *Admiral Lunin*. Stand by –' a moment's silence '– possible aspect change on Sierra-5, possible turn. Conn, we have a definite aspect change. Sierra-5 is now beam-on, definite beam-aspect on target.'

'Captain,' the XO said, 'that maximizes the effectiveness of his towed array.'

'Right. Sonar, conn. I want a self-noise check.'

'Sonar aye, stand by, sir.' Another few seconds. 'Conn, we're making some sort of noise ... not sure what, rattle, like, maybe something in the aft ballast tanks. Didn't show before, sir. Definitely aft ... definitely metallic.'

'Conn, maneuvering room, we got something screwy back here. I can hear something from aft, maybe in the ballast tanks.'

'Captain,' Shaw said next. 'Sierra-5 is now on a reciprocal heading. Target course is now southeasterly, roughly one-three-zero.'

'Maybe he can hear us,' Ricks growled. 'I'm taking us up through the layer. Make your depth one hundred feet.'

'One hundred feet, aye,' the diving officer responded immediately. 'Helm, five degrees up on the fairwater planes.'

'Five degrees up on the fairwater planes, aye. Sir, the fairwater planes are up five degrees, coming to one hundred feet.'

'Conn, maneuvering, the rattle has stopped. It stopped when we took the slight up-angle.'

The XO grunted next to the captain. 'What the hell does that mean ... ?'

'It probably means that some dumbass dockyard worker left his toolbox in the ballast tank. That happened to a friend of mine once.' Ricks was truly angry now, but if you had to have such incidents, here was the place for them. 'When we get above the layer, I want to go north and clear datum.'

'Sir, I'd wait. We know where the CZ is. Let him slide out of it, then we can maneuver clear while he can't hear us. Let him think he's got us scoped before we start playing tricks. He probably thinks we don't have him. By maneuvering radically, we're tipping our hand.'

Ricks considered that. 'No, we've cancelled the noise aft, we've probably dropped off his scopes already, and when we get above the layer, we can get lost in the surface noise and maneuver clear. His sonar isn't all that good. He doesn't even know what we are yet. He's just sniffing for something. This way we can put more distance between us.'

'Aye aye,' the XO responded neutrally.

Maine leveled off at one hundred feet, well above the thermocline layer, the boundary between relatively warm surface water and the cold deep water. It changed acoustical conditions drastically and, Ricks judged, should eliminate any chance that the Akula had him.

'Conn, sonar, contact lost in Sierra-5.'

'Very well. I have the conn,' Ricks announced.

'Captain has the conn,' the officer of the deck acknowledged.

'Left ten degrees rudder, come to new course three-five-zero.'

'Left ten degrees rudder, aye, coming to new course three-five-zero. Sir, my rudder is left ten degrees.'

'Very well. Engine room, conn, make turns for ten knots.'

'Engine room, aye, turns for ten knots. Building up slowly.'

Maine steadied up on a northerly course and increased speed. It took several minutes for her towed-array sonar to straighten out and be useful again. During this time, the American submarine was somewhat blinded.

'Conn, maneuvering, we got that noise again!' the speaker announced.

'Slow to five – all ahead one-third!'

'All ahead one-third, aye. Sir, engine room answers all ahead one-third.'

'Very well. Maneuvering, conn, what about that noise?'

'Still there, sir.'

'We'll give it a minute,' Ricks judged. 'Sonar, conn, got anything on Sierra-5?'

'Negative, sir, holding no contacts at this time.'

Ricks sipped at his coffee and watched the clock on the bulkhead for three minutes. 'Maneuvering, conn, what about the noise?'

'Has not changed, sir. It's still there.'

'Damn! X, bring her down a knot.' Claggett did as he was told. The skipper was losing it, he realized. Not good. Another ten minutes passed. The worrisome noise aft attenuated, but did not go away.

'Conn, sonar! Contact bearing zero-one-five, just appeared real sudden, like, it's Sierra-5, sir. Definite Akula-class, *Admiral Lunin*. Evaluate as direct-path contact, bow-on aspect. Probably just came up through the layer, sir.'

'Does he have us?' Ricks asked.

'Probably yes, sir,' the sonarman reported.

'Stop!' another voice announced. Commodore Mancuso walked into the room. 'Okay, we conclude the exercise at this point. Will the officers please come with me?'

Everyone let out a collective breath as the lights went up. The room was set in a large square building shaped not at all like a submarine, though its various other rooms duplicated most of the important parts of an Ohio-class boomer. Mancuso led the attack-center crew into a conference room and closed the door.

'Bad tactical move, Captain.' Bart Mancuso was not known for his diplomacy. 'XO, what advice was that you gave to your skipper?' Claggett recited it word for word. 'Captain, why did you reject that advice?'

'Sir, I estimated that our acoustical advantage was sufficient to allow me to do that in such a way as to maximize separation from the target.'

'Wally?' Mancuso turned to the skipper of the Red Team, Commander Wally Chambers, about to become the CO of USS *Key West*. Chambers had worked for Mancuso on *Dallas*, and had the makings of one hell of a fast-attack skipper. He had just proven that, in fact.

'It was too predictable, Captain. Moreover, by continuing course and changing depth course you presented the noise source to my towed array, and also gave me a hull-popping transient that ID'd you as a definite submarine contact. You would have been better off to turn bow-on, maintain depth, and slow down. All I had was a vague indication. If you'd slowed down, I would never have ID'd you. Since you didn't, I noted your hop on top the layer and sprinted in fast underneath as soon as I cleared the CZ. Captain, I didn't know I had you until you let me know, but you let me know, and you did let me get close. I floated my tail over the layer while I stayed right underneath it. There was a fairly good surface duct, and I had you at two-nine thousand yards. I could hear you, but you couldn't hear me. Then it was just a matter of continuing my sprint until I was close enough for a high-probability solution. I had you cold.'

'The point of the exercise was to show you what happened when you lost your acoustical advantage.' Mancuso let that sink in before going on. 'Okay, so it wasn't fair, was it? Who ever said life was fair?'

'Akula's a good boat, but how good is its sonar?'

'We assume it's as good as a second-flight 688.'

No way, Ricks thought to himself. 'What other surprises can I expect?'

'Good question. The answer is that we don't know. And if you don't know, you assume they're as good as you are.'

No way, Ricks told himself.

Maybe even better, Mancuso didn't add.

'Okay,' the Commodore told the assembled attack-center crew. 'Go over your own data and we do the wash-up in thirty minutes.'

Ricks watched Captain Mancuso exit the room sharing a chuckle with Chambers. Mancuso was a smart, effective sub-driver, but he was still a damned fast-attack jockey who didn't belong in command of a boomer squadron, because he simply didn't think the right way. Calling in his former shipmate from Atlantic Fleet, another fast-attack jockey – well, yeah, that's how it was done, but damn it! Ricks was sure he'd done the right thing.

It had been an unrealistic test. Ricks was sure of that. Hadn't Rosselli told the both of them that *Maine* was quiet as a black hole? Damn. This was his first chance to show the commodore what he could do, and he'd been faked out of making a favorable impression by an artificial and unfair test, and some goofs from his people – the ones Rosselli had been so damned proud of.

'Mr Shaw, let's see your TMA records.'

'Here, sir.' Ensign Shaw, who'd graduated sub school at Groton less than two months before, was standing in the corner, the chart and his notes grasped tightly in his tense hands. Ricks snatched them away and spread them on a work table. The Captain's eyes scanned the pages.

'Sloppy. You could have done this at least a minute faster.'

'Yes, sir,' Shaw replied. He didn't know how he might have gone faster, but the Captain said so, and the Captain was always right.

'That could have made the difference,' Ricks told him, a muted but still nasty edge on his voice.

'Sorry, sir.' That was Ensign Shaw's first real mistake. Ricks straightened, but still had to look up to meet Shaw's eyes. That didn't help his disposition either.

' "Sorry" doesn't cut it, Mister. "Sorry" endangers our ship and our mission. "Sorry" gets people killed. "Sorry" is what an unsatisfactory officer says. Do you understand me, Mr Shaw?'

'Yes, sir.'

'Fine.' The word came out as a curse. 'Let's make sure this never happens again.'

The rest of the half hour was spent going over the records of the exercise. The officers left the room for a larger one, where they would relive the exercise, learning what the Red Team had seen and done. Lieutenant Commander Claggett slowed the Captain down.

'Skipper, you were a little hard on Shaw.'

'What do you mean?' Ricks asked in annoyed surprise.

'He didn't make any mistakes. I couldn't have done

the track more than thirty seconds faster myself. The quartermaster I had with him has been doing TMAs for five years. He's taught it at sub school. I kept an eye on both of them. They did okay.'

'Are you saying the mistake was my fault?' Ricks asked in a deceptively gentle voice.

'Yes, sir,' the XO replied honestly, as he had been taught to do.

'Is that a fact?' Ricks walked out the door without another word.

To say that Petra Hassler-Bock was unhappy was an understatement of epic proportions. A woman in her late thirties, she'd lived over fifteen years on the run, hiding from the West German police before things had simply become too dangerous, precipitating her escape to the East Zone – what had been the East Zone, the *Bundes Kriminal Amt* investigator smiled to himself. Amazingly, she'd thrived on it. Every photo in the thick file showed an attractive, vital, smiling woman with a girl's unlined face framed by pretty brown hair. This same face had coldly watched three people die, one after several days of knife-work, the detective told himself. That murder had been part of an important political statement – it had been at the time of the vote on whether or not to allow the Americans to base their Pershing-2 and Cruise missiles in Germany, and the Red Army Faction had wanted to terrify people into seeing things their way. It hadn't worked, of course, though it had made the victim's death into a gothic exercise.

'Tell me, Petra, did you enjoy killing Wilhelm Manstein?' the detective asked.

'He was a pig,' she answered defiantly. 'An overweight, sweaty, whore-mongering pig.'

That was how they'd caught him, the detective knew. Petra had set up the kidnapping first by attracting his attention, then by establishing a brief but fiery relationship. Manstein had not been the most attractive example of German manhood, of course, but Petra's idea of women's liberation was rather more robust than the norm in Western countries. The nastiest members of Baader-Meinhof and the RAF had been the women. Perhaps it was a reaction to the *Kinder-Kuche-Kirche* mindset of German males, as some psychologists said, but the woman before him was the most coldly frightening assassin he'd ever met. The first body parts mailed to Manstein's family had been those which had offended her so greatly. Manstein had lived for ten days after that, the pathologist's report stated, providing noisy red entertainment for this still-young lady.

'Well, you took care of that, didn't you? I imagine Günther was somewhat unsettled by your passion, wasn't he? After all, you spent – what? Five nights with Herr Manstein before the kidnapping? Did you enjoy that part also, *mein Schatz*?' The insult scored, the detective saw. Petra had been attractive once, but no longer. Like a flower a day after cutting, she was no longer a living thing. Her skin was sallow, her eyes surrounded by dark rings, and she'd lost at least eight kilos. Defiance blazed out from her, but only briefly. 'I expect you did, giving in to him, letting him "do his thing." You must have enjoyed it enough that he kept coming back. It wasn't just baiting him, was it? It could not have been just an act. Herr Manstein was a discerning philanderer. He had so much experience, and he only frequented the most skillful whores. Tell me, Petra, how did you acquire so much skill? Did you practice beforehand with Günther – or with others? All in the name of revolutionary justice, of course, or revolutionary *Komaradschaft, nicht wahr*? You are a worthless slut, Petra. Even whores have morals, but not you.

'And your beloved revolutionary cause,' the detective sneered. '*Doch!* Such a cause. How does it feel to be rejected by the entire German *Volk*?' She stirred in her chair at that, but couldn't quite bring herself . . . 'What's the matter, Petra, no heroic words now? You always talked about your visions of freedom and democracy, didn't you? Are you disappointed now that we have real democracy – and the people detest you and your kind! Tell me, Petra, what is it like to be rejected? Totally rejected. And you know it's true,' the investigator added. 'You know it's no joke. You watched the people in the street from your windows, didn't you, you and Günther? One of the demonstrations was right under your apartment, wasn't it? What did you think while you watched, Petra? What did you and Günther say to each other? Did you say it was a counter-revolutionary trick?' The detective shook his head, leaning forward to stare into those empty, lifeless eyes, enjoying his own work as she had done.

'Tell me, Petra, how do you explain the votes? Those were free elections. You know that, of course. Everything you stood for and worked for and murdered for – all a mistake, all for *nothing*! Well, it wasn't a total loss, was it? At least you got to make love to Wilhelm Manstein.' The detective leaned back and lit a small cigar. He blew smoke up at the ceiling. 'And now, Petra? I hope you enjoyed that little tryst, *mein Schatz*. You will never leave this prison alive. Never, Petra. No one will ever feel pity for you, not even when you're confined to a wheelchair. Oh, no. They'll remember your crimes and tell themselves to leave you here with all the other vicious beasts. There is no hope for you. You will die in this building, Petra.'

Petra Hassler-Bock's head jerked at that. Her eyes went wide for an instant as she thought to say something, but stopped short.

The detective went on conversationally. 'We lost track of Günther, by the way. We nearly got him in Bulgaria – missed him by thirty hours. The Russians, you see, have been giving us their files on you and your friends. All those months you spent at those training camps. Well, in any case, Günther is still on the run. In Lebanon, we think, probably holed up with your old friends in that ratpack. They're next,' the detective told her. 'The Americans, the Russians, the Israelis, they're cooperating now, didn't you hear? It's part of this treaty business. Isn't *that* wonderful? I think we'll get Günther there . . . with luck he'll fight back or do something really foolish, and we can bring you a picture of his body . . . Pictures, that's right! I almost forgot!

'I have something to show you,' the investigator announced. He inserted a video cassette into a player and switched on the TV. It took a moment for the picture to settle down into what was plainly an amateur video taken with a hand-held camera. It showed twin girls, dressed in matching pink dirndl outfits, sitting side by side on a typical rug in a typical German apartment – everything was fully *in Ordnung*, even the magazines on the table were squared off. Then the action started.

'*Komm, Erika, Komm, Ursel!*' a woman's voice urged, and both infants pulled themselves up on a coffee table and tottered towards her. The camera followed their halting, unstable steps into the woman's arms.

'*Mutti, Mutti!*' they both said. The detective switched the TV off.

'They're talking and walking. *Ist das nicht wunderbar?* Their new mother loves them very much, Petra. Well, I thought you'd like to see that. That's all for today.' The detective pressed a hidden button, and a guard appeared to take the manacled prisoner back to her cell.

The cell was stark, a cubicle made of white-painted bricks. There was no outside window, and the door was of solid steel except for a spyhole and a slot for food trays. Petra didn't know about the TV camera that looked through what seemed to be yet another brick near the ceiling, but was really a small plastic panel transparent to red and infra-red light. Petra Hassler-Bock retained her composure all the way to the cell, and until the door was slammed shut behind her.

Then she started coming apart.

Petra's hollow eyes stared at the floor – that was painted white, also – too wide and horrified for tears at first, contemplating the nightmare that her life had become. It could not be real, part of her said with confidence that bordered on madness. All she'd believed in, all she'd worked for – gone! Günther, gone. The twins, gone. The cause, gone. Her life, gone.

The *Bundes Kriminal Amt* detectives only interrogated her for amusement. She knew that much. They had never seriously probed her for information, but there was a reason for that. She had nothing worthwhile to give them. They'd shown her copies of the files from Stasi headquarters. Nearly everything her erstwhile fraternal socialist brothers had had on her – far more than she had expected – was now in *West* German hands. Names, addresses, phone numbers, records dating back more than twenty years, things about herself that she'd forgotten, things about Günther that she'd never known. All in the hands of the BKA.

It was all over. All lost.

Petra gagged and started weeping. Even Erika and Ursel, her twins, the product of her own body, the physical evidence of her faith in the future, of her love for Günther. Taking their first steps in the apartment of strangers. Calling some stranger *Mutti*, mommy. The wife of a BKA captain – they'd told her that much. Petra wept for half an hour, not making noise, knowing that there had to be a microphone in the cell, this cursed white box that denied her sleep.

Everything lost.

Life – here? The first and only time she'd been in the exercise yard with other prisoners, they'd had to pull two of them off her. She could remember their screams as the guards had taken her for medical treatment – whore, murderess, animal . . . To live here for forty years or more, alone, always alone, waiting to go mad, waiting for her body to weaken and decay. For her life meant *life*. Of that she was certain. There would be no pity for her. The detective had made that clear. No pity at all. No friends. Lost and forgotten . . . except for the hate.

She made her decision calmly. In the manner of prisoners all over the world, she'd found a way of getting a piece of metal with an edge on it. It was, in fact, a segment of razor blade from the instrument with which she was allowed to shave her legs once a month. She removed it from its place of hiding, then pulled the sheet – also white – from the mattress. It was like any other, about ten centimeters thick, covered with heavy striped fabric. Its trim was a loop of fabric in which was inserted a rope-like stiffener, with the mattress fabric sewn tight around it to give the edge strength. With the razor edge she began detaching the trim from the mattress. It took three hours and not a small amount of blood, for the razor segment was small, and it cut her fingers many times, but finally she had two full meters of improvised rope. She turned one end of the rope into a noose. The free end of the rope she tied to the light fixture over the door. She had to stand on her chair to do that, but she'd have to stand on the chair in any case. It took three attempts to get the knot right. She didn't want too much length on the rope.

When she was satisfied with that, she proceeded without pause. Petra Hassler-Bock removed her dress and her bra. Next she knelt on the chair with her back to the door, getting its position and hers just right, placed the noose around her neck, and drew it tight. Then she drew up her legs, using her bra to secure them between her back and the door. She didn't want to flinch from this. She had to show her courage, her devotion. Without stopping for a prayer or lament, her hands pushed the chair away. Her body fell perhaps five centimeters before the improvised rope stopped her fall and drew tight. Her body rebelled against her will at this point. Her drawn-up legs fought against the bra holding them between the backs of her thighs and the metal door, but in fighting the restraint, they merely pushed Petra fractionally away from the door, and that increased the strangulation on her upper neck.

She was surprised by the pain. The noose fractured her larynx before sliding over it to a point under her jaw. Her eyes opened wide, staring at the white bricks of the far wall. That's when the panic hit her. Ideology has its limits. She couldn't die, didn't want to die, didn't want to –

Her fingers raced to her throat. It was a mistake. They fought to get under the mattress trim, but it was too thin, cutting so deeply into the soft flesh of her neck that she couldn't get a single finger under it. Still she fought, knowing that she had mere seconds before the blood loss to her brain . . . it was getting vague now, her vision was beginning to suffer. She couldn't see the lines of mortar between the even German-made brickwork on the far wall. Her hands kept trying, cutting into the surface blood vessels of her throat, drawing blood that only made the noose slick, able to sink in tighter, cutting off circulation through the carotid arteries even more. Her mouth opened wide and she tried to scream, no, she didn't want to die, didn't – needed help. Couldn't anyone hear her? Could no one help her? Too late, just two seconds, maybe only one, maybe not even that, the last remaining shred of consciousness told her that if she could just loosen the bra holding her legs, she could have stood and . . .

The detective watched the TV picture, saw her hands flutter towards the bra, searching limply for the clasp before they fell away, and twitched for a few more seconds, then stopped. *So close*, he thought. *So very close to saving herself*. It was a pity. She'd been a pretty girl, but she'd chosen to murder and torture, and she'd also chosen to die, and if she'd changed her mind at the end – didn't they all? Well, not quite all – that was merely renewed proof that the brutal ones were cowards after all, *nicht wahr*?

Aber naturlich.

'This television is broken,' he said, switching it off. 'Better get a new one to keep an eye on Prisoner Hassler-Bock.'

'That will take about an hour,' the guard supervisor said.

'That's fast enough.' The detective removed the cassette from the same tape recorder he'd used to show the touching family scene. It went into his briefcase with the other. He locked the case and stood. There was no smile on his face, but there was a look of satisfaction. It wasn't his fault that the *Bundestag* and *Bundesrat* were unable to pass a simple and effective death-penalty statute. That was because of the Nazis, of course. Damned barbarians. But even barbarians were not total fools. They hadn't ripped up the *autobahns* after the war, had they? Of course not. So just because the Nazis had executed people – well, some of them had even been ordinary murderers whom any civilized government of the era would have executed. And if anyone merited death, Petra Hassler-Bock did. Murder by torture. Death by hanging. That, the detective figured, was fair enough. The Wilhelm Manstein murder case had been his from the start. He'd been there when the man's genitals had arrived by mail. He'd watched the pathologists examine the body, had attended the funeral, and he remembered the sleepless nights when he'd been unable to wash the horrid spectacles from his mind. Perhaps now he would. Justice had been slow, but it had come. With luck, those two cute little girls would grow into proper citizens, and no one would ever know who and what their birth mother had once been.

The detective walked out of the prison towards his car. He didn't want to be near the prison when her body was discovered. Case closed.

'Hey, man.'

'Marvin. I hear that you did well with weapons,' Ghosn said to his friend.

'No big deal, man. I've been shooting since I was a kid. That's how you get dinner where I come from.'

'You outshot our best instructor,' the engineer pointed out.

'Your targets are a hell of a lot bigger than a rabbit, and they don't move. Hell, I used to hit jacks on the move with my .22. If you have to shoot what you eat, you learn right quick to hit what you aim at, boy. How'd you do with that bomb thing?' Marvin Russell asked.

'A lot of work for very little return,' Ghosn replied.

'Maybe you can make a radio from all that electrical stuff,' the American suggested.

'Perhaps something useful.'

CHAPTER 10

Last Stands

Flying west is always easier than flying east. The human body adjusts more easily to a longer day than a shorter one, and the combination of good food and good wine makes it all the easier. Air Force One had a sizable conference room that could be used for all manner of functions. In this case it was a dinner for senior administration officials and selected members of the press pool. The food, as usual, was superb. Air Force One may be the only aircraft in the world which serves something other than TV dinners. Its stewards shop daily for fresh foods, which are most often prepared at six hundred knots at eight miles altitude, and more than one of the cooks had left military service to become executive chef at a country club or posh restaurant. Having cooked for the President of the United States of America looks good on any chef's résumé.

The wine in this case was from New York, a particularly good blush Chablis that the President was known to like, when he wasn't drinking beer. The converted 747 had three full cases stowed below. Two white-coated sergeants kept all the glasses filled as the courses came in and out. The atmosphere was relaxed, and the conversations all off the record, on deep background, and be careful or you'll never eat in here again.

'So, Mr President,' the *New York Times* asked. 'How quickly do you think this will be implemented?'

'It is starting even as we speak. The Swiss army representatives are already in Jerusalem to look things over. Secretary Bunker is meeting with the Israeli government to facilitate the arrival of American forces in the region. We expect to have things actually moving inside of two weeks.'

'And the people who'll have to vacate their homes?' the *Chicago Tribune* continued the question.

'They will be seriously inconvenienced, but with our help the new homes will be constructed very rapidly. The Israelis have asked for and will get credits with which to purchase pre-fabricated housing made in America. We're also paying to set up a factory of that type for them to continue on their own. Many thousands of people will be relocated. That will be somewhat painful, but we're going to make it just as easy as we can.'

'At the same time,' Liz Elliot put in, 'let's not forget that quality of life is more than having a roof over your head. Peace has a price, but it also has benefits. Those people will know real security for the first time in their lives.'

'Excuse me, Mr President,' the *Tribune* reporter said with a raised glass. 'That was not meant as criticism. I think we all agree that this treaty is a godsend.' Heads nodded all around the table. 'The way it is implemented is an important story, however, and our readers want to know about it.'

'The relocations will be the hardest part,' Fowler responded calmly. 'We must salute the Israeli government for agreeing to it, and we must do the best we can to make the process just as painless as is humanly possible.'

'And what American units will be sent over to defend Israel?' another reporter asked.

'Glad you asked,' Fowler said. He was. The previous questioner had overlooked the most obvious potential obstacle to treaty-implementation – would the Israeli Knesset ratify the agreements? 'As you may have heard, we're reestablishing a new Army unit, the 10th United States Cavalry Regiment. It's being formed at Fort Stewart, Georgia, and at my direction ships of the National Defense Reserve Fleet are being mobilized right now to get them over to Israel just as quickly as we can.

The 10th Cavalry is a famous unit with a distinguished history. It was one of the black units that the westerns have almost totally ignored. As luck would have it –' luck had nothing to do with it '– the first commander will be an African American, Colonel Marion Diggs, a distinguished soldier, West Point grad and all that. That's the land force. The air component will be a complete wing of F-16 fighter-bombers, plus a detachment of AWACS aircraft, and the usual support personnel. Finally, the Israelis are giving us home-porting at Haifa, and we'll almost always have a carrier battle-group and a Marine Expeditionary unit in the Eastern Med to back up everything else.'

'But with the draw-down –'

'Dennis Bunker came up with the idea on the 10th Cavalry, and frankly I wish I could say that it's one of mine. As for the rest, well, we'll try to fit it in somehow or other with the rest of the defense budget.'

'Is it really necessary, Mr President? I mean, with all the budget battles, particularly on the matter of defense, do we really have to –'

'Of course we do.' The National Security Advisor cut the reporter off at his ugly knees. *You asshole*, Elliot's expression said. 'Israel has serious and very real security considerations, and our commitment to preserving Israeli security is the *sine qua non* of this agreement.'

'Christ, Marty,' another reporter muttered.

'We'll compensate for the additional expense in other areas,' the President said. 'I know I'm returning to one more round of ideologically-based wrangling over how we pay for the cost of government, but I think we have demonstrated here that government's costs do pay off. If we have to nudge taxes up a little to preserve world peace, then the American people will understand and support it,' Fowler concluded matter-of-factly.

Every reporter took note of that. The President was going to propose yet another tax increase. There had already been Peace Dividend I and II. This would be the first Peace Tax, one of them thought with a wry smile. That would sail through Congress, along with everything else. The smile had another cause as well. She noted the look in the President's eyes when he gazed over at his National Security Advisor. She'd wondered about that. She'd tried to get Liz Elliot at home twice, right before the trip to Rome, and both times all she'd gotten on her private line was the answering machine. She could have followed up on that. She could have staked out Elliot's townhouse off Kalorama Road and made a record of how often Elliot was sleeping at home, and how often she was not. But. But that was none of her business, was it? No, it wasn't. The President was a single man, a widower, and his personal life had no public import so long as he was discreet about it, and so long as it didn't interfere with his conduct of official business. The reporter figured she was the only one who'd noticed. What the hell, she thought, if the President and his National Security Advisor were that close, maybe it was a good thing. Look how well the Vatican Treaty had gone . . .

Brigadier General Abraham Ben Jakob read over the treaty text in the privacy of his office. He was not a man who often had difficulty in defining his thoughts. That was a luxury accorded him by paranoia, he knew. For all of his adult life – a life that had started at age 16 in his case, the first time he'd carried arms for his country – the world had been an exceedingly simple place to understand: there were Israelis and there were others. Most of the others were enemies or potential enemies. A very few of the others were associates or perhaps friends, but friendship for Israel was mostly a unilateral business. Avi had run five operations in America, 'against' the Americans. 'Against' was a relative term, of course. He'd never intended harm to come to America, he'd merely wanted to know some things the American government knew, or to obtain something the American government had and Israel needed. The information would never be used against America, of course, nor would the military hardware, but the Americans, understandably, didn't like having their secrets taken away. That did not trouble General Ben Jakob in any way. His mission in life was to protect the State of Israel, not to be pleasant to people. The Americans understood that. The Americans occasionally shared intelligence information with the Mossad. Most often this was done on a very informal basis. And on rare occasions, the Mossad gave information to the Americans. It was all very civilized – in fact, it was not at all unlike two competing businesses who shared both adversaries and markets, and sometimes cooperated but never quite trusted each other.

That relationship would now change. It had to. America was now committing its own troops to Israeli defense. That made America partly responsible for the defense of Israel – and reciprocally made Israel responsible for the safety of the Americans (something the American media had not yet noted). That was the Mossad's department. Intelligence-sharing would have to become a much wider street than it had been. Avi didn't like that. Despite the euphoria of the moment, America was not a country with which to entrust secrets, particularly those obtained after much effort and often blood by intelligence officers in his employ. Soon the Americans would be sending a senior intelligence representative to work out the details. They'd send Ryan, of course. Avi started making notes. He needed to get as much information as he could on Ryan so that he could cut as favorable a deal with the Americans as possible.

Ryan . . . was it true that he'd gotten this whole thing started? There was a question, Ben Jakob thought. The American government had denied it, but Ryan was not a favorite of President Fowler or his National Security Bitch, Elizabeth Elliot. The information on her was quite clear. While Professor of Political Science at Bennington, she'd had PLO representatives in to lecture on their view of the Middle East – in the name of fairness and balance! It could have been worse. She wasn't Vanessa Redgrave, dancing with an AK-47 held over her head, Avi told herself, but her 'objectivity' had stretched to the point of listening politely to the representatives of the people who'd attacked Israeli children at Ma'alot, and Israeli athletes at Munich. Like most members of the American government, she had forgotten what principle was. But Ryan wasn't one of those . . .

The treaty was *his work.* His sources were right. Fowler and Elliot would never have come up with an idea like this. Using religion as the key would never have occurred to them.

The Treaty. He went back to it, returning to his notes. How had the government ever allowed itself to be maneuvered into this?

We shall overcome . . .

That simple, wasn't it? The panicked telephone calls and cables from Israel's American friends, the way they were starting to jump ship, as though . . .

But how could it have been otherwise? Avi asked himself. In any case, the Vatican Treaty was a done deal. Probably a done deal, he told himself. The eruptions in the Israeli population had begun, and the next few days would be passionate. The reasons were simple enough to understand:

Israel was essentially vacating the West Bank. Army units would remain in place, much as American units were still based in Germany and Japan, but the West Bank was to become a Palestinian state, demilitarized, its borders guaranteed by the UN, which was probably a nice sheet of framed parchment, Ben Jakob reflected. The real guarantee would come from Israel and America. Saudi Arabia and its sister Gulf states would pay for the economic rehabilitation of the Palestinians. Access to Jerusalem was guaranteed, also – that's where most of the Israeli troops would be, with large and easily-secured base camps, and the right to patrol at will. Jerusalem itself became a dominion of the Vatican. An elected mayor – he wondered if the Israeli now holding the post would keep his post . . . Why not? he asked himself, he was the most even-handed of men – would handle civil administration, but international and religious affairs would be managed under Vatican authority by a troika of three clerics. Local security for Jerusalem was to be handled by a Swiss motorized regiment. Avi might have snorted at that, but the Swiss had been the model for the Israeli army, and the Swiss were supposed to train with the American regiment. The 10th Cavalry were supposed to be crack regular troops. On paper, it was all very neat.

Things on paper usually were.

On Israel's streets, however, the rabid demonstrations had already begun. Thousands of Israeli citizens were to be displaced. Two police officers and a soldier had already been hurt – at Israeli hands. The Arabs were keeping out of everyone's way. A separate commission run by the Saudis would try to settle which Arab family owned what piece of ground – a situation that Israel had thoroughly muddled when it had seized land that may or may not have been owned by Arabs, and – but that was not Avi's problem, and he thanked God for it. His given name was Abraham, not Solomon.

Will it work! he wondered.

It cannot possibly work, Qati told himself. Word that a treaty had been signed had thrown him into a ten-hour bout of nausea, and now that he had the treaty text, he felt himself at death's door itself.

Peace! And yet Israel will continue to exist! What, then, of his sacrifices, what of the hundreds, thousands, of freedom fighters sacrificed under Israeli guns and bombs? For what had they died? For what had Qati sacrificed his life? He might as well have died, Qati told himself. He'd denied himself everything. He might have lived a normal life, might have had a wife and sons and a house and comfortable work, might have been a doctor or engineer or banker or merchant. He had the intelligence to succeed at anything his mind selected as worthy of himself – but no, he had chosen the most difficult of paths. His goal was to build a new nation, to make a home for his people, to give them the human dignity they deserved. To lead his people. To defeat the invaders.

To be remembered.

That was what he craved. Anyone could recognize

injustice, but to remedy it would have allowed him to be remembered as a man who had changed the course of human history, if only in a small way, if only for a small nation . . .

That wasn't true, Qati admitted to himself. To accomplish his task meant defying the great nations, the Americans and Europeans who had inflicted their prejudices on his ancient homeland, and men who did that were not remembered as small men. Were he successful, he would be remembered among the great, for great deeds define great men, and the great men were those whom history remembered. But whose deeds would be remembered now? Who had conquered what – or whom?

It was not possible, the Commander told himself. Yet his stomach told him something else as he read over the treaty text with its dry, precise words. The Palestinian people, his noble, courageous people, could they possibly be seduced by this infamy?

Qati stood and walked back to his private bathroom to retch again. That, part of his brain said, even as he bent over the bowl, was the answer to his question. After a time, he stood and drank a glass of water to remove the vile taste from his mouth, but there was another taste that was not so easily removed.

Across the street, in another safe house run by the organization, Günther Bock was listening to *Deutsche Welle*'s German overseas radio service. Despite his politics and his location, Bock would never stop thinking of himself as a German. A German revolutionary-socialist, to be sure, but a German. It had been another warm day in his true home, the radio reported, with clear skies, a fine day to walk along the Rhein holding Petra's hand, and . . .

The brief news report stopped his heart. 'Convicted murderess Petra Hassler-Bock was found hanged in her prison cell this afternoon, the victim of an apparent suicide. The wife of escaped terrorist Günther Bock, Petra Hassler-Bock was convicted of the brutal murder of Wilhelm Manstein after her arrest in Berlin, and sentenced to life imprisonment. Petra Hassler-Bock was thirty-eight years of age.

'The resurgence of the Dresden football club has surprised many observers. Led by star forward Willi Scheer...'

Bock's eyes went wide in the unlit darkness of his room. Unable even to look at the lit radio dial, his eyes found the open window and stared at the stars of evening.

Petra, dead!

He knew it was true, knew better than to tell himself it was impossible. It was all too possible ... inevitable, in fact. *Apparent suicide!* Of course, just as all the Baader-Meinhof members had *apparently* committed suicide, one having reportedly shot himself in the head ... three times. 'A real death-grip on the gun,' had been the joke of the West German police community of the time.

They'd murdered his wife, Bock knew. His beautiful Petra was dead. His best friend, his truest comrade, his lover. Dead. It should not have hit him as hard as it did, Günther knew. What else might he have expected? They'd had to kill her, of course. She was both a link with the past, and a potentially dangerous link with Germany's socialist future. In killing her, they'd further secured the political stability of the new Germany, *Das Vierte Reich.*

'Petra,' he whispered to himself. She was more than a political figure, more than a revolutionary. He remembered every contour of her face, every curve of her youthful body. He remembered waiting for their children to be born, and the smile with which she'd greeted him after delivering Erika and Ursel. They, too, were gone, as totally removed from him as though they'd also died.

It was not a time to be alone. Bock dressed and walked across the street. Qati, he was glad to see, was still awake, though he looked ghastly.

'What is wrong, my friend?' the Commander asked.

'Petra is dead.'

Qati showed genuine pain on his face. 'What happened?'

'The report is that she was found dead in her cell – hanged.' His Petra, Bock thought in delayed shock, found strangled by her graceful neck. The image was too painful for contemplation. He'd seen that kind of death. He and Petra had executed a class enemy that way and watched his face turn pale, then darken, and ... The image was unbearable. He could not allow himself to see Petra that way.

Qati bowed his head in sorrow. 'May Allah have mercy on our beloved comrade.'

Bock managed not to frown. Neither he nor Petra had ever believed in God, but Qati had meant well by his prayer, even though it was nothing more than a waste of breath. At the very least, it was an expression of sympathy and good will – and friendship. Bock needed that right now, and so he ignored the irrelevancy and took a deep breath.

'It is a bad day for our cause, Ismael.'

'Worse than you think, this cursed treaty –'

'I know,' Bock said. 'I know.'

'What do you think?' One thing Qati could depend on was Bock's honesty. Günther was objective about everything.

The German took a cigarette from the Commander's desk and lit it from the table lighter. He didn't sit, but rather paced the room. He had to move about to prove to himself that he was still alive, as he commanded his mind to consider the question objectively.

'One must see this as merely one part of a larger plan. When the Russians betrayed World Socialism, they set in motion a series of events aimed at solidifying control over most of the world on the part of the capitalist classes. I used to think that the Soviets merely advanced this as a matter of clever strategy, to get economic assistance for themselves – you must understand that the Russians are a backward people, Ismael. They couldn't even make Communism work. Of course, Communism was invented by a German,' he added with an ironic grimace (that Marx had been a Jew was something he diplomatically left out). Bock paused for a moment, then went on with a coldly analytical voice. He was grateful for the chance to close the door briefly on his emotions and speak like the revolutionary of old.

'I was wrong. It was not a question of tactics at all. It is a complete betrayal. Progressive elements within the Soviet Union have been outmaneuvered even more thoroughly than in the DDR. Their rapprochement with America is quite genuine. They are trading ideological purity for temporary prosperity, yes, but there is no plan on their part to return to the socialist fold.

'America, for its part, is charging a price for the help they offer. America forced the Soviets to deny support for Iraq, to lessen support for you and your Arab brothers, and finally to accede to their plan to secure Israel once and for all. Clearly, the "Israel Lobby" in America has been planning this trick for some time. What makes it different is Soviet acquiescence. What we now face is not merely America, but conspiracy on a global scale. We have no friends, Ismael. We have only ourselves.'

'Do you say we are defeated?'

'No!' Bock's eyes blazed for a moment. 'If we stop now – they have advantage enough already, my friend. Give them one more and they will use the current state of affairs to hunt all of us down. Your relationship with the Russians is as bad as it has ever been. It will get worse still. Next, the Russians will begin cooperation with the Americans and Zionists.'

'Who would have ever thought that the Americans and Russians would . . .'

'Noone. Noone except those who brought it about, the American ruling elite and their bought dogs, Narmonov and his lackies. They were exceeding clever, my friend. We ought to have seen it coming, but we did not. You didn't see it coming here. I never saw it coming in Europe. The failure was ours.'

Qati told himself that the truth was precisely what he needed to hear, but his stomach told him something else entirely.

'What ideas do you have for remedying the situation?' the Commander asked.

'We are faced with an alliance of two very unlikely friends and their hangers-on. One must find a way to destroy the alliance. In historical terms, when an alliance is broken, the former allies are even more suspicious of each other than they were before the alliance was formed. How to do that?' Bock shrugged. 'I don't know. That will require time ... The opportunities are there. Should be there,' he corrected himself. 'There is much potential for discord. There are many people who feel as we do, many still in Germany who feel as I do.'

'But you say it must begin between America and Russia?' Qati asked, interested as always by his friend's meanderings.

'That is where it must lead. If there were a way to make it start there, so much the better, but that would seem unlikely.'

'Perhaps not as unlikely as you imagine, Günther,' Qati thought to himself, scarcely aware that he'd spoken aloud.

'Excuse me?'

'Nothing. We will discuss this later. I am tired, my friend.'

'Forgive me for troubling you, Ismael.'

'We will avenge Petra, my friend. They will pay for their crimes!' Qati promised him.

'Thank you.' Bock left. Two minutes later, he was back in his room. The radio was still on, now playing traditional music. It came back to him then, the weight of the moment. He did not manage tears, however. All Bock felt was rage. Petra's death was a wrenching personal tragedy, but his whole *world* of ideas had been betrayed. The death of his wife was just one more symptom of a deeper and more virulent disease. The whole world would pay for Petra's murder, if he could manage it. All in the name of revolutionary justice, of course.

*

Sleep came hard for Qati. Surprisingly, part of the problem was guilt. He too had his memories of Petra Hassler and her supple body – she hadn't been married to Günther then – and the thought of her dead, found at the end of a German rope ... How had she died? Suicide, the news report had said? Qati believed it. They were brittle, these Europeans. Clever, but brittle. They knew the passion of the struggle, but they did not know of endurance. Their advantage lay in their broader view. That came from their more cosmopolitan environment and their generally superior education. Whereas Qati and his people tended to be overly focused on their immediate problem, their European comrades could see the broader issues more clearly. The moment of perceptive clarity came as something of a surprise. Qati and his people had always regarded the Europeans as comrades but not as equals, as dilettantes in the business of revolution. That was a mistake. They had always faced a more rigorous revolutionary task because they lacked the ready-made sea of discontent from which Qati and his colleagues drew their recruits. That they had been less successful in their goals was due to objective circumstances, not a reflection on their intelligence or dedication.

Bock could have made a superb operations officer because he saw things clearly.

And now! Qati asked himself. That was a question, but one that would require time for contemplation. It was not a question for a hasty answer. He'd sleep on that one for several days ... more like a week, the Commander promised himself, as he tried to find sleep.

'... I have the great privilege and high honor of introducing the President of the United States.'

The assembled members of Congress stood as one person from their crowded seats in the House chamber. Arrayed in the front row were the members of the cabinet, the Joint Chiefs of Staff, and the Justices of the Supreme Court, who also rose. In the balconies were others, among them the Saudi and Israeli ambassadors sitting side-by-side for the first time in memory. The TV cameras panned the great room in which both history and infamy had been made. The applause echoed from wall to wall until hands grew red from it.

President Fowler rested his notes on the lectern. He turned to shake the hand of the Speaker of the House, the President Pro Tempore of the Senate, and his own Vice President, Roger Durling. In the euphoria of the moment, noone would comment that Durling came last. Next he turned to smile and wave at the assembled multitude, and the noise increased yet again. Every gesture in Fowler's repertoire came into play. The one-hand wave, the two-hand wave, hands at shoulder level, and hands over the head. The response was truly bi-partisan, and that was remarkable, Fowler noted. His most vociferous enemies in the House and Senate were assiduous in their enthusiasm, and he knew it to be genuine. There still was true patriotism in the Congress, much to the surprise of everyone. Finally, he waved for silence and the applause grudgingly subsided.

'My fellow Americans, I come to this house to report on recent events in Europe and the Middle East, and to lay before the United States Senate a pair of treaty documents which, I hope, will meet with your speedy and enthusiastic approval.' More applause. 'With these treaties, the United States, operating in close co-operation with many other nations – some trusted old friends, and some valuable new ones – has helped to bring about peace in a region that has helped to give peace to the world, but which has known all too little peace itself.

'One can search all of human history. One can trace the evolution of the human spirit. All of human progress, all the shining lights that have lit our way up from barbarism, all the great and good men and women who have prayed and dreamed and hoped and worked for this moment – this moment, this opportunity, this culmination, is the last page in the history of human conflict. We have reached not a starting point, but a *stopping* point. We –' More applause interrupted the President. He was very slightly annoyed, having not planned for this interruption. Fowler smiled broadly, waving for silence.

'We have reached a stopping point. I have the honor to report to you that America has led the way on the road to justice and peace.' Applause. 'It is fitting that this should be so . . .'

'A little thick, isn't it?' Cathy Ryan asked.

'A little.' Jack grunted in his chair and reached for his wine. 'It's just how things go, babe. There are rules for this sort of thing just as there are for opera. You have to follow the formula. Besides, it is a major – hell, a colossal development. Peace is breaking out again.'

'When are you leaving?' Cathy asked.

'Soon,' Jack replied.

'Of course, there is a price we must pay for this, but history demands responsibility from those who forge it,' Fowler said on the TV. 'It is our task to guarantee the peace. We must send American men and women to protect the State of Israel. We are sworn to defend that small and courageous country against all enemies.'

'What enemies are they?' Cathy asked.

'Syria isn't happy with the treaty as yet. Neither is Iran. As far as Lebanon goes, well, there isn't any Lebanon in any real sense of the word. It's just a place on the map where people die. Libya and all those terrorist groups. There are still enemies to be concerned about.' Ryan finished off the glass and walked into the kitchen to refill it. It was a shame to waste good wine like this, Jack told himself. The way he was guzzling it, he might as well drink anything . . .

'There will be a monetary cost as well,' Fowler was saying, as Ryan came back.

'Taxes are going up again,' Cathy observed crossly.

'Well, what did you expect?' *Fifty million of it is my fault, of course. A billion here, and a billion there . . .*

'Will this really make a difference?' she asked.

'It should. We'll find out if all those religious leaders believe in what they say, or if they're just bullshit artists. What we've done is to hoist them on their own petards, babe . . . Make that "principles,"' Jack said after a moment. 'Either they work things out in accordance with their beliefs or they reveal themselves as charlatans.'

'And . . . ?'

'I don't think they're charlatans. I think they'll be faithful to what they've always said. They have to be.'

'And soon you won't have any real work to do, will you?'

Jack caught the hopeful note in her voice. 'I don't know about *that*.'

After the end of the President's speech came the commentary. Speaking in opposition was Rabbi Solomon Mendelev, an elderly New Yorker who was one of Israel's most fervent – some would say rabid – supporters. Oddly, he'd never actually traveled to Israel. Jack didn't know why that was true and made a mental note to find out why tomorrow. Mendelev led a small but effective segment of the Israeli lobby. He'd been nearly alone in voicing approval – well, understanding – of the shootings on Temple Mount. The rabbi had a beard, and wore a black yarmulke over what looked like a well-rumpled suit.

'This is a betrayal of the State of Israel,' he said, after receiving the first question. Surprisingly, he spoke with calm reason. 'In forcing Israel to return what was rightfully hers, the United States has betrayed the Jewish people's historic right to the land of their fathers, and also gravely compromised the physical security of the country. Israeli citizens will be forced from their homes at gunpoint, just as happened fifty years ago,' he concluded ominously.

'Now wait a minute,' another commentator responded heatedly.

'God, these people are passionate,' Jack noted.

'I lost family members in the Holocaust,' Mendelev said, his voice still reasonable. 'The whole point of the State of Israel is to give Jews a place where they can be safe.'

'But the President is sending American troops –'

'We sent American troops to Vietnam,' Rabbi

Mendelev pointed out. 'And we made promises, and there was a treaty involved there, also. Israel's only possible security is within defensible borders behind her own troops. What America has done is to bully that country into accepting an agreement. Fowler cut off defense supplies to Israel as a means of "sending a message." Well, the message was sent and received: either give in or be cut off. That is what happened. I can prove it, and I will testify before the Senate Foreign Relations Committee to prove it.'

'Uh-oh,' Jack observed quietly.

'Scott Adler, Deputy Secretary of State, personally delivered that message while John Ryan, the Deputy Director of the CIA, made his own pitch to Saudi Arabia. Ryan promised the Saudi king that America would bring Israel to heel. That's bad enough, but for Adler, a Jew, to do what he did . . .' Mendelev shook his head.

'This guy's got some good sources.'

'Is what he says true, Jack?' Cathy asked.

'Not exactly, but what we were doing over there was supposed to be secret. It wasn't supposed to be widely-known that I was out of the country.'

'I knew you were gone –'

'But not where to. It won't matter. He can make a little noise, but it won't matter.'

The demonstrations began the next day. They'd bet everything on this. It was the last desperate throw. The two leaders were Russian Jews who'd only recently been allowed to leave a country that manifestly had little love for them. On arrival in their only true home, they'd been allowed to settle on the West Bank, that part of Palestine that had been taken from Jordan by force of arms in the Six Day War of 1967. Their pre-fabricated apartments – tiny by American standards, but incomprehensibly luxurious by Russian ones – stood on one of the hundreds of rocky slopes that defined the region. It was new and strange to them, but it was home, and home is something people fight to defend. The son of Anatoliy – he'd renamed himself Nathan – was already a regular officer in the Israeli army. The same was true of David's daughter. Their arrival in Israel so short a time before had seemed to all of them like salvation itself – and now they were being told to leave their homes? Again? Their lives had borne enough recent shocks. This was one too many.

The whole block of apartments was similarly occupied by Russian immigrants, and it was easy for Anatoliy and David to form a local *kollektiv* and get things properly organized. They found themselves an orthodox rabbi – the only thing they didn't have in their small community – to provide religious guidance and began their march towards the Knesset behind a sea of flags and a holy Torah. Even in so small a country, this took time, but the march was of such a nature as to attract the inevitable media coverage. By the time the sweating and weary marchers arrived at their destination, all the world knew of their trek and its purpose.

The Israeli Knesset is not the most sedate of the world's parliamentary bodies. The body of men and women ranges from the ultra-right to the ultra-left, with precious little room for a moderate middle. Voices are often raised, fists are often shaken or pounded on whatever surface presents itself, all beneath the black-and-white photo of Theodor Herzl, an Austrian whose ideal of Zionism in the mid-19th century was the guiding vision for what he hoped would be a safe homeland for his abused and mistreated people. The passion of the parliamentarians is such as to make many an observer wonder how it is possible, in a country where nearly everyone is a member of the army reserves and consequently has an automatic weapon in his (or her) closet, that some Knesset members have failed to be blasted to quivering fragments at their seats in the course of a spirited debate. What Theodor Herzl would have thought of the goings-on is anyone's guess. It was Israel's curse that the debates were too lively, the government too severely polarized both on political or religious grounds. Almost every religious sub-sect had its own special area of land, and consequently its own parliamentary representation.

It was a formula calculated to make France's often-fragmented assembly look well-organized, and it had for a generation denied Israel a stable government with a coherent national policy.

The demonstrators, joined by many others, arrived an hour before debate was to begin on the question of the treaties. It was already possible – likely – that the government would fall, and the newly-arrived citizens sent representatives to every member of the Knesset they could locate. Members who agreed with them came outside and gave fiery speeches denouncing the treaties.

'I don't like this,' Liz Elliot observed, watching the TV in her office. The political furor in Israel was much stronger than she had expected, and Elliot had called Ryan in for an assessment of the situation.

'Well,' the DDCI agreed, 'it is the one thing we couldn't control, isn't it?'

'You're a big help, Ryan.' On Elliot's desk was the polling data. Israel's most respected public-opinion firm had conducted a survey of five thousand people, and found the numbers were 38 percent in favor of the treaty, 41 percent opposed, and 21 percent undecided. The numbers roughly matched the political makeup of the Knesset, whose right-wing elements slightly outnumbered the left, and whose precarious center was always fragmented into small groupings, all of which waited for a good offer from one side or the other that would magnify their political importance.

'Scott Adler went over this weeks ago. We knew going in that the Israeli government was shaky. For Christ's sake, when in the last twenty years has it *not* been shaky?'

'But if the Prime Minister cannot deliver . . .'

'Then it's back to Plan B. You wanted to put pressure on their government, didn't you? You'll get your wish.' This was the one thing that hadn't been fully considered, Ryan thought, but the truth of the matter was that full consideration would not have helped. The Israeli government had been a model of anarchy in action for a generation. The treaty work had gone ahead on the assumption that, once transformed into a *fait accompli*, the treaty would have to be ratified by the Knesset. Ryan had not been asked for an opinion on that, though he still thought it a fair assessment.

'The political officer at the embassy says that the balance of power may be the little party controlled by our friend Mendelev,' Elliot noted, trying to be calm.

'Maybe so,' Jack allowed.

'It's absurd!' Elliot snarled. 'That little old fart hasn't even been there – '

'Some sort of religious thing. I checked. He doesn't want to go back until the Messiah arrives.'

'Jesus!' the National Security Advisor exclaimed.

'Exactly. You got it.' Ryan laughed and got a nasty look. 'Look, Liz, the man has his personal religious beliefs. We may think they're a little off, but the Constitution demands that we both tolerate and *respect* them. That's the way we do things in this country, remember?'

Elliot waved her fist at the TV set. 'But this crazy rabbi is screwing things up! Isn't there *anything* we can do about it?'

'Like what?' Jack asked quietly. There was more to her demeanor than panic.

'I don't know – *something* . . .' Elliot allowed her voice to trail off, leaving an opening for her visitor.

Ryan leaned forward and waited until he had her full attention. 'The historical precedent you're looking for, Dr Elliot, is, "Will no one rid me of this troublesome priest?" Now, if you're trying to tell me something, let's get it clear and in the open, shall we? Are you proposing that we interfere with the parliament of a friendly democratic country, or that we do something illegal within the borders of the United States of America?' A pause while her eyes focused a little more tightly. 'Neither one of those things will happen, Dr Elliot. We let them make up their own minds. If you even think of telling me to interfere with Israel's democratic processes, the President gets my resignation just as fast as I can drive down here to deliver it. If you're wishing out loud for us to hurt that little old guy in New York, remember that such wishes fall under at least two conspiracy statutes. My duty as an ordinary citizen, much less an official of the government of my country, is to report suspected violations of the law to the appropriate law-enforcement agencies.' The look Ryan got after his pronouncement was venomous.

'Damn you! I never said –'

'You just fell into the most dangerous trap in government service, ma'am. You started to think that your wishes to make the world a better place supersede the principles under which our government is supposed to operate. I can't stop you from having such thoughts, but I can tell you that my agency will not be a party to it, not as long as I'm there.' It sounded too much like a lecture, but Ryan felt that she needed it. She was entertaining the most dangerous of thoughts.

'*I never said that!*'

Bullshit. 'Fine, you never said or thought that. I was mistaken. You have my apology. Let the Israelis decide to ratify the treaties or not. They have a democratic government. It is their right to decide. We have the right to nudge them in the right direction, to tell them that our continued level of aid is contingent upon their agreeing to it, but not to interfere directly with their governmental processes. There are some lines you may not cross, even if "you" happen to be the U.S. government.'

The National Security Advisor managed a smile. 'Thank you for your views on the matter of proper government policy, Dr Ryan. That will be all.'

'Thank *you*, Dr Elliot. My assessment, by the way, is that we should let things be. The treaty will be approved, despite what you see here.'

'Why?' Elliot managed not to hiss.

'The treaties are good for Israel in any objective sense. The people will realize that as soon as they've had a chance to digest the information, and make their views known to their representatives. Israel *is* a democracy, and democracies generally do the smart thing. History, you see. Democracy has become popular in the world because it works. If we panic and take precipitous action, we'll only mess things up. If we let the process work as it's supposed to work, the right thing will probably happen.'

'Probably?'

'There are no certainties in life; there are only probabilities,' Ryan explained. Why didn't everyone understand that? he wondered to himself. 'But interference has a higher probability of failure than doing nothing. Doing nothing at all is often the right thing. This is such a case. Let their system work. I think it will work. That is my opinion.'

'Thank you for your assessment,' she said, turning away.

'A pleasure, as always.'

Elliot waited until she heard the door close before turning to look. 'You arrogant prick, I'll break you for that,' she promised.

Ryan climbed back into his car on West Executive Drive. *You went too far, man*, he told himself.

No, you didn't. She was starting to think that way, and you had to slam the door on it right there and then.

It was the most dangerous thought that a person in government could have. He'd seen it before. Some dreadful thing happened to people in Washington, D.C. They arrived in the city, usually full of ideals, and those fine thoughts evaporated so rapidly in what was in fact a muggy and humid environment. Some called it being captured by the system. Ryan thought of it as a kind of environmental pollution. The very atmosphere of Washington corroded the soul.

And what makes you immune, Jack?

Ryan considered that, unmindful of the look Clark gave him in the mirror as they drove towards the river. What had made him different to this point was the fact that he had never given in, not even once . . . or had he? There were things he might have done differently. There were some things that hadn't worked out quite as well as he might have wished.

You're not different at all. You just think you are.

As long as I can face the question and the answers, then I am safe.

Sure.

'So?'

'So, I can do many things,' Ghosn replied. 'But not alone. I will need help.'

'And security?'

'That is an important question. I have to make a serious assessment of what the possibilities are. At that point I will know my precise requirements. I know I will need help in some areas, however.'

'Such as?' the Commander asked.

'The explosives.'

'But you are an expert in such things,' Qati objected.

'Commander, this task requires precision such as we have never been forced to face. We cannot use ordinary plastic explosives, for example, for the simple reason that they are plastic – they change shape. The explosive blocks I use must be as rigid as stone, must be shaped to a thousandth of a millimeter, and the shape must be determined mathematically. The theoretical side of that is something I could assimilate, but it will take months. I would rather devote my time to refabricating the nuclear material . . . and . . .'

'Yes?'

'I believe I can improve the bomb, Commander.'

'Improve? How?'

'If my initial readings are correct, this type of weapon can be adapted to become not a bomb but a trigger.'

'Trigger for what?' Qati asked.

'A thermonuclear fusion bomb, a hydrogen bomb, Ismael. The yield of the weapon might be increased by a factor of ten, perhaps a hundred. We could destroy Israel, certainly a very large part of it.'

The commander paused for a few breaths, assimilating that bit of information. When he spoke, he spoke softly. 'But you need help. Where might be the best place?'

'Günther may have some valuable contacts in Germany. If he can be trusted,' Ghosn added.

'I have considered this. Günther can be trusted.' Qati explained why.

'We are sure the story is real?' Ghosn asked. 'I have no more faith in coincidences than you, Commander.'

'There was a photograph in a German newspaper. It appeared quite genuine.' A German tabloid had managed to get a graphic black-and-white photo that showed the results of a hanging in all its ghastly splendor. The fact that Petra was nude above the waist had ensured its publication. Such an end for a terrorist murderer was too juicy to be denied to the German males, one of whom had been castrated by this woman.

'The problem is simply that we must minimize the number of people who know about this, else — excuse me, Ismael.'

'But we need some help. Yes, I understand that.' Qati smiled. 'You are correct. It is time to discuss our plans with our friend. You propose to explode the bomb in Israel?'

'Where else? It is not my place to make such plans, but I assumed . . .'

'I have not thought about it. One thing at a time, Ibrahim. When are you leaving for Israel?'

'I planned to do so in the next week or so.'

'Let it wait until we see what this treaty business will do.' Qati thought. 'Begin your studies. We will make haste slowly on this matter. First you must determine your requirements. We will then try to meet them in the most secure location we can arrange.'

It took forever, it seemed, but forever in political terms can be a time period ranging from five minutes to five years. In this case, it took less than three days for the important part to happen. Fifty thousand more demonstrators arrived before the Knesset. Led by veterans of all of Israel's wars, the new crowd supported the treaties. There were more shouts and shaken fists, but for once there was no overt violence, as the police managed to keep the two passionate groups separated. Instead they labored to out-shout each other.

The cabinet met again in closed session, both ignoring and attending to the din outside their windows. The Defense Minister was surprisingly quiet during the discussion. On being asked, he agreed that the additional arms promised by the Americans would be hugely useful: 48 additional F-16 fighter-bombers; and for the first time, M-2/3 Bradley fighting vehicles, Hellfire anti-tank missiles, and access to the revolutionary new tank-gun technology America was developing. The Americans would underwrite most of the cost of building a high-tech training center in the Negev similar to their own National Training Center at Fort Irwin, California, where the 10th Cav unit would train constantly as the 'OpFor' or opposing force against Israeli units. The Defense Minister knew the effect the NTC had had for the U.S. Army, which was at its highest state of professionalism since World War II. With the new matériel and training base, he judged that the real effectiveness of Israel's defense forces would increase by 50 percent. To that he added the U.S. Air Force F-16 wing and the tank regiment, both of which, as spelled out in a secret codicil of the Mutual Defense Treaty, chopped to Israeli command in time of emergency – a situation that was defined by Israel. That was totally unprecedented in American history, the Foreign Minister pointed out.

'So, is our national security degraded or enhanced by the treaties?' the Prime Minister asked.

'It is somewhat enhanced,' the Defense Minister admitted.

'Then will you say so?'

Defense pondered that for a moment, his eyes boring in on the man seated at the head of the table. *Will you support me when I make my bid for the premiership?* his eyes asked.

The Prime Minister nodded.

'I will address the crowds. We can live with these treaties.'

The speech did not pacify everyone, but it was enough

to convince a third of the anti-treaty demonstrators to depart. The crucial middle element in the Israeli parliament observed the events, consulted its conscience, and made its decision. The treaties were ratified by a slim margin. Even before the United States Senate had a chance to clear the treaties through the Armed Services and Foreign Relations committees, implementation of both agreements began.

CHAPTER 11

Robosoldiers

They weren't supposed to look human. The Swiss guards were all over 185 centimeters in height and not one weighed less than 85 kilograms, which translated to about six-one and a hundred eighty pounds for American tourists. Their physical fitness was manifest. The guard encampment, just outside the city in what had been a Jewish settlement until less than two weeks before, had its own high-tech gymnasium, and the men were 'encouraged' to pump iron until their exposed skin looked as taut as a drumhead. Their forearms, exposed below rolled-up sleeves, were thicker than the lower legs of most men, and already tanned brown beneath what were often sun-bleached blond hairs. Their mostly blue eyes were always hidden behind dark glasses in the case of the officers, and tinted Lexan shields for the rest.

They were outfitted in fatigues of an urban-camouflage pattern, a curious design of black, white, and several shades of gray that allowed them to blend in with the stones and whitewashed stucco of Jerusalem in a way that was eerily effective, especially at night. Their boots were the same, not the spit-shined elegance of parade soldiers. The helmets were Kevlar, covered with cloth of the same pattern. Over the fatigues went camou-flaged flak jackets of American design that merely seemed to increase the physical bulk of the soldiers. Over the flak jackets came the web gear. Each man always carried four fragmentation grenades and two smokes, plus a one-liter canteen, first-aid packet, and ammo pouches for a light total load-out of about twelve kilos.

They traveled about the city in teams of five, one non-com and four privates per team, and twelve teams to each duty section. Each man carried a SIG assault rifle, two of which had grenade launchers slung underneath the barrel. The sergeant also carried a pistol, and two men in each team carried radios. The teams on patrol were in constant radio contact and regularly practiced mutual-support maneuvers.

Half of each duty section walked, while the other half moved about slowly and menacingly in American-built HMMWVs. Essentially an oversized jeep, each 'hummer' had at least a pintel-mounted machine-gun, and some had six-barreled miniguns, plus Kevlar armor to protect the crews against the casual enemy. At the commanding note of their horns, everyone cleared a path.

At the command post were several armored fighting vehicles – English-built armored cars that could just barely navigate the streets of the ancient city. Always on duty at the post was a platoon-sized unit commanded by a captain. This was the emergency-response team. They were armed with heavy weapons, like the Swedish Carl Gustav M-2 recoilless, just the right thing for knocking a hole in any building. Supporting *them* was an engineer section with copious quantities of high explosives; the 'sappers' ostentatiously practiced by knocking down those settlements which Israel had agreed to abandon. In fact, the entire regiment practiced its combat skills at those sites, and people were allowed to observe from a few hundred meters away in what was rapidly becoming a genuine tourist attraction. Already, Arab merchants were producing T-shirts with logos like ROBOSOLDIER! for anyone who cared to buy them. The commercial sense of the merchants was not unrewarded.

The Swiss guards did not smile, nor did they speak to the casual interrogator, a facility that came easily to them. Journalists were encouraged to meet with the commanding officer, Colonel Jacques Schwindler, and were occasionally allowed to speak with lower ranks in barracks or at training exercises, but never on the street. Some contact with the locals was inevitable, of course.

The soldiers were learning rudimentary Arabic, and English sufficed for everyone else. They occasionally issued traffic citations, though this was mainly a function of the local civil police force that was still forming up – with support from the Israelis who were phasing out of the function. More rarely a Swiss guard would step into a street fight or other disturbance. Most often the mere sight of a five-man team would reduce people to respectful silence and docile civility. The mission of the Swiss was intimidation, and it didn't require many days for people to appreciate how good they were at it. At the same time, their operations depended most of all on something other than the physical.

On the right shoulder of each uniform was a patch. It was in the shape of a shield. The centerpiece was the white cross on red background of the Swiss, to demonstrate the origin of the soldiers. Around it were the Star and Crescent of Islam, the six-pointed Judaic Star of David, and the Christian Cross. There were three versions of the patch, so that each religious emblem had an equal chance of being on top. It was publicly known that the patches were distributed at random, and the symbology indicated that the Swiss flag protected them all equally.

The soldiers deferred always to religious leaders. Colonel Schwindler met daily with the religious troika which governed the city. It was believed that they alone made policy, but Schwindler was a clever, thoughtful man, whose suggestions from the first had carried great weight with the Imam, the Rabbi, and the Patriarch. Schwindler had also traveled to the capitals of every Middle East nation. The Swiss had chosen well – he'd been known as the best colonel in their army. An honest and scrupulously fair man, he'd acquired an enviable reputation. Already on his office wall was a gold-mounted sword, a present from the King of Saudi Arabia. A stallion of equal magnificence was quartered at the guard force encampment. Schwindler didn't know how to ride.

It was up to the troika to run the city. They had proven

314

to be even more effective than anyone had dared to hope. Chosen for their piety and scholarship, each soon impressed the others. It had been agreed upon at once that each week there would be a public prayer service particular to one of the represented religions, and that each would attend, not actually participating, but demonstrating the respect that was at the foundation of their collective purpose. Originally suggested by the Imam, it had unexpectedly proven to be the most effective method of tempering their internal disagreements and also setting the example for the citizens of the city in their care. This was not to say that there were not disagreements. But those were invariably difficulties between two of the members, and in such cases the uninvolved third would mediate. It was in the interests of all to reach a peaceful and reasonable settlement. 'The Lord God' – a phrase each of the three could use without prejudice – required their good will, and after a few initial teething problems, that good will prevailed. Over coffee, after concluding one dispute over scheduling access to one shrine or another, the Greek Patriarch noted with a chuckle that perhaps this was the first miracle he had ever witnessed. No, the Rabbi had replied, it was no miracle that men of God should have the conviction to obey their own religious principles. All at once? the Imam had asked with a smile, perhaps not a miracle, but certainly it had required over a millennium to achieve. Let us not begin a new dispute, the Greek had said with a rumbling laugh, over the settlement of another – now, if you can only help me find a way to deal with my fellow Christians!

Outside on the streets, when clerics of one faith encountered those of another, greetings were exchanged to set an example for everyone. The Swiss Guards saluted each in their turn, and when speaking with the most senior, they would remove their glasses or helmets to show public respect.

That was the only humanity the Swiss Guards were allowed to demonstrate. It was said that they didn't even sweat.

'Scary sons of bitches,' Ryan observed, standing in shirt-sleeves at a corner. American tourists snapped pictures. Jews still looked a touch resentful. Arabs smiled. The Christians who'd largely been driven out of Jerusalem by increasing violence had barely started to return. Everyone got the hell out of their way as the five men moved briskly down the street, not quite marching, their helmeted heads turning left and right. 'They really do look like robots.'

'You know,' Avi said, 'there hasn't been a single attack on them since the first week. Not one.'

'I wouldn't want to fool with them,' Clark observed quietly.

In the first week, as though by Providence, an Arab youth had killed an elderly Israeli woman with a knife – it had been a street robbery rather than a crime with political significance – and had made the mistake of doing so in view of a Swiss private, who'd run him down and subdued him with a martial-arts blow right out of a movie. The Arab in question had been taken to the troika and given the choice of a trial by Israeli or Islamic law. He'd made the mistake of choosing the latter. After a week in an Israeli hospital to allow his injuries to heal, he'd faced a trial in accordance with the word of the Koran, chaired by Imam Ahmed bin Yussif. One day after that, he had been flown to Riyadh, Saudi Arabia, driven to a public square, and, after having had time to repent his misdeeds, publicly beheaded with a sword. Ryan wondered how you said *pour encourager les autres* in Hebrew, Greek, and Arabic. Israelis had been amazed at the speed and severity of justice, but the Muslims had merely shrugged and pointed out that the Koran had its own stern criminal code, and that it had proven highly effective over the years.

'Your people are still a little unhappy with this, aren't they?'

Avi frowned. Ryan had faced him with the necessity of expressing his personal opinion, or speaking the truth. 'They'd feel safer with our paratroops here . . . man-to-man, Ryan?' Truth won out, as it had to with Avi.

'Sure.'

'They'll learn. It will take a few more weeks, but they will learn. The Arabs like the Swiss, and the key to the peace on this street is how our Arab friends feel. Now, will you tell me something?' Clark's head moved fractionally at that.

'Maybe,' Ryan answered, looking up the street.

'How much did you have to do with this?'

'Nothing at all,' Jack replied with a neutral coldness that matched the pace of the soldiers. 'It was Charlie Alden's idea, remember? I was just the messenger boy.'

'So Elizabeth Elliot has told everyone.' Avi didn't have to say any more.

'You wouldn't have asked the question unless you knew the answer, Avi. So why ask the question?'

'Artfully done.' General Ben Jakob sat down and waved for the waiter. He ordered two beers before speaking again. Clark and the other bodyguard weren't drinking. 'Your president pushed us too hard. Threatening us with withholding our arms . . .'

'He could have gone a little easier, I suppose, but I do not make policy, Avi. Your people made it happen when they murdered those demonstrators. That reopened a part of our own history that we wish to forget. It neutralized your congressional lobby – a lot of those people were on the other side of our own civil rights movement, remember. You forced us to move, Avi. You know that. Besides –' Ryan stopped abruptly.

'Yes?'

'Avi, this thing just might work. I mean, look around!' Jack said, as the beers arrived. He was thirsty enough that a third of it disappeared in an instant.

'It is a slim possibility,' Ben Jakob admitted.

'You get better intel from Syria than we do,' Ryan pointed out. 'I've heard that they've started saying nice things about the settlement – very quietly, I admit. Am I right?'

'If it's true.' Avi grunted.

'You know the hard part about "peace" intel?'

Ben Jakob's eyes were focused on a distant wall as he contemplated – what? 'Believing it is possible?'

Jack nodded. 'That's one area where we have the advantage over you guys, my friend. We've been through all that.'

'True, but the Soviets never said – proclaimed – for two generations that they wanted to wipe you from the face of the earth. Tell the worthy President Fowler that such concerns are not so easily allayed.'

Jack sighed. 'I have. I did. Avi, I'm not your enemy.'

'Neither are you my ally.'

'Allies? We are now, General. The treaties are in force. General, my job is to provide information and analysis to my government. Policy is made by people senior to me, and smarter than me,' Ryan added with deadpan irony.

'Oh? And who might they be?' General Ben Jakob smiled at the younger man. His voice dropped a few octaves. 'You've been in the trade for what – not even ten years, Jack. The submarine business, what you did in Moscow, the role you played in the last election –'

Ryan tried to control his reaction, but failed. 'Jesus, Avi!' *How the hell did he find that out!*

'You cannot take the Lord's name in vain, Dr Ryan,' the deputy chief of the Mossad chided. 'This is the City of God. Those Swiss chaps might shoot you. Tell the lovely Miss Elliot that if she pushes too hard, we still have friends in your media, and a story such as that . . .' Avi smiled.

'Avi, if your people mention that to Liz, she will not know what you are talking about.'

'Rubbish!' General Ben Jakob snorted.

'You have my word on that, sir.'

It was General Ben Jakob's turn to be surprised. 'That is difficult to believe.'

Jack finished off the beer. 'Avi, I've said what I can. Has it ever occurred to you that your information may not have come from an entirely reliable source? I will tell you this: I have no personal knowledge of what you alluded to. If there was any kind of deal, I was kept out of it. Okay, I have reason to believe that something may have happened, and I can even speculate what it might have been, but if I ever have to sit in front of a judge and answer questions, all I can say is that I do not *know* anything. And you, my friend, cannot blackmail someone with something that person doesn't know about. You'd have to do a pretty good selling job just to convince them that something had happened in the first place.'

'My God, what Moore and Ritter set up really was elegant, wasn't it?'

Ryan set down his empty glass. 'Things like that never happen in real life, General. That's movie stuff. Look, Avi, maybe that report you have is a little on the thin side. The spectacular ones often are. Reality never quite keeps up with art, after all.' It was a good play. Ryan grinned to carry the point.

'Dr Ryan, in 1972 the Black September faction of the Palestine Liberation Organization contracted the Japanese Red Army to shoot up Ben Gurion Airport, which they did, killing off mainly American Protestant pilgrims from your island of Puerto Rico. The single terrorist taken alive by our security forces told his interrogators that his dead comrades and their victims would become a constellation of stars in the heavens. In prison he purportedly converted himself to Judaism, and even circumcised himself with his teeth, which speaks volumes for his flexibility,' Brigadier General Avi Ben Jakob added matter-of-factly. 'Do not ever tell me that there is something too mad to be true. I have been an intelligence officer for more than twenty years, and the only thing of which I am certain is that I have not yet seen it all.'

'Avi, even I'm not that paranoid.'

'You have never experienced a holocaust, Dr Ryan.'

'Oh? Cromwell and the Potato Famine don't count? Get off that horse, General. We're deploying the U.S. troops here. If it comes to that, there will be American blood on the Negev, or Golan, or whatever.'

'And what if —'

319

'Avi, you ask what if. If *that* what-if ever happens, General, I will fly here myself. I used to be a Marine. You know I've been shot at before. There will be no second Holocaust. Not while I live. My countrymen will not let it happen ever again. Not my government, Avi, my countrymen. We will not let that happen. If Americans have to die to help protect this country, then Americans will die to do so.'

'You said that to Vietnam.' Clark's eyes flared at that one, Ben Jakob noticed. 'You have something to say?'

'General, I'm no high official, just a grunt with pretensions. But I got more combat time than anybody in this country of yours, and I'm telling you, sir, that what really scares me about this place is how you guys always fuck up the same way we did over there – we learned, you didn't. And what Dr Ryan says is right. He'll come over. So will I, if it comes to that. I've killed my share of enemies, too,' Clark told him in a low, quiet voice.

'Another Marine?' Avi asked lightly, though he knew better.

'Close enough,' Clark said. 'And I've kept current, as they say,' he added with a smile.

'What about your associate?' Avi motioned towards Chavez, who stood casually at the corner, eyeing the street.

'Good as I ever was. So're those kids in the Cav. But this war talk is all bullshit. You guys both know that. You want security, sir, you settle your domestic problems. Peace will follow that like a rainbow after a storm.'

'Learn from your mistakes . . .'

'We had a four-thousand-mile buffer to fall back through, General. It isn't that far from here to the Med. You'd better learn from our mistakes. Good news is, you are better able to make a real peace than we ever were.'

'But to have it imposed –'

'Sir, if it works, you'll thank us. If it doesn't work, we have a lot of people to stand by you when the crap hits the fan.' Clark noticed that Ding had moved casually from his post across the street, moving aimlessly, it seemed, like a tourist . . .

'Including you?'

'Bet your ass, General,' Clark replied, alert now, watching the people on the street. What had Chavez spotted? What had he missed?

Who are they? Ghosn wondered. It took a second. *Brigadier General Abraham Ben Jakob, Deputy Director of the Mossad*, his brain answered after sorting through all the recognition photographs he'd memorized. *Talking to an American. I wonder who he is* . . . Ghosn's head turned slowly and casually. The American would have several bodyguards . . . the one close by was obvious. A very serious fellow that one was, old . . . late forties, perhaps. It was the hardness – no, not hardness, but alertness. One could control the face but not the eyes – ah, the man put sunglasses back on. More than one. Had to be more than one, plus Israeli security officers. Ghosn knew that he'd let his eyes linger a touch too long, but –

'Oops.' A man had bumped into him, a fraction smaller and slighter than Ghosn. Dark complexion, possibly even a brother Arab, but he'd spoken in English. Contact was broken before Ghosn had time to realize that he'd been quickly and expertly frisked. 'Sorry.' The man moved off. Ghosn didn't know, wasn't sure if it had been what it seemed to be or if he'd just been checked out by an Israeli, American, or other security officer. Well, he wasn't carrying a weapon, not even a pocket knife, just a shopping bag full of books.

Clark saw Ding give the all-clear sign, an ordinary gesture, like shooing an insect off his neck. Then why the eye-recognition from the target – anyone who took an interest in his protectee was a target – why had he stopped and looked? Clark turned around. There was a pretty girl just two tables away. Not Arab or Israeli, some sort of European, Germanic language, sounded like, maybe Dutch. Good-looking girl, and such girls attracted looks. Maybe he and the other two had just been between a looker and his lookee. Maybe. For a protective officer, the balance between awareness and paranoia was impossible to draw, even when you understood the tactical environment, and Clark had no such illusions here. On the other hand, they'd selected a random eatery on a random street, and the fact that Ryan was here, and that Ben Jakob and he had decided to look things over . . . nobody had intelligence that good, and nobody had enough troops to cover even a single city – except maybe the Russians in Moscow – to make the threat a real one. But why the eye-recognition?

Well. Clark recorded the face, and it went into the memory hopper with all the hundreds of others.

Ghosn continued his own patrol. He'd purchased all the books he needed, and was now observing the Swiss troops, how they moved, how tough they looked. Avi Ben Jakob, he thought. Missed opportunity. Targets like that one didn't appear every day. He continued down the rough, cobbled street, his eyes vacant as they appeared to scan at random. He'd take the next right, increase his pace, and try to get ahead of the Swiss before they made it to the next cross street. He both admired what he saw in them and regretted that he saw it.

'Nicely done,' Ben Jakob observed to Clark. 'Your subordinate is well-trained.'

'He shows promise.' As Clark watched, Ding Chavez looped back to his lookout point across the street. 'You know the face?'

'No. My people probably got a photograph. We'll check it out, but it was probably a young man with normal sexual drives,' Ben Jakob jerked his head towards the Dutch girl, if that's what she was.

Clark was surprised the Israelis hadn't made a move. A shopping bag could contain anything. And 'anything' had generally negative connotations in this environment. God, he hated this job. Looking out for himself was one thing. He typically used mobility, random paths, irregular pacing, always keeping an eye out for escape routes or ambush opportunities. But Ryan, while he might have had similar instincts – tactically speaking, the DDCI was pretty swift, Clark judged – had an over-developed sense of faith in the competence of his two bodyguards.

'So, Avi?' Ryan asked.

'Well, the first echelon of your cavalry troops is settling in. Our tank people like your Colonel Diggs. I must say I find their regimental crest rather odd – a bison is just a kind of wild cow, after all.' Avi chuckled.

'As with a tank, Avi, you probably don't want to stand in front of one.' Ryan wondered what would happen when the 10th Cav ran its first full-up training exercise with the Israelis. It was widely believed in the U.S. Army that the Israelis were overrated, and Diggs had a big reputation as a kick-ass tactician. 'It looks like I can report to the President that the local situation is showing real signs of promise.'

'There will be difficulties.'

'Of course there will. Avi, the millennium doesn't arrive for a few more years,' Jack noted. 'But did you think things would go so smoothly so fast?'

'No, I didn't,' Ben Jakob admitted. He fished out the cash to pay the check, and both men rose. Clark took his cue and went over to Chavez.

'Well?'

'Just that one guy. Heavy shopping bag, but it looked like books – textbooks, matter of fact. There was a sales slip still in one. Would you believe books on nuclear physics? The one title I saw was, anyway. Big, thick, heavy mother. Maybe he's a grad student or something, and that *is* one pretty lady over there, man.'

'Let's keep our minds on business, Mr Chavez.'

'She's not my type, Mr Clark.'

'What do you think of the Swiss guys?'

'They look awful pretty for track-toads. I wouldn't want to play with them unless I picked the turf and the time, man.' Chavez paused. 'You notice the guy I frisked eyeballed them real hard?'

'No.'

'He did . . . looked like he knew what he was –' Domingo Chavez paused. 'I suppose people around here seen a lot of soldiers. Anyway, he gave 'em a professional sorta look. That's what I noticed first, not the way he eyeballed you and the doc. The guy had smart eyes, y'know what I mean?'

'What else?'

'Moved good, decent shape. Hands looked soft, though, not hard like a soldier. Too old for a college kid, but maybe not for a grad student.' Chavez paused again. 'Jesucristo! this is a paranoid business we're in, man. He was not carrying a weapon. His hands didn't look like he was a martial-arts type. He just came down the street looking at those Swiss grunts, eyeballed over where the doc and his friend were, then he just kept going. End of story.' There were times when Chavez wished he'd opted to remain in the Army. He would have had his degree and his commission by now instead of cramming in night courses at George Mason while he played bodyguard to Ryan. At least the doc was a good guy, and working with Clark was . . . interesting. But this intelligence stuff was a strange life.

'Time to move,' Clark advised.

'I got the point.' Ding's hand checked the automatic clipped under his loose shirt. The Israeli guards were already moving up the street.

Ghosn caught them just as he'd planned. The Swiss had helped. An elderly Muslim cleric had stopped the squad sergeant to ask a question. There was a problem with translation, the imam didn't speak English, and the Swiss soldier's Arabic was still primitive. It was too good an opportunity to pass up.

'Excuse me,' Ghosn said to the imam, 'can I help with translation?' He absorbed the rapid-fire string of his native language and turned to the soldier.

'The imam is from Saudi Arabia. This is his first time in Jerusalem since he was a boy and he requires directions to the Troika's office.'

On recognizing the seniority of the cleric, the sergeant removed his helmet and inclined his head respectfully.

'Please tell him that we would be honored to escort him there.'

'Ah, there you are!' another voice called. It was obviously an Israeli. His Arabic was accented, but literate. 'Good day, Sergeant,' the man added in English.

'Greetings, Rabbi Ravenstein. You know this man?' the soldier asked.

'This is Imam Mohammed Al Faisal, a distinguished scholar and historian from Medina.'

'Is it all I have been told?' Al Faisal asked Ravenstein directly.

'All that and more!' the rabbi replied.

'Excuse me?' Ghosn had to say.

'You are?' Ravenstein asked.

'A student. I was attempting to assist with the language problem.'

'Ah, I see,' Ravenstein said. 'Very kind of you. Mohammed is here to look at a manuscript we uncovered at a dig. It's a scholarly Muslim commentary on a very old Torah, 10th Century, a fantastic find. Sergeant, I can manage things from here, and thank you also, young man.'

'Do you require escort, sir?' the sergeant asked. 'We are heading that way.'

'No, thank you, we are both too old to keep up with you.'

'Very well.' The sergeant saluted. 'Good day.'

The Swiss moved off. The few people who'd taken note of the brief encounter pointed and smiled.

'The commentary is by Al Qalda himself, and it seems to cite the work of Nuchem of Acre,' Ravenstein said. 'The state of preservation is incredible.'

'Then I must see it!' The two scholars began walking down the street as rapidly as their aged legs would carry them, oblivious to everything around them.

Ghosn's face didn't change. He'd shown wonder and amusement for the benefit of the Swiss infantrymen now halfway down the block, themselves with a trailing escort of small children. His discipline allowed him to sidle off to the side, take another turn, and vanish down a narrow alley, but what he had just seen was far more depressing.

Mohammed Al Faisal was one of the five greatest Islamic scholars, a highly-respected historian, and a distant member of the Saudi royal family, despite his unpretentious nature. Except for his age – the man was nearing eighty – he might have been one of the members of the troika running Jerusalem – that and the fact that they'd wanted a scholar of Palestinian ancestry for political reasons. No friend of Israel, and one of the most conservative of the Saudi religious leaders, had he become enamored of the treaty also?

Worse still, the Swiss had treated the man with the utmost respect. Worst of all, the Israeli rabbi had done the same. The people in the streets, nearly all of them Palestinians, had watched it all with amusement and . . . what? Tolerance? Acceptance, as though it were the most natural thing in the world. The Israelis had long ago given lip-service to respect for their Arab neighbors, but that promise had not even been written on sand for all the permanence it had carried.

Ravenstein wasn't like that, of course. Another scholar, living in his own little world of dead things and ideas, he'd often counseled moderation in dealings with Arabs, and handled his archaeological digs with Muslim consultation . . . and now . . .

And now he was a psychological bridge between the Jewish world and the Arab one. People like that would continue doing what they had always done, but now it was not an aberration, was it?

Peace. It was possible. It could happen. It wasn't just another mad dream imposed on the region by outsiders. How quickly the ordinary people were adapting to it. Israelis were leaving their homes. The Swiss had already taken over one settlement and demolished several others. The Saudi commission was set up, and was beginning to work on restoring land parcels to their rightful owners. A great Arab university was planned for the outskirts of Jerusalem, to be built with Saudi money. It was moving so fast! Israelis were resisting, but less than he had expected. In another week, he'd heard from twenty people, tourists would flood the city – hotel bookings were arriving as rapidly as satellite phone links could deliver them. Already two enormous new hotels were being planned for the influx, and on the basis of increased tourism alone the Palestinians here would reap fantastic economic benefits. They were already proclaiming their total political victory over Israel, and had collectively decided to be magnanimous in their triumph – it made financial sense to be so, and the Palestinians had the most highly developed commercial sense in the Arab world.

But Israel would still survive.

Ghosn stopped at a street cafe, set down his bag and ordered a glass of juice. He contemplated the narrow street as he waited. There were Jews and Muslims. Tourists would soon flood the place; the first wave had barely broken at local airports. Muslims, of course, to pray at the Dome of the Rock. Americans with their money, even Japanese, curious at a land even more ancient than their own. Prosperity would soon come to Palestine.

Prosperity was the handmaiden of peace, and the assassin of discontent.

But prosperity was not what Ibrahim Ghosn wanted for his people or his land. Ultimately, perhaps, but only after the other necessary preconditions had been met. He paid for his orange juice with American currency and walked off. Soon he was able to catch a cab. Ghosn had entered Israel from Egypt. He'd leave Jerusalem for Jordan, thence back to Lebanon. He had work to do, and he hoped the books he carried contained the necessary information.

Ben Goodley was a post-doctoral student from Harvard's Kennedy School of Government. A bright, good-looking academic of twenty-seven years, he was also possessed of enough ambition for the entire family after which the school had been named. His doctoral thesis had examined the folly of Vietnam from the intelligence side of the equation, and it had been sufficiently controversial that his professor had forwarded it to Liz Elliot for comment. The National Security Advisor's only beef with Goodley was that he was a man. Nobody was perfect.

'So, exactly what sort of research do you want to do?' she asked him.

'Doctor, I hope to examine the nature of intelligence decisions as they relate to recent changes in Europe and the Middle East. The problem is getting FOI'd into certain areas.'

'And what is your ultimate objective? I mean,' Elliot said, 'is it teaching, writing, government service, what?'

'Government service, of course. The historical environmental demands, I think, that the right people take the right action. My thesis made it clear, didn't it, that we've been badly served by the intelligence community almost continuously since the 1960s. The whole institutional mindset over there is geared in the wrong direction. At least –' he leaned back and tried to look comfortable '– that's how it often appears to an outsider.'

'And why is that, do you think?'

'Recruiting is one problem. The way CIA, for example, selects people really determines how they obtain and analyze data. They create a gigantic self-fulfilling prophecy. Where's their objectivity, where's their ability to see trends? Did they predict 1989? Of course not. What are they missing now? Probably a lot of things. It might be nice,' Goodley said, 'to get a handle on the important issues before they become crisis items.'

'I agree.' Elliot watched the young man's shoulders drop as he discreetly let out a deep breath. She decided to play him just a little, just enough to let him know whom he'd be working for. 'I wonder what we can do with you . . . ?' Elliot let her eyes trace across the far wall.

'Marcus Cabot has an opening for a research assistant. You'll need a security clearance, and you'll need to sign a very strict non-disclosure agreement. You cannot publish anything without having it cleared in advance.'

'That's almost prior-restraint,' Goodley pointed out. 'What about the Constitutional issue?'

'Government must keep some secrets if it is to function. You may have access to some remarkable information. Is getting published your goal, or is it what you said? Public service does require some sacrifices.'

'Well . . .'

'There will be some important openings at CIA in the next few years,' Elliot promised.

'I see,' Goodley said, quite truthfully. 'I never intended to publish classified information, of course.'

'Of course,' Elliot agreed. 'I can handle that through my office, I suppose. I found your paper impressive. I want a mind like yours working for the government, if you can agree to the necessary restrictions.'

'In that case, I guess I can accept them.'

'Fine.' Elliot smiled. 'You are now a White House Fellow. My secretary will take you across the street to the security office. You have a bunch of forms to fill out.'

'I already have a "secret" clearance.'

'You'll need more than that. You'll have to get a SAP/SAR clearance – that means "special-access programs/special access required." It normally takes a few months for that –'

'Months?' Goodley asked.

'I said "usually." We can fast-track part of that. I suggest you start apartment-hunting. The stipend is sufficient?'

'Quite sufficient.'

'Fine. I'll call Marcus over at Langley. You'll want to meet him.' Goodley beamed at the National Security Advisor. 'Glad to have you on the team.'

The new White House Fellow took his cue and stood. 'I will try not to disappoint you.'

Elliot watched him leave. It was so easy to seduce people, she knew. Sex was a useful tool for the task, but power and ambition were so much better. She'd already proven that, Elliot smiled to herself.

*

'An atomic bomb?' Bock asked.

'So it would seem,' Qati replied.

'Who else knows?'

'Ghosn is the one who discovered it. Only he.'

'Can it be used?' the German asked. *And why have you told me?*

'It was severely damaged and must be repaired. Ibrahim is now assembling the necessary information for evaluating the task. He thinks it possible.'

Günther leaned back. 'This is not some elaborate ruse? An Israeli trick, perhaps an American one?'

'If so, it is a very clever one,' Qati said, then explained the circumstances of the discovery.

'1973 . . . it does fit. I remember how close the Syrians came to destroying the Israelis . . .' Bock was silent for a moment. He shook his head briefly. 'How to use such a thing . . .'

'That is the question, Günther.'

'Too early to ask such a question. First, you must determine if the weapon can be repaired. Second, you must determine its explosive yield – no, before that you must determine its size, weight, and portability. That is the most important consideration. After that comes the yield – I will assume that –' He fell silent. 'Assume? I know little of such weapons. They cannot be too heavy. They can be fired from artillery shells of less than twenty-centimeter diameter. I know that much.'

'This one is much larger than that, my friend.'

'You should not have told me this, Ismael. In a matter like this one, security is everything. You cannot trust anyone with knowledge such as this. People talk, people boast. There could be penetration agents in your organization.'

'It was necessary. Ghosn knows that he will need some help. What contacts do you have in the DDR?'

'What sort?' Qati told him. 'I know a few engineers, people who worked in the DDR nuclear program . . . it's a dead program, you know.'

'How so?'

'Honecker was planning to build several reactors

of the Russian sort. When Germany reunited, their environmental activists took one look at the design and – well, you can imagine. The Russian designs do not have a sterling reputation, do they?' Bock grunted. 'As I keep telling you, the Russians are a backward people. Their reactors, one fellow told me, were designed mainly for production of nuclear material for weapons . . .'

'And . . .'

'And it is likely that there was a nuclear-weapons program within the DDR. Interesting, I never thought that through, did I?' Bock asked himself quietly. 'What exactly do you want me to do?'

'I need you to travel to Germany and find some people – we would prefer merely one, for obvious reasons – to assist us.'

Back to Germany? Bock asked himself. 'I'll need –'

Qati tossed an envelope into his friend's lap. 'Beirut has been a crossroads for centuries. Those travel documents are better than the real ones.'

'You will need to move your location immediately,' Bock said. 'If I am caught, you will have to assume that they will get every bit of information I have. They broke Petra. They can break me or anyone else they wish.'

'I will pray for your safety. In that envelope is a telephone number. When you return, we will be elsewhere.'

'When do I leave?'

'Tomorrow.'

CHAPTER 12

Tinsmiths

'And I'll raise you a dime,' Ryan said, after taking his draw.

'You're bluffing,' Chavez said after a sip of beer.

'I never bluff,' Jack replied.

'Out.' Clark tossed in his cards.

'They all say that,' the Air Force sergeant observed. 'See your dime and bump you a quarter.'

'Call,' Chavez said.

'Three jacks.'

'Beats my eights,' the sergeant groused.

'But not a straight, Doc.' Ding finished off his beer. 'Gee, that puts me five bucks ahead.'

'Never count your winnings at the table, son,' Clark advised soberly.

'I never did like that song.' Chavez grinned. 'But I like this game.'

'I thought soldiers were lousy gamblers,' the Air Force sergeant observed sourly. He was three bucks down, and he was a real poker player. He got to practice against politicians all the time on long flights when they needed a good dealer.

'One of the first things they teach you at CIA is how to mark cards,' Clark announced, as he went for the next round of drinks.

'Always knew I should have taken the course at The Farm,' Ryan said. He was about even, but every time he'd had a good hand, Chavez had held a better one. 'Next time, I'll let you play with my wife.'

'She good?' Chavez asked.

'She's a surgeon. She deals seconds so smooth she can

fool a professional mechanic. She plays with cards as a kind of dexterity exercise,' Ryan explained with a grin. 'I *never* let her deal.'

'Mrs Ryan would never do anything like that,' Clark said, when he sat back down.

'Your turn to deal,' Ding said.

Clark started shuffling, something he also did fairly well. 'So, what you think, Doc?'

'Jerusalem? Better than I hoped. How about you?'

'Last time I was there – '84, I think – God, it was like Olongapo in the P.I. You could smell it – the trouble, I mean. You couldn't actually see it, but, man, it was there. You could feel people watching you. Now? It's sure chilled out some. How about some five-card stud?' Clark asked.

'Dealer's choice,' the sergeant agreed.

Clark dealt the hole cards, then the first set of up cards. 'Nine of spades to the Air Force. Five of diamonds to our Latino friend. Queen of clubs to the doc, and the dealer gets – how about that? Dealer gets an ace. Ace bets a quarter.'

'Well, John?' Ryan asked after the first round of bets.

'You do put a lot of faith in my powers of observation, Jack. We'll know for sure in a couple of months, but I'd say it looks all right.' He dealt four more cards. 'Possible straight – possible straight flush to the Air Force. Your bet, sir.'

'Another quarter.' The Air Force sergeant felt lucky. 'The Israeli security guys have mellowed out some, too.'

'How so?'

'Dr Ryan, the Israelis really know about security. Every time we fly over here, they put a wall up around the bird, y'know? This time the wall wasn't so high. I talked to a couple of 'em, and they're more relaxed – not officially, but personal, y'know? Used to be they hardly talked at all. Looked like a big difference to me, anyway.'

Ryan smiled as he decided to fold. His eight, queen, and deuce weren't going anywhere. It never failed. You always got better data from sergeants than generals.

*

'What we have here,' Ghosn said, flipping his book to the right page, 'is essentially an Israeli copy of an American Mark-12 fission bomb. It's a boosted-fission design.'

'What does that mean?' Qati asked.

'It means that tritium is squirted into the core just as the act of firing begins. That generates more neutrons and greatly increases the efficiency of the reaction. As a result, you need only a small amount of fissionable material . . .'

'But?' Qati heard the 'but' coming.

Ghosn leaned back and stared at the core of the device. 'But the mechanism to insert the boost material was destroyed by the impact. The kryton switches for the conventional explosives are no longer reliable and must be replaced. We have enough intact explosive blocks to determine their proper configuration, but manufacturing new ones will be very difficult. Unfortunately, I cannot depend on simply reverse-engineering the entire weapon. I must duplicate the original design theoretically first, determine what it can and cannot do, then re-invent the processes for fabrication. Do you have any idea what the original cost for that was?'

'No,' Qati admitted, sure that he was about to learn.

'More than what it cost to land people on the moon. The most brilliant minds in human history were part of this process: Einstein, Fermi, Bohr, Oppenheimer, Teller, Alvarez, von Neumann, Lawrence – a hundred others! The giants of physics in this century. Giants.'

'You're telling me you cannot do it?'

Ghosn smiled. 'No, Commander, I am telling you that I can. What is the work of genius the first time is the work of a tinsmith soon thereafter. It required genius the first time because it *was* the first time, and also because technology was so primitive. All the calculations had to be done manually at first, on big mechanical calculators. All the work on the first hydrogen bomb was done on the first primitive computers – Eniac, I think it was called. But today?' Ghosn laughed. It really was absurd. 'A videogame has more computing power than Eniac ever did. I can run the calculations on a high-end personal computer in seconds and duplicate what took Einstein months. But the most important thing is that they did not really know if it was possible. It is, and I know *that*! Next, they made records of how they proceeded. Finally, I have a template, and though I cannot reverse-engineer it entirely, I can use this as a theoretical model.

'You know, given two or three years, I could do it all myself.'

'Do you think we have two or three years?'

Ghosn shook his head. He'd already reported on what he saw in Jerusalem. 'No, Commander. We surely do not.'

Qati explained what he had ordered their German friend to do.

'That is good. Where do we move to?'

Berlin was once more the capital of Germany. It had been Bock's plan that this should be so, of course, but not that it should be this sort of Germany. He'd flown in from Italy – via Greece, and, before that, Syria – and cleared passport control with scarcely a wave. From that point, he'd simply rented a car and driven out of Berlin on highway E-74 north towards Greifswald.

Günther had rented a Mercedes Benz. He rationalized this by telling himself that his cover was that of a businessman, and besides he hadn't rented the biggest one available. There were times when he thought he might as well have rented a bicycle. This road had been neglected by the DDR government, and now that the Federal Republic was fully in place, the highway was little more than a linear repair gang. It went without saying that the other side of the road was already fixed. His peripheral vision caught hundreds of big, powerful Benzes and BMWs streaking south towards Berlin as the capitalists from the West blazed about to reconquer economically what had collapsed under political betrayal.

Bock took his exit outside Greifswald, driving east through the town of Kemnitz. The attempts at road repair had not yet reached the secondary roads. After hitting half a dozen potholes Günther had to pull over and consult his map. He proceeded three kilometers, then made a series of turns, ending up on what had once been an up-scale neighborhood of professionals. In the driveway of the house he sought was a Trabant. The grass was still neatly trimmed, of course, and the house was neatly arranged, down to the even curtains in the windows – this was Germany, after all – but there was an air of disrepair and depression not so much seen as felt. Bock parked his car a block away and walked an indirect route back to the house.

'I am here to see Herr Doktor Fromm,' he told the woman, Frau Fromm, probably, who answered the door.

'Who may I say is calling?' she asked formally. She was in her middle forties, her skin tight over severe cheeks, with too many lines radiating from her dull blue eyes and tight, colorless lips. She examined the man on her front step with interest, and perhaps a little hope. Though Bock had no idea why this should be so, he took the chance to make use of it.

'An old friend,' Bock smiled to reinforce the image. 'May I surprise him?'

She wavered for a moment, then her face changed and good manners took hold. 'Please come in.'

Bock waited in the sitting room, and he realized that his impression was right – but why it was right struck him hard. The interior of the house reminded him of his own apartment in Berlin. The same specially-made furniture that had once looked so good in contrast to what was available for ordinary citizens in the German Democratic Republic did not impress as it once had. Perhaps it was the Mercedes he'd driven up, Bock told himself, as he heard footsteps approaching. But no. It was dust. Frau Fromm was not cleaning the house as a good German *Hausfrau* did. A sure sign that something was badly wrong.

'Yes?' Dr Manfred Fromm said, as a question before his eyes widened in delayed recognition. 'Ah, so good to see you!'

'I wondered if you'd remember your old friend Hans,' Bock said with a chuckle, stretching out his hand. 'A long time, Manfred.'

'A very long time indeed, *Junge*! Come to my study.' The two men walked off under the inquisitive eyes of Frau Fromm. Dr Fromm closed the door behind himself before speaking.

'I am sorry about your wife. It was unspeakable what happened.'

'That is past. How are you doing?'

'You haven't heard? The "Greens" have attacked us. We're about to shut down.'

Doktor Manfred Fromm was, on paper, the deputy assistant director of the Lubmin/Nord Nuclear Power Station. The station had been built twenty years earlier from the Soviet VVER Model 230 design, which, primitive as it was, had been adequate with an expert German operations team. Like all Soviet designs of the period, the reactor was a plutonium producer, which, as had been proven at Chernobyl, was neither terribly efficient nor especially safe, but did carry the benefit of producing weapons-grade nuclear material, in addition to 816 megawatts of electrical power from its two functioning reactors.

'The Greens,' Bock repeated quietly. 'Them.' The Green Party was a natural consequence of the German national spirit, which venerated all growing things on one hand, while trying very hard to kill them on the other. Formed from the extreme – or the consistent – elements of the environmental movement, it had fought against many things equally upsetting to the Communist Bloc. But where it had failed to prevent the deployment of theater nuclear weapons – and after their successful deployment had resulted in the INF Treaty, which had eliminated all such weapons on both sides of the line – it was now successfully raising the purest form of political hell in what had once been the German Democratic Republic. The nightmare of pollution in the East was now the obsession of the Greens, and number one on their hit list was the nuclear-power industry, which they called hideously unsafe. Bock reminded himself that the Greens had never truly been under proper political control. The party would never be a major power in German politics, and now it was being exploited by the same government that it had once annoyed. Whereas once the Greens had shrieked about the pollution of the Ruhr and the Rhein from Krupp, and howled about the deployment of NATO nuclear arms, now it was crusading in the East more fervently than Barbarossa had ever attempted in the Holy Land. Their incessant carping on the mess in the East was ensuring that socialism would not soon return to Germany. It was enough to make both men wonder if the Greens had not been a subtle capitalist ploy from the very beginning.

Fromm and the Bocks had met five years earlier. The Red Army Faction had come up with a plan to sabotage a West German reactor, and wanted technical advice on how to do so most efficiently. Though never revealed to the public, their plan had been thwarted only at the last minute. Publicity on the BND's intelligence success would conversely have threatened Germany's own nuclear industry.

'Less than a year until they shut us down for good. I only go in to work three days a week now. I've been replaced by a "technical expert" from the West. He lets me "advise" him, of course,' Fromm reported.

'There must be more, Manfred,' Bock observed. Fromm had also been the chief engineer in Erich Honecker's most cherished military project. Though allies within the World Socialist Brotherhood, the Russians and the Germans could never have been true friends. The bad blood between the nations stretched back a thousand years, and while Germany had at least made a go of socialism, the Russians had failed completely. As a result, the East German military had never been anything like the much larger force in the West. To the last, the Russians had feared Germans, even those on their own side, before incomprehensibly allowing the country to be unified. Erich Honecker had decided that such distrust might have strategic ramifications, and had drawn plans to keep some of the plutonium produced at Greifswald and elsewhere. Manfred Fromm knew as much about nuclear bomb design as any Russian or American, even if he'd never quite been able to put his expertise into play. The plutonium stockpile secretly accumulated over ten years had been turned over to the Russians as a final gesture of Marxist fealty, lest the Federal German government get it. That last honorable act had resulted in angry recriminations – angry enough that one other cache of material had never been turned over. What connections Fromm and his colleagues had once had with the Soviets were completely gone.

'Oh, I have a fine offer.' Fromm lifted a manila envelope on his cluttered desk. 'They want me to go to Argentina. My counterparts in the West have been there for years, along with most of the chaps I worked with.'

'What do they offer?'

Fromm snorted. 'One million D-Mark per year until the project is completed. No difficulties with taxes, numbered account, all the normal enticements,' Fromm said with an emotionless voice. And that, of course, was quite impossible. Fromm could no more work for Fascists than he could breathe water. His grandfather, one of the original Spartacists, had died in one of the first labor camps soon after Hitler's accession to power. His father had been part of the Communist underground and a player in a spy ring, had somehow survived the war despite the systematic hunting of the *Gestapo* and the *Sicherheitsdienst*, and been an honored local Party member to the day of his death. Fromm had learned Marxism-Leninism while he'd learned to walk, and the elimination of his profession had not enamored him of the new political system which he'd been educated to despise. He'd lost his job, had never fulfilled his prime ambition, and was now being treated like an office boy by some pink-cheeked engineer's assistant from Göttingen. Worst of all, his wife wanted him to take the job in Argentina and was making a further hell of his life so long as he refused to consider it. Finally he had to ask his question. 'Why are you here, Günther? The entire country is looking for you, and despite that fine disguise, you are in danger here.'

Bock smiled confidently. 'Isn't it amazing what new hair and glasses can do for you?'

'That does not answer my question.'

'I have friends who need your skills.'

'What friends might those be?' Fromm asked dubiously.

'They are politically acceptable to me and to you. I have not forgotten Petra,' Bock replied.

'That was a good plan we put together, wasn't it? What went wrong?'

'We had a spy among us. Because of her, they changed the security arrangements at the plant three days before we were supposed to go in.'

'A Green?'

Günther allowed himself a bitter smile. '*Ja*, she had second thoughts about possible civilian casualties and damage to the environment. Well, she is now part of the environment.' Petra had done the shooting, her husband remembered. There was nothing worse than a spy, and it was fitting that Petra should have done the execution.

'Part of the environment, you say? How poetic.' It was Fromm's first attempt at levity, and about as successful as all his attempts. Manfred Fromm was a singularly humorless man.

'I cannot offer you money. In fact, I cannot tell you anything else. You must decide on the basis of what I have already said.' Bock didn't have a gun, but he did have a knife. He wondered if Manfred knew the alternatives he faced. Probably not. Despite his ideological purity, Fromm was a technocrat, and narrowly focused.

'When do we leave?'

'Are you being watched?'

'No. I had to travel to Switzerland for the "business offer." Such things cannot be discussed in this country, even if it is united and happy,' he explained. 'I made my own travel arrangements. No, I do not think I am being watched.'

'Then we can leave at once. You need not pack anything.'

'What do I tell my wife?' Fromm asked, then wondered

why he'd bothered. It wasn't as though his marriage was a happy one.

'That is your concern.'

'Let me pack some things. It's easier that way. How long...?'

'I do not know.'

It took half an hour. Fromm explained to his wife that he was going to be away for a few days for further business discussions. She gave him a hopeful kiss. Argentina might be nice, and nicer still to be able to live *well* somewhere. Perhaps this old friend had been able to talk sense into him. He drove a Mercedes, after all. Perhaps he knew what the future really held.

Three hours later, Bock and Fromm boarded a flight to Rome. After an hour's layover, their next stop was Turkey, and from there to Damascus, where they checked into a hotel to get some needed rest.

If anything, Ghosn told himself, Marvin Russell was even more formidable-looking than he'd been before. What little excess weight he'd carried had sweated off, and his daily fitness exercises with the soldiers of the movement had only added to an already muscular physique, while the sun had bronzed him until he might almost have been mistaken for an Arab. The one discordant note was his religion. His comrades reported that he was a true pagan, an unbeliever, who prayed to the sun, of all things. It disquieted the Muslims, but people were working, gently, to show him the true faith of Islam, and it was reported that he listened respectfully. It was also reported that he was a dead shot with any weapon to any range; that he was the most lethal hand-to-hand fighter they'd ever encountered – he'd nearly crippled an instructor – and that he had field-craft skills that would impress a fox. A clever, cunning, natural warrior was the overall assessment. Aside from his religious eccentricities, the others liked and admired him.

'Marvin, if you get any tougher, you will frighten me!' Ghosn chuckled at his American friend.

'Ibrahim, this is the best thing I've ever done, coming

341

here. I never knew that there were other folks who been fucked over like my people, man – but you guys are better at fighting back. You guys got real balls.' Ghosn blinked at that – this from a man who'd snapped a policeman's neck like a twig. 'I really want to help, man, any way I can.'

'There is always a place for a true warrior.' If his language skills improved, he'd make a fine instructor, Ghosn thought. 'Well, I must be off.'

'Where are you going?'

'A place we have east of here.' It was to the north. 'Some special work I must do.'

'That thing we dug up?' Russell asked casually. Almost too casually, Ghosn thought, but that was not possible, was it? Caution was one thing. Paranoia was another.

'Something else. Sorry, my friend, but we must take our security seriously.'

Marvin nodded. 'It's cool, man. That's what killed my brother, fucking up security. See ya' when you get back.'

Ghosn left for his car and drove out of the camp. He took the Damascus road for an hour. Foreigners so often failed to appreciate how small the Middle East was – the important parts, at least. The drive from Jerusalem to Damascus, for example, would have been a mere two hours on decent roads, though the two cities were the proverbial worlds apart politically ... or had been, Ghosn reminded himself. He'd heard of some ominous rumblings from Syria of late. Was even that government tiring of the struggle? It was easy to call that an impossibility, but that word no longer had its prior meaning.

Five kilometers outside Damascus, he spotted the other car waiting at the prescribed place. He drove past it for two thousand meters, scanning for surveillance before he decided it was safe to turn around. A minute later, he pulled over close to it. The two men got out as they'd been directed to do, and their driver, a member of the Organization, simply drove away.

'Good morning, Günther.'

'And to you, Ibrahim. This is my friend, Manfred.'

Both men got into the back of the car, and the engineer drove off at once.

Ghosn eyed the newcomer in the mirror. Older than Bock, thinner, with deep-sunk eyes. He was poorly dressed for the environment and sweating like a pig. Ibrahim handed back a plastic water bottle. The newcomer wiped off the top with his handkerchief before drinking. *Arabs not sanitary enough for you?* Ghosn wondered. Well, that was not his concern, was it?

The drive to the new location took two hours. Ghosn deliberately took a circuitous route despite the fact that the sun would keep a careful observer informed of their direction. He didn't know what sort of training this Manfred fellow had, and while it was prudent to assume he knew every skill there was, it was also prudent to employ every trick in the book. By the time they arrived at their destination, only a trained reconnaissance soldier would have been able to duplicate the route.

Qati had chosen well. Until a few months earlier, it had been a command center for Hezbollah. Dug into the side of a steep hillside, the corrugated-iron roof was covered with earth and planted with the sparse local shrubbery. Only a skilled man who knew exactly what he was looking for could ever have spotted it, and that was unlikely. Hezbollah was particularly adept at routing out informers in its midst. A dirt track ran right past it to an abandoned farm whose land was too played-out even for opium and hashish production, which was the major cash crop in the area. Inside the structure was about a hundred square meters of concrete-floored shade, even with room to park a few vehicles. The only bad news was that this place would be a deathtrap in case of an earthquake, Ghosn told himself, not an unknown occurrence in the region. He pulled the car in between two posts, out of sight. On leaving the car, he dropped camouflage netting behind it. Yes, Qati had chosen well.

The hardest balance, as always, was choosing between the two aspects of security. On the one hand, the more people who knew that anything was happening, the worse it was. On the other, some people were necessary just to provide a guard force. Qati had brought most of his personal guard, ten men of known loyalty and skill. They knew Ghosn and Bock by sight, and their leader came forward to meet Manfred.

'This is our new friend,' Ghosn told the man, who looked closely at the German's face and walked away.

'*Was gibt's hier?*' Fromm asked in tense German.

'What we have here,' Ghosn answered in English, 'is very interesting.'

Manfred took his lesson from that.

'*Kommen Sie mit, bitte.*' Ghosn led them to a wall with a door in it. A man with a rifle stood outside of it, which made much better sense than a lock. The engineer nodded to the guard, who nodded curtly back. Ghosn led them into the room and pulled a cord to turn on the fluorescent lighting. There was a large metal work table covered with a tarp. Ghosn removed the tarp without further comment. He was tiring of the drama in any case. It was time for real work.

'*Gott im Himmel!*'

'I've never seen it myself,' Bock admitted. 'So that is what it looks like?'

Fromm put on some glasses and peered over the mechanism for perhaps a minute before looking up. 'American design, but not American manufacture.' He pointed. 'Wrong sort of wiring. Crude device, thirty years – no, older than that in design, but not in fabrication. These circuit boards are . . . 1960s, perhaps early '70s. Soviet? From the cache in Azerbaijan, perhaps?'

Ghosn merely shook his head.

'Israeli? *Ist das möglich?*' That question got a nod.

'More than possible, my friend. It is here.'

'Gravity bomb. Tritium injection into the pit to boost yield – 50 to 70 kilotons, I'd guess – radar and impact fusing. It has actually been dropped, but did not go off. Why?'

'Apparently it was never armed. Everything we recovered is before you,' Ghosn answered. He was already impressed with Manfred.

Fromm ran his fingers inside the bombcase, searching for connectors. 'You're correct. How interesting.' There

344

was a long pause. 'You know that it can probably be repaired . . . and even . . .'

'Even what?' Ghosn asked, knowing the answer.

'This design can be converted into a triggering device.'

'For what?' Bock asked.

'For a hydrogen bomb,' Ghosn answered. 'I suspected that.'

'Awfully heavy, nothing like the efficiency of a modern design. As they say, crude but effective . . .' Fromm looked up. 'You want my help to repair it, then?'

'Will you help?' Ghosn asked.

'Ten years – more, twenty years I have studied and thought . . . How will it be used?'

'Does that trouble you?'

'It will not be used in Germany?'

'Of course not,' Ghosn answered, almost in annoyance. What quarrel did the Organization really have with the Germans, after all?

Something in Bock's mind, however, went *click*. He closed his eyes for a moment to engrave the thought in his memory.

'Yes, I will help.'

'You will be well-paid,' Ghosn promised him. He saw a moment later that this was a mistake. But that didn't matter, did it?

'I do not do such things for money! You think I am a mercenary?' Fromm asked indignantly.

'Excuse me. I meant no insult. A skilled worker is someone to be rewarded for his time. We are not beggars, you know.'

Neither am I, Fromm almost said, before his good sense intervened. These were not the Argentines, were they? They were not Fascists, not capitalists, they were revolutionary comrades who had also fallen upon bad political times . . . though he was sure their fiscal situation was highly favorable indeed. The Soviets had never *given* arms to the Arabs. It had all been sold for hard currency, even under Brezhnev and Andropov, and if that had been good enough for the Soviets when they still held the true faith . . . then . . .

'Forgive me. I merely stated a fact, and I did not mean to insult you, either. I know you are not beggars. You are revolutionary soldiers, freedom fighters, and I will be honored to assist you in any way I can.' He waved his hand. 'You may feel free to pay me whatever you think fair –' it would be plenty, more than a mere million D-Mark! '– but please understand that I do not sell myself for money.'

'It is a pleasure to meet an honorable man,' Ghosn said, with a satisfied look.

Bock thought they had both laid it on rather thick, but kept his peace. He already suspected how Fromm would be paid.

'So,' Ghosn said next. 'Where do we begin?'

'First, we think. I need paper and pencil.'

'And who might you be?' Ryan asked.

'Ben Goodley, sir.'

'Boston?' Ryan asked. The accent was quite distinctive.

'Yes, sir. Kennedy School. I'm a post-doctoral fellow and, well, now I'm a White House Fellow also.'

'Nancy?' Ryan turned to his secretary.

'The Director has him on your calendar, Dr Ryan.'

'Okay, Dr Goodley,' Ryan said with a smile, 'come on in.' Clark took his seat after sizing the new guy up.

'Want some coffee?'

'You have decaf?' Goodley asked.

'You want to work here, boy, you'd better get used to the real stuff. Grab a seat. Sure you don't want any?'

'I'll pass, sir.'

'Okay.' Ryan poured his customary mug and sat down behind his desk. 'So, what are you doing in this puzzle palace?'

'The short version is, looking for a job. I did my dissertation on intelligence operations, their history and prospects. I need to see some things to finish my work at Kennedy, then I want to find out if I can do the real thing.'

Jack nodded. That sounded familiar enough. 'Clearances?'

'TS, SAP/SAR. Those are new. I already have a "secret", because some of my work at Kennedy involved going into some presidential archives, mainly in D.C., but some of the stuff in Boston is still sensitive. I was even part of the team that FOI'd a lot of stuff from the Cuban Missile Crisis.'

'Dr Nicholas Bledsoe, his work?'

'That's right.'

'I didn't buy all of Nick's conclusions, but that was a hell of a piece of research.' Jack raised his mug in salute.

Goodley had written nearly half of that monograph, including the conclusions. 'What did you take issue with – if I may ask?'

'Khrushchev's action was fundamentally irrational. I think – and the record bears this out – that his placing the missiles there was impulsive rather than reasoned.'

'I disagree. The paper pointed out that the principal Soviet concern was our IRBMs in Europe, especially the ones in Turkey. It seems logical to conclude that it was all a ploy to reach a stable situation regarding theater forces.'

'Your paper didn't report on everything,' Jack said.

'Such as?' Goodley asked, hiding his annoyance.

'Such as the intel we were getting from Penkovskiy and others. Those documents are still classified, and will remain so for another twenty years.'

'Isn't fifty years a long time?'

'Sure is,' Ryan agreed. 'But there's a reason. Some of that information is still – well, not exactly current, but it would reveal some tricks we don't want revealed.'

'Isn't that just a *little* extreme?' Goodley asked, as dispassionately as he could manage.

'Let's say we had Agent BANANA operating back then. Okay, he's dead now – died of old age, say – but maybe Agent PEAR was recruited by him, and he's still working. If the Sovs find out who BANANA was, that might give them a clue. Also you have to think about certain methods of message-transfer. People have been playing baseball for a hundred fifty years, but a change-up is still a change-up. I used to think the same way you do, Ben.

You learn that most of the things that are done here are done for a reason.'

Captured by the system, Goodley thought.

'By the way, you did notice that Khrushchev's last batch of tapes pretty much proved Nick Bledsoe wrong on some of his points – one other thing.'

'Yes?'

'Let's say that John Kennedy had hard intel in the spring of 1961, really good stuff that Khrushchev wanted to change the system. In '58, he'd effectively gutted the Red Army, and he was trying to reform the Party. Let's say that Kennedy had hard stuff on that, and he was told by a little bird that if he cut the Russkies a little slack, maybe we could have had a rapprochement in the 60s. *Glasnost*, say, thirty years early. Let's say all that happened, and the President blew the call, decided for political reasons that it was disadvantageous to cut Nikita a little slack . . . *That* would mean that the 1960s were all a great big mistake. Vietnam, everything, all a gigantic screwup.'

'I don't believe it. I've been through the archives. It's not consistent with everything we know about –'

'Consistency in a politician?' Ryan interrupted. 'There's a revolutionary concept.'

'If you're saying that really happened –'

'It was a hypothetical,' Jack said with a raised eyebrow. Hell, he thought, the information was all out there for anyone who wanted to pull it together. That it had never been done was just another manifestation of a wider and more troubling problem. But the part that worried him was right in this building. He'd leave history to historians . . . until, someday, he decided to rejoin their professional ranks. *And when will that be, Jack?*

'Nobody'd ever believe it.'

'Most people believe that Lyndon Johnson lost the New Hampshire primary to Eugene McCarthy because of the Tet Offensive, too. Welcome to the world of intelligence, Dr Goodley. You know what's the hard part of recognizing the truth?' Jack asked.

'What's that?'

'Knowing that something just bit you on the ass. It's not as easy as you think.'

'And the breakup of the Warsaw Pact?'

'Case in point,' Ryan agreed. 'We had all kinds of indicators, and we all blew the call. Well, that's not true, exactly. A lot of the youngsters in the DI – Directorate of Intelligence,' Jack explained unnecessarily, which struck Goodley as patronizing '– were making noise, but the section chiefs pooh-poohed it.'

'And you, sir?'

'If the Director's agreeable, we can let you see some of that. Most of it, in fact. The majority of our agents and field officers got faked out of their jockstraps, too. We all could have done better, and that's as true of me as it is of anybody else. If I have a weakness, it's that I have too tactical a focus.'

'Trees instead of the forest?'

'Yep,' Ryan admitted. 'That's the big trap here, but knowing about it doesn't always help a whole hell of a lot.'

'I guess that's why they sent me over,' Goodley observed.

Jack grinned. 'Hell, that's not terribly different from how I got started here. Welcome aboard. Where do you want to start, Dr Goodley?'

Ben already had a good idea on that, of course. If Ryan could not see it coming, that was not his problem, was it?

'So, where do you get the computers?' Bock asked. Fromm was closeted away with his paper and pencils.

'Israel for a start, maybe Jordan or Turkey,' Ghosn replied.

'This will be rather expensive,' Fromm warned.

'I have already checked out the computer-controlled machine tools. Yes, they are expensive.' *But not that expensive*. It occurred to Ghosn that he had access to hard-currency assets that might boggle the mind of this unbeliever. 'We will see what your friend requires. Whatever it is, we will get it.'

CHAPTER 13

Process

Why did I ever accept this job?

Roger Durling was a proud man. The upset winner of what was supposed to have been a secure Senate seat, then the youngest governor in the history of California, he knew pride to be a weakness, but he also knew that there was much to justify his.

I could have waited a few years, maybe returned to the Senate and earned my way into the White House, instead of cutting a deal, and delivering the election to Fowler . . . in return for this.

'This' was Air Force Two, the radio callsign for whatever aircraft the Vice President rode on. The implicit contrast with 'Air Force One' made just one more joke that attached to what was putatively the second most important political post in the United States, though not as earthily apt as John Nance Garner's observation: 'A pitcher of warm spit.' The whole office of Vice President, Durling judged, was one of the few mistakes made by the Founding Fathers. It had once been worse. Originally, the Vice President was supposed to have been the losing candidate who, after losing, would patriotically take his place in a government not his and preside over the Senate, setting aside petty political differences to serve the country. How James Madison had ever been that foolish was something scholars had never really examined, but the mistake had been corrected quickly enough by the 12th Amendment in 1803. Even in an age when gentlemen preparing for a duel referred to each other as 'sir,' that was something that pressed selflessness too far. And so the law had been changed, and the Vice President was now an appendage instead of a defeated enemy. That so many Vice Presidents had succeeded to the top job was less a matter of design than happenstance. That so many had done well – Andrew Johnson, Theodore Roosevelt, Harry Truman – was miraculous.

It was in any case a chance he would never have. Bob Fowler was physically healthy and politically as secure as any President had been since . . . Eisenhower? Durling wondered. Maybe even FDR. The important, almost co-equal role for the Vice President that Carter had initiated with Walter Mondale – something largely ignored but highly constructive – was a thing of the past. Fowler did not need Durling anymore. The President had made that quite clear.

And so Durling was relegated to subsidiary – not even secondary – duties. Fowler got to fly about in a converted 747 dedicated to his use alone. Roger Durling got whatever aircraft might be available, in this case one of the VC-20B Gulfstreams that were used by anyone who had the right credentials. Senators and House members on junkets got them if they were on the right committees, or if the President sensed a need to stroke their egos.

You're being petty, Durling told himself. *By being petty, you justify all the crap you have to put up with*.

His misjudgment had been at least as great as Madison's, the Vice President told himself as the aircraft taxied out. In deciding that a political figure would place country above his own ambition, Madison had merely been optimistic. Durling, on the other hand, had ignored an evident political reality, that the real difference in importance between President and Vice President was far greater than the difference between Fowler and any of a dozen committee chairmen in the House or Senate. The President had to deal with Congress to get any work done. He didn't *need* to deal with his Vice President.

How had he allowed himself to get here? That earned an amused grunt, though the question had occurred to Durling a thousand times. Patriotism, of course, or at least the political version of it. He'd delivered California, and without California he and Fowler would both still be

351

governors. The one substantive concession he'd gotten – the accession of Charlie Alden to the post of National Security Advisor – had been for naught, but he had been the deciding factor in changing the Presidency from one party to another. And his reward for that was drawing every crap detail in the executive branch, delivering speeches that would rarely make the news, though those of various cabinet officials did, speeches to keep faithful the party faithful, speeches to float new ideas – usually bad ones, and rarely his own – and wait for lightning to strike himself instead of the President. Today he was going out to talk about the need to raise taxes to pay for the peace in the Middle East. What a marvelous political opportunity! he thought. Roger Durling would outline the need for new taxes in St Louis before a convention of purchasing managers, and he was sure the applause would be deafening.

But he had accepted the job, had given his word to perform the duties of the office, and if he did any less, then what would he be?

The aircraft rolled unevenly past the hangars and various aircraft, including NEACP, the 747 configured as the National Emergency Airborne Command Post, known as 'Kneecap,' or more dramatically as 'The Doomsday Plane.' Always within two flying hours of wherever the President might be (a real headache when the President visited Russia or China), it was the only safe place the President might occupy in a nuclear crisis – but that didn't really matter anymore, did it? Durling saw people shuffling in and out of the aircraft. Funding hadn't been reduced on that yet – well, it was part of the President's personal fleet – and it was still kept ready for a rapid departure. He wondered how soon that might change. Everything else had.

'We're ready for departure. All buckled, sir?' the sergeant-attendant asked.

'You bet! Let's get this show on the road,' Durling replied with a smile. On Air Force One, he knew, people often showed their confidence in the aircraft and the crew by not buckling. More evidence that his airplane was second-best, but he could hardly growl at the sergeant for being a pro, and to this man Roger Durling was important. The Vice President reflected that this made the sergeant E-6 in the U.S. Air Force a more honorable man than most of the people in politics, but that wasn't much of a surprise, was it?

'That's a roger.'

'*Again!*' Ryan asked.

'Yes, sir,' the voice on the other end of the phone said.

'Okay, give me a few minutes.'

'Yes, sir.'

Ryan finished off his coffee and walked off towards Cabot's office. He was surprised to see Goodley in there again. The youngster was keeping his distance from the Director's cigar smoke, and even Jack thought that Marcus was overdoing the Patton act, or whatever the hell Cabot thought he was trying to look like.

'What is it, Jack?'

'CAMELOT,' Jack replied with visible annoyance. 'Those White House pukes have bowed out again. They want me to join in instead.'

'Well, are you that tied up?'

'Sir, we talked about that four months ago. It's important for the people at the White House to –'

'The President and his people are busy on some things,' the DCI explained tiredly.

'Sir, these things are scheduled weeks in advance, and it's the fourth straight time that –'

'I *know*, Jack.'

Ryan stood his ground. 'Director, somebody has to explain to them how important this is.'

'I've tried, dammit!' Cabot shot back. He had done so, Jack knew.

'Have you tried working through Secretary Talbot, or maybe Dennis Bunker?' Jack asked. *At least the President listens to them*, Jack didn't add.

He didn't have to. Cabot got the message. 'Look, Jack, we can't give orders to the President. We can only give advice. He doesn't always take it. You're pretty good at this, anyway. Dennis likes playing with you.'

'Fine, sir, but it's not my job – do they even *read* the wash-up notes?'

'Charlie Alden did. I suppose Liz Elliot does, too.'

'I bet,' Ryan observed icily, ignoring Goodley's presence. 'Sir, they are being irresponsible.'

'That's a little strong, Jack.'

'It's a little true, Director,' Ryan said, as calmly as he could.

'Can I ask what CAMELOT is?' Ben Goodley asked.

'It's a game,' Cabot answered. 'Crisis-management, usually.'

'Oh, like SAGA and GLOBAL?'

'Yeah,' Ryan said. 'The President never plays. The reason is that we cannot risk knowledge of how he would act in a given situation – and yes, that is overly Byzantine, but it's always been that way. Instead, the National Security Advisor or some other senior staff member takes his place, and the President is supposed to be briefed on how it goes. Except that President Fowler thinks that he doesn't have to bother, and now his people are starting to act the same dumb way.' Jack was sufficiently annoyed that he used the words 'President Fowler' and 'dumb' in the same sentence.

'Well, I mean, is it really necessary?' Goodley asked. 'Sounds like an anachronism to me.'

'You have car insurance, Ben?' Jack asked.

'Yes, sure.'

'Ever have an auto accident?'

'Not one that was my fault,' Goodley replied.

'Then why bother with insurance?' Jack answered the question: 'Because it's *insurance*, right? You don't expect to need it, you never want to need it, but because you *might* need it, you spend the money – or time, in this case – to have it.'

The Presidential Scholar made a dismissive gesture. 'Come on, it's a different thing altogether.'

'That's right. In a car, it's just your ass.' Ryan stopped the sermon. 'Okay, Director, I'm off for the rest of the day.'

'Your objections and recommendations are noted, Jack. I will bring them up at my first opportunity – oh, before you leave, about NIITAKA . . .'

Ryan stopped in his tracks and stared down at Cabot. 'Sir, Mr Goodley is not cleared for that word, much less that file.'

'We are not discussing the substance of the case. When will the people downstairs' – Ryan was grateful he didn't say MERCURY – 'be ready for the, uh, modified operations? I want to improve data-transfer.'

'Six weeks. Until then we have to use the other methods we discussed.'

The Director of Central Intelligence nodded. 'Very well. The White House is very interested in that, Jack. Good job to all concerned.'

'Glad to hear that, sir. See you tomorrow.' Jack walked out.

'NIITAKA?' Goodley asked after the door closed. 'Sounds Japanese.'

'Sorry, Goodley. You can forget that word at your earliest opportunity.' Cabot had only spoken it to remind Ryan of his place, and the honorable part of the man already regretted having done so.

'Yes, sir. May I ask an unrelated question?'

'Sure.'

'Is Ryan as good as people say?'

Cabot stubbed out the remains of his cigar, to the relief of his visitor. 'He's got quite a record.'

'Really? I've heard that. You know, that's the whole reason I'm here, to examine the personality types that really make a difference. I mean, how does someone grow into the job? Ryan's skyrocketed up the ladder here. I'd be very interested in seeing how he managed to do that.'

'He's done it by being right a lot more often than he's wrong, by making some tough calls, and with some field jobs that even I can hardly believe,' Cabot said, after a moment's consideration. 'And you can never, ever reveal that to anyone, Dr Goodley.'

'I understand, sir. Could I see his record, his personnel file?'

The DCI's eyebrows arched. 'Everything you see in there is classified. Anything you try to write about it —'

'Excuse me, but I know that, sir. Everything I write is subject to security review. I signed off on that. It's important that I learn how a person really fits in here, and Ryan would seem to be an ideal case study for examining how that process happens. I mean, that's why the White House sent me over here,' Goodley pointed out. 'I'm supposed to report to them on what I find.'

Cabot was silent for a moment. 'I suppose that's okay, then.'

Ryan's car arrived at the Pentagon's River entrance. He was met by an Air Force one-star and conducted inside, bypassing the metal detector. Two minutes later, he was in one of many subterranean rooms that lie under and around this ugliest of official buildings.

'Hello, Jack,' Dennis Bunker called from the far end of the room.

'Mr Secretary.' Jack nodded as he took his National Security Advisor's chair. The game started immediately. 'What seems to be the problem?'

'Aside from the fact that Liz Elliot has decided not to grace us with her presence?' The Secretary of Defense chuckled, then went serious. 'There has been an attack on one of our cruisers in the Eastern Med. The information is still sketchy, but the ship has been severely damaged and may be sinking. We presume heavy casualties.'

'What do we know?' Jack asked, settling into the game. He put on a color-coded nametag that identified which part he was playing. A card hanging from the ceiling over his chair had the same purpose.

'Not much.' Bunker looked up as a Navy lieutenant entered the room.

'Sir, USS *Kidd* reports that *Valley Forge* exploded and sank five minutes ago as a result of the initial damage.

There are no more than twenty survivors, and rescue operations are underway.'

'What is the cause of the loss?' Ryan asked.

'Unknown, sir. *Kidd* was thirty miles from *Valley Forge* at the time of the incident. Her helo is on the scene now. Commander Sixth Fleet has brought all his ships to full-alert status. USS *Theodore Roosevelt* is launching aircraft to sweep the area.'

'I know the CAG on *TR*, Robby Jackson,' Ryan said to nobody in particular. Not that it mattered. *Theodore Roosevelt* was actually in Norfolk, and Robby was still preparing for his next cruise. The names in the wargame were generic, and personal knowledge of the players didn't matter, since they were not supposed to be real people. But if it were real, Robby was Commander Air Group on USS *Theodore Roosevelt*, and his would be the first plane off the cats. It was well to remember that, though this might be a game, its purpose was deadly serious. 'Background information?' Jack asked. He didn't remember all of the pre-brief on the scenario being played out.

'CIA reports a possible mutiny in the Soviet Union by Red Army units in Kazakhstan, and disturbances in two Navy bases there also,' the game narrator, a Navy commander, reported.

'Soviet units in the vicinity of *Valley Forge*?' Bunker asked.

'Possibly a submarine,' the naval officer answered.

'Flash Message,' the wall speaker announced. 'USS *Kidd* reports that it has destroyed an inbound surface-to-surface missile with its Close-In Weapons System. Superficial damage to the ship, no casualties.'

Jack walked to the corner to pour himself a cup of coffee. He smiled as he did so. These games were fun, he admitted to himself. He really did enjoy them. They were also realistic. He'd been swept away from a normal day's routine, dumped in a stuffy room, given confused and fragmented information, and had no idea at all what the hell was supposed to be going on. That was reality. The old joke: How do crisis-managers resemble mushrooms? They're kept in the dark and fed horseshit.

'Sir, we have an incoming HOTLINE message . . .'

Okay, Ryan thought, *it's that kind of game today. The Pentagon must have come up with the scenario. Let's see if it's still possible to blow the world up . . .*

'More concrete?' Qati asked.

'Much more concrete,' Fromm answered. 'The machines each weigh several tons, and they must be totally stable. The room must be totally stable, and totally sealed. It must be clean like a hospital – no, much better than any hospital you have ever seen.' Fromm looked down at his list. *Not cleaner than a* German *hospital, of course.* 'Next, electrical power. We'll need three large backup generators, and at least two UPSs –'

'What?' Qati asked.

'Un-interruptible power supplies,' Ghosn translated. 'We'll keep one of the backup generators turning at all times, of course?'

'Correct,' Fromm answered. 'Since this is a primitive operation, we'll try not to use more than one machine at a time. The real problem with electricity is ensuring a secure circuit. So, we take the line current through the UPSs to protect against spikes. The computer systems on the milling machines are highly sensitive.

'Next!' Fromm said. 'Skilled operators.'

'That will be highly difficult,' Ghosn observed.

The German smiled, amazing everyone present. 'Not so. It will be easier than you think.'

'Really?' Qati asked. *Good news from this infidel?*

'We'll need perhaps five highly trained men, but you have them in the region, I am sure.'

'Where? There is no machine shop in the region that –'

'Certainly there is. People here wear spectacles, do they not?'

'But –'

'Of course!' Ghosn said, rolling his eyes in amazement.

'The degree of precision, you see,' Fromm explained

to Qati, 'is no different from what is required for eye-glasses. The machines are very similar in design, just larger, and what we are attempting to do is simply to produce precise and predictable curves in a rigid material. Nuclear bombs are produced to exacting specifications. So are spectacles. Our desired object is larger, but the principle is the same, and with the proper machinery it is merely a matter of scale, not of substance. So: can you obtain skilled lens-makers?'

'I don't see why not,' Qati replied, hiding his annoyance.

'They must be highly skilled,' Fromm said, like a schoolmaster. 'The best you can find, people with long experience, probably with training in Germany or England.'

'There will be a security problem,' Ghosn said quietly.

'Oh? Why is that?' Fromm asked, with a feigned bafflement that struck both of the others as the summit of arrogance.

'Quite so,' Qati agreed.

'Next, we need sturdy tables on which to mount the machines.'

Halfway point, Lieutenant Commander Walter Claggett told himself. In forty-five more days, USS *Maine* would surface outside Juan de Fuca Straits, link up with the tug boat, and follow Little Toot into Bangor, where she would then tie up and begin the hand-off process to the 'Blue' crew for the next deterrence-patrol cycle. *And not a moment too soon.*

Walter Claggett – friends called him Dutch, a nickname that had originated at the Naval Academy for a reason he no longer remembered; Claggett was black – was thirty-six years old, and it had been known to him before sailing that he was being 'deep-dipped' for early selection to commander and had a chance for an early crack at a fast-attack boat. That was fine with him. His two attempts at marriage had both ended in failure, which was not uncommon for submariners – thankfully, there were no kids involved in either union – and the

Navy was his life. He was just as happy to spend all of his time at sea, saving his carousing time for those not really brief intervals on the beach. To be at sea, to slide through black water in control of a majestic ship of war, that was the best of all things to Walter Claggett. The company of good men, respect truly earned in a most demanding profession, the acquired ability to know every time what the right thing to do was, the relaxed banter in the wardroom, the responsibility he had to counsel his men – Claggett relished every aspect of his career.

It was just his commanding officer he couldn't stand.

How the hell did Captain Harry Ricks ever make it this far? he asked himself for the twentieth time this week. The man was brilliant. He could have designed a submarine-reactor system on the back of an envelope, or maybe even in his head during a rare daydream. He knew things about submarine design that Electric Boat's shipwrights had never even thought about. He could discuss the ins and outs of periscope design with the Navy's chief optics expert, and knew more about satellite-navigation aids than NASA or TRW or whoever the hell was running *that* program. Surely he knew more about the guidance packages on their Trident-II D-5 sea-launched ballistic missiles than anyone this side of Lockheed's Missile Systems Division. Over dinner two weeks earlier, he'd recited a whole page from the maintenance manual. From a technical point of view, Ricks might have been the most thoroughly prepared officer in the United States Navy.

Harry Ricks was the quintessential product of the Nuclear Navy. As an engineer he was unequaled. The technical aspects of his job were almost instinctive to him. Claggett was good, and knew it; he also knew that he'd never be as good as Harry Ricks.

It's just that he doesn't know dick about submarining or submariners, Claggett reflected bleakly. It was incredible, but true, that Ricks had little feeling for seamanship and none at all for sailors.

'Sir,' Claggett said slowly, 'this is a very good chief. He's young, but he's sharp.'

'He can't keep control of his people,' Ricks replied.

'Captain, I don't know what you mean by that.'

'His training methods aren't what they're supposed to be.'

'He is a little unconventional, but he has cut six seconds off the average reload time. The fish are all fully functional, even the one that came over from the beach bad. The compartment is completely squared away. What more can we ask of the man?'

'I don't ask. I direct. I order. I expect things to be done my way, the right way. And they will be done that way,' Ricks observed in a dangerously quiet voice.

It made no sense at all to cross the skipper on issues like this, especially when he posed them in this way, but Claggett's job as executive officer was to stand between the crew and the captain, especially when the captain was wrong.

'Sir, I must respectfully disagree. I think we look at results, and the results here are just about perfect. A good chief is one who stretches the envelope, and this one hasn't stretched it very far. If you slap him down, it will have a negative effect on him and his department.'

'X, I expect support from all my officers, and especially from you.'

Claggett sat straight up in his chair as though from a blow. He managed to speak calmly. 'Captain, you have my support and my loyalty. It is not my job to be a robot. I'm supposed to offer alternatives. At least,' he added, 'that's what they told me at PXO School.' Claggett regretted the last sentence even before it was spoken, but somehow it had come out anyway. The CO's cabin was quite small, and immediately got smaller still.

That was a very foolish thing to say, Lieutenant-Commander Walter Martin Claggett, Ricks thought with a blank look.

'Next, the reactor drills,' Ricks said.

'Another one? So soon?' *For Christ's sake, the last one was friggin' perfect. Almost perfect,* Claggett corrected himself. *The kids might have saved ten or fifteen seconds somewhere.* The Executive Officer didn't know where that might have been, though.

'Proficiency means every day, X.'

'Indeed it does, sir, but they are proficient. I mean, the ORSE we ran right before Captain Rosselli left missed setting the squadron record by a whisker, and the last drill we ran beat *that!*'

'No matter how good drill results are, always demand better. That way you always *get* better. Next ORSE, I want the squadron record, X.'

He wants the Navy record, the world record, maybe even a certificate from God, Claggett thought. *More than that, he wants it on his record.*

The growler phone on the bulkhead rattled. Ricks lifted it.

'Commanding Officer. . . . yes, on the way.' He hung up. 'Sonar contact.'

Claggett was out the door in two seconds, the captain right behind him.

'What is it?' Claggett asked first. As executive officer, he was also the approach officer for tactical engagements.

'Took me a couple minutes to recognize it,' the leading sonarman reported. 'Real flukey contact. I think it's a 688, bearing about one-nine-five. Direct-path contact, sir.'

'Playback,' Ricks ordered. The sonarman took over another screen – his had grease-pencil marks on it and he didn't want to remove those yet – and ran the display back a few minutes.

'See here, Cap'n? Real flukey . . . right about here it started firming up. That's when I called in.'

The Captain stabbed his finger on the screen. 'You should have had it there, petty officer. That's two minutes wasted. Pay closer attention next time.'

'Aye aye, Cap'n.' What else could a twenty-three-year-old sonarman second-class say? Ricks left the sonar room. Claggett followed, patting the sonar operator on the shoulder as he went.

God damn it, Captain!

'Course two-seven-zero, speed five, depth five hundred even. We're under the layer,' the Officer of the Deck reported. 'Holding contact Sierra-Eleven at bearing one-nine-five, broad on the port beam. Fire-control tracking party is manned. We have fish in tubes one, three, and four. Tube two is empty for service. Doors closed, tubes dry.'

'Tell me about Sierra-Eleven,' Ricks ordered.

'Direct-path contact. He's below the layer, range unknown.'

'Environmental conditions?'

'Flat calm on the roof, a moderate layer at about one hundred feet. We have good isothermal water around us. Sonar conditions are excellent.'

'First read on Sierra-Eleven is over ten thousand yards.' It was Ensign Shaw on the tracking party.

'Conn, Sonar, we evaluate contact Sierra-Eleven is a definite 688-class, US fast-attack. I can guestimate speed at about fourteen-fifteen knots, sir.'

'Whoa!' Claggett observed to Ricks. 'We picked up a Los Angeles at 10-K plus! That's gonna piss somebody off . . .'

'Sonar, Conn, I want data, not guesses,' Ricks said.

'Cap'n, he did well to pick that contact out of the background,' Claggett said very quietly. Summer in the Gulf of Alaska meant fishing boats and baleen whales, both in large numbers, making noises and cluttering up sonar displays. 'That's one hell of a good sonarman in there.'

'We pay him to be good, X. We don't award medals for doing an adequate job. I want a playback later to see if there might have been a sniff earlier that he missed.'

Anybody can find something on playback, Claggett thought to himself.

'Conn, Sonar, I'm getting a very faint blade-count . . . seems to indicate fourteen knots, plus or minus one, sir.'

'Very well. That's better, Sonar.'

'Uh, Captain . . . may be a little closer than ten thousand . . . not much, but a little. Track is firming up . . .

best estimate now nine-five hundred yards, course roughly three-zero-five,' Shaw reported next, waiting for the sky to fall.

'So he's not over ten thousand yards off now?'

'No, sir, looks like nine-five hundred.'

'Let me know when you change your mind again,' Ricks replied. 'Drop speed to four knots.'

'Reduce speed four knots, aye,' the OOD acknowledged.

'Let him get ahead of us?' Claggett asked.

'Yep.' The Captain nodded.

'We have a firing solution,' the weapons officer said. The XO checked his watch. It didn't get much better than this.

'Very well. Glad to hear it,' Ricks replied.

'Speed is now four knots.'

'Okay, we have him. Sierra-Eleven is at bearing two-zero-one, range nine-one hundred yards, course three-zero-zero, speed fifteen.'

'Dead meat,' Claggett said. *Of course, he's making it easy by going this fast.*

'True enough. This will look good on the patrol report.'

'That's tricky,' Ryan observed. 'I don't like the way this is going.'

'Neither do I,' Bunker agreed. 'I recommend weapons release to the *TR* battlegroup.'

'I agree, and will so advise the President.' Ryan placed the call. Under the rules for this game, the President was supposed to be on Air Force One, somewhere over the Pacific, returning from an unspecified country on the Pacific Rim. The President's decision-making role was being played by a committee elsewhere in the Pentagon. Jack made his recommendation and waited for the reply.

'Only in self-defense, Dennis.'

'Bullshit,' Bunker said quietly. 'He listens to me.'

Jack grinned. 'I agree, but not this time. No offensive action, you may act only to defend the ships in the group.'

The SecDef turned to the action officer: 'Forward that

to *Theodore Roosevelt*. Tell them I expect full combat air patrols. Anything over two hundred miles I want reported to me. Under two hundred, the battlegroup commander is free to act at discretion. For submarines, the bubble radius is fifty – five-zero – miles. Inside that, prosecute to kill.'

'That's creative,' Jack said.

'We have that attack on *Valley Forge*.' The best estimate at the moment was that it had been a surprise missile attack from a Soviet submarine. It appeared that some units of the Russian fleet were acting independently, or at least under orders not emanating from Moscow. Then things got worse.

'HOTLINE message. There has just been a ground-force attack on a Strategic Rocket Regiment . . . SS-18 base in Central Asia.'

'Launch all the ready bombers right now! Jack, tell the President that I just gave the order.'

'Comm-link failure,' the wall speaker said. 'Radio contact with Air Force One has been interrupted.'

'Tell me more!' Jack demanded.

'That's all we have, sir.'

'Where's the Vice President now?' Ryan asked.

'He's aboard Kneecap Alternate, six hundred miles south of Bermuda. Kneecap Prime is four hundred miles ahead of Air Force One, preparing to land in Alaska for the transfer.'

'Close enough to Russia that an intercept is possible . . . but not likely . . . have to be a one-way mission,' Bunker thought aloud. 'Unless they strayed over a Soviet warship with SAMs . . . Vice President is temporarily in charge.'

'Sir, I –'

'That's my call to make, Jack. The President is either out of the loop or has had his comm links compromised. SecDef says that the Vice President is in charge until the comm links are reestablished and validated by code-word authentication. Forces are now at DEFCON-ONE on my authority.'

One thing about Dennis Bunker, Ryan thought, the

man never stopped being a fighter jock. He makes decisions and sticks to them. He was usually right, too, as he was here.

Ryan's file was a thick one. Almost five inches, Goodley saw in the privacy of his seventh-floor cubbyhole. Half an inch of that was background and security-clearance forms. The academic record was fairly impressive, especially his doctoral work in history at Georgetown University. Georgetown wasn't Harvard, of course, but it was a fairly respectable institution, Goodley told himself. His first Agency job had been as part of Admiral James Greer's Junior Varsity program, and his first report, 'Agents and Agencies,' had dealt with terrorism. Odd coincidence, Goodley thought, given what had happened later.

The documents on Ryan's encounter in London occupied thirty double-space pages, mainly police-report summaries and a few news photos. Goodley started making notes. *Cowboy*, he wrote first of all. Running into things like that. The academic shook his head. Twenty minutes later, he read over the executive summary of Ryan's second CIA report, the one which confidently predicted that the terrorists would probably never operate in America – delivered days before the attack on his family.

Guessed wrong there, didn't you, Ryan! Goodley chuckled to himself. As bright as they said he was, he made mistakes like everyone else . . .

He'd made a few while working in England, too. He hadn't predicted Chernenko's succession of Andropov, though he had predicted Narmonov was the coming man well in advance of nearly everyone, except Kantrowitz up at Princeton, who'd been the first to see star quality in Andrey Il'ych. Goodley reminded himself that he'd been an undergraduate then, bedding that girl at Wellesley, Debra Frost . . . wonder what ever happened to her . . . ?

'Son of a bitch . . .' Ben whispered a few minutes later. 'Son of a *bitch*.'

Red October, a Soviet ballistic missile submarine . . . defected. Ryan was one of the first to suspect it . . . Ryan, an analyst at London Station had . . . run the operation at sea! *Killed* a Russian sailor. That was the cowboy part again. Couldn't just arrest the guy, had to shoot him down like something in a movie . . .

Goddamn! A Russian ballistic-missile submarine defected . . . and they kept it quiet . . . oh, the boat was later sunk in deep water.

Back to London after that for a few more months before rotating home to be Greer's special assistant and heir-apparent. Some interesting work with the arms-control people . . .

That can't be right. The KGB Chairman was killed in a plane crash . . .

Goodley was taking furious notes now. Liz Elliot could not have known any of this, could she?

You're not looking for good stuff about Ryan, the White House Fellow reminded himself. Elliot had never really said that, of course, but she had made herself clear in a way that he'd understood . . . or thought he'd understood, Goodley corrected himself. He suddenly realized just how dangerous a game this might be.

Ryan kills people. He'd shot and killed at least three. You didn't get that from talking to the man. Life wasn't a Western. People didn't carry revolvers with notches cut in the handles. Goodley didn't feel a chill over his skin, but he did remind himself that Ryan was someone to be regarded warily. He'd never before met someone who had killed other men, and was not foolish enough to regard such people as heroic or somehow more than other men, but it was something to keep in mind, wasn't it?

There were blank spots around the time of James Greer's death, he noted . . . wasn't that the time when all that stuff was happening down in Colombia? He made some notes. Ryan had been acting DDI then, but just after Fowler took over, Judge Arthur Moore and Robert Ritter had retired to make way for the new presidential administration, and Ryan had been confirmed by the Senate as Deputy Director of Central Intelligence. So much for his work record. Goodley closed that portion and opened up the personal and financial side . . .

'Bad call . . .' Ryan said. Twenty minutes too late.

'I think you're right.'

'Too late. What did we do wrong?'

'I'm not sure,' Bunker replied. 'Tell the *TR* group to disengage and pull back, maybe?'

Ryan stared at the map on the far wall. 'Maybe, but we've backed Andrey Il'ych into a corner . . . we have to let him out.'

'How? How do we do that without cornering ourselves?'

'I think there was a problem with this scenario . . . not sure what, though . . .'

'Let's rattle his cage hard,' Ricks thought aloud.

'Like how, Cap'n?' Claggett asked.

'Status on tube two?'

'Empty, it was down for maintenance inspection,' the weapons officer replied.

'Is it okay?'

'Yes, sir, completed the inspection half an hour before we got the contact.'

'Okay . . .' Ricks grinned. 'I want a water slug out of tube two. Let's give him a real launch transient to wake him up!'

Damn! Claggett thought. It was almost something Mancuso or Rosselli would have done. Almost . . . 'Sir, that's kind of a noisy way to do it. We can shake him up enough with a "Tango" call on the Gertrude.'

'Weps, we have a solution on Sierra-Eleven?' *Mancuso wants aggressive skippers, well, I'll show him aggressive . . .*

'Yes, sir!' the weapons officer snapped back at once.

'Firing Point Procedures. Prepare to fire a water-slug on tube two.'

'Sir, I confirm torpedo tube two is empty. Weapons in tubes one, three and four are secure.' A call was made to the torpedo room to re-confirm what the electronic displays announced. In the torpedo room, the chief looked through the small glass port to make certain that they wouldn't be launching anything.

'Tube two is empty by visual inspection. High-pressure air is online,' the chief called over the communications circuit. 'We are ready to shoot.'

'Open outer door.'

'Open outer door, aye. Outer door is open.'

'Weps?'

'Locked in.'

'Match generated bearings and . . . *shoot!*'

The weapons officer pushed the proper button. USS *Maine* shuddered with the sudden pulse of high-pressure air out of the torpedo tube and into the sea.

Aboard USS *Omaha*, six thousand yards away, a sonarman had been trying for the past few minutes to decide if the trace on his screen was something other than clutter when a dot appeared on the screen.

'Conn, Sonar, transient, transient. Mechanical Transient bearing zero-eight-eight, dead aft!'

'What the hell?' the Officer of the Deck said. He was the boat's navigator, in the third week of duty in the new post. 'What's back there?'

'Transient, transient – launch transient bearing zero-eight-eight! I say again, launch transient dead aft!'

'All ahead flank!' the suddenly pale lieutenant said a touch too loudly. 'Battle stations! Stand by the five-inch room.' He lifted the command phone for the captain, but the general alarm was already sounding, and the Commanding Officer ran barefoot into the attack center, his coveralls still open.

'What the fuck is going on?'

'Sir, we had a launch transient dead aft – Sonar, Conn, what else do you have?'

'Nothing, sir, nothing after the transient. That was a launch-transient, HP air into the water, but . . . sounded a little funny, sir. I show nothing in the water.'

'Right full rudder!' The OOD ordered, ignoring the Captain. He hadn't been relieved yet, and conning the boat was his responsibility. 'Make your depth one hundred feet. Five-inch room, launch a decoy now-now-now!'

'Right full rudder, aye. Sir, my rudder is right full, no course given. Speed twenty knots and accelerating,' helmsman said.

'Very well. Come to course zero-one-zero.'

'Aye, coming to new course zero-one-zero!'

'Who's in this area?' the CO asked in a relaxed voice, though he didn't feel relaxed.

'*Maine*'s around here somewhere,' the navigator answered.

'Harry Ricks.' *That asshole*, he didn't say. It would have been bad for discipline. 'Sonar, talk to me!'

'Conn, sonar, there is nothing in the water. If there was a torpedo, I'd have it, sir.'

'Nav, drop speed to one-third.'

'Aye, all ahead one-third.'

'I think we scared the piss out of him,' Ricks observed, hovering over the sonar display. Seconds after the simulated launch, the 688 on the scope had floored his power plant, and now there was also the gurgling sound of a decoy.

'Just backed off on the power, sir, blade count is coming down.'

'Yeah, he knows there's nothing after him now. We'll give him a call on the Gertrude.'

'That dumbass! Doesn't he know that there may be an Akula around here?' the Commanding Officer of USS *Omaha* growled.

'We don't show him, sir, just a bunch of fishing boats.'

'Okay. Secure from general quarters. We'll let *Maine* have her little laugh.' He grimaced. 'My fault. We should have been trolling along at ten instead of fifteen knots. Make it so.'

'Aye, sir. Where to?'

'The boomer ought to have a feel for what's north of here. Go southeast.'

'Right.'

'Nice reaction, Nav. We might have evaded the fish. Lessons?'

'You said it, sir. We were going too fast.'

'Learn from your captain's mistake, Mr Auburn.'

'Always, sir.'

The skipper punched the younger man's shoulder on the way out.

Thirty-six thousand yards away, the *Admiral Lunin* was drifting at three knots just over the thermocline layer, her towed-array sonar drooping under it.

'Well?' her Captain asked.

'We have this burst of noise at one-three-zero,' the sonar officer said, pointing to the display, 'and nothing else. Fifteen seconds later, we have another burst of noise here . . . ahead of the first. The signature appears to be an American Los Angeles class going to full power, then slowing and disappearing off our screens.'

'An exercise, Yevgeniy . . . the first transient was an American missile submarine . . . an Ohio-class. What do you think of that?' Captain First Rank Valentin Borisso-vich Dubinin asked.

'No one has ever detected an Ohio in deep water . . .'

'For all things, there is a first time.'

'And now?'

'We will hover and wait. The Ohio is quieter than a sleeping whale, but at least we know now that there is one in the area. We will not chase after it. Very foolish of the Americans to make noise in this way. I've never seen that happen before.'

'The game has changed, Captain,' the sonar officer observed. It had changed quite a lot. He didn't have to say 'Comrade Captain' anymore.

'Indeed it has, Yevgeniy. Now it is a true game. Noone need get hurt, and we can test our skills as in the Olympics.'

*

'Critique?'

'I would have closed a little before shooting, sir,' the weapons officer said. 'Even money he might have evaded that one.'

'Agreed, but we were only trying to shake him up,' Ricks said comfortably.

Then what was the purpose of that exercise? Dutch Claggett wondered. *Oh, of course, to show how aggressive you are.*

'I guess we accomplished that,' the XO said to support his captain. There were grins all around the control room. Boomers and fast-attack subs often played games, mostly pre-planned. As usual, the Ohio had won this one, too. They'd known that Omaha was around, of course, and that she was looking for a Russian Akula that the P-3s had lost off the Aleutians a few days before. But the Russian 'Shark' class sub was nowhere to be heard.

'OOD, take her south. We went and made a datum with that launch transient. We'll clear datum back down where Omaha was.'

'Aye aye, sir.'

'Well done, people.' Ricks walked back to his cabin.

'New course?'

'South,' Dubinin said. 'He'll clear datum by going into the area already swept by the Los Angeles. We'll maintain position just over the layer, leave our "tail" under it, and try to reacquire.' There wasn't much chance, the Captain knew, but fortune still favored the bold. Or something like that. The submarine was due to go back to port in another week, and supposedly the new sonar array she was due to receive during his scheduled overhaul was a major improvement over the current one. He'd been here south of Alaska for three weeks. The submarine he'd detected, USS *Maine* or USS *Nevada*, if his intelligence reports were correct, would finish this patrol, refit, conduct another, refit again, then yet another patrol in February, which coincided with his deployment schedule after his overhaul. So, the next time he was back, he'd be up against the same captain, and this one had made a mistake. After a refit, *Admiral Lunin* would be quieter, and would have better sonar, and Dubinin was starting to wonder when he'd be able to play his game against the Americans . . . Wouldn't it be nice, he thought. All the time he'd spent to get here, the wonderful years learning his trade in Northern Fleet under Marko Ramius. What a pity, for such a brilliant officer to have died in an accident. But duty at sea was dangerous, always had been, always would be. Marko had gotten his crew off before scuttling . . . Dubinin shook his head. Today he might have gotten assistance from the Americans. Might? Would have, just as an American ship would get one from a Soviet. The changes in his country and the world made Dubinin feel much better about his job. It had always been a demanding game of skill, but its deadly purpose had changed. Oh, yes, the American missile submarines still had their rockets pointed at his country, and Soviet rockets were pointed at America, but perhaps they would be gone soon. Until they were, he'd continue to do his job, and it seemed ironic indeed that just as the Soviet Navy was on the threshold of becoming competitive – the Akula class was roughly equal with an early Los Angeles class in a mechanical sense – the need for it was diminishing. Like a friendly game of cards, perhaps? he asked himself. Not a bad simile . . .

'Speed, Captain?'

Dubinin considered that. 'Assume a range of twenty nautical miles and a target speed of five knots. We'll do seven knots, I think. That way we can remain very quiet and perhaps still catch him . . . every two hours we'll turn to maximize the capacity of the sonar . . . Yes, that is the plan.' *Next time, Yevgeniy, we'll have two new officer sonar operators to back you up*, Dubinin reminded himself. The drawdown of the Soviet submarine force had released a lot of young officers who were now getting specialist training. The submarine's complement of officers would double, and even more than the new equipment, that would make a difference in his abilities to hunt.

'We blew it,' Bunker said. 'I blew it. I gave the president bad advice.'

'You're not the only one,' Ryan admitted, as he stretched. 'But was that scenario realistic – I mean, really realistic?'

It turned out that the whole thing had been a ploy by a hard-pressed Soviet leader trying to get control over his military, and doing so by making it look as though some renegades had taken action.

'Not likely, but possible.'

'All things are possible,' Jack observed. 'What do you suppose their war-games say about us?'

Bunker laughed. 'Nothing good, I'm sure.'

At the end, America had had to accept the loss of its cruiser, USS *Valley Forge*, in return for the Charlie-class submarine that USS *Kidd*'s helicopter had found and sunk. That was not regarded as an even trade, rather like losing a rook to the other fellow's knight. Soviet forces had gone on alert in Eastern Germany, and the weaker NATO forces had been unsure of their ability to deal with them. As a result, the Soviets had won a concession on the troop-pullback schedule. Ryan thought the whole scenario contrived, but they often were, and the point in any case was to see how to manage an unlikely crisis. Here they had done badly, moving too rapidly in non-essential areas, and too slowly on the ones that mattered, but which had not been recognized in time.

The lesson, as always, was: Don't make mistakes. That was something known by any first-grader, of course, and all men made mistakes, but the difference between a first-grader and a senior official was that official mistakes carried far more weight. That fact was an entirely different lesson, and one often not learned.

CHAPTER 14

Revelation

'So, what have you found?'

'He's a most interesting man,' Goodley replied. 'He's done some things at CIA that are hardly believable.'

'I know about the submarine business, and the defection of the KGB head. What else?' Liz Elliot asked.

'He's rather well-liked in the international intelligence community, like Sir Basil Charleston over in England – well, it's easy to see why they like him – but the same is true in the NATO countries, especially in France. Ryan stumbled across something that enabled the DGSE to bag a bunch of *Action Directe* people,' Goodley explained. He was somewhat uncomfortable with his role of designated informer.

The National Security Advisor didn't like to be kept waiting, but there was no sense in pressing the young scholar, was there? Her face took on a wry smile. 'Am I to assume that you have started admiring the man?'

'He's done fine work, but he's made his mistakes, too. His estimate on the fall of East Germany and the progress of reunification was way off.' He had not managed to learn that everyone else was, as well. Goodley himself had guessed almost exactly right on this issue up at the Kennedy School, and the paper he'd published in an obscure journal was something else that had earned him attention at the White House. The White House fellow stopped again.

'And . . . ?' Elliot prodded.

'And there are some troubling aspects in his personal life.'

Finally! 'And those are?'

'Ryan was investigated by the SEC for possible insider-stock trading before he entered CIA employ. It seems there was a computer-software company about to get a Navy contract. Ryan found out about it before anyone else and made a real killing. The SEC found out – the reason is that the company executives themselves were also investigated – and examined Ryan's records. He got off on a technicality.'

'Explain,' Liz ordered.

'In order to cover their own backsides, the company officials arranged to have something published in a defense trade paper, just a little filler item, not even two column inches, but it was enough to show that the information upon which they and Ryan operated was technically in the public domain. That made it legal. What's more interesting is what Ryan did with the money after attention was called to it. He cut it out of his brokerage account – that's in a blind-trust arrangement now with four different money-managers.' Goodley stopped. 'You know what Ryan's worth now?'

'No, what is it?'

'Over fifteen million dollars. He's by far the richest guy at the Agency. His holdings are somewhat undervalued. I'd say he's worth closer to twenty myself, but he's been using the same accounting method since before he joined CIA, and you can't critique him there. How you figure net worth is kind of metaphysical, isn't it? Accountants have different ways of doing things. Anyway, what he did with that windfall: He split it off to a separate account. Then a short while ago it all moved out into an educational trust fund.'

'His kids?'

'No,' Goodley answered. 'The beneficiaries – no, let me back up. He used part of the money to set up a convenience store – a 7-Eleven – for a widow and her children. The rest of the money is set aside in T-Bills and a few blue-chip stocks to educate her children.'

'Who is she?'

'Her name is Carol Zimmer. Laotian by birth, she's the widow of an Air Force sergeant who got killed in a training accident. Ryan has been looking after the family. He even signed out of his office to attend the birth of the newest child – a girl, by the way. Ryan visits the family periodically,' Goodley concluded.

'I see.' She didn't, but this is what one says. 'Any professional connection?'

'Not really. Mrs Zimmer, as I said, was Laotian. Her father was one of those tribal chieftains that CIA supported against the North Vietnamese. The whole group was wiped out. I haven't discovered how she managed to escape. She married an Air Force sergeant and came to America. He died in an accident somewhere, rather recently. There is nothing in Ryan's file to show any previous connection to the family at all. The Laos connection is possible – to CIA, I mean – but Ryan wasn't in government employ then, he was an undergrad in college. There's nothing in the file to show a connection of any kind. Just one day, a few months before the last presidential election, he set up this trust fund, and ever since he visits them on the average of once a week. Oh, there was one other thing.'

'What's that?'

'I cross-referenced this from another file. There was some trouble at the 7-Eleven, some local punks were bothering the Zimmer family. Ryan's principal bodyguard is a CIA officer named Clark. He used to be a field officer, and now is a protective guy. I wasn't able to get his file,' Goodley explained. 'Anyway, this Clark guy evidently assaulted a couple of gang kids. Sent one to the hospital. I checked a newspaper clipping. It was in the news, a little item – concerned citizen sort of thing. Clark and another CIA guy – the paper identified them as federal employees, no CIA connection – were supposedly accosted by four street toughs. This Clark guy must be a piece of work. The gang leader had his knee broken and was hospitalized. One other was just knocked unconscious, and the rest just stood there and wet their pants. The local cops treated it as a gang problem – well, a former gang problem. No formal charges were pressed.'

'What else do you know about this Clark?'

'I've seen him a few times. Big guy, late forties, quiet, actually seems kind of shy. But he moves – you know what he moves like? I took karate courses once. The instructor was a former Green Beret, Vietnam veteran, all that stuff. Like that. He moves like an athlete, fluid, economical, but it's his eyes. They're always moving around. He looks at you sideways and decides if you're a threat or not a threat . . .' Goodley paused. At that moment he realized what Clark really was. Whatever else he was, Ben Goodley was no fool. '. . . that is one dangerous guy.'

'What?' Liz Elliot didn't know what he was talking about.

'Excuse me. I learned that from the karate teacher up at Cambridge. The really dangerous ones don't seem dangerous. You just sort of lose track of them in the room. My teacher, he was mugged on the subway station right there by Harvard. I mean, they tried to mug him. He left three kids bleeding on the bricks. They thought he was just a janitor or something – he's an African-American, about fifty now, I guess. Looks like a janitor or something the way he dresses, not dangerous at all. That's what Clark is like, just like my old *sensei* . . . Interesting,' Goodley said. 'Well, he's a SPO, and they're supposed to be good at their job.

'I speculate that Ryan found out that some punks were bothering Mrs Zimmer, and had his bodyguard straighten things out. The Anne Arundel County police thought it was just fine.'

'Conclusions?'

'Ryan has done some very good work, but he's blown some big ones, too. Fundamentally, he's a creature of the past. He's still a Cold War guy. He's got problems with the Administration, like a few days ago when you didn't attend the CAMELOT game. He doesn't think you take your job seriously, thinks that not playing those war-games is irresponsible.'

'He said that?'

'Almost a direct quote, I was in the room with Cabot when he came in and bitched.'

Elliot shook her head. 'That's a Cold Warrior talking. If the President does his job right, and if I do my job right, there won't be any crises to manage. That's the whole point isn't it?'

'And so far, you guys seem to be doing all right,' Goodley observed.

The National Security Advisor ignored the remark, looking at her notes.

The walls were in place, and weather-sealed with plastic sheeting. The air-conditioning system was already running, removing both humidity and dust from the air. Fromm was at work with the machine-tool tables. Table was too pedestrian a term. They were designed to hold several tons each, and had screw jacks on each sturdy leg. The German was leveling each machine with the aid of spirit-levels built into the frames.

'Perfect,' he said, after three hours of work. It had to be perfect. Now it was. Under each table was a full meter of reinforced concrete footings. Once leveled, the legs were bolted into place so that each was a solid part of the earth.

'The tools must be so rigid?' Ghosn asked. Fromm shook his head.

'Quite the reverse. The tools float on a cushion of air.'

'But you said they weigh over a ton each!' Qati objected.

'Floating them on an air cushion is trivial, you've seen photographs of hovercraft weighing a hundred tons. Floating them is necessary to dampen out vibrations from the earth.'

'What tolerances are we seeking?' Ghosn asked.

'Roughly what one needs for an astronomical telescope,' the German replied.

'But, the original bombs –'

Fromm cut Ghosn off. 'The original American bombs on Hiroshima and Nagasaki were crude embarrassments. They wasted almost all of their reaction mass, especially the Hiroshima weapon – you would not manufacture so crude a weapon any more than you would design a bomb with a burning gunpowder fuse, eh?

'In any case, you cannot use such a wasteful design,' Fromm went on. 'After the first bombs, the American engineers had to face the problem that they had limited supplies of fissile material. That few kilos of plutonium over there is the most expensive material in the world. The plant needed to make it through nuclear bombardment costs billions, then comes the additional cost of separation, another plant, and another billion. Only America had the money to do the initial project. Everyone in the world *knew* about nuclear fission – it was no secret, what real secrets are there in physics, eh? – but only America had the money and resources to make the attempt. And the people,' Fromm added. 'What people they had! So, the first bombs – they made three, by the way – were designed to use all the available material, and because the main criterion was reliability, they were made to be crude, but effective. And they required the largest aircraft in the world to carry them.

'*Also*, then the war was won, and bomb-design became a professional study and not a frantic wartime project, *ja*? The plutonium reactor they have at Hanford turned out only a few tens of kilos of plutonium per year at the time, and the Americans had to learn to use the material more efficiently. The Mark-12 bomb was one of the first really advanced designs, and the Israelis improved it somewhat. That bomb has five times the yield of the Hiroshima device for less than a fifth of the reaction mass – twenty-five-fold improvement in efficiency, *ja*? And we can improve that by almost a factor of ten.

'Now a really expert design team, with the proper facilities could advance that by another factor of . . . perhaps four. Modern warheads are the most elegant, the most fascinating –'

'Two megatons?' Ghosn asked. *Was it possible?*

'We cannot do it here,' Fromm said, the sorrow manifest in his voice. 'The available information is insufficient. The physics are straightforward, but there are engineering concerns, and there are no published articles

380

to aid us in the bomb-design process. Remember that warhead tests are being carried out even today to make the bombs smaller and yet more efficient. One must experiment in this field, as with any other, and we cannot experiment. Nor do we have the time or money to train technicians to execute the design. I *could* come up with a theoretical design for a megaton-plus device, but in truth it would have only a fifty-percent likelihood of success. Perhaps a little more, but it would not be a practical undertaking without a proper experimental-test program.'

'What can you do?' Qati asked.

'I can make this into a weapon with a nominal yield of between four hundred and five hundred kilotons. It will be roughly a cubic meter in size and weigh roughly five hundred kilos.' Fromm paused to read the looks on their faces. 'It will not be an elegant device, and it will be overly bulky and heavy. It will also be quite powerful.' It would be far more clever in design than anything American or Russian technicians had managed in the first fifteen years of the nuclear age, and that, Fromm thought, wasn't bad at all.

'Explosive containment?' Ghosn asked.

'Yes.' This young Arab was very clever, Fromm thought. 'The first bombs used massive steel cases. Ours will use explosives – bulky but light, and just as effective. We will squirt tritium into the core at the moment of ignition. As in the original Israeli design, that will generate large quantities of neutrons to boost the fission reaction; that reaction in turn will blast additional neutrons into another tritium supply, causing a fusion reaction. The energy budget is roughly fifty kilotons from the primary and four hundred from the secondary.'

'How much tritium?' While not a difficult substance to obtain in small amounts – watchmakers and gunsight manufacturers used it, but only in microscopic quantities – Ghosn knew supplies over ten miligrams were virtually unobtainable, as he had just discovered himself. Tritium – not plutonium despite what Fromm had said – was the most expensive commercially available material on the planet. You could *get* tritium, but not plutonium.

'I have fifty grams,' Fromm announced smugly. 'Far more than we can actually use.'

'Fifty *grams*!' Ghosn exclaimed. '*Fifty!*'

'Our reactor complex was manufacturing special nuclear material for our own bomb project. When the socialist government fell, it was decided to give the plutonium to the Soviets – loyalty to the world socialist cause, you see. The Soviets didn't see things that way. Their reaction –' Fromm paused '– they called it . . . well, I will leave that to your imagination. Their reaction was so strong that I decided to hide our tritium production. As you know it is very valuable commercially – my insurance policy, you might call it.'

'Where?'

'In the basement of my home, concealed in some nickel-hydrogen batteries.'

Qati didn't like that, not one small bit. The Arab chieftain was not a well man, the German could see, and that did not help him conceal his feelings.

'I need to return to Germany in any case to get the machine tools,' he said.

'You have them?'

'Five kilometers from my home is the Karl Marx Astrophysical Institute. We were supposed to manufacture astronomical telescopes there, visual and X-ray telescopes. Alas, it never opened. Such a fine "cover" wasted, eh? In the machine shop, in crates marked ASTROPHYSICAL INSTRUMENTS, are six high-precision, five-axis machines – the finest sort,' Fromm observed with a wolfish grin. 'Cincinnati Milacron, from the United States of America. Precisely what the Americans use at their Oak Ridge, Rocky Flats, and Pantex fabrication plants.'

'What about operators?' Ghosn asked.

'We were training twenty of them, sixteen men and four women, each with a university degree . . . No, that would be too dangerous. It is not really necessary in any case. The machines are "user-friendly," as they say. We could do the work ourselves, but that would take too much time. Any skilled lensmaker – even a master gunsmith, as a matter of fact – can operate them. What was the business of Nobel Prize winners fifty years ago is now the work of a competent machinist,' Fromm said. 'Such is the nature of progress, *ja*?'

'It could be, then again it could not,' Yevgeniy said. He'd been on duty for twenty hours straight, and only six hours of fitful sleep separated that from yet another, longer stint.

Finding it, if that indeed was what they'd done, had taken all of Dubinin's skill. He'd guessed that the American missile sub had headed south, and that her cruising speed was in the order of five knots. Next came environmental considerations. He'd had to stay close, within direct-path range, not allowing himself to come into a sonar convergence zone. The CZs were annular – donut – shaped areas around a vessel. Sound that went downward from a point within the convergence zone was refracted by the water temperature and pressure, traveling back and forth to the surface on a helical path at semi-regular intervals that in turn depended on environmental conditions. By staying out of them, relative to where he thought his target was, he could evade one means of detection. To do that meant that he had to stay within theoretical direct-path distance, the area in which sound simply traveled radially from its source. To accomplish that without detection, he had to remain on the top side of the thermocline layer – he figured that the American would remain under it – while allowing his towed-array sonar to hang below it. In this way, his own engine-plant noises would probably be deflected away from the American submarine.

Dubinin's tactical problem lay in his disadvantages. The American submarine was quieter than his, and possessed both better sonars and better sonar-operators. Senior Lieutenant Yevgeniy Nikolayevich Ryskov was a very bright young officer, but he was the only sonar expert aboard who might fairly be matched against the

American counterparts, and the boy was burning himself out. Captain Dubinin's only advantage lay in himself. He was a fine tactician, and knew it. And his American counterpart was not, Dubinin thought, and didn't know it. There was a final disadvantage. By staying on top of the layer, he made counter-detection by an American patrol aircraft easier, but Dubinin was willing to run that risk. What lay before him was a prize such as no Russian submarine commander had ever grasped.

Both captain and lieutenant stared at a 'waterfall' display, looking not at a strobe of light, but instead a disjointed, barely visible vertical line that wasn't as bright as it should have been. The American Ohio-class was quieter than the background noise of the ocean, and both men wondered if somehow environmental conditions were showing them the acoustical shadow of that most sophisticated of missile submarines. It was just as likely, Dubinin thought, that fatigue was playing hallucinatory games with both of their minds.

'We need a transient,' Ryskov said, reaching for his tea. 'A dropped tool, a slammed hatch . . . a mistake, a mistake . . .'

I could ping him . . . I could duck below the layer and hit him with a blast of active sonar energy and find out . . . NO! Ryskov turned away and nearly swore at himself. *Patience, Valentin. They are patient, we must be patient.*

'Yevgeniy Nikolay'ch, you look weary.'

'I can rest in Petropavlovsk, Captain. I will sleep for a week, and see my wife – well, I will not sleep entirely for that week,' he said with an exhausted grin. The lieutenant's face was illuminated by the yellow glow of the screen. 'But I will not turn away from a chance like this one!'

'There will be no accidental transients.'

'I know, Captain. Those damned American crews . . . I *know* it's him, I *know* it's an Ohio! What *else* could it be?'

'Imagination, Yevgeniy, imagination and too large a wish on our part.'

Lieutenant Ryskov turned. 'I think my captain knows better than that!'

'I think my lieutenant is right.' *Such a game this is! Ship against ship, mind against mind. Chess in three dimensions, played in an ever-changing physical environment.* And the Americans were the masters of the game. Dubinin knew that. Better equipment, better crews, better training. Of course, the Americans knew that, too, and two generations of advantage had generated arrogance rather than innovation . . . not in all, but certainly in some. A clever commander in the missile submarine would be doing things differently . . . *If I had such a submarine, not all the world could find me!*

'Twelve more hours, then we must break contact and turn for home.'

'Too bad,' Ryskov observed, not meaning it. Six weeks at sea was enough for him.

'Make your depth six-zero feet,' the Officer of the Deck said.

'Make my depth six-zero feet, aye,' the Driving Officer replied. 'Ten degrees up on the fairwater planes.'

The missile-firing drill had just begun. A regular occurrence, it was intended both to ensure the competence of the crew and desensitize them to their primary war-fighting mission, the launch of twenty-four UGM-93 Trident-II D-5 missiles, each with ten Mark 5 re-entry vehicles of 400 kilotons nominal yield. A total of two hundred forty warheads with a total net yield of 96 megatons. But there was more to it than that, since nuclear weapons depended on the interlocking logic of several physical laws. Small weapons employed their yield with greater efficiencies than larger ones. Most important of all, the Mark 5 RV had a demonstrated accuracy of ±50 meters CEP ('Circular Error Probable'), meaning that after a flight of over four thousand nautical miles, half the warheads would land within 164.041 *feet* of their targets, and nearly all the rest within 300 feet. The 'miss' distance was far smaller than the crater to be expected from such a warhead, as a result of which the

D-5 missile was the first sea-launched ballistic missile with counter-force capability. It was designed for a disarming first-strike. Given the normal two-at-one targeting, *Maine* could eliminate 120 Soviet missiles and/or missile-control bunkers, roughly ten percent of the current Soviet ICBM force, which was itself configured for a counter-force mission.

In the missile-control center – MCC – aft of the cavernous missile room, a senior chief petty officer lit up his panel. All twenty-four birds were on line. On-board navigation equipment fed data into each missile-guidance system. It would be updated in a few minutes from orbiting navigation satellites. To hit a target, the missile had to know not only where the target was, but also where the missile itself was starting from. The NAVSTAR Global Positioning System could do that with a tolerance of less than five meters. The senior chief watched status lights change as missiles were interrogated by his computers and reported their readiness.

Around the submarine, water pressure on the hull diminished at a rate of 2.2 tons per square foot for every 100 feet of rise towards the surface. *Maine*'s hull expanded slightly as the pressure was relieved, and there was a tiny amount of noise as steel relaxed from the compression.

It was only a groan, scarcely audible even over the sonar systems and seductively close to the call of a whale. Ryskov was so drunk with fatigue that had it come a few minutes later he would have missed it, but though his daydreams were getting the best of him, his mind retained enough of its sharpness to take note of the sound.

'Captain . . . hull-popping noise . . . right there!' His finger stabbed the screen, just at the bottom of the shadow he and Dubinin had been examining. 'He's coming shallow.'

Dubinin raced into the control room. 'Stand by to change depth.' He put on a headset that connected him to Lieutenant Ryskov.

'Yevgeniy Nikolay'ch, this must be done well, and done quickly. I will drop below the layer just as the American goes over it . . .'

'No, captain, you can wait. His array will hang below briefly, as ours would do!'

'Damn!' Dubinin almost laughed. 'Forgive me, Lieutenant. For that, a bottle of Starka.' Which was the best Russian-made vodka.

'My wife and I will drink your health . . . I'm getting an angle reading . . . Estimate target five degrees depression from our array . . . Captain, if I can hold him, the moment we lose him through the layer . . .'

'Yes, a quick range estimate!' It would be crude, but it would be something. Dubinin rasped quick orders to his tracking officer.

'Two degrees . . . hull noises are gone . . . this is very hard to hold, but he's occulting the background a little more now – GONE! He's through the layer now!'

'One, two, three . . .' Dubinin counted. The American must be doing a missile drill, or coming up to receive communications, in any case he'd go to twenty meters depth, and his towed array . . . five hundred meters long . . . speed five knots, and . . . Now!

'Helm, down five degrees on the bow planes. We're going just below the layer. *Starpom*, make note of outside water temperature. Gently, helm, gently . . .'

Admiral Lunin dipped her bow and slid below the undulating border that marked the difference between relatively warm surface water and colder deep water.

'Range?' Dubinin asked his tracking officer.

'Estimate between five and nine thousand meters, Captain! Best I can do with the data.'

'Well done, Kolya! Splendid.'

'We're below the layer now, water temperature down five degrees!' the *Starpom* – executive officer – called.

'Bow planes to zero, level out.'

'Planes to zero, captain . . . zero angle on the boat.'

Had there been enough overhead room, Dubinin would have leaped off his feet. He'd just done what no other Soviet submarine commander – and if his intelligence information was right, only a handful of Americans – had ever done. He'd established contact with and *tracked* an American Ohio-class fleet ballistic-missile submarine. In a war situation, he'd be able to fire off ranging pings with his active sonar and launch torpedoes. He'd stalked the world's most elusive game, and was close enough for a killing shot. His skin tingled from the excitement of the moment. Nothing in the world could match this feeling. Nothing at all.

'*Ryl nepravo,*' he said next. 'Right rudder, new course three-zero-zero. Increase speed slowly to ten knots.'

'But, Captain . . .' his *Starpom* said.

'We're breaking contact. He'll continue this drill for at least thirty minutes. It is very unlikely that we can evade counter-detection when he concludes it. Better to leave now. We do not want him to know what we have done. We will meet this one again. In any case, our mission is accomplished. We have tracked him, and we got close enough to launch our attack. At Petropavlovsk, men, there will be much drinking, and your captain will do the buying! Now, let's clear the area quietly so that he will not know that we were ever here.'

Captain Robert Jefferson Jackson wished he was younger, wished that his hair was still completely black, that he could again be a young 'nugget' fresh from Pensacola, ready to take his first hop in one of the forbidding fighter aircraft that sat like enormous birds of prey along the flight line at Oceana Naval Air Station. That all twenty-four of the F-14D Tomcats in the immediate area were his was not as satisfying as the knowledge that *one* was his and his alone. Instead, as Commander Air Group, he 'owned' two Tomcat squadrons, two more of F/A-18 Hornets, one of A-6E Intruder medium-attack aircraft, another of S-3 submarine hunters, and finally the less glamorous tankers, electronic-warfare Prowlers, and rescue/ASW helicopters. A total of seventy-eight birds with an aggregate value of . . . what? A billion dollars? Much more if you considered replacement cost. Then there were the three thousand men who flew and serviced the aircraft, each of whom was beyond price, of course. He was responsible for all of it. It was much more fun to be a new fighter pilot who drove his personal airplane and left the worrying to management. Robby was now management, the guy the kids talked about in their cabins on the ship. They didn't want to be called into his office, because that was like going to see the principal. They didn't really like flying with him, because a) he was too old to be good at it any more (they thought), and b) he'd tell them whatever he thought they were doing wrong (fighter pilots do not often admit mistakes, except among themselves).

There was a certain irony to it. His previous job had been in the Pentagon, pushing papers. He'd prayed and lusted for release from that job, whose main excitement every day was finding a decent parking spot. Then he'd gotten his command of his air wing – and been stuck with more admin crap than he'd ever faced in his life. At least he got to fly twice a week . . . if he were lucky. Today was such a day. His command master chief petty officer gave him a grin on the way out the door.

'Mind the store, Master Chief.'

'Roger that, skipper. It'll be here when you get back.'

Jackson stopped in his tracks. 'You *can* have someone steal all the paperwork.'

'I'll see what I can do, sir.'

A staff car took him to the flight line. Jackson was already in his Nomex flight suit, an old smelly one whose olive-drab color was faded from many washings, and threadbare at the elbows and seat from years of use. He could and should have gotten a new one, but pilots are superstitious creatures; Robby and this flight suit had been through a lot together.

'Hey, skipper!' called one of his squadron commanders.

Commander Bud Sanchez was shorter than Jackson. His olive skin and Bismarck mustache accentuated bright eyes and a grin right out of a toothpaste commercial. Sanchez, Commanding Officer of VF-1, would fly Jackson's wing today. They'd flown together when

Jackson had commanded VF-41 off the *John F. Kennedy*. 'Your bird is all dialed in. Ready to kick a little ass?'

'Who's the opposition today?'

'Some jarheads out of Cherry Point in 18-Deltas. We got a Hummer already orbiting a hundred miles out, and the exercise is BARCAP against low-level intruders.' BARCAP meant Barrier Combat Air Patrol. The mission was to prevent attacking aircraft from crossing a line that they were not supposed to cross. 'Up to some heavy ACM? Those Marines sounded a little cocky over the phone.'

'The Marine I can't take ain't been born yet,' Robby said, as he pulled his helmet off the rack. It bore his call-sign, Spade.

'Hey, you RIOs,' Sanchez called, 'quit holdin' hands and let's get it on!'

'On the way, Bud.' Michael 'Lobo' Alexander came from around the lockers, followed by Jackson's radar-intercept officer, Henry 'Shredder' Walters. Both were under thirty, both lieutenants. In the locker room, people talked by call-sign rather than rank. Robby loved the fellowship of squadron life as much as he loved his country.

Outside, the plane captains – petty officers – who were responsible for maintaining the aircraft walked the officers to their respective birds and helped them aboard. (On the dangerous area of a carrier flight deck, pilots are led virtually by the hand by enlisted men, lest they get lost or hurt.) Jackson's bird had a double-zero ID number on the nose. Under the cockpit was painted 'CAPT. R. J. Jackson "SPADE"' to make sure that everyone knew that this was the CAG's bird. Under that was a flag representing a MiG-29 fighter aircraft that an Iraqi had mistakenly flown too close to Jackson's Tomcat not so long before. There hadn't been much to it – the other pilot had forgotten, once, to check his 'six' and paid the price – but a kill was a kill, and kills were what fighter pilots lived for.

Five minutes later, all four men were strapped in, and engines were turning.

'How are you this morning, Shredder?' Jackson asked over his intercom.

'Ready to waste some Marines, skipper. Lookin' good back here. Is this thing gonna fly today?'

'Guess it's time to find out.' Jackson switched to radio. 'Bud, this is Spade, ready here.'

'Roger, Spade, you have the lead.' Both pilots looked around, got an all-clear from their plane captains, and looked around again.

'Spade has the lead.' Jackson tripped his brakes. 'Rolling now.'

'Hello, *mein Schatz*,' Manfred Fromm said to his wife.

Traudl rushed forward to embrace him. 'Where have you been?'

'That I cannot say,' Fromm replied, with a knowing twinkle in his eye. He hummed a few bars from Lloyd Webber's 'Don't Cry for Me, Argentina.'

'I knew you would see,' Traudl beamed at him.

'You must not talk of this.' To confirm her suspicion, he handed her a wad of banknotes, five packets of ten thousand D-Marks each. That should keep the mercenary bitch quiet and happy, Manfred Fromm told himself. 'And I will only be here overnight. I had some business to do, and of course –'

'Of course, Manfred.' She hugged him again, the money in her hands. 'If only you had called!'

Arrangements had been absurdly easy to make. A ship outbound for Latakia, Syria, was sailing from Rotterdam in seventy hours. He and Bock had arranged for a commercial trucking company to load the machine tools into a small cargo container which would be loaded on the ship and unloaded onto a Syrian dock in six more days. It would have been faster to send the tools by air, or even by rail to a Greek or Italian port for faster transshipment by sea, but Rotterdam was the world's busiest port, with overworked customs officials whose main task was searching for drug shipments. Sniffer dogs could go over that particular container to their hearts' content.

Fromm let his wife go into the kitchen to make coffee.

It would take a few minutes, and that was all he needed. He walked down into his basement. In the corner, as far from the water-heater as was possible was an orderly pile of lumber, on top of which were four black metal boxes. Each weighed about twelve kilograms, about twenty-five pounds. Fromm carried one at a time – on the second trip, he got a pair of gloves from his bureau drawer to protect his hands – and placed them in the trunk of his rented BMW. By the time the coffee was ready, his task was complete.

'You have a fine tan,' Traudl observed, carrying the tray out from the kitchen. In her mind, she'd already spent about a quarter of the money her husband had given her. So, Manfred had seen the light. She'd known he would, sooner or later. Better that it should be sooner. She'd be especially nice to him tonight.

'Günther?'

Bock didn't like leaving Fromm to his own devices, but he also had a task to perform. This was a far greater risk. It was, he told himself, a high-risk operational concept, even if the real dangers were in the planning stage, which was both an oddity and a relief.

Erwin Keitel lived on a pension, and not an especially comfortable one at that. Its necessity came from two facts. First, he was a former Lieutenant-Colonel in the East German Stasi, the intelligence and counter-intelligence arm of the defunct German Democratic Republic; second, he had liked his work of thirty-two years. Whereas most of his former colleagues had acknowledged the changes in their country and for the most part put their German identity ahead of whatever ideology they'd once held – and told literally everything they knew to the *Bundes Nachrichten Dienst* – Keitel had decided that he was not going to work for capitalists. That made him one of the 'politically unemployed' citizens of the united Germany. His pension was a matter of convenience. The new German government honored, after a fashion, pre-existing government obligations. It was at the least politically expedient, and what Germany now was was a matter of daily struggling with facts that were not and could not be reconciled. It was easier to give Keitel a pension than to leave him on the official dole, which was deemed more demeaning than a pension. By the government, that is. Keitel didn't see things quite that way. If the world made any sense at all, he thought, he would have been executed or exiled – exactly where he might have been exiled to, Keitel didn't know. He'd begun to consider going over to the Russians – he'd had good contacts in the KGB – but that thought had died a quick death. The Soviets had washed their hands of everything to do with the DDR, fearing treachery from people whose allegiance to world socialism – or whatever the hell the Russians stood for now, Keitel had no idea – was somewhat less than their allegiance to their new country. Keitel took his seat beside Bock's in the corner booth of a quiet *Gasthaus* in what had formerly been East Berlin.

'This is very dangerous, my friend.'

'I am aware of that, Erwin.' Bock waved for two liter glasses of beer. Service was quicker than it had been a few years before, but both men ignored that.

'I cannot tell you how I feel about what they did to Petra,' Keitel said, after the girl left them.

'Do you know exactly what happened?' Bock asked, in a level and emotionless voice.

'The detective who ran the case visited her in prison – he did so quite often – not for interrogation. They made a conscious effort to push her over the edge. You must understand, Günther, courage in a man or a woman is a finite quality. It was not weakness on her part. Anyone can break. It is simply a matter of time. They watched her die,' the retired colonel said.

'Oh?' Bock's face didn't change, but his knuckles went white on the stein handle.

'There was a television camera hidden in her cell. They have her suicide on videotape. They watched her do it, and did nothing to stop her.'

Bock didn't say anything, and the room was too dim to see how pale his face went. It was as though a hot blast from a furnace swept over him, followed by one from the North Pole. He closed his eyes for a brief second to get control of himself. Petra would not have wished him to be governed by emotion at a time like this. He opened his eyes to look at his friend.

'Is that a fact?'

'I know the name of the detective. I know his address. I still have friends,' Keitel assured Bock.

'Yes, Erwin, I am sure you do. I need your help to do something.'

'Anything.'

'You know, of course, what brought us to this.'

'That depends on how you mean it,' Keitel said. 'The people disappointed me in the way they allowed themselves to be seduced, but the common people always lack the discipline to know what is good for them. The real cause of our national misfortune . . .'

'Precisely, the Americans and the Russians.'

'*Mein lieber Günther*, even a united Germany cannot —'

'Yes, it can. If we are to remake the world into our image, Erwin, both of our oppressors must be damaged severely.'

'But how?'

'There is a way. Can you believe me that much, just for now?'

Keitel drained his beer and sat back. He'd helped train Bock. At fifty-six, it was too late for him to change his ideas of the world, and he was still a fine judge of character. Bock was a man such as himself. Günther had been a careful, ruthless, and very effective clandestine operator.

'What of our detective friend?'

Bock shook his head. 'As much satisfaction as that might give me, no. This is not a time for personal revenge. We have a movement and a country to save.' *More than one, in fact*, Bock thought, but this was not the time for that. What was taking shape in his mind was a grand stroke, a breathtaking maneuver that might — he was too intellectually honest to say *would*, even to himself — change the world into a more malleable shape.

Exactly what would happen after that, who could say? That would not matter at all if he and his friends were unable to take the first bold step.

'How long have we known each other – fifteen years, twenty?' Keitel smiled. '*Aber naturlich*. Of course I can trust you.'

'How many others can we trust?'

'How many do we need?'

'No more than ten, but we will need a total of ten.'

Keitel's face went blank. *Eight men we can trust absolutely . . . ?*

'That is too many for safety, Günther. What sort of men?' Bock told him. 'I know where to start. It should be possible . . . men of my age . . . and some younger, of your age. The physical skills you require are not difficult to obtain, but remember that much of this is beyond our control.'

'As some of my friends say, that is in God's hands,' Günther said with a smirk.

'Barbarians,' Keitel snorted. 'I have never liked them.'

'*Ja, doch*, they don't even let a man have a beer,' Bock smiled. 'But they are strong, Erwin, they are determined, and they are faithful to the cause.'

'Whose cause is that?'

'One we both share at the moment. How much time do you need?'

'Two weeks. I can be reached –'

'No.' Bock shook his head. 'Too risky. Can you travel, are you being watched?'

'Watch me? All of my subordinates have changed allegiance, and the BND knows that the KGB will have nothing to do with me. They would not waste the assets to watch me. I am a gelding, you see?'

'Some gelding, Erwin.' Bock handed over some cash. 'We will meet in Cyprus in two weeks. Make sure you are not followed.'

'I will – I do. I have not forgotten how, my friend.'

Fromm awoke at dawn. He dressed at leisure, trying not to wake Traudl. She'd been more of a wife in the past twelve hours than in the preceding twelve months, and his conscience told him that their nearly failed marriage had not been entirely her fault. He was surprised to find breakfast waiting on the table for him.

'When will you be back?'

'I'm not sure. Probably several months.'

'That long?'

'*Mein Schatz*, the reason I am there is that they need what I know, and I am being well-paid.' He made a mental note to have Qati send additional funds. So long as money kept coming in, she'd not be nervous.

'It is not possible for me to join you?' Traudl asked, showing real affection for her man.

'It is no place for a woman.' Which was honest enough that his conscience allowed itself to relax a little. He finished his coffee. 'I must be off.'

'Hurry back.'

Manfred Fromm kissed his wife and walked out the door. The BMW was not affected in the least by the fifty kilos of weight in the trunk. He waved to Traudl one last time before driving off. He gave the house a final look in the mirror, thinking, correctly, that he might not see it again.

His next stop was the Karl Marx Astronomical Institute. The single-story buildings were already showing their neglect, and it surprised him that vandals had not broken windows. The truck was already there. Fromm used his keys to let himself into the machine shop. The tools were still there, still in hermetically sealed crates, and the crates were still marked ASTROPHYSICAL INSTRUMENTS. It was just a matter of signing some forms he'd typed up the previous afternoon. The truck driver knew how to operate the propane-fueled forklift, and drove each crate into the container. Fromm took the batteries from the trunk of his car, and set them in a final, small box, which was loaded on last. It took him an additional half hour to chain things down in place, and then he drove off. He and 'Herr Professor Fromm' would meet again outside Rotterdam.

Fromm rendezvoused with Bock in Greifswald. They

drove west in the latter's car – Bock was a better driver.

'How was home?'

'Traudl liked the money a great deal,' Fromm reported.

'We'll send her more, at regular intervals . . . every two weeks, I think.'

'Good, I was going to ask Qati about that.'

'We take care of our friends,' Bock observed, as they passed over what had once been a border crossing. Now it was merely green.

'How long for the fabrication process?'

'Three months . . . maybe four. We could go faster,' Fromm said apologetically, 'but remember that I have never actually done this with real material, only in simulation. There is absolutely no margin for error. It will be complete by the middle of January. At that point, it is yours to use.' Fromm wondered, of course, what plans Bock and the others had for it, but that was not really his concern, was it? *Doch*.

CHAPTER 15

Development

Ghosn could only shake his head. He knew objectively that it resulted from the sweeping political changes in Europe, the effective elimination of borders attendant to the economic unification, the collapse of the Warsaw Pact and headlong rush to join in the new European family. Even so, the hardest part of getting these five machine tools out of Germany and into his valley had been finding a suitable track at Latakia, and that had actually been rather difficult, since negotiating the road into where his shop lay had incomprehensibly been overlooked by everyone – including, he thought with some satisfaction, the German. Fromm was now observing closely as a gang of men labored to move the last of the five tools onto its table. Arrogant as he may have been, Fromm was an expert technologist. Even the tables had been built to exactly the right size, with ten centimeters of extra space around each tool so that one could rest a notebook. The backup generators and UPSs were in place and tested. It was just a matter of getting the tools set up and fully calibrated, which would take about a week.

Bock and Qati were observing the whole procedure from the far end of the building, careful to keep out of the way.

'I have the beginnings of an operational plan,' Günther said.

'You do not intend the bomb for Israel, then?' Qati asked. He was the one who would approve or disapprove the plan. He would, however, listen to his German friend. 'Can you tell me of it yet?'

'Yes,' Bock did so.

'Interesting. What of security?'

'One problem is our friend, Manfred – more properly, his wife. She knows his skills, and she knows he is away somewhere.'

'I would have thought that killing her carries more risks than rewards.'

'Ordinarily it would appear so, but all of Fromm's fellow experts are also away – with their wives in most cases. Were she merely to disappear, it would be assumed by the neighbors that she'd joined her husband. His absence risks a comment by her, however casual it might be, that Manfred is off doing something. Someone might notice.'

'Does she actually know what his former job was?'

'Manfred is very security-conscious, but we must assume that she does. What woman does not?'

'Go on,' Qati said tiredly.

'Discovery of her body will force the police to search for her husband, and that is also a problem. She must disappear. Then it will seem that she has joined her husband.'

'Instead of the other way around,' Qati observed with a rare smile, 'at the end of the project.'

'Quite so.'

'What sort of woman is she?'

'A shrew, a money-grabber, not a believer,' Bock, an atheist, said, somewhat to Qati's amusement.

'How will you do it?'

Bock explained briefly. 'It will also validate the reliability of our people for that part of the operation. I'll leave the details to my friends.'

'Trickery? One cannot be overly careful in an enterprise like this one . . .'

'If you wish, a videotape of the elimination? Something unequivocal?' Bock had done that before.

'It is barbaric,' Qati said. 'But regrettably necessary.'

'I will take care of that when I go to Cyprus.'

'You'll need security for that trip, my friend.'

'Yes, thank you, I think I will.' Bock knew what that meant. If his capture looked imminent – well, he was in a profession that entailed serious risks, and Qati had to be careful. Günther's own operational proposal made that all the more imperative.

'The tools all have levelers for the air plates,' Ghosn said in annoyance, fifteen meters away. 'Very good ones – why all the trouble with the tables?'

'My young friend, this is something we can only do one time. Do you wish to take any chances at all?'

Ghosn nodded. The man was right, even if he was a patronizing son-of-a-bitch. 'And the tritium?'

'In those batteries. I've kept them in a cool place. You release the tritium by heating them. The procedure for recovering the tritium is delicate, but straightforward.'

'Ah, yes, I know how to do that.' Ghosn remembered such lab experiments from university.

Fromm handed him a copy of the manual for the first tool. 'Now, we both have new things to learn so that we can teach the operators.'

Captain Dubinin sat in the office of the Master Shipwright of the yard. Known variously as Shipyard Number 199, Leninskaya Komsomola, or simply Komsomol'sk, it was the yard at which the *Admiral Lunin* had been built. Himself a former submarine commander, the man preferred the title Master Shipwright to Superintendent and had changed the title on his office door accordingly on taking the job two years earlier. He was a traditionalist, but also a brilliant engineer. Today he was a happy man.

'While you were gone, I got hold of something wonderful!'

'What might that be, Admiral?'

'The prototype for a new reactor feed pump. It's big, cumbersome, and a cast-iron bastard to install and maintain, but it's . . .'

'Quiet?'

'As a thief,' the Admiral said with a smile. 'It reduces the radiated noise of your current pump by a factor of fifty.'

'Indeed? Who did we steal that from?'

The Master Shipwright laughed at that. 'You don't need to know, Valentin Borissovich. Now, I have a question for you: I have heard that you did something very clever ten days ago . . .'

Dubinin smiled. 'Admiral, that is something which I cannot –'

'Yes, you can. I spoke with your squadron commander. Tell me, how close did you get to USS *Nevada*?'

'I think it was actually *Maine*,' Dubinin said. The intelligence types disagreed, but he went with his instincts. 'About eight thousand meters. We identified him from a mechanical transient made during an exercise, then I proceeded to stalk on the basis of a couple of wild guesses –'

'Rubbish! Humility can be overdone, Captain. Go on.'

'And after tracking what we thought was our target, he confirmed it with a hull transient. I think he came up to conduct a rocket-firing drill. At that point, given our operational schedule and the tactical situation, I elected to break contact while it was possible to do so without counter-detection.'

'That was your cleverest move of all,' the Master Shipwright said, pointing a finger at his guest. 'You could not have decided better, because the next time you go out, you will be the most quiet submarine we've ever put to sea.'

'They still have the advantage over us,' Dubinin pointed out honestly.

'That is true, but for once the advantage will be less than the difference between one commander and another, which is as it should be. We both studied under Marko Ramius. If only he were here to see this!'

Dubinin nodded agreement. 'Yes, given current political circumstances, it is truly a game of skill, not one of malice anymore.'

'Would that I were young enough to play,' the Master Shipwright said.

'And the new sonar?'

'This is our design from the Severomorsk Laboratory, a large aperture array, roughly a forty-percent improvement in sensitivity. On the whole, you will be the equal of an American Los Angeles class in nearly all regimes.'

Except crew, Dubinin didn't say. It would be years before his country had the ability to train men as the Western navies did, and by that time Dubinin would no longer have command at sea – BUT! In three months time he'd have the best ship that his nation had ever given one of its captains. If he were able to cajole his squadron commander into giving him a larger officer complement, he could beach the more inept of his conscripts and begin a really effective training regimen for the rest. Training and leading the crew was his job. He was the commanding officer of *Admiral Lunin*. He took credit for what went well, and blame for what went badly. Ramius had taught him that from the first day aboard the first submarine. His fate was in his own hands, and what man could ask for more than that?

Next year, USS Maine, *when the bitterly cold storms of winter sweep across the North Pacific, we will meet again.*

'Not a single contact,' Captain Ricks said in the wardroom.

'Except for *Omaha*.' LCDR Claggett looked over some paperwork. 'And he was in too much of a hurry.'

'Ivan doesn't even try anymore. Like he's gone out of business.' It was almost a lament from the Navigator.

'Why even try to find us?' Ricks observed. 'Hell, aside from that Akula that got lost . . .'

'We did track the guy a while back,' Nav pointed out.

'Maybe next time we'll get some hull shots,' a lieutenant observed lightly from behind a magazine. There was general laughter. Some of the more extreme fast-attack skippers had, on very rare occasions, maneuvered close enough to some Soviet submarines to take flash photographs of their hulls. But that was a thing of the past. The Russians were a lot better at the submarine game than they'd been only ten years earlier. Being number two did make one try harder.

'Now, the next engineering drill,' Ricks said.

The Executive Officer noted that the faces around the table didn't change. The officers were learning not to groan or roll their eyes. Ricks had a very limited sense of humor.

'Hello, Robby!' Joshua Painter got up from his swivel chair and walked over to shake hands with his visitor.

'Morning, sir.'

'Grab a seat.' A steward served coffee to both men. 'How's the wing look?'

'I think we'll be ready on time, sir.'

Admiral Joshua Painter, USN, was Supreme Allied Commander Atlantic, Commander-in-Chief Atlantic, and Commander-in-Chief U.S. Atlantic Fleet – they only paid him one salary for the three jobs, though he did have three staffs to do his thinking for him. A career aviator – mainly fighters – he had reached the summit of his career. He would not be selected for Chief of Naval Operations. Someone with fewer politically rough edges would get that job, but Painter was content. Under the rather eccentric organization of the armed services, the CNO and other service chiefs merely advised the Secretary of Defense. The SecDef was the one who gave the orders to the area CINCs – commanders-in-chief. SACLANT-CINCLANT-CINCLANTFLT might have been an awkward, cumbersome, and generally bloated command, but it was a *command*. Painter owned real ships, real airplanes, and real marines, had the authority to tell them where to go and what to do. Two complete fleets, 2nd and 6th, came under his authority: seven aircraft carriers, a battleship – though an aviator, Painter rather liked battleships; his grandfather had commanded one – over a hundred destroyers and cruisers, 60 submarines, a division and a half of marines, thousands of combat aircraft. The fact of the matter was that only one country in the world had more combat power than Joshua Painter did, and that country was no longer a serious strategic threat in these days of international amity. He no longer had to look forward to the possibility of war. Painter was a happy man. A man who'd flown missions over Vietnam, he'd seen American power go from its post-World War II peak to its nadir in the 1970s, then bounce back again until America once more was the most powerful country on earth. He'd played his part in the best of times and the worst of times, and now the best of times were better still. Robby Jackson was one of the men to whom his Navy would be turned over.

'What's this I heard about Soviet pilots in Libya again?' Jackson asked.

'Well, they never really left, did they?' Painter asked rhetorically. 'Our friend wants their newest weapons, and he's paying with hard cash. They need the cash. It's business. That's simple enough.'

'You'd think he'd learn,' Robby observed with a shake of the head.

'Well, maybe he will . . . soon. It must be real lonely being the last of the hotheads. Maybe that's why he's loading up while he still can. That's what the intel people say.'

'And the Russians?'

'Quite a lot of instructors and technical people there on contract, especially aviators and SAM types.'

'Nice to know. If our friend tries anything, he's got some good stuff to hide behind.'

'Not good enough to stop you, Robby.'

'Good enough to make me write some letters.' Jackson had written enough of those. As a CAG, he could look forward on this cruise – as with every other he'd ever taken – to deaths in his air wing. To the best of his knowledge, no carrier had ever sailed for a deployment, whether in peace or war, without some fatalities, and as the 'owner' of the air wing, the deaths were his responsibility. Wouldn't it be nice to be the first, Jackson thought. Aside from the fact that it would look good on his record, not having to tell a wife or a set of parents that Johnny had lost his life in service of his country . . . possible, but not likely, Robby told himself. Naval aviation was too dangerous. Past forty now, knowing that immortality was something between a myth and a joke, he had already found himself staring at the pilots in the squadron ready rooms and wondering which of the handsome, proud young faces would not be around when *TR* again made landfall at the Virginia Capes, whose pretty, pregnant wife would find a chaplain and another aviator on her doorstep just before lunch, along with a squadron wife to hold her hand when the world ended in distant fire and blood. A possible clash with Libyans was just one more threat in a universe where death was a permanent resident. He'd gotten too old for this life, Jackson admitted quietly to himself. Still as fine a fighter pilot as any — he was too mature to call himself the world's best anymore, except over drinks — the sadder aspects of the life were catching up, and it would soon be time to move on, if he were lucky, to an admiral's flag, just flying occasionally to show he still knew how and trying to make the good decisions that would minimize the unwanted visits.

'Problems?' Painter asked.

'Spares,' Captain Jackson replied. 'It's getting harder to keep all the birds up.'

'Doing the best we can.'

'Yes, sir, I know. Going to get worse, too, if I'm reading the papers right.' Like maybe three carriers would be retired, along with their air wings. Didn't people ever learn?

'Every time we've won a war we've been punished for it,' CINCLANT said. 'At least winning this one didn't cost us a whole lot. Don't worry, there'll be a place for you when the time comes. You're my best wing commander, Captain.'

'Thank you, sir. I don't mind hearing things like that.'

Painter laughed. 'Neither did I.'

'There is a saying in English,' Golovko observed. '"With friends like these, who has need of enemies?" What else do we know?'

'It would appear that they turned over their entire supply of plutonium,' the man said. A representative of the weapons research and design institute at Sarova, south of Gorkiy, he was less a weapons engineer than a

405

scientist who kept track of what people outside the Soviet Union were up to. 'I ran the calculations myself. It is theoretically possible that they developed more of the material, but what they turned over to us slightly exceeds our own production of plutonium from plants of similar design here in the Soviet Union. I think we got it all from them.'

'I have read all that. Why are you here now?'

'The original study overlooked something.'

'And what might that be?' the First Deputy Chairman of the Committee for State Security asked.

'Tritium.'

'And that is?' Golovko didn't remember. He was not an expert on nuclear materials, being more grounded in diplomatic and intelligence operations.

The man from Sarova hadn't taught basic physics in years. 'Hydrogen is the simplest of materials. An atom of hydrogen contains a proton, which is positively charged, and an electron, which is negatively charged. If you add a neutron – that has no electrical charge – to the hydrogen atom, you get deuterium. Add another, and you get tritium. It has three times the atomic weight of hydrogen, because of the additional neutrons. In simple terms, neutrons are the stuff of atomic weapons. When you liberate them from their host atoms, they radiate outward, bombarding other atomic nuclei, releasing more neutrons. That causes a chain reaction, releasing vast amounts of energy. Tritium is useful because the hydrogen atom is not supposed to contain any neutrons at all, much less two of them. It is unstable, and tends to break down at a fixed rate. The half-life of tritium is 12.3 years,' he explained. 'Thus if you insert tritium in a fission device, the additional neutrons it adds to the initial fission reaction accelerate or "boost" the fission in the plutonium or uranium reaction mass by a factor of between five and forty, allowing a far more efficient use of the heavy fission materials, like plutonium or enriched uranium. Secondly, additional amounts of tritium placed in the proper location nearby the fission device – called a "primary" in this case – begin a fusion reaction. There are other ways of doing this, of course. The chemicals of choice are lithium-deuteride and lithium-hydride, which is more stable, but tritium is still extremely useful for certain weapons applications.'

'And how does one make tritium?'

'Essentially by placing large quantities of lithium-aluminum in a nuclear reactor and allowing the thermal neutron flux – that's an engineering term for the back-and-forth traffic of the particles – to irradiate and transform lithium to tritium by capture of some of the neutrons. It turns up as small, faceted bubbles inside the metal. I believe that the Germans also manufactured tritium at their Greifswald plant.'

'Why? What evidence do you have?'

'We analyzed the plutonium they sent us. Plutonium has two isotopes, plutonium 239 and 240. From the relative proportions, you can determine the neutron flux in the reactor. The German sample has too little 240. Something was attenuating the neutron flux. That something was probably – almost certainly – tritium.'

'You are certain of that?'

'The physics involved here are complex but straightforward. In fact you can in many cases identify the plant that produced a plutonium sample by examining the ratio of various materials. My team and I are quite certain of our conclusions.'

'Those plants were under international inspection, yes? Are there no controls on the production of tritium?'

'The Germans managed to circumvent some of the plutonium inspections, and there are no international controls on tritium at all. Even if there were such controls, concealing tritium production would be child's play.'

Golovko swore under his breath. 'How much?'

The scientist shrugged. 'Impossible to say. The plant is being completely shut down. We no longer have access to it.'

'Doesn't tritium have other uses?'

'Oh, yes. It's commercially very valuable. It's phosphorescent – glows in the dark. People use it for watch dials, gunsights, instrument faces, all manner of applications. It is commercially very valuable, on the order of fifty thousand American dollars per gram.'

Golovko was surprised at himself for the digression. 'Back up for a moment, please. You tell me that our Fraternal Socialist Comrades in the German Democratic Republic were working not only to make their own atomic bombs, but also hydrogen bombs?'

'Yes, that is likely.'

'And one element of this plan is unaccounted for?'

'Also correct – possibly correct,' the man corrected himself.

'Likely?' It was like extracting an admission from a child, the First Deputy Chairman thought.

'*Da*. In their place, given the directives they received from Erich Honecker, it is certainly something I would have done. It was, moreover, technically quite simple to do. After all, we gave them the reactor technology.'

'What in hell were we thinking about?' Golovko muttered to himself.

'Yes, we made the same mistake with the Chinese, didn't we?'

'Didn't anyone –' The engineer cut him off.

'Of course there were warnings voiced. From my institute and the one at Kyshtym. No one listened. It was judged politically expedient to make this technology available to our allies.' The last word was delivered evenly.

'And you think we should do something?'

'I suppose we could ask our colleagues in the Foreign Ministry, but it would be worthwhile to get something substantive done. So, I decided to come here.'

'You think, then, that the Germans – the new Germans, I mean – might have a supply of fissionable material and this tritium from which they might make their own nuclear arsenal?'

'That is a real possibility. There are, as you know, a sizable number of German nuclear scientists who are mainly working in South America at the moment. The best of all possible worlds for them. They are doing what may well be weapons-related research twelve thousand kilometers from home, learning that which they need to learn at a distant location, and on someone else's payroll. If that is indeed the case, are they doing so merely as a business venture? I suppose that is a possibility, but it would seem more likely that their government has some knowledge of the affair. Since their government has taken no action to stop them, one must assume that their government approves of that activity. The most likely reason for their government to approve is the possible application of the knowledge they are acquiring for German national interests.'

Golovko frowned. His visitor had just strung three possibilities into a threat. He was thinking like an intelligence officer, and an especially paranoid one at that. But those were often the best kind.

'What else do you have?'

'Thirty possible names.' He handed a file over. 'We've spoken with our people – those who helped the Germans set up the Greifswald plant, I mean. Based on their recollections, these are the people most likely to be part of the project, if any. Half a dozen of them are remembered as being very clever indeed, good enough to work with us at Sarova.'

'Any of them make overt inquiries into –'

'No, and not necessary. Physics is physics. Fission is fission. Laws of science do not respect rules of classification. You cannot conceal nature, and that's exactly what we're dealing with here. If these people can operate a reactor, then the best of them can design nuclear weapons, given the necessary materials – and our reactor design *gave* them the ability to generate the proper materials. I think it is something you need to look into – to see what they did, and what they have. In any case, that is my advice.'

'I have some very good people in Directorate T of the First Chief Directorate,' Golovko said. 'After we digest this information, some of them will come to speak with you.' Sarova was only a few hours away by train.

'Yes, I've met with some of your technology analysts.

A few of them are very good indeed. I hope you still have good contacts in Germany.'

Golovko didn't answer that. He had many contacts still in Germany, but how many of them had been doubled? He'd recently done a reliability assessment of former penetration agents in the Stasi, and concluded that none could be trusted – more properly, that those who could be trusted were no longer in positions of any use, and even those . . . He decided on the spot to make this an all-Russian operation.

'If they have the materials, how soon might they fabricate weapons?'

'Given their level of technical expertise, and the fact that they've had access to American systems under NATO, there is no reason whatever why they could not have home-made weapons already in their inventory. They would not be crude weapons, either. In their position, and given the special nuclear materials, I could easily have produced two-stage weapons within months of unification. More sophisticated three-stage weapons . . . maybe another year.'

'Where would you do it?'

'In East Germany, of course. Better security. Exactly where?' The man thought for a minute. 'Look for a place with extremely precise machine tools, the sort associated with high-precision optical instruments. The X-ray telescope we just orbited was a direct spin-off of H-Bomb research. Management of X-rays, you see, is very important in a multi-stage weapon. We learned much of American bomb technology from open-source papers on focusing X-rays for astrophysical observations. As I said, it's physics. It cannot be hidden, only discovered; once discovered, it is open for all who have the intelligence and the desire to make use of it.'

'That is so wonderfully reassuring,' Golovko observed crossly. But who could he be angry with – this man for speaking the truth, or nature for being so easy to discover? 'Excuse me, Professor. Thank you very much indeed for taking the time to bring this to our attention.'

'My father is a mathematics teacher. He has lived

his entire life in Kiev. He remembers the Germans.'

Golovko saw the man out the door, then walked back to stare out the window.

Why did we ever let them unify? he asked himself. *Do they still want land? Lebensraum? Do they still want to be the dominant European power? Or are you being paranoid, Sergey?* He was paid to be paranoid, of course. Golovko sat down and lifted his phone.

'It is a small thing, and if it is necessary nothing more needs to be said,' Keitel replied to the question.

'And the men?'

'I have what I need, and they are reliable. All have worked overseas, mainly in Africa. All are experienced. Three colonels, six lieutenant-colonels, two majors – all of them retired like me.'

'Reliability is all-important,' Bock reminded the man.

'I know that, Günther. Each of these men would have been a general someday. Each has impeccable Party credentials. Why do you think they were retired, eh? Our New Germany cannot trust them.'

'Agents provocateurs?'

'I am the intelligence officer here,' Keitel reminded his friend. 'I do not tell you your job. Don't you tell me mine. Please, my friend, either you trust me or you do not. That choice is yours.'

'I know that, Erwin. Forgive me. This operation is most important.'

'And I know that, Günther.'

'How soon can you do it?'

'Five days – I'd prefer that we take longer, but I am prepared to move quickly. The problem, of course, is disposing of the body in a suitable manner.'

Bock nodded. That was something he'd never had to worry about. The Red Army Faction had rarely had to worry about that – except in the case of the turncoat Green woman who'd blown that one operation. But that one had been happenstance rather than design. Burying her in a national forest had been done – out of humor actually, not that he had thought of it, putting her back into the ecology she'd loved so much. It had been Petra's idea.

'How will I deliver the videotape to you?'

'Someone will meet you here. Not me, someone else. Stay at the same hotel two weeks from today. You will be met. Conceal the tape cassette in a book.'

'Very well.' Keitel thought Bock was overdoing things. Cloak-and-dagger was such a game that amateurs enjoyed playing it more than the professionals, for whom it was merely the job. Why not simply put the thing in a box and wrap it in plastic like a movie cassette? 'I will soon need some funding.'

Bock handed over an envelope. 'A hundred thousand marks.'

'That will do nicely. Two weeks from today.' Keitel left Bock to pay the bill and walked off.

Günther ordered another beer, staring off to the sea, cobalt blue under a clear sky. Ships were passing out on the horizon – one was a naval vessel, whose he couldn't tell at that distance, and the rest were simply merchantmen plying their trade from one unknown port to another.

On a day like this, a warm sun and a cool ocean breeze. Not far away was a beach of powdery white sand where children and lovers could enjoy the water. He thought of Petra and Erika and Ursel. No one passing by could tell from his face. The overt emotions of his loss were behind him. He'd wept and raged enough to exorcise them, but within him were the higher emotions of cold fury and revenge. So fine a day it was, and he had no one with whom to enjoy it. Whatever fine days might come later would find him just as alone. There would never be another Petra for him. He might find a girl here to use, just as some sort of biological exercise, but that wouldn't change things. He would be alone for the remainder of his life. It was not a pleasant thought. No love, no children, no personal future. Around him the terrace bar was about half-full of people, mainly Europeans, mainly on vacation with their families, smiling and laughing as they drank their beer or wine or other local concoctions, thinking ahead to the entertainments the night might hold, the intimate dinners, and the cool cotton sheets that would follow, the laughter and the affection – all the things that the world had denied Günther Bock.

He hated them all, sitting there alone, his eyes sweeping over the scene as he might have done a zoo, watching the animals. Bock detested them for their laughter and their smiles . . . and their futures. It wasn't fair. He'd had a purpose in life, a goal to strive for. They had jobs. Fifty or so weeks per year, they left their homes and drove to their workplaces and did whatever unimportant thing it was that they did, and came home, and like good Europeans saved their money for the annual fling in the Aegean, or Majorca, or America, or someplace where there was sun and clean air and a beach. Pointless though their lives might have been, they had the happiness that life had denied to the solitary man sitting in the shade of a white umbrella, staring out to sea again and sipping at his beer. It was not fair, not the least bit fair. He had devoted his life to their welfare – and they had the life that he'd hoped to give them, while he had less than nothing.

Except his mission.

Bock decided that he would not lie to himself on this issue any more than he did on others. He hated them. Hated them all. If he didn't have a future, why should they? If happiness was a stranger to him, why should it be their companion? He hated them because they had rejected him and Petra, and Qati, and all the rest who fought against injustice and oppression. In doing that, they had chosen the bad over the good – and for that one was damned. He was more than they were, Bock knew, he was better than they could ever hope to be. He could look down on all of them and their pointless little lives, and whatever he did to them – for them, he still tried to believe – was for him alone to decide. If some of them were hurt, that was too bad. They were not really people. They were empty shadows of what could have been people if they'd lived lives of purpose. They had not cast him out, they'd cast themselves out, seeking the happiness that came from ... whatever lives they led. The lazy way. Like cattle. Bock imagined them, heads down in feeding troughs, making contented barnyard noises while he surveyed them. If some had to die – and some *did* have to die – should it trouble him? Not at all, Günther decided.

'*Mister* President ...'

'Yes, Elizabeth?' Fowler replied with a chuckle.

'When's the last time someone told you how good a lover you are?'

'I sure don't hear that in the Cabinet Room.' Fowler was speaking to the top of her head, which nestled on his chest. Her left arm was wrapped around his chest, while his left hand stroked her blonde hair. The fact of the matter, the President thought, was that he was indeed pretty good at this. He had patience, which he judged the most important talent for the business. Liberation and equal-rights issues notwithstanding, it was a man's job to make a woman feel cherished and respected.

'Not in the Press Room, either.'

'Well, you're hearing it from your National Security Advisor.'

'Thank you, Dr Elliot.' Both had a good laugh. Elizabeth moved up to kiss him, dragging her breast along his chest to do so. 'Bob, you don't know what you mean to me.'

'Oh, I think I might,' the President allowed.

Elliot shook her head. 'All those dry years in academe. Never had time, always too busy. I was so tied up with being a professor. So much time wasted ...' A sigh.

'Well, I hope I was worth waiting for, dear.'

'You were, and you are.' She rolled over, resting her head on his shoulder and drawing his hand across her chest until it rested on a convenient spot. His other hand found a similar place, and her hands held his in place.

What do I say next? Liz asked herself. She had spoken the truth. Bob Fowler was a gentle, patient, and talented lover. It was also true that on hearing such a thing, any man, even a President, was under control. *Nothing, for a while*, she decided. There was time to enjoy him further, and time to examine her own feelings, her eyes open and staring at a dark rectangle on the wall that was a fine oil painting whose artist she'd never bothered to note, some sweeping Western landscape of where the plains ended at the Front Range of the Rockies. His hands moved gently, not quite arousing again, but giving her subtle waves of pleasure which she accepted passively, occasionally adjusting the position of her head to show that she was still awake.

She was starting to love the man. Wasn't that odd? She paused, wondering if it was or wasn't. There was much to like and admire in him. There was also much to confuse. He was an irreconcilable mixture of coldness and warmth, and his sense of humor defied understanding. He cared deeply about many things, but his depth of feeling seemed always motivated by a logical understanding of issues and principles rather than true passion. He was often befuddled – genuinely so – that others didn't share his feelings on issues, in the same way that teachers of mathematics were never angered, but saddened and puzzled that others failed to see the beauty and symmetry of their calculations. Fowler was also capable of remarkable cruelty and total ruthlessness, both delivered without a trace of rancor. People stood in his way, and if he could destroy them, he did. It was like the line in *The Godfather*. It was never personal, just business. Perhaps he'd learned that from the *mafiosi* he'd sent to prison, Liz wondered. The same man could treat his true followers with a matter-of-fact coldness that rewarded efficiency and loyalty with . . . how could she describe it? . . . the gratitude of an accountant.

And yet he was also a wonderfully tender man in bed. Liz frowned at the wall. There was no understanding him, was there?

'Did you see that report from Japan?' the President asked, getting to business just as Elliot was on the verge of a conclusion.

'Ummm, glad you brought that up. Something disturbing came into the office the other day.'

'About what?' Fowler showed his interest by moving his hands in a more deliberate fashion, as though to coax information out of her that she'd been waiting to reveal for some time.

'Ryan,' Liz replied.

'Him again? What is it?'

'The reports we heard about improper financial dealings were true, but it looks like he weaseled out of them on a technicality. It would have been enough to keep him out of this Administration, but since he's grandfathered in from before . . .'

'There are technicalities and technicalities. What other thing do you have?'

'Sexual impropriety, and possibly using Agency personnel to settle personal scores.'

'Sexual impropriety . . . disgraceful . . .'

Elliot giggled. He liked that. 'There might be a child involved.' Fowler did not like that. He was a very seriously committed man on the issue of children's rights. His hands stopped moving.

'What do we know?'

'Not enough. It should be looked at, though,' Liz said, coaxing his hands back into motion.

'Okay, have the FBI do a quiet investigation,' the President said, ending the issue, he thought.

'That won't work.'

'Why?'

'Ryan has a very close relationship with the Bureau. They might balk on those grounds, might smooth the thing over.'

'Bill Shaw isn't like that. He's as good a cop as I've ever met – even *I* can't make him do things, and that's the way it should be.' Logic and principle again. The man was impossible to predict.

'Shaw worked personally on the Ryan Case – the terrorist thing, I mean. Prior personal involvement by the head of the investigative agency . . . ?'

'True,' Fowler admitted. It would look bad. Conflict of interest and all that.

'And Shaw's personal trouble-shooter is that Murray fellow. He and Ryan are pretty tight.'

A grunt. 'So, what then?'

'Somebody from the Attorney General's office, I think.'

'Why not Secret Service?' Fowler asked, knowing the answer, but wondering if she did.

'Then it looks like it's a witch hunt.'

'Good point. Okay, the A.G.'s office. Call Greg tomorrow.'

'Okay, Bob.' Time to change subjects. She brought one of his hands to her face, and kissed it. 'You know, at times like this I really miss cigarettes.'

'Smoke after sex?' he asked with a harder embrace.

'When you make love to me, Bob, I smoke during sex . . .' She turned to stare into his eyes.

'Maybe I should think about relighting the fire . . . ?'

'They say,' the National Security Advisor purred, moving to kiss him again, '. . . they say the President of the United States is the most powerful man in the world . . .'

'I do my best, Elizabeth.'

Half an hour later, Elliot decided that it was true. She was starting to love him. Then she wondered what he felt for her . . .

CHAPTER 16

Fueling the Fire

'*Guten Abend, Frau Fromm,*' the man said.

'And you are?'

'Peter Wiegler, from the *Berliner Tageblatt*. I wonder if I might speak with you briefly.'

'About what?' she asked.

'*Aber . . .*' He gestured at the rain he was standing in. She remembered that she was civilized after all, even to a journalist.

'Yes, of course, please come in.'

'Thank you.' He came in out of the rain and removed his coat, which she hung on a peg. He was a captain in the KGB's First Chief (Foreign) Directorate, a promising young officer of thirty years, handsome, gifted in language, the holder of a master's degree in psychology, and another in engineering. He already had Traudl Fromm figured out. The new Audi parked outside was comfortable but not luxurious, her clothing – also new – very presentable but not overpowering. She was proud and moderately greedy, but also parsimonious. Curious, but guarded. She was hiding something, also smart enough to know that turning him away would generate more suspicion than whatever explanation she might have. He took his seat on an overstuffed chair, and waited for the next move. She didn't offer coffee. She hoped the encounter would be a short one. He wondered if this third person on his list of ten names might be something worth reporting to Moscow Center.

'Your husband is associated with the Greifswald-Nord Nuclear Power Station?'

'He was. As you know, it is being closed down.'

'Quite so. I would like to know what you and he think of that. Is Dr Fromm at home?'

'No, he is not,' she answered uncomfortably. 'Wiegler' didn't react visibly.

'Really? May I ask where he is?'

'He is away on business.'

'Perhaps I might come back in a few days, then?'

'Perhaps. You might call ahead?' It was the way she said it that the KGB officer noticed. She was hiding something, and the captain knew that it had to be something –

There was another knock at the door. Traudl Fromm went to answer it.

'*Guten Abend, Frau Fromm,*' a voice said. 'We bring a message from Manfred.'

The captain heard the voice, and something inside his head went on alert. He told himself not to react. This was Germany, and everything was *in Ordnung*. Besides, he might learn something . . .

'I, ah, have a guest at the moment,' Traudl answered.

The next statement was delivered in a whisper. The captain heard approaching steps, and took his time before turning to look. It was a fatal error.

The face he saw might as easily have come from one of the endless World War II movies that he'd grown up on, just that it lacked the black-and-silver-trimmed uniform of an SS officer. It was a stern, middle-aged face with light blue eyes entirely devoid of emotion. A professional face that measured his as quickly as he –

It was time to –

'Hello. I was just about to leave.'

'Who is he?' Traudl didn't get a chance to answer.

'I'm a reporter with –' It was too late. A pistol appeared from nowhere. '*Was gibt's hier?*' he demanded.

'Where is your car?' the man behind the gun asked.

'I parked it down the street. I –'

'All those spaces right in front? Reporters are lazy. Who are you?'

'I'm a reporter with the –'

'I think not.'

419

'This one, too,' the one in black said. The captain remembered the face from somewhere . . . He told himself not to panic. That, too, was a mistake.

'Listen closely. You will be going on a short trip. If you cooperate, you will be returned here within three hours. If you do not cooperate, things will go badly for you. *Verstehen Sie?*'

They had to be intelligence officers, the captain thought, making a correct guess. And they had to be German, and that meant that they would play by the rules, he told himself, making the last mistake of what had been a promising career.

The courier arrived from Cyprus right on schedule, handing off his package to another man at one of five pre-selected transfer points, all of which had been under surveillance for twelve hours. The second man walked two blocks and started up his Yamaha motorcycle, tearing off into the countryside just as fast as he could in an area where motorcyclists were all certifiably mad. Two hours after that, he delivered the package, certain that he had not been followed, and kept going another thirty minutes before circling back to his point of origin.

Günther Bock took the package and was annoyed to see that it was to all appearances a movie cassette – *Chariots of Fire* – rather than the hollowed-out book he'd requested. Perhaps Erwin was delivering a message along with the cassette. Bock inserted it in a player and switched it on, catching the first few minutes of the feature movie, which was subtitled in French. Soon, he realized that Keitel's message was on what intelligence professionals really did. He fast-forwarded through ninety minutes of the film before the picture changed.

What?

'*Who* are you?' an off-camera voice asked harshly.

'I am Peter Wiegler, I am a reporter with –' The rest was a scream. The equipment used was crude, just an electrical cord ripped off a lamp or appliance, the insulation trimmed off the free end to expose a few centimeters of copper. Few understood just how effective crude instruments could be, especially if the user possessed some degree of sophistication. The man who called himself Peter Wiegler screamed as though his throat would split from the effort. He'd already bitten through his lower lip in previous efforts to keep silent. The only good thing about using electricity was that it wasn't especially bloody, just noisy.

'You must understand that you are being foolish. Your courage is impressive, but wasted here. Courage only has use when there is hope of rescue. We've already searched your car. We have your passports. We know that you are not German. So, what are you? Pole, Russian, what?'

The young man opened his eyes and took a long breath before speaking. 'I am an investigative reporter with the *Berliner Tageblatt*.' They hit him again with the electric cord, and this time he passed out. Bock watched a man's back approach the victim and check his eyes and pulse. The torturer appeared to be wearing a chemical-warfare-protective suit of rubberized fabric, but without the hood and gloves. It must have been awfully hot, Bock thought.

'Obviously a trained intelligence officer. Probably Russian. Not circumcised, and his dental work is stainless steel, not especially well-done. That means an East Bloc service, of course. Too bad, this lad is quite brave.' The voice was admirably clinical, Bock thought.

'What drugs do we have?' another voice asked.

'A rather good tranquilizer. Now?'

'Now. Not too much.'

'Very well.' The man went off camera, then returned with a syringe. He grasped the victim's upper arm, then injected the drug into a vein inside the elbow. It took three minutes before the KGB man regained consciousness, just enough for the rush of drugs to assault his higher brain functions.

'Sorry we had to do that to you. You have passed the test,' the voice said, this time in Russian.

'What test –' The answer was in Russian, just two words before his brain took hold and stopped him. 'Why did you ask me in Russian?'

'Because that was what we wished to know. Good night.'

The victim's eyes went wide as a small-caliber pistol appeared, was placed against his chest, and fired. The camera withdrew a bit to show more of the room. A plastic sheet – actually three of them – covered the floor to catch blood and other droppings under the metal chair. The bullet wound was speckled with black powder marks, and bulged outward from the intrusion of gun-gases below the skin. There wasn't much bleeding. Heart wounds never produced much. In a few more seconds, the body stopped quivering.

'We could have taken more time to ascertain additional information, but we have what we need, as I will explain later.' It was Keitel's voice, off camera.

'Now, Traudl . . .'

They brought her in front of the camera, hands bound in front of her, her mouth gagged with the same bandag-ing tape, her eyes wide in terror, naked. She was trying to say something around the gag, but no one there had been interested. The tape was a day and a half old, of course. Günther could tell that from the TV that was playing in the corner, tuned to an evening news broad-cast. The entire performance was a professional *tour de force* designed to meet his requirements.

Bock could almost hear the man thinking, *Now, how do we do this?* Günther momentarily regretted the instructions he'd given Keitel. But the evidence had to be positive. Magicians and other experts in illusion regu-larly consulted with intelligence agencies – but some things could not be faked, and he had to be sure that he could trust Keitel to do terrible and dangerous things. It was an objective necessity that this be graphic.

Another man looped a rope over a ceiling beam and hauled her hands up, then the first pressed his pistol into her armpit and fired a single shot. At least he wasn't a sadist, Bock thought. Such people were not reliable. It was quite sad to watch in any case. The bullet had punc-tured her heart, but she was too excited to die quickly, struggling for more than half a minute, eyes still wide, fighting for breath, still trying to speak, probably begging for help, asking why ... After she went limp, one checked the pulse at her neck, then lowered her slowly to the floor. They'd been as gentle about it as they could have been under the circumstances. The shooter spoke without facing the camera.

'I hope you are satisfied. I did not enjoy this.'

'You weren't supposed to,' Bock said to the television set.

The Russian was taken off the chair and laid beside Traudl Fromm. While the bodies were dismembered, Keitel's voice spoke. It was a useful diversion, as the visual scene simply got more horrible. Bock was not squeamish about many things, but it troubled his psyche when human bodies were abused after death. Necessary or not, it seemed gratuitous to him.

'The Russian is undoubtedly an intelligence officer, as you have seen. His automobile was a rental from Berlin, and is being driven tomorrow to Magdeburg, where it will be turned in. It was parked down the street, normal procedure for a professional, of course, but a give-away in the event of capture. In the car we found a list of names, all of them in the DDR nuclear-power industry. It would seem that our Russian comrades have suddenly become interested in Honecker's bomb project. A pity we didn't have another few years to follow up on that, no? I regret the complication involved, but it took us several days to set up arrangements for disposing of the bodies, and we had no idea Frau Fromm had her "guest" when we knocked on the door. At that point, of course, it was too late. Besides, with the rain we had ideal conditions for the kidnapping.' Two men were working on each body. All wore the protective suits, and now they had their hoods and masks on, doubtless to protect them from the smell as much as to protect their identity. As in a slaughterhouse, sawdust was applied in bucketfuls to soak up the copious amounts of blood being spilled. Bock knew from experience just how messy murders could be. They worked quickly as Keitel's voice-over went on, using powered industrial cutting tools. Arms and legs had been removed from the torsos, and then the heads were removed and held up to the camera. No one could fake this. Keitel's men had truly murdered two human beings. The dismemberment in front of a playing television made that absolutely certain, and would doubtless also make disposal easier. The pieces were assembled neatly for wrapping in plastic. One of the men started brushing the blood-soaked sawdust into a pile for yet another plastic bag.

'The body parts will be burned at two widely separated locations. This will be accomplished long before you get the tape. That ends our message. We await further instructions.' And the tape returned to the dramatization of the 1920 Olympics – or was it 1924? Bock wondered. Not that it mattered, of course.

'Yes, Colonel?'

'One of my officers has failed to check in.' The Colonel was from Directorate T, the technical branch of the First Chief Directorate. The holder of a doctor's degree in engineering, his personal specialty was missile systems. He had worked in America and France, ferreting out the secrets of various military weapons before being promoted to his current job.

'Details?'

'Captain Yevgeniy Stepanovich Feodorov, age thirty, married, one child, a fine young officer on the major's list. He was one of the three I sent into Germany at your direction to check out their nuclear facilities. He's one of my best.'

'How long?' Golovko asked.

'Six days. He flew into Berlin via Paris last week. He had German papers, good ones from downstairs, and a list of ten names to investigate. His instructions were to maintain a low profile unless he discovered something important, in which case he was to make contact with Station Berlin – what's left of it, I mean. We scheduled a periodic check-in, of course. He didn't make it, and after twenty-four hours, I got the alert.'

'Could it be that he's just careless?'

'Not this boy,' the Colonel said flatly. 'Does the name mean anything to you?'

'Feodorov ... wasn't his father ... ?'

'Stefan Yurievich, yes. Yevgeniy is his youngest son.'

'Good God, Stefan taught *me*,' Golovko said. 'Possibility of ... ?'

'Defection?' The Colonel shook his head angrily. 'Not a chance. His wife is in the chorus with the opera. No – they met in university and married young over the objections of both sets of parents. It's a love-match like we all wish we had. She's a stunningly beautiful girl, voice like an angel. Only a *zhopnik* would walk away from her. Then there's the child. He is by all reports a good father.' Golovko saw where this was leading.

'Arrested, then?'

'I haven't heard a whisper. Perhaps you might arrange to have that checked. I fear the worst.' The Colonel frowned and stared down at the rug. He didn't want to be the one who broke the news to Natalia Feodorova.

'Hard to believe,' Golovko said.

'Sergey Nikolay'ch, if your suspicions are correct, then this program we were tasked to investigate is a matter of grave importance to them, is it not? We may have confirmed something in the most expensive way possible.'

General-Lieutenant Sergey Nikolayevich Golovko was silent for several seconds. *It's not supposed to be like this*, he told himself. *The intelligence business is supposed to be civilized. Killing each other's officers is a thing of the distant past. We don't do that sort of thing anymore, haven't done it in years ... decades ...*

'None of the alternatives are credible, are they?'

The Colonel shook his head. 'No. But the most credible is that our man stumbled into something both real and extremely sensitive. Sensitive enough to kill for. A secret nuclear-weapons program is that sensitive, is it not?'

'Arguably, yes.' The Colonel was showing the sort of loyalty to his people that KGB expected, Golovko noted.

He was also thinking over the alternatives and presenting his best estimate of the situation.

'Have you sent your technical people to Sarova yet?'

'Day after tomorrow. My best man was sick, just got out of the hospital – broke his leg in a fall down some stairs.'

'Have him carried there if necessary. I want a worst-case estimate of plutonium production at the DDR power stations. Send another man to Kyshtym to back-check the people at Sarova. Pull in the other people you sent to Germany. We'll restart the investigation more carefully. Two-man teams, and the backup man is to be armed . . . that is dangerous,' Golovko said on reflection.

'General, it takes a lot of time and money to train my field people. I will need two years to replace Feodorov, two whole years. You can't just pull an officer out of another branch and drop him into this line of work. These people must understand what they are looking for. Assets like that should be protected.'

'You are correct. I will clear it with the Chairman and send experienced officers . . . maybe some people from the Academy . . . credential them like German police officials . . . ?'

'I like that, Sergey Nikolay'ch.'

'Good man, Pavel Ivan'ch. And on Feodorov?'

'Maybe he'll turn up. Thirty days before he's declared missing, then I'll have to see his wife. Very well, I'll pull my people in and start planning the next phase of the operation. When will I have a list of the escort officers?'

'Tomorrow morning.'

'Very well, General, thank you for your time.'

Golovko shook the man's hand and remained standing until the door closed. He had ten minutes until his next appointment.

'Damn,' he said to his desktop.

'More delays?'

Fromm did not quite manage to hide his disgust. 'We are saving time! The material we will be working on has machining characteristics similar to stainless steel. We must also manufacture blanks for the casting process. Here.'

Fromm unfolded his working drawings.

'We have here a folded cylinder of plutonium. Around the plutonium is a cylinder of beryllium, which is a godsend for our purposes. It is very light, very stiff, an X-ray window, and a neutron *reflector*. Unfortunately, it is also rather difficult to machine. We must use cubic boronnitride tools, essentially an analog to industrial diamond. Steel or carbon tools would have results you do not wish to contemplate. We also have health considerations.'

'Beryllium is not toxic,' Ghosn said. 'I checked.'

'True, but the dust resulting from the machining process converts to beryllium oxide, which when inspired converts again to beryllium hydroxide, and *that* causes berylliosis, which is uniformly fatal.' Fromm paused, staring at Ghosn like a schoolmaster before going on.

'Now, around the beryllium is a cylinder of tungsten-rhenium, which we need for its density. We will purchase twelve kilograms in powder form, which we will sinter into cylindrical segments. You know sintering? That is heating it just hot enough to form. Melting and casting is too difficult, and not necessary for our purposes. Around that goes the explosive-lens assembly. And this is just the primary, Ghosn, not even a quarter of our total energy budget.'

'And the precision required . . .'

'Exactly. Think of this as the world's largest ring or necklace. What we produce must be as finely finished as the most beautiful piece of jewelry you have ever seen – or perhaps a precision optical instrument.'

'The tungsten-rhenium?'

'Available from any major electrical concern. It's used in special filaments for vacuum tubes, numerous other applications, and it's far easier to work than pure tungsten.'

'Beryllium – oh, yes, it's used in gyroscopes and other instruments . . . thirty kilograms.'

427

'Twenty-five . . . yes, get thirty. You have no idea how lucky we are.'

'How so?'

'The Israeli plutonium is gallium-stabilized. Plutonium has four phase-transformations below melting point, and has the curious habit, in certain temperature regimes, of changing its density by a factor of over twenty percent. It is a multi-state metal.'

'In other words, a sub-critical mass can –'

'Exactly,' Fromm said. 'What appears to be a sub-critical mass can under certain circumstances convert itself into criticality. It will not explode, but the gamma- and neutron-flux would be lethal within a radius of . . . oh, anywhere from ten to thirty meters depending on circumstances. That was discovered during the Manhattan Project. They were – no, not lucky. They were brilliant scientists, and as soon as they had a gram or so of plutonium, it was decided to investigate its properties. Had they waited, or simply assumed that they knew more than they did – well . . .'

'I had no idea,' Ghosn admitted. *Merciful God* . . .

'Not everything is in books, my young friend, or should I say, not all the books have all the information. In any case, with the addition of gallium, the plutonium is a stable mass. It is actually quite safe to work, as long as we take the proper precautions.'

'So we start by machining out stainless-steel blanks to these specifications, then make our casting-molds – investment casting, of course.'

Fromm nodded. 'Correct. Very good, *mein Junge.*'

'Then when the casting is done, we will machine the bomb material . . . I see. Well, we seem to have good machinists.'

They'd 'drafted' – that was the term they used – ten men, all Palestinians, from local optical shops, and trained them on the use of the machine tools.

The tools were all that Fromm had said they were. Two years earlier, they'd been totally state-of-the-art, identical to the equipment used in the American Y-12 fabrication plant at Oak Ridge, Tennessee. Tolerances were measured by laser interferometry, and the rotating tool heads were computer-controlled in three dimensions through five axes of movement. Instructions were passed to the computers via touch-screens. The design itself had been done on a mini-computer and drawn out on an expensive drafting machine.

Ghosn and Fromm brought the machinists in and set them to work on their first task, making the stainless steel blank for the plutonium primary that would ignite the thermo-nuclear fire.

'Now,' Fromm said, 'for the explosive lenses . . .'

'I've heard much about you,' Bock said.

'I hope it was good,' Marvin Russell replied with a guarded smile.

My first Indian, Bock thought quickly. He was oddly disappointed. Except for the cheekbones, he might have easily been mistaken for any Caucasian, and even those could seem like a Slav with perhaps a taste of Tatar in his background . . . What color there was had come mainly from the sun. The rest of the man was formidable enough, the size and obvious strength.

'I hear you killed a police officer in Greece by snapping his neck.'

'I don't know why people make a big deal about that,' Russell said with weary honesty. 'He was a scrawny little fuck, and I know how to take care of myself.'

Bock smiled and nodded. 'I understand how you feel, but your method was impressive in any case. I have heard good things about you, Mr Russell and —'

'Just call me Marvin. Everybody else does.'

Bock smiled. 'As you wish, Marvin. I am Günther. Particularly your skill with weapons.'

'It's no big deal,' Russell said, genuinely puzzled. 'Anybody can learn to shoot.'

'How do you like it here?'

'I like it a lot. These people — I mean, they have heart, y'know? They ain't quitters. They work real hard at what they do. I admire that. And what they done for me, Gunther, it's like family, man.'

'We are a family, Marvin. We share everything, good and bad. We all have the same enemies.'

'Yeah, I seen that.'

'We may need your help for something, Marvin. It's for something fairly important.'

'Okay,' Russell replied simply.

'What do you mean?'

'I mean "yes," Gunther.'

'You haven't even asked what it is,' the German pointed out.

'Okay.' Marvin smiled. 'So tell me.'

'We need you to go back to America in a few months. How dangerous is that for you?'

'Depends. I've done time – in prison, I mean. You know that. My fingerprints are on file with the cops, but they don't have a picture of me – I mean, the one they have is pretty old. I've changed since then. They're looking for me up in the Dakotas, probably. If you send me there, it might be a little tricky.'

'Nowhere near there, Marvin.'

'Then it shouldn't be much of a problem, dependin' on what you need me to do.'

'How do you feel about killing people – Americans, I mean?' Bock watched his face for a reaction.

'Americans.' Marvin snorted. 'Hey, man, *I'm* a fuckin' American, okay? My country ain't what you think. *They* stole my country from me, just like what happened to these guys here, okay? It ain't just here shit like that happened, okay? You want me to do some people for you, yeah, I can do that, if you got a reason. I mean, I don't kill for fun, I ain't no psycho, but you got a reason, sure, I can do it.'

'Maybe more than one –'

'I heard you when you said "people," Gunther. I ain't so stupid that I think "people" means one guy. You just make sure some cops, maybe even some FBI guys are in there, yeah, I'll help kill all you want. One thing you need to know, though.'

'What's that?'

'The other side ain't dumb. They got my brother, remember. They're serious dudes.'

'We also are serious,' Bock assured him.

'I seen that, man. What can you tell me about the job?'

'What do you mean, Marvin?' Bock asked as casually as he could.

'I mean I grew up there, man, remember? I know stuff that maybe you don't. Okay, you got security and all that, and you ain't gonna tell me anything now. Fine, that's no problem. But you might need my help later on. These guys here are okay, they're smart and all, but they don't know dick about America — I mean, not what you need to get around and stuff. You go huntin', you gotta know the ground. I know the ground.'

'That is why we want your help,' Bock assured him, as though he'd already thought that part all the way through. Actually he had not, and now he was wondering just how useful this man might be.

Andrey Il'ych Narmonov saw himself as the captain of the world's largest ship of state. That was the good news. The bad news was that the ship had a leaky bottom, a broken rudder, and uncertain engines. Not to mention a mutinous crew. His office in the Kremlin was large, with room to pace about, something he found himself doing all too much of late. That, he thought, was a sign of an uncertain man, and the President of the Union of Soviet Socialist Republics could not afford that, especially when he had an important guest.

Union of Sovereign *Soviet Republics*, he thought. Though the official name-change had not yet been approved, that was how his people were starting to think. *That's the problem.*

The ship of state was breaking up. There was no precedent for it. The dissolution of the British Empire was the example that many liked to use, but that wasn't quite right, was it? Nor was any other example. The Soviet Union of old had been a unique political creation. What was now happening in the Soviet Union was also entirely without precedent. What had once been exhilarating to him was now more than frightening. He was the one who had to make the hard decisions, and he had no historical model to follow. He was completely on his own, as alone as any man had ever been, with a task larger than any man had ever faced. Lauded in the West as a consummate political tactician, he thought of it himself as an endless succession of crises. *Wasn't it Gladstone?* he thought. *Wasn't it he who described his job as being the man on a raft in the rapids, fending off rocks with a pole . . . ? How apt, how apt indeed.* Narmonov and his country were being swept along by overwhelming forces of history, somewhere down that river was an immense cataract, a falls that could destroy everything . . . but he was too busy with the pole and the rocks to look so far ahead. That was what being a political tactician meant. He devoted all his creative energy to day-to-day survival, and was losing sight of the next week . . . even the day after tomorrow . . .

'Andrey Il'ych, you are growing thin,' Oleg Kirilovich Kadishev observed from his leather seat.

'The walking is good for my heart,' the President replied wryly.

'Then perhaps you will join our Olympic team?'

Narmonov stopped for a moment. 'It would be nice indeed to compete merely against foreigners. *They* think I am brilliant. Alas, our own people know better.'

'What can I do to help my president?'

'I need your help, the help of those on the right.'

It was Kadishev's turn to smile. The press – Western as well as Soviet – never got that straight. The LEFT wing in the Soviet Union was that of the Communist hard-liners. For over eighty years reform in that country had always come from the right. All the men executed by Stalin for wanting to allow the merest bit of personal freedom had always been denounced as *Right*-Deviationists. But self-styled progressives in the West were always on the political left, and they called *their* reactionary enemies 'conservatives' and generally identified them as being on the political RIGHT. It seemed too great a stretch of imagination for Western journalists to adjust their ideological polarity to a different political reality. The newly-liberated Soviet journalists had merely aped their Western colleagues and used the foreign descriptions to muddle what was already a chaotic political scene. The same was true of 'progressive' Western politicians, of course, who were championing so many of the experiments of the Soviet Union in their own countries – all the experiments which had been taken to the limit and proven to be something worse than mere failures. Perhaps the blackest humor available in all the world was the carping from leftist elements in the West, some of whom were already observing that the *backward* Russians had failed because they had proven unable to covert socialism into a humanistic government – whereas *advanced* Western governments could accomplish just that (of course, Karl Marx himself had said that, hadn't he?). Such people were, Kadishev thought with a bemused shake of his head, no less idealistic than the members of the first Revolutionary Soviets, and just as addle-brained. The Russians had merely taken the revolutionary ideals to their logical limits, and found there only emptiness and disaster. Now that they were turning back – a move that called for political and moral courage such as the world had rarely seen – the West *still* didn't understand what was happening! *Khrushchev was right all along*, the parliamentarian thought. *Politicians are the same all over the world.*

Mostly idiots.

'Andrey Il'ych, we do not always agree on methods, but we *have* always agreed on goals. I know you are having trouble with our friends on the other side.'

'*And* with your side,' President Narmonov pointed out more sharply than he should have.

'And with my side, it is true,' Kadishev admitted casually. 'Andrey Il'ych, do you say that we must agree with you on *everything*?'

Narmonov turned, his eyes momentarily angry and wide. 'Please, not that, not today.'

'How may we help you?' *Losing control of your emo-*

tions, Comrade President! A bad sign, my friend . . .

'I need your support on the ethnic issue. We cannot have the entire Union break apart.'

Kadishev shook his head forcefully. '*That* is inevitable. Letting the Balts and the Azeris go eliminates many problems.'

'We need the Azerbaijani oil. If we let that go, our economic situation worsens. If we let the Balts go, the momentum will strip away half of our country.'

'Half our population, true, but scarcely twenty percent of our land. And most of our problems,' Kadishev said again.

'And what of the people who leave? We throw them into chaos and civil war. How many will die, how many deaths on our conscience, eh?' the President demanded.

'Which is a normal consequence of decolonization. We cannot prevent it. By attempting to, we merely keep the civil war within our own borders. *That* forces us to place too much power into the hands of the security forces, and that is too dangerous. I don't trust the Army any more than you do.'

'The Army will not launch a coup. There are no Bonapartists in the Red Army.'

'You have greater confidence in their fealty than I do. I think they see a unique historical opportunity. The Party has held the military down since the Tukhachevskiy business. Soldiers have long memories, and they may be thinking that this is their chance . . .'

'Those people are all dead! And their children with them,' Narmonov countered angrily. It had been over fifty years, after all. Those few with direct memory of the purges were in wheelchairs or living on pensions.

'But not their grandchildren, and there is institutional memory to consider as well.' Kadishev leaned back and considered a new thought that had sprung almost fully formed into his head. *Might that be possible . . . ?*

'They have concerns, yes, and those concerns are little different from my own. We differ on how to deal with the problem, not on the issue of control. While I am not sure of their judgment, I *am* sure of their loyalty.'

'Perhaps you are correct, but I am not so sanguine.'

'With your help, we can present a united front to the forces of early dissolution. That will discourage them. That will allow us to get through a few years of normalization, and then we can consider an orderly departure for the republics with a genuine commonwealth – association, whatever you wish to call it – to keep us associated economically while being separate politically.'

The man is desperate, Kadishev saw. *He really is collapsing under the strain. The man who moves about the political arena like a Central Army hockey forward is showing signs of fatigue . . . will he survive without my help . . . ?*

Probably, Kadishev judged. Probably. That was too bad, the younger man thought. Kadishev was the *de facto* leader of the forces on the 'left,' the forces that wanted to break up the entire country and the government that went with it, yanking the remaining nation – based on the Russian Federation – into the 21st century by its throat. If Narmonov fell . . . if he found himself unable to continue, then who . . . ?

Why, me, of course.

Would the Americans support him?

How could they fail to support Agent SPINNAKER of their own Central Intelligence Agency?

Kadishev had been working for the Americans since his recruitment by Mary Patricia Foley some six years before. He didn't think of it as treason. He was working for the betterment of his country, and saw himself as succeeding. He'd fed the Americans information on the internal workings of the Soviet government, some of it highly valuable, some material they could as easily have gotten from their own reporters. He knew that they regarded him as their most valuable source of political intelligence in the Soviet Union, especially now that he controlled fully forty percent of the votes in the country's bumptious new parliament, the Congress of People's Deputies. *Thirty-nine percent*, he told himself. *One must be honest*. Perhaps another eight percent could be his if he made the proper move. There were

435

many shades of political loyalty among the twenty-five hundred members. Genuine democrats, Russian nationalists of both democratic and socialist stripe, radicals of both left and right. There was also a cautious middle of politicians, some genuinely concerned about what course their country might take, others merely seeking to conserve their personal political status. How many could he appeal to? How many could he win over?

Not quite enough . . .

But there was one more card he could play, wasn't there?

Da. If he had the audacity to play it.

'Andrey Il'ych,' he said in a conciliatory voice, 'you ask me to depart from an important principle so that I can help you reach a goal we share – but to do so by a route that I distrust. This is a very difficult matter. I am not even sure that I can deliver the support you require. My comrades might well turn their backs on me.' It only agitated the man further.

'Rubbish! I know how well they trust you and your judgment.'

They are not the only ones who trust me . . . Kadishev told himself.

As with most investigations, this one was done mainly with paper. Ernest Wellington was a young attorney, and an ambitious one. As a law-school graduate and a member of the bar, he could have applied to the FBI and learned the business of investigation properly, but he considered himself a lawyer rather than a cop, besides which he enjoyed politics, and the FBI prided itself on avoiding political wrangling wherever possible. Wellington had no such inhibitions. He enjoyed politics, considered it the life's blood of government service, and knew it to be the path to speedy advancement both within and without the government. The contacts he was making now would make his value to any of a hundred 'connected' law firms jump five-fold, plus making him a known name within the Department of Justice. Soon he would be in the running for a 'special-assistant' job. After that – in five years or so – he'd have a crack at a section chief's office . . . maybe even U.S. Attorney in a major city, or head of a special DoJ strike force. That opened the door to political life, where Ernest Wellington could be a real player in the Great Game of Washington. All in all, it was heady wine indeed for an ambitious man of twenty-seven years, an honors graduate from Harvard Law who'd ostentatiously turned down lucrative offers from prestigious firms, preferring instead to devote his early professional years to public service.

Wellington had a pile of papers on his desk. His office was in what was almost an attic in the Justice Department's building on The Mall, and the view from the single window was of the parking lot that rested in the center of the Depression-era structure. It was small, and the air-conditioning was faulty, but it was private. It is little appreciated that lawyers avoid time in court as assiduously as the boastful avoid genuine tests of ability. Had he taken the jobs offered by the New York corporate firms – the best such offer was for over $100,000 per year – his real function would have been that of proof-reader, really a glorified secretary, examining contracts for typos and possible loopholes. Early life in the Justice Department was little different. Whereas in a real prosecutorial office he might have been tossed alive into a courtroom environment to sink or swim, here at headquarters he examined records, looking for inconsistencies, nuances, possible technical violations of the law, as though he were an editor for a particularly good mystery writer. Wellington started making his notes.

John Patrick Ryan. Deputy to the Director of Central Intelligence, nominated by the President – politics at work – and confirmed less than two years previously. Prior to that acting Deputy Director (Intelligence), following the death of Vice Admiral James Greer. Prior to that, Special Assistant to DDI Greer, and sometime special representative of the Directorate of Intelligence over in England. Ryan had been an instructor in history at the Naval Academy, a graduate student at Georgetown University, and a broker at the Baltimore office of

Merrill Lynch. Also, briefly, a second lieutenant in the United States Marine Corps. Clearly a man who enjoyed career changes, Wellington thought, noting all the important dates.

Personal wealth. The requisite financial statement was in the file, near the top. Ryan was worth quite a bit. Where had it come from? That analysis took several hours. In his days as a broker, J. P. Ryan had been a real cowboy. He'd bet over a hundred thousand dollars on the Chicago and North Western Railroad at the time of the employee takeover, and reaped . . . over six million from it. That was his one really big score – sixty-to-one opportunities were not all that common, were they? – but some of the others were also noteworthy. On hitting a personal net worth of eight million, he'd called it quits and gone to Georgetown for his doctorate in history. Continued to play the market on an amateur basis – that wasn't quite right, was it? – until joining government service. His portfolio was now managed by a multiplicity of investment counselors . . . their accounting methods were unusually conservative. Ryan's net worth looked to be twenty million, maybe a little more. The accounts were managed on a blind basis. All Ryan saw was quarterly earnings statements. There were ways around that, of course, but it was all strictly legal. Proving impropriety was virtually impossible unless they put a wiretap on the line of his brokers, and that was not something easily accomplished.

He had been investigated by the SEC, but that had actually been a spin-off of the SEC's look at the firm he'd bought into. The summary sheet noted in clipped bureaucratese that no technical violation had been made, but Wellington observed that this judgment was more technical than substantive. Ryan had balked at signing a consent order – understandably – and the government had not pressed him on the issue. That was less understandable, but explainable, since Ryan had not been the actual target of the investigation; someone had decided that it had all probably been a coincidence. Ryan had, however, broken that money out of his main account . . . *Gentleman's Agreement?* Wellington wrote on his legal pad. Perhaps. If asked, Ryan would respond that he'd done it out of an over-scrupulous sense of guilt. The money had gone into T-Bills, rolled over automatically for years and untouched until it had all been used to . . . *I see. That's interesting . . .*

Why an educational trust fund? Who was Carol Zimmer? What interest did Ryan have in her children? Timing? Significance?

It was amazing, as always, that so much paper could show so little. Perhaps, Wellington mused, that was the real point of government paperwork, to give the appearance of substance while saying as little as possible. He chuckled. That was also the point of most legal papers, wasn't it? For two hundred dollars per hour, lawyers loved to quibble over the placement of commas and other weighty matters. He paused, recycling his brain. He had missed something very obvious.

Ryan was not liked by the Fowler Administration. *Why*, then, had he been nominated for DDCI. Politics? But politics was the reason you selected people unqualified for . . . Did Ryan have any political connections at all? The file didn't show any. Wellington riffled through the papers and found a letter signed by Alan Trent and Sam Fellows of the House Select Committee. *That* was an odd couple, a gay and a Mormon. Ryan had sailed through confirmation much more easily than Marcus Cabot, even easier than Bunker and Talbot, the President's two star cabinet members. Part of that was because he was a second-level man, but that didn't explain it all. That meant political connections, and very fine ones. Why? What connections? Trent and Fellows . . . *what the hell could those two ever agree on?*

It was certain that Fowler and his people didn't like Ryan, else the Attorney General would not have personally placed Wellington on the case. Case? Was that the right term for his activities? If there were a *case*, why wasn't this being handled by the FBI? Politics, obviously. Ryan had worked closely with the FBI on several things . . . but . . .

439

William Connor Shaw, Director of the Federal Bureau of Investigation, was celebrated as the most honest man in government. Politically naïve, of course, but the man dripped integrity, and that wasn't always so bad a quality in a police agency, was it? Congress thought so. There was even talk of eliminating special prosecutors, the FBI had become so clean, especially after the special prosecutor had bungled the ... but the Bureau was being segregated from this one.

This was an interesting case, wasn't it? A man could win his spurs on something like this.

CHAPTER 17

Processing

The days were shorter now, Jack told himself. It wasn't that he was all that late, just that the days were shortening. The earth's orbit around the sun, and the way the axis of rotation was not perpendicular with the plane of the ... ecliptic? Something like that. His driver dropped him off in front of the door, and he walked tiredly in, wondering when the last day had been, outside of the weekends, when he'd seen his house in daylight and not outlined by electric lights. About the only good news was that he didn't bring work home – but that wasn't quite true either, was it? He brought no documents home, but it was less easy to clear out his mind than to clear off his desk.

Ryan heard the sounds of a normal house, the TV tuned to Nickelodeon. The washing machine was making noise. Have to have that fixed. He walked into the family room to announce himself.

'Daddy!' Jack Jr ran over to deliver a hug, followed by a plaintive look. 'Daddy, you promised to take me to a baseball game.'

Oh, shit ... The kids were back in school, and there couldn't be more than a dozen home games left up in Baltimore. He had to, had to, had to ... *When?* When could he break loose? The new communications center project was only half-done, and that was his baby, and the contractor was a week behind, and he had to get that back on line if it was going to be ready when it was supposed to be ...

'I'm going to try, Jack,' Ryan promised his son, who

was too young to understand about any obligation beyond a father's promise.

'Daddy, you promised.'

'I know.' *Shit!* Jack made a mental note. He had to do something about that.

'Bed time,' Cathy announced. 'Tomorrow's a school day.'

Ryan hugged and kissed both of his children, but the exercise in affection merely left an empty spot in his conscience. What sort of a father was he turning into? Jack Jr's First Communion was next April or May, and who could say if he'd be home for that? Better find out the date so that he could schedule it now. Try to schedule it now. Jack reminded himself that little things like promises to his kids were –

Little things?

God, how did this ever happen? Where has my life gone?

He watched the kids head to their rooms, then himself headed to the kitchen. His dinner was in the oven. He set the plate on the breakfast counter before walking to the refrigerator. He was buying wine in boxes now. It was much more convenient, and his taste in wine was getting far less selective of late. The cardboard boxes held a Mylar bag full of – Australian, wasn't it? About where California wines had been twenty years earlier. The vintage in question was very fruity, to mask its inadequacies, and had the proper alcohol content, which was what he was mainly after anyway. Jack looked at the wall clock. If he were very lucky, he might get six and a half, maybe seven hours of sleep before a new day started. He needed the wine to sleep. At the office, he lived on coffee, and his system was becoming saturated with caffeine. Once he'd been able to nap at his desk, but no longer. By eleven in the morning, his system was wired, and by late afternoon his body played a strange melody of fatigue and alertness that sometimes left him wondering if he were going a little mad. Well, as long as he asked himself that question . . .

A few minutes later, he finished his dinner. Pity the

oven had dried it out. Cathy had done this one herself. He'd been – he'd planned to be home at a decent hour, but . . . It was always something, wasn't it? When he stood, there was a twinge of discomfort from his stomach. On the way into the family room he opened the closet door to pull a packet of antacid tablets from his coat pocket. These he chewed and washed down with wine, starting off his third glass in less than thirty minutes at home.

Cathy wasn't there, though she'd left some papers on the table next to her customary chair. Jack listened and thought he heard a shower running. Fine. He took the cable controller and flipped to CNN for another newsfix. The lead story was something about Jerusalem.

Ryan settled back into his chair and allowed himself a smile. It was working. The story was about the resurgence of tourism. Shop owners were loading up in anticipation of their biggest Christmas in a decade. Jesus, explained a Jew who'd opted to stay in the town of Bethlehem, was after all a nice Jewish boy from a good family. His Arab partner toured the camera crew through the store. Arab partner? Jack thought. Well, why not?

It's worth it, Ryan told himself. *You helped bring that about. You helped make that happen. You have saved lives, and if nobody else knows it, the hell with it. You know. God knows. Isn't that enough?*

No, Jack told himself in a quiet flash of honesty.

So what if the idea had not been completely original? What idea ever was? It had been his thought that had brought it together, his contacts that had gotten the Vatican on board, his . . . He deserved something for it, some recognition, enough for a little footnote in some history book; but would he get it?

Jack snorted into his wine. No chance. Liz Elliot, that clever bitch, telling everybody that it was Charlie Alden who'd done it. If Jack ever tried to set the record straight, he'd look like a swine stealing credit from a dead man – and a good man, despite his mistake with that Blum girl. *Cheer up, Jack. You're still alive. You have a wife, you have kids.*

It still wasn't fair, was it? Fair? Why had he ever expected life to be fair? Was he turning into another one of *them*? Ryan asked himself. Another Liz Elliot, another grasping, small-minded ass with an ego-size inversely proportionate to her character. He'd so often worried and wondered about the process, how a person might be corrupted. He'd feared the overt methods, deciding that a cause or a mission was *so* vital that you might lose perspective on the important things, like the value of a single human life, even the life of an enemy. He hadn't lost that, not ever, and knew that he never would. It was the subtler things that were wearing at him. He was turning into a functionary, worrying about credit and status and influence.

He closed his eyes to remind himself of what he already had: a wife, two kids, financial independence, accomplishments that no one could ever take away.

You are *turning into one of them . . .*

He'd fought – he had *killed* – to defend his family. Maybe Elliot was offended by that, but in quiet moments like this, Jack remembered the times with a thin, grim smile. Not two hundred yards from where he now sat, he'd drilled three rounds into a terrorist's chest, coldly and efficiently – steel on target! – validating all the things they'd taught him at Quantico. That his heart had been beating a thousand times per second, that he'd come close to wetting his pants, that he'd had to swallow back his vomit, were small things. He'd done what he had to do, and because of that his wife and children were alive. He was a man who'd proven his manhood in every possible way – winning and marrying a wonderful girl, fathering two God-sent children, defending all of them with skill and courage. Every time fate had presented its challenge, Jack had met it and gotten the job done.

Yeah, he told himself, smiling at the TV. *Screw Liz Elliot.* That was a humorous thought. Who, he asked himself, would want to? That cold, skinny bitch, with her arrogance and . . . what else? Ryan's mind paused, seeking the answer to the question. What else? She was weak, wasn't she? Weak and timid. Beneath all the bluster and the hardness, what was really in there? Probably not much. He'd seen that sort of National Security Advisor before. Cutter, unwilling to face the music. Liz Elliot. Who'd want to screw her? Not very smart, and nothing in there to back up what smarts she did have. Good thing for her that the President had Bunker and Talbot to fall back on.

You're better than all of them. It was a satisfying thought to accompany the end of this glass of wine. *Why not have another? This stuff really isn't all that bad, is it?*

When Ryan returned, he saw Cathy was back also, going over her patient notes in the high-backed chair she liked.

'Want a glass of wine, honey?'

Dr Caroline Ryan shook her head. 'I have two procedures tomorrow.'

Jack came around to take his place in the other chair, almost not glancing at his wife, but he caught her out the corner of his eye.

'Wow.'

Cathy looked up from her paperwork to grin at him. Her face was nicely made-up. Jack wondered how she'd managed not to mess her hair up in the shower.

'Where did you get that?'

'Out of a catalog.'

'Whose, Fredericks?'

Dr Caroline Muller Ryan, M.D., F.A.C.S., was dressed in a black peignoir that was a masterpiece of revelation and concealment. He couldn't tell what held the robe portion in place. Underneath was something filmy and . . . very nice. The color was odd, though, Cathy's nighties were all white. He'd never forgotten the wonderful white one she'd worn on their wedding night. Not that she'd been a virgin at the time, but somehow that white silk had made her so . . . that, too, was a memory that would never go away, Jack told himself. She'd never worn it since, saying that like her wedding dress, it was something only to be used once. What have I done to earn this wonderful girl? Jack asked himself.

445

'To what do I owe this honor?' Jack asked.

'I've been thinking.'

'About what?'

'Well, Little Jack is seven. Sally is ten. I want another one.'

'Another what?' Jack set his glass down.

'Another baby, you dope!'

'Why?' her husband asked.

'Because I can, and because I want one. I'm sorry,' she went on with a soft smile, 'if that bothers you. The exercise, I mean.'

'I think I can handle that.'

'I have to get up at four-thirty,' Cathy said next. 'My first procedure is before seven.'

'So?'

'So.' She rose and walked over to her husband. Cathy bent down to kiss him on the cheek. 'See me upstairs.'

Ryan sat still for a minute or two, gunning down the rest of his drink, switching off the TV, and smiling to himself. He checked to make sure the house was locked and the security system armed. He stopped off in the bathroom to brush his teeth. A surreptitious check on her vanity drawer revealed a thermometer and a little index card with dates and temperatures on it. So. She wasn't kidding. She'd been thinking about this and, typically, keeping it to herself. Well, that was okay, wasn't it? Yeah.

Jack entered the bedroom and paused to hang up his clothes, donning a bathrobe before joining his wife at the bedside. She rose to wrap her arms around his neck, and he kissed her.

'You sure about this, babe?'

'Does it bother you?'

'Cathy, to please you – anything you want that I can get or give, honey. Anything.'

I wish you'd cut back on the drinking, Cathy didn't say. It wasn't the time. She felt his hands through the peignoir: Jack had strong but gentle hands that now traced her figure through the outfit. It was cheap and tarty, but every woman was entitled to look cheap and

446

tarty once in a while, even an associate professor of ophthalmic surgery at the Wilmer Eye Institute of the Johns Hopkins Hospital. Jack's mouth tasted like toothpaste and cheap white wine, but the rest of him smelled like a man, the man who'd made her life into a dream – mostly a dream. He was working too hard, drinking too much, not sleeping enough. But underneath all that was her man. And they didn't come any better, weaknesses, absences, and all.

Cathy made the proper noises when Jack's hands found the buttons. He got the message, but his fingers were clumsy. Annoying, the buttons were small and in those damned little fabric loops, but behind the buttons and the fabric were her breasts, and that fact ensured that he would not stop. Cathy took in a deep breath and smelled her favorite dusting powder. She didn't like perfume. A woman generated all the smells a man needed, she thought. There. Now his hands found her bare, smooth and still young skin. Thirty-six was not old, not too old for one more child. One more was all she craved, one more time to feel a new life growing within her. She'd accept the stomach upsets, the compressed bladder, the odd discomfort that merely gave detail to the wonder and the miracle of new life. The pain of birth – it was not fun, not at all, but to be able to do it, to have Jack at her side as he'd been with Sally and Little Jack, it was the most profound act of love that she had ever known. It was what being a woman meant, to be able to bring life to the world, to give a man the only kind of immortality there was, as he gave it to her.

And besides, she thought with a suppressed giggle, getting pregnant beat the hell out of jogging as a form of exercise.

Jack's hands removed her garment completely and eased her onto the bed. He was good at this, always had been, from their first nervous time, and at that moment she'd known that he would ask for her hand ... after he'd sampled the other parts. Another giggle of past and present, as his hands slid over skin that was now both hot and cold to the touch. And when he'd asked, when

447

he'd worked up the courage, she'd seen the fear in his eyes, the terror at the possibility of rejection, when she was the one who had worried – even cried once – for a week that he might not ask, might change his mind, might find someone else. From before their first love-making, Cathy had known. This was the one. Jack was the man with whom she would share her life, whose children she would bear, whom she would love to the grave, maybe beyond, if the priests were right. It wasn't his size or his strength, not even the bravery he'd had to show twice in her sight – and, she suspected, more than that in other places she'd never know about – it was his goodness, his gentleness, and a strength that only the perceptive knew about. Her husband was in some ways ordinary, in others unique, but in all ways a man, with all the strengths and few of the weaknesses . . .

And tonight he would give her another child. Her cycle, predictable as always, was confirmed by her morning temperature. Well, she admitted, it was mainly a statistical probability, but a very high probability in her case. Mustn't get too clinical, not with Jack, and not at a time like this.

Her skin was on fire now. Jack was *so* good at this. His kisses both gentle and passionate, his hands so wonderfully skilled. He was wrecking her hair, but that didn't matter. Surgical caps made perms a waste of time and money. Through the scent of the dusting powder now came the more significant smells of a woman who was nearly ready. Ordinarily she was more of a participant in these episodes, but tonight she was letting Jack take complete charge, searching over her silky skin for the . . . interesting parts. He liked that occasionally. He also liked it when she played a more active role. More than one way to do this. It came almost as a surprise. Cathy arched her back and whimpered the first time, not really saying anything. It wasn't necessary. They'd been married long enough that he knew all the signals. She kissed him hard and wantonly, digging her nails into his shoulders. That signal meant *now!*

But nothing happened.

She took his hand, kissed it, and moved it down so that he would know that she was ready.

He seemed unusually tense. Okay, she was rushing him ... why not let ... after all, she'd let him take charge, and if she changed now ... She moved the hand back to her breast and was not disappointed. Cathy paid closer attention to him now. Tried to. His skills in exciting her were unchanged. She cried out again, kissed him hard, gasping a little, letting him know that he was the one, that her world centered on him as his centered on her. But still his back and shoulders were tense and knotted. What was the matter?

Her hands moved again, running over his chest, pulling playfully on the black hairs. That always set him off ... especially as her hands followed the hairy trail down to ...

What!

'Jack, what's wrong?' It seemed forever before she heard him speak.

'I don't know.' Jack rolled over, away from his wife, onto his back, and his eyes stared at the ceiling.

'Tired?'

'I guess that's it.' Jack slurred the words. 'Sorry, honey.'

Damn damn damn! but before she could think to say something else, his eyes closed.

It's the hours he's working, and all that drinking. But it wasn't fair! This was the day, this was the moment, and –

You're being selfish.

Cathy rose from the bed and collected her peignoir from the floor. She hung it up neatly before getting another that was fit to sleep in and heading into the bathroom.

He's a man, not a machine. He's tired. He's been working too goddamned hard. Everyone has a bad day. Sometimes he wants it and you're not in the mood, and sometimes that makes him a little mad, and it's not his fault and it's not your fault. You have a wonderful marriage, but not a perfect one. Jack's as good a man

449

as you have ever known, but he is not perfect either.

But I wanted . . .

I want another baby, and the timing is so right, right now!

Cathy's eyes filled with tears of disappointment. She knew she was being unfair. But she was still disappointed. And a little angry.

'Well, Commodore, I can't knock the service.'

'Hell, Ron, you expect me to have an old shipmate pick up a rental?'

'As a matter of fact, yes.'

Mancuso snorted. His driver tossed the bags into the trunk of the Navy Plymouth while he and Jones let themselves into the back.

'How's the family?'

'Great, thank you, Commodore –'

'You can call me Bart now, Dr Jones. Besides, I just screened for Admiral.'

'All right!' Dr Ron Jones observed. 'Bart. I like that. Just don't call me Indy. Let's see, the family. Kim's back in school for her doctorate. The kids are all in school – day-care, whatever – and I'm turning into a damned businessman.'

'Entrepreneur, I believe, is the correct term,' Mancuso observed.

'Okay, be technical. Yeah, I own a big piece of the company. But I still get my hands dirty. I got a business guy to do the accounting bullshit. I still like to do real work. Last month I was down at AUTEC on the *Tennessee* checking out a new system.' Jones looked at the driver. 'Okay to talk here?'

'Petty Officer Vincent is cleared higher than I am. Isn't that right?'

'Yes, sir, Admiral's always right, sir,' the driver observed, as he headed off towards Bangor.

'You got a problem, Bart.'

'How big?'

'A unique problem, skipper,' Jones said, lapsing back to the time when he and Mancuso had done some interesting things aboard USS *Dallas*. 'It's never happened before.'

Mancuso read his eyes. 'Got pictures of the kids?'

Jones nodded. 'You bet. How are Mike and Dominic doing?'

'Well, Mike's looking at the Air Force Academy.'

'Tell him the oxygen rots your brain.'

'Dominic's thinking CalTech.'

'No kidding? Hell, I can help him out.'

The rest of the drive occupied itself with small talk. Mancuso swept into his office and closed the soundproof door behind Jones after ordering coffee from his steward.

'What's the problem, Ron?'

Jones hesitated just a fraction before answering. 'I think somebody was tracking *Maine*.'

'Track an *Ohio*? Come on.'

'Where is she now?'

'Heading back out to sea, as a matter of fact. Blue Crew is embarked. She links up with a 688 when she clears the strait for some noise checks, then clears to her patrol area.' Mancuso could discuss almost anything with Jones. His company consulted on the sonar technology for all submarines and anti-submarine platforms in the U.S. fleet, and that necessarily included a lot of operational information.

'Got any Gold Crew guys on base now?'

'The captain's off on vacation. XO's here, Dutch Claggett. Know him?'

'Wasn't he on the *Norfolk*? Black guy, right?'

'That's right.'

'I've heard good stuff about him. He did a nice job on a carrier group on his command quals. I was riding a P-3 when he kicked their ass.'

'You heard right. He's being deep-dipped. This time next year he'll be taking command of a fast-attack.'

'Who's his skipper?'

'Harry Ricks. Heard of him, too?'

Jones looked at the floor and muttered something. 'I got a new guy working for me, retired chief whose last tour was with Ricks. Is he as bad as I hear?'

'Ricks is a super engineer,' Mancuso said. 'I mean it. He's a genius at that stuff.'

'Fine, skipper, so are you, but does Ricks know how to drive?'

'Want some coffee, Ron?' Mancuso gestured at the pot.

'You might want Commander Claggett here, sir.' Jones rose and got his own coffee. 'Since when have you turned diplomat?'

'Command responsibilities, Ron. I never told outsiders about the crazy stuff you did on *Dallas*.'

Jones turned and laughed. 'Okay, you got me there. I have the sonar analysis in my briefcase. I need to see his course tracks, depth records, that stuff. I think there's a good chance *Maine* had a trailer, and that, Bart, is no shit.'

Mancuso lifted his phone. 'Find Lieutenant-Commander Claggett. I need him in my office at once. Thank you. Ron, how sure —'

'I did the analysis myself. One of my people looked it over and caught a whiff. I spent fifty hours massaging the data. One chance in three, maybe more, that she was being trailed.'

Bart Mancuso set his coffee cup down. 'That's really hard to believe.'

'I know. That very fact may be skewing my analysis. It is kinda incredible.'

It was an article of faith in the United States navy that its fleet ballistic-missile submarines had never, not ever, not once been tracked while on deterrence patrol. As with most articles of faith, however, it had caveats.

The location of American missile-sub bases was not a secret. Even the United Parcel Service deliverymen who dropped off packages knew what to look for. In its quest for cost-efficiency, the Navy mainly used civilian security officers — 'rentacops' — at its bases. Except that Marines were used wherever there were nuclear weapons. Wherever you saw Marines, there were nukes about. That was called a security measure. The missile boats themselves were unmistakably different from the smaller fast-attack subs. The ship names were on the

Navy register, and the sailors of those ships wore ballcaps identifying them by name and hull number. With knowledge available to anyone, the Soviets knew where to station their own fast-attack boats to catch the American 'boomers' on the way out to sea.

At first this had not been a problem. The first classes of Soviet fast-attack submarines had been equipped with 'Helen Keller' sonars that could neither see nor hear, and the boats themselves had been noisier than unmuffled automobiles. All that had changed with the advent of the Victor-III class, which approximated a late American 594-class in radiated noise levels, and began to approach adequacy in sonar performance. Victor-IIIs had occasionally turned up at the Juan de Fuca Strait – and elsewhere – waiting for a U.S. missile sub to deploy, and in some cases, since harbor entrances are typically restricted waters, they had established contact and held on tight. That occasionally had included active sonar-lashing, both unnerving and annoying to American sub crews. As a result, U.S. fast-attack subs often accompanied missile submarines to sea. Their mission was to force the Soviet subs off. This was accomplished by the simple expedient of offering an additional target for sonar, confusing the tactical situation, or sometimes by forcing the Russian submarine off-track by ramming – called 'shouldering,' to defuse that most obscene of marine terms. In fact, American boomers had been tracked, only in shallow water, only near well-known harbors, and only for brief periods of time. As soon as the American subs reached deep water, their tactics were to increase speed to degrade the trailing sub's sonar performance, to maneuver evasively, and then go quiet. At that point – every time – the American submarine broke contact. The Soviet sub lost its track, and became the prey instead of the hunter. Missile submarines typically had highly-drilled torpedo departments, and the more aggressive skippers would have all four of their tubes loaded with Mark 48 torpedoes with solutions set on the now-blinded Soviet sub as they watched it wander away in vulnerable befuddlement.

The simple fact was that American missile submarines were invulnerable in their patrol areas. When fast-attack boats were sent in to hunt them, care had to be given to operating depths – much like traffic control for commercial aircraft – lest an inadvertent ramming occur. American fast-attack boats, even the most advanced 688-class, had rarely tracked missile submarines, and the cases where Ohios had been tracked could be counted on the fingers of one hand. Nearly all involved a grievous mistake made by the missile-boat skippers, the ultimate 'black mark in the copybook,' and even then only a very good and very lucky fast-attack skipper had managed to pull it off – and never ever without being counter-detected. *Omaha* had one of the best drivers in the Pacific Fleet, and he had failed to find *Maine* despite having some good intelligence data provided – better than anything a Soviet commander would ever get.

'Good morning, sir,' Dutch Claggett said on his way through the door. 'I was right down the hall at personnel.'

'Commander, this is Dr Ron Jones.'

'This the Jonesy you like to brag on, sir?' Claggett took the civilian's hand.

'None of those stories are true,' Jones said.

Claggett stopped cold when he saw the looks. 'Somebody die or something?'

'Grab a seat,' Mancuso said. 'Ron thinks you might have been tracked on your last patrol.'

'Bullshit,' Claggett observed. 'Excuse me, sir.'

'You're pretty confident,' Jones said.

'*Maine* is the best submarine we own, Dr Jones. We are a black hole. We don't radiate sound, we suck it in from around us.'

'You know the party line, Commander. Now, can we talk business?' Ron unlocked his briefcase and pulled out a heavy sheaf of computer printouts. 'Right around the half-way point in your patrol.'

'Okay, yeah, that's when we snuck up behind *Omaha*.'

'I'm not talking about that. *Omaha* was in front of you,' Jones said, flipping to the right page.

'I still don't believe it, but I'll look at what you got.'

The computer pages were essentially a graphic printout of two 'waterfall' sonar displays. They bore time and true-bearing references. A separate set showed environmental data, mainly water temperature.

'You had a lot of clutter to worry about,' Jones said, pointing to notations on the pages. 'Fourteen fishing boats, half a dozen deep-draft merchant ships, and I see the humpbacks were up to thin out the krill. So, your sonar crew was busy, maybe a little overloaded. You also had a pretty hard layer.'

'All that's right,' Claggett allowed.

'What's this?' Jones pointed to a blossom of noise on the display.

'Well, we were tracking *Omaha*, and the captain decided to rattle their cage with a water slug.'

'No shit?' Jones asked. 'Well, that explains his reaction. I guess they changed their underwear and headed north. You never would have pulled that off on me, by the way.'

'Think so?'

'Yeah, I think so,' Jones replied. 'I always paid real good attention to what was aft of us. I've been out on Ohios, Commander, okay? You can be tracked. Anybody can. It isn't just the platform. Now, look here.'

The printout was a computer-generated cacophony of dots that seemed for the most part to show nothing but random noise, as though a convention of ants had walked across the pages for hours. As with all truly random events, this one had irregularities, places where for one reason or another the ants had never trod, or places where a large number had congregated and then dispersed.

'This line of bearing,' Jones said. 'This pattern comes back eight times, and it comes back only when the layer thins out.'

Commander Claggett frowned. 'Eight, you say? These two could be reverbs from the fishing boats, or really distant CZ-contacts.' He flipped through the pages. Claggett knew his sonar. 'This is thin.'

'That's why your people didn't catch it, either aboard or here. But that's why I got the contract to back-check your people,' Jones said. 'Who was out there?'

'Commodore?' Claggett asked, and got a nod. 'There was an Akula-class out there somewhere. The P-3s lost him south of Kodiak, so he was within maybe six hundred miles of us. That doesn't mean this is him.'

'Which one?'

'*Admiral Lunin*,' Claggett answered.

'Captain Dubinin?'

'Jesus, you *are* cleared pretty good,' Mancuso noted. 'They say he's very good.'

'Ought to be, we have a mutual friend. Is Commander Claggett cleared for that?'

'No. Sorry, Dutch, but that is really black.'

'He ought to be cleared for that,' Jones said. 'This secrecy crap goes way too far, Bart.'

'Rules are rules.'

'Yeah, sure. Anyway, this is the one that twigged me. Last page.' Ron flipped through to the end. 'You were coming up to antenna depth . . .'

'Yeah, practice on the missiles.'

'You made some hull noises.'

'We came up fast, and the hull's made of steel, not elastic,' Claggett said in some annoyance. 'So?'

'So, your hull went up through the layer faster than your "tail" did. Your towed array caught this.'

Claggett and Mancuso both went very quiet. What they saw was a fuzzy vertical line, but the line was in a frequency range that denoted a Soviet submarine's acoustical signature. It was by no means conclusive evidence, but it, like all the other things Jones had notated, was dead aft of *Maine*'s course.

'Now, if I was a betting man, which I'm not, of course, I'd give you two-to-one that while you were underneath the layer, someone might have been tooling along just over top, letting his tail hang under it. He caught your hull transient, saw you were going shallow, and ducked under the layer just as you came over it. Cute move, but your big up-angle meant that your tail stayed down longer than it should have, and that's where this signature came from.'

'But there's nothing after that.'

'Nothing at all,' Jones admitted. 'It never came back. From there on to the end of the tapes, nothing but random noise and otherwise-identified contacts.'

'It's pretty thin, Ron,' Mancuso said, standing up to straighten his back.

'I know. That's why I flew out. In writing it would never sell.'

'What do you know about Russian sonar that we don't?'

'Getting better ... approaching where we were, oh, ten or twelve years ago. They pay more attention to broad-band than we do – that's changing now. I sold the Pentagon on taking another look at the broad-band integration system Texas Instruments have been working on. Commander, what you said before about being a black hole. It cuts both ways. You can't *see* a black hole, but you *can* detect it. What if you track an Ohio by what should be there but isn't?'

'Background noise?'

'Yep.' Jones nodded. 'You make a hole in it. You make a black spot where there's no noise. If he can really isolate a line of bearing on his gear, and if he's got really good filters, and one dynamite sonar operator, I think it's possible – *if* something else cues you in.'

'That's *real* thin.'

Jones granted that observation. 'But it's not impossible. I ran the numbers. It's not good, but it's not impossible. Moreover, we can track below ambient now. Maybe they can, too. I'm hearing they've started turning out a new large-aperture tail – the one designed by the guys outside Murmansk. Good as a BQR-15 used to be.'

'I don't believe it,' Mancuso said.

'I do, skipper. It's not new technology. What do we know about *Lunin*?'

'She's in overhaul right now. Let's see.' Mancuso

turned to look at the polar-projection chart on his office wall. 'If that was him, then if he headed straight back to base . . . it's *possible*, technically speaking, but you're assuming a hell of a lot.'

'I'm saying that this bird was just in the neighborhood when you fired that water slug, that you headed south, and so did he, that you gave him a hull transient which he reacted to, and then he broke contact on his own. The data is thin, but it fits – maybe, I grant you, *maybe*. That's what they pay me for, guys.'

'I commended Ricks for rattling *Omaha*'s cage like that . . .' Mancuso said, after a moment. 'I want aggressive skippers.'

Jones chuckled to break the tension in the room. 'I wonder why, Bart?'

'Dutch knows about that job we had on the beach, that pickup we did.'

'That was a little exciting,' Jones admitted.

'One chance in three . . .'

'The probability increases if you assume the other skipper is smart. Dubinin had a great teacher.'

'What are you two talking about?' Lieutenant Commander Claggett asked in some exasperation.

'You know we have all sorts of data on the Russian Typhoon class, lots more on their torpedoes. Ever wonder how we got all that data, Commander?'

'Ron, God damn it!'

'I didn't break any rules, skipper, and besides, he needs to know.'

'I can't do that and you know it.'

'Fine, Bart.' Jones paused. 'Commander, you may speculate on how we got all that information in one great big lump. You might even guess right.'

Claggett had heard a few rumbles, like why the Eight-Ten dock at Norfolk had been closed so long a few years before. There was a story floated about, spoken only in submarine wardrooms far at sea and well below the surface, that somehow the U.S. Navy had gotten its hands on a Russian missile sub, how a very strange reactor had turned up at the Navy's nuclear-power school in Idaho for tests and then had disappeared, how complete drawings *and* some hardware from Soviet torpedoes had magically appeared in Groton, and how two night missile shots out of Vandenberg Air Force Base had not appeared to be American missiles at all. Lots of operational intelligence had come into the fleet, very good stuff, stuff that sounded like it had come from someone who knew what the hell he was talking about – not always the case with intelligence information – on Soviet submarine tactics and training. Claggett needed only to look at Mancuso's uniform to see the ribbon that denoted a Distinguished Service Medal, America's highest peace-time decoration. The ribbon had a star on it, indicating a second such award. Mancuso was rather young for a squadron command, and very young indeed to be selected for Rear Admiral (Lower Half). And here was a former enlisted man who'd sailed with Mancuso, and now called him *Bart*. He nodded to Dr Jones.

'I get the picture. Thanks.'

'You're saying operator error?'

Jones frowned. He didn't know all that much about Harry Ricks. 'Mainly bad luck. Call it good luck, even. Nothing bad happened, and we've learned something. We know more about the Akula than we used to. A weird set of circumstances came together. Won't happen again in a hundred years, maybe. Your skipper was a victim of circumstance, and the other guy – if there was another guy there – was very damned sharp. Hey, the important thing about mistakes is that you learn from them, right?'

'Harry gets back in ten days,' Mancuso said. 'Can you be back here then?'

'Sorry,' Jones said with a shake of the head. 'I'm going to be in England. I'm going out on HMS *Turbulent* for a few days of hide 'n' seek. The Brits have a new processor that we need to look at, and I drew the duty.'

'You're not going to ask me to present this to the CO, are you, sir?' Claggett asked after a minute's reflection.

'No, Dutch . . . you trying to tell me something?'

It was Claggett's turn to look unhappy. 'Sir, he's my

boss, and he's not a bad boss, but he is a little positive in his thinking.'

That was artfully done, Jones thought. . . . *not a bad boss . . . a little positive. He just called his skipper an idiot in a way that no one could ever call disloyal.* Ron wondered what sort of hyper-nuc-engineer this Ricks was. The good news was that this XO had his act together. And a smart skipper listened to his XO.

'Skipper, how's Mr Chambers doing?'

'Just took over *Key West*. Got a kid you trained as his leading sonarman. Billy Zerwinski, just made chief, I hear.'

'Oh, yeah? Good for him. I figured Mr Chambers was going places, but Billy Z as a chief? What is my Navy coming to?'

'This is taking forever,' Qati observed sourly. His skin was pasty white. The man was suffering again from his drug treatment.

'That is false,' Fromm replied sternly. 'I told you several months, and it will be several months. The first time this was done, it took three years and the resources of the world's richest nation. I will do it for you in an eighth of that time, and on a shoestring budget. In a few days we'll start to work on the rhodium. That will be much easier.'

'And the plutonium?' Ghosn asked.

'That will be the last metal work – you know why, of course.'

'Yes, Herr Fromm, and we must be extremely careful, since when you work with a critical mass you must be careful that it does not become critical while you are forming it,' Ghosn replied, allowing his exacerbation to show for a change. He was tired. He'd been at work for eighteen hours now, supervising the workers. 'And the tritium?'

'Last of all. Again, the obvious reason. It is relatively unstable, and we want the tritium we use to be as pure as possible.'

'Quite so.' Ghosn yawned, barely having heard the

answer to his question, and not troubling himself to wonder why Fromm had answered as he had.

For his part, Fromm made a mental note. Palladium. He needed a small quantity of palladium. How had he forgotten that? He grunted to himself. Long hours, miserable climate, surly workers and associates. A small price to pay, of course, for this opportunity. He was doing what only a handful of men had ever done, and he was doing it in such a way as to equal the work of Fermi and the rest in 1944–5. It was not often that a man could measure himself against the giants and come off well in the comparison. He found himself wondering idly what the weapon would be used for, but admitted to himself that he didn't care, not really. Well, he had other work to do.

The German walked across the room to where the milling machines were. Here another team of technicians were at work. The beryllium piece now on the machine had the most intricate shape and had been the hardest to program, with concave, convex, and other complex curves. The machine was computer-controlled, of course, but was kept under constant observation through the Lexan panels that isolated the machining area from the outside world. The area was ventilated upwards into an electro-static air-cleaner. There was no sense in just dumping the metallic dust into the external air – in fact doing so constituted a major security hazard. Over the electro-static collection plates was a solid two meters of earth. Beryllium was not radioactive, but plutonium was, and plutonium would presently be worked on this very same machine. The beryllium was both necessary to the device and good practice for later tasks.

The milling machine was everything Fromm had hoped for when he'd ordered it several years before. The computer-driven tools were monitored by lasers, producing a degree of perfection that could not have been achieved so quickly as recently as five years ago. The surface of the beryllium was jeweled from the machining, already looking like the finish on a particularly fine rifle bolt, and this was only the first stage of machining. The data read-out on the machine showed tolerances measured in angstroms. The tool-head was spinning at 25,000 RPM, not so much grinding as burning off irregularities. Separate instruments kept a computer eye on the work being done, both measuring tolerances and waiting for the tool-head to show signs of wear, at which point the machine would automatically stop and replace the tool with a fresh one. Technology was wonderful. What had once been the work of specially-trained master machinists overseen by Nobel Prize winners was now being done by microchips.

The actual casing for the device was already fabricated. Ellipsoidal in shape, it was 98 centimeters in length by 52 in extreme breadth. Made of steel one centimeter in thickness, it had to be strong, but not grossly so, just enough to hold a vacuum. Also ready for installation were curved blocks of polyethylene and polyurethane foam, because a device of this sort required the special properties of both the strongest and the flimsiest materials. They had gotten ahead of themselves in some areas, of course, but there was no sense in wasting time or idle hands. On another machine, workers were practicing yet again on a stainless-steel blank that simulated the folded-cylinder plutonium reaction-mass primary. It was their seventh such practice session. Despite the sophistication of the machines, the first two had gone badly, as expected. By number five, they had figured most of the process out, and the sixth attempt had been good enough to work – but not good enough for Fromm. The German had a simple mental model for the overall task, one formulated by America's National Aeronautics and Space Administration to describe the first moon landing. In order for the device to perform as desired, a complex series of individual events had to take place in an inhumanly precise sequence. He viewed the process as a walk through a series of gates. The wider the gates were, the easier it would be to walk through them quickly. Plus/minus tolerances reflected slight closure of the individual gates. Fromm wanted zero tolerances. He wanted every single part of the weapon to match his design criteria as exactly as the available technology made possible. The closer to perfection he could get, the more likely it was that the device would perform exactly as he predicted . . . or even better, part of him thought. Unable to experiment, unable to find empirical solutions to complex theoretical problems, he'd over-engineered the weapon, providing an energy budget that was several orders of magnitude beyond what was really necessary for the projected yield. That explained the vast quantity of tritium he planned to use, more than five times what was really needed in a theoretical sense. That carried its own problems, of course. His tritium supply was several years old, and some parts of it had decayed into ^{3}He, a decidedly undesirable isotope of helium, but by filtering the tritium through palladium he'd separate the tritium out, ensuring a proper total yield. American and Soviet bombmakers could get away with far less of it, because of their extensive experimentation, but Fromm had his own advantage. He did not have to concern himself with a long shelf-life for his device, and that was a luxury that his Soviet and American counterparts did not have. It was the only advantage he had over them, and Fromm planned to make full use of it. As with most parts of bomb design, it was an advantage that cut both ways, but Fromm knew he had full control over the device. *Palladium*, he told himself. *Mustn't forget that*. But he had plenty of time.

'Finished.' The head of the team waved for Fromm to look. The stainless-steel blank came off the machine easily, and he handed it to Fromm. It was thirty centimeters in length. The shape was complex, what one would get from taking a large water tumbler and bending its top outside and down towards the base. It would not hold water because of a hole in the center of what might have been the bottom – actually it would, Fromm told himself a second later, just in the wrong way. The blank weighed about three kilograms, and every surface was mirror-smooth. He held it up to the light to check for imperfections and irregularities. His eyes were not that good. The quality of the finish was easier to understand

463

mathematically than visually. The surface, so said the machine, was accurate to a thousandth of a micron, or a fraction of a single wavelength of light.

'It is a jewel,' Ghosn observed, standing behind Fromm. The machinist beamed.

'Adequate,' was Fromm's judgment. He looked at the machinist. 'When you've made five more equally as good, I will be satisfied. Every metal segment must be of this quality. Begin another,' he told the machinist. Fromm handed the blank to Ghosn and walked away.

'Infidel,' the machinist growled under his breath.

'Yes, he is,' Ghosn agreed. 'But he is the most skilled man I have ever met.'

'I'd rather work for a Jew.'

'This is magnificent work,' Ghosn said, to change the subject.

'I would not have believed it possible to polish metal so precisely. This machine is incredible. I could make anything with it.'

'That is good. Make another of these,' Ghosn told him with a smile.

'As you say.'

Ghosn walked to Qati's room. The Commander was looking at a plate of simple foods, but unable to touch it for fear of retching.

'Perhaps this will make you feel better,' Ghosn told him.

'That is?' Qati said, taking it.

'That is what the plutonium will look like.'

'Like glass . . .'

'Smoother than that. Smooth enough for a laser mirror. I could tell you the accuracy of the surface, but you've never seen anything that small in your life anyway. Fromm is a genius.'

'He's an arrogant, overbearing –'

'Yes, Commander, he is all of that, but he is exactly the man we need. I could never have done this myself. Perhaps, given a year or two, perhaps I might have been able to rework that Israeli bomb into something that would work – the problems were far more complex than

464

I knew only a few weeks ago. But this Fromm . . . what I am learning from him! By the time we are finished, I *will* be able to do it again on my own!'

'Really?'

'Commander, do you know what engineering is?' Ghosn asked. 'It is like cooking. If you have the right recipe, the right book, and the right ingredients, anyone can do it. Certainly this task is a hard one, but the principle holds. You must know how to use the various mathematical formulae, but they are all in books also. It is merely a question of education. With computers, the proper tools – and a good teacher, which this Fromm bastard is . . .'

'Then why haven't more –'

'The hard part is getting the ingredients, specifically the plutonium or U235. That requires a nuclear reactor plant of a specific type, or the new centrifuge technology. Either represents a vast investment, and one which is difficult to conceal. It also explains the remarkable security measures taken in the handling and transport of bombs and their components. The oft-told tale that bombs are hard to make is a lie.'

CHAPTER 18

Progress

Wellington had three men working for him. Each was an experienced investigator, accustomed to politically sensitive cases which demanded the utmost discretion. His job was to identify likely areas of field investigation, then to examine and correlate the information they returned to his office in the Justice Department. The tricky part was to gather the information without notice going back to the target of the probe, and Wellington correctly thought that that part of the task would be particularly difficult with a target like Ryan. The DDCI was nothing if not perceptive. His previous job had qualified him as a man who could hear the grass grow and read tea-leaves with the best of them. That meant going slow . . . but not too slow. It also seemed likely to the young attorney that the purpose of his investigation was not to produce data suitable for a grand jury, which gave him quite a bit more leeway than he might otherwise have had. He doubted that Ryan could have been so foolish as to have actually broken any law. The SEC rules had been grazed, perhaps bent, but on inspection of the SEC investigation documents, it was clear that Ryan's action had, arguably, been made in good faith and full expectation that he had not violated any statute. That judgment might have been technical on Ryan's part, but the law *was* technical. The Securities and Exchange Commission could have pushed, and might even have gotten an indictment, but they would never have gotten a conviction . . . maybe they could have muscled him into a settlement and/or a consent decree, but Wellington doubted that also. They'd suggested it as a sign of good faith, and he had answered with a flat *no*. Ryan was not a man to tolerate being pushed around. This man had killed people. That didn't frighten Wellington in any way. It was merely an indicator of the man's strength of character. Ryan was a tough, formidable son-of-a-bitch who met things head-on when he had to.

That's his weakness, Wellington told himself.

He prefers to meet things head-on. He lacks subtlety. It was a common failing of the honest, and a grievous weakness in a political environment.

Ryan had political protectors, however. Trent and Fellows were nothing if not canny political craftsmen.

What an interesting tactical problem . . .

Wellington saw his task as two-fold: to get something that could be used against Ryan, and something that would also neutralize his political allies.

Carol Zimmer. Wellington closed one file and opened another.

There was a photograph from the Immigration and Naturalization Service. That one was years old – she'd been a child-bride in the most literal sense of the word when she'd first come to America, a tiny little thing with a doll's face. A more recent photo taken by his field investigator showed a mature woman still short of forty, her face now showing some lines where once there had been the smoothness of china. If anything she was more beautiful than before. The timid, almost hunted look in the first photo – understandable, since it had been taken after her escape from Laos – had been replaced by that of a woman secure in her life. She had a cute smile, Wellington told himself.

The lawyer remembered a classmate in law school, Cynthia Yu. *Damn, hadn't she been quite a lay . . . same sort of eyes, almost, the Oriental coquette . . .*

Might that *be it!*

Something that simple?

Ryan was married: wife, Caroline Muller Ryan, M.D., eye surgeon. Photo: a quintessential Wasp, except that she was Catholic, slender and attractive, mother of two.

Well, just because a man has a pretty wife . . .

Ryan had established an educational trust fund ...
Wellington opened another file. It was a Xerox copy of
the document.

Ryan, he saw, had done it alone, through a lawyer –
not his regular lawyer! A D.C. guy. And Caroline Ryan
had not signed the papers ... did she even know about
it? The information on his desk suggested that she did
not.

Wellington next checked the birth records on the newest Zimmer child. Her husband had been killed in a 'routine training accident' – the timing was equivocal. She
might have gotten pregnant the very week her husband
had been killed. Then again, she might not have. It was
her seventh child – eighth? You couldn't tell with those,
could you? Gestation could be nine months, or less. First
kids were usually late. Later kids, as often as not, were
early. Birth weight of the child ... five pounds seven
ounces ... less than average, but she was an Asian, and
they were small ... did they have smaller-than-normal
babies? Wellington made his notes, recognizing that he
had a series of maybes, and not a single fact.

But, hell, was he really looking for facts?

The two punks. Ryan's bodyguards, Clark and Chavez,
had mangled one of them. His investigator had checked
that out with the Anne Arundel County Police Department. The local cops had signed off on Clark's story. The
punks in question had long but minor records, a few
summary probations, a few sessions with youth-
counselors. The cops were delighted at the way things
had turned out. 'Okay with me if he'd shot that worthless little fucker,' a police sergeant had said, with a laugh
recorded on the investigator's tape cassette. 'That Clark
guy looked like one very serious dude. His sidekick ain't
much different. If those punks were dumb enough to
hassle them, hey, it's a tough world, y'know? Two other
gang members confirmed the story the way the good
guys told it, and that's a closed case, man.'

But *why* had Ryan set his two bodyguards on them?
He's killed to protect his family, hasn't he . . . ? This

is not a guy who tolerates danger to his . . . friends . . .
family . . . lovers?

It *is possible.*

'Hmm . . .' Wellington observed to himself. The DDCI is getting a little on the side. Nothing illegal, just unsavory. Also out of character for the saintly Dr John Patrick Ryan. When his lover is annoyed by some local gang members, he simply sics his bodyguards on them, like a mafia *capo* might do, as a lordly public service that no cop would ever bother fooling with.

Might that be enough?

No.

He needed something more. Evidence, some sort of evidence. Not good enough for a grand jury . . . but good enough for – what? To launch an official investigation. Of course. Such investigations were never really secret, were they? A few whispers, a few rumors. Easily done. But first Wellington needed something to hang his hat on.

'There are those who say this could be a preview of the Superbowl: Three weeks into the NFL season, the Metrodome. Both teams are two and oh. Both teams look like the class of their respective conferences. The San Diego Chargers take on the Minnesota Vikings.'

'You know, Tony Wills's rookie season has started even more spectacularly than his college career. Only two games, and he has three hundred six yards rushing in forty-six carries – that's six-point-seven yards every time he touches the ball, and he did *that* against the Bears and the Falcons, two fine rushing defenses,' the color man observed. 'Can anybody stop Tony Wills?'

'And a hundred twenty-five yards in his nine pass receptions. It's no wonder that they call this kid the franchise.'

'Plus his doctorate from Oxford University.' The color man laughed. 'Academic All-American, Rhodes Scholar, the man who single-handedly put Northwestern University back on the map with two trips to the Rose Bowl. You suppose he's faster than a speeding bullet?'

'We'll find out. That rookie middle linebacker for the Chargers, Maxim Bradley, is the best thing I've seen since Dick Butkus came out of Illinois, the best middle linebacker Alabama ever turned out – and that's the school of Tommy Nobis, Cornelius Bennett, and quite a few other all-pros. They don't call him the Secretary of Defense for nothing.' It was already the biggest joke in the NFL, referring to the team owner, Dennis Bunker, the real SecDef.

'Tim, I think we got us a ball game!'

'I should be there,' Brent Talbot observed. 'Dennis is.'

'If I tried to keep him away from his games, he'd resign,' President Fowler said. 'Besides, he used his own plane.' Dennis Bunker owned his own small jet, and though he allowed others to fly him around, he still maintained a current commercial pilot's license. It was one of the reasons the military respected him. He could try his hand at almost anything that flew, having once been a distinguished combat flyer.

'What's the spread on this one?'

'Vikings by three,' the President answered. 'That's just because of the home field. The teams are pretty even. I saw Wills against the Falcons last week. He's some kid.'

'Tony's all of that. A wonderful boy. Smart, marvelous attitude, spends a lot of time with kids.'

'How about we get him to be a spokesman for the anti-drug campaign?'

'He already does that in Chicago. I can call him if you want.'

Fowler turned. 'Do it, Brent.'

Behind them Pete Connor and Helen D'Agustino relaxed on a couch. President Fowler knew them both to be football fans, and the President's TV room was large and comfortable.

'Anybody want a beer?' Fowler asked. He could not watch a ballgame without a beer.

'I'll get it,' D'Agustino said, heading for the refrigerator in the next room. It was the most curious thing about this most complex of men, 'Daga' thought to herself. The man looked, dressed, walked, and acted like a patrician. He was a genuine intellectual, with the arrogance to match. But in front of a TV watching a football game – Fowler only watched baseball when his presidential duties required it – he was Joe Six-Pack, with a bowl of popcorn and a glass of beer, or two, or three. Of course, even here, his 'anybody want a beer?' was a command. His bodyguards could not drink on duty, and Talbot never touched the stuff. Daga got herself a Diet Coke.

'Thank you,' Fowler said, when she handed the glass to her President. He was even more polite at football games. Perhaps, D'Agustino thought, because it was something he and his wife had done. She hoped that was true. It gave the man the humanity that he needed above all things.

'Wow! Bradley hit Wills hard enough that we heard it up here.' On the screen, both men got up and traded what looked like an emotional exchange but was probably a mutual laugh.

'Might as well get acquainted fast, Tim. They'll be seeing a lot of each other. Second and seven from the thirty-one, both teams just getting loosened up. That Bradley's a smart linebacker. He played off the center and filled the hole like he knew what was coming.'

'He certainly reads his keys well for a rook, and that Viking center made the Pro Bowl last year,' the color guy pointed out.

'Great ass on that Bradley kid,' Daga pointed out quietly.

'This women's lib stuff is going too far, Helen,' Pete said with a grin. He shifted positions on the couch to get his service revolver out of his kidney.

Günther Bock and Marvin Russell stood on the sidewalk just outside the White House grounds among a crowd of a hundred or so tourists, most of whom aimed cameras at the executive mansion. They'd arrived in the city the previous evening, and tomorrow they'd tour the Capitol. Both wore ballcaps to protect them from what still felt like a summer sun. Bock had a camera draped around his neck on a Mickey Mouse strap. He snapped a few photos, mainly to blend in with the rest of the tourists. The real observations came from his trained mind. This was a much harder target than people realized. The buildings around the White House were all large enough that sharpshooters were provided with excellent perches concealed by the stonework. He knew that he was probably under surveillance right now, but they couldn't have the time or money to compare his likeness to every photo they had on their books, and he'd taken the trouble to alter his appearance enough to dispense with that worry.

The President's helicopter flew in and landed only a hundred meters from where he stood. A man with a man-portable SAM might stand a good chance of taking it out – except for the practical considerations. To be there at the right time was much harder than it seemed. The ideal way would be to have a small truck, perhaps one with a hole cut in the roof so that the missileer could stand, fire, and attempt his escape. Except for the riflemen who certainly perched on the surrounding buildings, and Bock had no illusions that such snipers would miss their targets. Americans had invented sharpshooting, and their President would have the services of the best. Doubtless some of the people in this crowd of tourists were also Secret Service agents, and it was unlikely that he'd spot them.

The bomb could be driven here and detonated in a truck ... depending on the protective measures that Ghosn had warned him about. Similarly, he might be able to deliver the weapon by truck to the immediate vicinity of the Capitol Building, perhaps at the time of the President's State of the Union Address ... if the weapon were ready on time. That they weren't sure of, and there was also the question of shipping it here – three weeks, it would take. Latakia to Rotterdam, then transshipment to an American port. Baltimore was the closest major port. Norfolk/Newport News was next. Both handled lots of containerized shipping. They could fly it in, but airborne cargo was often X-rayed, and they could not risk that.

The idea was to catch the President on a weekend. It almost had to be a weekend for everything else to work. Everything else. Bock knew that he was violating one of his most important operational precepts – simplicity. But for this to have a chance of working, he had to arrange more than one incident, and he had to do it on a weekend. But the American President was only in the White House about half the time on weekends, and his movements between Washington, Ohio, and other places were unpredictable. The simplest security measure available to the President of the United States was the one they used: his movement schedule, as well-known as it might have been, was irregular and its precise details were often closely held. Bock needed at least a week's lead-time to set up his other arrangements – and that was optimistic – but it would be nearly impossible to get that seven days. It would actually have been easier to plan a simple assassination with conventional weapons. A small aircraft, for example, might be armed with SA-7 missiles . . . probably not. The President's helicopter undoubtedly had the best infra-red jammers available . . .

One chance. You get only one chance.

What if we are patient! What if we simply sit on the bomb for a year and bring it into the country for the next State of the Union speech . . . ? Getting the bomb close enough to the Capitol Building to destroy it and everyone in it should not be hard. He'd heard – and would see tomorrow – that the Capitol was a building of classical construction – lots of stone, but little structural ironwork . . . perhaps all they needed was patience.

But that wouldn't happen. Qati would not allow it. There was both the question of security, and the more important consideration that Qati thought himself a dying man, and dying men were not known for their patience.

And would it work in any case? How well did the Americans guard the areas where the President's presence was predictable well in advance? Were their radiological sensors in the area?

You'd put them there, wouldn't you?

Only one chance. You'll never be able to repeat this.

At least one week's advance notice, or you'll never achieve anything beyond mass-murder.

Must be a place without the likely presence of radiological sensors. That eliminated Washington.

Bock started walking away from the black iron fence. His face did not betray the anger he felt.

'Back to the hotel?' Russell asked.

'Yes, why not?' Both men were still tired from their traveling anyway.

'Good, wanted to catch the ballgame. You know, that's about the only thing Fowler and I see eye to eye on?'

'Humph? What's that?'

'Football.' Russell laughed. 'You know? Football. Okay, I'll teach it t'ya.'

Fifteen minutes later, they were in their rooms. Russell switched the TV to the local NBC channel.

'That was some drive, Tim. The Vikings had to convert six third downs, and two of them required measurements.'

'And one was a bad spot,' President Fowler said.

'Red didn't think so.' Talbot chuckled.

'They're holding Tony Wills to barely three yards a carry, and one of those was his twenty-yard break on the reverse that caught the Chargers napping.'

'A lot of work for three points, Tim, but they did get the three.'

'And now the Chargers get their chance at offense. The Vikings defense is a little iffy, with two of their starters out with minor injuries. I bet they're sorry to miss this one.'

The Chargers' quarterback took his first snap, faded back five steps and hurled the ball towards his flanker, slanting across the middle, but a hand tipped the ball, and it ended up in the surprised face of the Vikings' free safety, who pulled it in and fell at the forty.

*

Bock found the game exciting in a distant sort of way, but almost totally incomprehensible. Russell tried to explain, but it didn't really help very much. Günther consoled himself with a beer, stretching out on the bed while his mind rolled over what he'd seen. Bock knew what he wanted his plan to accomplish, but the exact details – especially here in America – were looking harder than expected. If only –

'What was that they said?'

'The Secretary of Defense,' Russell answered.

'A joke?'

Marvin turned. 'Sort of a joke. That's what they call the middle linebacker, Maxim Bradley, from the University of Alabama. But the real one owns the team. Dennis Bunker – there he is.' The camera showed Bunker in one of the stadium's sky-boxes.

How remarkable, Bock thought.

'What is this Superbowl they talked about?'

'That's the championship game. They have a playoff series of the most successful teams, and the last one is called the Superbowl.'

'Like the World Cup, you mean?'

'Yeah, something like that. 'Cept we do it every year. This year – actually next year, end of January – it's in the new stadium they built at Denver. The Skydome, I think they call it.'

'They expect these two teams to go there?'

Russell shrugged. 'That's the talk. The regular season is sixteen weeks, man, then three weeks of playoffs, then another week wait for the Superbowl.'

'Who goes to this last game?'

'Lots of people. Hey, man, it's *the* game. Everybody wants to go to it. Getting tickets is a mother. These two teams are the best to go all the way, but it's real unpredictable, y'know?'

'President Fowler is a football enthusiast?'

'That's what they say. He's supposed to go to a lot of Redskin games right here in D.C.'

'What about security?' Bock asked.

'It's tough. They put him in one of the special boxes.

Figure they have it rigged with bulletproof glass or something.'

How very foolish, Bock thought. Of course, a stadium was easier to secure than it might seem to the casual observer. A heavy crew-served weapon could only be fired from an entrance ramp, and watching those was relatively easy. On the other hand . . .

Bock closed his eyes. He was thinking in an unorganized way, vacillating between conventional and unconventional approaches to the problem. He was also allowing himself to focus on the wrong thing. Killing the American President was desirable, but not essential. What *was* essential was to kill the largest number of people in the most spectacular way imaginable, then to coordinate with other activities in order to foment . . .

Think! Concentrate on the real mission.

'The television coverage for these games is most impressive,' Bock observed after a minute.

'Yeah, they make a big deal of that. Satellite vans, all that stuff.' Russell was concentrating on the game. The Vikings had scored something called a touchdown, and the score was now ten to nothing, but it seemed now that the other team was moving rapidly in the other direction.

'Has the game ever been seriously disrupted?'

Marvin turned. 'Huh? Oh, during the war with Iraq, they had really tight security – and you remember the movie, right?'

'Movie?' Bock asked.

'*Black Sunday*, I think it was – some Middle East guys tried to blow up the place.' Russell laughed. 'Already been done, man. In Hollywood, anyway. They used a blimp. Anyway, during the Superbowl when we were fighting Iraq, they wouldn't let the TV blimp come near the place.'

'Is there a game at Denver today?'

'No, that's tomorrow night, Broncos and the Seahawks. Won't be much of a game. The Broncos are rebuilding this year.'

'I see.' Bock left the room and arranged for the concierge to get them tickets to Denver in the morning.

Cathy got up to see him off. She even fixed breakfast. Her solicitude over the past few days had not made her husband feel any better. Quite the reverse. But he couldn't say anything about it, could he? Even the way she overdid it, straightening his tie and kissing him on the way out the door. The smile, the loving look, all for a husband who couldn't get it up, Jack thought on his way out to the car. The same sort of smothering attention you might give to some poor bastard in a wheelchair.

'Morning, Doc.'

'Hello, John.'

'Catch the Vikings–Chargers game yesterday?'

'No, I, uh, took my son to see the Orioles. They lost six to one.' Success was following Jack everywhere, but at least he'd kept his word to his son. That was something, wasn't it?

'Twenty-four to twenty-one in overtime. God, that Wills kid is incredible. They held him to ninety-six yards, but when he had to deliver, he popped it for twenty yards and set up the field-goal,' Clark reported.

'You have money on the game?'

'Five bucks at the office, but it was a three-point spread. The education fund won that one.'

It gave Ryan something to chuckle about. Gambling was as illegal at CIA as it was in every other government office, but a serious attempt to enforce a ban on football betting might have started a revolution – the same was true at the FBI, Jack was sure, which enforced interstate gambling statutes – and the semi-official system was that half-point betting spreads were not allowed. All 'pushes' (odds-caused ties) forfeited into the Agency's in-house charity, the Education Aid Fund. It was something that even the Agency's own Inspector-General winked at – in fact, he liked to lay money on games as much as the next guy.

'Looks like you at least got some sleep, Jack,' Clark noted, as they made their way towards Route 50.

'Eight hours,' Jack said. He'd wanted another chance the previous night, but Cathy had said no. *You're too tired, Jack. That's all it is. You're working too hard, and I want you to take it easy, okay!*

Like I'm a goddamned stud horse that's been overworked.

'Good for you,' Clark said. 'Or maybe your wife insisted, eh?'

Ryan stared ahead at the road. 'Where's the box?'

'Here.'

Ryan unlocked it and started looking at the weekend's dispatches.

They caught an early direct flight from Washington National to Denver Stapleton International. It was a clear day most of the way across the country, Bock got a window seat and looked at the country, his first time in America. As with most Europeans, he was surprised, almost awed by the sheer size and diversity. The wooded hills of Appalachia; the flat farmlands of Kansas, speckled with the immense circular signature of the traveling irrigation systems; the stunning way the plains ended and the Rockies began within easy sight of Denver. No doubt Marvin would say something when they arrived about how this had all been the property of his people. What rubbish. They'd been nomadic barbarians, following the herds of bison, or whatever had once been there before civilization arrived. America might be his enemy, but it was a civilized country, and all the more dangerous for it. By the time the aircraft landed, he was squirming with his need for a smoke. Ten minutes after landing, they'd rented a car and were examining a map. Bock's head was dizzy from the lack of oxygen here. Nearly fifteen hundred meters of altitude, he realized. It was a wonder that people could play American football here.

They'd landed behind the morning rush hour, and driving to the stadium was simple. Southwest of the city, the new Skydome was a distinctive structure located on an immense plot of ground to allow ample room for parking. He parked the car close to a ticket window and decided that the simple approach would be best.

'Can I get two tickets for tonight's match?' he asked the attendant.

'Sure, we have a few hundred left. Where do you want them?'

'I don't know the stadium at all, I'm afraid.'

'You must be new here,' the lady observed with a friendly smile. 'All we got's in the upper deck, Section Sixty-Six and Sixty-Eight.'

'Two, please. Is cash all right?'

'Sure is. Where are you from?'

'Denmark,' Bock replied.

'Really? Well, welcome to Denver! Hope you enjoy the game.'

'Can I look around to see where my seat is?'

'Technically, no, but nobody really minds.'

'Thank you.' Bock smiled back at the simpering fool.

'They had seats for tonight?' Marvin Russell asked. 'I'll be damned.'

'Come, we will see where they are.'

Bock walked through the nearest open gate, just a few meters from the big ABC vans that carried the satellite equipment for the evening broadcast. He took the time to notice that the stadium was hard-wired for the equipment. So, the TV vans would always be in the same place, just by Gate 5. Inside, he saw a team of technicians setting up their equipment, then he headed up the nearest ramp, deliberately heading in the wrong direction.

The stadium had to seat sixty thousand people, perhaps a little more. It had three primary levels, called lower, mezzanine, and upper, plus two complete ranks of enclosed boxes, some of which looked quite luxurious. Structurally, it was quite impressive. Massive reinforced-concrete construction, all the upper decks were cantilevered. There were no pillars to block a spectator's view. A fine stadium. A superb target. Beyond the parking lot to the north were endless hectares of low-rise apartment buildings. To the east was a government office center. The stadium was not in the city center, but that couldn't be helped. Bock found and took his seat, orienting himself with the compass and the TV equipment. The latter was quite easy. An ABC banner was being hung below one of the press boxes.

'Hey!'

'Yes?' Bock looked down at a security guard.

'You're not supposed to be here.'

'Sorry.' He held up his tickets. 'I just bought them, and I wanted to see where my seats were, so that I would know where to park. I've never seen an American football game,' he added, heavy on the accent. Americans, he'd heard, were always nice to people with European accents.

'You want to park in Area A or B. Try to arrive early, like before five. You want to beat the rush-hour traffic. It can be a bear out there.'

Günther bobbed his head. 'Thank you. I'll be leaving now.'

'No problem, sir. It's no big deal. I mean, it's the insurance, y'know? You have people wandering around, they might get hurt and sue.'

Bock and Russell left. They circled the bottom level, just so that Günther could be sure he had the configuration memorized. Then that became unnecessary when he found a stadium diagram printed on a small card.

'Seen what you wanted?' Marvin asked, when they got back to the car.

'Yes, possibly.'

'You know, that's pretty subtle,' the American mused aloud.

'What do you mean?'

'Dickin' with the TV. The really dumb thing about revolutionaries is that they overlook the psychological stuff. You don't have to kill a lot of people, just pissin' them off, scarin' them, that's enough, isn't it?'

Bock stopped at the parking-lot exit and looked at his companion. 'You have learned much, my friend.'

'This is pretty hot stuff,' Ryan said, leafing through the pages.

'I didn't know it was that bad,' Mary Patricia Foley agreed.

'How are you feeling?'

The senior field officer's eyes twinkled. 'Clyde has dropped. Waiting for my water to break.'

Jack looked up. 'Clyde?'

'That's what I'm calling him – her – whatever.'

'Doing your exercises?'

'Rocky Balboa should be in the shape I'm in. Ed's got the nursery all painted up. The crib is put back together. All ready, Jack.'

'How much time will you be taking off?'

'Four weeks, maybe six.'

'I may want you to go over some of this at home,' Ryan said, lingering on page two.

'Long as you pay me,' Mary Pat laughed.

'What do you think, MP?'

'I think SPINNAKER is the best source we have. If he says it, it's probably true.'

'We haven't caught a whiff of this anywhere else . . .'

'That's why you recruit good penetration agents.'

'True,' Ryan had to agree.

The report from Agent SPINNAKER wasn't quite earth-shaking, but it was like the first rumble that got people worrying about a major quake. Since the Russians had taken the cork out of the bottle, the Soviet Union had developed an instant case of political schizophrenia. Wrong term, Ryan reflected. Multiple-personality disorder, perhaps. There were five identifiable political areas: the true-believing communists, who thought that any divergence from the True Path was a mistake (the Forward-to-the-Past crowd, some called them); the progressive socialists who wanted to create socialism with a human face (something that had singularly failed in Massachusetts, Jack thought wryly); the middle-of-the-roaders who wanted some free-market capitalism, backed up with a solid safety net (or craved the worst of both worlds, as any economist could say); the reformists, who wanted a thin net and a lot of capitalism (but no one knew what capitalism was yet, except for a rapidly expanding criminal sector); and on the far right, those who wanted a right-wing authoritarian government (which was what had put Communism in place over seventy years before). The groups on the extreme ends of the spectrum had perhaps 10 percent each in the Congress of People's Deputies. The remaining 80 percent of the votes were fairly evenly split among the three vaguely centrist positions. Naturally enough, various issues scrambled allegiances – environmentalism was particularly hot and divisive – and the biggest wild card was the incipient break-up of the republics that had always chafed under Russian rule, all the more so because of the political *coda* imposed from Moscow. Finally, each of the five groupings had its own political sub-sets. For example, there was currently a lot of talk from the political right of inviting the most likely Romanov heir-presumptive back to Moscow – not to take over, but merely to accept a semi-official apology for the murder of his ancestors. Or so the cover-story went. Whoever had come up with that idea, Jack thought, was either the most naive son of a bitch since Alice went down the rabbit hole or a politician with a dangerously simplistic mindset. The good news, CIA's Station Paris reported, was that the Prince of all the Russias had a better feel for politics and his own safety than his sponsors did.

The bad news was that the political and economic situation in the Soviet Union looked utterly hopeless. SPINNAKER's report merely made it look more ominous. Andrey Il'ych Narmonov was desperate, running out of options, running out of allies, running out of ideas, running out of time, and running out of maneuvering room. He was, the report said, overly concerned with his waffling on the nationalities problem, to the point that he was trying to strengthen his hold on the security apparatus – MVD, KGB, and the military – so that he could keep the empire together by force. But the military, SPINNAKER said, was both unhappy with that mission, and unhappy with the half-hearted way Narmonov planned to implement it.

There had been speculation about the Soviet military and its supposed political ambitions since the time of Lenin. It wasn't new. Stalin had taken a scythe through his officer corps in the late 1930s; it was generally agreed that Marshal Tukhashevskiy had not really posed a political threat, that it had been yet another case of Stalin's malignant paranoia. Khrushchev had done the same in the late '50s, but without the mass executions; that had been done because Khrushchev had wanted to save money on tanks and depend on nuclear arms instead. Narmonov had retired quite a few generals and colonels also; in this case, the move had been exclusively one of economizing on military expense across the board. But this time also, the military reductions had been accompanied by a political renaissance. For the first time there was a true political opposition movement in the country, and the fact of the matter was that the Soviet Army had all the guns. To counter that worrisome possibility, the KGB's Third Chief Directorate had existed for generations – KGB officers who wore military uniforms and whose mission it was to keep an eye on everything. But the Third Chief Directorate was a mere shadow of what it had been. The military had persuaded Narmonov to remove it, as a precondition to its own goal of a truly professional force, loyal to the country and the new constitution.

Historians invariably deemed the age in which they lived to be one of transition. For once they were right, Jack thought. If this were not an age of transition, then it was hard to imagine what the hell was. In the case of the Soviets, they were poised between two political and economic worlds, teetering, not quite balanced, not quite sure which way they would go. And that made their political situation dangerously vulnerable to . . . what? Jack asked himself.

Damned near anything.

SPINNAKER said Narmonov was being pressured to make a deal with the military, which, he said, was part of the Forward-to-the-Past mob. Group One. The danger existed, he said, that the Soviet Union would revert to a quasi-military state that repressed its progressive elements; that Narmonov had lost his nerve.

'He says he's had one-on-one meetings with Andrey Il'ych,' Mary Pat pointed out. 'Intel doesn't come any better than that.'

'Also true,' Jack replied. 'It is worrisome, isn't it?'

'I'm not really concerned about a reversion to Marxist rule . . . What worries me —'

'Yeah, I know. Civil war.' *Civil war in a country with thirty thousand nuclear warheads. There's a cheery thought.*

'Our position has been to cut Narmonov as much slack as he needs, but if our guy is right, that might be the wrong policy.'

'What's Ed think?'

'Same as me. We trust Kadishev. I recruited him. Ed and I have seen every report he's ever sent in. He delivers. He's smart, well-placed, very perceptive, a ballsy son-of-a-gun. When's the last time he gave us bad stuff?'

'I don't know that he ever has,' Jack replied.

'Neither do I, Jack.'

Ryan leaned back in his chair. 'Christ, I just love these easy calls . . . I don't know, MP. The time I met Narmonov . . . that is one tough, smart, agile son-of-a-bitch. He's got real brass ones.' Jack stopped. *More than you can say for yourself, boy.*

'We all have our limitations. Even the brass ones go soft.' Mrs Foley smiled. 'Oops, wrong metaphor. People run out of steam. Stress, hours, time in the saddle. Reality grinds us all down. Why do you think I'm taking time off? Being pregnant gives me a great excuse. Having a newborn isn't exactly a picnic, but I get a month or so of the fundamentals, real life instead of the stuff we do here every day. That's one advantage we have over men, doc. You guys can't break away like we women can. That may be Andrey Il'ych's problem. Who can he turn to for advice? Where can he go for help? He's been there a long time. He's dealing with a deteriorating situation, and he's running out of gas. That's what SPINNAKER tells us, and it is consistent with the facts.'

'Except that we haven't heard anything like this from anyone else.'

'But he's our best guy for the inside stuff.'

'Which completes the circularity of the argument, Mary Pat.'

'Doc, you have the report, and you have my opinion,' Mrs Foley pointed out.

'Yes, ma'am.' Jack set the document on his desk.

'What are you going to tell them?' 'Them' was the top row of the executive branch: Fowler, Elliot, Talbot.

'I guess I go with your evaluation. I'm not entirely comfortable with it, but I don't have anything to counter your position with. Besides, the last time I went against you, turned out I was the one who blew the call.'

'You know, you're a pretty good boss.'

'And you're pretty good at letting me down easy.'

'We all have bad days,' Mrs Foley said, as she got awkwardly to her feet. 'Let me waddle back to my office.'

Jack rose also and walked to open the door for her. 'When are you due?'

She smiled back at him. 'October thirty-first – Halloween, but I'm always late, and they're always big ones.'

'You take care of yourself.' Jack watched her leave, then walked in to see the Director.

'You'd better look this over.'

'Narmonov? I heard another SPINNAKER came in.'

'You heard right, sir.'

'Who's doing the write-up?'

'I will,' Jack said. 'I want to do some cross-checking first, though.'

'I go down tomorrow. I'd like to have it then.'

'I'll have it done tonight.'

'Good. Thanks, Jack.'

This is the place, Günther told himself halfway into the first quarter. The stadium accommodated sixty-two thousand seven hundred twenty paying fans. Bock figured another thousand or so people selling snacks and

485

beverages. The game was not supposed to be an important one, but it was clear that Americans were as serious about their football as Europeans were. There was a surprising number of people with multi-colored paint on their faces – the local team colors, of course. Several were actually stripped to the waist and had their chests painted up like football sweaters, complete with the huge numbers the Americans used. Various exhortatory banners hung from the rails at the front of the upper decks. There were women on the playing field selected for their dancing ability and other physical attributes, leading the fans in cheers.

He also learned about the sovereignty of American television. This large raucous crowd meekly accepted stoppage of the game so that ABC could intersperse the play with commercials – that would have started a riot in the most civilized European soccer crowd. TV was even used to regulate play. The field was littered with referees in striped shirts, and even they were supervised by cameras and, Russell pointed out, another official whose job it was to look at videotape recordings of every play and rule on the rightness or wrongness of every official ruling on the field. And to supervise *that*, two enormous TV screens made the same replays visible to the crowd. If all that had been tried in Europe, there would have been dead officials and fans at every game. The combination of riotous enthusiasm and meek civilization here was remarkable to Bock. The game was less interesting, though he saw Russell genuinely enjoyed it. The ferocious violence of American football was broken by long periods of inactivity. The occasional flaring of tempers was muted by the fact that each player wore enough protective equipment as to require a pistol to inflict genuine harm. And they were so big. There could hardly be a man down there under a hundred kilos. It would have been easy to call them oafish and awkward, but the running backs and others demonstrated speed and agility that one might never have guessed. For all that, the rules of the game were incomprehensible. Bock had never been one to enjoy sporting contests anyway.

He'd played soccer as a boy, but that was far in his past.

Günther returned his attention to the stadium. It was a massive and impressive structure with its arching steel roof. The seats had rudimentary cushions. There was an adequate number of toilets, and a massive collection of concession stands, most serving weak American beer. A total of sixty-five thousand people here, counting police, concessionaires, TV technicians. Nearby apartments . . . He realized that he'd have to educate himself on the effects of nuclear weapons to come up with a proper estimate of expected casualties. Certainly a hundred thousand. Probably more. Enough. He wondered how many of these people would be here. Most, perhaps. Sitting in their comfortable chairs, drinking their cold, weak beer, devouring their hot dogs and peanuts. Bock had been involved in two aircraft incidents. One airliner blown out of the sky, another attempted hijacking that had not gone well at all. He'd fantasized at the time about the victims, sitting in comfortable chairs, eating their mediocre meals, watching their in-flight movie, not knowing that their lives were completely in the control of others whom they did not know. Not knowing. That was the beauty of it, how he could know and they could not. To have such control over human life. It was like being God, Bock thought, his eyes surveying the crowd. A particularly cruel and unfeeling God, to be sure, but history was cruel and unfeeling, wasn't it?

Yes, this was the place.

CHAPTER 19

Development

'Commodore, I have real trouble believing that,' Ricks said as evenly as he could manage. He was tanned and refreshed from his trip to Hawaii. He'd stopped in at Pearl Harbor while there, of course, to look over the sub base and dream about having command of Submarine Squadron One. That was a fast-attack squadron, but if a fast-attack guy like Mancuso could take over a boomer squadron, then surely turn-about was fair play.

'Dr Jones is a really good man,' Bart Mancuso replied.

'I don't doubt it, but our own people have been over the tapes.' It was normal operating procedure and had been so for more than thirty years. Tapes from missile-sub patrols were always examined by a team of experts on shore as a back-check to the sub's crew. They wanted to make sure that no one might have been trailing a missile boat. 'This Jones guy was one hell of a sonar operator, but now he's a contractor, and he has to justify his fees somehow, doesn't he? I'm not saying he's dishonest. It's his job to look for anomalies, and in this case what he did was to string a bunch of coincidences into a hypothesis. That's all there is here. The data is equivocal – hell, the data is almost entirely speculative – but the bottom line is that for this to be true, you have to assume that the same crewmen who tracked a 688 were unable to detect a Russian boat at all. Is that plausible?'

'That's a good point, Harry. Jones doesn't say that it's certain. He gives it a one-in-three chance.'

Ricks shook his head. 'I'd say one in a thousand, and that's being generous.'

'For what it's worth, Group agrees with you, and I had

some people from OP-02 here three days ago who said the same thing.'

So, why are we having this conversation? Ricks wanted to ask, but couldn't. 'The boat was checked for noise on the way out, right?'

Mancuso nodded. 'Yep, by a 688 right out of overhaul, all the bells and whistles.'

'And?'

'And she's still a black hole. The attack boat lost her at a range of three thousand yards at five knots.'

'So how are we writing it up?' Ricks asked, as casually as he could manage. This was going into his record, and that made it important.

It was Mancuso's turn to squirm. He hadn't decided. The bureaucrat part of him said that he'd done everything right. He'd listened to the contractor, booted the data up the chain of command to Group, to Force, and to the Pentagon experts. Their analysis had all been negative: Dr Jones was being overly paranoid. The problem was that Mancuso had sailed with Jones for three very good years in USS *Dallas*, and had never known him to make a bad call. Never. Not once. That Akula *had* been somewhere out there in the Gulf of Alaska. From the time the P-3 patrol aircraft had lost her to the moment she'd appeared outside her base, the *Admiral Lunin* had just fallen off the planet. Where had she been? Well, if you drew speed/time circles, it was possible that she'd been in *Maine*'s patrol area, possible that she'd left *Maine* at the proper time and made homeport at the proper time. But it was also possible – and very damned likely – that she'd never been in the same area as the American missile sub. *Maine* hadn't detected her, and neither had *Omaha*. How likely was it that a Russian sub could have evaded detection by both top-of-the-line warships?

Not very.

'You know what worries me?' Mancuso asked.

'What's that?'

'We've been in the missile-sub business for over thirty years. We've never been tracked in deep water. When I was XO on *Hammerhead*, we ran exercises against *Georgia* and had our heads handed to us. I never tried tracking an Ohio when I had *Dallas*, and the one exercise I ran against *Pulaski* was the toughest thing I ever did. But I've tracked Deltas, Typhoons, everything the Russians put in the water. I've taken hull shots of Victors. We're so good at this business . . .' The squadron commander frowned. 'Harry, we're used to being the best.'

Ricks continued to speak reasonably. 'Bart, we *are* the best. The only people close to us are the Brits, and I think we have them faded. Nobody else is in the same ballpark. I got an idea.'

'What's that?'

'You're worried about Mr Akula. Okay, I can understand that. It's a good boat, like a late 637-class even, for damned sure the best thing they've ever put in the water. Okay, we have standing orders to evade everything that comes our way – but you gave Rosselli a nice write-up for tracking this same Akula. You probably got a little heat from Group for that.'

'Good guess, Harry. A couple of noses went decidedly out of joint, but if they don't like the way I run my squadron, they can always pick a new squadron boss.'

'What do we know about *Admiral Lunin*?'

'She's in the yard for overhaul now, due out late January.'

'Going by past performance, it'll come out a little quieter.'

'Probably. Word is that she'll have a new sonar suite, say about ten years behind us,' Mancuso added.

'And that doesn't allow for the operators. It's still not a match for us, not even close to one. We can prove that.'

'How?'

'Why not recommend to Group that any boat that comes across an Akula is supposed to track him aggressively. Let the fast-attack guys really try to get in close. *But* if a boomer gets close enough to track without risk of counter-detection, let's go for that, too. I think we need better data on this bird. If he's a threat, let's upgrade what information we have on him.'

'Harry, that will really put Group into the overhead. They're not going to like this idea at all.' But Mancuso already did, and Harry could see it.

Ricks snorted. 'So? We're the best, Bart. You know it. I know it. They know it. We set some reasonable guidelines.'

'Like what?'

'The farthest anyone has ever tracked an Ohio is – what?'

'Four thousand yards, Mike Heimbach on *Scranton* against Frank Kemeny on *Tennessee*. Kemeny detected Heimbach first – difference was about one minute on detection. Everything closer than that was a pre-arranged test.'

'Okay, we multiply that by a factor of . . . five, say. That's more than safe, Bart. Mike Heimbach had a brand-new boat, the first rendition of the new sonar integration system, and three extra sonarmen out of Group Six, as I recall.'

Mancuso nodded. 'Right, it was a deliberate test, and they worst-cased everything to see if anyone could detect an Ohio. Isothermal water, below the layer, everything.'

And still *Tennessee* won,' Ricks pointed out. 'Frank was under orders to make it easy, and he still detected first, and as I recall he had a solution three minutes before Mike did.'

'True.' Mancuso thought for a moment. 'Make it twenty-five thousand yards separation. No closer than that.'

'Fine. I know I can track an Akula at that range. I have a very good sonar department – hell, we all do. If I stumble across this guy, I hover out there and gather all the signature data I can. I draw a twenty-five-thousand-yard circle around him and keep outside of it. There is no chance in *hell* that I'll get counter-detected.'

'Five years ago, Group would have shot both of us even for talking like this,' Mancuso observed.

'The world's changed. Look, Bart, you can run a 688

in close, but what does it prove? If we're really worried about boomer vulnerability, why dick around?'

'You're sure you can handle this?'

'Hell, yes! I'll write up the proposal for your operations staff, and you can send it up the flagpole to Group.'

'This'll end up in Washington, you know that.'

'Yeah, no more "We hide with pride," eh? What are we, a bunch of little old ladies? Damn it, Bart, I'm the commanding officer of a *war*ship. Somebody wants to tell me I'm vulnerable, well, I'm going to prove that's a load of horseshit. Nobody has ever tracked me. Nobody ever will, and I'm prepared to prove that.'

This interview had not gone the way Mancuso had expected at all. Ricks was talking like a real submarine-driver. It was the kind of talk Mancuso liked to hear.

'You're sure you're comfortable with this? It's really going to light a fire up the line. You're going to take some heat.'

'So are you.'

'I'm the squadron commander. I'm supposed to take heat.'

'I'll take my chances, Bart. Okay, I'm going to have to drill the hell out of my people, especially the sonar troops, tracking party, like that. I have the time, and I have a pretty good crew.'

'Okay. You write up the proposal. I'll give it a favorable endorsement and send it up.'

'See how easy it is?' Ricks grinned. If you want to be number one in a squadron of good skippers, he thought, you have to stand out from the crowd. OP-02 in the Pentagon would get excited about this, but they'd see that it was Harry Ricks who'd made the suggestion, and they knew his reputation as a smart, careful operator. On that basis, plus Mancuso's endorsement, it would be approved after some hemming and hawing. Harry Ricks: the best submarine engineer in the Navy, and a man willing to back up his expertise with deeds. Not a bad image. Certainly an image that would be noted and remembered.

'So, how was Hawaii?' Mancuso asked, surprised and

very pleased with the Commanding Officer (Gold) of USS *Maine*.

'This is very interesting. The Karl Marx Astrophysical Institute.' The KGB colonel handed the black-and-whites over to Golovko.

The First Deputy Chairman looked over the photos and set them down. 'Empty building?'

'Nearly so. Inside, we found this. It's a delivery manifest for five American machine tools. Very good ones, extremely expensive.'

'Used for?'

'Used for many things, like the fabrication of telescope mirrors, which fits very nicely with the institute's cover. The same instruments, our friends at Sarova tell us, are used to shape components for nuclear weapons.'

'Tell me about the institute.'

'Much of it appears to be entirely legitimate. Its head was to have been the DDR's leading cosmologist. It's been absorbed by the Max Planck Institute in Berlin. They're planning to build a large telescope complex in Chile, and are designing an X-ray observation satellite with the European Space Agency. It is noteworthy that X-ray telescopes have a rather close relationship with nuclear-weapons research.'

'How does one tell the difference between scientific research and –'

'You can't,' the colonel admitted. 'I've done some checking. We have leaked information on this ourselves.'

'What? How?'

'There have been a number of articles published in various professional journals about stellar physics. One begins, "Imagine the center of a star with an X-ray flux of such and such," except for one small thing: the star the author described has a flux much higher than the center of any star – by fourteen orders of magnitude.'

'I don't understand.' Golovko was having trouble with all this scientific gibberish.

'He described a physical environment in which the activity was one hundred thousand *billion* times the intensity inside *any* star. He was, in fact, describing the interior of a thermonuclear bomb at the moment of detonation.'

'And how the hell did that get past censors!' Golovko demanded in amazement.

'General, how scientifically literate do you think our censors are? As soon as that one saw "imagine the center of a star," he decided that it was not a matter of state security at all. That article was published fifteen years ago. There are others. In the past week I've discovered just how useless our secrecy measures are. You can imagine what it's like from the Americans. Fortunately, it requires a very clever chap to assimilate all the data. But it is by no means impossible. I've talked to a team of young engineers at Kyshtym. With a little push from here, we can initiate an in-depth study of how extensive the open scientific literature is. That will take five to six months. It does not directly affect this particular project, but I think it would be a most useful study to undertake. I think it likely that we have systematically underestimated the danger of third-world nuclear weapons.'

'But that's not true,' Golovko objected. 'We know that –'

'General, I helped write that study three years ago. I am telling you that I was grossly optimistic in my assessments.'

The First Deputy Chairman thought about that for a few seconds. 'Poor Ivan'ch, you are an honest man.'

'I am a frightened man,' the colonel replied.

'Back to Germany.'

'Yes. Of the people we suspect were part of the DDR bomb project, three are unaccounted for. All three men and their families are gone. The rest have found other work. Two could possibly be involved in nuclear research with weapons applications, but again, how does one tell? Where is the dividing line between peaceful physics and weapons-related activity? I do not know.'

'The three missing ones?'

'One is definitely in South America. The other two are merely missing. I am recommending that we launch a major operation to examine what's happening in Argentina.'

'What about the Americans . . .' Golovko mused.

'Nothing definite. I expect they're as much in the dark as we are.' The colonel paused. 'It is difficult to see how they would have an interest in wider proliferation of nuclear weapons. It's contrary to their government policy.'

'Explain Israel, then.'

'The Israelis obtained nuclear material from the Americans over twenty years ago, plutonium from their Savannah River plant, and enriched uranium from a depot in Pennsylvania. In both cases the transfers were apparently illegal. The Americans themselves launched an investigation. They believe that the Israeli Mossad pulled off one of the greatest operations in history, aided by Jewish American citizens in sensitive positions. There was no prosecution. What evidence they had came from sources that could not be revealed in court, and it was deemed politically inadvisable to reveal security leaks in so sensitive a government activity. Everything was handled quietly. The Americans and Europeans have been lax in selling nuclear technology to various countries – capitalism at work, there is a huge amount of money involved – but we made the same mistake with China and Germany, did we not? No,' the colonel concluded. 'I do not believe the Americans have any more interest in seeing German-made nuclear weapons than we do.'

'Next step?'

'I don't know, General. We've run all our leads down as well as we can without risk of detection. I think we need to look at activity in South America. Next, some careful inquiries within the German military establishment to see if there is any indication of a nuclear program there.'

'If there were, we'd have known by now.' Golovko

frowned. 'Good Lord, did I really say that? What delivery systems are likely?'

'Aircraft. There is no need for ballistic launchers. From Eastern Germany to Moscow is not all that far. They know our air-defense capabilities, don't they? We left enough of our equipment behind.'

'Pyotr, just how much more good news will you leave me this afternoon?'

The colonel smiled very grimly indeed. '*Nu*, and all those Western fools are rhapsodizing about how safe the world has become.'

The sintering process for the tungsten-rhenium was simplicity itself. They used a radio-frequency furnace much like a microwave oven. The metallic powder was poured into a mold and slid into the furnace for heating. After it became dazzlingly white hot – unfortunately not hot enough actually to melt the tungsten, which had a very high thermal tolerance – pressure was applied, and the combination of heat and pressure formed it into a mass that while not quite metallically solid was firm enough to treat as such. A total of twelve curved sections were made one after the other. They required machining to modest tolerances of shape and smoothness, and were set aside on their own section of shelving installed in the fabrication plant.

The big milling machine was working on the final large beryllium component, a large metallic hyperboloid about fifty centimeters in length, with a maximum width of twenty. The eccentric shape made for difficult machining, even with computer-assisted tools, but that could not be helped.

'As you see, the initial neutron flux will be a simple spherical expansion from the Primary, but it will be trapped by the beryllium,' Fromm explained to Qati. 'These metallic elements actually reflect neutrons. They are gyrating about at approximately twenty percent of the speed of light, and we will leave them with only this exit into the core. Inside the hyperboloid will be this cylinder of tritium-enriched lithium deuteride.'

'It happens so fast?' the Commander asked. 'The explosives will be destroying everything.'

'It requires a new way of thinking. As fast as the actions of the explosives are, you must remember that we require only three shakes for the bomb to complete the detonation process.'

'Three what?'

'Shakes.' Fromm allowed himself another of his rare smiles. 'You know what a nanosecond is – that is one billionth of a second, *ja*? In that span of time, a beam of light goes only thirty centimeters. The time it takes a beam of light to go from here to here.' He held his hands out about a foot apart.

Qati nodded. Surely that was a very brief time indeed.

'Good. A "shake" is ten nanoseconds. The time for light to go three meters. The term was invented by the Americans in the 1940s. They mean the time for a shake of a lamb's tail – a technical joke, you see. In other words, three shakes, the time needed for a beam of light to go approximately nine meters, the bomb has begun and ended the detonation process. That is many thousands of times the time required for chemical explosives to do anything.'

'I see,' Qati said, speaking both the truth and a lie. He left the room, allowing Fromm to return to his ghastly reveries. Günther was waiting out in the open air.

'Well?'

'I have the American side of the plan,' Bock announced. He opened up a map and set it on the ground. 'We will place the bomb here.'

'What is this place?' Bock answered the question. 'How many?' the Commander asked next.

'Over sixty thousand here. If the bomb's yield is as promised, the lethal radius will encompass all of this. Total dead will number between one and two hundred thousand.'

'That is all? For a nuclear bomb, that is all?'

'Ismael, this is merely a large explosive device.'

Qati closed his eyes and swore under his breath. Having only a minute before been told that it was something completely out of his experience, now he was being told the reverse. The Commander was bright enough to understand that both experts were correct.

'Why this place?' Bock explained that, too.

'It would be very gratifying indeed to kill their President.'

'Gratifying, but not necessarily beneficial. We could take the bomb into Washington, but I evaluate the risks of detection as serious, far too serious. Commander, my plan must take into consideration the fact that we have only one device and only one chance. We must therefore minimize the risk of detonation and base our target-selection on convenience more than any other factor.'

'And the German end of the operation?'

'That is more easily accomplished.'

'Will it work?' Qati asked, staring off at the dusty hills of Lebanon.

'It should. I give it a sixty percent chance.'

At the very least, we will punish the Americans and the Russians, the Commander told himself. The question came next: *Is that enough?* Qati's face became hard as he considered the answer to that.

But there was more than one question. Qati thought himself a dying man. The disease process had its ebbs and flows, like an inexorable tide, but a tide that never quite restored itself to where it had been a year or a month before. Though today he felt well, he knew that this was a relative thing. There was as much chance that his life would end in the next year as there was that Bock's plan would succeed. Could he allow himself to die and *not* do everything he could to see his mission accomplished?

No, and if his own death was likely, what importance should he give to the lives of others? Were they not all unbelievers?

Günther is an unbeliever, a true infidel. Marvin Russell is another, a pagan. The people you propose to kill ... they are not unbelievers. They are People of the Book, misguided followers of Jesus the Prophet, but also people who believe in the one God.

Yet Jews were also people of the Book. The Koran proclaimed it. They were the spiritual ancestors of Islam, as much the children of Abraham as the Arabs. So much in their religion was the same as his. His war against Israel was not about religion. It was about his people, cast out of their own land, displaced by another people who also claimed to be motivated by a religious imperative when it was really something else.

Qati faced his own beliefs in all their contradictions. Israel was his enemy. The Americans were his enemy. The Russians were his enemy. That was his personal theology, and though he might claim to be a Muslim, what ruled his life had precious little to do with God, however much he might proclaim the opposite to his followers.

'Proceed with your planning, Günther.'

CHAPTER 20

Competition

At the halfway point of the NFL season, the Vikings and Chargers were still the class of the league. Shrugging off their overtime loss to Minnesota, San Diego took their revenge the next week at home against doormat Indianapolis, whom they buried 45–3, while the Vikings had to struggle against the Giants in a Monday Night game, emerging on the sweet side of a 21–17 score. Tony Wills passed a thousand rushing yards in the third quarter of the season's eighth game, and was already consensus rookie of the year, plus becoming the official NFL spokesman for the President's Campaign Against Substance Abuse (CASA). The Vikings stumbled against the Forty-Niners, losing 24–16, which evened their record with San Diego's 7–1, but their nearest competition in the NFL Central – 'Black and Blue' – division was the Bears at 4–3. Parity in the National Football League had come and gone. The only serious challenge in the American Conference came, as always, from the Dolphins and Raiders, both of which were on the Chargers' dance card for the tail end of the season.

None of this was the least comfort to Ryan. Sleep came hard, despite the enveloping fatigue that seemed to define what his life had become. Before when thoughts had plagued his night, he'd come to the windows facing the Chesapeake Bay and stood, watching the ships and boats pass a few miles away. Now he sat and stared. His legs were weary and weak, always tired, until standing took a conscious effort. His stomach rebelled at the acid produced by stress and augmented by caffeine and alcohol. He needed sleep, slumber to relax his muscles, dreamless oblivion to loosen his mind from the day-to-day decisions. He needed exercise. He needed many things. He needed to be a man again. Instead he got wakefulness, a mind that would not stop turning over the thoughts of the day and the failures of the night.

Jack knew that Liz Elliot hated him. He even thought he knew why, that first meeting a few years before in Chicago where she'd been in a bad mood and he'd been in one also, and their introduction had been one of harsh words. The difference was that he tended to forget slights – most of them, anyway – and she did not; and she had the ear of the President. Because of her, his role in the Vatican Treaty would never be known. The one thing he had done that was untainted by his work at the Agency – Ryan was proud of what he'd done in CIA, but knew that it was narrowly political or strategic, aimed at the betterment of his own country, while the Vatican Treaty had been for the betterment of the whole world. That one proud insight. Gone, credited to others. Jack didn't want sole credit. It had not been exclusively his work, but he did want fair mention as one of the players. Was that asking too much? Fourteen-hour days, much of them spent in cars, the three times he'd risked his life for his country – for what? So that some political bitch from Bennington could tear up his evaluations.

Liz, you wouldn't even be *there except for me and what I did, and neither would your boss, the Iceman, Jonathan Robert Fowler of Ohio!*

But they could not know that. Jack had given his word. Given his word to what? For what?

The worst part of all, it was now affecting him in a way that was both new and totally unexpected. He'd disappointed his wife again this night. It was incomprehensible to him. Like throwing a light switch and getting no light, like turning the key to start the car and –

Like not being a man. That was the simple description.

I am a man. I've done all the things a man can do.

Try explaining that to your wife, chump!

I've fought for my family, for my country, killed for my family and my country. I've won respect among the

*best of men. I've done things that can never be known
and kept the secrets that had to be kept. I've served as
well as any man can.*

*So why are you looking out at the water at two in the
morning, ace?*

I've made a difference! Jack's mind raged.

Who knows? Who cares?

But what of my friends?

*A whole lot of good they do you — besides, what
friends? When's the last time you saw Skip Tyler or
Robby Jackson? Your friends at Langley — why not confide your problems to them?*

Dawn came as a surprise, but not so much a surprise
as that he'd actually slept, sitting alone in the living
room. Jack rose, feeling the aches in his muscles
unhelped by whatever number of hours he'd not been
awake. It hadn't been sleep, he told himself on the way
to the bathroom. It was just that he hadn't been awake.
Sleep was rest, and he felt singularly unrested, with a
pounding headache from the cheap wine of the previous
night. The only good news — if that's what it was — was
that Cathy didn't get up. Jack fixed his own coffee and
was waiting at the door when Clark drove up.

'Another great weekend, I see,' the man said, as Ryan
got into the car.

'*Et tu*, John?'

'Look, Deputy Director, you want to take a swing at
me, go right ahead. You looked like shit a couple of
months back and you're getting worse instead of better.
When's the last time you took a vacation, got away for
more than a day or two, you know, maybe pretended you
were a real person instead of some fuckin' government
ticket-puncher who's afraid that if he leaves nobody'll
notice?'

'Clark, you do have a way of brightening my
mornings.'

'Hey, man, I'm just a SPO, but don't bitch if I take the
"protective" part seriously, 'kay?' John pulled the car
over and parked it. 'Doc, I've seen this before. People
burn out. You're burning out. You're burning the candle

both ends and the middle. That's hard to do when you're in your twenties, and you ain't in your twenties anymore, in case nobody bothered telling you.'

'I'm quite aware of the infirmities that come with age.' Ryan tried a wry smile to show that it wasn't that big a deal, that Clark was overdoing it.

It didn't work. Suddenly it occurred to John that his wife hadn't been at the door. Trouble at home? Well, he couldn't ask about that, could he? What he saw in Ryan's face was bad enough. It wasn't just fatigue. He was tiring from within, all the shit he was taking from up the chain of command, the strain of backstopping Director Cabot on damned near everything that went out the front door. Cabot – not a bad guy, he meant well, but the truth of the matter was that he just didn't know what the hell he was doing. So Congress depended on Ryan, and the Operations and Intelligence Directorates depended on Ryan for leadership and coordination. He couldn't escape his responsibilities, and didn't have the good sense to realize that some were really things he could leave to others. The directorate chiefs could have taken up more of the slack, but they were letting Ryan do it all. A strong bark from the Deputy Director's office could have set that right, but would Cabot back him up – or would those White House pukes take it as a sign that Jack was trying a takeover?

Fuckin' politics! Clark thought as he pulled back onto the road. Office politics. Political politics. And something was wrong at home, too. Clark didn't know what, but he knew it was something.

Doc, you're too damned good a man for this!

'Can I lay a piece of advice on you?'

'Go ahead,' Jack replied, looking through dispatches.

'Take two weeks, go to Disney World, Club Med, find a beach and walk it. Get the hell out of town for a while.'

'The kids are in school.'

'So take them out of school, for Christ's sake! Better yet, maybe, leave them and get away, you and your wife. No, you're not that kind. Take them to see Mickey.'

'I can't. They're in school –'

'They're in *grammar* school not graduate school, Doc. Missing two weeks of long-division and learning to spell "squirrel" won't stunt their intellectual growth. You need to get away, recharge the batteries, smell the fucking roses!'

'Too much work, John.'

'You listen to me! You know how many friends I've buried? You know how many people I went out with who never got the chance to have a wife and kids and a nice house on the water? A lot, pal, a whole lot, never came close to having what you have. You got all that, and you're trying very damned hard to end up dead – and that's what's gonna happen, Doc. One way or another, give it maybe ten years.'

'I have a job to do!'

'It ain't important enough to wreck your fucking life for, you dumb ass! Can't you see that?'

'And then who runs the shop?'

'Sir, you might be hard to replace when you're at your best, but the shape you're in now, that Goodley kid can do your job at least as well as you can.' And that, Clark saw, scored for points. 'Just how effective do you think you are right now?'

'Will you do me a favor and just drive the car.' There was another SPINNAKER report waiting for him, according to coded phrases in the morning's dispatches, along with one from NIITAKA. This would be a busy day.

Just what he needed, Jack thought to himself, closing his eyes for a moment's rest.

It got worse. Ryan was surprised to find himself at work, more surprised that fatigue had defeated morning coffee and allowed him to sleep for forty minutes or so on the way in. He accepted Clark's told-you-so look and made his way up to the 7th floor. A messenger brought in the two important files, along with a note that Director Cabot was going to be late. The guy was keeping banker's hours. Spies were supposed to work harder, Jack thought. *I sure as hell do.*

NIITAKA came first. The Japanese, the report said, were planning to renege on a rare trade concession made only six months earlier. It would be explained away as 'unfortunate and unforeseen' circumstances, part of which might be true, Ryan thought as he read down the page – the Japanese had as many domestic political problems as everyone else – but there was something else: they were going to coordinate something in Mexico . . . something to do with the state visit of their Prime Minister to Washington the coming February. Instead of buying American farm goods, they were opting to buy them cheaper from Mexico, playing that off against reduced tariff barriers into that country. That was the plan, in any case. They weren't sure they could get the concession from Mexico, and they were planning . . .

. . . a bribe?

'Jesus,' Ryan breathed. The Mexican Institutional Revolutional Party – PRI – didn't exactly have an exemplary record for integrity, but this . . . ? It would be handled in face-to-face talks in Mexico City. If they got the concession, trading access to Mexican markets for opening Japan to Mexican foodstuffs, then the amount of American foodstuffs they had committed to buy the previous February would be reduced. It made good business sense. Japan would get food a little cheaper than they could in America while at the same time opening up a new market. Their excuse to American farmers would have to do with agricultural chemicals that their food-and-drug agency would decide, much to everyone's surprise, not to like for reasons of public health.

The bribe was fully in proportion to the magnitude of the target. Twenty-five million dollars, to be paid in a roundabout, quasi-legal fashion. When the Mexican president left office the following year, he would head a new corporation that . . . no, they would buy out a corporation he already owned for fair market value, and the new ownership would keep him on, while inflating the value of the business and paying his impressive salary in return for his obvious expertise at public relations.

'Nice separation,' Ryan said aloud. It was almost comical, and the funny part was that it might even be legal in America, if someone hired a sharp enough lawyer. Maybe not even that much. Plenty of people from State and Commerce had hired themselves out to Japanese interests immediately after leaving government service.

Except for one little thing: what Ryan held in his hand was evidence of conspiracy. In one way they were foolish: the Japanese thought that some counsels were sacrosanct, that some words spoken aloud would never be heard outside the four enclosing walls that heard them. They didn't know that a certain cabinet member had a certain mistress who in turn had a personal beef that matched her ability to loosen a man's tongue; and that America now had access to all that information, courtesy of a KGB officer . . .

'Think, boy.'

If they could get harder evidence, and give that over to Fowler . . . But how? You couldn't exactly cite the report of a spy in court . . . a Russian national, a KGB officer working in a third country.

But they weren't talking about an open court with rules of evidence, were they? Fowler could discuss this in his own face-to-face meet with their PM.

Ryan's phone rang. 'Yes, Nancy?'

'The Director just called in. He's got the flu.'

'Lucky him. Thanks. Flu, my ass,' Ryan said, after hanging up. The man was lazy.

. . . Fowler could play it one of two ways: 1, face-to-face, tell him that we know what he's up to and we won't stand for it, that we will inform the proper congressional people and . . . or, 2, just leak it to the press.

Option 2 would have all sorts of evil consequences, not the least of which would be in Mexico. Fowler didn't like the Mexican president, and liked the PRI even less. Whatever you said about Fowler, he was an honest man who loathed corruption in all its forms.

Option 1 . . . Ryan had to report this to Al Trent, didn't he? He had to let Trent know about the new operation, but Trent had his personal axe to grind on trade issues, and Fowler would worry that he might be leaky on this

issue. On the other hand, could he legally *not* tell Trent?
Ryan lifted his phone again.

'Nancy, could you tell the general counsel that I need
to see him? Thanks.'

Next came SPINNAKER. What, Ryan thought, does Mr
Kadishev have to say today . . . ?

'Dear God in heaven.' Ryan forced himself to relax.
He read through the complete report, then stopped and
read through it again. He picked up his phone and
punched the button to speed-dial Mary Pat Foley.

But the phone just rang for thirty seconds until someone picked it up.

'Yes?'

'Who is this?'

'Who is this?'

'This is Deputy Director Ryan. Where's Mary Pat?'

'In labor, sir. Sorry, I didn't know who you were,' the
man's voice went on. 'Ed's with her, of course.'

'Okay, thanks.' Ryan hung up. 'Shit!' On the other
hand, he couldn't be angry about that, could he? He got
up and walked out to his secretary's office.

'Nancy, Mary Pat's in labor,' Jack told Mrs Cummings.

'Oh, wonderful – well, not wonderful, it's not all that
much fun,' Nancy observed. 'Flowers?'

'Yeah, something nice – you know that stuff better
than I do. Put it on my American Express.'

'Wait until we're sure everything's okay?'

'Yeah, right.' Ryan returned to his office. 'Now what?'
he asked himself.

*You know what you have to do. The only question is
whether or not you really want to do it.*

Jack lifted his phone again and punched yet another
speed-dial button.

'Elizabeth Elliot,' she said, picking up her direct line,
the one known only to a handful of government insiders.

'Jack Ryan.'

The cold voice grew yet colder. 'What is it?'

'I need to see the President.'

'What about?' she asked.

'Not over the phone.'

'It's a secure phone, Ryan!'

'Not secure enough. When can I come over? It's important.'

'How important?'

'Important enough to bump his appointment schedule, Liz!' Ryan snapped back. 'You think I'm playing games here?'

'Calm down and wait.' Ryan heard pages turning. 'Be here in forty minutes. You can have fifteen minutes. I'll fix the schedule.'

'Thank you, Dr Elliot.' Ryan managed not to slam the phone down. *God damn that woman!* Ryan got up again. Clark was back in Nancy's office. 'Warm the car up.'

'Where to?' Clark asked, rising.

'Downtown.' Jack turned. 'Nancy, call the Director. Tell him I have to get something to the Boss, and, with all due respect, he should get his tail in here.' That would be inconvenient. Cabot's place was an hour away, in fox country.

'Yes, sir.' One of the few things he could depend on was Nancy Cummings' professionalism.

'I need three copies of this. Make one more for the Director, and return the original to secure storage.'

'Take two minutes,' Nancy said.

'Fine.' Jack walked off to the washroom. Looking in the mirror, he saw that Clark was as right as ever. He really did look like hell. But that couldn't be helped. 'Ready?'

'If you are, Doc.' Clark was already holding the documents in a zipped leather case.

The perversity of life did not abate this Monday morning. Somewhere around the I-66 cutoff, some fool had managed to cause an accident, and that backed traffic up. What should have been a ten or fifteen minute drive took thirty-five. Even senior government officials have to deal with D.C. traffic. The Agency car pulled into West Executive Drive barely on time. Jack managed not to run into the west entrance to the White House only because someone might notice. Reporters used this entrance, too. A minute later, he was in Liz Elliot's corner office.

'What gives?' the National Security Advisor asked.

'I'd prefer to go over this just once. We have a report from a penetration agent that you're not going to like very much.'

'You have to tell me something,' Elliot pointed out, reasonably for once.

'Narmonov, his military, and nukes.'

She nodded. 'Let's go.' It was a short walk down two corridors, past eight Secret Service agents who guarded the President's office like a pack of very respectful wolves.

'I hope this is good,' President Fowler said, without rising. 'I'm missing a budget brief for this.'

'Mr President, we have a very highly-placed penetration agent inside the Soviet government,' Ryan began.

'I know that. I have asked you not to reveal his name to me, as you recall.'

'Yes, sir,' Ryan said. 'I'm going to tell you his name now. Oleg Kirilovich Kadishev. We call him SPINNAKER. He was recruited some years ago by Mary Patricia Foley, when she and her husband were in Moscow.'

'Why did you give me that?' Fowler asked.

'So that you can evaluate what he says. You've seen his reports before under the codenames RESTORATIVE and PIVOT.'

'PIVOT . . . ? That's the one back in September that talked about problems with Narmonov's – I mean, that he was having trouble with his security apparatus.'

'Correct, Mr President.' *Good for you*, Ryan thought. *You remember what we send down.* It was not always so, Ryan knew.

'I gather his problems are worsening or you would not be here. Go on,' Fowler ordered, leaning back in his chair.

'Kadishev says he had a meeting with Narmonov last week – late last week –'

'Wait a minute. Kadishev – he's a member of their parliament, head of one of the opposition groups, right?'

'Also correct, sir. He has a lot of one-on-ones with Narmonov, and that's why he's so valuable to us.'

'Fine, I can see that.'

'In their most recent meeting, he says, Narmonov said that his problems are indeed getting worse. He's allowed his military and security forces to increase their internal clout, but it would seem that this is not enough. There may be opposition to the arms-reduction treaty implementation. According to this report, the Soviet military wants to hold onto all of its SS-18s instead of eliminating six regiments of them as agreed. Our man says that Narmonov may be ready to give in to them on that point. Sir, that would be treaty violation, and that's why I'm here.'

'How important is it?' Liz Elliot asked. 'The technical side, I mean.'

'Okay, we've never been able to make this very clear. Secretary Bunker understands, but Congress has never quite figured it out: since we're in the process of reducing nuclear arms by a little more than half, we've changed the nuclear equation. When both sides had ten thousand RVs it was pretty clear to everyone that nuclear war was a difficult – virtually impossible – thing to win. With so many warheads to hit, you'd never get them all, and there would always be enough left to launch a crippling counter-attack.

'But with the reductions, the calculus changes. Now, depending on the mix of forces, such an attack becomes theoretically possible, and that's why the mix of forces was so carefully spelled out in the treaty documents.'

'You're saying that the reduction makes things more dangerous rather than less?' Fowler asked.

'No, sir, not exactly. I've said all along – I consulted with the treaty team back some years ago, back when Ernie Allen was running it – that the net strategic improvement from a fifty percent reduction was illusory, mere symbolism.'

'Oh, come on,' Elliot observed scathingly. 'It's a reduction by half of –'

'Dr Elliot, if you ever bothered to sit in on the

CAMELOT games you'd understand this a little better.'
Ryan turned away before he noticed her reaction to this
rebuke. Fowler noticed her flush briefly and almost
smiled in amusement at her discomfort at being cut
down in front of her lover. The President returned his
attention to Ryan, sure that he and Elizabeth would
speak further on the matter.

'This issue gets very technical. If you don't believe me,
ask Secretary Bunker or General Fremont out at SAC
Headquarters. The deciding factor is the mix of forces,
not the number. If they hold onto those extra SS-18 regiments, the mix is changed to the point at which the
Soviets have a genuine advantage. The effect on the
treaty is substantive, not merely numerical. But there's
more.'

'Okay,' the President said.

'According to this report, there appears to be some
collusion between the military and the KGB. As you
know, while the Soviet military owns and maintains
the strategic launchers, the warheads have always been
under KGB control. Kadishev thinks that those two
agencies are getting a little too cozy, and further that
security on the warheads might be problematic.'

'Meaning what?'

'Meaning that an inventory of tactical warheads is
being withheld.'

'Missing nukes?'

'Small ones. It's possible, he says.'

'In other words,' Fowler said, 'their military may be
blackmailing Narmonov, and it's possible that they are
holding some small weapons as their trump cards?'

Not bad, Mr President. 'Correct, sir.'

Fowler was quiet for thirty seconds or so, turning that
over in his head as he stared into space. 'How reliable is
this Kadishev?'

'Mr President, he's been in our employ for five years.
His advice has been very valuable to us, and to the best
of our knowledge he's never misled us.'

'Possible that he's been turned?' Elliot asked.

'Possible but not likely. We have ways of dealing with

that. There are pre-arranged code-phrases which warn us of trouble. Good-news phrases accompany each report, and did in this case also.'

'What about confirming the report through other sources?'

'Sorry, Dr Elliot, but we have nothing to confirm this.'

'You came down here with an unconfirmed report?' Elliot asked.

'That is correct,' Ryan admitted, not knowing how tired he looked. 'There aren't too many agents who could make me do that, but this is one of them.'

'What can you do to confirm that?' Fowler asked.

'We can make discreet inquiries through our own networks, and with your permission we can have careful discussions with some foreign services. The Brits have someone in the Kremlin who's giving them some really good stuff. I know Sir Basil Charleston, and I can make approaches, but that means revealing something of what we know. You don't do something like this on the old-boy net. At this level you have to make a real *quid pro quo*. We never do that without getting executive approval.'

'I can understand that. Give me a day to think about it. Does Marcus know about this?'

'No, Mr President. He has the flu. Ordinarily, I would not have come here without consulting with the Director first, but I figured you would want to know about this quickly.'

'You've said previously that the Soviet military was more politically reliable than this,' Elliot observed.

'Also correct, Dr Elliot. Action such as Kadishev reports is completely unprecedented. Historically, our worries about political ambition within the Soviet military have been as groundless as they've been continuous. It would seem that this may have changed. The possibility of a *de facto* alliance between the military and the KGB is most disturbing.'

'So, you were wrong before?' Elliot pressed.

'That is a possibility,' Ryan admitted.

'And now?' Fowler asked.

'Mr President, what do you want me to say? Might I

be wrong on this also? Yes, I may. Am I sure this report is accurate? No, I am not, but the import of the information compels me to bring it to your attention.'

'I'm less concerned with the missile issue than with the missing warheads,' Elliot said. 'If Narmonov is facing real blackmail . . . wow.'

'Kadishev is a potential political rival to Narmonov,' Fowler noted speculatively. 'Why confide in him?'

'You meet regularly with the congressional leadership, sir. So does he. The political dynamic in the Congress of People's Deputies is more confused than on The Hill. Moreover, there's genuine respect between the two. Kadishev has supported Narmonov more often than he's opposed the man. They may be rivals, but there is also a commonality of views on many key issues.'

'Okay, I want this information confirmed any way you can, and as quickly as you can.'

'Yes, Mr President.'

'How's Goodley working out?' Elliot asked.

'He's a bright kid. He's got a good feel for the Eastern Bloc. I read over a paper he did up at the Kennedy School a while back, and it was better than our people did at the time.'

'Get him in on this. A fresh mind might be useful,' Liz opined.

Jack shook his head emphatically. 'This is too sensitive for him.'

'Goodley is that Presidential Fellow you told me about? Is he that good, Elizabeth?' Fowler wanted to know.

'I think so.'

'My authority, Ryan, let him in,' the President ordered.

'Yes, sir.'

'Anything else?'

'Sir, if you have a minute, we did have something else come in about Japan.' Jack explained further for a few minutes.

'Is that a fact . . . ?' Fowler smiled in his clever way. 'What do you think of them?'

'I think they like to play games,' Ryan answered. 'I do

not envy the folks who have to negotiate with them.'

'How can we find out if this is true?'

'It comes from a good source. It's another one we guard closely.'

'Wouldn't it be nice if . . . how would we find out if the deal is struck?'

'I don't know, Mr President.'

'I could ram something like that right down his throat. I'm getting tired of this trade impasse, and I'm tired of being lied to. Find a way to do it.'

'We'll try, Mr President.'

'Thanks for coming in.' The President didn't rise or extend his hand. Ryan stood and left.

'What do you think?' Fowler asked as he scanned over the report.

'It confirms what Talbot says about Narmonov's vulnerability . . . but worse.'

'I agree. Ryan looks harried.'

'He shouldn't be playing both sides of the street.'

'Hmph?' the President grunted without looking up.

'I have a preliminary report from the investigation Justice has been running. It looks as though he is playing around, as we suspected, and there is a kid involved. She's the widow of an Air Force guy who died in a training accident. Ryan has spent a lot of money to take care of the family, and his wife doesn't know.'

'I don't need that sort of scandal, not another womanizer on top of Charlie's affairs.' *Good thing they haven't found out about us*, he didn't have to say. That was, in any case, a different matter. Alden had been a married man. Ryan still was. Fowler was not. That made it different. 'How sure are you of this? You said a preliminary report?'

'That's right.'

'Firm it up and let me know what you find out.'

Liz nodded and went on. 'This thing with the Soviet military . . . scary.'

'Very scary,' Fowler agreed. 'We'll talk about it over lunch.'

'And that is the halfway point,' Fromm said. 'Might I ask a favor?'

'What favor is that?' Ghosn asked, hoping that it was not to go back to Germany for time with his wife. That might be sticky.

'I have not had a drink in two months.'

Ibrahim smiled. 'You understand that I am not permitted such things.'

'But do the same rules apply to me?' The German smiled. 'I am an infidel, after all.'

Ghosn laughed heartily. 'Quite true. I'll talk to Günther about it.'

'Thank you.'

'Tomorrow, we begin on the plutonium.'

'It will take so long?'

'Yes, that and the explosive blocks. We are precisely on schedule.'

'That is good to know.' *January 12 was the day.*

'Who do we have good in the KGB?' Ryan asked himself back in his office. The big problem with SPINNAKER's report was that much, maybe most, of the KGB was loyal to Narmonov. The part that might not be was the Second Chief Directorate, which concerned itself with the country's internal security. The First Chief – a/k/a Foreign – Directorate definitely was, especially with Golovko in his position as First Deputy Chairman to keep an eye on things. That man was a pro, and reasonably non-political. Ryan had a wild thought that a direct call might – no, he'd have to set up a meet . . . but where?

No, that was too dangerous.

'You want me?' It was Goodley, sticking his head through Jack's door. Ryan waved him in.

'Want a promotion?'

'What do you mean?'

'I mean that at the direction of the President of the United States you are in on something that I think you're not ready for.' Jack handed him the SPINNAKER report. 'Read.'

'Why me, and why did you say –'

'I also said you did a nice job predicting the breakup of the Pact. It was better than anything we did in-house, by the way.'

'You mind if I say that you're a strange guy to work with?'

'How do you mean that?' Jack asked.

'You don't like my attitude, but you commend my work.'

Ryan leaned back in his chair and closed his eyes. 'Ben, believe it or not, I am not always right. I make mistakes. I've made some whoppers even, but I am smart enough to know that, and because I'm that smart, I look for people with opposing views to backstop me. That's a good habit to get into. I learned it from Admiral Greer. If you learn anything from your time here, Dr Goodley, learn that. We can't afford fuckups here. They happen anyway, but we still can't afford them. That paper you did at Kennedy was better than what I did. It's theoretically possible that you might again one day be right when I am wrong. Fair enough?'

'Yes, sir,' Goodley replied quietly, surprised at the statement. Of course he'd be right when Ryan was wrong. That's why he was here.

'Read.'

'Mind if I smoke?'

Jack's eyes opened. 'You a smoker?'

'I quit a couple of years ago, but since I've been here . . .'

'Try to break that habit, but before you do, give me one.'

They both lit up and puffed away in silence, Goodley reading over the report, Ryan watching his eyes. The Presidential Fellow looked up.

'Damn.'

'Good first reaction. Now, what do you think?'

'It's plausible.'

Ryan shook his head. 'That's what I just told the President an hour ago. I'm not sure, but I had to take it to him.'

'What do you want me to do?'

'I want to play on this a little. The DI's Russian people will chew on it for a couple of days. I want you and me to do our own analysis, but I want a different spin on it.'

'Meaning what?'

'Meaning that you think it's plausible, and I have my doubts. Therefore, you will look for reasons it might not be true, and I'll look for reasons that it is.' Jack paused. 'The Intelligence Directorate will play this conventionally. They're too organized down there. I don't want that.'

'But you want me to —'

'I want you to exercise that brain. I think you're smart, Ben. I want you to prove it. That's an order, by the way.'

Goodley considered that. He wasn't accustomed to getting or taking orders. 'I don't know that I can do that.'

'Why not?'

'It's contrary to my views. It's not the way I see this, it's . . .'

'Your beef with me and a lot of people here is the corporate mind of CIA, right? Part of that is correct, we do have a corporate mind, and there are drawbacks to that. It's also true that your way of thinking has its own pitfalls. If you can prove to me that you are no more a prisoner of your views than I try to be of mine, then you have a future here. Objectivity isn't easy. You have to exercise it.'

It was a very clever challenge, Goodley thought. He wondered next if he'd perhaps misjudged the DDCI.

'Will Russell cooperate?'

'Yes, Ismael, he will,' Bock said, sipping at a beer. He'd gotten a case of a good German export brew for Fromm, and kept a few for himself. 'He thinks we'll be setting off a large conventional bomb to eliminate television coverage of the game.'

'Clever, but not actually intelligent,' Qati observed. He wanted a beer himself, but could not ask. Besides, he told himself, it would probably upset his stomach, and he'd actually enjoyed three consecutive days of relative health.

'His outlook is limited to tactical matters, yes. On tactical matters he is quite useful, however. His assistance will be crucial to that phase of the operation.'

'Fromm is working out well.'

'As I thought he would. It really is a pity that he will not see it to fruition. The same with the machinists?'

'Unfortunately, yes.' Qati frowned. Not a man who blanched at the sight of blood, neither was he one to kill unnecessarily. He'd had to kill people for reasons of security before, though never this many. It was almost becoming a habit. But, he asked himself, why worry about a few when you plan to kill so many more?

'Have you planned for the consequences of failure or discovery?' Bock asked.

'Yes, I have,' Qati replied with a sly smile, followed by an explanation.

'That is ingenious. Good to plan for every contingency.'

'I thought you'd like it.'

CHAPTER 21

Connectivity

It took two weeks, but something finally came back. A KGB officer in the employ of CIA nosed around and heard something: there might be an ongoing operation about nuclear weapons in Germany. Something being run out of Moscow Center. Golovko himself was overseeing things. People working in KGB Station Berlin were cut out of it. End of report.

'Well?' Ryan asked Goodley. 'What do you think?'

'It fits the SPINNAKER report. If the story about a flukey inventory of tactical nukes is correct, it certainly makes sense that it would have something to do with the pullbacks of their forward-deployed forces. Things get lost in transit all the time. I lost two boxes of books when I moved down here myself.'

'I'd like to think that people take closer care of nuclear weapons than that,' Ryan said dryly, noting that Goodley still had a hell of a lot to learn. 'What else?'

'I've been looking for data to counter the report. The Soviet reason for their inability to deactivate the SS-18s on schedule is that the factory they built for the purpose is inadequate. Our on-site inspectors can't decide if it's true or not – engineering question. I find it hard to believe that if the Russians actually built the thing – and, hell, they've been building SS-18s for quite a while, haven't they? – they should be able to design a place to dismantle them safely. They say the problem is in the fueling systems, and the wording of the treaty documents. The -18 uses storable liquids and has a pressurized body – that is, the missile structure depends on pressurization to remain rigid. They can de-fuel in the silos, but then they can't extract the birds without damaging them, and the treaty requires that they be taken intact to the disposal facility. But the disposal facility isn't designed right for de-fueling, they say. Something about a design flaw and possible environmental contamination. The storable liquids are nasty, they say, and you have to take all sorts of precautions to keep from poisoning people, and the facility is only three kilometers from a city, etc., etc.' Goodley paused. 'The explanation is plausible, but you have to wonder how people could have screwed up so badly.'

'Structural problem,' Jack said. 'They have trouble placing facilities out in the boonies for the simple reason that there few people have cars, and getting people from their homes to their place of work is more complicated there than here. It's subtle stuff like that that drives us crazy trying to figure the Russians out.'

'On the other hand, they can point to a basic mistake like that and try to explain all kinds of things away.'

'Very good, Ben,' Jack observed. 'Now you're thinking like a real spook.'

'This is a crazy place to work.'

'Storable liquids are nasty, by the way. Corrosive, reactive, toxic. Remember all the problems we had with the Titan-II missiles?'

'No,' Goodley admitted.

'Maintenance of the things is a bastard. You have to take all sorts of precautions, despite which you routinely get leaks. The leaks corrode things, injure the maintenance people . . .'

'Have we exchanged positions on this?' Ben asked lightly.

Ryan smiled, eyes closed. 'I'm not sure.'

'We're supposed to have better data than this. We're supposed to be able to find things out.'

'Yeah, I thought that way once myself. People expect us to know everything there is about every rock, puddle, and personality in the whole world.' His eyes opened. 'We don't. Never have. Never will. Disappointing, isn't it? The all-pervasive CIA. We have a fairly important question here, and all we have are probabilities, not certainties. How is the President supposed to make a decision if we can't give him facts instead of possibly learned opinions? I've said it before – in writing, even. What we provide people with, most of the time, is official guesses. You know, it's embarrassing to have to send something like this out.' Jack's eyes fell on the Directorate of Intelligence report. Their teams of Russian experts had chewed on SPINNAKER for a week and decided that it was probably true, but could represent a misunderstanding.

Jack's eyes closed again, and he wished his headache would go away. 'That's our structural problem. We look at various probabilities. If you give people a firm opinion, you run the risk of being wrong. Guess what? People remember when you're wrong a lot more often than when you're right. So the tendency is to include all the possibilities. It's intellectually honest, even. Hell of a good dodge. Problem is, it doesn't give people what they think they need. On the user end, people as often as not need probabilities rather than certainties, but they don't always know that. It can drive you crazy, Ben. The outside bureaucracies ask for things we often as not cannot deliver, and our inside bureaucracy doesn't like sticking its neck out on the line any more than anyone else. Welcome to the real world of intelligence.'

'I never figured you for a cynic.'

'I'm not a cynic. I'm a realist. Some things we know. Some things we don't. The people here are not robots. They're just people looking for answers and finding more questions instead. We have a lot of good people in this building, but bureaucracy mutes individual voices, and facts are discovered more often by individuals than committees.' There was a knock on the door. 'Come in.'

'Dr Ryan, your secretary isn't –'

'She's having a late lunch.'

'I have something for you, sir.' The man handed the envelope over. Ryan signed for it and dismissed the messenger.

'Good old All Nippon Airlines,' Ryan said after

opening the envelope. It was another NIITAKA report. He snapped upright in his chair. 'Holy shit!'

'Problem?' Goodley asked.

'You're not cleared for this.'

'What seems to be the problem?' Narmonov asked.

Golovko was in the uncomfortable position of having to announce a major success with unpleasant consequences. 'President, we have for some time been working on a project to penetrate American cipher systems. We've had some successes, particularly with their diplomatic systems. This is a message that was sent to several of their embassies. We've recovered all of it.'

'And?'

'Who sent this out?'

'Look, Jack,' Cabot said, 'Liz Elliot took the last SPINNAKER seriously, and she wants State's opinion.'

'Well, that's just great. What we've learned from it is that KGB has penetrated our diplomatic ciphers. NIITAKA read the same cable that our ambassador got. So now Narmonov knows what we're worried about.'

'The White House will say that it's not all that bad. Does it really hurt that he knows what our concerns are?' the Director asked.

'The short version is – yes, it does. Sir, you realize that I didn't know about this cable, and how do I read it? I get the text from a KGB officer in Tokyo. Jesus Christ, did we send this inquiry out to Upper Volta, too?'

'They got it all?'

Jack's voice turned to acid. 'Care to check the translation?'

'Go see Olson.'

'On the way.'

Forty minutes later, Ryan and Clark breezed into the outer office of Lieutenant General Ronald Olson, Director of the National Security Agency. Located at Fort Meade, Maryland, between Washington and Baltimore, it had the atmosphere of another Alcatraz, but without the pleasant view of San Francisco Bay. The main building was surrounded by a double fence patrolled by dogs at night – something even CIA didn't bother with, considering it overly theatrical – as physical evidence of their mania for security. NSA's job was to make and break ciphers, to record and interpret every bit of electronic noise on the planet. Jack left his driver reading a *Newsweek* as he strode into the top-floor office of the man who ran this particular outfit which was several times the size of CIA.

'Ron, you got one big problem.'

'What, exactly?'

Jack handed over the NIITAKA dispatch. 'I've warned you about this.'

'When did this go out?'

'Seventy-two hours ago.'

'Out of Foggy Bottom, right?'

'Correct. It was read in Moscow precisely eight hours later.'

'Meaning that someone in State might have leaked it, and their embassy could have sent it over by satellite,' Olson said. 'Or it could have leaked from a cipher clerk or any one of fifty foreign-service officers . . .'

'Or it could mean that they've broken the whole encoding system.'

'STRIPE is secure, Jack.'

'Ron, why haven't you just expanded TAPDANCE?'

'Get me the funding and I will.'

'This agent has warned us before that they've penetrated our cipher systems. They're reading our mail, Ron, and this is a pretty good piece of evidence.'

The General stood his ground. 'It's equivocal and you know it.'

'Well, our guy is saying that he wants personal assurance from the Director that we haven't, don't, and will never use comm links to transmit his material. As proof of that necessity, he sends us this, which he got at some significant hazard to his own ass.' Jack paused. 'How many people use this system?'

'STRIPE is exclusively for the State Department. Similar systems are used by the Defense Department. More or less the same machine, slightly different keying systems. The Navy especially likes it. It's very user-friendly,' Olson said.

'General, we've had the random-pad technology available for over three years. Your first version, TAPDANCE, used tape cassettes. We're moving over to CD-ROM. It works, it's easy to use. We'll have our systems up and running in another couple of weeks.'

'And you want us to copy it?'

'Looks sensible to me.'

'You know what my people will say if we copy a system from CIA?' Olson asked.

'God damn it! We stole the idea from you, remember?'

'Jack, we're working on something similar, easier to use, little bit more secure. There are problems, but my back-room boys are almost ready to try it out.'

Almost ready, Ryan thought. *That means anywhere from three months to three years.*

'General, I'm putting you on official notice. We have indications that your communications links are compromised.'

'And?'

'And I will make that report to Congress and the President as well.'

'It's much more likely that there's someone at State who leaked this. Further, it is possible that you're the victim of disinformation. What does this agent give us?' the NSA Director asked.

'Some very useful material – us and Japan.'

'But nothing on the Soviet Union?'

Jack hesitated before answering, but there was no question of Olson's loyalty. Or his intelligence. 'Correct.'

'And you're saying that you're certain this *isn't* a false-flag operation? I repeat – certain?'

'You know better than that, Ron. What's certain in this business?'

'Before I request a couple hundred million dollars' worth of funding, I need something better than this. It's happened before, and we've done it, too – if the other side has something you can't break, get them to change it. Make it appear that they're penetrated.'

'That might have been true fifty years ago, but not anymore.'

'Repeat, I need better evidence before I go to see Trent. We can't slap something together as quickly as you can with MERCURY. We have to make thousands of the god-damned things. Supporting that is complex and costly as hell. I need hard evidence before I stick my neck out that far.'

'Fair enough, General. I've had my say.'

'Jack, we'll look into it. I have a tiger team that does that, and I'll have them examining the problem tomorrow morning. I appreciate your concern. We're friends, remember?'

'Sorry, Ron. Long hours.'

'Maybe you need some time off. You look tired.'

'That's what everybody tells me.'

Ryan's next stop was at the FBI.

'I heard,' Dan Murray said. 'That bad?'

'I think so. Ron Olson isn't so sure.' Jack didn't have to explain. Of all the possible disasters for a government to face, short of war, none was worse than leaky communications links. Literally everything depended on secure methods of moving information from one place to another. Wars had been won and lost on the basis of a single message that had been leaked to the other side. One of America's most stunning foreign-policy coups, the Washington Naval Treaty, had been the direct result of the State Department's ability to read the cipher traffic between all of the participating diplomats and their governments. A government that had no secrets could not function.

'Well, there's the Walkers, Pelton, the others . . .' Murray observed. The KGB had been remarkably suc-cessful at recruiting people within the American com-munications agencies. Cipher clerks held the most sensitive jobs in the embassies, but were so poorly paid and regarded that they were still called 'clerks,' not even 'technicians.' Some resented that. Some resented it enough that they had decided that they could make money from what they knew. They all learned eventually that intelligence agencies pay poorly (except for CIA, which rewarded treason with real money), but by then it was always too late to turn back. From Walker the Russians had learned how American cipher machines were designed and how their keying systems worked. The basics of the cipher machines hadn't really changed all that much in the preceding ten years. Improved technology had made them more efficient and much more reliable than their stepping-switch and pin-disc ancestors, but they all worked on a mathematical area called Complexity Theory, which had been developed by telephone engineers sixty years earlier to predict the working of large switching systems. And the Russians had some of the best mathematical theorists in the world. It was believed by many that knowledge of the structure of cipher machines might enable a really clever mathematician to crack a whole system. Had some unknown Russian made a theoretical breakthrough? If so . . .

'We have to assume there are more we haven't caught. Add that to their technical expertise, and I'm really worried.'

'Doesn't affect the Bureau directly, thank God.' Most of the FBI encrypted communications were voice links, and though they could be broken, the data recovered was both too time-sensitive and further disguised by the use of code-names and slang that mostly concealed what agents were up to. Besides which, the opposition had real limits on how many things they could examine.

'Can you have your people do some scratching around?'

'Oh, yeah. You're going up the chain on this?'

'I think I have to, Dan.'

'You're bucking a couple of major bureaucracies.'

Ryan leaned against the doorframe. 'My cause is just, isn't it?'

'You never learn, do you?' Murray shook his head and laughed.

*

'Those bastard Americans!' Narmonov raged.

'What's the problem now, Andrey Il'ych?'

'Oleg Kirilovich, have you any idea what it is like dealing with a suspicious foreign country?'

'Not yet,' Kadishev answered. 'I only deal with suspicious domestic elements.' The effective abolition of the Politburo had perversely eliminated the apprenticeship period during which an up-and-coming Soviet political figure might learn the international version of statecraft. Now they were no better off than Americans were. And that, Kadishev reminded himself, was something to keep in mind. 'What seems to be the problem?'

'This must be kept absolutely secret, my young friend.'

'Understood.'

'The Americans have circulated a memorandum around their embassies to make discreet inquiries concerning my political vulnerability.'

'Indeed?' Kadishev did not allow himself to react beyond the single word. He was immediately struck by the dichotomy of the situation. His report had had the proper effect on the American government, but the fact that Narmonov knew of it made his discovery as an American agent possible. Wasn't that interesting? he asked himself in a moment of clear objectivity. His maneuvers were now a genuine gamble, with a downside as enormous as the upside. Such things were to be expected, weren't they? He was not gambling a month's wages. 'How do we know this?' he asked, after a moment's reflection.

'That I cannot reveal.'

'I understand.' *Damn! Well, he is confiding in me . . . though that might be a clever ploy on Andrey Il'ych's part, mightn't it!* 'But we are sure of it?'

'Quite sure.'

'How can I help?'

'I need your help, Oleg. Again, I ask for it.'

'This business with the Americans concerns you greatly, then?'

'Of course it does!'

'I can understand that it is something to be considered, but what real interest do they have in our domestic politics?'

'You know the answer to that.'

'True.'

'I need your help,' Narmonov repeated.

'I must discuss this with my colleagues.'

'Quickly, if you please.'

'Yes.' Kadishev took his leave and walked out to his car. He drove himself, which was unusual for a senior Soviet politician. Times had changed. Such officials now had to be men of the people, and that meant that the reserved center lanes of the broad Moscow streets were gone, along with most of the other traditional perks. That was too bad, Kadishev thought, but without the other changes that made it necessary, he'd still be a lonely voice in some distant *oblast* instead of the leader of a major faction in the Congress of People's Deputies. So, he was willing to do without the dacha in the woods east of Moscow, and the luxury apartment, and the chauffeur-driven, hand-made limousine, and all the other things that had once attached to the rulers of this vast and unhappy country. He drove to his legislative office, where at least he had a reserved parking place. Once behind the closed door of his office, he composed a brief letter on his personal typewriter. This he folded into a pocket. There was work to do this day. He walked down the street to the immense lobby of the Congress, and checked his coat. The attendant was female. She took his coat and handed him a numbered token. He thanked her politely. As she took the coat to its numbered hook, the attendant removed the note from the inside pocket and tucked it into the pocket of her own jacket. Four hours later, it arrived in the American Embassy.

'Panic attack?' Fellows asked.

'You might call it that, gentlemen,' Ryan said.

'Okay, tell us about the problem.' Trent sipped at his tea.

'We've had more indications that our communications links may be penetrated.'

'Again?' Trent rolled his eyes.

'Come on, Al, we've heard that song before,' Fellows grumbled. 'Details, Jack, details.'

Ryan went through the data.

'And what's the White House think?'

'I don't know yet. I'm heading up the street after I leave here. Frankly, I'd rather discuss it with you guys first, and I had to come down on some other stuff anyway.' Jack went on to describe the SPINNAKER report on Narmonov's problems.

'How long have you had this?'

'A couple of weeks —'

'Why haven't we heard it?' Trent demanded.

'Because we've been running around in circles trying to confirm it,' Jack answered.

'And?'

'Al, we've been unable to confirm directly. There are indications that the KGB is up to something. There seems to be a very discreet operation in Germany, looking for some lost tactical nukes.'

'Good Lord!' Fellows noted. 'What do you mean by "lost"?'

'We're not sure. If it ties in with SPINNAKER, well, maybe there's been some creative accounting on the part of the Soviet Army.'

'Your opinion?'

'I don't know, guys, I just don't know. Our analysis people are about evenly divided — those that are willing to offer an opinion.'

'We know their army isn't real happy,' Fellows said slowly. 'The loss of funding, loss of prestige, loss of units and billets . . . but *that* unhappy?'

'Pleasant thought,' Trent added. 'A power-struggle in a country with all those nukes . . . How reliable has SPINNAKER been?'

'Very. Five years of devoted service.'

'He's a member of their parliament, right?' Fellows asked.

'Correct.'

'Evidently a very senior one to get stuff like this . . . that's okay, I don't think either one of us wants to know his name,' Fellows added.

Trent nodded. 'Probably somebody we've met.' *Good guess, Al*, Jack didn't say. 'You're taking this seriously also?'

'Yes, sir, and also trying very hard to confirm it.'

'Anything new on NIITAKA?' Trent asked.

'Sir, I —'

'I heard from up the street that there's something to do with Mexico,' Al Trent said next. 'The President evidently wants my support on something. You are cleared to tell us. Honest, Jack, the President has authorized it.'

It was a technical rules violation, but Ryan had never known Trent to break his word. He went through that report also.

'Those little bastards!' Trent breathed. 'You know how many votes it cost me to roll over on that trade deal, and now they're planning to *break* it! So, you're saying we've been rolled again?'

'A possibility, sir.'

'Sam? The farmers in your district use all those nasty agricultural chemicals. Might cost 'em.'

'Al, free trade is an important principle,' Fellows said.

'So's keeping your goddamned word!'

'No argument, Al.' Fellows started thinking about how many of his farmers might lose expected export income from a flip-flop on the deal that he'd fought for on the floor of the House. 'How can we confirm this one?'

'Not sure yet.'

'Bug his airplane?' Trent suggested with a chuckle. 'If we can confirm this, I'd like to be there when Fowler shoves it up his ass! God *damn* it! I lost *votes* over this!' That he'd carried his district 58–42 was, for the moment, beside the point. 'Well, the President wants us to back him up on this one. Problems from your side of the aisle, Sam?'

'Probably not.'

'I'd just as soon stay clear of the political side of this, gentlemen. I'm just here as a messenger, remember?'

'Jack Ryan, last of the virgins.' Trent laughed. 'Good report, thanks for coming down. Let us know if the President wants us to authorize the new and improved TAPDANCE.'

'He'll never try. You're looking at two or three hundred million bucks, and bucks are tight,' Fellows noted. 'I want to see better data before we spring for it. We've dropped too much money down these black holes.'

'All I can say, Congressman, is that I'm taking it very seriously. So is the FBI.'

'And Ron Olson?' Trent asked.

'He's circling his wagons.'

'You'll have a better chance if he asks,' Fellows told Ryan.

'I know. Well, at least we'll have our system up and running in three more weeks. We've started turning out the first set of discs and doing preliminary tests now.'

'How so?'

'We use a computer to look for non-randomness. The big one, the Cray YMP. We brought in a consultant from MIT's Artificial Intelligence Laboratory to do a new kind of type-token program. In another week – ten days, call it – we'll know if the system is what we expect it to be. Then we'll start sending the hardware out.'

'I really hope you're wrong on this,' Trent said, as the meeting closed.

'So do I, man, but my instincts say otherwise.'

'And how much is it going to cost?' Fowler asked over lunch.

'From what I gather, two or three hundred million.'

'No. We've got budget problems enough.'

'I agree,' Liz Elliot said. 'But I wanted to discuss it with you first. It's Ryan's idea. Olson at NSA says he's full of it, says the systems are secure, but Ryan's really crazed about this new encoding system. You know he pushed the same thing through for the Agency – even went to Congress directly.'

'Oh, really?' Fowler looked up from his plate. 'He didn't go through OMB? What gives?'

'Bob, he delivered his pitch for the new NSA system to Trent and Fellows before he came to see me!'

'Who the hell does he think he is!'

'I keep telling you, Bob.'

'He's out, Elizabeth. Out. O-U-T. Get moving on it.'

'Okay, I think I know how to do it.'

Circumstances made it easy. One of Ernest Wellington's investigators had been staking out the 7-Eleven for a week. The Zimmer family business was just off U.S. Route 50 between Washington and Annapolis, and was adjacent to a large housing development, from which it drew much of its business. The investigator parked his van at the end of a street that gave him both a view of the business building and the family house which was only fifty yards away from it. The van was a typical covert-surveillance vehicle, custom-built by one of several specialty firms. The roof vent concealed a sophisticated periscope, whose two lenses were connected respectively to a TV camera and a 35mm Canon. The investigator had a cooler full of soft drinks, a large Thermos of coffee and a chemical toilet. He thought of the cramped van as his own personal space vehicle, and some of its high-tech gadgetry was at least as good as NASA had installed on the Shuttle.

'Bingo!' the radio crackled. 'Subject vehicle is taking the exit. Breaking off now.'

The man in the van lifted his own microphone. 'Roger, out.'

Clark had noticed the Mercury two days earlier. One of the problems with commuting was that the same vehicles kept showing up from time to time, and he'd decided that's all it was. It never got close, and never followed them off the main road. In this case, as he took the exit, it didn't follow. Clark shifted his attention to other matters. He hadn't noticed that the guy was using a microphone . . . but those new cellular things had you talking into the visor, and – wasn't technology wonderful? A good chase car need not tip himself off anymore. He pulled into the 7-Eleven parking lot, his eyes scanning for trouble. He saw none. Clark and Ryan exited the car at the same instant. Clark's topcoat was unbuttoned, as was his suit jacket, the easier to allow access to the Beretta 10mm pistol riding on his right hip. The sun was setting, casting a lovely orange glow in the western sky, and it was unseasonably warm, shirt-sleeve weather that made him regret the raincoat he was wearing. D.C.-area weather was as predictably unpredictable as anywhere in the world.

'Hello, Dr Ryan,' one of the Zimmer kids said. 'Mom's over at the house.'

'Okay.' Ryan walked back outside, and headed for the flagstone walk to the Zimmer residence. He spotted Carol in the back, with her youngest on the new swing seat. Clark trailed, alert as ever, seeing nothing but still-green lawns and parked cars, a few kids throwing a football. Such temperate weather in the beginning of December worried Clark. He believed it heralded a bastard of a winter.

'Hi, Carol!' Jack called. Mrs Zimmer was closely observing her youngest in the swing seat.

'Doc Ryan, you like the new swing seat?'

Jack nodded a little guiltily. He should have helped get it together. He was an expert on assembling toys. He leaned over. 'How's the little munchkin?'

'She won't get out, and it's dinnertime,' Carol said. 'You help?'

'How's everyone else?'

'Peter accepted in college, too! Full scholarship MIT.'

'Great!' Jack gave her a congratulatory hug. *What's the old joke? 'The doctor is five and the lawyer is three!' God, wouldn't Buck be proud of how these kids are turning out?* It was little more than the normal Asian obsession with education, of course, the same thing that had stood Jewish Americans in such good stead. If an opportunity presents itself, grab it by the throat. He bent down to the newest Zimmer, who held her arms up for her Uncle Jack.

'Come on, Jackie.' He picked her up, and got a kiss for his trouble. Ryan looked up when he heard the noise.

'Gotcha.' It's a simple trick, and an effective one. Even if you know it's coming, you can't do much to prevent it. The van had several buttons which, when pressed, beeped the horn. It was a sound the human brain recognized as a danger signal, and one instinctively looked towards whatever direction it had come from to see if there was any cause for concern. The investigator hit the nearest one, and, sure enough, Ryan looked up towards the sound, with an armful of kid. He'd caught the hug for the woman, and the kiss from the kid, and now he had a full-face shot on the 1200-speed film in his camera to backup the videotape. That simple. He had the goods on this Ryan guy. Amazing that a man with such a lovely wife would feel the need to screw around, but that was life, wasn't it? A CIA bodyguard to keep everything nice and secure. A kid involved, too. What a shit, the man thought, as the motor-drive whirred away on the Canon.

'You stay for dinnah! This time you stay. We celebrate Peter scholarship.'

'Can't say no to that one, Doc,' Clark observed.

'Okay.' Ryan carried Jacqueline Theresa Zimmer into the house. Neither he nor Clark noticed that the van parked fifty yards away pulled off a few minutes later.

It was the most delicate part of the process. The plutonium was set into ceriumsulfide ceramic crucibles. The crucibles were carried to the electric furnace. Fromm closed and locked the door. A vacuum pump evacuated the enclosure and replaced argon.

'Air has oxygen,' Fromm explained. 'Argon is an inert gas. We take no chances. Plutonium is highly reactive and pyrophoric. The ceramic crucibles are also inert and non-reactive. We use more than one crucible to avoid the possibility of forming a critical mass and starting a premature atomic reaction.'

'The phase-transformations?' Ghosn asked.

'Correct.'

'How long?' This question from Qati.

'Two hours. We take our time in this part. On removal from the furnace, the crucibles will be covered, of course, and we make the pour in an inert-gas enclosure. Now you know why we needed this sort of furnace.'

'No danger when you make the pour?'

Fromm shook his head. 'None at all, so long as we are careful. The configuration of the mold absolutely prevents forming a critical mass. I've done this many times in simulation. There have been accidents, but those invariably involved larger masses of fissile material and took place before all the hazards of handling plutonium were fully understood. No, we will move slowly and carefully. Pretend it is gold,' Fromm concluded.

'The machining process?'

'Three weeks, and two more of assembly and testing of the components.'

'The tritium extraction?' Ghosn asked.

Fromm bent down to look into the furnace. 'I'll do that right before completion, and that will conclude the exercise . . .'

'See any resemblance?' the investigator asked.

'Hard to tell,' Wellington thought. 'In any case, he sure seems to like the little tyke. Cute enough. I watched them build the swing set last weekend. The little one – name's Jackie, by the way, Jacqueline Theresa –'

'Oh? That's interesting.' Wellington made a note.

'Anyway, the little one loves the damned thing.'

'Seems right fond of Dr Ryan, also.'

'You suppose he really is the father?'

'Possible,' Wellington said, watching the videotape and comparing the picture there with the still shots. 'Light wasn't very good.'

'I can have the back-room boys enhance it. Take a few

days for the tape, though. They have to do it frame by frame.'

'I think that's a good idea. We want this to be solid.'

'It will be. So, what's going to happen to him?'

'He'll be encouraged to leave government service, I suppose.'

'You know, if we were private citizens, you might call this blackmail, invasion of privacy . . .'

'But we're not, and it isn't. This guy holds a security clearance, and it appears that his personal life isn't what it should be.'

'I suppose that's not our fault, is it?'

'Exactly.'

CHAPTER 22

Repercussions

'Damn it, Ryan, you can't do that!'

'Do what?' Jack responded.

'You went over my head to The Hill.'

'What do you mean? All I did was suggest to Trent and Fellows that there might be a problem. I'm supposed to do that.'

'It's not confirmed,' the Director insisted.

'So, what ever is fully confirmed?'

'Look at this.' Cabot handed over a new file.

'This is SPINNAKER. Why haven't I seen it yet?'

'Just read it!' Cabot snapped back.

'Confirms the leak . . .' It was a short one, and Jack raced through it.

'Except he thinks it's a leak in the Moscow embassy. Like a code clerk, maybe.'

'Pure speculation on his part – all he really says is that he wants his reports transported by hand now. That's the only definite thing this tells us.'

Cabot dodged. 'I know we've done that before.'

'Yes, we have,' Ryan admitted. It would even be easier now with the direct air service from New York to Moscow.

'What's the rat-line look like now?'

Ryan frowned at that. Cabot liked to use Agency jargon, though the term 'rat line,' meaning the chain of people and methods that transported a document from agent to case officer, had actually gone out of favor. 'It's a fairly simple one. Kadishev leaves his messages in a coat pocket. The check-room attendant at their Congress retrieves the messages and gets them off to one of our

537

people by brush-pass. Simple and direct. Also rather fast. I've never been comfortable with it, but it works.'

'So now we have two top agents who're unhappy with our communications systems, and I have to fly all the way to Japan – personally! – to meet with one.'

'It's not all that unusual for an agent to want to meet a high Agency official, Director. These people get twitchy, and knowing that some higher-up cares about them is what they need.'

'It'll waste a whole week of my time!' Cabot objected.

'You have to go to Korea in late January anyway,' Ryan pointed out. 'Catch our friend on the way back. He's not demanding to see you immediately, just soon.' Ryan returned to the SPINNAKER report, wondering why Cabot allowed himself to be sidetracked by irrelevancies. The reason, of course, was that the man was a dilettante, and a lazy one, who disliked losing arguments.

The new report said that Narmonov was very worried indeed that the West would find out just how desperate his situation with the Soviet military and KGB was. There was no further information on missing nuclear weapons, but plenty on new changes in parliamentary loyalties. The report gave Ryan the impression of having been slapped together. He decided to have Mary Pat look at it. Of all the people in the Agency, she was the only one who really understood the guy.

'I presume you're taking it to the President.'

'Yes, I think I have to.'

'If I may make a suggestion, remember to tell him that we have not really confirmed anything Kadishev has said.'

Cabot looked up. 'So?'

'So, it's true, Director. When you single-source something, especially something that's apparently highly important, you tell people that.'

'I believe this guy.'

'I'm not so sure.'

'The Russian department buys it,' Cabot noted.

'True, they've signed off on it, but I'd feel a hell of a

lot better if we had independent confirmation,' Jack said.

'Do you have any firm basis to doubt this information?'

'Nothing I can show to you, no. It's just that we ought to have been able to confirm something by now.'

'So, you expect me to go all the way down to the White House, present this, and then admit that it might be wrong?' Cabot stamped out his cigar, much to Jack's relief.

'Yes, sir.'

'I won't do that!'

'You have to do that, sir. You have to do that because it happens to be true. It's the rule.'

'Jack, it can get slightly tedious when you tell me what the rules of this place are. I am the Director, you know.'

'Look, Marcus,' Ryan said, trying to keep the exasperation out of his voice, 'what we have with this guy is some really hot information, something which, if true, could affect the way we deal with the Soviets. But it is not confirmed. It just comes from one person, okay? What if he's wrong? What if he misunderstands something. What if he's lying, even?'

'Do we have any reason to believe that?'

'None at all, Director, but on something this important – is it prudent or reasonable to affect our government's policy on the basis of a short letter from a single person?' That was always the best way to get to Marcus Cabot, prudence and reason.

'I hear what you're saying, Jack. Okay. My car is waiting. I'll be back in a couple of hours.'

Cabot grabbed his coat and walked out to the executive elevator. His Agency car was waiting. As Director of Central Intelligence, he got a pair of bodyguards, one driving, and the other in the front-passenger seat. Otherwise he had to deal with traffic the same as everyone else. Ryan, he thought on the drive down the George Washington Parkway, was becoming a pain in the ass. Okay, so he himself was new here. Okay, so he was inexperienced. Okay, so he liked to leave day-to-day stuff to his subordinates. He was the Director, after all, and didn't need to deal with every little damned thing. He was getting tired of having the rules of conduct explained to him once or twice a week, tired of having Ryan go over his head, tired of having analysis explained to him every time something really juicy came in. By the time he entered the White House, Cabot was quite annoyed.

'Morning, Marcus,' Liz Elliot said in her office.

'Good morning. We have another SPINNAKER report. President needs to go over it.'

'So, what's Kadishev up to?'

'Who told you his name?' the DCI growled.

'Ryan – didn't you know?'

'God damn it!' Cabot swore. 'He didn't tell me that.'

'Sit down, Marcus. We have a few minutes. How happy are you with Ryan?'

'Sometimes he forgets who's the Director and who's the Deputy.'

'He is a little on the arrogant side, isn't he?'

'Slightly,' Cabot agreed frostily.

'He's good at what he does – within limitations – but personally I'm getting a little tired of his attitude.'

'I know what you mean. He likes telling me what I have to do – with this, for example.'

'Oh, he doesn't trust your judgment?' the National Security Advisor asked, selecting her needle with care.

Cabot looked up. 'Yeah, that's the attitude he conveys.'

'Well, we weren't able to change everything from the previous administration. Of course, he *is* a pro at this . . .' her voice trailed off.

'And I'm not?' Cabot demanded.

'Of course you are, Marcus, you know I never meant it that way!'

'Sorry, Liz. You're right. Sometimes he rubs me the wrong way. That's all.'

'Let's go see the boss.'

'How solid is this?' President Fowler asked five minutes later.

'As you've already heard, this agent has been working

for us over five years, and his information has invariably been accurate.'

'Have you confirmed it?'

'Not completely,' Cabot replied. 'It's unlikely that we can, but our Russian department believes it, and so do I.'

'Ryan had his doubts.'

Cabot was getting a little tired of hearing about Ryan. 'I do not, Mr President. I think Ryan is trying to impress us with his new views on the Soviet government, trying to show us that he's not a cold-warrior anymore.' Again Cabot had dwelt on irrelevancies, Elliot thought to herself.

Fowler's eyes shifted. 'Elizabeth?'

'It's certainly plausible that the Soviet security apparatus is trying to stake out an improved position,' her voice purred at its most reasonable timbre. 'They're unhappy with the liberalization, they're unhappy with their loss of power, and they're unhappy with what they think is a failure of leadership on Narmonov's part. This information, therefore, is consistent with a lot of other facts we have. I think we should believe it.'

'If this is true, then we have to ease off on our support for Narmonov. We cannot be party to a reversion to more centralized rule, particularly if it results from elements who so clearly dislike us.'

'Agreed,' Liz said. 'Better to lose Narmonov. If he can't break their military to his will, then someone else will have to. Of course, we have to give him a fair chance . . . how we do that is rather tricky. We don't want to dump the country into the hands of their military, do we?'

'Are you kidding?' Fowler observed.

They stood on a catwalk inside the massive boat-shed where the Trident submarines were prepared for sea, watching the crew of USS *Georgia* load up for their next cruise.

'Talked his way out of it, Bart?' Jones asked.

'His explanation made a lot of sense, Ron.'

'When's the last time you caught me wrong?'

'For all things there is a first time.'

'Not this one, skipper,' Dr Jones said quietly. 'I got a feeling.'

'Okay, I want you to spend some more time on the simulator with his sonar troops.'

'Fair enough.' Jones was quiet for a few seconds. 'You know, it might be fun to go out, just one more time . . .'

Mancuso turned. 'You volunteering?'

'No. Kim might not understand my being away for three months. Two weeks is long enough. Too long, as a matter of fact. I'm getting very domesticated, Bart, getting old and respectable. Not young and bright-eyed like those kids.'

'What do you think of them?'

'The sonar guys? They're good. So's the tracking party. The guy Ricks replaced was Jim Rosselli, right?'

'That's right.'

'He trained them well. Can we go off the record?'

'Sure.'

'Ricks is not a good skipper. He's too tough on the troops, demands too much, too hard to satisfy. Not like you were at all, Bart.'

Mancuso dodged the compliment. 'We all have different styles.'

'I know that, but I wouldn't want to sail with him. One of his chiefs asked for a transfer off. So did half a dozen petty officers.'

'They all had family problems.' Mancuso had approved all the transfers, including the young chief torpedoman.

'No, they didn't,' Jones said. 'They needed excuses, and they used them.'

'Ron, look, I'm the squadron commander, okay? I can only elevate my COs on the basis of performance. Ricks didn't get here by being a loser.'

'You look from the top down. I look from the bottom up. From my perspective, this man is not a good skipper. I wouldn't say that to anybody else, but we were ship-mates. Okay, I was a peon, just a lowly E-6, but you never treated me that way. You were a good boss. Ricks isn't. The crew doesn't like him, does not have confidence in him.'

'Damn it, Ron, I can't allow stuff like that to affect my judgment.'

'Yeah, I know. Annapolis, old school tie – ring, whatever matters to you Canoe U. grads. You have to approach it a different way. Like I said, I wouldn't talk this way with anybody else. If I was on that boat, I'd try to transfer off.'

'I sailed with some skippers I didn't like. It's mainly a matter of style.'

'You say so, Commodore.' Jones paused. 'Just remember one thing, okay? There's lots of ways to impress a senior officer, but there's only one way to impress a crew.'

Fromm insisted that they take their time. The mold had long since cooled and was now broken open in the inert atmosphere of the first machine tool. The roughly-formed metal mass was set in place. Fromm personally checked the computer codes that told the machine what it had to do and punched the first button. The robotic system activated. The moving arm selected the proper tool head, secured it on the rotating spindle, and maneuvered itself into place. The enclosed area was flooded with argon gas, and Freon began spraying on the plutonium to keep everything to the proper isothermal heat environment. Fromm touched the computer screen, selecting the initial program. The spindle started turning, reaching over a thousand RPM, and approached the plutonium mass with a motion that was neither human nor mechanistic, but something else entirely, like a caricature of a man's action. As they watched from behind the Lexan shield, the first shavings of the silvery metal thread peeled off the main mass.

'How much are we losing?' Ghosn asked.

'Oh, the total will be less than twenty grams,' Fromm estimated. 'It's nothing to worry about.' Fromm looked at another gauge, the one that measured relative pressures. The machine tool was totally isolated from the rest of the room, with the pressure inside its enclosure marginally less than outside. The fact that argon gas was heavier than air would keep oxygen away from the plutonium. That prevented possible combustion. Combustion would generate plutonium dust, which was every bit as lethal as Fromm had told them. A toxic heavy metal, the additional hazard of radioactivity — mainly low-energy alphas — merely made death more rapid and marginally less pleasant. The machinists moved in to take over supervision of the process. They had worked out extremely well, Fromm thought. The skills they'd brought with them had grown with remarkable speed under his tutelage. They were nearly as good as the men he'd trained in Germany, despite their lack of formal education. There was much to be said for practical instead of theoretical work.

'How long?' Qati asked.

'How many times do I have to tell you? We are precisely on schedule. This phase of the project is the most time-consuming. The product we are now producing must be perfect. Absolutely perfect. If this part of the device fails to function, nothing else will.'

'That's true of everything we've done!' Ghosn pointed out.

'Correct, my young friend, but this is the easiest thing to get wrong. The metal is hard to work, and the metallic phase transformations make it all the more delicate. Now, let's see those explosive blocks.'

Ghosn was right. Everything had to work. The explosives had been almost entirely his problem after Fromm had set the design specifications. They'd taken normal TNT and added a stiffener, a plastic that made the material quite rigid, but without affecting its chemical properties. Normally explosives are plastic and easily malleable by their nature. That property had to be eliminated, since the shape of the blocks was crucial to the way in which their explosive energy was delivered. Ghosn had shaped six hundred such blocks, each a segment of a full ellipsoid. Seventy of them would nest together exactly, forming an explosive ring with an outside diameter of 35 centimeters. Each block had a squib fired from kryton switches. The wires leading from the power supply to the switches all had to be of exactly the same length. Fromm lifted one of the blocks.

'You say that these are all identical?' Fromm asked.

'Completely. I followed your directions exactly.'

'Pick seventy at random. I'll take one of the stainless-steel blanks, and we will test your work.'

The spot was already prepared, of course. It was, in fact, the eroded crater from an American-made Mark 84 bomb dropped by an Israeli F-4 Phantom some years before. Qati's men had erected a pre-fabricated structure of timber posts and beams whose roof was three layers of sandbags. Camouflage netting had been added to reduce the chance of notice. Test assembly took three hours, and an electronic strain-gauge was inserted in the steel blank and a wire run to the next crater down – two hundred meters away – where Fromm waited with an oscilloscope. They were finished just before dusk.

'Ready,' Ghosn said.

'Proceed,' Fromm replied, concentrating on his scope.

Ibrahim pressed the button. The structure disintegrated before their eyes. A few sandbags survived, flying through the air, but mainly there was a shower of dirt. On the O-scope, the peak pressure was frozen in place well before the *crump* of the blast wave passed over their heads. Bock and Qati were somewhat disappointed in the physical effects of the explosion, most of which had been attenuated by the sandbags. Was such a small detonation enough to ignite a nuclear device?

'Well?' Ghosn asked, as a man ran off to the newly-deepened crater.

'Ten percent off,' Fromm said, looking up. Then he smiled. 'Ten percent too much.'

'What does that mean?' Qati demanded, suddenly worried that they'd done something wrong.

'It means that my young student has learned his lessons well.' Fifteen minutes later, they were sure. It took two men to find it, and half an hour to remove the tungsten casing from the core. What had been a nearly solid steel mass as big around as a man's fist was now a distorted cylinder no wider than a cigar. Had it been plutonium, a nuclear reaction would have taken place. Of that the German was sure. Fromm hefted it in his hand and presented it to Ibrahim.

'Herr Ghosn,' he said formally. 'You have a gift with explosives. You are a fine engineer. In the DDR, it took us three attempts to get it right. You have done it in one.'

'How many more?'

Fromm nodded. 'Very good. We shall do another tomorrow. We will test all the stainless-steel blanks, of course.'

'That is why we made them,' Ghosn agreed.

On the way back, Bock ran over his own calculations. According to Fromm the force of the final explosion would be more than four hundred fifty thousand tons of TNT. He therefore based his estimates on a mere four hundred thousand. Bock was always conservative on casualty estimates. The stadium and all in it would be vaporized. No, he corrected himself. That wasn't really true. There was nothing magical about this weapon. It was merely a large explosive device. The stadium and all in it would be totally destroyed, but there would be a great deal of rubble flung ballistically hundreds, perhaps thousands of meters. The ground nearest the device would be pulverized down to pieces of molecular size. Dust particles would then be sucked up into the fireball. Bits of the bomb-assembly residue would affix themselves to the rising, boiling dust. That's what fallout was, he'd learned, dirt with bomb-residue attached. The nature of the blast – being set off at ground level – would maximize the fallout, which would be borne downwind. The majority would fall within thirty kilometers of the blast site. The remainder would be a plaything of the winds, to fall over Chicago or St Louis or maybe even Washington. How many would die from that?

Good question. He estimated roughly two hundred thousand from the blast itself, certainly no more than that. Another fifty to one hundred thousand from secondary effects, that number including long-term deaths from cancers which would take years to manifest themselves. As Qati had noted earlier, the actual death count was somewhat disappointing. It was so easy to think of nuclear bombs as magical engines of destruction, but they were not. They were merely highly powerful bombs with some interesting secondary effects. It also made for the finest terrorist weapon yet conceived.

Terrorist? Bock asked himself. *Is that what I am?*

It was, of course, in the eye of the beholder. Bock had long since decided his measure of respect for the judgment of others. This event would be the best expression of it.

'John, I need an idea,' Ryan said.

'What's that?' Clark asked.

'I've drawn a blank. The Japanese prime minister is going to be in Mexico in February, then he's flying up here to see the President. We want to know what he's going to be saying on his airplane.'

'I don't have the legs to dress up as a stew, Doc. Besides, I've never learned to do the tea ceremony either.' The field officer turned SPO paused and became serious. 'Bug an airplane . . . ? That sounds like a real technical challenge.'

'What do you know about this?'

John examined his coffee. 'I've placed intelligence-gathering devices before, but always on the ground. With an aircraft you have lots of ambient noise to worry about. You also have to sweat where your subject intends to sit. Finally, with a presidential aircraft you need to worry about security. The technical side is probably the hardest,' he decided. 'The greatest personal threat to the guy is probably at home – unless he's going to stopover at Detroit, right? Mexico City. Okay, people speak Spanish there, and my Spanish is pretty good. I'd take Ding down with me, of course . . . What sort of aircraft will he be using?'

'I checked. He'll be flying a JAL 747. The upper deck behind the cockpit is laid out as his conference room.

They put in beds, too. That's where he'll be. Their PM likes to kibbitz with the drivers. He's pretty smart about traveling, sleeps as much as he can to handle the jet-lag.'

Clark nodded. 'People have to wipe the windows. Not like he's got an air force base to handle all the ground-service requirements like we do it. If JAL flies into there regularly, they'll have Mexican ground crews. I'll check out data on the 747 . . . Like I said, that's the easy part. I can probably talk my way there. Might even get Ding to head down with a good set of papers and get a job. That would make it easier. I presume this has executive approval?'

'The President said "find a way." He'll have to approve the final op-plan.'

'I need to talk to the S&T guys.' Clark referred to the CIA's Directorate of Science and Technology. 'The real problem is noise . . . How fast, Doc?'

'Fast, John.'

'Okay.' Clark rose. 'Gee, I get to be a field-spook again. I'll be over in the new building. It may take me a few days to figure if it's possible or not. This means I can't go on the U.K. trip?'

'Bother you?' Jack asked.

'Nope. Just as soon stay home.'

'Fair enough. I get to do some Christmas shopping at Hamley's.'

'You know how lucky you are to have 'em little? All my girls want now is clothes, and I can't pick girl clothes worth a damn.' Clark lived in horror of buying women's clothing.

'Sally has her doubts now, but little Jack still believes.'

Clark shook his head. 'After you stop believing in Santa Claus, the whole world just goes downhill.'

'Ain't it the truth?'

CHAPTER 23

Opinions

'Jack, you look bloody awful,' Sir Basil Charleston observed.

'If one more person tells me that, I'm going to waste him.'

'Bad flight?'

'Bumpy as hell all the way across. Didn't sleep much.' As the even darker than usual circles under his eyes proclaimed.

'Well, we'll see if lunch helps.'

'It is a pretty day,' Ryan noted as they walked up Westminster Bridge Road towards Parliament. It was a rare early-winter English day with a blue, cloudless sky. A brisk wind swept down the Thames, but Ryan didn't mind. He had on a heavy coat and a scarf around his neck, and the frigid blast on his face woke him up. 'Trouble at the office, Bas?'

'Found a bug, a bloody bug, two floors down from my office! The whole building's being swept.'

'Things are tough all over. KGB?'

'Not sure,' Charleston said as they crossed the bridge. 'Trouble with the façade, you see, bloody thing began crumbling – same as happened to Scotland Yard a few years ago. The workers replacing it found an unexplained wire, and followed it . . . Our Russian friends have not cut back on their activities, and there are other services as well. See anything like that in your shop?'

'No. It helps that we're more isolated than Century House.' Jack meant that the British Secret Intelligence Service was in so densely populated an area – there was a nearby apartment block, for example – that a very

549

low-power bug could get data out. That was less likely at the Agency's Langley headquarters, which sat alone on a large wooded campus. In addition to that, the newer construction had allowed installation of elaborate protections against internal radio sources. 'You should do what we've done and install waveguides.'

'That would cost a bloody fortune, which we do not have at the moment.'

'What the hell, it gives us a chance to take a walk. If anyone can bug us out here, we've already lost.'

'It never ends, does it? We win the Cold War, but it never, ever ends.'

'Which Greek was it? The one whose personal hell was rolling a big rock up a hill, and every time he got it there the son-of-a-bitch rolled down the other side.'

'Sisyphus . . . ? Tantalus, perhaps? Long time since I bade farewell to Oxford, Sir John. In either case, you're right. Get to the top of one hill and all you see is another damned hill.' They continued walking down the embankment, away from Parliament, but towards lunch. Meetings like this one had rules. You couldn't get down to business until after the small talk and a pregnant pause. In this case, there were some off-season American tourists snapping pictures. Charleston and Ryan walked around to avoid them.

'We have a problem, Bas.'

'What's that?' Charleston said, without turning. Behind them were three security officers. Two more preceded them.

Jack didn't turn either. 'We have a guy inside the Kremlin. Spends some time with Narmonov. Says Andrey Il'ych is worried about a military/KGB coup. Says that they might renege on the strategic-arms treaty. Also says that some tactical nuclear devices may be missing from their inventories in Germany.'

'Indeed? That's cheery news. How good is your source?'

'Extremely good.'

'Well, I can say it's news to me, Dr Ryan.'

'How good is your guy?' Jack asked.

'Quite good.'

'Nothing like this?'

'Some rumbles, of course. I mean, Narmonov does have a full plate, doesn't he? Ever since that dreadful affair with the Balts, and the Georgians, *and* his Muslims. What is it you Yanks say, "one-armed paper hanger"? He's that busy and more. He's had to make a deal with his security forces, but a *coup d'état*?' Charleston shook his head. 'No. The tea leaves don't appear that way to us.'

'That's precisely what our agent is telling us. What about the nuclear thing?'

'I'm afraid our chap isn't well-placed for that sort of information. More the civilian side, you see.' And that, Jack knew, was as far as Basil would go. 'How seriously are you taking this?'

'Very seriously. I have to. This agent has been giving us good stuff for a lot of years.'

'One of Mrs Foley's recruits?' Charleston asked with a chuckle. 'What a marvelous young lady. I understand she recently delivered another child?'

'Little girl, Emily Sarah, looks just like her mom.' Jack thought he'd dodged the first question rather adroitly. 'Mary Pat will be back at work right after New Year.'

'Ah, yes, you do have that fortress nursery on your grounds, don't you?'

'One of the smartest investments we ever made. Wish I'd thought of it.'

'You Americans!' Sir Basil laughed. 'Missing nuclear weapons. Yes, I suppose one must take that very seriously indeed. Possible collusion between the army and KGB and a tactical-nuclear trump. Quite frightening, I must say, but we have not heard a whisper. Rather a difficult secret to keep, wouldn't you say? I mean, blackmail doesn't work terribly well unless people know they're being blackmailed.'

'We've also caught a rumble that KGB is running some nuclear-oriented operation in Germany. That's all, just a rumble.'

'Yes, we've heard that too,' Charleston said, as they

turned to walk down the brow to the *Tattersall Castle*, an old paddle steamer long since converted to a restaurant.

'And?'

'And we've run our own op. It seems that Erich Honecker had his own little Manhattan Project underway. Fortunately, it died in the womb. Ivan was quite upset to learn of it. The DDR returned a goodly supply of plutonium to their former socialist colleagues just before the change. I speculate that KGB is investigating the same thing.'

'Why didn't you tell us?' *Jesus, Bas.* Jack thought. *You guys just don't forget, do you!*

'Nothing to tell, Jack.' Charleston nodded at the head waiter, who took them to a table well aft. The security officers situated themselves between their charges and the rest of luncheoning humanity. 'Our German friends have been very forthcoming. The project, they say, has been quashed, completely and for all time. We've had our technical people over everything, and they confirmed everything our German colleagues told us.'

'When was this?'

'Several months ago. Ever eat here, Jack?' Charleston asked, as the waiter appeared.

'Not this one, a few of the other ferry boats.' Basil ordered a pint of bitter. Jack decided on a lager. They watched the waiter withdraw. 'The KGB op is more recent.'

'Interesting. Could be the same thing, you know, could be that they had the same interests we had and were just a little slower to move.'

'On nukes?' Ryan shook his head. 'Our Russian friends are pretty smart, Bas, and they pay much closer attention to nuclear issues than we do. It's one of the things I admire about them.'

'Yes, they did learn their lesson from China, didn't they?' Charleston set his menu down and waved for the waiter to bring the drinks. 'You think this is a serious matter, then?'

'Sure do.'

'Your judgment is generally rather good, Jack. Thank you,' Basil told the waiter. Both men made their orders. 'You think we should poke about?'

'I think that might be a good idea.'

'Very well. What else can you tell me?'

'I'm afraid that's it, Bas.'

'Your source must be very good indeed.' Sir Basil sipped at his beer. 'I think you have reservations.'

'I do, but . . . hell, Basil, when do we not have reservations?'

'Any contrary data?'

'None, just that we've been totally unable to confirm. Our source is good enough that we may not be able to confirm elsewhere. That's why I came over. Your guy must be pretty good, too, judging by what you've sent us. Whoever he is, he might be the best chance to back our guy up.'

'And if we can't confirm?'

'Then probably we'll go with it anyway.' Ryan didn't like that.

'And your reservations?'

'Probably don't matter. Two reasons. Number one, I'm not sure myself whether to sign off on this or not. Number two, not everyone cares what I think.'

'And that's why you've not received credit for your work on the treaty?'

Ryan grinned rather tiredly, having not had much sleep in the preceding thirty-six hours. 'I refuse to be surprised by that, and I won't ask how you pulled that one out of the hat.'

'But?'

'But I wish somebody would leak it to the press or something!' Ryan allowed himself a laugh.

'I'm afraid we don't do that here. I've only leaked it to one person.'

'PM?'

'His Royal Highness. You're having dinner with him tonight, correct? I reckoned he might like to know.'

Jack thought about that. The Prince of Wales wouldn't

let it go any farther. Ryan could never have told him . . . but . . . 'Thanks, pal.'

'We all crave recognition in one way or another. You and I are both denied it as a matter of course. Not really fair, but there you are. In this case I broke one of my own rules, and if you ask why, I'll tell you: what you did was bloody marvelous, Jack. If there were justice in the world, Her Majesty would enter you in the Order of Merit.'

'You can't tell her, Basil. She just might do it all on her own.'

'She might indeed, and that would let out the little secret, mightn't it?' Dinner arrived, and they had to wait again.

'It wasn't just me. You know that, Charlie Alden did a lot of good work. So did Talbot, Bunker, Scott Adler, a bunch of others.'

'Your modesty is as comprehensive as ever, Dr Ryan.'

'Does that mean "stupid," Bas?' Ryan got a smile instead of an answer. The Brits were good at that.

Fromm would never have believed it. They'd made five stainless-steel blanks to duplicate the size and configuration of the plutonium. Ghosn had made all the necessary explosive blocks. They'd tested the explosives on all five blanks, and in every case the explosives had done their job. This was one very talented young man. Of course he'd had exact plans to follow, and Fromm had generated them with the help of a fine computer, but even so, getting something so difficult right the first time was hardly the norm in engineering.

The plutonium was now through the first part of the machining process. It actually looked rather good, like a high-quality steel forging machined to be part of an automotive engine. That was a good beginning. The robot arm of the milling machine removed the plutonium from its spindle and set it in an enclosed box. The box was, of course, filled with argon gas. The arm sealed it and moved it to a door, then Fromm removed it from the machine enclosure and walked over to the air-bearing lathe. The process was reverse-duplicated. He slid the box into the enclosure. Vacuum pumps were activated and while the air was sucked out the top of the enclosure, argon gas was added at the bottom. When the internal atmosphere was totally inert, the robot arm of this tool opened the box, and extracted the plutonium. The next programmed set of movements set it precisely on a new spindle. The degree of precision was hugely important. Under Fromm's supervision, the spindle was activated, building its speed up slowly to fifteen thousand RPM.

'It would appear that – no!' Fromm swore. He'd thought he'd gotten it perfect. The spindle slowed back down, and a tiny adjustment was made. Fromm took his time checking the balance, then powered it up again. This time it was perfect. He took the RPMs all the way to twenty-five thousand and there was no jitter at all.

'You men did the first machining very nicely,' Fromm said over his shoulder.

'How much mass did we lose?' Ghosn asked.

'Eighteen-point-five-two-seven grams.' Fromm switched the spindle off and stood. 'I can scarcely praise our workers enough. I suggest that we wait until tomorrow to begin final polishing. It is foolish to rush about. We're all tired, and I think dinner is called for.'

'As you say, Herr Fromm.'

'Manfred,' the German said, surprising the younger man. 'Ibrahim, we must talk.'

'Outside?' Ghosn led the German out the door. Night was falling.

'We mustn't kill these men. They are too valuable. What if this opportunity presents itself again?'

'But you agreed . . .'

'I never expected things would go this well. The schedule I worked up assumed that you and I – no, I shall be honest, that I would have to supervise everything. You, Ibrahim, have astounded me with your skill. What we have done here is to have assembled a superb team. We must keep this team together!'

And where else will we get ten kilos of plutonium?
Ghosn wanted to ask.

'Manfred, I think you are correct. I will discuss this with the Commander. You must remember –'

'Security. *Ich weiß schön*. We can take no chances at this stage. I merely entreat you, as a matter of justice – of professional recognition, *ja?* – that consideration must be given. Do you understand?'

'Quite well, Manfred, I agree with you.' The German was acquiring humanity, Ghosn thought. A pity it came so late. 'In any case, I also agree with your desire for a decent dinner before we begin the final phase. Tonight there is fresh lamb, and we've obtained some German beer. Bitberger, I hope you like it.'

'A good regional lager. A pity, Ibrahim, that your religion denies it to you.'

'On this night,' Ghosn said, 'I hope Allah will forgive me for indulging.' Just as well, Ibrahim thought, to earn the infidel's confidence.

'Jack, it would appear that you are working too hard.'

'It's the commute, sir. Two or three hours a day in a car.'

'Find a place closer?' His Royal Highness suggested gently.

'Give up Peregrine Cliff?' Ryan shook his head. 'Then what about Cathy and Johns Hopkins? Then there's the kids, taking them out of school. No, that's no solution.'

'You doubtless recall that the first time we met, you commented rather forcefully on my physical and psychological condition. I rather doubt that I looked as dreadful as you do now.' The Prince had received more than one bit of information from Sir Basil Charleston, Jack noted, as a result of which there was no alcohol being served with dinner.

'It blows hot and cold at work. At the moment, it's blowing rather hot.'

'Truman, then? "If you can't stand the heat, get out of the kitchen"?'

'Yes, sir, something like that, but it'll cool off. Just

that we have some things happening now. It's like that. When you were driving your ship, it was like that, too, wasn't it?'

'That was much healthier work. I also had a far shorter distance to commute. About fifteen feet, as a matter of fact,' he added with a chuckle.

Ryan laughed rather tiredly. 'Must be nice. For me it's that far to see my secretary.'

'And the family?'

There was no sense in lying. 'Could be better. My work doesn't help.'

'Something is troubling you, Jack. It's quite obvious, you know.'

'Too much stress. I've been hitting the booze too hard, not enough exercise. The usual. It'll get better, just I've had a longer than usual stretch of bad times at the office. I appreciate your concern, sir, but I'll be all right.' Jack almost convinced himself that it was true. Almost.

'As you say.'

'And I must say that's the best dinner I've had in a very long time. So, when's the next time you're coming over to our side of the pond?' Ryan asked, grateful for the chance to change subjects.

'Late spring. A breeder in Wyoming will have some horses for me. Polo ponies, actually.'

'You gotta be crazy to play that game. Lacrosse on horses.'

'Well, it gives me a chance to enjoy the countryside. Magnificent place, Wyoming. I plan to tour Yellowstone also.'

'Never been there,' Jack said.

'Perhaps you could come with us, then? I might even teach you how to ride.'

'Maybe,' Jack allowed, wondering how he'd look on a horse, and wondering how the hell he'd be able to get away from the office for a week. 'Just so you don't wave one of those hammers at me.'

'Mallet, Jack, mallet. I shan't try to involve you in polo. You'd probably end up killing some unfortunate horse. I presume you'll be able to find the time.'

'I can sure try. If I'm lucky, the world will settle down a little by then.'

'It's settled down quite a bit, thanks in large part to your work.'

'Sir, Basil may have placed a little too much emphasis on what I did. I was just one cog in the machine.'

'Modesty can be overdone. I find it disappointing that you failed to receive any recognition,' the Prince observed.

'That's life, isn't it?' Jack was surprised at how it came out. For once, he'd been unable to hide his feelings completely.

'I thought as much. Yes, Jack, that's life, and life is not always fair. Have you thought perhaps about changing your line of work – take leave, perhaps?'

Jack grinned. 'Come on, I don't look all that bad. They need me at the office.'

His Royal Highness became very serious. 'Jack, are we friends?'

Ryan sat upright in his chair. 'I don't have all that many, but you're one of them.'

'Do you trust my judgment?'

'Yes, sir, I do.'

'Get out. Leave. You can always come back to it. A person of your talents never really leaves. You know that. I don't like the way you look. You've been at it too long. Have you any idea how lucky you are that you *can* leave? You have a degree of freedom I do not. Use it.'

'Nice try, man. If you were in my position, you wouldn't leave. Same reason, even. I'm not a quitter. Neither are you. It's that simple.'

'Pride can be a destructive force,' the Prince pointed out.

Jack leaned forward. 'It's not pride. It's fact. They do need me. I wish they didn't, but they do. Problem is, they don't know it.'

'Is the new director that bad?'

'Marcus is not a bad person, but he's lazy. He likes his position better than he likes his duties. I don't suppose that's a problem limited to the American government, is it? I know better. So do you. Duty comes first. Maybe you're stuck with your job because you were born into it, but I'm just as stuck with mine because I'm the guy best able to do it.'

'Do they listen to you?' His Highness asked sharply.

Jack shrugged. 'Not always. Hell, sometimes I'm wrong, but there has to be somebody there who does the right thing, at least tries to. That's me, sir. That's why I can't bug out. You know that just as well as I do.'

'Even if it harms you?'

'Correct.'

'Your sense of duty is admirable, Sir John.'

'I had a couple of good teachers. You didn't run and hide when you knew you were a target. You could have done that –'

'No, I could not have done so. If I had –'

'The bad guys would have won,' Jack finished the thought. 'My problem isn't very different, is it? I learned part of this from you. Surprised?' Jack asked.

'Yes,' he admitted.

'You don't run away from things. Neither do I.'

'Your verbal maneuvering is as skillful as ever.'

'See? I haven't lost it yet.' Jack was rather pleased with himself.

'I will insist that you bring the family out to Wyoming with us.'

'You can always go over my head – talk to Cathy.'

His Highness laughed. 'Perhaps I will. Flying back tomorrow?'

'Yes, sir. I'm going to hit Hamley's for some toys.'

'Get yourself some sleep, Jack. We'll have this argument again next year.'

It was five hours earlier in Washington. Liz Elliot stared across her desk at Bob Holtzman, who covered the White House. Like the permanent staffers here, Holtzman had seen them come and go, outlasting them all. His greater experience in the building was something of a paradox. Though necessarily cut out of the really good stuff – Holtzman knew that there were some secrets he'd never see until years too late to make a story of them; that was the work of historians – his skill at reading nuances and catching whiffs would have earned him a senior place at any intelligence agency. But his paper paid much better than any government agency, especially since he'd also penned a few best-selling books on life at the highest levels of government.

'This is deep background?'

'That's right,' the National Security Advisor said.

Holtzman nodded and made his notes. That set the rules. No direct quotes. Elizabeth Elliot could be referred to as an 'administration official,' or in the plural as 'sources within.' He looked up from his notebook – tape recorders were also out for this sort of interview – and waited. Liz Elliot liked her drama. She was a bright woman, somewhat elitist – not an uncommon trait in White House officialdom – and definitely the person closest to the President, if he was reading the signals right. But that was none of the public's business. The probable love affair between the President and his National Security Advisor was no longer a complete secret. The White House staffers were as discreet as ever – more, in fact. He found it odd that they should be so. Fowler was not the most lovable of men. Perhaps they felt sympathy for what had to be a lonely man. The circumstances of his wife's death were well-known, and had probably added a percentage point of sympathy votes in the last election. Maybe the staffers thought he'd change with a steady romance in his life. Maybe they were just being good professionals. (That distinguished them from political appointees, Holtzman thought. Nothing was sacred to them.) Maybe Fowler and Elliot were just being very careful. In any case, the White House press had discussed it off and on at 'The Confidential Source,' the bar at the National Press Club building, just two blocks away, and it had been decided that Fowler's love life was not properly a matter of public interest, so long as it did not injure his job performance. After all, his foreign-policy performance was pretty good. Euphoria from the Vatican Treaty and its stunningly favorable aftermath had never gone away. You couldn't slam a president who was doing so fine a job.

'We may have a problem with the Russians,' Elliot began.

'Oh?' Holtzman was caught by surprise for once.

'We have reason to believe that Narmonov is having considerable difficulty dealing with his senior military commanders. That could have effects on final compliance with the arms treaty.'

'How so?'

'We have reason to believe that the Soviets will resist elimination of some of their SS-18 stocks. They're already behind in destruction of the missiles.'

Reason to believe. Twice. Holtzman thought about that for a moment. A very sensitive source, probably a spy rather than an intercept. 'They say that there's a problem with the destruct facility. The inspectors we have over there seem to believe them.'

'Possibly the factory was designed with — what do you call it? Creative incompetence.'

'What's the Agency say?' Holtzman asked, scribbling his notes just as fast as he could.

'They gave us the initial report, but so far they've been unable to get us a real opinion.'

'What about Ryan? He's pretty good on the Soviets.'

'Ryan's turning into a disappointment,' Liz said. 'As a matter of fact — and this is something you can't say, you can't use his name — we have a little investigation going that's turned up some disturbing data.'

'Like?'

'Like, I think we're getting skewed data. Like, I think a senior Agency official is having an affair with a person of foreign birth, and there may be a child involved.'

'Ryan?'

The National Security Advisor shook her head. 'Can't confirm or deny. Remember the rules.'

'I won't forget,' Holtzman replied, hiding his annoyance. Did she think she was dealing with Jimmy Olsen?

'The problem is, it looks like he knows we don't like what he's telling us, and as a result he's trying to put a spin on the data to please us. This is a time when we really need good stuff from Langley, but we're not getting it.'

Holtzman nodded thoughtfully. That was not exactly a new problem at Langley, but Ryan wasn't that sort, was he? The reporter set that aside. 'And Narmonov?'

'If what we're getting is in any way correct, he may be on the way out, whether from the right or the left, we can't say. It may be that he's losing it.'

'That's solid?'

'It appears so. The part about blackmail from his security forces is very disturbing. But with our problems at Langley . . .' Liz held up her hands.

'Just when things were going so well, too. I guess you're having problems with Cabot?'

'He's learning his job pretty well. If he had better support, he'd be okay.'

'How worried are you?' Holtzman asked.

'Very much so. This is a time when we need good intel, but we're not getting it. How the hell can we figure out what to do about Narmonov unless we get good information? So, what do we get?' Liz asked in exasperation. 'Our hero is running around doing stuff that really doesn't concern his agency – he's gone over people's heads to The Hill on some things – doing a Chicken Little act on one thing while at the same time he's not getting Cabot good analysis on what appears to be a major issue. Of course, he has his distractions . . .'

Our hero, Holtzman thought. *What an interesting choice of words. She really hates the guy, doesn't she!* Holtzman knew the fact, but not the reason. There was no reason for her to be jealous of him. Ryan had never shown great ambition, at least not in a political sense. He was a pretty good man, by all accounts. The reporter remembered his one public *faux pas*, a confrontation with Al Trent which, Holtzman was certain, must have been staged. Ryan and Trent got along very well now by all accounts. What could possibly have been important enough to stage something like that? Ryan had two intelligence stars – what for, Holtzman had never been able to find out. Just rumors, five different versions of four different stories, probably all of them false. Ryan wasn't all that popular with the press. The reason was that he had never really leaked anything. He took secrecy a little too seriously. On the other hand, he didn't try to curry favor either, and Holtzman respected anyone who avoided that. Of one thing he was sure: he had gravely underestimated the antipathy for Ryan in the Fowler Administration.

I'm being manipulated. That was as obvious as a peacock in a barnyard. Very cleverly, of course. The bit about the Russians was probably genuine. The Central Intelligence Agency's inability to get vital information to the White House wasn't exactly new either, was it? That was probably true also. So, where was the lie? Or was there a lie at all? Maybe they just wanted to get truthful but sensitive information out . . . in the normal way. It wasn't the first time he'd learned things in the northwest-corner office of the White House West Wing.

Could Holtzman *not* do a story on this?

Not hardly, Bobby boy, the reporter told himself.

The ride home was smooth as silk. Ryan caught as much sleep as he could, while the sergeant who took care of the cabin read through assembly instructions for some of the toys Jack had picked up.

'Yo, sarge.' The pilot was back in the cabin for a stretch. 'Whatcha doin'?'

'Well, Maj, our DV here picked up some stuff for the kiddies.' The NCO handed over a page of directions. Tab-1 into Slot-A, use 7/8ths bolt, tighten with a wrench, using . . .

'I think I'd rather tinker with broke engines . . .'

'Roger that,' the sergeant agreed. 'This guy's got some bad times ahead.'

CHAPTER 24

Revelation

'I don't like being used,' Holtzman said, leaning back with his hands clasped at the base of his neck.

He sat in the conference room with his Managing Editor, another long-term Washington-watcher who'd won his spurs in the feeding frenzy that had ended the presidency of Richard Nixon. Those had been heady times. It had given the entire American media a taste for blood that had never gone away. The only good part about it, Holtzman thought, was that they didn't cozy up to anyone now. Any politician was a potential target for the righteous wrath of America's investigatorial priesthood. The fact of it was healthy, though the extent of it occasionally was not.

'That's beside the point. Who does? So, what do we know is true?' the editor asked.

'We have to believe her that the White House isn't getting good data. That's nothing new at CIA, though it's not as bad as it used to be. The fact of the matter is that Agency performance has improved somewhat — well, there is the problem that Cabot has lopped off a lot of heads. We also have to believe what she says about Narmonov and his military.'

'And Ryan?'

'I've met him at social functions, never officially. He's actually a fairly nice guy, good sense of humor. He must have a hell of a record. Two Intelligence Stars — what for, we do not know. He fought Cabot on downsizing the Operations Directorate, evidently saved a few jobs. He's moved up very fast. Al Trent likes him, despite that run-in they had a few years ago. There's gotta be a story in that, but Trent flatly refused to discuss it the only time I asked him. Supposedly they kissed and made up, and I believe that like I believe in the Easter Bunny.'

'Is he the sort to play around?' the editor asked next.

'What sort is that? You expect they're issued a scarlet "A" for their shirts?'

'Very clever, Bob. So, what the hell are you asking me?'

'Do we run a story on this or not?'

The editor's eyes widened in surprise. 'Are you kidding? How can we *not* run a story on this?'

'I just don't like being used.'

'We've been through that! I don't, either. Granted that it's obvious in this case, but it's still an important story, and if we don't run it, then the *Times* will. How soon will you have it ready?'

'Soon,' Holtzman promised. Now he knew why he'd declined a promotion to Assistant Managing Editor. He didn't need the money, his book income absolved him of the necessity of working at all. He liked being a journalist, still had his idealism, still cared about what he did. It was a further blessing, he thought, that he was absolved of the necessity of making executive decisions.

The new feed-water pump was everything the Master Shipwright had promised on the installation side, Captain Dubinin noted. They'd practically had to dismantle a whole compartment to get it in, plus torch a hole through the submarine's double hull. He could still look up and see sky through what should have been a curved steel overhead, something very unnerving indeed for a submarine officer. They had to make sure that the pump worked satisfactorily before they welded shut the 'soft patch' through which it had arrived. It could have been worse. This submarine had a steel hull. Those Soviet submarines made of titanium were the devil to weld shut.

The pump/steam-generator room was immediately aft of the reactor compartment. In fact the reactor vessel abutted the bulkhead on the forward side, and the pump assembly on the after side. The pump circulated water in and out of the reactor. The saturated steam went into the steam-generator, where it ran through an interface. There its heat caused water in the 'outside' or non-radioactive loop to flash to steam, which then turned the submarine turbine engines (in turn driving the propeller through reduction gears). The 'inner loop' steam, with most of its energy lost, then ran through a condenser that was cooled by seawater from outside the hull, and was pumped as water back into the bottom of the reactor vessel for reheating to continue the cycle. The steam-generator and condenser were actually the same large structure, and the same multi-stage pump handled all of the circulation. This one mechanical object was the acoustical Achilles heel of all nuclear-powered ships. The pump had to exchange vast quantities of water that was 'hot' both thermally and radioactively. Doing that much mechanical work had always meant making a large amount of noise. Until now.

'It's an ingenious design,' Dubinin said.

'It should be. The Americans spent ten years perfecting it for their missile submarines, then decided not to use it. The design team was crushed.'

The captain grunted. The new American reactor designs were able to use natural convection-circulation. One more technical advantage. They were so damnably clever. As both men waited, the reactor was powering up. Control rods were being withdrawn, and free neutrons from the fuel elements were beginning to interact, starting a controlled nuclear chain-reaction. At the control panel behind the captain and the Admiral, technicians called off temperature readings in degrees Kelvin, which started at absolute zero and used Celsius measurements.

'Any time now . . .' the Master Shipwright breathed.

'You've never seen it in operation?' Dubinin asked.

'No.'

Marvelous, the captain thought, looking up at the sky. *What a horrible thing to see from inside a submarine* . . . 'What was that?'

'The pump just kicked in.'

'You're joking.' He looked at the massive, multi-barrel assembly. He couldn't – Dubinin walked over to the instrument panel and –

Dubinin laughed out loud.

'It works, Captain,' the chief engineer said.

'Keep running up the power,' Dubinin said.

'Ten percent now, and rising.'

'Take it all the way to one-ten.'

'Captain . . .'

'I know, we never go over a hundred.' The reactor was rated for fifty thousand horsepower, but like most such machines, the maximum power rating was conservative. It had been run at nearly fifty-eight thousand – once, on builder's trials, resulting in minor damage to the steam generator's internal plumbing – and the maximum useful power was fifty-four-point-nine-six. Dubinin had only done that once, soon after taking command. It was something a ship's commander did, just as a fighter pilot must find out at least one time how fast he can make his aircraft lance through the air.

'Very well,' the engineer agreed.

'Keep a close eye on things, Ivan Stepanovich. If you see any problems, shut down at once.' Dubinin patted him on the shoulder and walked back to the front of the compartment, hoping the welders had done their jobs properly. He shrugged at the thought. The welds had all been X-rayed for possible faults. You couldn't worry about everything, and he had a fine chief engineer to keep an eye on things.

'Twenty percent power.'

The Master Shipwright looked around. The pump had also been mounted on its own small raft structure, essentially a table with spring-loaded legs. They largely prevented transmission of whatever noise the pump generated into the hull, and from there into the water. That, he thought, had been poorly designed. Well, there were always things to be done better. Building ships was one of the last true engineering art forms.

'Twenty-five.'

'I can hear something now,' Dubinin said.

'Speed equivalent?'

'With normal hotel load –' that meant the power required to operate various ship's systems ranging from air conditioning to reading lights '– ten knots.' The Akula class required a great deal of electric power for her internal systems. That was due mainly to the primitive air-conditioning systems, which alone ate up ten percent of reactor output. 'We need seventeen percent power for hotel loadings before we start turning the screw. Western systems are much more efficient.'

The Master Shipwright nodded grumpily. 'They have a vast industry concerned with environmental engineering. We do not have the infrastructure to do the proper research yet.'

'They have a much hotter climate. I was in Washington once, in July. Hell could scarcely be worse.'

'That bad?'

'The embassy chap who took me around said it was once a malarial swamp. They've even had Yellow Fever epidemics there. Miserable climate.'

'I didn't know that.'

'Thirty percent,' the engineer called.

'When were you there?' the Admiral asked.

'Over ten years ago, for the Incidents at Sea negotiations. My first and last diplomatic adventure. Some headquarters fool thought they needed a submariner. I was drafted out of Frunze for it. Total waste of time,' Dubinin added.

'How was it?'

'Dull. The American submarine types are arrogant. Not very friendly back then.' Dubinin paused. 'No, that's not fair. The political climate was very different. The hospitality was cordial, but reserved. They took us to a baseball game.'

'And?' the Admiral asked.

The captain smiled. 'The food and beer were enjoyable. The game was incomprehensible, and their explanations just made things worse.'

'Forty percent.'

'Twelve knots,' Dubinin said. 'The noise is picking up...'

'But?'

'But it's a fraction of what the old pump put out. My men have to wear ear protection in here. At full speed the noise is terrible.'

'We'll see. Did you learn anything interesting in Washington?'

Another grunt. 'Not to walk the streets alone. I went out for a stroll and saw some poor woman attacked by a street hooligan, and, you know, that was only a few blocks from the White House!'

'Really?'

'The young crook tried to run right past me with her purse. Like something from a film. It was quite amazing.'

'Tried to?'

'Did I ever tell you I was a good football player? I tackled him, a little too enthusiastically. Broke his kneecap, as a matter of fact.' Dubinin smiled, remembering the injury he'd inflicted on the worthless bastard. Concrete sidewalks were so much harder than a grassy football pitch...

'Fifty percent.'

'Then what happened?'

'The embassy people went mad about it. The ambassador screamed a lot. Thought they'd send me right home. But the local police talked about giving me a medal. It was hushed up, and I was never asked to be a diplomat again.' Dubinin laughed out loud. 'I won. Eighteen knots.'

'Why did you interfere?'

'I was young and foolish,' Dubinin explained. 'Never occurred to me that it might all be some CIA trick — that's what the ambassador was worried about. It wasn't, just a young criminal and a frail black woman. His kneecap shattered quite badly. I wonder how well he runs now...? And if he really were CIA, that's one less spy we have to worry about.'

'Sixty percent power, still very steady,' the engineer called. 'No pressure fluctuations at all.'

'Twenty-three knots. The next forty percent power doesn't do very much for us . . . and the flow noise off the hull starts building up at this point. Run it up smartly, Vanya!'

'Aye, Captain!'

'What's the fastest you've ever had him?'

'Thirty-two at max-rated power. Thirty-three on overload.'

'There's talk about a new hull paint . . .'

'The stuff the English invented? Intelligence says it adds more than a knot to the American hunter submarines.'

'That's right,' the Admiral confirmed. 'I hear we have the formula, but actually making it is very difficult, and applying it properly is even more so.'

'Anything over twenty-five and you run the risk of stripping the anechoic tiles off the hull. Had that happen once when I was *Starpom* on the *Sverdlovskiy Komsomolets* . . .' Dubinin shook his head. 'Like being inside a drum, the way those damned rubber slabs pounded the hull.'

'Not much we can do about that, I'm afraid.'

'Seventy-five percent power.'

'Take those tiles off and I get another knot.'

'You don't really advocate that?'

Dubinin shook his head. 'No. If a torpedo goes into the water, that could be the difference between life and death.'

Conversation stopped at that point. In ten minutes, power had reached a hundred percent, fifty-thousand horsepower. The pump noise was quite loud now, but it was still possible to hear a person speaking. With the old pump this power level was like listening to a rock band, Dubinin remembered, you could feel the sound rippling through your body. Not now, and the rafting of the pump body . . . the yard commander had promised him a vast reduction in radiated noise. He had not been boasting. Ten minutes later, he'd seen and heard everything he'd needed.

'Power down,' Dubinin commanded.

'Well, Valentin Borissovich?'

'KGB stole this from the Americans?'

'That is my understanding,' the Admiral said.

'I may kiss the next spy I meet.'

The motor vessel *George McReady* lay alongside the pier loading cargo. She was a large ship, ten years old, driven by large, low-speed marine diesels, and designed as a timber carrier. She could carry thirty thousand tons of finished lumber or, as was the case now, logs. The Japanese preferred to process the lumber themselves for the most part. It kept the processing money in their country instead of having to export it. At least an American-flag vessel was being used to do the delivery, a concession that had required ten months of negotiations. Japan could be a fun place to visit, though rather expensive.

Under the watchful eyes of the First Officer, gantry cranes lifted the logs from trucks and lowered them into the built-for-the-purpose holds. The process was remarkably speedy. Automation of cargo-loading was probably the most important development in the commercial shipping business. *George M* could be fully loaded in less than forty hours, and off-loaded in thirty-six, allowing the ship to return to sea very rapidly, but denying her crew the chance to do very much in whatever port they might be visiting. The loss of income for waterfront bars and other businesses that catered to sailors was not a matter of great concern to the shipowners, who did not make money when their hulls were tied alongside the pier.

'Pete, got the weather,' the Third Officer announced. 'Could be better.'

The First Officer looked at the chart. 'Wow!'

'Yeah, a monster Siberian low forming up. Gonna get bumpy a couple of days out. It's gonna be too big to dodge, too.'

The First Officer whistled at the numbers. 'Don't forget your 'scope patch, Jimmy.'

'Right. How much deck cargo?'

'Just those boys over there.' He pointed.

The other man grunted, then picked up a pair of binoculars from the holder. 'Christ, they're chained together!'

'That's why we can't strike 'em below.'

'Outstanding,' the junior man observed.

'I already talked to the bosun about it. We'll have them tied down nice and tight.'

'Good idea, Pete. If this storm builds like I expect, you'll be able to surf down there.'

'Captain still on the beach?'

'Right, he's due back at fourteen hundred.'

'Fueling complete. ChEng will have his diesels on line at seventeen hundred. Depart at sixteen-thirty?'

'That's right.'

'Damn, a guy hardly has time to get laid anymore.'

'I'll tell the captain about the weather forecast. It might make us late in Japan.'

'Cap'n'll love that.'

'Won't we all?'

'Hey, if it screws up our alongside time, maybe I can . . .'

'You and me both, buddy.' The First Officer grinned. Both men were single.

'Beautiful, isn't it?' Fromm asked. He leaned down, staring at the metallic mass through the Lexan sheeting. The manipulator arm had detached the plutonium from the spindle and moved it for a visual inspection that wasn't really necessary, but the plutonium had to be moved for the next part of the finishing process anyway, and Fromm wanted to see the thing close up. He shone a small, powerful flashlight on the metal, but then switched it off. The reflection of the overhead lights was enough.

'It really is amazing,' Ghosn said.

What they looked at might easily have been a piece of blown glass, so smooth it appeared. In fact it was far smoother than that. The uniformity of the outside surface was so exact that the greatest distorting effect came from gravity. Whatever imperfections there might have been were far too small to see with the naked eye, and were definitely below the design tolerances Fromm had established when he'd worked the hydrocodes on the minicomputer.

The outside of the folded cylinder was perfect, reflecting light like some sort of eccentric lens. As the arm rotated it around the long axis, the placement and size of the reflected ceiling lights did not move or waver. Even the German found that remarkable.

'I would never have believed we could do so well,' Ghosn said.

Fromm nodded. 'Such things were not possible until quite recently. The air-bearing-lathe technology is hardly fifteen years old, and the laser-control systems are newer still. The main commercial application is still for ultra-fine instruments like astronomical telescopes, very high-quality lenses, special centrifuge parts . . .' The German stood. 'Now, we must also polish the inside surfaces. Those we cannot visually inspect.'

'Why do the outside first?'

'This way we can be sure that the machine is performing properly. The laser will control the inside – we know now, you see, that it is giving us good data.' That explanation wasn't really true, but Fromm didn't want to give the real one: he truly thought this beautiful. The young Arab might not understand. *Das ist die schwarze Kunst* . . . It actually *was* rather Faustian, Fromm thought, wasn't it?

How very strange, Ghosn thought, *that something so wonderfully shaped could* . . .

'Things continue to go well.'

'Indeed,' Fromm replied. He gestured to the interior of the enclosure. When run properly, the lathe trimmed off something almost like metallic thread, but thinner, visible mainly because of its reflectivity. A singularly valuable thread, it was collected for remelting and possible future use.

'A good stopping place,' Fromm said, turning away.

'I agree.' They'd been at it for fourteen hours. Ghosn dismissed the men. He and Fromm walked out, too, leaving the room to the custody of the two security guards.

The guards were not highly educated men. Selected from the Commander's personal retinue of followers, each was the veteran of many years of combat operations. Perversely, their fighting had been more against fellow Arabs than their putative Zionist enemies. There was a plethora of terrorist groups, and since each drew its support from the Palestinian community, there was competition for the limited pool of followers. Competition among men with guns not infrequently led to confrontation and death. In the case of the guards, it also proved their loyalty. Each of the men on duty was an expert shot, about good enough to be on a par with the new American addition to the organization, the infidel Russell.

One of the guards, Achmed, lit up a cigarette and leaned against the wall. He faced yet another boring night. Walking guard on the outside, or patrolling the block on which Qati slept, at least gave them a variety of things to observe. One might imagine that there was an Israeli agent behind every parked car or behind every window, and such thoughts kept one awake and alert. Not here. Here they guarded machines that sat dumbly still. For diversion, and also in keeping with their duties, the guards kept an eye on the machinists, following them around the room, to and from their eating and sleeping spaces, and even on some of their less complicated jobs. Though not well-educated, Achmed was a bright man, quick to learn, and he fancied that he could have done any of these machinist jobs, given a few months to learn the trade properly. He was very good with weapons, able to diagnose a problem or fix an improper sight as quickly and well as a master gunsmith.

As he walked around, he listened to the drone of the blowers for the various air systems, and on each circuit he looked at the instrument panels that reported their status. The panels also monitored the backup generators, making sure each night that there was sufficient fuel in the tanks.

'They are awfully worried about the schedule, aren't

they?' Achmed mused. He continued his walk around, hoping the indicator light would blink off. He and his companion stopped to look at the same metallic bar that had so interested Fromm and Ghosn.

'What do you suppose that is?'

'Something wondrous,' Achmed said. 'Certainly they are keeping it as secret as they can.'

'I think it's part of an atomic bomb.'

Achmed turned. 'Why do you say that?'

'One of the machinists said it could be nothing else.'

'Wouldn't that be something to give to our Israeli friends?'

'After all the Arabs who've died in the last few years – the Israelis, the Americans, all the rest ... Yes, it would be a fine gift.' They continued their walk past the idle machines. 'I wonder what the rush is?'

'Whatever it is, they want it finished on time.' Achmed paused again, looking at the plethora of metal and plastic parts on the assembly table. An atomic bomb? he asked himself. But some of these things looked like ... like soda straws, long, thin ones, wrapped in tight bundles and twisted slightly ... Soda straws – in an atomic bomb? That was not possible. An atomic bomb had to be ... what? He admitted to himself that he had no idea at all. Well, he was able to read the Koran, and the newspapers, and weapons manuals. It wasn't his fault he hadn't had the chance to have proper schooling like Ghosn, whom he liked in a distant and slightly jealous way. Such a fine thing, an education. If only his own father had been something more than a displaced peasant, a shopowner, perhaps, someone able to save a little money ...

On his next circuit, he saw the – paint can? That's what it looked like. The metal shavings from the lathe were collected from the Freon sump. Achmed had seen the process often enough. The scrap – it looked mainly like very fine metallic thread – was collected mechanically and loaded into the container, which did look very much like a paint can, using a window and thick rubber gloves. The can was then placed into a double-door chamber and removed, taken to the next room, and opened in another similar chamber and put into one of those odd crucibles.

'I'm going outside for a piss,' his companion said.

'Enjoy the fresh air,' Achmed observed.

Achmed slung his weapon and watched his friend go out the double doors. He'd take a stroll soon himself, when it was time to check the perimeter security. He was the senior man, and was responsible for the outside guards, in addition to the security of the shop itself. It was worth it just to get out of the controlled environment of the machine shop. This was no way for a man to live, Achmed thought, stuck inside a sealed enclosure like a space station or submarine. He craved an education, but not to be an office worker, sitting down all the time and staring at papers. No, to be an engineer, the sort who built roads and bridges, that was an ambition he might once have held. Perhaps his son would be one, if he ever had the chance to marry and have a son. Something to dream for. His dreams were more limited now. For this to end, to be able to set his gun down, to have a real life, that was his primary dream.

But the Zionists had to die first.

Achmed stood alone in the room, bored to death. At least the outside guards could look at the stars. Something to do, something to do . . .

The paint can sat there, inside the enclosure. It appeared to be ready for the transfer. He'd watched the machinists do it often enough. What the hell. Achmed removed the can from the air lock and walked it into the furnace room. They put it inside the electric furnace, and . . . it was simple enough, and he was glad to be able to do something different, maybe something helpful to whatever project this was.

The can was light, might only have held air for all he could tell. Was it empty? The top was held on with clamps, and . . . no, he decided. He'd just do what the machinists did. Achmed walked to the furnace, opened the door, checked to see that the power was off – this thing got *hot*, he knew. It melted metal! Next he put on the thick rubber gloves they used and, forgetting to switch on the argon-flooding system, loosened the clamps on the can. He rotated the can backwards so that he could see what it looked like. He saw.

As he removed the top, the oxygen-laden air entered the can and attacked the plutonium filaments, some of which reacted at once, essentially exploding in his face. There was a flash, as though from a rifle primer, just a tiny puff of heat and light, certainly nothing to endanger a man, he knew at once. Not even any smoke that he noticed immediately, though he did sneeze once.

Despite that, Achmed was seized with terror. He'd done something he ought not to have done. What would the Commander think of him? What might the Commander do *to* him? He listened to the air-conditioning system, and thought he saw a puff of thin smoke rising into the exhaust vent. That was good. The electric dust-collector plates would take care of that. All he had to do . . .

Yes. He resealed the can and carried it back into the machine shop. His fellow guard hadn't returned yet. Good. Achmed slid the can back where it had been and made sure that things looked as they had looked a few minutes earlier. He lit another cigarette to relax himself, vexed with himself that he was as yet unable to quit the habit. It was starting to impede his running.

Achmed didn't know that he was already a corpse whose death had not yet been registered, and that his cigarette might as easily have been the breath of life itself.

'I can do it,' Clark announced, striding through the door like John Wayne into the Alamo.

'Tell me about it,' Jack said, waving to a chair.

'I just got back from Dulles, talked to a few people. The JAL 747s set up for Trans-Pac flights are arranged very conveniently for us. The upstairs lounge is set up with beds, like an old Pullman car. It helps us. The room is very lively acoustically, and that makes for easy pickup.' He laid out a diagram. 'There's a table here and here. We use two wireless bugs, and four broadcast channels.'

'Explain,' Jack said.

'The wireless bugs are omnidirectional. Okay, they transmit to the SHF transmitter, and that one gets it out of the airplane.'

'Why four channels?'

'The big problem is cancelling out the airplane noise, the engine whine, the air, all that stuff. Two channels are interior sound. The other two are for background noise only. We use that to cancel out the crap. We have people down in S&T who have been working on that for quite a while. You use the recorded background noise to establish what the interference is, then just change its phase to cancel it out. Pretty simple stuff if you have the right computer backup equipment. We do. Okay? The transmitter goes in a bottle. We aim it out of the window. Easy to do, I checked. Now, we will need a chase plane.'

'Like what?'

'With the right equipment, a business jet like a Gulfstream, better yet an EC-135. I'd recommend more than one, have them form up and break off.'

'How far away?'

'As long as its line of sight . . . up to thirty miles, and doesn't have to be the same altitude. Not like we have to fly formation on the guy.'

'How hard to build it?'

'Simple. The hardest part is the battery, and that'll fit in a liquor bottle, like I said. We'll make it a brand that you usually find in a duty-free store – I have a guy checking that – one with a ceramic bottle 'stead of a glass one. Like an expensive bottle of Chivas, maybe. The Japanese like their scotch.'

'Detection?' Ryan asked.

Clark grinned like a teenager who'd just snookered a teacher. 'We build the system exclusively from Japanese components, *and* we place a receiver tuned to the right freqs in the aircraft. He'll be traveling with the usual mob of newsies. I'll set a receiver in the waste bin of one of the downstairs heads. If the op gets burned, they'll think it was one of their own. It'll even look like a journalist did it.'

Ryan nodded. 'Nice touch, John.'

'I thought you'd like that. When the bird lands, we have a guy recover the bottle. We'll fix it – I mean, we'll see to it that you can't get the cork out. Superglue, maybe.'

'Getting aboard in Mexico City?'

'I have Ding looking at that. Time he got a taste of planning operations, and this is the soft side. My Spanish is good enough to fool a Mexican national.'

'Back to the bugging equipment. We won't be reading this in real-time?'

'No way.' Clark shook his head. 'What'll come across will be garbled, but we'll use high-speed tape machines to record, then we can wash it through the 'puters downstairs to get clean copy. It's an additional operational safeguard. The guys in the chase birds won't know what they're listening to, and only the drivers need to know who they're shadowing ... maybe not even that, as a matter of fact. I have to check on that.'

'How long to produce clean copy?'

'Have to do it at this end ... say a couple of hours. That's what the S&T guys say, anyway. You know the real beauty of this?'

'Tell me.'

'Airplanes are about the last place you can't bug. Our S&T guys have been playing with it for a long time. What made the breakthrough came from the Navy – very black project. Nobody knows we can do this. The computer codes are very complex. Lots of people are playing with it, but the actual breakthrough is on the theoretical side of the math. Came from a guy at NSA. I repeat, Sir John, nobody knows this is possible. Their security guys will be asleep. If they find the bug, they'll think it's an amateur attempt to do something. The receiver I put aboard won't actually recover anything usable to anyone but us –'

'And we'll have a guy recover that also, to back up the aerial transmissions.'

'That's right. So we have double-redundancy – or triple, I never have figured what the right terminology is. Three separate channels for the information, one in the plane, and two being beamed out from it.'

Ryan raised his coffee mug in salute. 'Okay, now that the technical side looks possible, I want an operational feasibility evaluation.'

'You got it, Jack. Goddamn! It's good to be a real spy again. With all due respect, watching out for your ass does not test my abilities all that much.'

'I love you, too, John.' Ryan laughed. It was his first in too long a time. If they could pull this one off, maybe that Elliot bitch would get off his back for once. Maybe the President would understand that field operations with real live field officers were still useful. It would be a small victory.

CHAPTER 25

Resolution

'So, what's the story on the things?' the Second Officer asked, looking down at the cargo deck.

'Supposed to be the roof beams for a temple. Small one, I guess,' the First Officer noted. 'How much more will these seas build . . . ?'

'I wish we could slow down, Pete.'

'I've talked to him twice about it. Captain says he has a schedule to meet.'

'Tell that to the fuckin' ocean.'

'Haven't tried that. Who do you call?'

The Second Officer, who had the watch, snorted. The First Officer – the ship's second in command – was on the bridge to keep an eye on things. That was actually the captain's job, but the ship's Master was asleep in his bed.

MV *George McReady* was pounding through thirty-foot waves, trying to maintain twenty knots, but failing, despite full cruising power on her engines. The sky was overcast, with occasional breaks in the clouds for the full moon to peek through. The storm was actually breaking up, but the wind was holding steady at sixty knots and the seas were still increasing somewhat. It was a typical North Pacific storm, both officers had already decided. Nothing about it made any sense. The air temperature was a balmy ten degrees Fahrenheit, and the flying spray was freezing to ice that impacted the bridge windows like birdshot in duck season. The only good news was that the seas were right on the bow. *George M* was a freighter, not a cruise liner, and lacked anti-roll stabilizers. In fact, the ride wasn't bad at all. The superstructure was set on the after portion of the ship, and that damped out most of the pitching motion associated with heavy seas. It also had the effect of reducing the officers' awareness of events at the forward end of the ship, a fact further accentuated by the reduced visibility from flying spray.

The ride also had a few interesting characteristics. When the bow plowed into an especially high wave, the ship slowed down. But the size of the ship meant that the bow slowed quicker than the stern, and as the deceleration forces fought to reduce the ship's speed, the hull rebelled by shuddering. In fact, the hull actually bent a few inches, something difficult to believe until it was seen.

'I served on a carrier once. They flex more than a foot in the middle. Once we were –'

'Look dead ahead, sir!' the helmsman called.

'Oh shit!' the Second Officer shouted. 'Rogue wave!'

Suddenly there it was, a fifty footer just a hundred yards from the *George M*'s blunt bow. The event was not unexpected. Two waves would meet and add their heights for a few moments, then diverge . . . The bow rose on the medium-size crest, then dropped before the onrushing green wall.

'Here we go!'

There wasn't time for the bow to climb over this one. The green water simply stepped over the bow as though it had never been there and kept rolling aft the five hundred feet to the superstructure. Both officers watched in detached fascination. There was no real danger to the ship – at least, they both told themselves, no immediate danger. The solid green mass came past the heavy cargo-handling masts and equipment, advancing at a speed of thirty miles per hour. The ship was already shuddering again, the bow having hit the lower portion of the wave, slowing the ship. In fact, the bow was still under water, since this wave was far broader than it was high, but the top portion was about to hit a white-painted steel cliff that was perpendicular to its axis of advance.

'Brace!' the Second Officer told the helmsman.

The crest of the wave didn't quite make the level of the bridge, but it did hit the windows of the senior officers' cabins. Instantly, there was a white vertical curtain of spray that blotted out the entire world. The single second it lasted seemed to stretch into a minute, then it cleared, and the ship's deck was exactly where it was supposed to be, though covered with seawater that was struggling to drain out the scuppers. *George M* took a fifteen-degree roll, then settled back down.

'Drop speed to sixteen knots, my authority,' the First Officer said.

'Aye,' the helmsman acknowledged.

'We're not going to break this ship while I'm on the bridge,' the senior officer announced.

'Makes sense to me, Pete.' The Second Officer was on his way to the trouble board, looking for an indicator light for flooding or other problems. The board was clear. The ship was designed to handle seas far worse than this, but safety at sea demanded vigilance. 'Okay here, Pete.'

The growler phone rang. 'Bridge, First Officer here.'

'What the hell was that?' the Chief Engineer demanded.

'Well, it was sorta a big wave, ChEng,' Pete answered laconically. 'Any problems?'

'No kidding. It really clobbered the forward bulkhead. I thought I was gonna eat my window – looks like a porthole is cracked. I really think we might want to slow down some. I hate getting wet in bed, y'know?'

'I already ordered that.'

'Good.' The line clicked off.

'What gives?' It was the Captain in pajamas and bathrobe. He managed to see the last of the seawater draining off the main deck.

'Fifty-sixty-footer. I've dropped speed to sixteen. Twenty's too much for the conditions.'

'Guess you're right,' the Captain grumbled. Every extra hour alongside the dock meant fifteen thousand dollars, and the owners did not like extra expenses. 'Build it back up soon as you can.' The captain withdrew before his bare feet got too cold.

'Will do,' Pete told the empty doorway.

'Speed fifteen point eight,' the helmsman reported.

'Very well.' Both officers settled back down and sipped at their coffee. It wasn't really frightening, just somewhat exciting, and the moonlit spray flying off the bow was actually rather beautiful to see. The First Officer looked down at the deck. It took a moment for him to realize.

'Hit the lights.'

'What's the problem?' The Second Officer moved two steps to the panel and flipped on the deck floods.

'Well, we still have one of them.'

'One of –' the junior officer looked down. 'Oh. The other three . . .'

The First Officer shook his head. How could you describe the power of mere water? 'That's strong chain, too, the wave snapped it like yarn. Impressive.'

The Second Officer picked up the phone and punched a button. 'Bosun, our deck cargo just got swept over the side. I need a damage check on the front of the superstructure.' He didn't have to say that the check should be done from inside the structure.

An hour later, it was clear that they'd been lucky. The single strike from the deck cargo had landed right on a portion of the superstructure backed by sturdy steel beams. Damage was minor, some welding and painting to be done. That didn't change the fact that someone would have to cut down a new tree. Three of the four logs were gone, and that Japanese temple would have to wait.

The three logs, still chained together, were already well aft of the *George M.* They were still green, and started soaking up sea water, making them heavier still.

Cathy Ryan watched her husband's car pull out of the driveway. She was now past the stage of feeling bad for him. Now she was hurt. He wouldn't talk about it – that is, he didn't try to explain himself, didn't apologize, tried to pretend that . . . what? And then part of the time he said he didn't feel well, was too tired. Cathy wanted to talk it over, but didn't know how to begin. The male ego was a fragile thing, Dr Caroline Ryan knew, and this had to be its most fragile spot. It had to be a combination of stress and fatigue and booze. Jack wasn't a machine. He was wearing down. She'd seen the symptoms months earlier. As much the commute as anything else. Two and a half, sometimes three hours every day in the car. The fact that he had a driver was something, but not much. Three more hours a day that he was away, thinking, working, not home where he belonged.

Am I helping or hurting? she asked herself. *Is part of it my fault?*

Cathy walked into the bathroom and looked at herself in the mirror. Okay, she wasn't a pink-cheeked kid anymore. There were worry lines around her mouth and squint lines around her eyes. She should have her spectacle prescription looked at. She was starting to get headaches during procedures, and she knew it could be a problem with her eyes – she was, after all, an ophthalmic surgeon – but like everyone else she was short of time and was putting off having her eyes looked at by another member of the Wilmer Eye Institute staff. Which was pretty dumb, she admitted to herself. She still had rather pretty eyes. At least the color didn't change, even though their refractive error might suffer from all the close work that her job mandated.

She was still quite slim. Wouldn't hurt to sweat off three or four pounds – better yet, to transfer that weight into her breasts. She was a small-breasted woman from a small-breasted family in a world that rewarded women for having udders to rival Elsie the Borden cow. Her usual joke that bust size was inversely proportional to brain size was a defense mechanism. She craved larger ones as a man always wanted a larger penis, but God or the gene pool had not chosen to give her those, and she would *not* submit to the vain ignominy of surgery – besides which she didn't like the numbers on that kind of surgery. Too many silicon implant cases developed complications.

The rest of her ... her hair, of course, was always a mess, but surgical discipline absolutely prevented her from paying great attention to that. It was still blonde and short and very fine, and when Jack took the time to notice, he liked her hair. Her face was still pretty, despite the squint lines and worry lines. Her legs had always been pretty nice, and with all the walking she did at Hopkins/Wilmer, they had actually firmed up slightly. Cathy concluded that her looks were not the sort to make dogs bark when she passed. She was, in fact, still rather attractive. At least the other docs at the hospital thought so. Some of her senior medical students positively swooned over her, she liked to think. Certainly no one fought to escape her rounds.

She was also a good mother. Though Sally and Little Jack were still asleep, she never failed to look after them. Especially with Jack gone so much, Cathy filled in, even to the point of playing catch with her son during T-ball season (that was something that made her husband uncomfortably guilty whenever he learned of it). She cooked good meals when she had the time. Whatever the house needed, she either did herself or 'contracted out' – Jack's phrase – to others.

She still loved her husband, and she let him know it. She had a good sense of humor, Cathy thought. She didn't let most things bother her. She never failed to touch Jack whenever the opportunity presented itself; she was a doctor, with a delicate touch. She talked to him, asked what he thought of something or other, let him know that she cared about him, cared about his opinions on things. There could be no doubt in his mind that he was still her man in every way. In fact, she loved him in every way a wife could. Cathy concluded that she wasn't doing anything wrong.

So, why didn't he – couldn't he . . . ?

The face in the mirror was more puzzled than hurt, she thought. *What else can I do!* she asked it.

Nothing.

Cathy tried to set that aside. A new day was beginning. She had to get the kids ready for school. That meant setting breakfast up before they awoke. This part of life wasn't fair, of course. She was a surgeon, a professor of surgery, as a matter of fact, but the simple facts of life also said she was a mother, with mother's duties that her husband did not share, at least not on the early morning of a work day. So much for women's lib. She got into her robe and walked down to the kitchen. It could have been worse. Both kids liked oatmeal, and actually preferred the flavored instant kind. She boiled the water for it, then turned the range to low heat while she walked back to wake the little ones up. Ten minutes later, Sally and Little Jack were washed and dressed on their way to the kitchen. Sally arrived first, setting the TV to the Disney Channel in time for Mousercise. Cathy took her ten minutes of peace to look at the morning paper and drink her coffee.

On the bottom right-hand side of the front page was an article about Russia. *Well, maybe that's one of the things that's bothering Jack.* She decided to read it. Maybe she could talk to him, find out why he was so . . . distracted? Was it just that, maybe?

'. . . disappointed with the ability of CIA to deliver data on the problem. There are further rumors of an underway investigation. An administration official confirms the rumors that a senior CIA official is suspected of financial misconduct and also of sexual improprieties. The name of this official has not been revealed, but he is reportedly very senior and responsible for coordinating information for the administration . . .'

Sexual improprieties! What did that mean? Who was it?

He.

Very senior and responsible for . . .

That was Jack. That was her husband. That was the phrase they used for someone at his level. In a quiet moment of total clarity, she knew that it had to be.

Jack . . . playing around? My Jack!

It wasn't possible.

Was it?

His inability to perform, his tiredness, the drinking, the distraction? Was it possible that the reason he didn't . . . someone else was exciting him?

It wasn't possible. Not Jack. Not her Jack.

But why else . . . ? She was still attractive – everyone thought so. She was still a good wife – there was no doubt of that? Jack wasn't ill. She would have caught any gross symptoms; she was a doctor, and a good one, and she knew she would not have missed anything important. She went out of her way to be nice to Jack, to talk to him, to let him know that she loved him, and . . .

Perhaps it wasn't *likely*, but was it *possible*?

Yes.

No. Cathy set the paper down and sipped at her coffee. Not possible. Not her Jack.

It was the last hour of the last leg in the manufacturing process. Ghosn and Fromm watched the lathe with what looked like detachment, but was in both cases barely controlled excitement. The Freon liquid being sprayed on the rotating metal prevented their seeing the product whose final manufacture was underway. That didn't help, even though both knew that seeing would not have helped in the least. The part of the plutonium mass being machined was hidden from their sight by other metal, and even if *that* had been otherwise, they both knew that their eyes were too coarse an instrument to detect imperfections. Both watched the machine read-out of the computer systems. Tolerances indicated by the machine were well within the twelve angstroms specified by Herr Doktor Fromm. They had to believe the computer, didn't they?

'Just a few more centimeters,' Ghosn said, as Bock and Qati joined them.

'You've never explained the Secondary part of the unit,' the Commander said. He'd taken to calling the bomb 'the unit'.

Fromm turned, not really grateful for the distraction, though he knew he should be. 'What do you wish to know?'

'I understand how the Primary works, but not the Secondary,' Qati said, simply and reasonably.

'Very well. The theoretical side of this is quite straightforward, once you understand the principle. That was the difficult part, you see, discovering the principle. It was thought at first that making the Secondary work was simply a matter of temperature – that is what distinguishes the center of a star, *ja*? Actually it is not, the first theoreticians overlooked the matter of pressure. That is rather strange in retrospect, but pioneering work is often that way. The key to making the Secondary work is managing the energy in such a way as to convert energy into pressure at the same time as you use its vast heat, and also to change its direction by ninety degrees. That is no small task when you are talking about redirecting seventy kilotons of energy,' Fromm said smugly. 'However, the belief that to make Secondary function is a matter of great theoretical difficulty, that is a fiction. The real insight Ulam and Teller had was a simple one, as most great insights are. Pressure *is* temperature. What they discovered – the secret – is that there is no secret. Once you understand the principles involved, what remains is just a question of engineering. Making the bomb work is computationally, not technically, demanding. The difficult part is to make the weapon portable. That is pure engineering,' Fromm said again.

'Soda straws?' Bock asked, knowing that his countryman wanted to be asked about that. He was a smug bastard.

'I cannot know for sure, but I believe this to be my personal innovation. The material is perfect. It is light, it is hollow, and it is easily twisted into the proper configuration.' Fromm walked over to the assembly table and returned with one. 'The base material is polyethylene, and as you see, we have coated the outside with copper and the inside with rhodium. The length of the "straw" is sixty centimeters, and the inside diameter is just under three millimeters. Many thousands of them surround the Secondary, in bundles twisted one hundred eighty degrees into a geometric shape called a helix. A helix is a useful shape. It can direct energy while retaining its ability to radiate heat in all directions.'

Inside every engineer, Qati thought, was a frustrated teacher. 'But what do they do?'

'*Also*, the first emission off the Primary is massive gamma radiation. Just behind that are the X-rays. In both cases, we are talking about high-energy photons, quantum particles which carry energy but which have no mass –'

'Light waves,' Bock said, remembering his *Gymnasium* physics. Fromm nodded.

'Correct. Extremely energetic light waves of a different – higher – frequency. Now, we have this vast amount of energy radiating from the Primary. Some we can reflect or warp towards the Secondary by use of the channels we have built. Most is lost, of course, but the fact is that we will have so much energy at our fingertips that we need only a small fraction of it. The X-rays sweep down the straws. Much of their energy is absorbed by the metallic coatings, while the oblique surfaces reflect some further down, allowing further energy absorption. The polyethylene also absorbs a good deal of energy. And what do you suppose happens?'

'Absorb that much energy, and it must explode, of course,' Bock said, before Qati could.

'Very good, Herr Bock. When the straws explode – actually they convert into plasma, but having split straws, we will not split hairs, eh? – the plasma expands radially to their axes, thus converting the axial energy from the Primary into radial energy imploding on the Secondary.'

The lightbulb went on in Qati's head. 'Brilliant, but you lose half of the energy, that part expanding outward.'

'Yes and no. It still makes an energy barrier, and that is what we need. Next, the uranium fins around the body of the Secondary are also converted to plasma – from the same energy flux, but more slowly than the straws due to their mass. This plasma has far greater density, and is pressed inward. Within the actual Secondary casing, there is two centimeters of vacuum, since that space will be evacuated. So, we have a "running start" for the plasma that is racing inward.'

'So, you use the energy from the Primary, redirected into a right-angle turn to perform the same function on the Secondary that is first done by chemical explosives?' Qati saw.

'Excellent, Commander!' Fromm replied, just patronizingly enough to be noticed. 'We now have a relatively heavy mass of plasma pressing inward. The vacuum gap gives it room to accelerate before slamming into the Secondary. This compresses the Secondary. The secondary assembly is lithium-deuteride and lithium-hydride, both doped with tritium, surrounded by uranium 238. This assembly is crushed violently by the imploding plasma. It is also being bombarded by neutrons from the Primary, of course. The combination of heat, pressure, and neutron bombardment causes the lithium to fission into tritium. The tritium immediately begins the fusion process, generating vast quantities of high-energy neutrons along with the liberated energy. The neutrons attack the U238, causing a fast-fission reaction, adding to the overall Secondary yield.'

'The key, as Herr Fromm said,' Ghosn explained, 'is managing the energy.'

'Straws,' Bock noted.

'Yes, I said the same thing,' Ghosn said. 'It is truly brilliant. Like building a bridge from paper.'

'And the yield from the Secondary?' Qati asked. He didn't really understand the physics, but he did understand the final number.

'The Primary will generate approximately seventy kilotons. The Secondary will generate roughly four hundred sixty-five kilotons. The numbers are approximate because of possible irregularities within the weapon, and also because we cannot test to measure actual effects.'

'How confident are you in the performance of the weapon?'

'Totally,' Fromm said.

'But without testing, you said . . .'

'Commander, I knew from the beginning that a proper

test program was not possible. That is the same problem we had in the DDR. For that reason the design is over-engineered, in some cases by a factor of forty percent, in others by a factor of more than one hundred. You must understand that an American, British, French, or even Soviet weapon of the same yield would not be a fifth the size of our "unit." Such refinements of size and efficiency can only come from extensive testing. The physics of the device are entirely straightforward. Engineering refinements come only from practice. As Herr Ghosn said, building a bridge. The Roman bridges of antiquity were very inefficient structures. By modern standards they use far too much stone, and as a result far too much labor to build them, *ja*? Over the years we have learned to build bridges more efficiently, using fewer materials and less labor to perform the same task. But do not forget that some Roman bridges still stand. They are still bridges, even if they are inefficient. This bomb design, though inefficient and wasteful of materials, is still a bomb, and it *will* work as I say.'

Heads turned, as the beeper on the lathe went off. An indicator light blinked green. The task was finished. Fromm walked over, telling the technicians to flush the Freon out of the system. Five minutes later, the object of so much loving care was visible. The manipulator arm brought it into view. It was finished.

'Excellent,' Fromm said. 'We will carefully examine the plutonium, and then we will commence assembly. *Meine Herren*, the difficult part is behind us.' He thought that called for a beer, and made another mental note that he hadn't gotten the palladium yet. Details, details. But that's what engineering was.

'What gives, Dan?' Ryan asked, over his secure phone. He had missed the morning paper at home, only to find the offending article waiting on his desk as part of *The Bird*.

'It sure as hell didn't come from here, Jack. It must be in your house.'

'Well, I just tore our security director a brand-new asshole. He says he doesn't have anything going. What the hell does a "very senior" official mean?'

'It means that this Holtzman guy got carried away with his adjectives. Look, Jack, I've already gone too far. I'm not supposed to discuss on-going investigations, remember?'

'I'm not concerned about that. Somebody just leaked material that comes from a closely-held source. If the world made any sense, we'd bring Holtzman in for questioning!' Ryan snarled into the phone.

'You want to rein in a little, boy?'

The DDCI looked up from the phone and commanded himself to take a deep breath. It wasn't Holtzman's fault, was it? 'Okay, I just simmered down.'

'Whatever investigation is underway, it isn't the Bureau running it.'

'No shit?'

'You have my word on it,' Murray said.

'That's fair enough, Dan.' Ryan calmed down further. If it wasn't the FBI and it wasn't his own in-house security arm, then that part of the story was probably fiction.

'Who could have leaked it?'

Jack barked out a laugh. 'Could have? Ten or fifteen people on The Hill. Maybe five in the White House, twenty – maybe forty here.'

'So the other part could just be camouflage, or somebody who wants a score settled.' Murray did not make it a question. He figured at least a third of all press leaks were aimed at settling grudges in one way or another. 'The source is sensitive?'

'This phone isn't all that secure, remember?'

'Gotcha. Look, I can approach Holtzman quietly and informally. He's a good guy, responsible, a pro. We can talk to him off the record and let him know that he may be endangering people and methods.'

'I have to go to Marcus for that.'

'And I have to talk to Bill, but Bill will play ball.'

'Okay, I'll talk to my Director. I'll be back.' Ryan hung up and walked again to the Director's office.

'I've seen it,' Director Cabot said.

'The Bureau doesn't know about this investigation, and neither do our people. From that we can surmise that the scandal part of the story is pure bull, but somebody's been leaking the take from SPINNAKER, and that sort of thing gets agents killed.'

'What do you suggest?' the DCI asked.

'Dan Murray and I approach Holtzman informally and let him know that he's stepping on sensitive toes. We ask him to back off.'

'Ask?'

'Ask. You don't give orders to reporters. Not unless you sign their paychecks, anyway,' Jack corrected himself. 'I've never actually done this, but Dan has. It was his idea.'

'I have to go upstairs on this,' Cabot said.

'God damn it, Marcus, we *are* upstairs!'

'Dealing with the press – it has to be decided elsewhere.'

'Super, get in your car and drive down and make sure you ask very nicely.' Ryan turned and stormed out before Cabot had a chance to flush at the insult.

By the time he'd walked the few yards to his private office, Jack's hands were quivering. *Can't he back me up on* anything? Nothing was going right lately. Jack pounded once on his desk, and the pain brought things back under control. Clark's little operation, that seemed to be heading in the right direction. That was one thing, and one thing was better than nothing.

Not much better. Jack looked at the photo of his wife and kids.

'God damn it,' he swore to himself. He couldn't get that guy to back him up on anything, he'd become a lousy father to his kids, and sure as hell he was no great shakes as a husband lately.

Liz Elliot read the front-page article with no small degree of satisfaction. Holtzman had delivered exactly what she had expected. Reporters were so easy to manipulate. It opened a whole new world for her, she had belatedly realized. With Marcus Cabot being so weak, and no one within the CIA bureaucracy to back him up, she would have effective control of that, as well. Wasn't that something?

Removing Ryan from his post was now more than a mere exercise in spite, as desirable as so simple a motive might have been. Ryan was the one who had said 'no' to a few White House requests, who occasionally went directly to Congress on internal matters . . . who prevented her from having closer contact with the Agency. With him out of the way, she could give orders – couched as 'suggestions' – to Cabot, who would then carry them out with a total absence of resistance. Dennis Bunker would still have Defense and his dumb football team. Brent Talbot would have the State Department. Elizabeth Elliot would have control of the National Security apparatus – because she also had the ear, and all the other important parts, of the President. Her phone beeped.

'Director Cabot is here.'

'Send him in,' Liz said. She stood and walked towards the door. 'Good morning, Marcus.'

'Hello, Dr Elliot.'

'What brings you down?' she asked, waving him to a seat on the couch.

'This newspaper article.'

'I saw it,' the National Security Advisor said sympathetically.

'Whoever leaked this might have endangered a valuable source.'

'I know. Somebody at your end? I mean, what's this about an in-house investigation?'

'It isn't us.'

'Really?' Dr Elliot leaned back and played with her blue silk cravat. 'Who, then?'

'We don't know, Liz.' Cabot looked even more uncomfortable than she had expected. Maybe, she thought playfully, he thought he was the target of the investigation . . . ? There was an interesting idea. 'We want to talk to Holtzman.'

'What do you mean?'

595

'I mean we and the FBI talk to him, informally of course, to let him know that he may be doing something irresponsible.'

'Who came up with that, Marcus?'

'Ryan and Murray.'

'Really?' She paused, as though considering the matter. 'I don't think that's a good idea. You know how reporters are. If you have to stroke them, you have to stroke them properly . . . hmm. I can handle that if you wish.'

'This really is serious. SPINNAKER is very important to us.' Cabot tended to repeat himself when he got excited.

'I know it. Ryan was pretty clear in his briefing, back when you were ill. You still haven't confirmed his reports?'

Cabot shook his head. 'No. Jack went off to England to ask the Brits to nose around, but we don't expect anything for a while.'

'What do you want me to tell Holtzman?'

'Tell him that he may be jeopardizing a highly important source. The man could die over this, and the political fallout might be very serious,' Cabot concluded.

'Yes, it could have undesired effects on their political scene, couldn't it?'

'If SPINNAKER is right, then they're in for a huge political shakeup. Revealing that we know what we know could jeopardize him. Remember that —'

Elliot interrupted. 'That Kadishev is our main fallback position. Yes. And if he gets "burned," then we might have no fall-back position. You've made yourself very clear, Marcus. Thank you. I'll work on this myself.'

'That should be quite satisfactory,' Cabot said, after a moment's pause.

'Fine. Anything else I need to know this morning?'

'No, that's why I came down.'

'I think it's time to show you something. Something we've been working on here. Pretty sensitive,' she added. Marcus got the message.

'What is it?' the DCI asked guardedly.

'This is absolutely confidential.' Elliot pulled a large manila envelope from her desk. 'I mean absolutely, Marcus. It doesn't leave the building, okay?'

'Agreed.' The DCI was already interested.

Liz opened the envelope and handed over some photographs. Cabot looked them over.

'Who's the woman?'

'Carol Zimmer, she's the widow of an Air Force crewman who got himself killed somehow or other.' Elliot filled in some additional details.

'Ryan, screwing around? I'll be damned.'

'Any chance we could get more information from inside the Agency?'

'If you mean accomplishing that without any suspicion on his part, it would be very difficult.' Cabot shook his head. 'His two SPOs, Clark and Chavez, no way. They're very tight. Good friends, I mean.'

'Ryan's friendly with bodyguards? You serious?' Elliot was surprised. It was like being solicitous towards furniture.

'Clark's an old field officer. Chavez is a new kid, working as an SPO while he finishes his college degree, looking to be a field officer. I've seen the files. Clark'll retire in a few more years, and keeping him around as an SPO is just a matter of being decent. He's done some really interesting things. Good man, good officer.'

Elliot didn't like that, but from what Cabot said, it seemed that it couldn't be helped. 'We want Ryan eased out.'

'That might not be easy. They really like him on The Hill.'

'You just said he's insubordinate.'

'It won't wash on The Hill. You know that. You want him fired, the President just has to ask for his resignation.'

But that wouldn't wash on The Hill either, Liz thought, and it seemed immediately clear that Marcus Cabot wouldn't be much help. She hadn't really expected that he would be. Cabot was too soft.

'We can handle it entirely from this end, if you want.'

'Probably a good idea. If it became known at Langley that I had a hand in this, it might look like spite. Can't have that,' Cabot demurred. 'Bad for morale.'

'Okay.' Liz stood, and so did Cabot. 'Thanks for coming down.'

Two minutes later, she was back in her chair, her feet propped up on a drawer. This was going *so* well. Exactly as planned. *I'm getting good at this . . .*

'So?'

'This was published in a Washington paper today,' Golovko said. It was seven in the evening in Moscow, the sky outside dark and cold as only Moscow could get cold. That he had to report on something in an American newspaper did not warm the night very much.

Andrey Il'ych Narmonov took the translation from the First Deputy Chairman and read through it. Finished, he tossed the two pages contemptuously onto his desktop. 'What rubbish is this?'

'Holtzman is a very important Washington reporter. He has access to very senior officials in the Fowler Administration.'

'And he probably writes a good deal of fiction, just as our reporters do.'

'We think not. We think the tone of the report indicates that he was given the data by someone in the White House.'

'Indeed?' Narmonov pulled out a handkerchief and blew his nose, cursing the cold that the sudden weather change had brought with it. If there was anything for which he did not have time, it was an illness, even a minor one. 'I don't believe it. I've told Fowler personally about the difficulty with the missile destruction, and the rest of this political twaddle is just that. You know that I've had to deal with uniformed hotheads – those fools who went off on their own in the Baltic region. So do the Americans. It's incredible to me that they should take such nonsense seriously. Surely their intelligence services tell them the truth – and the truth is what I've told Fowler myself!'

'Comrade President.' Golovko paused for a beat. *Comrade* was too hard a habit to break. 'Just as we have political elements who distrust the Americans, so they have elements who continue to hate and distrust us. Changes between us have come and gone very rapidly. Too rapidly for many to assimilate. I find it plausible that there might be American political officials who believe this report.'

'Fowler is vain, he is far weaker as a man than he would like people to know, he is personally insecure – but he is not a fool, and only a fool would believe this, particularly after meeting me and talking with me.' Narmonov handed the translation back to Golovko.

'My analysts believe otherwise. We think it possible that the Americans really believe this.'

'Thank them for their opinion. I disagree.'

'If the Americans are getting a report saying this, it means that they have a spy within our government.'

'I have no doubt that they have such people – after all, we do also, do we not? – but I do not believe it in this case. The reason is simple, no spy could have reported something which I did not say, correct? I have not said this to anyone. It is not true. What do you do to a spy who lies to us?'

'My President, it is not something we look upon kindly,' Golovko assured him.

'That is doubtless true of the Americans also.' Narmonov paused for a moment, then smiled. 'Do you know what this could be?'

'We are always open to ideas.'

'Think like a politician. This could easily be a sign of some sort of power-play within their government. Our involvement would then be merely incidental.'

Golovko thought about that. 'We have heard that there is – that Ryan, their deputy director, is unloved by Fowler . . .'

'Ryan, ah, yes, I remember him. A worthy adversary, Sergey Nikolay'ch?'

'He is that.'

Definitely something a politician would remember, Golovko thought.

'Why are they unhappy with him?' Narmonov asked.

'Reportedly a clash of personalities.'

'That I can believe. Fowler and his vanity.' Narmonov held up his hands. 'There you have it. Perhaps I might have made a good intelligence analyst?'

'The finest,' Golovko agreed. He had to agree, of course. Moreover, his President had said something that his own people had not examined fully. He left the august presence of his chief of state with a troubled expression. The defection of KGB Chairman Gerasimov a few years ago – an event that Ryan had himself engineered, if Golovko read the signs correctly – had inevitably crippled KGB's overseas operations. Six complete networks in America had collapsed, along with eight more in Western Europe. Replacement networks were only now beginning to take their place. That left major holes in KGB's ability to penetrate American government operations. The only good news was that they were starting to read a noteworthy fraction of American diplomatic and military communications – as much as four or five percent in a good month. But code-breaking was no substitute for penetration agents. There was something very strange going on here. Golovko didn't know what it was. Perhaps his President was right. Perhaps this was merely the ripples from an internal power-play. But it could also have been something else. The fact that Golovko didn't know what it was did not help matters.

'Just made it back in time,' Clark said. 'Did they sweep the wheels today?'

'If it's Wednesday . . .' Jack replied. Every week, his official car was examined for possible electronic bugs.

'Can we talk about it, then?'

'Yes.'

'Chavez was right. It's easy, just a matter of dropping a nice little *mordida* on the right guy. The regular maintenance man will be taken sick that day, the two of us get tapped to service the 747. I get to play maid, scrub the sinks and the crappers, replenish the bar, the whole thing. You'll have the official evaluation on your desk tomorrow, but the short version is, yeah, we can do it, and the likelihood of discovery is minimal.'

'You know the down-side?'

'Oh, yeah. Major International Incident. I get early retirement. That's okay, Jack. I can retire whenever I want. It would be a shame for Ding, though. That kid is showing real promise.'

'And if you're discovered?'

'I say in my best Spanish that some Japanese reporter asked me to do it, and paid me a lot of pesos to do it. That's the hook, Jack. They won't make a big deal about it if they think it's one of their own. Looks too bad, loss of face and all that.'

'John, you're a tricky, underhanded son of a bitch.'

'Just want to serve my country, sir.' Clark started laughing. A few minutes later, he took the turn. 'Hope we're not too late.'

'It was a long one at the office.'

'I saw that thing in the paper. What are we doing about it?'

'The White House will be talking to Holtzman, telling him to lay off.'

'Somebody dipping his pen in the company ink-well?'

'Not that we know about, same with the FBI.'

'Camouflage for the real story, eh?'

'Looks that way.'

'What bullshit,' Clark observed as he pulled into the parking place.

It turned out that Carol was in her home, cleaning up after dinner. The Zimmer family Christmas tree was up. Clark began ferrying the presents in. Jack had picked some of them up in England; Clark and Nancy Cummings had helped to wrap them – Ryan was hopeless at wrapping presents. Unfortunately, they'd walked into the house just in time to hear crying.

'No problem, Dr Ryan,' one of the kids told him in

the kitchen. 'Jackie had a little accident. Mom's in the bathroom.'

'Okay.' Ryan walked that way, careful to announce his presence.

'Okay, okay, come in,' Carol said.

Jack saw Carol leaning over the bathtub. Jacqueline was crying in the piteous monotone of a child who knows that she has misbehaved. There was a pile of kid's clothes on the tile floor, and the air positively reeked of crushed flowers. 'What happened?'

'Jackie think my perfume is same as her toy perfume, pour whole bottle.' Carol looked up from scrubbing.

Ryan lifted the little girl's shirt. 'You're not kidding.'

'Whole bottle – expensive! Bad girl!'

Jacqueline's crying increased in pitch. She'd probably had her backside smacked already. Ryan was just as happy not to have seen that. He disciplined his own kids as necessary, but didn't like to see other people smack theirs. That was one of several weak spots in his character. Even after Carol lifted her youngest out of the tub, the smell had not gone away.

'Wow, it is pretty strong, isn't it?' Jack picked Jackie up, which didn't mute her crying very much.

'Eighty dollar!' Carol said, but her anger was now gone. She had ample experience with small children, and knew that they were expected to do mischief. Jack carried the little one out to the living room. Her attitude changed when she saw the stack of presents.

'You too nice,' her mother noted.

'Hey, I just happened to be doing some shopping, okay?'

'You no come here Christmas, you have you own family.'

'I know, Carol, but I can't let Christmas go by without stopping in.' Clark came in with a final pile. These were his, Jack saw. Good man, Clark.

'We have nothing for you,' Carol Zimmer said.

'Sure you do. Jackie gave me a good hug.'

'What about me?' John asked.

Jack handed Jackie over. It was funny. Quite a few

men were wary of John Clark on the basis of looks alone, but the Zimmer kids thought of him as a big teddy bear. A few minutes later, they drove away.

'Nice of you to do that, John,' Ryan said as they drove off.

'No big deal. Hey, man, you know how much fun it was to shop for little kids? Who the hell wants to buy his kid a Bali bra – that's what Maggie wanted, put it on her list – a sexy bra, for Christ's sake. How the hell can a father walk into a department store and buy something like that for his own daughter?'

'They get a little big for Barbie dolls.'

'More's the pity, Doc, more's the pity.'

Jack turned and chuckled. 'That bra –'

'Yeah, Jack, if I ever find out, he's dogmeat.'

Ryan had to laugh at that, but he knew he could afford to laugh. His little girl wasn't dating yet. That would be hard, watching her leave with someone else, beyond his protective reach. Harder still for a man like John Clark.

'Regular time tomorrow?'

'Yep.'

'See ya' then, Doc.'

Ryan walked into his house at eight fifty-five. His dinner was in its usual place. He poured his usual glass of wine, took a sip, then removed his coat and hung it in the closet before walking upstairs to change clothes. He caught Cathy going the other way and smiled at her. He didn't kiss her. He was just too tired. That was the problem. If he could only get time to relax. Clark was right, just a few days off to unwind. That's all he needed, Jack told himself as he changed.

Cathy opened the closet door to get some medical files she'd left in her own topcoat. She almost turned away when she noticed something. Not sure what it was, Cathy Ryan leaned in, puzzled, then caught it. Where was it? Her nose searched left and right in a way that might have appeared comical except for the look on her face when she found it. Jack's camel-hair coat, the expensive one she'd gotten for him last year.

It wasn't her perfume.

CHAPTER 26

Integration

The assembly had begun with the purchase of additional instruments. An entire day was spent attaching one heavy block of spent uranium to the inside of the far end of the case.

'This is tedious, I know,' Fromm said, almost apologetically. 'In America and elsewhere there are special jigs, specially designed tools, people assemble many individual weapons of the same design, all advantages that we do not have.'

'And here everything must be just as exact, Commander,' Ghosn added.

'My young friend is correct. The physics are the same for all of us.'

'Then don't let us stop you,' Qati said.

Fromm went immediately back to work. Part of him was already counting the money he'd receive, but most concerned itself with the job at hand. Only half of the machinists had actually worked on the bomb's physics package itself. The rest had been employed entirely with manufacturing other fittings, most of which could be called cradles. These would hold the bomb components in place, and were mainly made from stainless steel for strength and compactness. Each was set in place according to a precise sequence, as the bomb was more complex than most machines, and required assembly according to a rigid set of instructions. Here again the process was made simpler by the quality of the design and the precision of the machine tools. Even the machinists were amazed that the parts all fit, and they murmured among themselves that whatever Fromm might be – and on this subject their speculation had been wide-ranging and colorful – he was an inhumanly skilled designer. The hardest part was installing the various uranium blocks. Installation of the lighter and milder materials went much more smoothly.

'The procedure for the tritium transfer?' Ghosn asked.

'We'll leave that for last, of course,' Fromm said, backing off from checking a measurement.

'Just heat the battery to release the gas, correct?'

'Yes,' Fromm said with a nod. 'But – no, no, not that way!'

'What did I do wrong?'

'This must twist in,' Fromm told the machinist. He stepped forward to demonstrate. 'Like that, do you see?'

'Yes, thank you.'

'The elliptical reflectors hang on these –'

'Yes, thank you, I know.'

'Very good.'

Fromm waved to Ghosn. 'Come over here. You see how this works now?' Fromm pointed to two series of elliptical surfaces which nested together one after the other – there was a total of nineteen – each made of a different material. 'The energy off the Primary impacts of these surfaces, destroying each in its turn, but in the process . . .'

'Yes, it is always more clear to see the physical model than to extract it from a sheet of figures.' This portion of the weapon derived its utility from the fact that light waves had no mass but did carry momentum. They were not 'light' waves at all, technically speaking, but since the energy was all in the form of photons the same principle held. The energy would immolate each of the elliptical surfaces, but in the process each surface would transfer a small but reliable percentage of the energy in another direction, adding to the energy already headed that way from the Primary itself.

'Your energy budget is lavish, Herr Fromm,' Ghosn observed not for the first time.

The German shrugged. 'Yes, it must be. If you cannot test, you must over-engineer. The first American bomb

– the one used on Hiroshima – was an untested design. It was wasteful of materials and disgustingly inefficient, but it was over-engineered. And it did work. With a proper test program . . .' With a proper test program he could measure the empirical effects, determine exactly what the necessary energy budget was, and how well he managed it, determine the exact performance of each component, improve those that needed improvement, and reduce the size of those which were too large or too massive for the task at hand, just as the Americans, and Russians, and British, and French had done over a period of decades, constantly refining their designs, making them more and more efficient, and because of that, smaller, lighter, simpler, more reliable, less expensive. This, Fromm thought, was the ultimate engineering discipline, and he was immeasurably grateful that he had finally gotten the chance to try his hand at it. This design was crude and heavy, no masterpiece of design. It would function – of that he was certain – but with time he could have done so much better . . .

'Yes, I see. A man of your skill could reduce this entire unit to the size of a large bucket.'

It was a vast compliment. 'Thank you, Herr Ghosn. Probably not that small, but small enough for the nose of a rocket.'

'If our Iraqi brothers had taken the time . . .'

'Indeed, there would be no Israel. But they were foolish, were they not?'

'They were impatient,' Ibrahim said, silently cursing them for it.

'One must be cold and clear-headed about such things. Such decisions must be made on the basis of logic, not emotion.'

'Indeed.'

Achmed was feeling very poorly indeed. He'd made his excuses and taken his leave, heading off to see the Commander's own physician, as per orders from Qati. Achmed had little experience of doctors. It was, he thought, something to be avoided if possible. He'd seen combat action and seen death and wounds, but never to himself. Even that was preferable to his current situation. One could understand injury from a bullet or a grenade, but what had made him ill so quickly and unexpectedly?

The doctor listened to his description of his condition, asked a few questions that were not entirely foolish, and noted that Achmed was a smoker – that had earned the fighter a head-shake and a cluck, as though cigarettes had anything to do with his situation. What rubbish, Achmed thought. Didn't he run six kilometers each day – or had, until very recently?

The physical examination came next. The doctor placed a stethoscope on his chest and listened. Instantly, Achmed noted, the doctor's eyes became guarded in a way not unlike the expression of a courageous fighter who didn't wish to betray his feelings.

'Breathe in,' the physician ordered. Achmed did so. 'Now, out slowly.'

The stethoscope moved. 'Again please.' The procedure was repeated six more times, front and back.

'Well?' Achmed asked, when the examination was finished.

'I don't know. I want to take you to see someone who understands these lung problems better.'

'I have no time for that.'

'You have time for this. I will talk to your Commander, if necessary.'

Achmed managed not to grumble. 'Very well.'

It was a measure of Ryan's own situation that he took no note of it, or more correctly that he was grateful for the diminished attention his wife accorded him. It helped. It took some of the pressure off. Maybe she understood that he just needed to be left alone for a while. He'd make it up to her, Jack promised himself. He sure as hell would, when he got it all back together. He was sure of that, or told himself that he was, though a distant part of his mind was less sure and announced the fact to a consciousness that preferred not to listen.

He tried to cut back on the drinking, but with the reduced demands he could, he decided, get a little more sleep, and the wine helped him sleep. In the spring, when things warmed up, he'd get back into a healthier routine. Yeah, that was it. He'd jog. He'd take the time at work, at lunch he'd get outside with the rest of the local sweat squad and run around the perimeter road inside the CIA enclosure. Clark would be a good trainer for this. Clark was a rock. Better him than Chavez, who was disgustingly fit and singularly unsympathetic to those who failed to keep in good shape – doubtless a carryover from his time in the infantry, Ryan thought. Ding would learn as he got closer to thirty. That number was the great equalizer, when you stopped being young and had to face the fact that everything had limits.

Christmas could have gone better, he thought, sitting at his desk. But it had been in the middle of the week, which meant that the kids were home two full weeks. It also meant that Cathy had to miss time at work, and that was a little hard on her. She liked her work, and as much as she loved the kids, and as fine a mother as she was, she resented the time away from Hopkins and her patients. Strictly speaking, it wasn't fair for her, Jack admitted to himself. She, too, was a professional and a fine one, despite which she was the one who always got tapped with kid duty while he never got relief from his work. But there were thousands of eye surgeons, and even a few hundred professors of eye surgery, but there was only one DDCI, and that was that. Not fair, perhaps, but a fact.

So much the better if he were able to accomplish something, Ryan told himself. Letting Elizabeth Elliot handle that damned newsie had been a mistake. Not that he'd expected much else from Marcus Cabot. The man was a drone. It really was that simple. He enjoyed the prestige that went with his post, but he didn't do anything. Ryan got most of the work, none of the credit, and all of the blame. Maybe that would change. He had the Mexican operation fully in hand, had taken that over entirely from the Directorate of Operations, and, by God, he'd get the credit for this. Maybe then things would get better. He pulled out the file for the operation and decided that he'd go over every detail, check every possible contingency. This one would work, and he'd make those White House bastards respect him.

'Go to your room!' Cathy shouted at Little Jack. Both an order and an admission of failure. Then she walked out of the room, tears in her eyes. She was acting stupidly, shouting at the kids when she should be confronting her own husband. *But how?* What could she say? What if – what if it were true? Then what? She kept telling herself that it couldn't be, but that was too hard to believe. How else to explain it? Jack had never failed at anything in his life. She remembered with pride the fact that he'd risked his life for her and the children. She'd been terrified, the breath frozen in her throat, walking along the beach, watching her man advance towards men with guns with his life and others in the balance. How could a man who had done that betray his own wife? It didn't make any sense.

But what other explanation was there? Didn't he find her exciting anymore? If so, why not? Wasn't she pretty enough? Didn't she do everything – and more – that a wife could? The simple rejection was bad enough – but to be set aside, to know that his energy and vigor was serving some other, unknown woman with cheap perfume was more than she could bear.

She had to confront him, had to get it into the open, had to find out.

How? she asked herself. That was the question. Could she discuss it with someone at Hopkins ... a psychiatrist, perhaps? Get professional advice ... ?

And risk having it get out, risk having her shame widely known? Caroline Ryan, Associate Professor, pretty, bright Cathy Ryan can't even hold onto her own husband? What do you suppose she did wrong? her friends would whisper when she was elsewhere. Sure, they'd all say that it couldn't be *her* fault, but then they'd pause and look embarrassed, and after a moment they'd wonder aloud what she might have done differently, why she hadn't noticed the signals, because, after all, a failed marriage was rarely the work of a single partner, and Jack wasn't really the sort to play around, was he? The embarrassment of it would be worse than anything in her life, she thought, forgetting for the moment times that had been far worse.

It didn't make any sense. But she didn't know what to do about it, though at the same time she knew that doing nothing was probably the worst thing of all. Was it all a trap? Did she have any choices at all?

'What's the matter, Mommy?' Sally asked, a Barbie in her hands.

'Nothing, honey, just leave Mommy alone for a while, okay?'

'Jack says he's sorry and can he come out of his room?'

'Yes, if he promises to be good.'

'Okay!' Sally ran out of the room.

Was it that simple? Cathy wondered. She could forgive him almost anything. Could she forgive him this? Not because she would want to forgive him. Because there was more to it than her pride. There were also kids, and kids needed a father, even a neglectful one. Was her pride more important than their needs? The other side of that – what sort of household would they have if Mom and Dad didn't get along? Wasn't that even more destructive? After all, she could always find . . .

. . . another Jack?

She started crying again. She cried for herself, for her own inability to make a decision, for the injury to her character. It was the sort of weeping that did nothing for the problem, except make it worse. Part wanted him gone. Part wanted him back. No part knew what to do.

'You understand that this is strictly confidential,' the investigator said, rather than asked. The man before him was short and overweight, with soft, pink hands. The Bismarck mustache was obviously an affectation to make him look manly. In fact he didn't look terribly impressive at all, until you took a close look at his face. Those dark eyes didn't miss a thing.

'Doctors are accustomed to confidentiality,' Bernie Katz replied, handing the credentials back. 'Make it fast. I have rounds in twenty minutes.'

The investigator thought that his assignment did have a certain elegance to it, though he wasn't sure that he approved. The problem was that playing around wasn't exactly a felony, though it did usually disqualify a man from a high security clearance. After all, if a man could break a promise made in a church, then why not one made merely on paper?

Bernie Katz leaned back, waiting as patiently as he was able, which wasn't very patient. He was a surgeon, accustomed to doing things and making his own decisions, not waiting for others. One hand twirled at his mustache as he rocked in the chair.

'How well do you know Dr Caroline Ryan?'

'Cathy? I've worked with her on and off for eleven years.'

'What can you tell me about her?'

'She's a brilliant surgeon, technically speaking, exceptional judgment, superbly skilled. She's one of the best instructors we have on staff. She's also a good friend. What seems to be the problem here?' Katz's eyes narrowed on his visitor.

'Sorry, I'm the guy asking the questions.'

'Yeah, I can tell. Get on with it,' Katz said coldly, examining the man, watching body language, expression, demeanor. He didn't like what he saw.

'Has she made any comments lately ... I mean, trouble at home, that sort of thing?'

'You do understand, I hope, that I am a physician, and things said to me are privileged.'

'Is Cathy Ryan your patient?' the man asked.

'I've examined her in the past. We all do that here.'

'Are you a psychiatrist?'

Katz nearly growled back an answer. Like most surgeons, he had a temper. 'You know the answer to that.'

The investigator looked up from his notes and spoke

matter-of-factly. 'In that case privilege does not apply. Now, could you answer the question, please?'

'No.'

'No, what?'

'No, she has made no such comments, to the best of my knowledge.'

'Comments on her husband, his behavior, changes in the way he's acting?'

'No. I know Jack pretty well, too. I really like the guy. He's evidently a good husband. They have two great kids, and you know the story on what happened to them some years back as well as I do, right?'

'Correct, but people change.'

'Not them.' Katz's comments had the finality of a death sentence.

'You seem quite certain.'

'I'm a doctor. I live by my judgment. What you are alleging is crap.'

'I'm alleging nothing,' the investigator said, knowing it was a lie, and knowing that Katz knew it for a lie. He'd judged the man correctly from the first moment. Katz was a hotheaded, passionate man unlikely to keep any secret he deemed unworthy of being kept. Probably one hell of a doctor, too.

'I return to my original question. Has Caroline Ryan acted in any way different from, say, a year ago?'

'She's a year older. They have kids, the kids are growing up, and kids can be a bother. I have a few of my own. Okay, so she's gained a pound or two, maybe – not a bad thing, she tries to be too thin – and she's a little tireder than she ought to be. She has a long commute, and work is hard here, especially for a mother with kids.'

'That's all, you think?'

'Hey, I'm an eye-cutter, not a marriage counselor. Not my field.'

'Why did you say you're not a marriage counselor? I never brought that up, did I?'

Clever son of a bitch, aren't you? Katz thought, letting go of his mustache. *Degree in psychology, maybe . . . more likely self-taught. Cops were pretty good at read-*

ing people. Reading me, even! 'Trouble at home for a married person generally means a troubled marriage,' Katz said slowly. 'No, there has been no such comment.'

'You're sure?'

'Quite sure.'

'Okay, thank you for your time, Dr Katz. Sorry to have bothered you.' He handed over a card. 'If you hear anything like that, I'd appreciate it if you called me.'

'What gives?' Katz asked. 'If you want my cooperation, I want an answer. I don't spy on people for the fun of it.'

'Doctor, her husband holds a very high and very sensitive government position. We routinely keep an eye on such people for reasons of national security. You do the same thing, even if you don't think much about it. If a surgeon shows up with liquor on his breath, for example, you take note of it and you take action, correct?'

'That doesn't happen here, ever,' Katz assured him.

'But you would take note of such a thing if it did happen.'

'You bet we would.'

'Glad to hear it. As you know, John Ryan has access to all sorts of highly sensitive information. Were we not to keep an eye on such people, we would be irresponsible. We've – this is a highly sensitive matter, Dr Katz.'

'I understand that.'

'We have indications that her husband might be acting . . . irregularly. We have to check that out. Understand? We *have* to.'

'Okay.'

'That's all we ask.'

'Very well.'

'Thank you for your cooperation, sir.' The investigator shook hands and left.

Katz managed not to flush until the man was gone. He didn't really know Jack all that well. They'd met at parties perhaps five or six times, traded a few jokes, talked about baseball or the weather or maybe international relations. Jack had never begged off on an answer, had never said *I can't discuss that* or anything.

Pleasant enough guy, Bernie thought. A good father by all accounts. But he didn't *know* the man at all.

Katz did, however, know Cathy as well as he knew any other doctor. She was a thoroughly wonderful person. If one of his kids should ever need eye surgery, she was one of the three people in the world whom he would trust to do the fix, and that was the highest compliment he could pay to anyone. She'd backed him up on cases and procedures, and he'd backed her up. When one needed advice, it was the other who got asked. They were friends, and associates. If they'd ever decided to leave the Hopkins/Wilmer faculty, they would have set up an office together, because a medical partnership is even harder to maintain than a good marriage. He might have married her, Katz thought, if he'd had the chance. She would have been an easy girl to love. She had to be a good mother. She drew a disproportionate number of kids as patients because in some cases the surgeon needed small hands, and hers were small, dainty, and supremely skillful. She lavished attention on her little patients. The floor nurses loved her for it. Everyone loved her, as a matter of fact. Her surgical team was extremely loyal to her. They didn't come any better than Cathy.

Trouble at home? Jack's playing around behind her back . . . hurting my friend?

'That worthless son of a bitch.'

He was late again, Cathy saw. After nine this time. Couldn't he ever get home at a decent hour?

And if not, why not?

'Hi, Cath,' he said on his way through to the bedroom. 'Sorry I'm late.'

When he was out of sight, she walked towards the closet and opened the door to check the coat. Nothing. He'd had it cleaned the very next day, claiming that it had been spotted. It had been spotted, Cathy remembered, but, but, but . . .

What to do?

She almost started crying again.

Cathy was back in her chair when Jack came through

614

on his way towards the kitchen. He didn't notice the look, didn't notice the silence. His wife stayed in her place, not really seeing the television picture her eyes were fixed on while her mind kept going over and over it, searching for an answer but finding only more anger.

She needed advice. She didn't want her marriage to end, did she? She could feel the process by which emotion and anger were taking over from reason and love. She knew that she ought to be worried about that, ought to resist the process, but she found herself unable to do either as the anger simply fed on itself. Cathy walked quietly into the kitchen and got herself a drink. She didn't have any procedures tomorrow. It was okay to have one drink. Again she looked over at her husband, and again he didn't notice. Didn't notice her? *Why* didn't he notice her? She'd put up with so much. Okay, the time they'd spent in England had been all right, she'd had a fairly good time teaching on staff at Guy's Hospital; it hadn't hurt her tenure at Hopkins a bit. But the other stuff – he was away so damned much! All that time back and forth to Russia when he was messed up with the arms treaty, so many other things, playing spy or something, leaving her at home with the kids, forcing her to lose time at work. She'd missed a couple of good procedures for that reason, when she'd been unable to get a sitter and had been forced to stick Bernie with something that she ought to have done.

And what had Jack been up to all that time? She had once accepted the fact that she couldn't even ask. What *had* he been doing? Maybe having a good laugh? A little fling with some sultry female agent somewhere? Like in the movies. There he was, in some exotic setting, a quiet, darkly-lit bar, having a meeting with some agent, and one thing might have led to another . . .

Cathy settled back in front of the TV and gulped at her drink. She nearly sputtered it back out. She wasn't accustomed to drinking bourbon straight.

This is all a mistake.

It seemed as though there were a war within her mind, the forces of good on one side, and the forces of evil on the other – or was it the forces of naiveté and those of reality? She didn't know, and she was too upset to judge.

Well, it didn't matter for tonight, did it? She was having her period, and even if Jack had asked – which he wouldn't, she knew – she'd say no. Why should he ask, if he was getting it somewhere else? Why should she say yes if he was? Why get the leavings? Why be second-string?

She sipped more carefully at her drink this time.

Need to get advice, need to talk to somebody! But who?

Maybe Bernie, she decided. She could trust Bernie. Soon as she got back. Two days.

'That takes care of the preliminaries.'

'Sure does, boss,' the coach said. 'How goes the Pentagon, Dennis?'

'Not as much fun as you're having, Paul.'

'That's the choice, isn't it? Fun or importance?'

'Everybody all right?'

'Yes, sir! We're pretty healthy for this far into the season, and we have this week to get everybody up to speed. I want another crack at those Vikings.'

'So do I,' Secretary Bunker said from his E-Ring office. 'Think we can really stop Tony Wills this time?'

'We can sure try. Isn't he one great kid? I haven't seen running like that since Gayle Sayers. Defensing him is a bitch, though.'

'Let's not try to think too far ahead. I want to be in Denver in a few weeks.'

'We play 'em one at a time, Dennis, you know that. Just we don't know who we're playing yet. I'd prefer LA. We can handle them easy enough,' the coach thought. 'Then we'll probably have to handle Miami in the division game. That'll be harder, but we can do it.'

'I think so, too.'

'I have films to look at.'

'Fair enough. Just remember, one at a time – but three more wins.'

'You tell the President to come on out to Denver. We'll

be there to see him. This is San Diego's year. The Chargers go all the way.'

Dubinin watched the water invade the graving dock as the sluices were opened. *Admiral Lunin* was ready. The new sonar array was rolled up on its spool inside the teardrop-shaped fairing that sat atop the rudder post. The seven-bladed screw of manganese-bronze had been inspected and polished. The hull was restored to full watertight integrity. His submarine was ready for sea.

As was the crew. He'd gotten rid of eighteen conscript sailors and replaced them with eighteen new officers. The radical down-sizing of the Soviet submarine fleet had eliminated a large number of officer billets. It would have been a waste of skilled manpower to return them to civilian life – besides which there were not enough jobs for them – and as a result they'd been retrained and assigned to the remaining submarines as technical experts. His sonar department would now be almost exclusively officers – two *michmaniy* would assist with the maintenance – and all of them were genuine experts. Surprisingly, there was little grumbling among them. The Akula class had what was for Soviet submarines very comfortable accommodations, but more important than that was the fact that the new members of the wardroom had been fully briefed on their mission, and what the boat had done – probably done, Dubinin corrected himself – on the previous cruise. It was the sort of thing that appealed to the sportsman in them. This was for the submariner the ultimate test of skill. For that they would do their best.

Dubinin would do the same. Pulling in a lot of old professional debts, and leaning heavily on the yard's Master Shipwright, he'd performed miracles during the refit. Bedding had all been replaced. The ship had been scrubbed surgically clean, and repainted with bright, airy colors. Dubinin had worked with the local supply officers and obtained the best food he could find. A well-fed crew was a happy crew, and men responded to a commander who worked hard for them. That was the whole point of the new professional spirit in the Soviet Navy. Valentin Borissovich Dubinin had learned his trade from the best teacher his navy had ever had, and he was determined that he would be the new Marko Ramius. He had the best ship, had the best crew, and he would on this cruise set the standard for the Soviet Pacific Fleet.

He would also have to be lucky, of course.

'That's the hardware,' Fromm said. 'From now on . . .'

'Yes, from now on we are assembling the actual device. I see you've changed the design somewhat . . . ?'

'Yes. Two tritium reservoirs. I prefer the shorter injection piping. Mechanically, it is no different. The timing is not critical, and the pressurization ensures that it will function properly.'

'Also makes loading the tritium easier,' Ghosn observed. 'That's why you did it.'

'Correct.'

The inside of the device made Ghosn think of the half-assembled body of some alien airplane. There was the delicacy and precision of aircraft parts, but the almost baffling configuration in which they were placed. Something from a science-fiction movie, Ghosn thought, whimsical for a brief moment . . . but then this was science-fiction, or had been until recently. The first public discussion of nuclear weapons had been in H. G. Wells, hadn't it? That hadn't been so long ago.

'Commander, I saw your doctor,' Achmed said in the far corner.

'And – you still look ill, my friend,' Qati noted. 'What is the problem?'

'He wants me to see another doctor in Damascus.'

Qati instantly did not like that. Did not like it at all. But Achmed was a comrade who had served the movement for years. How could he say no to someone who had twice saved his life, once stopping a bullet himself to do so?

'You know that what goes on here . . .'

'Commander, I will die before I speak of this place.

618

Even though I know nothing of this – this project. I will die first.'

There was no doubting the man, and Qati knew what it was to be seriously ill at a young and healthy age. He could not deny the man medical care while he himself regularly visited a physician. How could his men respect him if he did such a thing?

'Two men will go with you. I will select them.'

'Thank you, Commander. Please forgive my weakness.'

'Weakness?' Qati grabbed the man by the shoulder. 'You are the strongest among us! We need you back, and we need you healthy! Go tomorrow.'

Achmed nodded and withdrew to another place, embarrassed and shamed by his illness. His commander, he knew, faced death. It had to be cancer, he had so often visited the physician. Whatever it was, the Commander had not let it stop him. There was courage, he thought.

'Break for the night?' Ghosn asked.

Fromm shook his head. 'No, let's take another hour or two to assemble the explosive bed. We should be able to get part of it in place before we're too weary.' Both men looked up as Qati approached.

'Still on schedule?'

'Herr Qati, whatever arrangements you have in mind, we will be ready a day early. Ibrahim saved us that day with his work on the explosives.' The German held one of the small, hexagonal blocks. The squibs were already in place, the wire trailing off. Fromm looked at the other two, then bent down, setting the first block in its nesting place. Fromm made sure the block was exactly in place, then attached a numbered tag on the wire, and draped it into a plastic tray that held a number of dividers, like the trays of a tool box. Qati attached the wire to a terminal, checking three times to make sure the number on the wire was the same as that on the terminal. Fromm watched also. The process took four minutes. The electrical components had already been pre-tested. They could not be tested again. The first part of the bomb was now live.

619

CHAPTER 27

Data Fusion

'I've had my say, Bart,' Jones said on the way to the airport.

'That bad?'

'The crew hates him – the training they just went through didn't help. Hey, I was there, okay? I was in with the sonar guys, in the simulator, and he was there, and I wouldn't want to work for him. He almost yelled at me.'

'Oh?' That surprised Mancuso.

'Yeah, he said something that I didn't like – something plain wrong, skipper – and I called him on it, and you should have seen his reaction. Shit, I thought he'd have a stroke or something. And he was wrong, Bart. It was my tape. He was hassling his people for not cueing on something that wasn't there, okay? It was one of my trick tapes, and they saw that it was bogus, but he didn't and he started raisin' hell. That's a good sonar department. He doesn't know how to use it, but he sure likes to kibbitz like he does. Anyway, after he left, the guys started talking, okay? That isn't the only bunch he gives a hard time to. I hear the engineers are going nuts trying to keep this clown happy. Is it true they maxed an ORSE?'

Mancuso nodded, despite the fact he didn't like hearing this. 'They came within a whisker of setting a record.'

'Well, the guy doesn't want a record, he wants a perfect. He wants to redefine what perfect is. I'm telling you, man, if I was stuck on that boat, after the first cruise the first thing up through the hatch would be my sea bag. I'd fuckin' *desert* before I worked for that guy!' Jones paused. He'd gone too far. 'I caught the signal his XO gave you, I even thought he might have been a little out of line, maybe. I was wrong. That's one very loyal XO. Ricks hates one of his JOs, the kid does tracking-party duty. The quartermaster who's breaking him in – Ensign Shaw, I think his name is – says he's a real good kid, but the skipper's riding him like a broke-down horse.'

'Great, what am I supposed to do about it?'

'Beats me, Bart. I retired as an E-6, remember?' *Relieve the son of a bitch*, Jones thought, though he knew better. You could only relieve for cause.

'I'll talk to him,' Mancuso promised.

'You know, I heard about skippers like that. Never did believe the stories. Guess I got spoiled working for you,' Dr Jones observed as they approached the terminal. 'You haven't changed a bit, you know that? You still listen when somebody talks to you.'

'You have to listen, Ron. You can't know it all yourself.'

'I got news: not everyone knows that. I got one more suggestion.'

'Don't let him go hunting?'

'If I were in your position, I wouldn't.' Jones opened the door. 'I don't want to rain on the parade, skipper. That's my professional observation. He isn't up to the game. Ricks is nothing near the captain you used to be.'

Used to be. A singularly poor choice of words, Mancuso thought, but it was true. It was a hell of a lot easier to run a boat than to run a squadron, and a hell of a lot more fun, too.

'Better hustle if you want to catch that flight.' Mancuso held out his hand.

'Skipper, always a pleasure.'

Mancuso watched him walk into the terminal. Jones had never once given him bad advice, and if anything he'd gotten smarter. A pity he hadn't stayed in and gone for a commission. That wasn't true, the Commodore thought next. Ron would have made one hell of a CO, but he would never have had a chance. The system didn't allow it, and that was that.

The driver headed back without being told, leaving Mancuso in his rear seat with his thoughts. The system hadn't changed enough. He'd come up the old way, power school, an engineer tour before he got command. There was too much engineering in the Navy, not enough leadership. He'd made the transition, as did most of the skippers — but not all. Too many people made it through who thought that other people were just numbers, machines to be fixed, things to order, who measured people by numbers that were more easily understood than real results. Jim Rosselli wasn't like that. Neither was Bart Mancuso, but Harry Ricks was.

So. Now what the hell do I do?

First and foremost, he had no basis for relieving Ricks. Had the story come from anyone except Jones, he would have dismissed it as personality clashes. Jones was too reliable an observer for that. Mancuso considered what he'd been told and matched it with the higher-than-usual rate of transfer requests, the rather equivocal words he'd heard from Dutch Claggett. The XO was in a very touchy spot. Already selected for command . . . one bad word from Ricks and he'd lose that; against that possibility he had his loyalty to the Navy. His job demanded loyalty to his CO even while the Navy demanded truth. It was an impossible position for Claggett, and he'd done all that he could.

The responsibility was Mancuso's. He was the squadron commander. The boats were his. The skippers and crews were his. He rated the COs. That was it, wasn't it?

But was it right? All he had was anecdotal information and coincidence. What if Jones was just pissed off at the guy? What if the transfer requests had just been a statistical blip?

Dodging the issue, Bart. They pay you to make the tough decisions. Ensigns and chiefs get the easy ones. Senior captains are supposed to know what to do. That was one of the Navy's more entertaining fictions.

Mancuso lifted his car-phone. 'I want *Maine*'s XO in my office in thirty minutes.'

'Yes, sir,' his yeoman responded.

Mancuso closed his eyes and dozed for the rest of the ride. Nothing like a catnap to clear the mind. It had always worked on USS *Dallas*.

Hospital food, Cathy thought. Even at Hopkins, it was still hospital food. There had to be a special school somewhere for hospital chefs. The curriculum would be devoted to eliminating whatever fresh ideas they had, along with any skills they might have with spices, knowledge of recipes ... About the only thing they couldn't ruin was the Jell-O.

'Bernie, I need some advice.'

'What's the problem, Cath?' He knew already what it had to be, just from the look on her face and the tone of her voice. He waited as sympathetically as he could. Cathy was a proud woman, as she had every right to be. This had to be dreadfully hard on her.

'It's Jack.' The words came out rapidly, as though by a spasm, then stopped again.

The pain Katz saw in her eyes was more than he could bear. 'You think he's . . .'

'What? No – I mean – how, why did you . . . ?'

'Cathy, I'm not supposed to do this, but you're too important a friend for that. Screw the rules! Look, I had a guy in here last week, asking about you and Jack.'

The hurt only got worse. 'What do you mean? Who was here? Where from?'

'Government guy, some kind of investigator. Cathy, I'm sorry, but he asked me if there – if you had said anything about trouble at home. This guy was checking up on Jack, and he wanted to know if I knew anything that you were saying.'

'What did you say?'

'I told him I didn't know anything. I told him that you're one of the best people I know. You are, Cathy. You're not alone. You have friends, and if there is anything I can do – that any of us can do – to help you, we

623

will help you. Cathy, you're like family. You're probably feeling very hurt, and you're probably feeling very embarrassed. That is stupid, Cathy, that is very stupid. You know it's stupid, don't you?' Those pretty blue eyes were covered in tears, Katz saw, and in this moment he craved the chance to kill Jack Ryan, maybe do it on a table with a very sharp, very small surgical knife. 'Cathy, being alone doesn't help. This is what friends are really for. You are not alone.'

'I just can't believe it, Bernie. I just *can't*.'

'Come on, let's talk in my office, where it's private. Food's crummy today anyway.' Katz got her out of there, and he was sure that no one noticed. Two minutes later they were in his private office. He moved a stack of case files from the only other chair and sat her in it.

'He's just been acting different lately.'

'Do you really think it's possible that Jack is fooling around?' It took half a minute. Katz watched her eyes go up and down, finally staying down as she faced reality.

'It's possible. Yes.'

Bastard! 'Have you talked to him about it?' Katz kept his voice low and reasonable, but not dispassionate. She needed a friend now, and friends had to share pain to be useful.

A shake of the head. 'No, I don't know how.'

'You know that you have to do that.'

'Yeah.' Not so much a word as a gasp.

'It's not going to be easy. Remember,' Katz said with gentle hope in his voice, 'it could all be a mistake. Just some crazy misunderstanding.' Which Bernie Katz didn't believe for a moment.

She looked up, and her eyes were streaming now. 'Bernie, is there something wrong with me?'

'No!' Katz managed not to shout. 'Cathy, if there's a better person in this hospital than you, goddamn if I've ever met them! There is *nothing* wrong with you! You hear me? Whatever the hell this is, it is *not your fault*!'

'Bernie, I want another baby, I don't want to lose Jack –'

'Then if you really think that you have to win him back.'

'I *can't!* He isn't, he doesn't –' She broke down completely.

Katz learned then and there that anger has few limits. Having to keep it in, being denied a target, didn't help, but Cathy needed a friend more than she needed anything else.

'Dutch, this whole conversation is off the record.'

Lieutenant Commander Claggett was instantly on guard. 'As you say, Commodore.'

'Tell me about Captain Ricks.'

'Sir, he's my CO.'

'I'm aware of that, Dutch,' Mancuso said. 'I'm the squadron commander. If there's a problem with one of my skippers, there's a problem with one of my boats. Those boats cost a billion a copy, and I have to know about the problems. Is that clear, Commander?'

'Yes, sir.'

'Talk. That's an order.'

Dutch Claggett sat ramrod straight and spoke rapidly. 'Sir, he couldn't lead a three-year-old to the crapper. He treats the troops like they're robots. He demands a lot, but he never praises even when the guys put out. That's not the way I was taught to officer. He doesn't listen, sir. He doesn't listen to me, doesn't listen to the troops. Okay, fine, he's the CO. He owns the boat, but a smart skipper listens.'

'That's the reason for the transfers?'

'Yes, sir. He gave the chief torpedoman a bad time – I think he was wrong. Chief Getty was showing some initiative. He had the weapons on line, he had his people well-trained, but Captain Ricks didn't like the way he did it, and came down on him. I counseled against it, but the CO didn't listen. So Getty put in for transfer, and the skipper was glad to get rid of him, and endorsed it.'

'Do you have confidence in him?' Mancuso asked.

'Technically he's very good. Engineering-wise, he's

brilliant. He just doesn't know people and he doesn't know tactics.'

'He told me he wants to prove otherwise. Can he?'

'Sir, you're going too far now. I don't know that I have the right to answer that.'

Mancuso knew it was true, but pressed on anyway. 'You're supposed to be qualified for command, Dutch. Get used to making some hard calls.'

'Can he do it? Yes, sir. We have a good boat and a good crew. What he can't do the rest of us will do for him.'

The Commodore nodded and went silent for a moment. 'If you have any trouble with your next FitRep, I want to know about it. I think you may be a better XO than he's entitled to, Commander.'

'Sir, he's not a bad guy. I hear he's a good father and all that. His wife's a sweetie. It's just that he never learned to handle people, and nobody ever bothered teaching him right. Despite that he is a capable officer. If he'd only give an inch on the humanity side, he'd be a real star.'

'Are you comfortable with your op-orders?'

'If we sniff out an Akula to go in and track him – safe distance and all that. Am I comfortable? Hell, yes. Come on, Commodore, we're so quiet there's not a thing to worry about. I was surprised Washington approved this thing, and all, but that's bureaucratic stuff. The short version is, anybody can drive this boat. Okay, maybe Cap'n Ricks isn't perfect, but unless our boat breaks, Popeye could do the mission.'

They put the Secondary assembly in before the Primary. The collection of lithium compounds was contained in a metal cylinder roughly the size of a 105mm artillery casing, sixty-five centimeters high and eleven centimeters in diameter. It even had a rim machined on the bottom end so that it would fit exactly the right spot. There was a small curved tube at the bottom that attached to what would soon be the tritium reservoir. On the outside of the casing were the fins made of spent ^{238}U. They looked like rows of thick, black soda crackers, Fromm thought. Their mission, of course, was to be immolated to plasma. Beneath the cylinder were the first bundles of 'soda-straws' – even Fromm was calling them that now, though they actually were not; they were of the wrong diameter. Sixty centimeters in length, each bundle of a hundred was held together by thin but strong plastic spacers, and the bottom of each had been given a half-turn to make each bundle into a helix, a shape rather like that of a spiral staircase. The hard part in this segment of the design was to arrange the helixes to nest together perfectly. Seemingly trivial, it had taken fully two days for Fromm to figure out, but as with all aspects of his design, the pieces all fit into proper place until that portion of the design seemed a perfectly assembled mass of . . . soda straws. It almost made the German laugh. With tape measure, micrometer, and an expert eye – gradation marks had been machined into many of the parts, a small detail that had impressed Ghosn very greatly indeed. When Fromm was satisfied, they went on. First came the plastic foam blocks, each cut to precise specifications. They fit into the elliptical bomb-case. Ghosn and Fromm were now doing all the work. Slowly, carefully, they eased the first block into place within the flanges on the interior of the case. The straw bundles came next, one at a time, nesting perfectly with those immediately under them. At every step both men stopped to check the work. Fromm and Ghosn both checked the work, checked the plans, checked the work again, and checked the plans again.

For Bock and Qati, watching a few meters away, it was the most tedious thing they had ever seen.

'The people who do this work in America and Russia must die of boredom,' the German said quietly.

'Perhaps.'

'Next bundle, number thirty-six,' Fromm said.

'Thirty-six,' Ghosn replied, examining the three tags on the next batch of a hundred straws. 'Bundle thirty-six.'

'Thirty-six,' Fromm agreed, looking at the tags. He took it and maneuvered it into place. It fit perfectly, Qati

627

saw, coming closer. The German's skilled hands moved it slightly, so that the slits on its plastic jigs dropped into the slots on the jigs directly underneath. When Fromm was satisfied, Ghosn looked.

'Correct position,' Ibrahim said, for what must have been the hundredth time of the day.

'I agree,' Fromm announced, and both men wired it firmly into place.

'Like assembling a gun,' Qati whispered to Günther, as he walked away from the work table.

'No.' Bock shook his head. 'Worse than that. More like a child's toy.' The two men looked at each other and started laughing.

'Enough of that!' Fromm said in annoyance. 'This is serious work! We need silence! Next bundle, number thirty-seven!'

'Thirty-seven,' Ghosn dutifully replied.

Bock and Qati walked out of the room together.

'Watching a woman having a baby cannot be as dreadful as this!' Qati raged when they got outside.

Bock lit a cigarette. 'It isn't. I know. Women move faster than this.'

'Indeed, that is unskilled labor.' Qati laughed again. The humor vanished, and the Commander became serious. 'It's a pity.'

'Yes, it is. They have all served us well. When?'

'Very soon.' Qati paused. 'Günther, your part in the plan . . . it is very dangerous.'

Bock took a long pull on his cigarette, blowing the smoke out into the chilled air. 'It is my plan, is it not? I know the risks.'

'I do not approve of suicidal plans,' Qati observed after a moment.

'Nor do I. It is dangerous, but I expect to survive. Ismael, if we wanted a safe life, we would be working in offices – and we would never have met. What binds us is the danger and the mission. I've lost my Petra, my daughters, but I still have my mission. I do not say that this is enough, but is it not more than most men have?' Günther looked up at the stars. 'I have thought often of

628

this, my friend. How does one change the world? Not in safety. The safe ones, the timid ones, they benefit from our work. They rage at life, but they lack the courage to act. We are the ones who act. We take the risks, we face the danger, we deny ourselves for others. It is our task. My friend, it is far too late to have second thoughts.'

'Günther, it is easier for me. I am a dying man.'

'I know.' He turned to look at his friend. 'We're all dying men. We've cheated death, you and I. Eventually death will win, and the death we face lies not in bed. You chose this path, and so did I. Can we turn back now?'

'I cannot, but facing death is a hard thing.'

'That is true.' Günther flipped his cigarette into the dirt. 'But at least we have the privilege of knowing. The little people do not. In choosing not to act, they choose not to know. That is their choice. One can either be an agent of destiny or a victim of it. Everyone has that choice.' Bock led his friend back in. 'We have made ours.'

'Bundle thirty-eight!' Fromm commanded as they entered.

'Thirty-eight,' Ghosn acknowledged.

'Yes, Commodore?'

'Sit down, Harry, we need to talk over some things.'

'Well, I have the crew all ready. The sonar troops are hot.'

Mancuso looked at his subordinate. *At what point*, he wondered, *does a positive can-do attitude become a lie?* 'I'm a little concerned with the transfer rate from your ship.'

Ricks didn't go defensive. 'Well, we had some guys with family concerns. No sense holding onto people whose minds are in the wrong place. A statistical blip. I had it happen once before.'

I bet you did. 'How's morale?' Mancuso asked next.

'You've seen the results of our drills and exams. That must tell you something,' Captain Ricks replied.

Clever son of a bitch. 'Okay, let me make it clear, Harry. You had a run-in with Dr Jones.'

'So?'

'So, I talked with him about it.'

'How formal is this?'

'Informal as you like, Harry.'

'Fine. Your Jones fellow is a pretty good technician, but he seems to have forgotten the fact that he left the Navy as an enlisted man. If he wants to talk to me as an equal, it would help if he'd bothered to accomplish something.'

'That man has a doctor's degree in physics from Cal-Tech, Harry.'

Ricks took on a puzzled expression. 'So?'

'So, he's one of the smartest people I know, and he was the best enlisted man I ever met.'

'That's fine, but if enlisted were as smart as officers, we'd pay them more.' It was the supreme arrogance of the statement that angered Bart Mancuso.

'Captain, when I was driving *Dallas*, and Jones talked, I listened. If life had worked out a little different, he'd be on his XO tour right now and on his way to command of a fast-attack. Ron would have made a superb CO.'

Ricks dismissed that. 'We'll never know that, will we? I always figured that those who can, do. Those who can't, make excuses. Okay, fine, he's a good technician. I don't dispute that. He did good work with my sonar department, and I'm grateful for that, but let's not get too excited. There are lots of technicians, and lots of contractors.'

This was going nowhere, Mancuso saw. It was time to lay the law down. 'Look, Harry, I'm catching rumbles about morale on your boat. I see that many transfer requests, and it tells me there might be a problem. So, I nose around, and my impression is confirmed. You have a problem whether you know it or not.'

'That, sir, is bullshit. It's like the alcohol-counseling weenies. People with no drinking problem say they have no drinking problem, but the counselors say that denial of a problem is the first indication there is one. It's a circular argument. If I had a morale problem on my boat, performance figures would show it. But they *don't*. My record is pretty clear. I drive submarines for a living. I've been in the top one percent of the top one percent since I put this suit on. Okay, my style isn't the same as the next guy's. I don't kiss butt, and I don't mollycoddle. I demand performance, and I get it. You show me one hard indicator that I'm not doing it right, and I'll listen, but until you do, sir, it isn't broke, and I'm not going to try and fix it.'

Bartolomeo Vito Mancuso, Captain (Rear Admiral selectee), United States Navy, did not come out of his chair only because his mainly Sicilian ancestry had been somewhat diluted in America. In the old country, he was instantly sure, his great-great-grandfather would have leveled his *lupara* and blown a wide, bloody hole through Rick's chest for that. Instead he kept his face impassive and coldly decided on the spot that Ricks would never get beyond captain's rank. It was in his power to do that. He had a large collection of COs working for him. Only the top two, maybe the top three, would screen for flag rank. Ricks would be rated no higher than fourth in that group. It might be dishonest, Mancuso told himself in a moment of dispassionate integrity, but it was still the right thing to do. This man could not be trusted with command higher than he now held and he had probably come too far already. It would be so easy. Ricks would object loudly and passionately to being rated fourth in a group of fourteen, but Mancuso would simply say, *Sorry, Harry – I'm not saying there's anything wrong with you, just that Andy, Bill, and Chuck are a little better. Just bad luck to be in a squadron of aces, Harry. I have to make an honest call, and they're just a whisker better.*

Ricks was just fast enough to realize that he had crossed over a line, that there really were no 'off the record' talks in the Navy. He had defied his squadron commander, a man already on the fast track, a man trusted and believed by the Pentagon and the Op-02 bureaucracy.

'Sir, excuse me for being so positive. It's just that nobody likes to be called down when –'

Mancuso smiled as he cut the man off. 'No problem,

Harry. We Italians tend to be a little passionate, too.'
Too late, Harry . . .

'Maybe you're right. Let me think it over. Besides, if I
tangle with that Akula, I'll show you what my people
can do.'

Little late to talk about 'my people,' fella. But Mancuso had to give him the chance, didn't he? Not much
of a chance, but a little one. If there were a miracle, then
he might reconsider. *Might.* Bart told himself, *if this
arrogant little prick decides to kiss my ass at the main
gate at noon on the Fourth of July while the marching
band passes by.*

'Sessions like this are supposed to be uncomfortable
for everybody,' the squadron commander said. Ricks
would end up as an engineering expert, and a good one,
once Mancuso got rid of him, and there was no disgrace
in topping out as a captain, was there? Not for a good
man, anyway.

'Nothing else?' Golovko asked.

'Not a thing,' the Colonel replied.

'And our officer?'

'I saw his widow two days ago. I told her that he was
dead, but that we were unable to recover the body. She
took the news badly. It is a hard thing to see so lovely a
face in tears,' the man reported quietly.

'What about the pension, other arrangements?'

'I am seeing to it myself.'

'Good, those damned paper-pushers don't seem to care
about anyone or anything. If there's a problem, let me
know.'

'I have nothing more to suggest from the technical-
intelligence side,' the Colonel went on. 'Can you follow
up elsewhere?'

'We're still rebuilding our network inside their defense
ministry. Preliminary indications are that there is
nothing, that the new Germany has disavowed the
whole DDR project,' Golovko said. 'There is a hint that
American and British agencies have made similar inquiries and come away satisfied.'

'It is unlikely, I think, that German nuclear weapons would be a matter of immediate concern to the Americans or the English.'

'True. We are carrying on, but I do not expect to find anything. I think this is an empty hole.'

'In that case, Sergey Nikolayevich, why was our man murdered?'

'We still don't *know* that, damn it!'

'Yes, I suppose he might now be working for the Argentinians . . .'

'Colonel, remember your place!'

'I have not forgotten it. Nor have I forgotten that when someone troubles to murder an intelligence officer there is a good reason for it.'

'But there's nothing there! At least three intelligence services are looking. Our people in Argentina are still working –'

'Oh, yes, the Cubans?'

'Correct, that was their area of responsibility, and we can scarcely depend on their assistance now, can we?'

The colonel closed his eyes. What had KGB come to? 'I still think we should press on.'

'Your recommendation is noted. The operation is not over.'

Exactly what he could do now, Golovko thought after the man left, exactly what new avenues he should explore . . . he didn't know. He had a goodly percentage of his field force sniffing for leads, but as yet there was nothing. This miserable profession was so much like police work, wasn't it?

Marvin Russell went over his requirements. Certainly these were generous people. He still had almost all of the money he'd brought over. He'd even offered to make use of it, but Qati would have none of that. He had a briefcase in which were forty thousand dollars in crisp twenties and fifties, and on setting himself up in America he'd take in a direct bank transfer from an English bank. His tasks were fairly simple. First he needed new identities for himself and the others. That was child's play. Even doing the driver's licenses was not difficult, if you had the right hardware, and he'd be purchasing that for cash. He'd even be able to set the equipment up in the safe house. Now, exactly why he had to do hotel reservations in addition to setting up the safe house was another question. These characters sure liked to keep things complicated.

On the way to the airport, he'd taken a day to stop at a good tailor shop – Beirut might have been at war, but life still went on. By the time he boarded the British Airways jet for Heathrow he looked quite distinguished. Three very nice suits – two of them packed. A conservative haircut, expensive shoes that cramped his feet.

'Magazine, sir?' the stew asked.

'Thank you.' Russell smiled.

'American?'

'That's right. Going home.'

'It must be rather difficult in Lebanon.'

'Did get kind of exciting, yes.'

'Drink?'

'A beer would be very nice.' Russell grinned. He was even getting the businessman lingo down. The plane was not even a third full, and it seemed like this stewardess was going to adopt him. Maybe it was the tan, Russell thought.

'There you go, sir. Will you be staying long in London?'

''Fraid not. Connecting to Chicago. Two-hour layover.'

'That is too bad.' She even looked disappointed for him. The Brits, Russell thought, sure were nice people. Almost as hospitable as those Arabs.

The last bundle went in just after three in the morning, local time. Fromm didn't alter his demeanor a dot. He checked this one as carefully as he had checked the first, fixing it in place only after he was fully satisfied. Then he stood straight up and stretched.

'Enough!'

'I agree, Manfred.'

634

'This time tomorrow we'll have the assembly finished. What remains is simple, not fourteen hours' work.'

'In that case, let's get some sleep.' On the way out of the building, Ghosn gave the Commander a wink.

Qati watched them depart, then walked over to the senior guard. 'Where's Achmed?'

'Went to see the doctor, remember?'

'Hmmm. When's he back?'

'Tomorrow, maybe the day after, I'm not sure.'

'Very well. We will have a special job for you soon.'

The guard watched the men walking away from the building and nodded dispassionately. 'Where do you want us to excavate the hole?'

CHAPTER 28

Contractual Obligations

Jet lag could be a real bitch, Marvin thought. Russell had left O'Hare in a rented Mercury and driven west to a motel just east of Des Moines. He surprised the clerk by paying cash for his room, explaining that his wallet and credit cards had been stolen. He had an obviously brand-new wallet to support that statement, besides which the clerk honored cash as readily as any businessman. Sleep came easily that night. He awoke just after five, after a good ten hours of slumber, had himself a big American breakfast – as hospitable as people were in Lebanon, they didn't know how to eat; he wondered how they managed to live without bacon – and set off for Colorado. By lunch, he was halfway across Nebraska, and going over his plans and requirements again. Dinner found him in the town of Roggen, an hour northeast of Denver, which was close enough. Stiff from travel, he found yet another motel and crashed for the night. This time he was able to watch and enjoy some American TV, including a recap of the NFL season on ESPN. It was surprising how much he'd missed football. Almost as surprising as how much he'd missed having a drink whenever he wanted. That craving was fixed with a bottle of Jack Daniel's he'd gotten along the way. By midnight, he was feeling pretty mellow, looking around at his surroundings, glad to be back in America, and also glad for the reason he was back. It was time for some payback. Russell had not forgotten who had once owned Colorado, and hadn't forgotten the massacre at Sand Creek.

*

It should have been expected. Things had gone too smoothly, and reality does not often allow perfection. A small mistake in one of the fittings for the Primary had been detected, and that fitting had to be removed and remachined, a process that set them back by thirty hours, of which forty minutes had been required for the machining, and the rest for disassembly and reassembly of the weapon. Fromm, who should have been philosophical, had been livid during the whole procedure, and insisted on doing the fix himself. Then had come the laborious replacement of the explosive blocks, all the more onerous for having already been done once.

'Only three millimeters,' Ghosn noted. Just a mistaken setting on one of the controls. Since it had been a manual job, the computers hadn't caught it. One of Fromm's figures had been misread, and the first visual inspection of the assembly hadn't caught it. 'And we had that extra day.'

Fromm merely grumbled behind his protective mask, as he and Ghosn lifted the plutonium assembly and gently set it in place. Five minutes later, it was clear that they had it correctly located. The bars of tungsten-rhenium next fit into their own places, then the beryllium segments, and finally, the heavy depleted-uranium hemisphere that separated the Primary from the Secondary. Fifty more explosive blocks, and they were done. Fromm ordered a pause – what they had just accomplished was heavy work, and he wanted a short rest. The machinists were already gone, their services no longer required.

'We should have been done by now,' the German said quietly.

'It is unreasonable to expect perfection, Manfred.'

'The ignorant bastard couldn't read!'

'The number on the plans was smudged.' *And that was your fault*, Ghosn did not have to say.

'*Then he should have asked!*'

'As you say, Manfred. You pick a poor time to be impatient. We are on schedule.'

The young Arab just didn't understand, Fromm knew.

The culmination of his life's ambitions, and it should have been done by now! 'Come on.'

It required ten additional hours until the seventieth and last explosive block sat in its resting place. Ghosn attached its wire lead to the proper terminal, and that was that. He extended his hand to the German, who took it.

'Congratulations, *Herr Doktor* Fromm.'

'*Ja*. Thank you, *Herr* Ghosn.'

'Now we only need to weld the case shut, draw the vacuum – oh, excuse me, the tritium. How did I forget that? Who does the welding?' Manfred asked.

'I will. I'm very good at that.' The top half of the bombcase had a wide flange to ensure the safety of that procedure, and it had already been checked for a perfect fit. The machinists had not merely handled the precise work on the explosive part of the device. Every single part – except for the single mis-trimmed fitting – had been cut and shaped to Fromm's specifications, and the bomb-case had already been checked. It fit as tightly as the back of a watch.

'Doing the tritium is easy.'

'Yes, I know.' Ghosn motioned for the German to go outside. 'You are fully satisfied with the design and the assembly?'

'Completely,' Fromm said confidently. 'It will function exactly as I predict.'

'Excellent,' Qati said, waiting outside with one of his bodyguards.

Fromm turned, noting the Commander's presence, along with one of his ubiquitous guards. Dirty, scruffy people, but he had to admire them, Fromm told himself, as he turned to look at the darkened valley. There was a quarter moon, and he could just make out the landscape. It was so dry and harsh. Not these people's fault that they looked as they did. The land here was hard. But the sky was clear. Fromm looked up at the stars on this cloudless night. More stars than one could see in Germany, especially the Eastern part, with all its air pollution, and he thought about astrophysics, the path he might have taken, so closely related to the path he had.

Ghosn stood behind the German. He turned to Qati and nodded. The Commander made the same gesture to his bodyguard, whose name was Abdullah.

'Just the tritium remains,' Fromm said, his back to them.

'Yes,' Ghosn said, 'I can do that myself.'

Fromm was about to say that there was one more thing. He let it wait a moment, and didn't pay attention to Abdullah's footsteps. There was no sound at all as the guard removed a silenced pistol from his belt and pointed it at Fromm's head from a range of one meter. Fromm began to turn, to make sure that Ghosn knew about the tritium, but he never made it around. Abdullah had his orders. It was supposed to be merciful, as it had been for the machinists. It was a pity that it had been necessary at all, Qati thought, but it was necessary, and that was that. None of that mattered to Abdullah, who merely followed his orders, squeezing on the trigger smoothly and expertly until the round fired. The bullet entered the back of Fromm's skull, soon thereafter exiting through his forehead. The German dropped in a crumpled mass. Blood fountained out, but sideways, without reaching Abdullah's clothing. The guard waited until the blood flow stopped, then summoned two comrades to carry the body to the waiting truck. He'd be buried with the machinists. That, at least, was fitting, Qati thought. All the experts in the same place.

'A pity,' Ghosn observed quietly.

'Yes, but do you really think we would have further use of him?'

Ibrahim shook his head. 'No. He would have been a liability. We could not trust him. An infidel and a mercenary. He fulfilled his contract.'

'And the device?'

'It will work. I have checked the numbers twenty times. It is far better than anything I might have designed.'

'What's this about tritium?'

'In the batteries. I only need to heat them up and bleed

off the gas. Then the gas is pumped into the two reservoirs. You know the rest.'

Qati grunted. 'You have explained it, but I do not know it.'

'This part of the job is work for a high-school chemistry lab, no more than that. Simple.'

'Why did Fromm leave it for last?'

Ghosn shrugged. 'Something has to be last. This is an easy task rather than a hard one. Perhaps that is why. I can do it now if you wish.'

'Good.'

Qati watched the procedure. One after another, Ghosn loaded the batteries into the furnace, which he set for very low heat. A metal tube and a vacuum pump drew off the gas emitted by each in turn. It took less than an hour.

'Fromm lied to us,' Ghosn observed when he was done.

'What?' Qati asked in alarm.

'Commander, there is almost fifteen percent more tritium than he promised. So much the better.'

The next step was even simpler. Ghosn carefully checked that each reservoir was air- and pressure-tight – it was the sixth such test; the young engineer had learned from his German teacher – then transferred the tritium gas. The valves were closed and locked shut with cotter pins, so that any vibration in transit could not open them.

'Finished,' Ghosn announced. The guards lifted the top of the bombcase and lowered it into place from an overhead winch. It fit precisely into place. Ghosn took an hour to weld it shut. Another test confirmed that the bombcase was pressure-tight. He next attached a Leyboold vacuum pump to the case.

'What exactly do you need to achieve?'

'A millionth of an atmosphere is what we specified.'

'Can you do that? Won't it harm –'

Ghosn spoke not unlike Fromm, surprising the both of them. 'Commander, please? All that presses in is *air*. It does not crush you, and it will not crush this steel case, will it? It will take a few hours, and we can also

640

test the integrity of the bombcase again.' Which had also been done five times. Even without being welded, the case held well. Now one piece of metal, it would be as perfect as the mission required. 'We can get some sleep. It doesn't hurt the pump to run.'

'When will it be ready to transport?'

'In the morning. When is the ship leaving?'

'Two days.'

'There you have it,' Ghosn smiled broadly. 'Time to spare.'

First, Marvin visited the local branch of Colorado Federal Bank and Trust Company. He amazed and delighted the branch vice president by placing a call to England and having five hundred thousand dollars transferred by wire. Computers made things so much easier. In seconds, he had confirmation that Mr Robert Friend was every bit as substantial as he claimed to be.

'Can you recommend a good local realtor?' Russell asked the very solicitous banker.

'Right down the street, third door on the right. I'll have your checks ready when you get back.' The banker watched him leave and placed a rapid phone call to his wife, who worked in the real-estate office. She was waiting for him at the door.

'Mr Friend, welcome to Roggen!'

'Thank you, good to be back.'

'You've been away?'

'Spent some time in Saudi Arabia,' Russell/Friend explained. 'But I missed my winters.'

'What are you looking for?'

'Oh, a medium-sized ranch, place where I might raise some beef.'

'House, barns?'

'Yeah, a good-sized house. Not that big, don't need it – there's just me, you see – say about three thousand square feet. I can go smaller for good land.'

'You originally from around here?'

'The Dakotas, actually, but I need to be close to Denver for the transportation – air travel, I mean. I do a lot of that. My old homestead is too far from things.'

'Will you want help to run your ranch?'

'Yeah, I'll need that, say a place enough for two hands – maybe a couple. I really should have a place closer to town, but, damn it, I just want a place where I can eat my own beef.'

'I know what you mean,' the realtor agreed. 'I have a couple of places you might like.'

'Then let's go see them.' Russell smiled at the lady.

The second one was perfect. Just off Exit 50, five hundred acres, a nice old farm house with a new kitchen, a two-car garage, and three sturdy outbuildings. There was clear land in all directions, a pond with some trees half a mile from the house, and plenty of room for the cattle that Russell would never see.

'This one's been on the market for five months. The owner's estate is asking four hundred,' the realtor said, 'but we can probably get them to go for three-fifty.'

'Okay,' Russell said, checking access to Interstate 76. 'Tell them if they sign the contract this week, I'll make a fifty-thousand cash deposit, settlement in, oh, say four or five weeks. No problem on financing. I'll pay cash for the whole thing when I get the rest of my funds transferred. But – I want to start moving in immediately. God, I hate living in hotels, done way too much of that. You think we get all that done?'

The realtor beamed at him. 'I think I can guarantee it.'

'Great. So, how did the Broncos do this year?'

'Eight and eight. They're rebuilding. My husband and I have season tickets. You going to try and get tickets for the Superbowl?'

'I'd sure like to.'

'Going to be pretty hard,' the realtor warned him.

'I'll find a way.' An hour and one telephone call later, the realtor took a cashier's check for fifty thousand dollars from her banker husband. Russell had directions to the local furniture and appliance store. After an hour there, Marvin purchased a white Ford van from the local dealership and drove it to the ranch. He parked it in one of the barns. He'd be keeping the rental for a while. He would spend one more night in the motel, then settle into his new house. He did not feel any sense of accomplishment. There was much left to do.

Cathy Ryan found herself paying closer attention to the newspapers now. They were good for reporting scandals and leaks, and she now had the interest in such things that she had lacked before, especially for the byline of Robert Holtzman. Unfortunately, the new articles on the problems at CIA were more general, concentrating mainly on changes within the Soviet Union that she had difficulty understanding. It just wasn't an area in which she had much interest – as Jack didn't much care about the developments in eye surgery that his wife was very excited about. Finally, there did come a piece about financial impropriety and a 'very senior official.' That was the second such item and she realized that if it were Jack, she had all the investigatorial documents there in her own home. It was a Sunday, and Jack was away at work again, leaving her at home with the kids again. The kids enjoyed this chilly morning in front of the TV. Cathy Ryan went into the financial files.

They were a disaster. Money management was another thing that failed to interest Dr Caroline Ryan, and Jack assumed the duties more or less by default, just as cooking fell into her domain. She didn't even know the filing system, and was certain that Jack never expected her to wade into this colossal mess of documents. Along the way, she learned that the blind trust that managed their stock portfolio was doing rather well at the moment. Ordinarily, she just saw the year-end earnings statements. Money didn't interest her very much. The house was paid off. The kids' education funds were already set up. The Ryan family actually lived off the combined income of the two Doctors Ryan, which allowed their investments to grow, while complicating their annual taxes, which was also something that Jack – who still had his CPA certification – took care of, with the aid of the family's attorney. The most recent statement of net worth drew a gasp. Cathy decided to add the money manager to the Christmas card list. But that was not what she was after. She found it at two-thirty in the afternoon. The file was simply marked 'Zimmer,' and was naturally enough in the last drawer she got to.

The Zimmer file was several inches thick. She sat cross-legged on the floor before opening it, her head already aching from eyestrain and the Tylenol which she should have taken but hadn't. The first document was a letter from Jack to an attorney — not their regular attorney, the one who did their wills and taxes and the other routine work — instructing him to set up an educational trust fund for seven children, a number which had been changed to eight several months later, Cathy saw. The trust fund had been set up with an initial investment of over half a million dollars, and managed as a stock portfolio through the same managers who did part of the Ryan family account. Cathy was surprised to see that Jack did actually make recommendations for this account, something that he did not do for his own. He hadn't lost his touch, either. The yield from the Zimmer portfolio was twenty-three percent. Another hundred thousand dollars had been invested in a business — a Sub-Chapter-S corporation, she saw, whatever that was — with Southland Corporation as — oh, she realized, a 7-Eleven. It was a Maryland corporation, with the address given as . . .

That's only a few miles from here! It was, in fact, right off of Route 50, and that meant that Jack passed it twice a day on his way to and from work.

How convenient!

So, who the hell was Carol Zimmer?

Medical bills? Obstetrics?

Dr Marsha Rosen! *I know her!* Had Cathy not been on the faculty at Hopkins, she would have used Marsha Rosen for her own pregnancies; Rosen was a Yale graduate with a very fine reputation.

A baby! Jacqueline Zimmer! Jacqueline? Cathy thought, her face flushed scarlet. Then the tears began streaming down her cheeks.

You bastard! You can't give me a baby, but you gave one to her, didn't you!

She checked the date, then searched her memory, Jack hadn't been home that day until very late. She remembered, because she'd had to cancel out on a dinner party over at . . .

He was there! He was there for the delivery, wasn't he! What more proof do I need? The triumph of the discovery changed at once into black despair.

The world could end so easily, Cathy thought. Just a slip of paper could do it, and that was it. It was over.

Is it over?

How could it not be? Even if he still wanted — did she want him?

What about the kids? Cathy asked herself. She closed the file and replaced it without rising. 'You're a doctor,' she said to herself. 'You're supposed to think before you act.'

The kids needed a father. But what sort of father was he? Gone thirteen or fourteen hours a day, sometimes seven days a week. He managed to take his son to one — just one! — baseball game, despite constant pleas. He was lucky to make half of Little Jack's T-Ball games. He missed *every* school affair, the Christmas plays, all the other things. Cathy had been half surprised that he'd been home Christmas morning. The night before, assembling the toys, he'd gotten drunk again, and she hadn't even bothered trying to attract him. What was the point? His present to her . . . well, it was nice enough, but the sort of thing a man could get in a few minutes of shopping, no big deal —

Shopping.

Cathy rose and checked through the mail on Jack's desk. His credit card bills were sitting in the pile. She opened one and found a bunch of entries from Hamley's in London. Six hundred dollars? But he'd only gotten one thing for Little Jack, and two small items for Sally. Six hundred dollars!

Christmas shopping for two families, Jack?

'Just how much more evidence do you need, Cathy

girl?' she asked herself aloud again. 'Oh God oh God oh God –'

She didn't move for a very long time, nor did she see or hear anything outside of her own misery. Only the mother in her kept subconscious track of the sound of the kids in the playroom.

Jack got home just before seven that evening, actually rather pleased with himself to be an hour early, and further pleased that he had the Mexico operation set in concrete now. All he had to do was take it to the White House, and then after he got it approved – Fowler would go for this; risks and all, distaste for covert operations and all, this was too juicy for the politician in him to turn down – and after Clark and Chavez brought it off, his stock would go up. And things would change. Things would get better. He would get things straightened out. For starters, he'd plan a vacation. It was time for one. A week off, maybe two, and if some CIA puke showed up with daily briefing documents, Ryan would kill the son-of-a-bitch. He wanted freedom from the job, and he'd get it. Two good weeks. Take the kids out of school and go see Mickey, just as Clark had suggested. He'd make the reservations tomorrow.

'I'm home!' Jack announced. Silence. That was odd. He went downstairs and found the kids in front of the TV. They were doing too damned much of that, but that was their father's fault. He'd change that, too. He'd cut back on his hours. It was time Marcus held up his end instead of working banker's hours and leaving Jack with all the goddamned work.

'Where's Mommy?'

'I don't know,' Sally said, without turning away from the green slime and orange guck.

Ryan walked back upstairs and into the bedroom to change. Still no sign of his wife. He found her carrying a basket of wash. Jack stood in her path, leaning forward to kiss her, but she leaned back and shook her head. Okay, that was no big thing.

'What's for dinner, babe?' he inquired lightly.

'I don't know. Why don't you fix something?' It was

her tone, the snappy way she fired back without provocation.

'What did I do?' Jack asked. He was already surprised, but he hadn't had time enough to grasp her demeanor. The look in her eyes was an alien thing, and when she answered to this question, her voice made him shrivel.

'Nothing, Jack, you haven't done anything at all.' She pushed past him with the basket and disappeared around the corner.

He just stood there, flat against the wall, his mouth open, not knowing what to say, and not understanding why his wife had suddenly decided to despise him.

It took only a day and a half from Latakia to Pireus. Bock had found a ship heading to the right port, eliminating the need to transship at Rotterdam. Qati disliked deviation from the plan, but a careful check of shipping schedules showed that the five days saved might be important, and he agreed to it. He and Ghosn watched the gantry crane lift up the cargo container and move it onto the deck of the *Carmen Vita*, a Greek-flag container ship on the Mediterranean run. She would sail on the evening tide, and arrive in the United States in eleven days. They could have chartered a jet aircraft and done this, Qati thought, but it would have been too dangerous. Eleven days. He'd be able to see his physician again, and still have time to fly to America and make certain that all the arrangements were satisfactory. The workers secured the container box in place. It would be well-protected, in the center of the ship, with other boxes atop it, and well aft, so that winter storms would not buffet it directly. The two men retired to a waterfront bar and waited for the ship to sail, then flew to Damascus, and drove from there to their headquarters. The bomb shop was already gone — mothballed would have been a more accurate term. The power cables had been cut, and dirt pushed over all the entrances. If someone ever drove a heavy truck over the concealed roof there would be a major surprise, but that was unlikely. It *was* possible that they might use the facility again, and against that slim possibility was the inconvenience of removing the machines to another burial place. Simply covering the facility over was the most logical alternative.

Russell flew to Chicago to catch the first round of playoff games. He took with him a camera, an expensive Nikon F4, and burned up two rolls of ASA-100 color prints photographing the ABC trucks – the *Monday Night Football* team was doing this particular wild-card game – before catching a cab back to the airport. He was lucky enough on the flight that he caught part of the game on the radio during the drive from Stapleton International to his new house off Interstate 76. The Bears pulled it out in overtime, 23–20. That meant that Chicago would have the honor of losing the following week to the Vikings in the Metrodome. Minnesota had a by during the first week of wildcard games. Tony Wills' pulled groin would be fully healed, and that rookie, the announcer pointed out, had barely missed making two thousand rushing yards in his first NFL season, plus eight hundred yards as a receiver. Russell managed to catch nearly all of the AFC game, because it was played on the West Coast. There were no surprises, but it was still football.

USS *Maine* left the shed without incident. Tugs turned her around, pointing the submarine down the channel, and continued to stand by if assistance were required. Captain Ricks stood atop the sail, actually aft of the cockpit, leaning against rails set in the very top of the structure. Lieutenant Commander Claggett stood his watch in the control room. The navigator actually did the work, using the periscope to mark positions, which a quartermaster dutifully checked off on the chart, ensuring that the submarine was in the center of the channel and headed in the proper direction. The trip to sea was a fairly lengthy one. Throughout the boat, men continued to stow gear. Those not actually on watch settled into their bunks and tried to nap. Soon *Maine* would be on her regular six-hour watch cycle. The sailors all made the conscious effort to get their minds from land-mode into at-sea-mode. Families and friends might as well have been on another planet. For the next two months their entire world was contained within the steel hull of their submarine.

Mancuso watched the sailing as he always did for each of his boats. It was a shame, he decided, that there was no way to get Ricks off the boat. But there was no such way. He'd meet with Group in a few days to go over routine business. At that meeting, he'd express his misgivings about Ricks. He would not be able to go too far this first time, just to let Group know that he had his doubts about the 'Gold' CO. The quasi-political nature of the exercise grated on Mancuso, who liked things in the open and above board, the Navy Way. But the Navy Way had its own rules of behavior, and in the absence of substantive cause for action, all he could do now was to express concern with Ricks and his way of running things. Besides, Group was headed by yet another hyper-engineering type who would probably have a little too much sympathy with Harry.

Mancuso tried to find an emotion for the moment, but failed. The slate-grey shape diminished in the distance, gliding across the oily-calm waters of the harbor, heading out for her fifth deterrence patrol, as U.S. Navy submarines had been doing for over thirty years. Business as usual, world changes and all, that's all it was. *Maine* sailed out to keep the peace through the threat of the most inhuman force known to man. The Commodore shook his head. What a hell of a way to run a railroad. That was why he'd always been a fast-attack man. But it worked, had worked, probably would continue to work for a lot more years, Bart told himself, and while not every boomer skipper was another Mush Morton, they'd all brought their boats back. He got into his navy-blue official car and told the driver to take him back to the office. Paperwork beckoned.

At least the kids didn't notice. Jack took some comfort in that. Kids lived as spectators in a highly complex world which required years of schooling to appreciate, as a result of which they took note mainly of the parts that they understood, and that did not include a Mom and Dad who simply didn't talk. It wouldn't last forever, of course, but it might last long enough for things to be smoothed over. Probably would, Jack thought. Sure it would.

He didn't know what was wrong, nor did he know what to do about it. What he ought to have done, of course, was get home at a decent hour, maybe take her out to dinner at a nice place and – but that was not possible with two kids in school. Getting a sitter in the middle of the week and this far out of town was impractical. Another option was simply to get home and pay closer attention to his wife, leading to a –

But he couldn't depend on his ability to do that, and one more failure could only make things worse.

He looked up from his desk, out at the pines that lay beyond the CIA boundary fence. The symmetry was perfect. His work was messing up his family life, and now his family life was messing up his work. So, now, he had nothing at all that he could do properly. Wasn't that nice? Ryan got up from his desk and left the office, wandering to the nearest kiosk. Once there he purchased his first pack of cigarettes in . . . five years? Six? Whatever, he stripped off the cellophane top and tapped one out. One luxury of having a private office was that he could smoke without interference – CIA had become just like all government offices in that respect; for the most part, people could only smoke in the rest rooms. He pretended not to see the disapproving look on Nancy's face on his way back in, then went rooting in his desk for an ashtray before lighting up.

It was, he decided a minute later – just as the initial dizziness hit him – one of the dependable pleasures of life. Alcohol was another. You ingested these substances and you got the desired result, which explained their popularity, in spite of the dangers to health that everyone knew about. Alcohol and nicotine, the two things that make intolerable life into something else. While they shortened it.

Wasn't that just great? Ryan almost laughed at his incredible stupidity. Just what else of himself would he destroy? But did it matter?

His work mattered. That he was sure of. That was what had landed him in this mess, one way or another. That was the prime destructive factor in his life, but he could no more leave that than he could change anything else.

'Nancy, please ask Mr Clark to come in.'

John appeared two minutes later. 'Aw, hell, Doc!' he observed almost immediately. 'Now, what's the wife gonna say?'

'Not a thing.'

'Bet you're wrong on that.' Clark turned to open a window for ventilation. He'd quit a long time before. It was the one vice that he feared. It had killed his father. 'What do you want?'

'How's the hardware?'

'Waiting for your go-ahead to build it.'

'Go,' Jack said simply.

'You got a go-mission order?'

'No, but I don't need it. We'll call it part of the feasibility study. How long to slap things together?'

'Three days, they say. We'll need some cooperation from the Air Force.'

'What about the computer side?'

'That program has already been validated. They've taken tapes from six different aircraft, and smoothed out the noise. It's never taken them more than two or three hours to do an hour of tape.'

'Mexico City to D.C. is . . .'

'Depending on weather, just under four hours, max. Doing the full tape will be an overnighter,' Clark estimated. 'The President's schedule is what?'

'Arrival ceremony is Monday afternoon. The first business session is the following morning. State dinner Tuesday night.'

'You going?'

Ryan shook his head. 'No, we're going to the one a week earlier – geez, that's not too far off, is it? I'll call the 89th Wing at Andrews. They do training hops all the time. Getting your team aboard won't be hard.'

'I have three capture teams selected. They're all ex-Air Force and Navy elint spooks,' Clark said. 'They know the business.'

'Okay, run with it.'

'You got it, Doc.'

Jack watched him leave and lit up another.

CHAPTER 29

Crossroads

MV *Carmen Vita* cleared the Straits of Gibraltar right on schedule, her Pielstick diesels driving her at a constant nineteen knots. The crew of forty officers and men (this ship did not have any women in the crew, though three of the officers had their wives with them) settled down for the normal sailing routine of watch-keeping and maintenance. They were seven days out from the Virginia Capes. On her deck and stowed below were a goodly number of standard-sized container boxes. These actually came in two sizes, and they were all loaded with various types of cargo which the captain and crew neither knew nor cared very much about. The whole point of containerization was that the ship was used exclusively as a contract-hauler, much as a trucker was used by various businesses. All the ship's crew needed to worry about was the weight of the containers, and that always seemed to work out rather uniformly, since the containers themselves were always loaded to reflect what a commercial truck could legally pull along a public highway.

The ship's southerly routing also made for a fairly sedate and uneventful passage. The really bitter winter storms followed a more northerly track, and the ship's master, a native of India, was happy for it. A youngish man for such a substantial command – he was only thirty-seven – he knew that good weather made for a fast and fuel-efficient voyage. He aspired to a larger and more sumptuous ship, and by keeping *Carmen Vita* on schedule and under budget, he'd get that in due course.

*

It was the tenth day in a row that Clark hadn't seen Mrs Ryan. John Clark had a good memory for such things, honed by years of field operations of one sort or another, in which one stayed alive by keeping track of everything, whether it seemed important or not. He'd never seen her more than twice in a row. Jack worked an inconvenient schedule – but so did she, with early-morning surgery at least twice a week . . . and she was awake this morning. He saw her head through the kitchen window, sitting at a table, probably drinking coffee and reading the paper or watching TV. But she hadn't even turned her head to look at her husband when he left, had she? Ordinarily she got up to kiss him goodbye like any wife. Ten days in a row.

Not a good sign, was it? What was the problem? Jack came out to the car, his face dark and looking down. There was the grimace again.

'Morning, Doc!' Clark greeted him cheerily.

'Hi, John,' was the subdued reply. He hadn't brought his paper again, either. He started reading from the dispatch box as usual, and by the time they reached the DC Beltway, he'd just be staring, a grim thousand-yard stare in his eyes as he lit a continuous chain of cigarettes. Clark decided that he just couldn't stand it anymore:

'Problem at home, Doc?' he asked quietly, watching the road.

'Yeah, but it's my problem.'

'Guess so. The kids are okay?'

'It's not the kids, John. Leave it, okay?'

'Right.' Clark concentrated on his driving while Ryan went through the message traffic.

What the hell is the problem. Be analytical, Clark told himself, *think it through*.

His boss had been depressed for over a month now, but it had really gotten worse – the news article, that thing from Holtzman? A family problem, not involving the kids. That meant trouble with the wife. He made a mental note to recheck that piece and any subsequent pieces when he got into the office. Seventy minutes after picking Ryan up – traffic was light this morning – he headed for CIA's rather impressive library and got the staff there busy. It wasn't hard for them. The Agency kept a special file for all the pieces that concerned it, arranged in folders by the authors' by-lines. The problem, Clark thought, was immediately clear.

Holtzman had talked about financial and sexual misconduct. Right after that article came out . . .

'Aw, shit,' Clark whispered to himself. He made copies of the various recent pieces – there were four of them – and went for a walk to clear his head. One nice thing about being an SPO, especially an SPO assigned to Ryan, was that he had very little work to do. Ryan was a homebody while in Langley. He didn't really move around all that much. As he took a quick walking tour of the grounds, he reread the news articles and made another connection. The Sunday piece. Ryan had gone home early that day. He'd been upbeat, talking about getting away right after the Mexican job, taking John's advice for a trip to Florida – but the next morning he'd looked like a corpse. And he wasn't bringing the paper out with him. His wife must have been reading it, and something had gone very bad between Ryan and his wife. That seemed reasonably clear. Clear enough for Clark.

Clark came back into the building, going through the normal routine of passing through the computer-controlled gates, then setting off to locate Chavez, who was in the New Headquarters Building. John found him in an office, going over schedules.

'Ding, get your coat.' Ten minutes later, they were on the D.C. Beltway. Chavez was checking a map.

'Okay,' Chavez said. 'I have it. Broadway and Monument, up from the harbor.'

Russell was dressed in coveralls. The photos of the ABC vans in Chicago had turned out very well, and he'd had a lab in Boulder blow them up to poster size. These he compared to his van – it was exactly the same model of utility van – to make precise measurements. What came next wasn't easy. He'd purchased a dozen large sheets of semi-rigid plastic, and he began carving them to make an exact match of the ABC logo. As he finished each, he taped it to the side of his van and used a marker pencil to scribe in the letters. It required six attempts to get it right, and Russell next used the knife to make reference marks on the van. It seemed a pity to score the paint on the van, but he reminded himself that the van would be blown up anyway, and there was no sense in getting sentimental about a truck. On the whole, he was proud of his artistic talents. He hadn't had a chance to exercise them since he'd learned a trade in the prison shop, many years before. When the logo was painted on, black letters on the white-painted truck, nobody would be able to tell the difference.

The next job of the day was to drive to the local motor-vehicle agency to get commercial tags for the van. He explained that he would use it for his electronics business, installing and servicing commercial phone systems. He walked out with temporary tags, and they promised delivery of the real ones in four working days, which struck Russell as unnecessarily efficient. Getting the license was even easier. The international licensing documents that Ghosn had provided to go along with his passport were honored by the State of Colorado, after he passed a written test, and he had a photo-certified license card to go along with the tags. His only 'mistake' was messing up one of the forms, but the clerk let him sign a fresh one while Russell dumped the first in the trash can. Or appeared to. The blank form slid into the pocket of his parka.

Johns Hopkins Hospital is not located in the best of neighborhoods. As compensation for that fact the Baltimore City Police guarded it in a way that reminded Clark of his time in Vietnam. He found a parking place on Broadway, just across from the main entrance. Then he and Chavez went in, walking around the marble statue of Jesus which both found rather admirable in size and execution. The large complex – Hopkins is a vast facility – made finding the right part difficult, but ten minutes later they were sitting outside the Wilmer Eye Institute office of Associate Professor Caroline M. Ryan, M.D., F.A.C.S. Clark relaxed and read a magazine while Chavez cast his lecherous eyes on the receptionist whom Mrs Ryan evidently rated. The other Dr Ryan, as Clark thought of her, showed up at twelve-thirty-five with an armful of documents. She gave the two CIA officers a *who-are-you* look and breezed into her office without a word. It didn't take much of a look on his part either. She'd always appeared to him a very attractive and dignified female. Not now. Her face, if anything, was in worse shape than her husband's. This really was getting out of hand, John thought. Clark gave it a ten-count and just walked past the open-mouthed receptionist to begin his newest career, marriage counsellor.

'What is this?' Cathy asked. 'I don't have any appointments today.'

'Ma'am, I need a few minutes of your time.'

'Who are you? Are you going to ask me about Jack?'

'Ma'am, my name is Clark.' He reached into his shirt pocket and pulled out the card-sized CIA photo-pass, attached as most were, to a metal chain that went around his neck. 'There may be some things you need to know about.'

Cathy's eyes went hard almost at once, the anger taking over from the hurt. 'I know,' she said. 'I've heard it all.'

'No, ma'am, I think that you do not know. This isn't a good place to talk. May I invite you to lunch?'

'Around here? The streets aren't all that –'

'Safe?' Clark smiled to show just how absurd her observation was.

For the first time, Caroline Ryan applied a professional eye to her visitor. He was about Jack's height, but bulkier. Whereas she had once found her husband's face manly, Clark's was rugged. His hands looked large and powerful, and his body language proclaimed that he could deal with anything. More impressive was his demeanor. The man could have intimidated almost anyone, she realized, but he was going out of his way to appear gentlemanly, and succeeding, like the ballplayers

657

who sometimes came here to see the kids. *Teddy bear* was what she thought. Not because he was, but because he wanted to be.

'There's a place right down Monument Street.'

'Fine.' Clark turned and lifted her overcoat from the clothes tree. He held it almost daintily for her to put it on. Chavez joined them outside. He was much smaller than Clark, but more overtly dangerous, like a gang kid who was trying to smooth off his edges. Chavez, she saw, took the lead as they walked outside, preceding them up the sidewalk in a way that was almost comical. The streets here were not what she thought safe – at least not for a woman walking alone, though that was more a problem at night than during the day – but Chavez moved like a man in battle. That, she thought, was interesting. They found the small restaurant quickly, and Clark steered everyone into a corner booth. Both the men had their backs to the wall so that they could stare outward at any incoming threat. Both had their coats unbuttoned, though they both seemed outwardly relaxed.

'Who exactly are you?' she asked. The whole affair was like something from a bad movie.

'I'm your husband's driver,' John replied. 'I'm a field officer, paramilitary type. I've been with the agency for almost twenty years.'

'You're not supposed to tell people stuff like that.'

Clark just shook his head. 'Ma'am, we haven't even started breaking laws yet. Now I'm mainly a Security and Protective Officer, an SPO. Ding Chavez here is also an SPO.'

'Hello, Doctor Ryan. My real name is Domingo.' He held out his hand. 'I work with your husband also. John and I drive him around and protect him on trips and stuff.'

'You're both carrying guns?'

Ding almost looked embarrassed. 'Yes, ma'am.'

With that, the adventurous part of the meeting ended, Cathy thought. Two obviously very tough men were trying to charm her. They had even succeeded. But that didn't change her problem. She was about to say something, but Clark started off first.

'Ma'am, there seems to be a problem between you and your husband. I don't know what it is – I think I know some of it – but I do know that it's hurting the guy. That's bad for the Agency.'

'Gentlemen, I appreciate your concern, but this is a private matter.'

'Yes, ma'am,' Clark responded in his eerily polite voice. He reached into his pocket and pulled out Xerox copies of the Holtzman articles. 'Is this the problem?'

'That's not any of your . . .' Her mouth clamped shut.

'I thought so. Ma'am, none of this is true. I mean, the sexual impropriety part. That's definitely not true. Your husband hardly goes anywhere without one of us. Because of where he works and who he is, he has to sign out for every place he goes to – like a doctor on call, okay? If you want, I can get you copies of his itinerary for as far back as you want.'

'That can't be legal.'

'No, it probably isn't,' Clark agreed. 'So?'

She so wanted to believe, Cathy thought, but she couldn't, and it was best to tell them why. 'Look, your loyalty to Jack is very impressive – but I *know*, okay? I went through the financial records, and I know about that Zimmer woman, and I know about the kid!'

'What exactly do you know?'

'I know that Jack was there for the delivery. I know about the money, and how he tried to hide it from me and everybody else. I know that he's being investigated by the government.'

'What do you mean?'

'A government investigator was here at Hopkins! I know that!'

'Dr Ryan, there is no such investigation at CIA, and no investigation at the FBI, either. That's a fact.'

'Then who was here?'

'I'm afraid I don't know that,' Clark answered. It wasn't entirely true, but Clark figured this lie was not pertinent to the matter at hand.

'Look, I know about Carol Zimmer,' she said again.

'What do you know?' Clark repeated quietly. The response he got surprised him.

The answer almost came out as a scream. 'Jack's playing around, and she's the one! And there's a kid involved, and Jack is spending so much time with her that he doesn't have any time for me and he can't even –' She stopped, at the point of sobbing.

Clark waited for her to settle down. His eyes didn't leave her face for an instant, and he saw it all as clearly as though it had been printed on a page. Ding merely looked embarrassed. He wasn't old enough to understand.

'Will you hear me through?'

'Sure, why not? It's over, the only reason I haven't just walked out is the kids. So go ahead, make your pitch. Tell me that he still loves me and all that. He doesn't have the guts to talk about it to me himself, but I'm sure he had something to do with this,' she concluded bitterly.

'First of all, he does not know we are here. If he finds out, I'll probably lose my job, but that's no big thing. I have my retirement. Besides, I'm about to break bigger rules than that one. Where do I begin?' Clark paused before going on.

'Carol Zimmer is a widow. Her husband was Chief Master Sergeant Buck Zimmer, U.S. Air Force. He died in the line of duty. As a matter of fact, he died in your husband's arms. I know. I was there. Buck took five rounds in the chest. Both lungs. It took him five or six minutes to die. He left behind seven children – eight, if you count the one his wife was carrying. Buck didn't know about that one when he died. Carol was waiting to surprise him.

'Sergeant Zimmer was the crew chief on an Air Force special-operations helicopter. We took that aircraft into a foreign country to rescue a group of U.S. Army soldiers who were conducting a covert mission.'

'I was one of 'em, ma'am,' Ding announced, somewhat

to Clark's displeasure. 'I wouldn't be here if the doc hadn't put it out on the line.'

'The soldiers had been deliberately cut off from support from this end of the operation –'

'Who?'

'He's dead now,' Clark answered in a way that left no doubt at all. 'Your husband uncovered what was an illegal operation. He and Dan Murray of the FBI set up the rescue mission. It was a bad one, really tough. We were very lucky to get it done. I'm surprised you haven't noticed something – nightmares, maybe?'

'He doesn't sleep well – well, yes, sometimes he . . .'

'Dr Ryan missed having a bullet take his head off by . . . oh, maybe two inches, maybe three. We had to rescue a squad of soldiers off a hilltop, and they were under attack. Jack worked one machinegun. Buck Zimmer had another one. Buck took hits as we lifted out, went down hard. Jack and I tried to help him, but I don't even think you Hopkins guys could have done very much. It wasn't real pretty. He died –' Clark stopped for a moment, and Cathy could see that he wasn't faking the pain. 'He was talking about his kids. Worried about 'em, like any man would be. Your husband held Zimmer in his arms and promised him that he would look after them, that he'd see they were all educated, that he would take care of the family. Ma'am, I've been in this business a long time, back before you learned how to drive a car, okay? I've never seen anything better than what Jack did.

'After we got back, Jack did what he promised. I mean, of course. I'm not surprised he kept it a secret from you. There are aspects to the total operation that I do not know myself. But this much I do know: that man gives his word, he keeps it. I helped. We got the family moved up here from Florida. He set them up a little business. One of the kids is already in college, at Georgetown, and the second-oldest is already accepted into MIT. I forgot to tell you, Carol Zimmer – well, Carol ain't her name. She was born in Laos. Zimmer got her out when everything went to hell there, married her, and they started punching out kids like movie tickets. Anyway, she's a typical Asian mom. She thinks education is a gift from God Himself, and those kids really study hard. They all think your husband's a saint. We stop in to see them at least once a week, every week.'

'I want to believe you,' Cathy said. 'What about the baby?'

'You mean when it was born? Yeah, we were both there. My wife was the coach for the delivery – Jack didn't think it was right for him to be in the room, and I've never been there for one. It kind of scares me,' Clark admitted. 'So we waited in the usual place with all the other wimps. If you want, I can introduce you to the Zimmer family. You can also confirm the story through Dan Murray at the FBI, if you think that is necessary.'

'Won't that get you into trouble?' Cathy knew at once that she could trust Murray. He was straight-laced on moral issues; it came from being a cop.

'I will definitely lose my job. I suppose they could prosecute me – technically, I have just committed a federal felony – but I doubt it would go that far. Ding would lose his job, too, because he hasn't had the sense to keep his mouth shut like I told him to.'

'Shit,' Ding commented, then looked embarrassed. 'Excuse me, ma'am. John, this is a matter of honor. 'Cept for the Doc, I'd be fertilizer on some Colombian hilltop. I owe him my life. That counts more than a job, *'mano.'*

Clark handed over an index card. 'These are the dates of the operation. You may remember that when Admiral Greer died, Jack didn't make the funeral.'

'Yes! Bob Ritter called me, and – '

'That's when it was. You can verify all of this with Mr Murray.'

'God!' It all hit her at once.

'Yes, ma'am. All the garbage in these articles. It's all a lie.'

'Who's doing it?'

'I don't know, but I am going to find out. Doctor, I've been watching your guy come apart for the past six months. I've seen it happen before, in combat – I spent quite some time in Vietnam – but this has been worse.

That Vatican Treaty, the way the Middle East is settling down. Jack had a big part in that, but he isn't getting any credit at all. Exactly what part he played, I'm not sure. He's pretty good at keeping secrets. That's part of his problem. He keeps it all inside. You do that too much and it's like cancer, like acid or something. It eats you up. It's eating him up, and this crap in the papers has made it a lot worse.

'All I can say, Doc, is this: I don't know a better man than your husband, and I've been around the block a few times. He's put it on the line more than the times you know about, but there's people around who don't like him very much, and those people are trying to get him in a way that he can't deal with. It's typical, dirty, under-handed crap, but Jack's not the kind of guy who can deal with that. He plays by the rules, you see. So, it's eating him up.'

Cathy was weeping now. Clark handed her a hand-kerchief.

'I figured you should know. If you think it's necessary, I want you to check it out as much as you think you have to. That's your decision, and I want you to make the call without worrying about me or Ding or anybody else, okay? I'll take you to see Carol Zimmer and the kids. If I lose my job – the hell with it. I've been in the business too damned long anyway.'

'Christmas presents?'

'For the Zimmer kids? Yeah, I helped wrap them. Your husband can't wrap presents worth a damn, but I suppose you know that. I even delivered some of my own. My two are too grown for fun presents, and they're great kids, the Zimmers. It's nice being an uncle,' John added, with a genuine smile.

'All a lie?'

'I don't know about the financial stuff, just the other things. And they tried to get at him through you, judging by what you just said.'

The tears stopped at that moment. Cathy wiped her eyes and looked up. 'You're right. You said you don't know who's doing this?'

'I'm planning to find out,' Clark promised her. Her demeanor had changed completely. This was some broad.

'I want you to let me know. And I want to meet the Zimmer family.'

'When do you get off work?'

'I have to make a few phone calls and some notes – say an hour?'

'I can squeeze that in, but I may have to leave early. They have a 7-Eleven about ten miles from your place.'

'I know it's close, but not exactly where.'

'You can follow me down.'

'Let's go.' Cathy led them out, or tried to. Chavez beat her out the door, and held the point all the way back to the hospital. He and Clark decided to stay outside and get some air, then spotted two youths sitting on their car.

It was strange, John Clark thought as he crossed the street. At the beginning Caroline Ryan had been the angry one, angry and betrayed. He'd been the voice of understanding. Now she was feeling much better – though worse in another way – but he had absorbed all of her anger. It was a little too much to bear, and there in front of him was an outlet for it.

'Off the car, punk!'

'Christ, John!' Ding said behind him.

'Says who!' the youth said, hardly turning to see the man approaching. He got his head around just in time to see the hand grasp his shoulder. Then the world rotated and the brick wall of a building approached his face very rapidly. Fortunately, his boom-box absorbed most of the impact, which, however, had a negative effect on the boom-box.

'Motherfucker!' the kid snarled, coming out with a knife. His companion was six feet away, and also had a knife out.

Clark just smiled at them. 'Who's first?'

The thought of avenging his appliance died a quick death. Both youths knew danger when they saw it.

'You lucky I don't have my gun, man!'

'You can leave the knives, too.'

'You a cop?'

'No, I am not a policeman,' Clark said, walking over with his hand out. Chavez backed him up, his coat opened, as both youths noticed. They dropped their knives and started walking away.

'What the hell is —'

Clark turned to see a policeman approaching, with a large dog. Both were fully alert. John pulled out his CIA pass. 'I didn't like their attitude.'

Chavez handed the knives over. 'They dropped these, sir.'

'You really should leave that sort of thing to us.'

'Yes, sir,' Clark agreed. 'You're right. Nice dog you have there.'

The cop pocketed the knives. 'Have a good one,' he said, wondering what the hell this had been about.

'You, too, officer.' Clark paused and turned to Chavez. 'God damn, that felt good.'

'Ready to go to Mexico, John?'

'Yeah. I just hate leaving unfinished business behind, you know?'

'So, who's trying to fuck him over?'

'Not sure.'

'Bull,' Ding observed.

'Won't be sure until I talk to Holtzman.'

'You say so, man. I like her,' he added. 'That's some lady.'

'Yeah, she is. Just what he needs to set things straight.'

'You think she'll call that Murray guy?'

'Does it matter?'

'No.' Chavez looked up the street. 'A question of honor, Mr C.'

'I knew you'd understand, Ding.'

Jacqueline Zimmer was a beautiful child, Cathy thought, holding her. She wanted another, must have another. Jack would give her one, maybe another girl if they were lucky.

'We hear so much 'bout you!' Carol said. 'You doctor?'

'Yes, I teach doctors, I'm a professor of surgery.'

'My oldes' son must meet you. He want to be doctor. He student at Georgetown.'

'Maybe I can help him a little. Can I ask you a question?'

'Yes.'

'Your husband . . .'

'Buck? He die. I don't know all the things, just that he die – on duty, yes? Is secret thing. Very hard for me,' Carol said soberly, but without overt grief. She was over that now. 'Buck was a very good man. So your husban'. You be nice to him,' Mrs Zimmer added.

'Oh, I will,' Cathy promised. 'Now, we have to make this a secret?'

'What secret?'

'Jack doesn't know that I know about you.'

'Oh? I know there are many secret, but – okay, I un'erstan'. I keep this secret, too.'

'I will talk to Jack about that. I think you should come to our house and meet our children. But for now, we keep the secret?'

'Yes, okay. We surprise him?'

'Right.' Cathy smiled as she handed the child back. 'I will see you again, soon.'

'Feel better, Doc?' Clark asked her out in the parking lot.

'Thank you . . . ?'

'Call me John.'

'Thanks, John.' It was the warmest smile since his kids at Christmas.

'Any time.'

Clark drove west on Route 50. Cathy turned east for home. Her knuckles were white on the steering wheel of her car. The anger was back now. For the most part, she was angry at herself. How could she have thought that of Jack? She'd been very foolish, very small, and so disgustingly selfish. But it wasn't really her fault. Someone else had invaded their household, she decided as she pulled into the garage. She was on the phone almost immediately. She had to do one more thing. She had to be completely certain.

'Hi, Dan.'

'Cathy! How's the eye business, kid?' Murray asked.

'Got a question for you.'

'Shoot.'

She'd already decided how to do it. 'There's a problem with Jack . . .'

Murray's voice became guarded. 'What is it?'

'He's having nightmares,' Cathy said. It wasn't a lie, but what followed was. 'Something about a helicopter, and Buck somebody . . . I can't ask him about it, but –'

Murray cut her off. 'Cathy, I can't talk about it over the phone. That's a business matter, kid.'

'Really?'

'Really, Cathy. It's something I know about, but I cannot discuss it with you. I'm sorry, but that's the way it has to be. It's business.'

Cathy went on with a touch of alarm in her voice. 'It's not something that's happening now – I mean –'

'It's way in the past, Cathy. That's all I can say. If you think Jack needs professional help, then I can make a few calls and –'

'No, I don't think so. It was really bad a few months ago, but it does seem to be getting better. I was just worried that it might be something at the office . . .'

'All behind him, Cathy. Honest.'

'You sure, Dan?'

'Positive. I would not kid around on something like this.'

And that, Cathy knew, was that. Dan was every bit as honest as Jack was. 'Thanks, Dan. Thanks a lot,' she said in her best medical voice, the one that revealed nothing at all.

'Any time, Cathy.' By the time he hung up, Murray wondered if he'd just been had in some way. No, he decided, there was no way she could have found out about that.

Had he seen the other end of the disconnected phone line, he would have been surprised to discover how

667

wrong he was. Cathy sat alone in the kitchen, crying one last time. She'd had to check, there had not been a choice to purge all the emotions from her soul, but now she was completely certain that Clark had spoken the truth; that someone was trying to hurt her husband, that whoever it was was willing to use his wife and his family against him. *Who could ever hate a man so much that they would try that?* she wondered.

Whoever it was was her enemy. Whoever it was had attacked her and her family just as coldly as those terrorists had done, but much more cravenly.

Whoever it was would pay for that.

'Where have you been?'

'Sorry, Doc. I had some errands to run.' Clark had come back through the S&T office. 'Here.'

'What's this?' Ryan took the bottle. It was an expensive container of Chivas Regal in a ceramic bottle. The sort you couldn't see through.

'That's our transceiver. They made up four of them. Nice job, isn't it? Here's the pickup.' Clark handed over a green stick, almost the thickness of a cocktail straw, but not quite. 'It'll look like a plastic doodad to hold the flowers in place. We decided to use three of them. The technies say they can multiplex the outbound transmissions, and for some reason or other they can crunch the computer time down to one-to-one. They also say that if we had another few months to play with the comm links, we could almost real-time the whole thing.'

'What we have is enough,' Jack said. Here and now 'almost' was better than perfect too late. 'I've funded enough research projects.'

'I agree. What about the test flights?'

'Tomorrow, ten o'clock.'

'Super.' Clark stood. 'Hey, Doc, how about you call it a day? You look wasted.'

'I think you're right. Give me another hour, and I'm out of here.'

'Fair enough.'

*

Russell met them at Atlanta. They'd come across through Mexico City, thence through Miami, where the customs people were very interested in drugs, but not particularly interested in Greek businessmen who opened their bags without being asked. Russell, who was now Robert Friend of Roggen, Colorado – with the driver's license to prove it – shook hands with both of them and helped to collect their baggage.

'Weapons?' Qati asked.

'Not here, man. I have everything you need at home.'

'Any problems?'

'Not one.' Russell was silent for a moment. 'Maybe there is one.'

'What?' Ghosn asked with concealed alarm. Being on foreign soil always made him nervous, and this was his first trip to America.

'Cold as hell where we're going, guys. You might want to get some decent coats.'

'That can wait,' the Commander decided. He was feeling very bad now. The latest batch of chemotherapy had denied him food for nearly two days, and as much as he craved nourishment, his stomach rebelled at the mere sight of it in one of the airport fast-food stands. 'What about our flight?'

'Hour and a half. How about you get some sweaters, okay? Follow me. I'm not foolin' about the weather. It's like zero where we're going.'

'Zero? That is not so –' Ghosn stopped. 'You mean, below zero, centigrade?'

Russell stopped for a second. 'Oh. Yeah, that's right. Zero here means something different. Zero's cold, guys, okay?'

'As you say,' Qati agreed. Half an hour later they had thick woolen sweaters to go under their thin raincoats. The mostly empty Delta flight to Denver left on time. Three hours later, they walked off their last jetway for a while. Ghosn had never seen so much snow in his life.

'I can hardly breathe,' Qati said.

'It'll take you a day to get used to the altitude. You guys go get the luggage. I'll get the car and warm it up for you.'

'If he's betrayed us,' Qati said, as Russell walked away, 'we'll know it in the next few minutes.'

'He has not,' Ghosn replied. 'He is a strange man, but a faithful one.'

'He is an infidel, a pagan.'

'That is true, but he also listened to an imam in my presence. At least he was polite. I tell you, he is faithful.'

'We will see,' Qati said, walking tiredly and breathlessly to the baggage-claim level. Both men looked around as they moved, searching for eyes. That was always the giveaway, the eyes that fixed on you. It was hard even for the most professional of men to keep from looking at their targets.

They collected their luggage without incident, and Marvin was waiting. He could not stop the blast of air from hitting them, and thin as the air was, it was also colder than either had ever experienced. The heat of the car was welcome indeed.

'How go the preparations?'

'Everything is on schedule, Commander,' Russell said. He drove off. The Arabs were quietly impressed by the vast open space, the broad interstate highway – they found the speed-limit signs very strange – and the obvious wealth in the area. They were also impressed with Russell, who had manifestly done quite well. Both men rested easier that he had not betrayed them. It was not that Qati had actually expected it, rather that he knew that his vulnerability increased as they got closer to the final part of the plan. That, he knew, was normal.

The farm was of a good size. Russell had thoughtfully overheated it somewhat, but what Qati noted most of all was its obvious defensibility, with a clear field of fire in all directions. He got them inside and carried the bags for them.

'You guys have to be pretty tired,' Marvin observed. 'Why don't you just bed down? You're safe here, okay?' Qati took the advice. Ghosn did not. He and Russell went to the kitchen. Ibrahim was happy to learn that Marvin was a skilled cook.

'What is this meat?'

'Venison – deer meat. I know you can't eat pork, but you got any problems with deer?' the American asked.

Ghosn shook his head. 'No, but I have never had it.'

'It's okay, I promise. I found this at a local store this morning. Native-American soul food, man. This is good mule deer. There's a game-rancher around here who grows them commercially. I can try you out on beefalo, too.'

'What the devil is that?'

'Beefalo? Another thing you can only get around here. It's a cross between beef cattle and buffalo. Buffalo is what my people used to eat, man, biggest damned cow you're ever gonna see!' Russell grinned. 'Good lean meat, healthy and everything. But venison's the best, Ismael.'

'You must not call me that,' Ghosn said tiredly. It had been a twenty-seven hour day for him, counting the time zones.

'I got the IDs for you and the Commander.' Russell pulled the envelopes from a drawer and tossed them on the table. 'Names are exactly what you wanted, see? We just have to do the photos and put them on the cards. I have the equipment to do it.'

'Was this hard to get?'

Marvin laughed. 'Naw, it's standard commercial stuff. I used my own license form as a master, ginned up the copies, then I got the hardware to do first-class dupes. Lots of companies use photo-passes, and the equipment is standardized. Three hours work. I figure we have all day tomorrow and the day after to go over everything.'

'Excellent, Marvin.'

'You want a drink?'

'Alcohol, you mean?'

'Hey, man, I saw you have a beer with that German guy – what was his name?'

'Herr Fromm, you mean.'

'Come on, it's not as bad as eatin' pork, is it?'

'Thank you, but I will pass on that – is that how you say it?'

'"Pass on the drink"? – yeah, that's fine, man. How's that Fromm guy doing?' Marvin asked casually, looking at the meat. It was almost done.

'Doing well,' Ghosn answered just as casually. 'He went off to see his wife.'

'Exactly what were you guys working on, anyway?' Russell poured himself a shot of Jack Daniel's.

'He helped us with the explosives, some special tricks, you see. He's an expert in the field.'

'Great.'

It was the first hopeful sign in a few days, maybe a few weeks, Ryan thought. Dinner was fine, all the better to make it home in time to have it with the kids. Cathy had evidently gotten home from work at a reasonable hour and had taken the time to fix a good one. Best of all, they'd talked. Afterwards, Jack had helped her clean up. Finally, the kids went off to bed, and they were alone.

'I'm sorry I snapped at you,' Cathy said.

'It's okay, I guess I deserved it.' Ryan was willing to say almost anything to calm things down.

'No, I was wrong, Jack. I was feeling bitchy, and I had cramps, and my back hurt. What's wrong with you is that you're working too hard and drinking too much.' She came over to kiss him. 'Smoking, Jack?'

He was amazed. He hadn't expected to be kissed. More than that, he expected an explosion if she discovered that he'd smoked. 'Sorry, babe. Bad day at the office. I wimped.'

Cathy held his hands. 'Jack, I want you to cut back on the drinking, and get your rest. That's your problem, that and the stress. We'll worry about the smoking later, just so you don't smoke around the kids. I haven't been very sympathetic, and I've been a little wrong myself, but you have to clean up your act. What you've been doing is bad for you, and bad for us.'

'I know.'

'Go to bed. You need sleep more than anything else.'

Being married to a physician had its drawbacks. Chief among those was that you couldn't argue with one. Jack kissed her on the cheek and did as he was told.

CHAPTER 30

East Room

Clark arrived at the house at the proper time and had to do something unusual. He waited. After a couple of minutes, he was ready to knock on the door, but then it opened. Dr Ryan (male) came out partway, then stopped and turned to kiss Dr Ryan (female), who watched him walk off, and, after his back was fully turned, fired off a beaming smile at the car.

All right! Clark thought. Maybe he did have a new career set up. Jack also looked fairly decent, and Clark told him so as soon as he got in the car.

'Yeah, well, I got sent to bed early,' Jack chuckled, tossing his paper on the front seat. 'Forgot to have a drink, too.'

'Couple more days like that and you just might be human again.'

'Maybe you're right.' But he still lit up a cigarette, somewhat to Clark's annoyance. Then he realized just how smart Caroline Ryan was. One thing at a time. Damn, Clark told himself, that *is* some broad.

'I'm set up for the test flight. Ten o'clock.'

'Good. It is nice to put you to some real work, John. Playing SPO must be boring as hell,' Ryan said, opening the dispatch box.

'It has its moments, sir,' Clark replied, pulling onto Falcon's Nest Road. It was another quiet day on the dispatches, and soon Ryan had his head buried in the morning *Post*.

Three hours later, Clark and Chavez arrived at Andrews Air Force Base. A pair of VC-20Bs had already been scheduled for routine training flights. The pilots and crews of the 89th Military Airlift – 'The President's' – Wing had a strict regimen for maintaining proficiency. The two aircraft took off a few minutes apart and headed east to perform various familiarization maneuvers to acquaint two new co-pilots with air-traffic control procedures – which the drivers already knew backwards and forwards, of course, but that was beside the point.

In the back, an Air Force technical sergeant was doing his own training, playing with the sophisticated communications equipment that the plane carried. He occasionally looked aft to see that civilian, whoever the hell he was, talking into a flower pot, or just into a little green stick. There are some things, the sergeant thought, that a guy just isn't supposed to understand. He was entirely correct.

Two hours later, the two Gulfstreams landed back at Andrews and rolled to a halt at the VIP terminal. Clark gathered up his gear and walked out to meet another civilian who'd been aboard the other aircraft. The pair walked off to their car, already talking.

'I could understand part of what you were saying – clear, I mean,' Chavez reported. 'Say about a third of it, maybe a little less.'

'Okay, we'll see what the techies can do with it.' The drive back to Langley took thirty-five minutes, and from there Clark and Chavez drove back into Washington for a late lunch.

Bob Holtzman had gotten the call the previous evening. It had come on his unlisted home line. A curt, short message, it had also perked his interest. At two in the afternoon, he walked into a small Mexican place in Georgetown called Esteban's. Most of the business crowd had gone, leaving the place about a third full, mainly with kids from Georgetown University. A wave from the back told him where to go.

'Hello,' Holtzman said, sitting down.

'You Holtzman?'

'That's right,' the reporter said. 'And you are?'

'Two friendly guys,' the older one said. 'Join us for lunch?'

'Okay.' The younger one got up and started feeding quarters into a jukebox that played Mexican music. In a moment, it was certain that his tape recorder wouldn't have a chance of working.

'What do you want to see me about?'

'You've been writing some pieces on the Agency,' the older one started off. 'The target of your articles is the Deputy Director, Dr John Ryan.'

'I never said that,' Holtzman replied.

'Whoever leaked all that shit to you lied. It's a set-up.'

'Says who?'

'Just how honest a reporter are you?'

'What do you mean?' Holtzman asked.

'If I tell you something totally off the record, will you print it?'

'That depends on the nature of the information. What exactly is your intention?'

'What I mean, Mr Holtzman, is that I can prove to you that you've been lied to, but the proof of that can never be revealed. It would endanger some people. It would also prove that somebody's been using you to grind an axe or two. I want to know who that person is.'

'You know that I can never reveal a source. That violates our code of ethics.'

'Ethics in a reporter,' the man said, just loudly enough to be heard over the music. 'I like that. Do you also protect sources who lie to you?'

'No, we don't do that.'

'Okay, then I'm going to tell you a little story, but the condition is that you may never, ever reveal what I am going to tell you. Will you honor such a condition?'

'What if I find out you are misleading me?'

'Then you will be free to print it. Fair enough?' Clark got a nod. 'Just remember, I will be very unhappy if you ever print it, 'cuz I ain't lying. One more thing, you can't ever use what I am going to tell you as a lead to do your own digging.'

'That's asking a lot.'

'You make the call, Mr Holtzman. You have the reputation of an honest reporter, and a pretty smart one.

There are some things that can't be reported — well, that's going too far. Let's say that there are things that have to remain secret for a very long time. Like years. What I'm getting at is this: you've been used. You have been conned into printing lies in order to hurt someone. Now, I'm not a reporter, but if I were, that would bother me. It would bother me because it's wrong, and it would bother me because someone took me for a sucker.'

'You have it figured out. Okay, I agree to your conditions.'

'Fair enough.' Clark told his story. It took ten minutes.

'What about the mission? Where exactly did the man die?'

'Sorry, pal. And you can forget about finding that one out. Less than ten people can answer that.' Clark's lie was a clever one. 'If you even manage to figure out who they are, they won't talk — they can't. Not too many people voluntarily leak information about breaking laws.'

'And the Zimmer woman?'

'You can check out most of that story. Where she lives, the family business, where the kid was born, who was there, who the doctor was.'

Holtzman checked his notes. 'There's something really, really big behind all this, isn't there?'

Clark just stared at him. 'All I want is a name.'

'What will you do with it?'

'Nothing that concerns you.'

'What will Ryan do with it?'

'He doesn't know we're here.'

'Bullshit.'

'That, Mr Holtzman, is the truth.'

Bob Holtzman had been a reporter a very long time. He'd been lied to by experts. He'd been the target of very organized and well-planned lies, had been the instrument of political vendettas. He didn't like that part of his job, not in the least. The contempt he felt for politicians came mainly from their willingness to break any rule. Whenever a politician broke his word, told the most outrageous of lies, took money from a contributor and

676

left the room at once to perform a service for that contributor, it was called 'just politics.' That was wrong, and Holtzman knew it. There was still in him something of the idealist who had graduated from Columbia's journalism school, and though life had made him a cynic, he was one of those few people in Washington who remembered his ideals and occasionally mourned for them.

'Assuming I can verify this story you've told, what's in it for me?'

'Maybe just satisfaction. Maybe nothing more than that. I honestly doubt there will be any more, but if there is, I'll let you know.'

'Just satisfaction?' Holtzman asked.

'Ever want to get even with a bully?' Clark asked lightly.

The reporter brushed that aside. 'What do you do at the Agency?'

Clark smiled. 'I'm really not supposed to talk about that.'

'Once upon a time, the story goes, a very senior Soviet official defected, right off the tarmac at Moscow airport.'

'I've heard that story. If you ever printed it . . .'

'Yes, it would fuck up relations, wouldn't it?' Holtzman observed.

'How long have you had it?'

'Since right before the last election. The President asked me not to run it.'

'Fowler, you mean?'

'No, the one Fowler beat.'

'And you played ball.' Clark was impressed.

'The man had a family, a wife and a daughter. Were they killed in a plane crash, like the press release said?'

'You ever going to print this?'

'I can't, not for a lot of years, but someday I'm going to do a book . . .'

'They got out, too,' Clark said. 'You're looking at the guy who got them out of the country.'

'I don't believe in coincidences.'

'The wife's name is Maria. The daughter's name is Katryn.'

Holtzman didn't react, but he knew that only a handful of people in the Agency could possibly have known the details to that one. He'd just asked his own trick question, and gotten the right answer.

'Five years from today, I want the details of the bust-out.'

Clark was quiet for a moment. Well, if the reporter was willing to break a rule, then Clark had to play ball, too. 'That's fair. Okay, you have a deal.'

'Jesus Christ, John!' Chavez said.

'The man needs a quid pro quo.'

'How many people inside know the details?'

'Of the operation? Not many. My end . . . if you mean all the details, maybe twenty, and only five of them are still in the Agency. Ten of them are not Agency employees.'

'Then who?'

'That would give too much away.'

'Air Force Special Ops,' Holtzman said. 'Or maybe the Army, Task Force 160, those crazy guys at Fort Campbell, the ones who went into Iraq the first night –'

'You can speculate all you want, but I'm not going to say anything. I will say this, when I tell you my end, I want to know how the hell you figured out that we even had this operation.'

'People like to talk,' Holtzman said simply.

'True enough. Do we have a deal, sir?'

'If I can verify what you've told me, if I'm sure I've been lied to, yes, I will reveal the source. You have to promise that it will never get to the press.'

Jesus, this is like diplomacy, Clark reflected. 'Agreed. I'll call you in two days. For what it's worth, you're the first reporter I've ever talked to.'

'So, what do you think?' Holtzman asked with a grin.

'I think I ought to stick with spooks.' John paused. 'You might have been a pretty good one.'

'I am a pretty good one.'

*

'Just how heavy is this thing?' Russell asked.

'Seven hundred kilos.' Ghosn did the mental arithmetic. 'Three quarters of a ton – your ton, that is.'

'Okay,' Russell said. 'The truck'll handle that. How do we get it from the truck into my truck?' The question turned Ghosn pale.

'I had not considered that.'

'How was it loaded on?'

'The box is set on a wooden . . . platform?'

'You mean a pallet? They put it in with a fork-lift?'

'Yes,' Ghosn said, 'that is correct.'

'You're lucky. Come on, I'll show you.' Russell led the man out into the cold. Two minutes later, he saw that one of the barns had a concrete loading dock and a rusty propane-powered forklift. The only bad news was that the dirt path leading up to it was covered with snow and frozen mud. 'How delicate is the bomb?'

'Bombs can be very delicate, Marvin,' Ghosn pointed out.

Russell had a good laugh at that one. 'Yeah, I guess so.'

It was fully ten hours earlier in Syria. Dr Vladimir Moiseyevich Kaminiskiy had just started work, early as was his custom. A professor at Moscow State University, he'd been sent to Syria to teach in his specialty, which was respiratory problems. It was not a specialty to make a man an optimist. Much of what he saw in the Soviet Union and also here in Syria was lung cancer, a disease as preventable as it was lethal.

His first case of the day had been referred by a Syrian practitioner whom he admired – the man was French-trained and very thorough – and also one who only referred interesting cases.

On entering the examining room, Kaminiskiy found a fit-looking man in his early thirties. A closer look showed someone with a gray, drawn face. His first impression was, *cancer*, but Kaminiskiy was a careful man. It could be something else, something contagious. His examination took longer than he'd expected, necessitating several X-ray films, and some additional tests, but he was called back to the Soviet embassy before the results arrived.

It required all of Clark's patience, but he let it go almost three days, on the assumption that Holtzman didn't get right on the case. John left his house at eight-thirty in the evening and drove to a gas station. There he told the attendant to fill up the car – he hated pumping it himself – and walked over to the pay phone.

'Yeah,' Holtzman said, answering his unlisted line.

Clark didn't identify himself. 'You have a chance to run the facts down?'

'Yeah, as a matter of fact. Got most of 'em, anyway. Looks like you were right. Really is annoying when people lie to you, isn't it?'

'Who?'

'I call her Liz. The President calls her Elizabeth. Want a freebie?' Holtzman added.

'Sure.'

'Call this evidence of good faith on my part. Fowler and she are getting it on. Nobody's reported it because we figure it's not the public's business.'

'Good for you,' Clark observed. 'Thanks. I owe you one.'

'Five years, man.'

'I'll be around.' Clark hung up. So, John thought, I thought that's who it was. He dropped another quarter in the phone. He got lucky on the first try. It was a woman's voice.

'Hello?'

'Dr Caroline Ryan?'

'Yes, who's this?'

'The name you wanted, ma'am, is Elizabeth Elliot. The President's National Security Advisor.' Clark decided not to add the other part. It was not relevant to the situation, was it?

'You're sure?'

'Yes.'

'Thank you.' The line clicked off.

Cathy had sent Jack to bed early again. The man was being sensible. Well, that wasn't a surprise, was it? she thought. After all, he married me.

The timing could have been a little better. A few days earlier, she had planned to skip the official dinner, claiming work as an excuse, but now . . .

How do I do this . . . ?

'Morning, Bernie,' Cathy Ryan said as she scrubbed her hands, as usual, all the way to the elbows.

'Hi, Cath. How's it going?'

'A lot better, Bernie.'

'Really?' Dr Katz started scrubbing.

'Really.'

'Glad to hear it,' Katz observed dubiously.

Cathy finished, shutting off the water with taps from her elbows. 'Bernie, it turns out I overreacted rather badly.'

'What about the guy who came to see me?' Katz asked, his head down.

'It was not true. I can't explain now, maybe some other time. Need a favor.'

'Sure, what?'

'The cornea replacement I have scheduled for Wednesday, can you take it?'

'What gives?'

'Jack and I have to go to a formal dinner in the White House tomorrow night. State dinner for the Prime Minister of Finland, would you believe? The procedure is straightforward, no complications I know about. I can have you the file this afternoon. Jenkins is going to do the procedure – I'm just supposed to ride shotgun.' Jenkins was a bright young resident.

'Okay, I'll do it.'

'Okay, thanks. Owe you one,' Cathy said on her way through the door.

The *Carmen Vita* pulled into Hampton Roads barely an hour late. She turned to port and proceeded south past the Navy piers. The captain and pilot rode the port-side bridge wing, noting the carrier that was even now departing from the pier with a few hundred wives and children waving goodbye to USS *Theodore Roosevelt.* Two cruisers, two destroyers, and a frigate were already moving. They, the pilot explained, were the screening ships for 'The Stick,' as *TR* was called by her crew. The Indian-born captain grunted and returned to business. Half an hour later, the container ship approached her pier at the end of Terminal Boulevard. Three tugs took their position and eased the *Carmen Vita* alongside. The ship had barely been tied up when the gantry cranes started moving cargo.

'Roggen, Colorado?' the trucker asked. He flipped open his large book map and looked on I-76 for the right place. 'Okay, I see it.'

'How fast?' Russell asked.

'From the time I leave here? Eighteen hundred miles. Oh, two days, maybe forty hours if I'm lucky. Gonna cost you.'

'How much?' Russell asked. The trucker told him. 'Cash all right?'

'Cash is fine. I knock ten percent off for that,' the trucker said. The IRS never found out about cash transactions.

'Half in advance.' Russell peeled off the bills. 'Half on delivery, a grand bonus if you break forty hours.'

'Sounds good to me. What about the box?'

'You bring that right back here. We'll be getting more stuff in a month,' Russell lied. 'We can make this a sort of regular run for you.'

'Sounds good to me.'

Russell returned to his friends, and together they watched the unloading process from the comfort of a block building with a large coffee urn.

Teddy Roosevelt cleared the harbor in record time, bending on twenty knots before they reached the sea buoy. Already, the aircraft were orbiting overhead, first among them the F-14 Tomcat fighters that had lifted off from Oceana Naval Air Station. As soon as there was sea room, the carrier came into the northerly wind to commence flight operations. The first plane down had the Double-Zero number of the CAG, Captain Robby Jackson. His Tomcat caught a gust over the fantail, and as a result caught the number-two wire when it landed – 'trapped' – somewhat to Jackson's annoyance. The next aircraft, flown by Commander Rafael Sanchez, made a perfect trap on the number-three arrestor wire. Both aircraft taxied out of harm's way. Jackson left the fighter and immediately sprinted to his place on Vulture's Row, high up on the carrier's island structure, so that he could observe the arrival of the rest of his aircraft. This was how a deployment started, with the CAG and squadron commanders watching their troops land. Each trap would be recorded on videotape for critiques. The cruise had not gotten off to a very good start, Jackson noted as he sipped his first mug of shipboard coffee. He'd missed his customary 'OK' grade, as the Air Boss had informed him with a twinkling eye.

'Hey, Skipper, how my kids doing?' Sanchez asked, taking his seat behind Robby.

'Not bad, I see you kept your record going, Bud.'

'It's not hard, Captain. You just keep an eye on the wind as you turn in. I saw that gust you took. Guess I should have warned you.'

'Pride goeth before the fall, Commander,' Robby observed. Sanchez had seventeen consecutive OKs. Maybe he could see the wind, Jackson thought. Seventy uneventful minutes later, *TR* turned back east, taking the great-circle route for the Straits of Gibraltar.

The trucker made sure the container box was firmly secured to the bed of his truck, then climbed into the cab of his Kenworth diesel tractor. He started his engine and waved to Russell, who waved back.

'I still think we should follow him,' Ghosn said.

'He'd notice and wonder why,' Marvin replied. 'And if something goes wrong, what would you do, fill in the hole it makes in the highway? You didn't follow the ship, did you?'

'True.' Ghosn looked at Qati and shrugged. Then they walked off to their car for the drive to Charlotte, from which they would fly directly to Denver.

Jack was ready early, as he usually was, but Cathy took her time. It was so unusual for her to look in a mirror and see hair that looked like it belonged to a real woman, as opposed to a surgeon who didn't give a damn. That had entailed the waste of two hours, but there were prices that one had to pay. Before she went downstairs, Cathy took two suitcases out from her closet and set them in the middle of the bedroom.

'Here, can you do this?' she asked her husband.

'Sure, babe.' Ryan took the gold necklace and clasped it around her neck. It was one he'd given her on the Christmas before Little Jack was born. Some good memories went along with this necklace, Jack remembered. Then he stood back. 'Turn around.'

Cathy did as she was told. Her evening dress was royal-blue silk that caught and reflected light like glass. Jack Ryan was not a man who understood women's fashions – figuring the Russians out came more easily to him – but he approved whatever the new rules were. The rich blue of the dress and the gold jewelry she wore with it set off the blush of her fair skin and the buttery yellow of her hair. 'Nice,' Jack said. 'All ready, babe?'

'Sure am, Jack.' She smiled back at him. 'Go warm the car up.'

Cathy watched him head off into the garage, then said a few words to the sitter. She put on her fur – surgeons typically have little use for animal-rights activists – and followed Jack a minute later. Jack backed out of the garage, and headed off.

Clark had to laugh to himself. Ryan still didn't know beans about counter-surveillance techniques. He watched the taillights of the car diminish, then disappear entirely around the bend of the road before heading into the Ryan driveway.

'You're Mr Clark?' the sitter asked.

'That's right.'

'They're in the bedroom.' The sitter pointed.

'Thank you.' Clark returned a minute later. Typical woman, he thought, they all overpack. Even Caroline Ryan wasn't perfect. 'Good night.'

'Night.' The sitter was already entranced with the TV.

It takes just under an hour to drive from Annapolis, Maryland, into Central D.C. Ryan missed having an official car, but his wife had insisted that they drive themselves. They turned off of Pennsylvania Avenue, through the gate into East Executive Drive, where uniformed police directed them to a parking place. Their wagon looked a little humble mixed in with Caddys and Lincolns, but that was all right with Jack. The Ryans walked up the gentle slope to the East Entrance, where Secret Service personnel checked their invitations against the guest list, and checked them off. Jack's car keys set off the metal detector, evoking an embarrassed smile.

No matter how many times one goes there, there is always something magical about visiting the White House, especially at night. Ryan led his wife westward. They handed off their coats, and took their numbered tokens right next to the White House's own small theater, then continued. At the chicane turn there were the usual three social reporters, women in their sixties who stared you in the face while making their notes and generally looked like the witches from *Macbeth* with their open-mouth, drooly smiles. Officers from all the military services decked out in their full-dress – what Ryan used to call 'Head Waiter' – uniforms waited in files to provide escort duty. As usual, the Marines looked best with their scarlet sashes, and a disgustingly good-looking captain motioned them up the stairs to the main level. Jack noted the admiring glance cast at his wife and decided to smile about it.

At the top of the marble stairs, another officer, this one a female Army lieutenant, directed them into the East Room. They were announced into the room – as though anyone were listening – and a liveried usher approached at once with a silver tray of drinks.

'You're driving, Jack,' Cathy whispered. Jack took a Perrier and a twist. Cathy got champagne.

The East Room of the White House is the size of a small gymnasium. The walls are ivory-white, its false columns decorated with gold leaf. There was a string quartet in one corner, along with a grand piano that was being played, rather well, Ryan thought, by an Army sergeant. Half the people were already here, the men in black tie and the women in dresses. Perhaps there were people who were totally comfortable at such affairs, Ryan told himself, but he wasn't one of them. He started circulating, and soon found Defense Secretary Bunker and his wife, Charlotte.

'Hello, Jack.'

'Hi, Dennis, you know my wife?'

'Caroline,' Cathy said, sticking her hand out.

'So, what do you think about the game?'

Jack laughed. 'Sir, I know how you and Brent Talbot have been fighting over this. I was born in Baltimore. Somebody stole our team.'

'You didn't lose that much, did you? This is our year.'

'But the Vikings say the same thing.'

'They were lucky to get past New York.'

'The Raiders gave you a brief scare, as I recall.'

'They got lucky,' Bunker grumbled. 'We buried 'em in the second half.'

Caroline Ryan and Charlotte Bunker traded a woman-to-woman look: *Football!* Cathy turned, and there she was. Mrs Bunker made off, while the boys talked about boy things.

Cathy took a deep breath. She wondered if this were the right time and the right place, but she could no more have stopped herself now than she could have given up surgery. She left Jack facing the other way, and headed across the floor in a line as direct as a falcon's.

Dr Elizabeth Elliot was dressed almost identically to Dr Caroline Ryan. The cuts and pleats were a little different, but the expensive garments were close enough to make a fashion editor wonder if they had shopped at the same store. A triple string of pearls graced her neck, and she was talking with two others. Her head turned as she saw the approaching shape.

'Hello, Dr Elliot. You remember me?' Cathy asked with a warm smile.

'No. Should I?'

'Caroline Ryan. That help?'

'Sorry,' Liz replied, knowing at once who she was, but not knowing anything else that might be of interest. 'Do you know Bob and Libby Holtzman?'

'I've read your material,' Cathy said, taking Holtzman's extended hand.

'It's always nice to hear that.' Holtzman noted the delicacy of her touch and could feel the guilt shoot up his arm. Was this the woman whose marriage he had attacked? 'This is Libby.'

'You're a reporter, too,' Cathy observed. Libby Holtzman was taller than she, and dressed in an outfit that emphasized her ample bosom. One of hers is worth both of mine, Cathy noted, managing not to sigh. Libby had the sort of bust on which men yearned to lay their heads.

'You operated on a cousin of mine a year or so ago,' Libby Holtzman said. 'Her mom says you're the best surgeon in the world.'

'All doctors love to hear that.' Cathy decided that she would like Mrs Holtzman, despite her physical handicap.

'I know you're a surgeon, but where have we met?' Liz Elliot asked, with the offhand interest she might have shown a dog breeder.

'Bennington. In my freshman year, you taught PoliSci 101.'

'Is that a fact? I'm surprised you remember.' She made it clear that she did not.

'Yes. Well, you know how it is.' Cathy smiled. 'Freshman Pre-Med is a real bear. We really have to concentrate on the important stuff. So the unimportant courses are all throwaways, easy A's.'

Elliot's expression didn't change. 'I was never an easy grader.'

'Sure you were. It was just a matter of repeating it all back to you.' Cathy smiled even more broadly.

Bob Holtzman was tempted to take a step back, but managed not to move at all. His wife's eyes went a touch wider, having caught the signals more quickly than her husband. A war had just begun. It would be nastier than most.

'What ever happened to Dr Brooks?'

'Who?' Liz asked.

Cathy turned to the Holtzmans. 'Times really were different back in the 70s, weren't they? Dr Elliot just had her masters, and the PoliSci department was – well, kind of radical. You know, the fashionable kind.' She turned back. 'Surely you haven't forgotten Dr Brooks and Dr Hemmings! Where was that house you shared with them?'

'I don't remember.' Liz told herself to maintain control. This would be all over soon. But she couldn't walk away.

'Wasn't it on that three-way corner, a few blocks from the campus . . . ? We used to call them the Marx Brothers,' Cathy explained with a giggle. 'Brooks never wore socks – in Vermont, remember, he must have gotten terrible colds from that – and Hemmings never washed his hair. That was some department. Of course, Dr Brooks went off to Berkeley, and then you went out there, too, to finish your doctorate. I guess you liked working under him. Tell me, how is Bennington now?'

'Just as nice as ever.'

'I never get back there for the alum meetings,' Cathy said.

'I haven't been back there myself in over a year,' Liz replied.

'What ever happened to Dr Brooks?' Cathy asked again.

'He teaches at Vassar now, I think.'

'Oh, you've kept track of him? Still trying to bed every skirt in sight, too, I bet. Radical-chic. How often do you see him?'

'Not in a couple of years.'

'We never understood what you saw in them,' Cathy observed.

'Come now, Caroline, none of us were virgins back then.'

Cathy sipped at her champagne. 'That's true, times were different, and we did lots of very dumb things. But I got lucky. Jack made an honest woman of me.'

Zing! Libby Holtzman thought.

'Some of us haven't had time.'

'I don't know how you manage without a family. I don't think I could handle the loneliness.'

'At least I never have to worry about an unfaithful husband,' Liz observed icily, finding her own weapon, not knowing it wasn't loaded anymore.

Cathy looked amused. 'Yes, I suppose some women have to worry about that. But I don't, thank God.'

'How can any woman be sure?'

'Only a fool is unsure. If you know your man,' Cathy explained, 'you know what he can and cannot do.'

'And you really feel that secure?' Liz asked.

'Of course.'

'They say the wife is always the last to know.'

Cathy's head cocked to one side. 'Is this a philosophical discussion, or are you trying to say something to my face instead of behind my back?'

Jesus! Holtzman felt that he was a spectator at a prize-fight.

'Did I give you that impression? Oh, I'm so sorry, Caroline.'

'That's okay, Liz.'

'Excuse me, but I prefer –'

'I go by "professor," too you know, medical doctor, Johns Hopkins, and all that.'

'I thought you were an *associate* professor.'

Dr Ryan nodded. 'That's right. I got offered a full professorship at the University of Virginia, but that meant moving away from the house we like, moving the kids out of school, and, of course, there's the problem with Jack's career. So, I turned it down.'

'I guess you are pretty tied down.'

'I do have responsibilities, and I like working at Hopkins. We're doing some pioneer work, and it's good to be where the action is. It must have been much easier for you to come to Washington, what with nothing to hold you anywhere – and besides, what's new in political science?'

'I'm quite satisfied with my life, thank you.'

'I'm sure you are,' Cathy replied, seeing the chink, and knowing how to exploit it. 'You can always tell when a person is happy in their work.'

'And you, Professor?'

'Life couldn't be much better. As a matter of fact, there's only one real difference between us,' Caroline Ryan said.

'And that is?'

'I don't know where my wife wandered off to. There's yours with Liz Elliot and the Holtzmans. I wonder what they're talking about?' Bunker said.

'At home, at night, I sleep with a man,' Cathy said sweetly. 'And the nice thing about it is that I never have to change the batteries.'

Jack turned to see his wife and Elizabeth Elliot, whose pearl necklace seemed to turn brown before his eyes, she went so pale. His wife was shorter than the National Security Advisor, and she looked like a pixie next to Libby Holtzman, but whatever the hell had just happened, Cathy was holding her ground like a mommabear on her kill, her eyes locked on the taller Elliot. He moved over to see what the problem was.

'Hi, honey.'

'Hello, Jack,' Cathy said, her eyes fixed on her target. 'Do you know Bob and Libby?'

'Hi.' Ryan shook hands with both, catching looks from them that he could only guess at. Mrs Holtzman seemed about to explode, but then she took a breath and controlled herself.

'You're the lucky guy who married this woman?' Libby asked. That comment made Elliot turn away first from the confrontation.

'Actually she's the one who married me, I think,' Jack said, after a further moment's confusion.

'If you'll excuse me,' Elliot said, departing from the battlefield as gracefully as she could. Cathy took Jack's arm and steered him towards the corner with the piano.

'What in the *hell* was that all about?' Libby Holtzman asked her husband. She thought she knew most of it already. Her successful struggle not to laugh aloud had nearly strangled her.

'What it's about, my dear, is that I broke an ethical rule. And you know something?'

'You did the right thing,' Libby announced. 'The Marx Brothers? "Three-way corner." Liz Elliot, the Queen Radical WASP. My God.'

'Jack, I have a terrible headache, I mean, a really terrible one,' Cathy whispered to her husband.

'That bad?'

She nodded. 'Can we get out of here before I get nauseous?'

'Cathy, you don't just walk out of these things . . .' Jack pointed out.

'Sure you do.'

'What were you and Liz talking about?'

'I don't think I like her very much.'

'You're not the only one. Okay.' Jack headed for the door with Cathy on his arm. The Army captain at the stairs was very understanding. Five minutes later, they were outside. Jack helped his wife into the car and headed back up the drive towards Pennsylvania.

'Go straight,' Cathy said.

'But –'

'Go straight, Jack.' It was her surgeon's voice. The one that told people what to do. Ryan pulled past Lafayette Park. 'Now left.'

'Where are we supposed to be going?'

'Now turn right – and left into the driveway.'

'But –'

'Jack, please?' Cathy said softly.

The doorman of the Hay Adams Hotel helped Caroline from the car. Jack handed the keys to the parking attendant, then followed his wife in. He watched the concierge hand her a key, then she breezed off to the elevators. He followed her onto and off the elevator, and from there to a corner suite.

'What gives, Cathy?'

'Jack, there's been too much work, too much kids, and not enough us. Tonight, my darling, there is time for us.' She wrapped her arms around his neck, and there was nothing for her husband to do but kiss her. She put the key in his hand. 'Now get the door open before we scare somebody.'

'But what about –'

'Jack, shut up. Please,' she added.

'Yes, dear.' Ryan led his wife into the room.

Cathy was gratified to see that her instructions had been carried out as perfectly as the staff of this most excellent of hotels could arrange. A light dinner was set on the table, along with a chilled bottle of Möet. She draped her coat on the sofa in confidence that everything else was as it should be.

'Could you pour the champagne? I'll be back in a moment. You might want to take your coat off and relax,' she said over her shoulder on the way into the bedroom.

'Sure,' Jack said to himself. He didn't know what was going on, or what Cathy had in mind, but he didn't really care all that much either. After dropping his dinner jacket atop his wife's mink, he peeled the foil off the champagne, then twisted off the wire, and gently worked the cork free. He poured two glasses, and set the bottle back in the silver bucket. He decided to trust the wine untasted, then walked to look out the window at the White House. Jack didn't hear her come back into the room. He felt it, felt the air change somehow. When he turned she was standing there in the doorway.

It was the second time she'd worn it, the floor-length gown of white silk. The first time had been their honeymoon. Cathy walked barefoot across the carpet to her husband, gliding through space like an apparition.

'Your headache must have gone away.'

'I'm still thirsty, though,' Cathy said, smiling up at Jack's face.

'I think I can handle that.' Jack lifted the glass and held it to her lips. She took a single sip, then moved it to his.

'Hungry?'

'No.'

She leaned against him, taking both his hands in hers. 'I love you, Jack. Shall we?'

Jack turned her around, and walked behind, his hands at her waist. The bed, he saw, was turned down, and the light out, though the glare from the flood-lit White House washed in through the windows.

'Remember the first time, the first night we were married?'

Jack chuckled. 'I remember both, Cathy.'

'This is going to be another first time, Jack.' She reached behind him and flipped off the cummerbund. Her husband took the cue. When he was naked, she embraced him as fiercely as she could manage, and the silk of her nightgown rustled against his skin. 'Lie down.'

'You're more beautiful than ever, Cathy.'

'I wouldn't want anyone to steal you from me.' Cathy joined him on the bed. He was ready, and so was she. Caroline pulled the nightgown up to her waist and mounted him, then let it fall down around her. His hands found her breasts. She held them in place, rocking up and down on him, knowing that he couldn't last very long, but neither could she.

No man should be so lucky, Jack told himself, straining, trying to control himself, and though he failed miserably, he was rewarded with a smile that nearly broke his heart.

'Not bad,' Cathy said a minute later, kissing his hands.

'Out of practice.'

'The night is young,' she said, as she lay down beside him, 'and that's the best I've had in a while, too. Now, are you hungry?'

Ryan looked around the room. 'I, uh . . .'

'Wait.' She left the bed and returned with a bathrobe with the hotel monogram. 'I want you to stay warm.'

Dinner passed in silence. There was nothing that

needed to be said, and for the following hour they silently pretended that they were both in their twenties again, young enough to experiment in love, to explore it like a new and wonderful place where every turn in the road revealed something never before seen. It had been far too long, Jack told himself, but he dismissed the thought from a mind that for once was untroubled. Dessert was finished, and he poured the last of the champagne.

'I have to stop drinking.' *But not tonight.*

Cathy finished off her glass, and set it on the table. 'It wouldn't hurt you to stop, but you're not an alcoholic. We proved that last week. You needed rest, and you got your rest. And now, I want more of you.'

'If there's any left.'

Cathy stood and took his hand. 'There's plenty more where that came from.'

This time Jack did the leading. Once in the bedroom, he reached down and pulled the nightgown over her head, then tossed his robe on the floor next to it.

The first kiss lasted for some eternal period of time. He lifted her in his arms and laid her on the bed, joining her a moment later. The urgency had not passed for either of them. Soon he was atop her, feeling her warmth under and around him. He did better this time, controlling himself until her back arched and her face took on the curious look of pain that every man wants to give his wife. At the end, his arms reached under her and lifted her off the bed, up against his chest. Cathy loved it when he did that, loved her man's strength almost as much as his goodness. And then it was over, and he lay at her side. Cathy pulled him against her, his face to her regrettably flat chest.

'There never was anything wrong with you,' she whispered into her ear. She was not surprised by what came next. She knew the man so well, though she'd been foolish enough to forget the fact. She hoped that she'd be able to forgive herself for that. Jack's whole body shook with his sobs. Cathy held him fast to her, feeling his tears on her breasts. Such a fine, strong man.

'I've been a lousy husband, and a lousy father.'

Her cheek came down on the top of his head. 'Neither one of us has set any records lately, Jack, but that's over, isn't it?'

'Yeah.' He kissed her breast. 'How did I ever find you?'

'You won me, Jack. In the great lottery of life, you got me. I got you. Do you think that married people always deserve each other? All the ones I see at work who just can't make it. Maybe they just don't try, maybe they just forget.'

'Forget?'

What I almost forgot. 'For richer, for poorer, for better, for worse; in sickness and in health, as long as we both shall live.' Remember? I made the promise, too. Jack, I know how good you can be, and that's plenty good enough. I was so bitchy to you last week . . . I'm sorry for all the terrible things I did. But that's all over.'

Presently the weeping stopped. 'Thanks, babe.'

'Thank you, Jack.' She ran a finger down his back.

'You mean?' His head moved back to see her face. He got another smile, the gentle kind that a woman saves for her husband.

'I think so. Maybe this one will be another girl.'

'That might be nice.'

'Go to sleep.'

'In a minute.' Jack rose to head for the bathroom, then into the sitting room before coming back. Ten minutes later, he was still. Cathy rose to put her nightie back on, and on her way back from the bathroom she cancelled the wake-up call that Jack had just ordered. It was her turn to stare out the windows at the home of the President. The world had never seemed prettier. Now, if she could just get Jack to quit working for those people . . .

The truck made a fuel stop outside of Lexington, Kentucky. The driver paused ten minutes to load up on coffee and pancakes – he found breakfasts best for staying awake on the road – then pressed on. The thousand-dollar bonus sounded pretty good, and to be sure of it he had to cross the Mississippi before the rush hour in St Louis.

CHAPTER 31

Dancers

Ryan knew it was too late when the traffic woke him up and he saw that the windows were flooded with light. A look at his watch showed eight-fifteen. That almost set off a panic attack, but it was too late to panic, wasn't it? Jack rose from the bed and walked into the sitting room to see his wife already working on her morning coffee.

'Don't you have to work today?'

'I was supposed to assist with a procedure that started a few minutes ago, but Bernie is covering for me. I think you ought to put some clothes on, though.'

'How do I get to work?'

'John'll be here at nine.'

'Right.' Ryan walked off to shower and shave. On the way, he looked in the closet and noted that a suit, shirt, and tie were waiting for him. His wife had certainly planned this one carefully. He had to smile. Jack had never thought of his wife as a master – mistress? – of conspiracy. By eight-forty, he was washed and shaved.

'You know I have an appointment right across the street at eleven.'

'No, I didn't. Say hi to that Elliot bitch for me.' Cathy smiled.

'You don't like her, either?' he asked.

'Not much there to like. She was a crummy college teacher. She's not as smart as she thinks. Major ego problems.'

'I've noticed. She doesn't like me very much.'

'I did get that impression. We had a little fight yesterday. I think I won,' Cathy observed.

'What was it all about anyway?'

'Oh, just a girl-to-girl thing.' Cathy paused. 'Jack . . . ?'

'Yeah, babe?'

'I think it's time for you to leave.'

Ryan examined his breakfast plate. 'I think you may be right. I have a couple more things to do . . . but when they're done . . .'

'How long?' she asked.

'Two months at the outside. I can't just leave, babe. I'm a presidential appointee. I had to be confirmed by the Senate, remember? You can't just walk away from that – it's like desertion if you do. There are rules you have to follow.'

Cathy nodded. She'd won her point already. 'I understand, Jack. Two months is good enough. What would you like to do?'

'I could get a research job almost anywhere, Center for Strategic and International Studies, Heritage, maybe the Johns Hopkins Center for Advanced International Studies. I had this talk in England with Basil. When you get to my level, you're never really gone. Hmph. I might even write another book . . .'

'We'll start off with a nice long vacation, soon as the kids are out of school.'

'I thought . . . ?'

'I won't be too pregnant then, Jack.'

'You really think it happened last night?'

Her eyes arched wickedly. 'The timing was just about right, and you had two chances, didn't you? What's the matter? You feel used?'

Her husband smiled. 'I've been used worse.'

'See me tonight?'

'Did I ever tell you how much I like that nightie?'

'My wedding dress? It's a little formal, but it did have the desired effect. Shame we don't have more time now, isn't it?'

Jack decided he'd better get out of here while he still could. 'Yeah, babe, but I have work to do, and so do you.'

'Awww,' Cathy observed playfully.

'I can't tell the President that I was late because I was boffing my wife across the street.' Jack came to his wife and kissed her. 'Thanks, honey.'

'A pleasure, Jack.'

Ryan emerged from the front door to see Clark waiting in the drive-through. He got right in.

''Morning, Doc.'

'Hi, John. You only made one mistake.'

'What's that?'

'Cathy knew your name. How?'

'You don't need to know,' Clark replied, handing over the dispatch box. 'Hell, sometimes I like to sack in myself, y'know?'

'I'm sure you broke some kind of law.'

'Yeah, right.' Clark headed out. 'When do we get the go-ahead on the Mexico job?'

'That's what I'm going into the White House for.'

'Eleven?'

'Right.'

It was gratifying to see that the CIA could in fact operate without his presence. Ryan arrived on the seventh floor to see that everyone was at work. Even Marcus was where he belonged.

'Ready for your trip?' Jack asked the Director.

'Yeah, heading off tonight. Station Japan is setting up the meet with Lyalin.'

'Marcus, please remember that he is Agent MUSHASHI, and his information is NIITAKA. Using his real name, even here, is a bad habit to get into.'

'Yeah, Jack. You're heading down to see the President soon for the Mexico thing?'

'That's right.'

'I like the way you set that thing up.'

'Thanks, Marcus, but the credit goes to Clark and Chavez. Open to a suggestion?' Jack asked.

'Go ahead.'

'Put them back in Operations?'

'If they bring this one off, the President will go along with it. So will I.'

'Fair enough.' That was pretty easy, Jack thought. He wondered why.

*

Dr Kaminiskiy went over the films and swore at himself for his error of the previous day. It hardly seemed possible, but —

But it wasn't possible. Not here. Was it? He had to run some additional tests, but first he spent an hour tracking down his Syrian colleague. The patient was moved to another hospital, one with a laminar room. Even if Kaminiskiy were wrong, this man had to be totally isolated.

Russell fired up the forklift and took several minutes to figure out the controls. He wondered what the previous owner had needed with one, but there was no point in that. There was enough remaining pressure in the propane tanks that he didn't have to worry about that either. He walked back to the house.

The people here in Colorado were friendly enough. Already, the local newspaper distributors had set up the delivery boxes at the end of the drive. Russell had the morning paper to read with his coffee. A moment later, he realized how good a thing that was.

'Uh-oh,' he observed quietly.

'What is the problem, Marvin?'

'I've never seen this before. The Vikings fans are planning a convoy . . . over a thousand cars and buses. Damn,' he noted. 'That'll screw the roads up . . .' He turned to see the extended weather forecast.

'What do you mean?'

'They have to come down I-76 to get to Denver. That might mess things up some. We want to arrive about noon, maybe a little later . . . about the same time the convoy is supposed to arrive . . .'

'Convoy — what do you mean? Convoy defending against what?' Qati asked.

'Not a real convoy,' Russell explained. 'More like a, uh, a motorcade. The fans from Minnesota have a big deal laid on . . . Tell you what, let's get a motel room for us. One close to the airport. When's our flight?' He paused. 'Jesus, I really haven't been thinking very clear, have I?'

'What do you mean?' Ghosn asked again.

'Weather,' Russell replied. 'This is Colorado, and it is January. What if we get another snowstorm?' He scanned the page. *Uh-oh* . . .

'For driving, you mean?'

'That's right. Look, what we ought to do is get rooms reserved, one of the motels right by the airport, say. We can go down the night before . . . or I'll get the rooms for two – no, three nights, so there won't be any suspicion. Christ, I hope there's vacancies.' Russell walked to the phone and flipped open the Yellow Pages right next to it. It took him four tries to find a room with twin doubles in a little independent place a mile from the airport. This he had to guarantee with a credit card that he'd managed not to use until now. He didn't like having to do that. One more bit of paper for his trail.

'Good morning, Liz.' Ryan walked into the office and sat down. 'How are you today?'

The National Security Advisor didn't like being baited any more than the next person. She'd had a little battle with this bastard's wife – in front of reporters! – and taken her lumps publicly. Whether Ryan had had anything to do with it or not, he must have had a good laugh about it last night. Worse than that, what that skinny little bitch had said also went after Bob Fowler, didn't it? The President had thought so on being told last night.

'You ready for the brief?'

'Sure am.'

'Come on.' She'd let Bob handle this.

Helen D'Agustino watched the two officials enter the Oval Office. She'd heard the story, of course. A Secret Service agent had heard the whole thing, and the vicious put-down administered to Dr Elliot had already been the subject of a few discreet chuckles.

'Good morning, Mr President,' she heard Ryan say, as the door closed.

'Morning, Ryan. Okay, let's hear it.'

'Sir, what we plan to do is actually fairly simple. Two CIA officers will be in Mexico, at the airport, covered as

airline maintenance personnel. They'll do the normal
stuff, emptying ashtrays, cleaning the johns. Before they
leave they will place fresh flower arrangements in the
upstairs lounge. Concealed in the arrangements will be
microphones like this one.' Ryan pulled the plastic spike
from his pocket and handed it over. 'These will transmit
what they pick up to a second transmitter, concealed in
a bottle. That device will broadcast a multi-channel EHF
– that's extremely high frequency – signal out of the
aircraft. A series of three other aircraft will fly parallel
courses with the 747 to receive that signal. An additional
receiver with a tape-recorder attached will be concealed
on the 747, both as a backup to the air-to-air links and
as a cover for the operation. If it's located, the bugs will
seem to be something done by the news people accom-
panying the Prime Minister. We don't expect that, of
course. We'll have people at Dulles to recover our
gadgets. In either case, the electronic transmission will
be processed and the transcripts presented to you a few
hours after the aircraft lands.'

'Very well. What are the chances for success?' Chief
of Staff Arnold van Damm asked. He had to be there,
of course. This was more an exercise in politics than
statecraft. The down-side political risk was serious, just
as the reward for success would be more than noteworthy.

'Sir, there are no guarantees for operations of this kind.
If something is said, it is likely that we'll know what it
is, but he might not even discuss the matter at all. The
equipment has all been tested. It works. The field officer
running this operation is well experienced. He's done
touchy ones before.'

'Like?' van Damm asked.

'Like getting Gerasimov's wife and daughter out a few
years ago.' Ryan explained on for a minute or so.

'Is the operation worth the risk?' Fowler asked.

That surprised Ryan quite a bit. 'Sir, that decision is
yours to make.'

'But I asked you for an opinion.'

'Yes, Mr President, it is. The take we've been getting

from NIITAKA shows a considerable degree of arrogance on their part. Something like this might have the net effect of shocking them into playing honest ball with us.'

'You approve of our policy of dealing with Japan?' van Damm asked, just as surprised as Ryan had been a moment earlier.

'My approval or disapproval is beside the point, but the answer to your question is, yes.'

The Chief of Staff was openly amazed. 'But the previous administration – how come you never told us?'

'You never asked, Arnie. I don't make government policy, remember? I'm a spook. I do what you tell me to do, as long as it's legal.'

'You're satisfied on the legality of the operation?' Fowler asked, with a barely suppressed smile.

'Mr President, you're the lawyer, not me. If I do not know the legal technicalities – and I don't – I must assume that you, as an officer of the court, are not ordering me to break the law.'

'That's the best dance number I've seen since the Kirov Ballet was in the Kennedy Center last summer,' van Damm observed, with a laugh.

'Ryan, you know all the moves. You have my approval,' Fowler said, after a brief pause. 'If we get what we expect, then what?'

'We have to go over that with the State Department guys,' Liz Elliot announced.

'That is potentially dangerous,' Ryan observed. 'The Japanese have been hiring a lot of the people from the trade-negotiation section. We have to assume that they have people inside.'

'Commercial espionage?' Fowler asked.

'Sure, why not? NIITAKA has never given us hard evidence of that, but if I were a bureaucrat looking to leave government service and make half a mill' a year representing them – like a lot of them do – how would I present myself to them as a potentially valuable asset? I'd do it the same way a Soviet official or spook presents bonafides to us. You deliver something juicy up-front.

That's illegal, but we're not devoting any assets to looking at the problem. For that reason, wide dissemination of the information from this operation is very dangerous. Obviously you'll want the opinion of Secretary Talbot and a few others, but I'd be really careful how much farther you spread it. Also, remember that if you tell the P.M. that you know what he said – and if he knows he only said it in one place – you run the risk of compromising this intelligence-gathering technique.' The President accepted that without anything more than a raised eyebrow.

'Make it look like a leak in Mexico?' van Damm asked.

'That's the obvious ploy,' Ryan agreed.

'And if I confront him with it directly?' Fowler asked.

'Kind of hard to beat a straight-flush, Mr President. And if this were ever to leak, Congress would go ballistic. That's one of my problems. I'm required to discuss this operation with Al Trent and Sam Fellows. Sam will play ball, but Al has political reasons to dislike the Japanese.'

'I could order you not to tell him . . .'

'Sir, that's one law I may not break for any reason.'

'I might have to give you that order,' Fowler observed.

Ryan was surprised again. Both he and the President knew what the consequences of that order would be. Just what Cathy had in mind. It might, in fact, be a fine excuse to leave government service.

'Well, maybe that won't be necessary. I'm tired of playing patty-cake with these people. They made an agreement, and they're going to keep it or have to deal with a very irate President. Worse than that, the idea that someone can suborn the President of a country in so venal a way is contemptible. God damn it! I hate corruption.'

'Right on, boss,' van Damm commented. 'Besides, the voters will like it.'

'That bastard,' Fowler went on, after a moment. Ryan couldn't tell how much of this was real and how much feigned. 'He tells me he's coming over to work out a few details, get acquainted some more, and what he's really planning is to welsh on a deal. Well, we'll see about that. I guess it's time he learned about hardball.' The discourse stopped. 'Ryan, I missed you last night.'

'My wife got a headache, sir. Had to leave. Sorry.'

'Feeling all right now?'

'Yes, sir, thank you.'

'Turn your people loose.'

Ryan stood. 'Will do, Mr President.'

Van Damm followed him out and walked him to the West Entrance. 'Nice job, Jack.'

'Gee, they going to start liking me?' Jack asked wryly. The meeting had gone much too well.

'I don't know what happened last night, but Liz is really pissed at your wife.'

'They talked about something, but I don't know what.'

'Jack, you want it straight?' van Damm asked.

Ryan knew that the friendly walk to the door was just too convenient, and the symbolism was explicit enough, wasn't it? 'When, Arnie?'

'I'd like to say it's just business and not personal, but it is personal. I'm sorry, Jack, but it happens. The President will give you a glowing send-off.'

'Nice of him,' Jack replied matter-of-factly.

'I tried, Jack. You know I like you. These things happen.'

'I'll go quietly. But —'

'I know. No back-shots on the way out or after you're gone. You'll be asked in periodically, maybe draw some special missions, liaison stuff. You get an honorable discharge. On that, Jack, you have my word of honor, and the President's. He's not a bad guy, Jack, really he isn't. He's a tough-minded son-of-a-bitch and a good politician, but he's as honest as any man I know. It's just that your way of thinking and his way of thinking are different — and he's the President.'

Jack could have said that the mark of intellectual honesty is the solicitation of opposing points of view. Instead, he said, 'Like I said, I'll go quietly. I've been doing this long enough. It's time to relax a little, smell the roses and play with the kids.'

'Good man.' Van Damm patted his arm. 'You bring this job off and your going-away statement from the Boss will sparkle. We'll have Callie Weston write it, even.'

'You stroke like a pro, Arnie.' Ryan shook his hand and walked off to his car. Van Damm would have been surprised to see the smile on his face.

'Do you have to do it that way?'

'Elizabeth, ideological differences notwithstanding, he has served his country well. I disagree with him on a lot of things, but he's never lied to me, and he's always tried to give me good advice,' Fowler replied, looking at the plastic-stick microphone. He suddenly wondered if it was working.

'I *told* you what happened last night.'

'You got your wish. He's on the way out. At this level, you do not throw people out the door. You do it in a civilized and honorable way. Anything else is small-minded and decidedly stupid, politically. I agree with you that he's a dinosaur, but even dinosaurs get a nice spot in the museums.'

'But –'

'That's all. Okay, you had words with his wife last night. I'm sorry about that, but what kind of person penalizes someone for what their wife did?'

'Bob, I have a right to expect your support!'

Fowler didn't like that, but responded reasonably. 'And you have it, Elizabeth. Now, this is neither the time nor the place for this sort of discussion.'

Marcus Cabot arrived at Andrews Air Force Base just after lunch for his flight to Korea. The arrangements were more luxurious than they looked. The aircraft was a U.S. Air Force C-141B Starlifter, an aircraft with four engines and an oddly serpent-like fuselage. Loaded into the cargo area, he saw, was essentially a house trailer complete with kitchen, living and bed rooms. It was also heavily insulated – the C-141 is a noisy aircraft, especially aft. He went out the front door to meet the flight crew. The pilot, he saw, was a blond captain of thirty years. There were, in fact, two complete flight crews. The flight would be long, with a fueling stop at Travis Air Force Base in California, followed by three mid-air 'tankings' over the Pacific. It would also be singularly boring, and he would sleep through it as much as possible. He wondered if government service were really worth it, and the knowledge that Ryan would soon be gone – Arnold van Damm had gotten the word to him – didn't improve his outlook. The Director of Central Intelligence strapped himself in and started to read through his briefing documents. An Air Force non-com offered him a glass of wine, which he started on as the aircraft taxied off the ramp.

John Clark and Domingo Chavez boarded their own flight later that afternoon for Mexico City. It was better, the senior man thought, to get settled in and acclimated. Mexico City was yet another high-altitude metropolis whose thin air was made all the worse by air pollution. Their mission gear was carefully packed away, and they expected no trouble with customs clearance. Neither carried a weapon, of course, as this sort of mission did not require it.

The truck pulled off the Interstate exactly thirty-eight hours and forty minutes after leaving the cargo terminal at Norfolk. That was the easy part. It took fifteen minutes and all the driver's skill to back his rig up to the concrete loading dock outside the barn. A warm sun had thawed the ground into a six-inch-deep layer of gooey mud that almost prevented him from completing the maneuver, but on the third try he made it. The driver jumped down and walked back towards the dock.

'How do you open this thing?' Russell asked.

'I'll show you.' The driver paused to scrape the mud off his boots, then worked the latch on the container. 'Need help unloading?'

'No, I'll do it myself. There's coffee over in the house.'

'Thank you, sir. I could use a cup.'

'Well, that was easy enough,' Russell said to Qati, as

they watched the man go away. Marvin opened the doors and saw a single large box with 'SONY' printed on all four sides, along with arrows to show which side was up, and the image of a champagne glass to tell the illiterate it was delicate. It was also sitting on a wooden pallet. Marvin removed the fasteners that held it in place, then fired up the fork-lift. The task of removing the bomb and putting it inside the barn was completed in another minute. Russell shut the fork-lift down, then draped a tarp over the box. By the time the trucker came back, the cargo box was again closed.

'Well, you got your bonus,' Marvin told him, handing over the cash.

The driver riffled through the bills. Now he got to drive the box back to Norfolk, but first he'd hit the nearest truck-stop for eight hours of sleep. 'A pleasure doing business with you, sir. You said you might have another job for me in a month or so?'

'That's right.'

'Here's how you reach me.' The trucker handed over his card.

'Heading right back?'

'After I get some sack time. I just heard on the radio there's snow coming tomorrow night. A big one, they say.'

'That time of year, isn't it?'

'Sure is. You have a good one, sir.'

'Be careful, man,' Russell said, shaking his hand one more time.

'It's a mistake to let him go,' Ghosn observed to the Commander in Arabic.

'I think not. The only face he has really seen is Marvin's, after all.'

'True.'

'Have you checked it?' Qati asked.

'There is no damage to the packing box. I will do a more detailed check tomorrow. I would say that we are almost ready.'

'Yes.'

*

'You want the good news or the bad news?' Jack asked.

'Good first,' Cathy said.

'They're asking me to resign my position.'

'What's the bad news?'

'Well, you never really leave. They'll want me to come back occasionally. To consult, stuff like that.'

'Is that what you want?'

'This work does get in your blood, Cathy. Would you like to leave Hopkins and just be a doc with an office and patients and glasses to prescribe?'

'How much?'

'Couple times a year, probably. Special areas I happen to know a lot about. Nothing regular.'

'Okay, that's fair – and, no, I couldn't give up teaching young docs. How soon?'

'Well, I have two things I have to finish up with. Then we have to pick someone for the job . . .' *How about the Foleys*, Jack thought. *But which one . . . ?*

'Conn, sonar.'

'Conn, aye,' the navigator answered.

'Sir, I got a possible contact bearing two-nine-five, very faint, but it keeps coming back.'

'On the way.' It was a short five steps into the sonar room. 'Show me.'

'Right here, sir.' The sonarman pointed to a line on the display. Though it looked fuzzy, it was in fact composed of discrete yellow dots in a specific frequency range, and as the time-scale moved vertically upward, more dots kept appearing, regular only in that they seemed to form a vague and fuzzy line. The only change in the line was a slight drift in direction. 'I can't tell you what it is yet.'

'Tell me what it isn't.'

'It ain't no surface contact, and I don't think it's random noise either, sir.' The petty officer traced it all the way to the top of the tube with a grease pencil. 'Right about here, I decided it might actually be something.'

'What else you got?'

'Sierra-15 over here is a merchant, heading southeast

and way the hell away from us – that's a third-CZ contact we been trackin' since before turn of the last watch, and that's about it, Mr Pitney. I guess it's too bumpy topside for the fishermen to be out this far.'

Lieutenant Pitney tapped the screen. 'Call it Sierra-16, and I'll get a track started. How's the water?'

'Deep channel seems very good today, sir. Surface noise is a little tough, though. This one's tough to hold.'

'Keep an eye on it.'

'Aye aye.' The sonarman turned back to his scope.

Lieutenant Jeff Pitney returned to the control room, lifted the growler phone, and punched the button for the Captain's cabin. 'Gator here, Cap'n. We have a possible sonar contact bearing two-nine-five, very faint. Our friend might be back, sir ... yes, sir.' Pitney hung up and hit the 1-MC speaker system. 'Man the fire-control tracking party.'

Captain Ricks appeared a minute later, wearing sneakers and his blue overalls. His first stop was to control, to check course, speed, and depth. Then he went into sonar.

'Let's see it.'

'Damn thing just faded on me again, sir,' the sonarman said sheepishly. He used a piece of toilet paper – there was a roll over each scope – to erase the previous mark, and penciled in another. 'I think we have something here, sir.'

'I hope you didn't interrupt my sleep for nothing,' Ricks noted. Lieutenant Pitney caught the look the two other sonarmen exchanged at that.

'Coming back, sir. You know, if this is an Akula, we should be getting a little pump noise in this spectrum over here...'

'Intelligence says he's coming out of overhaul. Ivan is learning how to make them quieter,' Ricks said.

'Guess so ... slow drift to the north, call the current bearing two-nine-seven.' Both men knew that figure could be off by ten degrees either way. Even with the enormously expensive system on *Maine*, really long-distance bearings were pretty vague.

'Anybody else around?' Pitney asked.

'*Omaha* is supposed to be around somewhere south of Kodiak. Wrong direction. It's not her. Sure it's not a surface contact?'

'No way, Cap'n. If it was diesel, I'd know it, and if it was steam, I'd know that, too. There's no pounding from surface noise. Has to be a submerged contact, Cap'n. Only thing makes sense . . .'

'Pitney, we're on two-eight-one?'

'Yessir.'

'Come left to two-six-five. We'll set up a better baseline for the target-motion analysis, try to get a range estimate before we turn in.'

Turn in, Pitney thought. *Jesus, boomers aren't supposed to do this stuff.* He gave the order anyway, of course.

'Where's the layer?'

'One-five-zero feet, sir. Judging by the surface noise, there's twenty-five-footers up there,' the sonarman added.

'So he's probably staying deep to smooth the ride out.'

'Damn, lost him again . . . we'll see what happens when the tail straightens back out . . .'

Ricks leaned his head out of the sonar room and spoke a single word: 'Coffee.' It never occurred to him that the sonarmen might like some, too.

It took five more minutes of waiting before the dots started appearing again in the right place.

'Okay, he's back. I think,' the sonarman added. 'Bearing looks like three-zero-two now.'

Ricks walked out to the plotting table. Ensign Shaw was doing his calculations along with a quartermaster. 'Has to be a hundred-thousand-plus yards. I'm assuming a north-easterly course from the bearing drift, speed of less than ten. Has to be a hundred-K yards or more.' That was good, fast work, Shaw and the petty officer thought.

Ricks nodded curtly and went back to sonar.

'Firming up, getting some stuff on the fifty-herz line now. Starting to smell like Mr Akula, maybe.'

'You must have a pretty good channel.'

'Right, Captain, pretty good and improving a little. That storm's gonna change it when the turbulence gets down to our depth, sir.'

Ricks went into control again: 'Mr Shaw?'

'Best estimate is one-one-five-K yards, course north-easterly, speed five knots, maybe one or two more, sir. If his speed's much higher than that, the range is awfully far.'

'Okay, I want us to come around very gently, come right to zero-eight-zero.'

'Aye aye, sir. Helm, right five degrees rudder, come to new course zero-eight-zero.'

'Right five degrees rudder, aye. Sir, my rudder is right five degrees, coming to new course zero-eight-zero.'

'Very well.'

Slowly, so as not to make too great a bend in the towed array, USS *Maine* reversed course. It took three minutes before she settled down on the new course, doing something no US fleet ballistic-missile submarine had ever done before. Lieutenant-Commander Claggett appeared in the control room soon thereafter.

'How long you figure he's going to hold this course?' he asked Ricks.

'What would you do?'

'I think I'd troll along in a ladder pattern,' Dutch answered, 'and my drift would be south instead of north, reverse of how we do it in the Barents Sea, right? Interval between sweeps will be determined by the performance of his tail. That's one hard piece of intel we can develop, but depending on how that number looks, we'll have to be real careful how we trail him, won't we?'

'Well, I can't approach to less than thirty thousand yards under any circumstances. So ... we'll close to fifty-K until we have a better feel for him, then ease it in as circumstances permit. One of us should be in here at all times as long as he's in the neighborhood.'

'Agreed.' Claggett nodded. He paused for a beat before going on. 'How the hell,' the XO asked very quietly indeed, 'did OP-02 ever agree to this?'

'Safer world now, isn't it?'

'I s'pose, sir.'

'You're jealous that boomers can do a fast-attack job?'

'Sir, I think that OP-02 slipped a gear, either that or they're trying to impress some folks with our flexibility or something.'

'You don't like this?'

'No, Captain, I don't. I know we can do it, but I don't think we should.'

'Is that what you talked to Mancuso about?'

'What?' Claggett shook his head. 'No, sir. Well, he did ask me that, and I said we could do it. Not my place to enter into that yet.'

Then what did you talk to him about? Ricks wanted to ask. He couldn't, of course.

The Americans were a great disappointment to Oleg Kirilovich Kadishev. The whole reason they'd recruited him was to get good inside information on the Soviet government, and he'd delivered precisely that for years. He'd seen the sweeping political changes coming for his country, seen them early because he'd known Andrey Il'ych Narmonov for what he was. And for what he was not. The President of his country was a man of stunning political gifts. He had the courage of a lion and the tactical agility of a mongoose. It was a plan that he lacked. Narmonov had no idea where he was going, and that was his weakness. He had destroyed the old political order, eliminated the Warsaw Pact through inaction, merely by saying out loud, only once, that the Soviet Union would not interfere with the political integrity of other countries, and had done so in the knowledge that the only thing that kept Marxism in place was the threat of Soviet force. The Eastern European communists had foolishly played along, actually thinking themselves secure in the love and respect of their people in one of history's most colossal and least understood acts of lunacy. But what made the irony sublime was that Narmonov could not see the same thing in his own country, to which was added one more, fatal, variable.

The Soviet people – a term that never had any meaning, of course – were held together only by the threat of force. Only the guns of the Red Army guaranteed that Moldavians, and Latvians, and Tadzhiks and so many others would follow the Moscow line. They loved the communist leadership even less than the great-grandfathers had loved the czars. And so while Narmonov had dismantled the Party's central role in managing the country, he'd eliminated his ability to control his people, but left himself no ethos with which to supplant what had gone before. The plan – in a nation which for over eighty years had always had The Plan – simply did not exist. So, necessarily, when turmoil began to replace order, there was nothing to do, nothing to point to, no goal to strive for. Narmonov's dazzling political maneuvers were ultimately pointless. Kadishev saw that. Why didn't the Americans, who had gambled everything on the survival of 'their man' in Moscow?

The forty-six-year-old parliamentarian snorted at the thought. He was their man, wasn't he? He'd warned them for years, and they hadn't listened, but instead used his reports to buttress a man who was rich in skill but bereft of vision – and how could a man lead without vision?

The Americans, just as foolish, just as blind, had actually been surprised by the violence in Georgia, and the Baltic states. They actually ignored the nascent civil war that had already begun in the arc of Southern republics. Half a million military weapons had vanished in the withdrawal from Afghanistan. Mostly rifles, but some were *tanks!* The Soviet Army could not begin to deal with the situation. Narmonov struggled with it on a day-to-day basis like some kind of desperate juggler, barely managing to keep up, taking his effort from one place to another, keeping his plates in the air, but barely. Didn't the Americans understand that some fine day all the plates would fall at the same time? The consequences of that were frightening to everyone. Narmonov needed a vision, needed a plan, but he didn't have one.

Kadishev did, and that was the entire point of his exercise. The Union had to be broken up. The Muslim republics had to go. The Balts had to go. Moldavia had to go. The Western Ukraine had to go – he wanted to keep the Eastern part. He had to find a way to protect the Armenians, lest they be massacred by the local Muslims, and had to find a way to keep access to the oil of Azerbaijan, at least long enough until, with help from the West, he could exploit all the resources of Siberia.

Kadishev was a Russian. It was part of his soul. Russia was the mother of the Union, and like a good mother, she would let her children go at the proper time. The proper time was now. That would leave a country stretching from the Baltic to the Pacific, with a largely homogeneous population, and immense resources that were scarcely catalogued, much less tapped. It could and should be a great, strong country, powerful as any, rich in history and arts, a leader in the sciences. That was Kadishev's vision. He wished to lead a Russia that was a true superpower, a friend and associate to other countries of European heritage. It was his task to bring his country into the light of freedom and prosperity. If that meant dismissing almost half of the population and twenty-five percent of the land – so be it.

But the Americans weren't helping. Why this should be so, he simply did not understand. They had to see that Narmonov was a street without an exit, a road that merely stopped . . . or perhaps stopped at the brink of a great abyss.

If the Americans couldn't help, then it was within his power to force them to help. That was why he had allowed himself to be recruited by Mary Foley in the first place.

It was early morning in Moscow, but Kadishev was a man who had long since disciplined himself to live on a minimum of sleep. He typed his report on an old, heavy, but quiet machine. Kadishev used the same cloth ribbon many times. No one would ever be able to examine the ribbon to see what had been written on it, and the paper was from a sheaf taken from the office central supply room. Several hundred people had access to it. Like all professional gamblers, Kadishev was a careful man.

When he was finished, he used leather gloves to wipe the paper clean of whatever fingerprints he might have accidentally left on it, then, using the same gloves, he folded the copy into a coat pocket. In two hours, the message would be passed. In less than twenty, the message would be in other hands.

Agent SPINNAKER needn't have bothered, KGB was under orders not to harass the People's Deputies. The coat-check girl pocketed the paper, and soon thereafter passed it across to an individual whose name she did not know. That man left the building and drove to his own work place. Two hours after that, the message was in another container in the pocket of a man driving to the airport, where he boarded the 747 for New York.

'Where to this time, Doctor?' the driver asked.

'Just drive around.'

'What?'

'We need to talk,' Kaminiskiy said.

'About what?'

'I know you are KGB,' Kaminiskiy said.

'Doctor,' the driver chuckled, 'I am an embassy driver.'

'Your embassy medical file is signed by Dr Feodor Il'ych Gregoriyev. He is a KGB doctor. We were classmates. May I go on?'

'Have you told anyone?'

'Of course not.'

The driver sighed. Well, what could one do about that? 'What is it you wish to talk about?'

'You are KGB – foreign directorate?'

There was no avoiding it. 'Correct. I hope this is important.'

'It may be. I need someone to come down from Moscow. There's a patient I'm treating. He has a very unusual lung problem.'

'Why should it interest me?'

'I've seen a similar problem before – a worker from Beloyarskiy. Industrial accident, I was called in to consult on it.'

'Yes? What is at Beloyarskiy?'

'They fabricate atomic weapons there.'

The driver slowed the car. 'Are you serious?'

'It could be something else – but the tests I need to run now are very specific. If this represents a Syrian project, we will not get the proper cooperation. Therefore, I need some special equipment from Moscow.'

'How quickly?'

'The patient isn't going anywhere, except into the ground. I'm afraid his condition is quite hopeless.'

'I have to go through the *rezident* on this. He won't be back until Sunday.'

'Fast enough.'

CHAPTER 32

Closure

'Can I help?' Russell asked.

'Thank you, Marvin, but I would really prefer to do this myself, without distractions,' Ghosn said.

'I understand. Yell if you need anything.'

Ibrahim donned his heaviest clothing and walked out into the cold. The snow was falling quite hard. He'd seen snow in Lebanon, of course, but nothing like this. The storm had scarcely begun half an hour before and there was already more than three centimeters of it. The northerly wind was the most bitter he'd ever experienced, cutting into his very bones as he walked the sixty meters or so to the barn. Visibility was restricted to no more than two hundred meters. He could hear the traffic on the nearby highway, but could not even see the lights of the vehicles. He entered the barn through a side door and already regretted the fact that this building had no heating. Ghosn told himself very forcefully that he could not allow such things to affect him.

The cardboard box that shielded the device from casual view was not actually attached, and came off easily. What lay under that was a metal box with dials and other accoutrements for what it pretended to be, a commercial video-tape machine. The suggestion had come from Günther Bock, and the actual body of the machine had been purchased as scrap from a Syrian TV news agency which had replaced it with a new model. The access doors built into the metal body were almost perfectly suited to Ghosn's purpose, and the ample void space held the vacuum pump, in case that was needed. Ghosn instantly saw that it was not. The gauge that was part of the bomb case showed that the body had not leaked any air at all. That hardly came as a surprise – Ghosn was just as skilled a welder as he had told the late Manfred Fromm – but it was gratifying to the young engineer. Next he checked the batteries. There were three of these, all new, all nickel-cadmium, and all, he saw, fully charged, according to the test circuit. The timing device was next to the batteries. Making sure that its firing terminals were vacant, he checked its time – it was already set on local – against his watch, and saw that either one or the other (probably his watch) was a total of three seconds off. That was close enough for his purposes. Three glasses placed inside the box to illustrate any rough handling in transit were still intact. The shippers had taken their care, as he had hoped.

'You are ready, my friend,' Ghosn said quietly. He closed the inspection door, made sure it was properly latched, then replaced the cardboard cover. Ghosn blew warm breath on his hands, then walked back to the house.

'How will the weather affect us?' Qati asked Russell.

'There's another storm behind this one. I figure we'll drive down tomorrow evening, right before it starts. The second one will be short, maybe another inch or two, they say. If we go in between the two, the road should be all right. Then we check into the motel, and wait for the right time, right?'

'Correct. And the truck?'

'I'll do the painting today, soon as I have the heaters rigged. That's only two hours work. I have the templates all done,' Russell said as he finished his coffee. 'Load the bomb after I paint, okay?'

'How long for the paint to dry?' Ghosn asked.

'Three hours, tops. I want the paint job to be good, okay?'

'That is fine, Marvin.'

Russell laughed as he collected the breakfast dishes. 'Man, I wonder what the people who made that movie would think?' He turned to see puzzlement on the faces of his guests.

'Didn't Gunther tell you?' The faces were blank. 'I saw the movie on television once. *Black Sunday*. A guy came up with an idea of killing the whole Superbowl crowd from a blimp.'

'You're joking,' Qati observed.

'No, in the movie they had a big anti-personnel thing on the bottom of the blimp, but the Israelis found out what was going on, and their CIA guys got there in the nick of time – you know, how it usually happens in the movies. With my people, it was always the cavalry that got there in the nick of time, so's they could kill all the savage Indians.'

'In this movie, the objective was to kill the entire stadium?' Ghosn asked, very quietly.

'Huh – oh, yeah, that's right.' Russell was loading the dishes into the dishwasher. 'Not like we're doing.' He turned. 'Hey, don't feel bad. Just taking out the TV coverage is going to piss people off like you wouldn't believe. And this stadium is covered, okay? That blimp-thing wouldn't work. You'd need like a nuke or something to do the same thing.'

'There's an idea,' Ghosn observed with a chuckle, wondering what reaction he'd get.

'Some idea. Yeah, you might start a real nuclear war – shit, man, guess whose people lives up in the Dakotas, where all those SAC bases are? I don't think I could play that kind of a game.' Russell dumped in the detergent and started the wash cycle. 'What exactly do you have in that thing anyway?'

'A very compact and powerful high-explosive compound. It will do some damage to the stadium, of course.'

'I figured that. Well, taking out the TV won't be hard – that's delicate shit, y'know? – and just doing that – man, I'm telling you, it's going to have an effect like you wouldn't believe.'

'I agree, Marvin, but I would like to hear your reasoning on this,' Qati said.

'We've never had a really destructive terrorist act over here. This one will change things. People won't feel safe. They'll install check points and security stuff everywhere. It'll really piss people off, make people think. Maybe they'll see what the real problems are. That's the whole point, isn't it?'

'Correct, Marvin,' Qati replied.

'Can I help you with the painting?' Ghosn asked. He might get curious, Ibrahim thought, and they couldn't have that.

'I'd appreciate it.'

'You must promise to turn the heat on,' the engineer observed with a smile.

'Depend on it, man, or else the paint won't dry right. I guess this is kinda cold for ya.'

'Your people must be very hard to live in such a place.'

Russell reached for his coat and gloves. 'Hey, man, it's our place, y'know?'

'Do you really expect to find him?' the *Starpom* asked.

'I think we have a fine chance,' Dubinin replied, leaning over the chart. 'He'll be somewhere in here, well away from the coastal waters – too many fishermen with nets there – and north of this area.'

'Excellent, Captain, only two million square kilometers to search.'

'And we will cover only two-thirds of that. I said a fine chance, not a certainty. In three or four more years, we'll have the RPV the designers are working on, and we can send our sonar receptors down into the deep sound channel.' Dubinin referred to the next step in submarine technology, a robot mini-sub, which would be controlled from the mother ship by a fiber-optic cable. It would carry both sensors and weapons, and by diving very deep it could find out if sonar conditions in the thousand-to-two-thousand-meter regime were really as good as the theorists suggested. That would change the game radically.

'Anything on the turbulence sensors?'

'Negative, Captain,' a lieutenant answered.

'I wonder if those things are worth the trouble . . .' the executive officer groused.

'They worked the last time.'

'We had calm seas overhead then. How often are the seas calm in the North Pacific in winter?'

'It could still tell us something. We must use every trick we have. Why are you not optimistic?'

'Even Ramius only tracked an Ohio once, and that was on builder's trials, when they had the shaft problem. And even then, he only held the contact for – what? Seventy minutes.'

'We had this one before.'

'True enough, Captain.' The *Starpom* tapped a pencil on the chart.

Dubinin thought about his intelligence briefing on the enemy – old habits were hard to break. Harrison Sharpe Ricks, Captain, Naval Academy, in his second missile-submarine command, reportedly a brilliant engineer and technician, a likely candidate for higher command. A hard and demanding taskmaster, highly regarded in his navy. He'd made a mistake before, and was unlikely to make another, Dubinin told himself.

'Fifty thousand yards, exactly,' Ensign Shaw reported.

'This guy's not doing any Crazy Ivans,' Claggett thought for the first time.

'He's not expecting to be hunted himself, is he?' Ricks asked.

'I guess not, but his tail's not as good as he thinks it is.' The Akula was doing a ladder-search pattern. The long legs were on a roughly south-west-to-north-east vector, and at the end of each he shifted down south-east to the next leg, with an interval between search legs of about fifty thousand yards, twenty-five nautical miles. That gave a notional range of about thirteen miles to the Russian's towed-array sonar. At least, Claggett thought, that's what the intelligence guys would have said.

'You know, I think we'll hold at fifty-K yards, just to play it on the safe side,' Ricks announced, after a moment's reflection. 'This guy is a lot quieter than I expected.'

'Plant noises are down quite a bit, aren't they? If this guy was creeping instead of trying to cover ground . . .'

Claggett was pleased that his Captain was speaking like his conservative-engineer self again. He wasn't especially surprised. When push came to shove, Ricks reverted to type, but that was all right with the XO, who didn't think it was especially prudent to play fast-attack with a billion-dollar boomer.

'We could still hold him at forty, thirty-five tops.'

'Think so? How much will his tail's performance improve with a slower speed?'

'Good point. It'll be some, but intelligence calls it a thin-line array like ours . . . probably not all that much. Even so, we're getting a good profile on this bird, aren't we?' Ricks asked rhetorically. He'd get a gold star in his copybook for this.

'So, what do you think, MP?' Jack asked Mrs Foley. He held the translation in his hand. She'd opted for the original Russian-language document.

'Hey, I recruited him, Jack. He's my boy.'

Ryan checked his watch; it was just about time. Sir Basil Charleston was nothing if not punctual. His secure direct-line phone rang right on the hour.

'Ryan.'

'Bas here.'

'What gives, man?'

'That thing we talked out, we had our chap look into it. Nothing at all, my boy.'

'Not even that our impressions were incorrect?' Jack asked, his eyes screwed tightly shut, as though to keep the news out.

'Correct, Jack, not even that. I admit I find that slightly curious, but it is plausible, if not likely, that our chap should not know this.'

'Thanks for trying, pal. We owe you one.'

'Sorry we could not be of help.' The line went dead.

It was the worst possible news, Ryan thought. He stared briefly at the ceiling.

'The Brits have been unable to confirm or deny SPIN-NAKER's allegations,' Jack announced. 'What's that leave us with?'

'It's really like this?' Ben Goodley asked. 'It all comes down to *opinion*?'

'Ben, if we were really that smart at reading fortunes, we'd be *making* fortunes in the stock market,' Ryan said gruffly.

'But you did!' Goodley pointed out.

'I got lucky on a few hot issues.' Ryan dismissed the observation. 'Mary Pat, what do you think?'

Mrs Foley looked tired, but then she had an infant to worry about. Jack thought he should tell her to take it easier. 'I have to back up my agent, Jack. You know that. He's our best source of political intelligence. He gets in to see Narmonov alone. That's why he's so valuable, and that's why his stuff has always been hard to back up – but it's never been wrong, has it?'

'The scary part is that he's starting to convince me.'

'Why scary, Dr Ryan?'

Jack lit a cigarette. ''Cause I know Narmonov. That man could have made me disappear one cold night outside o' Moscow. We cut a deal, shook on it, and that was that. Takes a very confident man to do something like that. If he has lost that confidence, then ... then the whole thing could come apart, rapidly and unpredictably. Can you think of anything scarier than that?' Ryan's eyes swept the room.

'Not hardly,' agreed the head of the Intelligence Directorate's Russian Department. 'I think we have to go with it.'

'So do I,' Mary Pat agreed.

'Ben?' Jack asked. 'You believed this guy from the beginning. What he says backs up your position from up at Harvard.'

Dr Benjamin Goodley didn't like being cornered like that. He had learned a hard but important lesson in his months in CIA: it was one thing to form an opinion in an academic community, to discuss options around the lunch tables in the Harvard faculty club, but it was different here. From these opinions national policy was made. And that, he realized, was what being captured by the system actually meant.

'I hate to say this, but I've changed my mind. There may be a dynamic here we haven't examined.'

'What might that be?' the head of the Russian Department asked.

'Just consider this abstractly. If Narmonov goes down, who replaces him?'

'Kadishev is one of the possibilities, say one chance in three or so,' Mary Pat answered.

'In academia – hell, anywhere – isn't that a conflict of interest?'

'MP?' Ryan asked, shifting his eyes.

'Okay, so what? When has he ever lied to us before?'

Goodley decided to run with it, pretending this was an academic discussion. 'Mrs Foley, I was detailed to look for indications that SPINNAKER was wrong. I've checked everything I've had access to. The only thing I've found is a slight change in the tone of his reports over the last few months. The way he uses language is subtly different. His statements are more positive, less speculative in some areas. Now, that may fit his reports – the content of them, I mean – but ... there may be some meaning in that.'

'You're basing your evaluation on how he dots his i's?' The Russian expert demanded with a snort. 'Kid, we don't do that sort of work here.'

'Well, I have to take this one downtown,' Ryan said. 'I have to tell the President that we think he's right. I want to get Andrews and Kantrowitz in here to backstop us – objections?' There were none. 'Okay, thank you. Ben, could you stay for a moment? Mary Pat, take a long weekend. That's an order.'

'She's colicky, and I haven't been getting much sleep,' Mrs Foley explained.

'So, have Ed take the night duty,' Jack suggested.

'Ed doesn't have tits. I nurse, remember?'

'MP, has it ever occurred to you that nursing is a conspiracy of lazy men?' Ryan asked with a grin.

The baleful look in her eyes concealed her good humor. 'Yeah, at about two every morning. See you Monday.'

Goodley got back in his chair after the other two left. 'Okay, you can yell at me now.'

Jack waved for him to light up. 'What do you mean?'

'For bringing up a dumb idea.'

'Dumb idea, my ass. You were the first to suggest it. You've been doing good work.'

'I haven't found beans,' the Harvard scholar grumbled.

'No, but you've been looking in all the right places.'

'If this stuff was for real, how likely is it that you'd be able to confirm through other sources?' Goodley asked.

'A little better than even money, maybe sixty percent, tops. Mary Pat was right. This guy's been giving us stuff we can't always get somewhere else. But you're also correct: he stands to profit from being right. I have to run this one down to the White House before the weekend starts. Then I'm going to call Jake Kantrowitz and Eric Andrews and get them to fly in here for a look-see next week. Got any particular plans for the weekend?' Jack asked.

'No.'

'You do now. I want you to sweep through all your notes and do us a position paper, a good one.' Ryan tapped his desk. 'I want it here Monday morning.'

'Why?'

'Because you're intellectually honest, Ben. When you look at something, you really look.'

'But you never agree with my conclusions!' Goodley objected.

'Not very often, but your supporting data is first-rate. Nobody's right all the time. Nobody's wrong all the time, either. The process is important, the intellectual discipline, and you have that locked down pretty tight, Dr Goodley. I hope you like living in Washington. I'm going to offer you a permanent position here. We're setting up a special group in the DI. Their mission will be to take contrarian positions, an in-house Team-B that reports directly to the DDI. You'll be the number-two man in the Russian section. Think you can handle it? Think carefully, Ben,' Jack added hastily. 'You'll take a lot of heat from the A-Team. Long hours, mediocre pay, and not a hell of a lot of satisfaction at the end of the day. But you'll see a lot of good stuff, and every so often someone's going to pay attention to you. Anyway, the position paper I want will be your entrance exam – if you're interested. I don't give a good goddamn what your conclusions are, but I want something I can contrast with what I'm going to get from everybody else. You game or not?'

Goodley squirmed in his seat and hesitated before talking. Christ, was this going to abort his career? But he couldn't *not* say it, could he? He let out his breath, and spoke. 'There's something you should know.'

'Okay.'

'When Dr Elliot sent me here –'

'You were supposed to critique me. I know.' Ryan was very amused. 'I did a pretty good job of seduction, didn't I?'

'Jack, there was more to it than that . . . she wanted me to do a personal check . . . to look for stuff that she could use against you.'

Ryan's face went very cold. 'And?'

Goodley flushed, but went on rapidly. 'And I delivered. I checked your file for the SEC investigation, and passed on some things about other financial dealings – the Zimmer family, stuff like that.' He paused. 'I'm pretty ashamed of myself.'

'Learn anything?'

'About you? You're a good boss. Marcus is a lazy asshole, looks good in a suit. Liz Elliot is a prissy, mean-spirited bitch; she really likes manipulating people. She used me like a bird-dog. I learned something, all right. I'll never, ever do that again. Sir, I've never apologized like this to anyone before, but you ought to know. You have a right to know.'

Ryan stared into the young man's eyes for more than a minute, wondering if he'd flinch, wondering what sort of stuff was in there. Finally, he stubbed out his cigarette. 'Make sure it's a good position paper, Ben.'

'You'll get the best I have.'

'I think I already have, Dr Goodley.'

*

'Well?' President Fowler asked.

'Mr President, SPINNAKER reports that there is definitely a number of tactical nuclear weapons missing from Soviet Army inventories, and that the KGB is conducting a frantic search for them.'

'Where?'

'All over Europe, including inside the Soviet Union itself. Supposedly, KGB is loyal to Narmonov, at least most of it, Narmonov thinks – our man says he's not so sure. The Soviet military is definitely not; he says that a coup is a serious possibility, but Narmonov is not taking strong enough action to deal with it. The possibility of blackmail is quite real. If this report is correct, there is the possibility of a rapid power shift over there whose consequences are impossible to estimate.'

'And what do you think?' Dennis Bunker asked soberly.

'The consensus at Langley is that this may be reliable information. We're beginning a careful check of all relevant data. The two best outside consultants are at Princeton and Berkeley. I'll have them in the office Monday to look over our data.'

'When will you have a firm estimate?' Secretary Talbot asked.

'Depends on what you mean by firm. End of next week, we'll have a preliminary estimate. "Firm" is going to take a while. I've tried getting this confirmed by our British colleagues, but they came up blank.'

'Where could those things show up?' Liz Elliot asked.

'Russia's a big country,' Ryan replied.

'It's a big world,' Bunker said. 'What's your worst-case estimate?'

'We haven't started that process yet,' Jack answered. 'When you're talking about missing nuclear weapons, worst-cases can be pretty bad.'

'Is there any reason to suspect a threat directed against us?' Fowler asked.

'No, Mr President. The Soviet military is rational, and that would be an act of lunacy.'

'Your faith in the uniformed mentality is touching,' Liz Elliot noted. 'You really think theirs are more intelligent than ours?'

'They deliver when we ask them to,' Dennis Bunker said sharply. 'I wish you would have just a little respect for them, Dr Elliot.'

'We will save that for another day,' Fowler observed. 'What could they possibly gain from threatening us?'

'Nothing, Mr President,' Ryan answered.

'Agreed,' Brent Talbot said.

'I'll feel better when those SS-18s are gone,' Bunker noted, 'but Ryan's right.'

'I want an estimate on that, too,' Elliot said. 'I want it fast.'

'You'll get it,' Jack promised.

'What about the Mexico operation?'

'Mr President, the assets are in place.'

'What is this?' the Secretary of State asked.

'Brent, I think it's time you got briefed in on this. Ryan, commence.'

Jack ran through the background information and the operational concept. It took several minutes.

'I can't believe they'd do such a thing: it's outrageous,' Talbot said.

'Is this why you're not coming out to the game?' Bunker asked with a smile. 'Brent, I can believe it. How quickly will you have the transcripts from the aircraft?'

'Given his ETA into Washington, plus processing time . . . say around ten that night.'

'You can still come out to the game then, Bob,' Bunker said. It was the first time Ryan had ever seen someone address the President that way.

Fowler shook his head. 'I'll catch it at Camp David. I want to be bright-eyed for this meet. Besides, the storm that just hit Denver might be here Sunday. Getting back into town could be tough, and the Secret Service spent a couple hours explaining how bad football games are for me – meaning them, of course.'

'Going to be a good one,' Talbot said.

'What's the point spread?' Fowler asked.

Jesus! Ryan thought.

'Vikings by three,' Bunker said. 'I'll take all of that action I can get.'

'We're flying out together,' Talbot said. 'Just so Dennis doesn't drive the airplane.'

'Leaving me up the hills of Maryland. Well, somebody has to mind the government.' Fowler smiled. He had an odd smile, Jack thought. 'Back to business. Ryan: you said this is not a threat to us?'

'Let me backtrack, sir. First, I must emphasize that the SPINNAKER report remains totally unconfirmed.'

'You said the CIA backs it.'

'There is a consensus of opinion that it is probably reliable. We're checking that very hard right now. That's the whole point of what I said earlier.'

'Okay,' Fowler said. 'If it's not true, there is nothing for us to worry about, correct?'

'Yes, Mr President.'

'And if it is?'

'Then the risk is one of political blackmail in the Soviet Union, worst-case, a civil war with the use of nuclear weapons.'

'Which is not good news – possible threats to us?'

'No direct threat to us is likely.'

Fowler leaned back in his chair. 'That makes sense, I suppose. But I want a really, *really* good estimate of that just as fast as you can get it to me.'

'Yes, sir. Believe me, Mr President, we're checking every aspect of this development.'

'Good report, Dr Ryan.'

Jack stood to take his dismissal. It was so much more civilized now that they'd gotten rid of him.

The markets had sprung up of their own accord, mainly in the eastern sections of Berlin. Soviet soldiers, never the most free of individuals, now found themselves in an undivided *Western* city that offered each the chance simply to walk away, to disappear. The amazing thing was that so few did it, despite the controls kept on them, and one reason for it was the availability of open-air markets. The individual Soviet soldiers were continuously surprised at the desire of Germans, Americans and so many others to buy memorabilia of the Red Army – belts, *shapka* fur hats, boots, whole uniforms, all manner of trinkets – and the fools paid *cash*. Hard-currency cash, dollars, pounds, Deutschmarks, whose value at home in the Soviet Union was multiplied tenfold. Other sales to more discriminating buyers had included such big-ticket items as a T-80 tank, but that had required the connivance of a regimental commander, who'd justified it in his paperwork as the accidental destruction of a vehicle by fire. The colonel had gotten a Mercedes 560SEL from that, with plenty of cash left over for his retirement fund. Western intelligence agencies had gotten all they wished by this point, leaving the markets to amateurs and tourists; they assumed that the Soviets tolerated it for the simple reason that it brought a good deal of hard currency into their economy, and did so at bargain prices. Westerners typically paid more than ten times the actual production cost of what they purchased. The introductory course in capitalism, some Russians thought, would have other payoffs when the troops concluded their conscripted service.

Erwin Keitel approached one such Soviet soldier, a senior sergeant by rank. 'Good day,' he said in German.

'*Nicht spreche,*' the Russian answered 'English?'

'English is okay, yes?'

'Da.' The Russian nodded.

'Ten uniforms.' Keitel held up both hands to make the number unambiguous.

'Ten?'

'Ten, all large, big like me,' Keitel said. He could have spoken in perfect Russian, but that would have caused more trouble than it was worth. 'Colonel uniforms, all colonel, okay?'

'Colonel – *povodnik*. Regiment officer, yes? Three stars here?' the man tapped his shoulders.

'Yes.' Keitel nodded. 'Tank uniform, must be for tank.'

'Why you want?' the sergeant asked, mainly to be

polite. He was a tanker, and getting the right garb was not a problem.

'Make movie – television movie.'

'Television?' The man's eyes lit up. 'Belts, boots?'

'Yes.'

The man checked left and right, then lowered his voice. 'Pistol?'

'You can do that?'

The sergeant smiled and nodded emphatically to show that he was a serious broker. 'Take money.'

'Must be Russian pistol, correct pistol,' Keitel said, hoping that this pidgin exchange was clear.

'Yes, I can get.'

'How soon?'

'One hour.'

'How much?'

'Five thousand mark, no pistol. Ten pistol, five thousand mark more.' And that, Keitel thought, was highway robbery.

He held up his hands again. 'Ten thousand mark, yes. I pay.' To show he was serious, he displayed a sheaf of hundred-mark notes. He tucked one in the soldier's pocket. 'I wait one hour.'

'I come back here, one hour.' The soldier left the area rapidly. Keitel walked into the nearest *Gasthaus* and ordered a beer.

'If this were any easier,' he observed to a colleague, 'I'd say it was a trap.'

'You heard about the tank?'

'The T-80, yes, why?'

'Willi Heydrich did that for the Americans.'

'Willi?' Keitel shook his head. 'What was his fee?'

'Five hundred thousand D-Mark. Damned-fool Americans. Anyone could have set that up.'

'But they didn't know that at the time.' The man laughed bleakly. DM500,000 had been enough to set the former *Oberst-Leutnant* Wilhelm Heydrich up in a business – a *Gasthaus* like this one – which made for a much better living than he'd ever gotten from the Stasi. Heydrich had been one of Keitel's most promising subordinates, and now he had sold out, quit his career, turned his back on his political heritage, and turned into one more new-German citizen. His intelligence training had merely served as a vehicle, to take one last measure of spite out on the Americans.

'What about the Russian?'

'The one who made the deal? Ha!' the man snorted. 'Two *million* marks. He undoubtedly paid off the division commander, got his Mercedes, and banked the rest. That unit rotated back to the Union soon thereafter, and one tank more or less from a division . . . ? The inspectorate might not even have noticed.'

They had one more round, while watching the TV over the bar – a disgusting habit picked up from the Americans, Keitel thought. When forty minutes had passed, he went back outside, with his colleague in visual contact. It might be a trap, after all.

The Russian sergeant was back early. He wasn't carrying anything but a smile.

'Where is it?' Keitel asked.

'Truck, around . . .' the man gestured.

'*Ecke*? Corner?'

'*Da*, that word, corner. *Um die Ecke*.' The man nodded emphatically.

Keitel waved to the other man, who went to get the car. Erwin wanted to ask the soldier how much of the money was going to his lieutenant, who typically skimmed a sizable percentage of every deal for their own use, but that really was beside the point, wasn't it?

The Soviet Army GAZ-69 light truck was parked a block away. It was a simple matter of backing up the agent's car to the tailgate and popping the trunk. But first, of course, Keitel had to inspect the merchandise. There were ten camouflage battle-dress uniforms, lightweight, but of better than normal quality, because these were for officers' use. Headwear was a black beret with the red star and rather antique-looking tank badge that showed them to be for an armor officer. The shoulderboards of each uniform had the three stars of a full colonel. Also included were the uniform belts and boots.

'*Pistolen*?' Keitel asked.

First, eyes swept the street. Then ten cardboard boxes appeared. Keitel pointed to one, and it opened to reveal a Makarov PM. That was a nine-millimeter automatic modeled on the German Walther PP. The Russians, in a gesture of magnanimity, even tossed in five boxes of 9mm-x-18 ball ammunition.

'*Ausgezeichnet*,' Keitel observed, reaching for his money. He counted out ninety-nine hundred-mark bills.

'Thank you,' the Russian said. 'You need more, you see me, yes?'

'Yes, thank you.' Keitel shook his hand and got into the car.

'What has the world become?' the driver said as he headed off. As recently as three years before, those soldiers would have been court-martialed – perhaps even shot – for what they had done.

'We have enriched the Soviet Union to the tune of ten thousand marks.'

The driver grunted. '*Doch*, and that "merchandise" must have cost at least two thousand to manufacture! What is it they call that . . . ?'

'A "volume discount".' Keitel couldn't decide whether to laugh or not. 'Our Russian friends learn fast. Or perhaps the *muzhik* cannot count past ten.'

'What we plan to do is dangerous.'

'That is true, but we are being well paid.'

'You think I do this for money?' the man asked, an edge on his voice.

'No, nor do I. But if we must risk our lives, we might as well be rewarded for it.'

'As you say, Colonel.'

It never occurred to Keitel that he really did not know what he was doing, that Bock had not told him everything. For all his professionalism, Keitel had neglected to remind himself that he was doing business with a terrorist.

*

The air was wonderfully still, Ghosn thought. He'd never experienced really heavy snow. The storm was lingering longer than expected, was expected to continue for another hour or so. It had dropped half a meter, which, along with the flakes still in the air, muffled sound to a degree he had never known. It was a silence you could hear, he told himself standing on the porch.

'Like it, eh?' Marvin asked.

'Yes.'

'When I was a boy, we got really big storms, not like this one, storms that dropped *feet* of snow – like a whole meter at once, man – and then it would really get cold, like twenty or thirty below. You go outside, and it's like you're on another planet or something, and you wonder what it was like a hundred years ago, living in a tipi with your woman and your babies and your horses outside, everything clean and pure like it's supposed to be. It must have been something, man, it must have really been something.'

The man was poetic, but foolish, Ibrahim thought. So primitive a life, most of your children died before their first year had ended, starving in winter because there was no game to hunt. What fodder was there for the horses, and how did they get to it under the snow? How many people and animals froze to death? Yet he idolized the life. That was foolish. Marvin had courage. He had tenacity, and strength, and devotion, but the fact of the matter was that he didn't understand the world, didn't know God, and lived according to a fantasy. It really was unfortunate. He could have been a valuable asset.

'When do we leave?'

'We'll give the highway boys a couple of hours to scrape the roads. You take the car – it has front-wheel drive and you won't have any problem driving. I'll take the van. There's no hurry, right? We don't want to take chances?'

'That is right.'

'Let's go inside 'fore we both freeze.'

*

'They really gotta clean up the air in this place,' Clark said, when he finished coughing.

'It is pretty bad,' Chavez agreed.

They'd rented a small place near the airport. Everything they needed was tucked away in closets. They'd made their contacts on the ground. The usual service team would be sick when the 747 came in. It would be a fiscal illness, of course. It turned out that getting the two CIA officers aboard wasn't all that hard. The Mexicans did not especially like the Japanese, at least not the government kind, whom they regarded as more arrogant than Americans – which, to a Mexican citizen, was remarkable. Clark checked his watch. Nine more hours until it swooped in through the pollution. Just a brief courtesy visit to see the Mexican president, supposedly, then off to Washington to see Fowler. Well, that made things easy for Clark and Chavez.

They started off for Denver just at midnight. The Colorado state-roads teams had done their usual professional job. What could not be scraped was salted and sanded, and the usual one-hour drive took merely an additional fifteen minutes. Marvin handled the check-in, paying for three nights with cash, and making a show of getting a receipt for his expense account. The desk clerk noted the ABC logo on the truck, and was disappointed that the rooms he'd given them were around back. Had they parked in front, maybe he could get more business. As soon as he left, the clerk went back to dozing in front of the TV. The Minnesota fans would be arriving the next day, and they promised to be a raucous, troublesome crowd.

The meet with Lyalin proved easier to arrange than expected. Cabot's brief get-acquainted session with the new head of the Korean CIA had gone even more smoothly than he'd dared to hope – the Koreans were quite professional – allowing him to fly off to Japan twelve hours early. The Chief of Station Tokyo had a favorite spot, a hostess house located in one of the innumerable meandering backstreets within a mile of the embassy, and also a place very easy to secure and surveil.

'Here is my latest report,' Agent MUSHASHI said, handing over the envelope.

'Our President is most impressed with the quality of your information,' Cabot replied.

'As I am impressed with the salary.'

'So, what can I do for you?'

'I wanted to be sure that you are taking me seriously,' Lyalin said.

'We do that,' Marcus assured him. *Does this fellow think we pay in the millions for the fun of it?* he wondered. It was Cabot's first face-to-face with an agent. Though he'd been briefed to expect a conversation just like this one, it still came as a surprise.

'I plan to defect in a year, with my family. What exactly will you do for me?'

'Well, we will debrief you at length, then assist you in finding a comfortable place to live and work.'

'Where?'

'Anywhere you wish, within reason.' Cabot managed to conceal his exasperation. This was work for a junior case officer.

'What do you mean, "within reason"?'

'We won't let you live right across the street from the Russian Embassy. What exactly do you have in mind?'

'I don't know yet.'

Then why did you bring this up? 'What sort of climate do you like?'

'Warm, I think.'

'Well, there's Florida, lots of sun.'

'I will think about that.' The man paused. 'You do not lie to me?'

'Mr Lyalin, we take good care of our guests.'

'Okay. I will continue to send you information.' And with that, the man simply got up and left.

Marcus Cabot managed not to swear, but the look he gave to the station chief ignited a laugh.

'First time you've done a touchy-feely, right?'

'You mean, that's all?' Cabot could scarcely believe it.

'Director, this is a funny business. Crazy as it sounds, what you just did was very important,' Sam Yamata said. 'Now he knows that we really care about him. Bringing up the President was a good move, by the way.'

'You say so.' Cabot opened the envelope and started reading. 'Good Lord!'

'More on the Prime Minister's trip?'

'Yes, the details we didn't get before. Which bank, payoffs to other officials. We may not even need to bug the airplane . . .'

'Bug an airplane?' Yamata asked.

'You never heard me say that.'

The station chief nodded. 'How could I? You were never here.'

'I need to get this off to Washington fast.'

Yamata checked his watch. 'We'll never catch the direct flight in time.'

'Then we'll fax it secure.'

'We're not set up for that. Not on the Agency side, I mean.'

'How about the NSA guys?'

'They have it, Director, but we've been warned about the security of their systems.'

'The President needs this. It has to go out. Do it, my authority.'

'Yes, sir.'

CHAPTER 33

Passages

It was nice to wake up at a decent hour – eight o'clock – at home on a Saturday. Without a headache. That was something he hadn't done in months. He fully planned to spend the day at home doing precisely nothing more than shave, and he planned that only because he'd be going to Mass that evening. Ryan soon learned that on Saturday mornings his children were glued to the TV set, watching various cartoons, including something concerning turtles that he'd heard about but never seen. On reflection, he decided to pass on it this morning also.

'How are you this morning?' he asked Cathy, on his way into the kitchen.

'Not bad at all. I – oh, damn!'

The noise she heard was the distinctive trilling of the secure phone. Jack ran into the library to catch it.

'Yeah?'

'Dr Ryan, this is the ops room. Swordsman,' the watch officer said.

'Okay.' Jack hung up. 'Damn.'

'What's the matter?' Cathy asked from the doorway.

'I have to go in. By the way, I have to be in tomorrow, too.'

'Jack, come on –'

'Look, babe, there are a couple of things I have to do before I leave. One's happening right about now – and you can forget that, okay? – and I have to be in on it.'

'Where do you have to go this time?'

'Just into the office. I don't have any overseas stuff planned at all, as a matter of fact.'

'Supposed to snow tonight, maybe a big one.'

'Great. Well, I can always stay over.'

'I'm going to be so happy when you leave that god-damned place for good.'

'Can you stick with me just a couple of months more?'

'"Couple of months"?'

'April first, I'm out of there. Deal?'

'Jack, it's not that I don't like what you do, just that –'

'Yeah, the hours. Me, too. I'm used to the idea of leaving now, turning into a normal person again. I gotta change.'

Cathy bowed to the inevitable and went back to the kitchen. Jack dressed casually. On weekends you didn't have to wear a suit. He decided that he could even dispense with a tie, and also that he'd drive himself. Thirty minutes later, he was on the road.

It was a gloriously clear afternoon over the Straits of Gibraltar. Europe to the north, Africa to the south. The narrow passage had once been a mountain range, the geologists said, and the Mediterranean a dry basin until the Atlantic had broken in. This would have been the perfect place to watch from, too, thirty thousand feet up.

And best of all, he would not have had to worry about commercial air traffic back then. Now he had to listen to the guard circuit make sure some airliner didn't blunder into his path. Or the other way around, which was actually more honest.

'There's our company,' Robby Jackson observed.

'Never seen her before, sir,' Lieutenant Walters said.

'Her' was the Soviet carrier *Kuznetzov*, the first real carrier in the Russian fleet. Sixty-five thousand tons, thirty fixed-wing aircraft, ten or so helicopters. Escorting her were the cruisers *Slava* and *Marshal Ustinov*, plus what looked like one Sovremenny- and two Udaloy-class destroyers. They were coming east in a compressed tactical formation, and were two hundred forty miles behind the *TR* battlegroup. Half a day back, Robby thought, or half an hour, depending on how you looked at it.

'We give 'em a fly-by?' Walters asked.

'Nope, why piss 'em off?'

'Looks like they're in a hurry . . .' the RIO said, looking through a pair of binoculars. 'I'd say about twenty-five knots.'

'Maybe they're just trying to clear the strait as quick as they can.'

'I doubt that, skipper. What do you suppose they're here for?'

'Same as us, according to intel. Train, show the flag, make friends and influence people.'

'Didn't you have a run-in once . . . ?'

'Yeah, a Forger put a heat-seeker up my ass a few years back. Got my Tom back all right, though.' Robby paused for a moment. 'They said it was an accident, supposedly the pilot was punished.'

'Believe it?'

Jackson gave the Russian battlegroup a last look. 'Yeah, as a matter of fact.'

'First time I saw a picture of that thing I said to myself, there's a Navy Cross that hasn't happened yet.'

'Chill out, Shredder. Okay, we seen 'em. Let's head back.' Robby moved the stick to turn back east. This he did in a leisurely maneuver rather than the hard bank and pull a younger fighter jock might try. Why stress the airframe unnecessarily? Jackson would have thought if he'd bothered to think about it. In the back seat, Lieutenant Henry 'Shredder' Walters thought the CAG was just turning into an old guy.

Not that old. Captain Jackson was as alert as ever. His seat was jacked up about as far as it would go, because Robby was on the short side. This gave him a good field of view. His eyes swept in a constant pattern left-right, up-down, and in to look at his instruments about once a minute. His main concern was commercial air traffic, and also private planes, since this was a weekend, and people liked to orbit the Rock to take pictures. A civilian in a Lear Jet, Robby thought, could be more dangerous than a loose Sidewinder . . .

'Jesus! Coming up at nine!'

Captain Jackson's head snapped to the left. Fifty feet away was a MiG-29 Fulcrum-N, the new naval variant

of the Russian air-superiority fighter. The visored face of
the pilot was staring at him. Robby saw that four
missiles were hanging on the wings. The Tomcat only
had two at the moment.

'Came up from underneath,' Shredder reported.

'Clever of him.' Robby took the news with equa-
nimity. The Russian pilot waved. Robby returned the
gesture.

'Damn, if he wanted to —'

'Shredder, will you cool it? I've been playing games
with Ivan for almost twenty years. I've intercepted more
Bears than you've had pussy. We're not tactical. I just
wanted to fly back here and get a look at their formation.
Ivan over there decided to come up to look at us. He's
being neighborly about it.' Robby edged his stick forward, taking his aircraft down a few feet. He wanted to
eyeball the Russian's underside. No extra fuel tanks, just
the four missiles, AA-11 'Archers,' NATO called them.
The tail hook looked flimsier than the one the Americans had on their planes, and he remembered reports of
landing problems the Russians had experienced. Well,
carrier aviation was new to them, wasn't it? They'd
spend years learning all the lessons. Other than that, the
aircraft looked impressive. Newly painted, the pleasant
gray the Russians used instead of the high-tech infra-
red-suppressive gray that the US Navy had adopted a few
years ago. The Russian version was prettier; the USN
paint was more effective in concealment, though it did
give the planes a painfully leprous appearance. He
memorized the tail number to report to the wing intelligence troops. He couldn't see any of the pilot. The
helmet and visor covered his face, and he wore gloves.
Fifty-foot closure was a little tight, but not that big a
deal. Probably the Russian was trying to show him that
he was good, but not crazy. That was fair enough. Robby
came back up level and waved to thank the Russian for
holding a steady line. Again the gesture was returned.

What's your name, boy? Robby thought. He also wondered what the Russian thought about the victory flag
painted under the cockpit, under which was printed in

small letters, MiG-29, 17-1-91. *Let's not get too cocky over there.*

The 747 landed after its long trans-Pacific flight, much to the relief of the flight crew, Clark was sure. Twelve-hour flights must have been a bitch, the CIA officer was sure, especially flying into a smog-filled bowl at the end of it. The aircraft taxied out, then turned and finally stopped at a space marked by a military band, several rows of soldiers and civilians, and the customary red carpet.

'You know, after that much time in an airplane I'm too dogshit to do anything intelligent,' Chavez observed quietly.

'So remember never to run for President,' Clark replied.

'Right, Mr C.'

The stairs were rolled up, and presently the door opened. The band struck up something or other – the two CIA officers were too far away to hear it clearly. The normal TV crews flitted about. The arriving Japanese Prime Minister was met by the Mexican foreign minister, listened to a brief speech, made a brief one of his own, walked past the troops who'd been standing in place for ninety minutes, then did the first sensible thing of the day. He got into a limo and drove off to his embassy for a shower – or more likely, Clark thought, a hot bath. The way the Japs did it was probably the perfect cure for air travel, a long soak in hundred-plus-degree water. It was sure to take the wrinkles out of the skin and the stiffness out of the muscles, John thought. Pity that Americans hadn't learned that one. Ten minutes after the last dignitary left, and the troops marched off, and the carpet was rolled back up, the maintenance people were summoned to the aircraft.

The pilot spoke briefly with the head mechanic. One of the big Pratt and Whitney engines was running just a hair warm. Other than that he had no beefs at all. Then the flight crew departed for a rest. Three security people took station around the outside of the aircraft. Two more paced the interior. Clark and Chavez entered, showing their passes to Mexican and Japanese officials, and went to work. Ding started in the washrooms, taking his time because he'd been told the Japanese were particular about having spotless latrines. It required only one sniff of the air inside the airplane to note that Japanese citizens were allowed to smoke. Each ashtray had to be checked, and more than half of those required emptying and cleaning. Newspapers and magazines were collected. Other cleaning staff handled the vacuuming.

Forward, Clark checked the booze locker. Half the people aboard must have arrived with hangovers, he decided. There were some serious drinkers aboard. He was also gratified to see that the technical people at Langley had guessed right on the brand of scotch that JAL liked to serve. Finally he went up to the lounge area behind the cockpit. It exactly matched the computer mock-up he'd examined for hours prior to coming down. By the time he'd finished his cleaning duties, he was sure that bringing this one off would be a snap. He helped Ding with the trash bags and left the aircraft in time to catch a dinner. On the way out to his car, he passed a note to a CIA officer from Station Mexico.

'God damn it!' Ryan swore. 'This came in through State?'

'Correct, sir. Director Cabot's orders to use a fax line. He wanted to save transcription time.'

'Didn't Sam Yamata bother to explain about date-lines and time-zones?'

' 'Fraid not.'

There was no sense swearing further at the man from the Japan Department. Ryan read through the pages again. 'Well, what do you think?'

'I think the Prime Minister is walking into an ambush.'

'Isn't that too damned bad?' Ryan observed. 'Messenger this down to the White House. The President's going to want it PDQ.'

'Right.' The man left. Ryan dialed up operations next. 'How's Clark doing?' Jack asked, without preamble.

'Okay, he says. He's ready to make the plant. The

monitor aircraft are all standing by. We know of no changes in the PM's schedule.'

'Thanks.'

'How long are you going to be in?'

Jack looked outside. The snow had already started. 'Maybe all night.'

It was developing into a big one. The eastbound cold-weather storm from the Midwest was linking into a low-pressure area coming up the coast. The really big snow storms in the D.C. area always came in from the south, and the National Weather Service was saying six-to-eight inches. That prediction was up from two-to-four only a few hours earlier. He could leave work right now, then try to fight his way back in the morning, or he could stay. Staying, unfortunately, looked like the best option.

Golovko was also in his office, though the time in Moscow was eight hours ahead of Washington. That fact did not contribute to Sergey's humor, which was poor.

'Well?' he asked the man from the communications-intelligence watch staff.

'We got lucky. This document was sent by facsimile printer from the U.S. Embassy Tokyo to Washington.' He handed the sheet over.

The slick thermal paper was covered mainly with gibberish, some discrete but disordered letters, and even more black-and-white hash from the random noise, but perhaps as much as twenty percent was legible English, including two complete sentences and one full paragraph.

'Well?' Golovko asked again.

'When I delivered it to the Japanese section for comment, they handed me this.' Another document was passed. 'I've marked the paragraph.'

Golovko read the Russian-language paragraph, then compared it to the English –

'It's a fucking translation. How was our document sent in?'

'By embassy courier. It wasn't transmitted because

two of the crypto machines in Tokyo were being repaired, and the *Rezident* decided it was unimportant enough to wait. It ended up in the embassy bag. So, they are not reading our ciphers, but they got this anyway.'

'Who's working this case . . . ? Lyalin? Yes.' Golovko said, almost to himself. He next called the senior watch officer for the First Chief Directorate. 'Colonel, this is Golovko. I want a Flash-priority to *Rezident* Tokyo. Lyalin to report to Moscow immediately.'

'What's the problem?'

'The problem is, we have another leak.'

'Lyalin is a very effective officer. I know the material he's sending back.'

'So do the Americans. Get that message off at once. Then, I want everything we have from THISTLE on my desk.' Golovko hung up and looked at the major standing in front of his desk. 'That mathematician who figured this all out – good God, I wish we'd had him five years ago!'

'He spent ten years devising this theory on ordering chaos. If it's ever made public, he'll win the Planck Medal. He took the work of Mandelbrot at Harvard University in America and MacKenzie at Cambridge, and –'

'I will take your word for it, Major. The last time you tried to explain this witchcraft to me I merely got a headache. How is the work going?'

'We grow stronger every day. The only thing we cannot break is the new CIA system that's starting to come on line. It seems to use a new principle. We're working on it.'

President Fowler boarded the Marine VH-3 helicopter before the snow got too bad. Painted a shiny olive-drab on the bottom, with white on top, and little else in the way of markings, it was his personal bird, with the call-sign Marine-One. Elizabeth Elliot boarded just behind him, the press corps noted. Pretty soon they'd have to break the story on the two, some thought. Or maybe the President would do the job for them by marrying the bitch.

The pilot, a Marine lieutenant-colonel, brought the twin turbine engines to full power, then eased up on the collective, rising slowly and turning northwest. He was almost instantly on instruments, which he didn't like. Flying blind and on instruments didn't trouble him. Flying blind and on instruments with the President aboard did. Flying in snow was about the worst thing there was. All external visual references were gone. Staring out the windshield could turn the most seasoned airman into a disoriented and airsick feather-merchant in a matter of seconds. As a result, he spent far more time scanning his instruments. The chopper had all manner of safety features, including collision-avoidance radar, plus having the undivided attention of two senior air-traffic controllers. In some perverse ways, this was a safe way to fly. In clear air, some lunatic with a Cessna might just try to perform a mid-air with Marine-One, and maneuvering to avoid such things was a regular drill for the colonel, both in the air and in the aircraft simulator at Anacostia Naval Air Station.

'Wind's picking up faster than I 'spected,' the co-pilot, a major, observed.

'May get a little bumpy when we hit the mountains.'

'Should have left a little sooner.'

The pilot switched settings on his intercom box, linking him with the two Secret Service agents in back. 'May want to make sure everybody's strapped in tight. Picking up a little chop.'

'Okay, thanks,' Pete Connor replied. He looked to see that everyone's seatbelt was securely fastened. Everyone aboard was too seasoned a flyer to be the least bit concerned, but he preferred a smooth ride as much as the next person. The President, he saw, was fully relaxed, reading over a folder that had just arrived a few minutes before they'd left. Connor settled back also. Connor and D'Agustino loved Camp David. A company of hand-picked Marine riflemen provided perimeter security. They were backed up and augmented by the best electronic surveillance systems America had ever built. Backing everyone up were the usual Secret Service agents. Nobody was scheduled to come in or out of the place this weekend, except, possibly, one CIA messenger who would drive. Everyone could relax, including the President and his lady friend, Connor thought.

'This is getting bad. Better tell the weather pukes to stick their head out the window.'

'They said eight inches.'

'I got a buck says more than a foot.'

'I never bet against you on weather,' the co-pilot reminded the colonel.

'Smart man, Scotty.'

'Supposed to clear tomorrow night.'

'I'll believe that when I see it, too.'

'Temp's supposed to drop to zero, too, maybe a touch under.'

'*That* I believe,' the colonel said, checking his altitude, compass, and artificial horizon. His eyes went outboard again, seeing only snowflakes being churned by the downwash of the rotor tips. 'What do you call visibility?'

'Oh, in a clear spot ... maybe a hundred feet ... maybe one-fifty ...' The major turned to grin at the colonel. The grin stopped when he started thinking about the ice that might build up on the airframe. 'What's the outside temp?' he murmured to himself.

'Minus 12 centigrade,' the colonel said, before he could look at the thermometer.

'Coming up?'

'Yeah. Let's take her down a little, ought to be colder.'

'Goddamned D.C. weather.'

Thirty minutes later, they circled over Camp David. Strobe lights told them where the landing pad was – you could see down better than in any other direction. The co-pilot looked aft to check the fairing over the landing gear. 'We got a little ice now, Colonel. Let's get this beast down before something scary happens. Wind is thirty knots at three-zero-zero.'

'Starting to feel a touch heavy.' The VH-3 could pick up as much as four hundred pounds of ice per minute under the right – wrong – weather conditions. 'Fuckin' weather weenies. Okay, I got the LZ in sight.'

'Two hundred feet, airspeed thirty,' the major read off the instruments. 'One fifty at twenty-five . . . one hundred at under twenty . . . looking good . . . fifty feet and zero ground-speed . . .'

The pilot eased down on the collective. The snow on the ground started blowing up from the rotor-wash. It created a vile condition called a white-out. The visual references which had just reappeared – vanished instantly. The flight crew felt themselves to be inside a ping-pong ball. Then a gust of wind swung the helicopter around to the left, tilting it also. The pilot's eyes immediately flicked down to the artificial horizon. He saw it tilt, knowing that the danger that had appeared was as severe as it was unexpected. He moved the cyclic to level the aircraft, and dropped the collective to the floor. Better a hard landing than catching a rotor in the trees he couldn't see. The helicopter dropped like a stone – exactly three feet. Before people aboard realized that something was wrong, the helicopter was down and safe.

'And that's why they let you fly the Boss,' the major said over the intercom. 'Nice one, Colonel.'

'I think I broke something.'

'I think you're right.'

The pilot keyed the intercom. 'Sorry about that. We caught a gust over the pad. Everybody okay back there?'

The President was already up, leaning into the cockpit. 'You were right, Colonel. We should have left sooner. My mistake,' Fowler said graciously. What the hell, he thought, he wanted this weekend.

The Camp David detachment opened the chopper's door. An enclosed HMMWV pulled up to it so that the President and his party didn't have to get too cold. The flight crew watched them pull away, then checked for damage.

'Thought so.'

'Metering pin?' The major bent down to look. 'Sure enough.' The landing had just been hard enough to snap the pin that controlled the hydraulic shock-absorber on the right-side landing gear. It would have to be fixed.

'I'll go check to see if we have a spare,' the crew chief said. Ten minutes later, he was surprised to learn that they didn't. That was annoying. He placed a phone call to the helicopter base at the old Anacostia Naval Air Station to have a few driven up. Until it arrived, there was nothing that could be done. The aircraft could still be flown in an emergency, of course. A fire-team of Marine riflemen stood close guard on the helicopter, as always, while another squad walked perimeter guard in the woods around the landing pad area.

'What is it, Ben?'

'Does this place have a dorm?' Goodley asked.

Jack shook his head. 'You can use the couch in Nancy's office if you want. How's your paper coming?'

'I'm going to be up all night anyway. I just thought of something.'

'What's that?'

'Going to sound a little crazy – nobody ever checked to make sure that our friend Kadishev actually met with Narmonov.'

'What do you mean?'

'Narmonov was out of town most of last week. If there was no meet, then the guy was lying to us, wasn't he?'

Jack closed his eyes and cocked his head to one side. 'Not bad, Dr Goodley, not bad.'

'We have Narmonov's itinerary. I have people checking on Kadishev's now. I'm going all the way back to last August. If we're going to do a check, it might as well be a comprehensive one. My position piece might be a little late, but this hit me last – this morning, actually. I've been chasing it down most of the day. It's harder than I thought.'

Jack motioned to the storm outside. 'Looks like I'm going to be stuck here a while. Want some help?'

'Sounds good to me.'

'Let's get some dinner first.'

Oleg Yurievich Lyalin boarded his flight to Moscow with mixed feelings. The summons was not all that irregular.

It was troublesome that it had come so soon after his meeting with the CIA Director, but that was probably happenstance. More likely, it had to do with the information he'd been delivering to Moscow about the Japanese Prime Minister's trip to America. One surprise he had not told CIA concerned Japanese overtures to the Soviet Union to trade high-technology for oil and lumber. That deal would have upset the Americans greatly only a few years earlier, and marked the culmination of a five-year project that Lyalin had worked on. He settled into his airline seat and allowed himself to relax. He had never betrayed his country, after all, had he?

The satellite up-link trucks were in two batches. There were eleven network vehicles, all parked just at the stadium wall. Two hundred meters away were thirty-one more, smaller Ku-band up-links for what looked like regional TV stations, as opposed to the bigger network vans. The first storm had passed, and what looked like a tank division's worth of heavy equipment was sweeping up the snow from the stadium's enormous parking lot.

There was the spot, Ghosn thought, right next to the ABC 'A' unit. There was a good twenty meters of open space. The absence of security astounded him. He counted only three police cars, just enough to keep drunks away from men trying to get their work done. The Americans felt so secure. They'd tamed the Russians, crushed Iraq, intimidated Iran, pacified his own people, and now they were as totally relaxed as a people could be. They must love their comforts, Ibrahim told himself. Even their stadia had roofs and heat to keep the elements out.

'Gonna knock those things over like dominos,' Marvin observed from the driver's seat.

'Indeed we will,' Ghosn agreed.

'See what I told you about security?'

'I was wrong to doubt you, my friend.'

'Never hurts to be careful.' Russell started another drive around the perimeter. 'We'll come in this gate right here, and just drive right up.' The headlights of the van illuminated the few flakes of this second storm. It was too cold to snow a lot, Russell had explained. This Canadian air mass was heading south. It would warm up as it hit Texas, dropping its moisture there instead of on Denver, which had half a meter, Ghosn estimated. The men who cleared the roads were quite efficient. As with everything else, the Americans liked their conveniences. Cold weather – build a stadium with a roof. Snow on the highways – get rid of it. Palestinians – buy them off. Though his face didn't show it, he had never hated America more than at this moment. Their power and their arrogance showed in everything they did. They protected themselves against everything, no matter how big or small, knew that they did, and proclaimed it to themselves and the whole world.

Oh, God, to bring them down!

The fire was agreeably warm. The President's cabin at Camp David was in the classic American pattern, heavy logs laid one atop the other, though on the inside they were reinforced with Kevlar fiber, and the windows were made of rugged polycarbonate to stop a bullet. The furniture was an even more curious mix of ultra-modern and old-comfortable. Before the couch he sat on were three printers for the major news services, because his predecessors liked to see the wire copy, and there were three full-sized televisions, one of which was usually tuned to CNN. But not tonight. Tonight it was on Cinemax. Half a mile away was a discreetly-sited antenna farm that tracked all of the commercial satellites, along with most of the military ones, a benefit of which was access to every commercial satellite channel – even the X-rated ones, which Fowler didn't bother with – creating the world's most expensive and exclusive cable system.

Fowler poured himself a beer. It was a bottle of Dortmunder Union, a popular German brew that the Air Force flew over – being President did carry some useful and unofficial perks. Liz Elliot drank a French white, while the President's left hand toyed with her hair.

The movie was a sappy comedic romance that appealed to Bob Fowler. The female lead, in fact, reminded him of Liz in looks and mannerisms. A little too snappy, a little too domineering, but not without redeeming social value. Now that Ryan was gone – well, on the way to being gone – maybe things would settle down.

'We've certainly done well, haven't we?'

'Yes, we have, Bob.' She paused for a sip of wine. 'You were right about Ryan. Better to let him go honorably.' *So long as he's gone, along with that little shrew he married.*

'I'm glad to hear you say that. He's not a bad guy, just old-fashioned. Out of date.'

'Obsolete,' Liz added.

'Yeah,' the President agreed. 'Why are we talking about him?'

'I can think of better things.' She turned her face into his hand and kissed it.

'So can I,' the President murmured as he set his glass down.

'The roads are covered,' Cathy reported. 'I think you made the right decision.'

'Yeah, there was just a bad one on the Parkway just outside the gate. I'll be home tomorrow night. I can always steal one of the four-by-fours they have downstairs.'

'Where's John?'

'He's not here right now.'

'Oh,' Cathy observed. *And what might he be up to?*

'While I'm here, I might as well get some work done. Call you in the morning.'

'Okay, bye.'

'That's one aspect of this place that I won't miss,' Jack told Goodley. 'Okay, what have you developed?'

'We've been able to verify all the meetings through September.'

'You look like you're ready to drop. How long have you been up?'

'Since yesterday, I guess.'

'Must be nice to be still in your twenties. Grab a piece of the couch outside,' Ryan ordered.

'What about you?'

'I want to read over this stuff again.' Jack tapped the file on his desk. 'You're not into this one yet. Go get some Z's.'

'See you in the morning.'

The door closed behind Goodley. Jack started to read through the NIITAKA documents, but soon lost concentration. He locked the file in his desk and found a piece of his own couch, but sleep wouldn't come. After a few minutes of staring at the ceiling, Ryan decided that he might as well stare at something less boring. He switched on the TV. Jack worked the controller to catch a news broadcast, but he hit the wrong button and found himself staring at the tail end of a commercial on Channel 20, an independent Washington station. He almost corrected the mistake when the movie came back. It took a moment. Gregory Peck and Ava Gardner . . . black and white . . . Australia.

'Oh yeah,' Ryan said to himself. It was *On the Beach*. He hadn't seen that in years, a Cold War classic from . . . Nevil Shute, wasn't it? A Gregory Peck movie was always worth the trouble. Fred Astaire, too.

The aftermath of a nuclear war. Jack was surprised at how tired he was. He'd been getting his rest lately, and . . .

. . . he went to sleep, but not all the way. As sometimes happened to him, the movie entered his mind, though the dream was in color, and that was better than the black-and-white print on the TV, his mind decided, then decided further to watch the movie in its entirety. From the inside. Jack Ryan began to take over various roles. He drove Fred Astaire's Ferrari in the bloody and last Australian Grand Prix. He sailed to San Francisco in the USS *Sawfish*, SSN-623 (except, part of his mind objected, that 623 was the number of a different submarine, USS *Nathan Hale*, wasn't it?). And the Morse signal, the Coke bottle on the windowshade, that wasn't very funny at all, because it meant that he and his wife would have to have that cup of tea, and he really didn't want to do that because it meant he had to put the pill in the baby's formula so that he could be sure that the baby would die and his wife wasn't up to it – understandable, his doctor was a wife – and he had to take the responsibility because he was the one who always did and wasn't it a shame that he had to leave Ava Gardner on the beach watching him sail so that he and his men could die at home if they made it which they probably wouldn't and the streets were so empty now. Cathy and Sally and Little Jack were all dead and it was all his fault because he made them take their pills so that they wouldn't die of something else that was even worse but that was still dumb and wrong even though there wasn't much of a choice was there so instead why not use a gun to do it and –

'What the fuck!' Jack snapped upright as though driven by a steel spring. He looked at his hands, which were shaking rather badly, until they realized that his mind was under conscious control now. 'You just had a nightmare, boy, and this one wasn't the helicopter with Buck and John.

'It was worse.'

Ryan reached for his cigarettes and lit one, standing up after he did so. The snow was still coming down. The scrapers weren't keeping pace with it, down on the parking lot. It took time to shake one of these off, watching his family die like that. So many of the goddamned things. *I've gotta get away from this place!* There were just too many memories, and not all of them were good. The wrong call he'd made before the attack on his family, the time in the submarine, being left on the runway at Sheremetyevo Airport and looking at good old Sergey Nikolayevich from the wrong side of a pistol, and worst of all that helicopter ride out of Colombia. It was just too much. It was time to leave. Fowler and even Liz Elliot were doing him a favor, weren't they?

Whether they knew it or not.

Such a nice world lay out there. He'd done his part.

He'd made parts of it a little better, and had helped others to do more. The movie he'd just lived in, hell, it might have come to pass in one way or another. But not now. It was clean and white out there, the lights over the parking lot just illuminating it enough, so much better than it usually looked. He'd done his part. Now it was someone else's turn to try his or her hand at the easier stuff.

'Yeah.' Jack blew his smoke out at the window. First, he'd have to break this habit again. Cathy would insist. And then? Then an extended vacation, this coming summer, maybe go back to England – maybe by ship instead of flying? Take the time to drive around Europe, maybe blow the whole summer. Be a free man again. Walk the beach. But then he'd have to get a job, do something. Annapolis – no, that was out. Some private group? Maybe teach? Georgetown, maybe?

'Espionage 101,' he chuckled to himself. That was it, he'd teach how to do all the illegal stuff.

'How the hell did James Greer ever last so long in this crummy racket?' How had he handled the stress? That was one lesson he'd never passed on.

'You still need sleep, man,' he reminded himself. This time he made sure the TV was off.

CHAPTER 34

Placement

Ryan was surprised to see that the snow hadn't stopped. The walkway outside his top-floor window had almost two feet piled up, and the maintenance crews had failed completely to keep up with things through the night. High winds were blowing and drifting snow across the roads and parking lots more quickly than it could be removed, and even the snow that they did manage to move simply found another inconvenient place to blow over. It had been years since a storm like this had hit the Washington area. The local citizenry was already beyond panic into desperation, Jack thought. Cabin fever would already be setting in. Food stocks would not easily be replaced. Already some husbands and some wives were looking at their spouses and wondering how hard to cook they might be . . . It was one thing to laugh about as he went to get water for his coffee machine. He grabbed Ben Goodley's shoulder on the way out of the office.

'Shake it loose, Dr Goodley.'

The eyes opened slowly. 'What time is it?'

'Seven-twenty. What part of New England are you from originally?'

'New Hampshire, up north, place called Littleton.'

'Well, take a look out the window and it might remind you of home.'

By the time Jack returned with fresh water, the younger man was standing at the windows. 'Looks like about a foot and a half out there, maybe a little more. So, what's the big deal? Where I come from this is called a flurry.'

'In D.C., it's called The Ice Age. I'll have coffee ready

in a few minutes.' Ryan decided to call the security desk of the lobby. 'What's the situation?'

'People calling in saying they can't make it. But what the hell – most of the night staff couldn't get out. The G.W. Parkway is closed. So's the Beltway on the Maryland side, and the Wilson Bridge – again.'

'Outstanding. Okay, this is important, so listen up – that means anybody who makes it in is probably KGB-trained. Shoot 'em.' Goodley could hear the laughter on the phone from ten feet away. 'Keep me posted on the weather situation. And reserve me a four-by-four, the GMC, in case I have to go somewhere.' Jack hung up and looked at Goodley. 'Rank hath its privileges. Besides, we have a couple of them.'

'What about people who have to get in?'

Jack watched the coffee start to come out of the machine. 'If the Beltway and G.W. are closed, that means that two-thirds of our people can't get in. Now you know why the Russians have invested so much money in weather-control programs.'

'Doesn't anybody down here –'

'No, people down here pretend that snow is something that happens on ski slopes. If it doesn't stop soon, it'll be Wednesday before anything starts moving in this town.'

'It's really that bad here?'

'You'll see for yourself, Ben.'

'And I left my cross-country skis up in Boston.'

'We didn't hit that hard,' the major objected.

'Major, the breaker board seems to disagree with you,' the crew chief replied. He pushed the breaker back in position. The small black plastic tab hesitated for a moment, then popped right back out. 'No radio because of this one, and no hydraulics 'cause of that one. I'm afraid we're grounded for a while, sir.'

The metering pins for the landing gear had arrived at two in the morning, on the second attempt. The first, aborted, attempts had been by car, until someone had decided that only a military vehicle could make it. The parts had arrived by HMMWV, and even that had been held up by the various stopped cars on the highways between Washington and Camp David. Repairs on the helicopter were supposed to have started in another hour or so – it was not a difficult job – but suddenly they were more complicated.

'Well?' the major asked.

'Probably a couple of loose wires in there. I gotta pull the whole board, sir, inspect the whole thing. That's a whole day's work at best. Better tell 'em to warm up a back-up aircraft.'

The major looked outside. This was not a day he wanted to fly anyway. 'We're not supposed to go back until tomorrow morning. When'll it be fixed?'

'If I start now ... say around midnight.'

'Get breakfast first. I'll take care of the back-up bird.'

'Roge-o, Major.'

'I'll have them run some power out here for a heater, and a radio, too.' The major knew the crew chief was from San Diego.

The major trudged back to the cabin. The helicopter pad was on a high spot, and the wind was trying very hard to blow it clear of snow. As a result, there was only six inches to worry about. Down below, the drifts were as much as three feet deep. The grunts out walking the woods must be having a fine time, he thought.

'How bad?' the pilot asked, shaving.

'Circuit panel is acting up. The chief says he needs all day to get it back on line.'

'We didn't hit that hard,' the colonel objected.

'I already said that. Want me to make the call?'

'Yeah, go ahead. Have you checked the threat board?'

'The world's at peace, Colonel, sir. I checked.'

The 'threat board' was mainly an expression. The alert level of the government agencies that dealt with various problems depended on the expected level of danger in the world. The greater the possible danger, the more assets were kept ready to deal with them. At the moment there was no perceived threat to the United States of America, and that meant that only a single aircraft was kept ready to back-stop the President's VH-3. The major placed the call to Annacostia.

'Yeah, let's keep dash-two warm. Dash-one is down with electrical problems . . . no, we can handle it here. Oughta be back on line by midnight. Right. Bye.' The major hung up just in time for Pete Connor to enter their cabin.

'What gives?'

'Bird's broke,' the colonel replied.

'I didn't think we hit that hard,' Connor objected.

'Well, that makes it official,' the major observed. 'The only one who thinks we did hit that hard's the friggin' airplane.'

'The back-up's on alert status,' the colonel said, as he finished shaving. 'Sorry, Pete. Electrical problem, maybe has nothing to do with the touchdown. The back-up can be here in thirty-five minutes. Our threat board is blank. Anything we need to know about?'

Connor shook his head. 'No, Ed. We know of no particular threat.'

'I can bring the back-up bird here, but it means exposing it to the weather. We can take better care of it down at Annacostia. That's your call, sir.'

'You can leave it down there.'

'The Boss still wants to watch the game up here, right?'

'Correct. We all get a day off. Lift off for D.C. tomorrow about six-thirty. Problem with that?'

'No, ought to be fixed before then.'

'Okay.' Connor left and walked back to his cabin.

'What's it like out there?' Daga asked.

'About how it looks,' Pete said. 'The chopper's broke.'

'I wish they'd be more careful,' Special Agent Helen D'Agustino observed as she brushed her hair.

'Not their fault.' Connor lifted the phone to the Secret Service command center, located a few blocks west of the White House. 'This is Connor. The chopper is down with a mechanical problem. Back-up is being kept at Annacostia because of weather conditions. Anything on the board I need to know about?'

'No, sir,' the junior agent responded. On his status board, in LED characters he could see that the President of the United States – designated 'POTUS' on his display – was shown to be at Camp David. The First Lady of the United States – 'FLOTUS' – space was blank. The Vice President was at his official residence on the ground of the U.S. Naval Observatory off of Massachusetts Avenue, North West, along with his family. 'Everything's nice and calm, far as we know.'

'How are the roads down there?' Pete asked.

'Bad. Every Carryall we have is out retrieving people.'

'Thank God for Chevrolet.' Like the FBI, the Secret Service used the big Chevy four-wheel-drive trucks to get around. Heavily armored and with roughly the fuel-efficiency of a tank, the Carryall was able to do things that only a tank could excel. 'Okay, it's nice and snug up here.'

'I bet the Marines are freezing their *cojones* off.'

'What about Dulles?'

'The Prime Minister is due in at eighteen hundred. The guys say Dulles has one runway open now. They expect to have everything clear by afternoon. Storm's slacking off a little here, finally. You know, the funny thing . . .'

'Yeah.' Connor didn't need to hear the rest. The funny thing was that weather like this made the job of the Secret Service easier. 'Okay, you know where to reach us.'

'Right. See ya tomorrow, Pete.'

Connor looked outside when he heard the noise. A Marine was driving a snow-plow, trying to clear the paths between the cabins. Two more were working on the roads. It seemed rather odd. The equipment was painted in the Pentagon's woodland camouflage pattern of greens and browns, but the Marines were in their whites. There were even white pull-over covers for their M-16A2 rifles. Anyone who tried to get in here today would find, too late, that the perimeter guard force was totally invisible, and these Marines were all combat veterans. At times like this, even the Secret Service could relax, and that came rarely enough. There came a knock on the door. Daga got it.

'Morning papers, ma'am.' A Marine corporal handed them over.

'You know,' D'Agustino observed after she closed the door, 'sometimes I think the guys who deliver these things are the only people you can really depend on.'

'What about the Marines?' Pete asked with a laugh.

'Oh, them, too.'

'Aspect change in Sierra-16!' the sonarman called. 'Target is coming left.'

'Very well,' Dutch Claggett replied. 'Mr Pitney, you have the conn.'

'Aye aye, sir, I have the conn,' the navigator said as the XO went into the sonar room. The fire-control tracking party perked up, waiting to restart their calculations.

'Right there, sir,' the sonarman tapped the screen with his pencil. 'Looks like a beam aspect now. Conn, sonar, bearing is now one-seven-zero, target is coming left. Radiated noise level is constant, estimate target speed is unchanged.'

'Very well, thank you.'

It was the third such turn they had tracked – Claggett's estimation appeared to be correct. The Russian was conducting a very methodical, very conservative – and very smart – search pattern of this patrol area, just like the 688s did in looking for Russian subs. The interval between the rungs of this ladder seemed to be about forty thousand yards.

'X, that new feed pump they have is a beaut,' the sonarman observed. 'His plant noise is way the hell down, and the sucker's doing ten knots according to the tracking party.'

'Couple more years and we're going to have to worry about these guys.'

'Transient, transient – mechanical transient on Sierra-16, bearing is now one-six-four, still drifting left. Speed constant.' The petty officer circled the noise blip

761

on the screen. 'Maybe, sir, but they still got a lot to learn.'

'Range to target is now four-eight thousand yards.'

'Mr Pitney, let's open the range some. Bring her right,' the executive officer commanded.

'Aye, helm, left five degrees rudder, come to new course two-zero-four.'

'Turning for another leg?' Captain Ricks asked as he entered sonar.

'Yeah, looks like the legs are pretty regular, Cap'n.'

'Methodical son of a bitch, isn't he?'

'Turned within two minutes of our estimate,' Claggett replied. 'I just ordered us right to maintain distance.'

'Fair enough.' Ricks was actually enjoying this. He hadn't been aboard a fast-attack boat since his first assistant-department-head tour. Playing tag with Russian submarines was something he had not done in the past fifteen years. On the rare occasions he'd heard them at all, his action had always been the same: track long enough to determine the other sub's course, then turn perpendicular to it and head away until it faded back to random noise.

Necessarily, the game was changing somewhat. It wasn't as easy as it used to be. The Russian subs were getting quieter. What had been an annoying trend a few years ago was rapidly turning into something genuinely troubling. And maybe we just had to change the way we do business . . .

'You know, X, what if this becomes the standard tactic?'

'What do you mean, Cap'n?'

'I mean, as quiet as these guys are getting, maybe this is the smart move . . .'

'Huh?' Claggett was lost.

'If you're tracking the guy, at least you always know where he is. You can even launch a SLOT buoy and call in assets to help you dispose of him. Think about it. They're getting pretty quiet. If you break off as soon as you detect the guy, what's to say you don't blunder into him again? So, instead, we track at a nice, safe distance and just keep an eye on him.'

'Uh, Captain, that's fine as far as it goes, but what if the other guy gets a sniff of us, or what if he just reverses course and boogies backwards at high speed?'

'Good point. So, we trail on his quarter instead of just off his stern ... that will make an accidental closure less likely. Banging straight aft for a trailer is a logical defensive measure, but he can't go punching holes all over the ocean, can he?'

Jesus, this guy is trying to develop tactics ... 'Sir, let me know if you sell that one to OP-02.'

'Instead of trailing dead aft, I'm going to hold off his northern quarter now. It gives us better performance off the tail anyway. It should actually be safer.'

That part of it made sense, Claggett thought. 'You say so, Cap'n. Maintain fifty-K yards?'

'Yes, we still want to be a little cautious.'

The second storm, as predicted, hadn't done very much, Ghosn saw. There was a light dusting – that seemed to be the term they used – on the vehicles and parking lot. Hardly enough to bother with, it duplicated the most severe winter storm he'd ever seen in Lebanon.

'How about some breakfast?' Marvin asked. 'I hate to work on an empty stomach.'

The man was remarkable, Ibrahim thought. He was completely free of jitters. Either very brave or ... something else. Ghosn considered that. He'd killed the Greek policeman without a blink, had taught a brutal lesson to one of the organization's combat instructors, shown his prowess with firearms, and been completely contemptuous of danger when they'd uncovered the Israeli bomb. There was something missing in this man, he concluded. The man was fearless, and such men were not normal. It wasn't that he was able to control his fear as most soldiers learned to do. Fear simply wasn't there. Was it merely a case of trying to impress people? Or was it real? Probably real, Ghosn thought, and if it were, this man was truly mad, and therefore more dangerous than useful. It made things easier for Ghosn to think that.

The motel didn't offer room service from its small coffee shop. All three walked out into the cold to get their breakfasts. Along the way, Russell picked up a paper to read about the game.

Qati and Ghosn only needed a brief look to find one more reason to hate Americans. They ate eggs with bacon or ham, and pancakes with sausage – in all three cases, products of the most unclean of animals, the pig. Both men found the sight and smell of pork products repulsive. Marvin didn't help when he ordered some as unconsciously as he'd ordered coffee. The Commander, Ghosn noted, ordered oatmeal, and halfway through breakfast he went suddenly pale and left the table.

'What's the matter with him anyway? Sick?' Russell asked.

'Yes, Marvin, he is quite ill.' Ghosn looked at the greasy bacon on Russell's plate and knew the smell of it had set Qati's stomach off.

'I hope he's able to drive.'

'That will not be a problem.' Ghosn wondered if that were true. Of course it was, he told himself, the Commander had been through tougher times – but such bluster was for others, not for times like this. No, because there had never been such a time as this, the Commander would do what must be done. Russell paid for the breakfast with cash, leaving a large tip because the waitress looked like a Native American.

Qati was pale when they got back to the rooms, and wiping his face after a long bout of nausea.

'Can I get you something, man?' Russell asked. 'Milk, something good for your stomach?'

'Not now, Marvin. Thank you.'

'You say so, man.' Russell opened his paper. There was nothing to do for the next few hours but wait. The morning line on the game, he saw, was Minnesota by six and a half. He decided that if anyone asked, he'd take the Vikings and give the points.

*

Special Agent Walter Hoskins, Assistant Special Agent in Charge (Corruption and Racketeering), of the Denver Field Division knew that he would miss the game despite the fact that his wife had given him a ticket for Christmas. This he had sold to the S-A-C for two hundred dollars. Hoskins had work to do. A confidential informant had scored at the annual NFL Commissioner's party last night. That party – like the ones preceding the Kentucky Derby – always attracted the rich, powerful, and important. This one had been no exception. Both U.S. Senators from Colorado and California, a gaggle of congressmen, the states' governors, and approximately three hundred others had attended. His CI had been at the table with Colorado's governor, senators, and the congresswoman from the third district, all of whom were targets of his corruption case. Liquor had flowed, and in the *vino* had been the usual amount of *veritas*. A deal had been made last night. The dam would be built. The payoffs had been agreed upon. Even the head of the Sierra Club's local branch had been in on it. In return for a large donation from the contractor and a new park to be authorized by the governor, the environmentalists would mute their objections to the project. The sad part, Hoskins thought, was that the area really needed the water project. It would be good for everyone, including the local fishermen. What made it illegal was that bribes were being made. He would have his choice of five federal statutes to apply to the case, the nastiest of which was the RICO law, the Racketeer-Influenced and Corrupt Organization Act that had been passed over twenty years before without a thought about its possible scope of coverage. He already had one governor in a federal penitentiary, and to that he would add four more elected officials. The scandal would rip Colorado state politics asunder. The confidential informant in question was the governor's personal aide, an idealistic young woman who had decided eight months earlier that enough was enough. Women were always best for wearing a wire, especially if they had large breasts, as this one did. The mike went right in the bra, and the geometry of the location made for good sound quality. It was also a safe spot, because the governor had already sampled her charms and found them lacking. The old saw was right: hell really did have no fury like a woman scorned.

'Well?' Murray asked, annoyed to have to be in his office on another Sunday. He'd had to ride the subway in, and now that was broken down. He might be stuck all day here.

'Dan, we have enough to prosecute already, but I want to wait until the money gets passed to do the bust. My CI really delivered for us. I'm doing the transcript myself right now.'

'Can you fax it?'

'Soon as I'm done. Dan, we've got them all by the ass, all of 'em.'

'Walt, we just might put up a statue to you,' Murray said, forgetting his annoyance. Like most career cops he loathed public corruption almost as much as he loathed kidnappers.

'Dan, the transfer here is the best thing that ever happened to me.' Hoskins laughed into the phone. 'Maybe I'll run for one of the vacant Senate seats.'

'Colorado could do worse,' Dan observed. *Just so you don't carry a gun anywhere*, Murray thought unkindly. He knew that was unfair. Though Walt wasn't worth beans on the muscle end of the business, the other side of his assessment the previous year had also been correct: Hoskins was a brilliant investigator, a chessmaster to equal Bill Shaw, even. Walt just couldn't bring down a bust worth a damn. Well, Murray corrected himself, this one wouldn't be very hard. Politicians hid behind lawyers and press-spokesmen, not guns. 'What about the U.S. Attorney?'

'He's a good, sharp kid, Dan. He's on the team. Backup from the Department of Justice won't hurt, but the fact of the matter is that this guy can do it if he has to.'

'Okay. Shoot me the transcript when it's done.' Murray switched buttons on his phone, calling Shaw's home in Chevy Chase.

'Yeah.'

'Bill, Dan here,' Murray said over the secure phone. 'Hoskins scored last night. Says he's got it all on tape – all five principal subjects cut the deal over their roast beef.'

'You realize that we might have to promote the guy now?' the FBI Director noted with a chuckle.

'So, make him a deputy-assistant director,' Dan suggested.

'That hasn't kept you out of trouble. Do I need to come in?'

'Not really. What's it like there?'

'I'm thinking of putting up a ski-jump in the driveway. Roads really look bad.'

'I took the Metro in, then it shut down – ice on the tracks or something.'

'Washington, D.C., the City that Panics,' Shaw replied. 'Okay, I plan to relax and watch the game, Mr Murray.'

'And I, Mr Shaw, will forgo my personal pleasures and work for the greater glory of the Bureau.'

'Good, I like dedication in my subordinates. Besides, I got my grandson here,' Shaw reported, watching his daughter-in-law feed him from a bottle.

'How is Kenny Junior?'

'Oh, we just might make an agent out of him. Unless you really need me, Dan . . .'

'Bill, enjoy the kid, just remember to hand him back when he messes the diapers.'

'Right. Keep me posted on this. I'll have to take this to the President myself, you know.'

'You expect problems there?'

'No. He's a stand-up guy on corruption stuff.'

'I'll be back.' Murray walked out of his office towards communications. He found Inspector Pat O'Day heading the same way.

'Were those your sled dogs I saw in the drive-thru, Pat?'

'Some of us drive decent cars.' O'Day had a four-wheel-drive pickup. 'The 9th Street barrier is frozen in the up position, by the way. I've told 'em to leave the other one down.'

'What are you in for?'

'I have the watch in the command center. My relief lives out in Frederick. I don't expect to see him until half-past Thursday. I-270 is closed until spring, I think.'

'Christ, this is a wimpy town when it snows.'

'Tell me about it.' O'Day's last field assignment had been in Wyoming, and he still missed the hunting out there.

Murray told the communications staff that the inbound fax from Denver was code-word material. Nobody would get to see it but him for the moment.

'I can't match this one,' Goodley said, just after lunch.

'Which one?'

'The first one that shook us up – no, excuse me, the second one. I cannot reconcile Narmonov's and SPINNAKER's schedules.'

'That doesn't necessarily mean anything.'

'I know. The odd thing is, remember what I said about linguistic differences in his reports?'

'Yeah, but remember my Russian is pretty thin. I can't catch nuances like you can.'

'This is the first place it shows up, and it's also the first one where I can't satisfy myself that they definitely met.' Goodley paused. 'I think I might have something here.'

'Remember that you have to sell it to our Russian department.'

'That's not going to be easy.'

'That's right,' Ryan agreed. 'Back it up with something, Ben.'

One of the security guys helped Clark with the case of bottles. He restocked the bar supplies, then headed to the upper level with the remaining four bottles of Chivas. Chavez tagged behind with the flowers. John Clark put the bottles in their places and looked around the compartment to be sure that everything was in order. He fussed with a few minor items to show that he was being sincere. The bottle with the transceiver in it had a cracked top. That should make sure that nobody tried to open it, he thought. Clever of the S&T guys, he thought. The simple things usually worked best.

The flower arrangements had to be fastened in place. They were mainly white roses, nice ones, Chavez thought, and the little green sticks that held them in place looked like they belonged. Ding next went downstairs and looked at the forward washrooms. In the trash bin of one he dropped a very small, Japanese-made, tape recorder, making sure beforehand that it was operating properly. He met Clark at the base of the spiral stairs, and then both left the aircraft. The advance security people were just starting to arrive as they disappeared into the terminal's lower-level.

Once inside, both men found a locked room and used it to change clothes. They emerged dressed like businessmen, hair recombed, both wearing sunglasses.

'They always this easy, Mr C?'

'Nope.' Both men walked to the opposite side of the terminal. This put them half a mile from the JAL 747, but with a direct line of sight to it. They could also see a Gulfstream-IV business jet liveried as a private aircraft. It was supposed to take off right before the Japanese aircraft, but would head on a diverging course. Clark took a Sony Walkman from his briefcase, inserted a tape cassette, and donned the earphones. In fact, he heard the murmurs of the security men on the aircraft, and the tape was recording their words as his eyes scanned a paperback book. It was a pity that he couldn't understand Japanese, Clark thought. As with most covert operations, the main component was sitting around and doing precisely nothing while he waited for something to happen. He looked up to see the red carpet being rolled out again, and the troops forming up, and a lectern being set up. It must have been a real pain in the ass for the people who had to handle these things, he thought.

Things picked up rapidly. The President of Mexico personally accompanied the Japanese Prime Minister to the aircraft, shaking his hand warmly at the base of the stairs. That might have been evidence right there, Clark thought. There was elation that the job was going well, but sadness that such things as this really happened. The party went up the stairs, the door closed, the stairs were hauled off, and the 747 started its engines.

Clark heard the conversation pick up in the airplane's upstairs lounge. Then sound quality went immediately to hell when the engines fired up. Clark watched the Gulfstream begin taxiing off. The 747 began rolling two minutes later. It made sense. You had to be careful sending aircraft into the sky behind a jumbo. The big wide-bodies left behind wake turbulence that could be very dangerous. The two CIA officers remained in the observation lounge until the JAL airliner lifted off, and then their job was done.

Aloft, the Gulfstream climbed out to its crushing altitude of forty-one thousand feet on a heading of zero-two-six, inbound to New Orleans. The pilot eased off on the throttle somewhat, coached by the men in the back. Off to their right, the 747 was leveling off at the same altitude, on a course of zero-three-one. Inside the bigger aircraft, the supposed bottle of scotch was pointed out a window, and its EHF transmissions were scattering out towards the Gulfstream's receptors. The very favorable data-bandwidth of the system guaranteed a good signal, and no less than ten tape recorders were at work, two for each separate side-band channel. The pilot eased his course as far east as he dared until the two aircraft were over the water, then he turned back left as a second aircraft, this one an EC-135 that had struggled to get out of Tinker Air Force Base in Oklahoma, took up station thirty miles east, and two thousand feet below the larger Boeing product.

The first aircraft landed at New Orleans, unloaded its men and equipment, refueled, then lifted off to head back to Mexico City.

Clark was at the embassy. One of his additions to the operation was a Japanese-speaker from the Agency's Intelligence Directorate. Reasoning that his test reception would be useful to determine the effectiveness of the system, he had further decided that it would be better still to get an immediate read on what was being said. Clark thought that this was a reasonable demonstration of operational initiative. The linguist took his time, listening to the taped conversation three times before he started typing. He generated less than two pages. It annoyed him that Clark was reading over his shoulder.

'"I wish it was this easy to make a deal with the opposition in the Diet,"' Clark read aloud. '"We merely must take care of some of his associates also."'

'Looks to me that we got what we want,' the linguist observed.

'Where's your communications guy?' Clark asked the Station Chief.

'I can do it myself.' It was, indeed, easy enough. The Station Chief transcribed the two typed pages into a computer. Attached to the computer was a small machine that looked like a video-disc machine. On the large disc were literally billions of random digital numbers. Each letter he typed was randomly transformed into something else and transmitted to the MERCURY room at Langley. Here the incoming signal was recorded. A communications technician selected the proper description disc from the secure library, slid it into his own machine, and pressed a button. Within seconds, a laser printer generated two pages of cleartext message. This was sealed in an envelope and handed to a messenger, who made for the seventh-floor office of the Deputy Director.

'Dr Ryan, the dispatch you were waiting for.'

'Thank you.' Jack signed for it. 'Dr Goodley, you're going to have to excuse me for a moment.'

'No problem.' Ben went back to his pile of papers.

Ryan pulled the dispatch out and read it slowly and carefully twice. Then he picked up the phone and asked for a secure line to Camp David.

'Command center,' a voice answered.

'This is Dr Ryan at Langley. I need to talk to the Boss.'

'Wait one, sir,' the Navy chief petty officer replied. Ryan lit a cigarette.

'This is the President,' a new voice said.

'Mr President, this is Ryan. I have a fragment of conversation off the 747.'

'So soon?'

'It was made before engine start-up, sir. We have an unidentified voice – we think it's the PM – saying that he made the deal.' Jack read off three lines verbatim.

'That son-of-a-bitch,' Fowler breathed. 'You know, with evidence like that I could prosecute a guy.'

'I thought you'd want this fast, sir. I can fax you the initial transcript. The full one will take until twenty-one hundred or so.'

'It'll be nice to have something to read after the game. Okay, send it up.' The line went dead.

'You're welcome, sir,' Jack said into the phone.

'It is time,' Ghosn said.

'Okay.' Russell stood up and got into his heavy coat. It would be a really cold one outside. The predicted high temperature was six above, and they were not there yet. A bitter northeast wind was sweeping down out of Nebraska, where it was even colder. The only good thing about that was the clear sky it brought. Denver is also a city with a smog problem, made all the worse by winter-temperature inversions. But today the sky was literally cloudless, and to the west Marvin could see streams of snow being blown off the Front Range peaks like white banners. Surely it was auspicious, and the clear weather meant that the flight out of Stapleton would not be delayed as he had feared a few days before. He started the engine of the van, rehearsing his lines and going over the plan as he allowed the vehicle to heat. Marvin turned to look at the cargo. Almost a ton of super-high explosives, Ibrahim had said. That would really piss people off. Next he got into the rental car and started that one, too, flipping the heater all the way on. Shame that Commander Qati felt so bad. Maybe it was nerves, Russell thought.

A few minutes later, they came out. Ghosn got in next to Marvin. He was nervous, too.

'Ready, man?'

'Yes.'

'Okay.' Russell dropped the van into reverse and backed out of the parking place. He pulled forward, checking that the rental car was following, then headed off the parking lot onto the highway.

The drive to the stadium required only a few uneventful minutes. The police were out in force, and he saw that Ghosn was eyeing them very carefully. Marvin was not concerned. The cops were only there for traffic control, after all, and they were just standing around, since the traffic had scarcely begun. It was almost six hours till game time. He turned off the road onto the parking lot at the media entrance, and there was a cop he had to talk to. Qati had already broken off, and was now circling a few blocks away. Marvin stopped the van and rolled his window down.

'Howdy,' he said to the cop.

Officer Pete Dawkins of the Denver City Police was already cold, despite the fact that he was a native Coloradan. He was supposed to guard the media and VIP gate, a post he'd been stuck with only because he was a very junior officer. The senior guys were in warmer spots.

'Who are you?' Dawkins asked.

'Tech staff,' Russell replied. 'This is the media gate, right?'

'Yeah, but you're not on my list.' There was a limited number of available spaces in the VIP lot, and Dawkins couldn't just let anyone in.

'Tape machine broke in the "A" unit over there,' Russell explained with a wave. 'We had to bring down a backup.'

'Nobody told me,' the police officer observed.

'Nobody told me either until six last night. We had to bring the goddamned thing down from Omaha.' Russell waved his clipboard rather vaguely. Out of sight in the back, Ghosn was scarcely breathing.

'Why didn't they fly it down?'

'Cause FedEx don't work on Sunday, man, and the damned thing's too big to get through the door of a Lear. I ain't complaining, man. I'm Chicago tech staff, okay?

773

I'm Network. I get triple-time-and-a-half for this shit, away from home, special event, weekend overtime.'

'That sounds pretty decent,' Dawkins observed.

'Better'n a week's normal pay, man. Keep talking, officer.' Russell grinned. 'This is a buck and a quarter a minute, y'know?'

'You must have a hell of a union.'

'We sure do.' Marvin laughed.

'You know where to take it?'

'No problem, sir.' Russell pulled off. Ghosn let out a long breath as the van started moving again. He'd listened to every word, sure that something would go disastrously wrong.

Dawkins watched the van pull away. He checked his watch and made a notation of his own on his own clipboard. For some reason, the captain wanted him to keep track of who arrived when. It didn't make sense to Dawkins, but the captain's ideas didn't always make sense, did they? It took a moment for him to realize that the ABC van had Colorado tags. That was odd, he thought, as a Lincoln town car pulled up. This one was on his list. It was the commissioner of the NFL's American Conference. The VIPs were supposed to be pretty early, probably, Dawkins thought, so they could settle into their sky boxes and start their drinking early. He'd also drawn security at the Commissioner's party the night before and watched every rich clown in Colorado get sloppy drunk, along with various politicians and other Very Important People – mostly assholes, the young cop thought, having watched them – from all over America. He supposed that F. Scott Fitzgerald was right after all.

Two hundred yards away, Russell parked the van, set the brake, and left the engine on. Ghosn went in back. The game was scheduled to start at 4:20 local time. Major affairs always ran late, Ibrahim judged. He'd assumed a start time of 4:30. To that he added another half hour, setting T-Zero at 5:00, Rocky Mountain Standard Time. Arbitrary numbers always had zeros in them, after all, and the actual time of the detonation had been set weeks before: precisely on the first hour after game start.

The device did not have a very sophisticated anti-tamper device. There was a crude one set on each access door, but there hadn't been time to do anything complicated, and that, Ghosn thought, was a good thing. The gusting northeast wind was rocking the van, and a delicate tumbler switch might not have been a good idea after all.

For that matter, he realized rather belatedly, just slamming the door closed on the van might have ... *What else have you failed to consider?* he wondered. Ghosn reminded himself that all such moments brought up the most frightening of thoughts. He swiftly ran over everything he had done to this point. Everything had been checked a hundred times and more. It was ready. Of course it was ready. Hadn't he spent months of careful preparation for this?

The engineer made a last check of his test circuits. All were fine. The cold had not affected the batteries that badly. He connected the wires to the timer – or tried to. His hands were stiff from the cold, and quivered from the emotion of the moment. Ghosn stopped. He took a moment to get control of himself and attached them on the second try, screwing down the nut to hold them firmly in place.

And that, he decided, was that. Ghosn closed the access door, which set the simple tamper switch, and backed away from the device. No, he said to himself. It is no longer a 'device'.

'That it?' Russell asked.

'Yes, Marvin,' Ghosn answered quietly. He moved forward into the passenger seat.

'Then let's leave.' Marvin watched the younger man get out, and reached across to lock the door. Then he exited the van, and locked his. They walked west, past the big network up-link vans with their huge dish antennas. They had to be worth millions each, Marvin thought, and every one would be wrecked, along with the TV weenies, just like the ones who had made a sporting event of his brother's death. Killing them didn't worry him a bit, not one little bit. In a moment, the bulk of the stadium shielded them from the wind. They continued across the parking lot, past the ranks of early-arriving fans and the cars which were pulling onto the lot, many of them from Minnesota, full of fans dressed warmly, carrying peanuts and wearing hats, some of them adorned with horns.

Qati and the rental car were on a side-street. He simply slid over from the driver's seat, allowing Marvin to get behind the wheel. Traffic was now becoming thick, and, to avoid the worst of it, Russell took an alternate route he'd scouted out the previous day.

'You know, it really is a shame, messing with the game like this.'

'What do you mean?' Qati asked.

'This is the fifth time the Vikings have made it to the Superbowl. This time it looks like they're going to win. That Wills kid they have running for them is the best since Sayers, and because of us nobody'll see it happen. Too bad.' Russell shook his head and grinned at the irony of it all. Neither Qati nor Ghosn bothered to reply, but Russell hadn't expected them to. They just didn't have much sense of humor, did they? The motel parking lot was nearly empty. Everyone staying there must have been a fan of one sort or another, Marvin thought as he opened the door.

'All packed?'

'Yes.' Ghosn traded a look with the Commander. It was too bad, but it could not be helped.

The room hadn't been made up yet, but that was no big thing. Marvin went into the bathroom, closing the door behind him. When the American emerged, he saw that both Arabs were standing.

'Ready?'

'Yes,' Qati said. 'Could you get my bag down, Marvin?'

'Sure.' Russell turned and reached for the suitcase that lay on the metal shelf. He didn't hear the steel bar that struck the back of his neck. His short but powerful frame dropped to the cheap all-weather carpet on the floor. Qati had struck hard, but not hard enough to kill, the Commander realized. He was weakening by the day. Ghosn helped him move the body back into the bathroom, where they laid him face up. The motel was a cheap one, and the bathroom was small, too small for their purposes. They'd hoped to set him in the tub, but there wasn't room for both men to stand. Instead, Qati simply knelt by the American's side. Ghosn shrugged his disappointment and reached for a towel from the rack.

He wrapped the towel around Russell's neck. The man was more stunned than unconscious, and his hands were beginning to move. Ghosn had to move quickly. Qati handed him the steak knife that he'd removed from the coffee shop after dinner the previous night. Ghosn took it and cut deeply into the side of Russell's neck, just below the right ear. Blood shot out as though from a hose, and Ibrahim pushed the towel back down to keep it from splashing on his clothes. Then he did the same thing to the carotid artery on the left side. Both men held the towel down, almost as though to staunch the bloodflow.

It was at that moment that Marvin's eyes came completely open. There was no comprehension in them, there was no time for him to understand what was happening. His arms moved, but each man used all his weight to hold them down and prevented the American from accomplishing anything. He didn't speak, though his mouth opened, and, after a last accusing look at Ghosn, the eyes went dreamy for a moment, then rolled back. By this time, Qati and Ghosn were leaning back to avoid the blood that now filled the grooves between the bathroom tiles. Ibrahim pulled back the towel. The blood was trickling out now, and was not a concern. The towel was quite sodden, however. He tossed it into the tub. Qati handed him another.

'I hope God will be merciful to him,' Ghosn said quietly.

'He was a pagan.' It was too late for recriminations.

'Is it his fault that he never met a godly man?'

'Wash,' Qati said. There were two sinks outside the bathroom. Each man lathered his hands thoroughly, checking his clothes for any sign of blood. There was none.

777

'What will happen to this place when the bomb goes off?' Qati asked.

Ghosn thought about that. 'This close ... it will be outside the fireball, but – ' he walked to the windows and pulled the drapes back a few centimeters. The stadium was readily visible, and a direct line of sight made it easy to say what would happen. 'The thermal pulse will set it afire, and then the blast wave will flatten the building. The whole building will be consumed.'

'You're sure?'

'Completely. The effects of the bomb are easy to predict.'

'Good.' Qati removed all the travel documents and identification he and Ghosn had used to this point. They'd have to clear customs inspection, and they had already tempted fate enough. The surplus documents they tossed in a trash can. Ghosn got both bags and took them out to the car. They checked the room once more. Qati got into the car. Ghosn closed the door for the last time, leaving the 'Do Not Disturb' card on the knob. It was a short drive to the airport, and their flight left in two hours.

The parking lot filled up rapidly. By three hours before game time, much to Dawkins' surprise, the VIP lot was filled. Already the pre-game show had begun. He could see a team wandering around the lot with a minicam, interviewing the Vikings fans, who had converted one entire half of the parking lot into a giant tail-gate party. There were white vapor trails rising from charcoal grills. Dawkins knew that the Vikings fans were slightly nutty, but this was ridiculous. All they had to do was walk inside. They could have any manner of food and drink, and consume it in sixty-eight-degree air, sitting on a cushioned seat, but no – they were proclaiming their toughness in air that couldn't be much more than five degrees Fahrenheit. Dawkins was a skier and had worked his way through college as a ski patrol at one of the Aspen slopes. He knew cold and he knew the value of warmth. You couldn't impress cold air with anything. The air and wind simply didn't notice.

'How are things going, Pete?'

Dawkins turned. 'No problems, Sarge. Everybody on the list is checked off.'

'I'll spell you for a few minutes. Go inside and warm up for a while. You can get coffee at the security booth just inside the gate.'

'Thanks.' Dawkins knew that he'd need something. He was going to be stuck outside for the whole game, patrolling the lot to make sure nobody tried to steal something. Plainclothes officers were on the lookout for pickpockets and ticket-scalpers, but most of them would get to go inside and watch the game. All Dawkins had was a radio. That was to be expected, he thought. He had less than three years on the force. He was still almost a rookie. The young officer walked up the slope towards the stadium, right past the ABC minivan he'd checked through. He looked inside and saw the Sony tape machine. Funny, it didn't seem to be hooked up to anything. He wondered where those two techies were, but getting coffee was more important. Even polypropylene underwear had its limits, and Dawkins was as cold as he had ever remembered.

Qati and Ghosn returned the car to the rental agency and took the courtesy bus to the terminal, where they checked in their bags for the flight, then headed in to check their flight's status. Here they learned that the American MD-80 for Dallas-Fort Worth was delayed. Weather in Texas, the clerk at the desk explained. There was ice on the runways from the storm that had just skirted past Denver the previous night.

'I must make my connection to Mexico. Can you book me through another city?' Ghosn asked.

'We have one leaving for Miami, same departure time as your flight to Dallas. I can book you a connecting flight in Miami . . .' the ticket agent tapped the data into her terminal. 'There's a one-hour layover. Oh, okay, it's only a fifteen-minute difference into Mexico City.'

'Could you do that, please? I must make my connection.'

'Both tickets?'

'Yes, excuse me.'

'No problem.' The young lady smiled at her computer. Ghosn wondered if she'd survive the event. The huge glass windows faced the stadium and even at this distance the blast wave ... maybe, he thought, if she ducked fast enough. But she'd already be blinded from the flash. Such pretty dark eyes, too. A pity. 'Here you go. I'll make sure they switch the bags over,' she promised him. That Ghosn took with a grain of salt.

'Thank you.'

'The gate is that way.' She pointed.

'Thank you once more.'

The ticket agent watched them head off. The young one was pretty cute, she thought, but his big brother — or boss? she wondered — looked like a sourpuss. Maybe he didn't like to fly.

'Well?' Qati asked.

'The connecting flight roughly duplicates our schedule. We've lost a quarter hour buffer time in Mexico. The weather problem is localized. There should be no further difficulty.'

The terminal was very nearly empty. Those people who wished to leave Denver were evidently waiting for later flights so that they might watch the game on TV, and the same appeared to be true of arriving flights, Ibrahim saw. There were scarcely twenty people in the departure lounge.

'Okay, I can't reconcile the schedules here either,' Goodley said. 'In fact, I'd almost say we have a smoking gun.'

'How so?' Ryan asked.

'Narmonov was only in Moscow two days last week, Monday and Friday. Tuesday, Wednesday, and Thursday he was in Latvia, Lithuania, the Western Ukraine, and then a trip down to Volgograd for some local politicking. Friday's out because of when the message came over, right? But Monday, our friend was in the Congress build-

780

ing practically all day. I don't think they met last week, but the letter implies that they did. I think we got a lie here.'

'Show me,' Jack said.

Goodley spread his data out on Ryan's desk. Together they went over the dates and itineraries.

'Well, isn't that interesting,' Jack said after a few minutes. 'That son-of-a-bitch.'

'Persuasive?' Goodley wanted to know.

'Completely?' The Deputy Director shook his head. 'No.'

'Why not?'

'It's possible that our data is incorrect. It's possible that they met on the sly, maybe last Sunday when Andrey Il'ych was out at his dacha. One swallow doesn't make a spring,' Jack said with a nod towards the snow outside. 'We need to make a detailed check on this before it goes any farther, but what you've uncovered here is very, very interesting, Ben.'

'But, damn it —'

'Ben, you go slow on stuff like this,' Jack explained. 'You don't toss out the work of a valuable agent on the basis of equivocal data, and this is equivocal, isn't it?'

'Technically, yes. You think he's been turned?'

'Doubled, you mean?' Ryan grinned. 'You're picking up on the jargon, Dr Goodley. You answer the question for me.'

'Well, if he'd been doubled on us, no, he wouldn't send this sort of data. They wouldn't want to send us this kind of signal, unless elements within the KGB —'

'Think it through, Ben,' Jack cautioned.

'Oh, yeah. It compromises them, too, doesn't it? You're right, it's not likely. If he'd been turned, the data should be different.'

'Exactly. If you're right, and if he's been misleading us, the most likely explanation is the one you came up with. He stands to profit from the political demise of Narmonov. It helps to think like a cop in this business. Who profits — who has motive, that's the test you apply here. Best person to look at this is Mary Pat.'

'Call her in?' Goodley asked.
'Day like this?'

Qati and Ghosn boarded the flight on the first call, taking their first-class seats and strapping in. Ten minutes later the aircraft pulled back from the gate and taxied out to the end of the runway. They'd made a smart move, Ghosn thought. The flight to Dallas had still not been called. Two minutes after that, the airliner lifted off and soon turned southeast towards the warmer climes of Florida.

The maid was having a bad day already. Most of the guests had left late and she was way behind on her schedule. She clucked with disappointment at seeing the keep-out card on one doorknob, but it was not on the other, connecting room, and she thought it might be a mistake. The flip side of the card was the green 'Make Up Room NOW' message, and guests often made that mistake. First she went into the unmarked one. It was easy. Only one of the beds had been used. She stripped off the linen and replaced it with the speed that came from doing the same job more than fifty times per day. Then she checked out the bathroom, replaced the soiled towels, put a new bar of soap in the holder, and emptied the trashcan into the bag that hung from her cart. Then she had to make a decision – whether to make up the other room or not. The card on the knob said no, but if they didn't want it, why didn't they do the same thing for this room? It was worth a look at least. If anything obviously important was laid out, she'd stay clear. The maid looked through the open connecting door and saw two ordinarily messed-up beds. No clothing was on the floors. In fact, the room was as neat today as it had been the day before. She stuck her head through the door and looked back towards the wash area. Nothing remarkable there either. She decided to clean it, too. The maid got behind her cart and turned it to push through the door. Again she did the beds, then headed back to –
  How had she missed that before? A man's legs. What? She walked forward and –

It took the manager over a minute to calm her down enough to understand what she was saying. Thank God, he thought, that there were no guests on that side of the motel now; all were off to see the game. The young man took a deep breath and walked outside, past the coffee shop and around to the back side of the motel. The door had closed automatically, but his pass-key fixed that.

'My God,' he said simply. At least he'd been prepared for it. The manager was no fool. He didn't touch anything, but rather walked into the connecting room and out that door. The desk phone in his office had all the emergency numbers printed on a small card. He punched up the second one.

'Police.'

'I want to report a murder,' the manager said, as calmly as he could manage.

President Fowler set the fax down on the corner table and shook his head. 'It really is unbelievable that he'd try something so blatant.'

'What are you going to do about it?' Liz asked.

'Well, we have to verify it, of course, but I think we'll be able to do that. Brent is flying back from the game tonight. I'll want him in my office early for his advice, but I figure we'll just confront him with it. If he doesn't like it, that's just too damned bad. This is Mafia stuff.'

'You really do have a thing about this, don't you?'

Fowler opened a bottle of beer. 'Once a prosecutor, always a prosecutor. A hood is a hood is a hood.'

The JAL 747 touched down at Dulles International Airport three minutes early. Out of deference to the weather, and with the approval of the Japanese Ambassador, the arrival ceremony was abbreviated. Besides, the sign of a really important arrival in Washington was informality. It was one of the local folkways that the ambassador had explained to the current Prime Minister's predecessor. After a brief but sincere greeting from Deputy Secretary of State Scott Adler, the official party was loaded into all the four-wheel-drive vehicles that the embassy had been able to assemble on such short notice, and headed off to the Madison Hotel, a few blocks from the White House. The President, he learned, was at Camp David, and would be coming back to Washington the following morning. The Japanese Prime Minister, still suffering from the lingering effects of travel, decided to get a few more hours of sleep. He'd not yet taken off his coat when another clean-up crew boarded the aircraft yet again. One man retrieved the unused liquor, including one bottle with a cracked neck. Another emptied the wastebaskets of the various washrooms into a large trash bag. They were soon on their way to Langley. All of the chase aircraft except the first landed at Andrews Air Force Base, where the flight crews also began their mandated rest periods – in this case at the base officers' club. The recordings started their trip to Langley by car, arriving later than the tape recorder from Dulles. It turned out that the machine off the 747 had the best sound quality, and the technicians started on that tape first.

The Gulfstream returned to Mexico City, also on time. The aircraft rolled out to the general-aviation terminal and the flight crew of three – it was an Air Force crew, though no one knew that – walked into the terminal for dinner. Since they were Air Force, it was time for some crew rest. Clark was still at the embassy, and planned to catch the first quarter at least, before heading back to D.C. and all that damned snow.

'Be careful or you're going to fall asleep during the game,' the National Security Advisor warned.

'It's only my second beer, Elizabeth,' Fowler replied.

There was a cooler next to the sofa, and a large silver tray of munchies. Elliot still found it quite incredible. J. Robert Fowler, President of the United States, so intelligent and hard-minded in every possible way, but a rabid football fan, sitting here like Archic Bunker, waiting for the kickoff.

*

'I found one, but the other one's a son-of-a-bitch,' the crew chief reported. 'Can't seem to figure this one out, Colonel.'

'Come on inside and warm up,' the pilot said. 'You've been out there too long anyway.'

'Some kind of drug deal, I'll bet you,' the junior detective said.

'Then it's amateurs,' his partner observed. The photographer had snapped his customary four rolls of film, and now the coroner's men were lifting the body into the plastic bag for transport to the morgue. There could be little doubt on the cause of death. It was a particularly brutal murder. It seemed that the killers – there had to be two, the senior man already thought – had to have held the man's arms down before they slashed his throat, and then they had watched him bleed out while using the towel to keep their clothes clean. Maybe they were paying off a debt somehow or other. Perhaps this guy had done a rip-off, or there was some old grudge that they had settled. This was clearly not a crime of passion; it was far too cruel and calculated for that.

The detectives noted their good luck, however. The victim's wallet had still been in his pocket. They had all his ID, and better than that, they had two complete sets of other ID, all of which were now being checked out. The motel records had noted the license numbers of both vehicles associated with these rooms, and those also were being checked on the motor-vehicle-records computer.

'The guy's an Indian,' the coroner's rep said as they picked him up. 'Native American, I mean.'

'I've seen the face somewhere before,' the junior detective thought. 'Wait a minute.' Something caught his eye. He unbuttoned the man's shirt, revealing the top of a tattoo.

'He's done time,' the senior man said. The tattoo on the man's chest was a crude one, spit-and-pencil, and it showed something that he'd seen before ... 'Wait a minute ... this means something ...'

'Warrior Society!'

'You're right. The Feds had something out on – oh, yeah, remember? The shooting up in North Dakota last year?' The senior man thought for a second. 'When we get the information from the license, make sure they send it right off to Washington. Okay, you can take him out now.' The body was lifted and carried out. 'Bring in the maid and the manager.'

Inspector Pat O'Day had the good luck of drawing watch duty in the FBI's command center, Room 5005 of the Hoover Building. The room was oddly shaped, roughly triangular, with the desks of the command staff in the angle, and screens on the long wall. The quiet day they were having – there was adverse weather across half the country, and adverse weather is more of an obstacle to crime than any police agency – meant that one of the screens was showing the teams lining up for the coin toss in Denver. Just as the Vikings won the toss and elected to receive, a young lady from communications walked in with a couple of faxes from the Denver P.D.

'A murder case, sir. They think we might know who this is.'

The quality of photographs on driver's licenses is not the sort to impress a professional anything, and blowing them up – then sending them via fax – didn't improve matters very much. He had to stare at it for a few seconds, and almost decided that he didn't know the face, until he remembered some things from his time in Wyoming.

'I've seen this guy before . . . Indian . . . Marvin Russell?' He turned to another agent. 'Stan, have you ever seen this guy?'

'Nope.'

O'Day looked over the rest of the faxes. Whoever he was, he was dead, with a slashed throat, the Denver cops said. 'Probable drug-related killing' was the initial read from the Denver homicide guys. Well, that made sense, didn't it? John Russell had been part of a drug deal. The other initial data was that there had been other IDs at the scene of the crime, but that the licenses had been fakes – very good ones, the notes said. However, they had a truck registered to the victim, and also a car at the scene was a rental that had been signed out to Robert Friend, which was the name on the victim's license. The Denver P.D. was now looking for the vehicles, and wanted to know if the Bureau had anything useful on the victim and any likely associates.

'Get back to 'em, and tell 'em to fax us the photos from the other IDs they found.'

'Yes, sir.'

Pat watched the teams get onto the field for the kick-off, then lifted the phone. 'Dan? Pat. You want to come on down here? I think an old friend of ours just might have turned up dead . . . No, not that kind of friend.'

Murray showed up just in time for the kickoff, which took precedence over the faxes. Minnesota got the ball out of the twenty-four-yard line, and their offense went to work. The network immediately had the screen covered with all sorts of useless information so that the fans couldn't see the players.

'This look like Marvin Russell to you?' Pat asked.

'Sure as hell does. Where is he?'

O'Day waved at the TV screen. 'Would you believe Denver? They found him about ninety minutes ago with his throat cut. Local P.D. thinks it's drug-related.'

'Well, that's what did his brother in. What else?' Murray took the faxes from O'Day's hand.

Tony Wills got the first handoff, taking the ball five yards off tackle – almost breaking it for more. On second down, both men saw Wills catch a swing pass for twenty yards.

'That kid is really something,' Pat said. 'I remember seeing a game where Jimmy Brown . . .'

Bob Fowler had just started his third beer of the after-noon, wishing he'd been at the game instead of being stuck here. Of course, the Secret Service would have gone ape, and the security at the game would have to have been beefed up to the point that people would still be trying to get in. That was not a good political move, was it? Liz Elliot, sitting next to the President, flipped one of the other TVs to HBO to catch a movie. She donned a set of headphones so that she could hear it without disturbing the Commander in Chief. It just made no sense at all, she thought, none. How this man could get so enthusiastic about something as dumb as a little-boy's game . . .

Pete Dawkins finished his pre-game duties by pulling a chain across his gate. Anyone who wanted to get in now would have to use one of the two gates that were still open, but guarded. At the last Superbowl, a very clever gang of thieves had prowled the parking lot and come away with two hundred thousand dollars' worth of goods from the parked cars – mainly tape decks and radios – and that was not going to happen in Denver. He started his patrol, along with the three other officers. By agreement, they'd circulate all around the lot instead of sticking to specific areas. It was too cold for that. Moving around would at least keep them warm. Dawkins' legs felt as stiff as cardboard, and moving would loosen them up. He didn't really expect to stop any crimes. What car thief would be so dumb as to prowl around in zero-degree weather? Soon he found himself in the area the Minnesota fans had occupied. They were certainly well-organized. The tailgate parties had all ended on time. The lawn chairs were all stowed away, and they'd done a very effective job of cleaning up the area. Except for a few puddles of frozen coffee, you could hardly tell that they had done something here. Maybe the Minnesota fans weren't such idiots after all.

Dawkins had a radio plugged into his ear. Listening to a game on the radio was like having sex with your clothes on, but at least he knew what the cheers were about. Minnesota scored first. Wills took it in by sweeping left end from fifteen yards out. The Vikings' first drive had taken only seven plays and four minutes fifty seconds. Minnesota sounded pretty tough today.

*

'God, Dennis must be sick,' Fowler observed. Liz didn't hear him, concentrating instead on her movie. The Secretary of Defense immediately had cause to feel sicker. The kickoff was fielded at the five, and the reserve running back who handled that duty for the Chargers made it all the way to the forty – but there he fumbled, and a Viking fell on the ball.

'They say Marvin was a clever little bastard. Look at the numbers on the other licenses. Except for the first couple of digits, they're the same as his . . . I bet he got – well, somebody got – one of these ID machines,' Murray said.

'Passports and everything,' O'Day replied, watching Tony Wills do it again for eight yards. 'If they don't figure a way to key on that kid, this game's going to be a blowout.'

'What kind of passports?'

'They didn't say. I've asked for more information. They'll fax the photos when they get back into the office.'

In Denver the computers were humming. The rental car company was identified, and a check of their system revealed that the car had been returned to Stapleton International Airport just a few hours earlier. That made a really hot trail, and the detectives drove directly there from the motel, after taking initial statements from the first pair of 'witnesses.' The descriptions of the other two matched the photos on the passports. These were on their way to police headquarters. Already, they knew, the FBI was yelling for information. That made it sound more and more like a major drug case. Both detectives wondered where the victim's van was.

Dawkins finished his first circuit of the stadium just as Minnesota made its second touchdown. Again it was Wills, this time a four-yard pass out of the backfield. The guy already had fifty-one yards rushing and two receptions. Dawkins found himself looking at the ABC van he'd checked through. Why the Colorado tags? They'd said they were from Chicago, and that they had brought the tape widget in from Omaha. But the truck was painted like an official network truck. The local TV stations were not network-owned. They all showed network affiliation, but the big letters on them were for the local call-letters for the stations. Something to ask the sarge about. Dawkins circled the entry on his clipboard and wrote a question-mark next to it. He walked inside to the security booth.

'Where's the sarge?'

'Out walking the lot,' the officer at the booth replied. 'The dumbass has twenty bet on the Chargers. I don't think he can take it.'

'I'll see if I can get him to lay a little more,' Dawkins replied with a grin. 'Which way did he go?'

'North, I think.'

'Thanks.'

The Vikings kicked off again, with the score 14–0. The same return man took the kick, this time three yards deep in the endzone. He ignored the safety man's advice to down the ball and went up the middle like a shot. Breaking one tackle at the sixteen, he took advantage of a picture-book block and broke for the sidelines. Fifteen yards later it was clear that only the kicker had a chance, but the kicker was slow. At one hundred three yards, it was the longest kick return in Superbowl history. The point after was good, and the game was now 14–7.

'Feeling better, Dennis?' the Secretary of State asked the Secretary of Defense.

Bunker set his coffee down. He had decided not to drink. He wanted to be stone sober when he accepted the Lombardi Trophy from the Commissioner.

'Yeah, now we just have to figure a way to stop your boy.'

'Good luck.'

'He's a great kid, Bruce. Goddamn if he can't run.'

'He isn't just an athlete. Kid's got brains, and a good heart.'

'Bruce, if you educated him, I know he's smart,' Bunker said generously. 'I just wish he'd pull a hamstring right about now.'

Dawkins found his sergeant a few minutes later. 'Something funny here,' he said.

'What's that?'

'This truck – little white van on the east end of the row of big satellite trucks, "ABC" painted on it. Colorado commercial tags, but supposedly it's from Chicago or maybe Omaha. I check 'em through, said they had a tape deck to replace a broken one, but when I walked past it a few minutes ago, it wasn't hooked up, and the guys who brought it in were gone.'

'What are you telling me?' the sergeant asked.

'I think it might be a good idea to check it out.'

'Okay, call it in. I'll give it a walk-past.' The sergeant looked at the clipboard to check the tag number. 'I was headed off to help out the Wells Fargo guys at the loading dock. You take that for me, okay?'

'Sure, Sarge.' Dawkins headed off.

The watch supervisor lifted his Motorola radio. 'Lieutenant Vernon, this is Sergeant Yankevich, could you meet me down at the TV place?'

Yankevich started walking back south around the stadium. He had his own personal radio, but it lacked an earpiece. San Diego stopped the Vikings on downs. Minnesota punted – a good one that required a fair catch at the Chargers' thirty. Well, maybe his team could get the game even. Somebody ought to shoot that Wills kid, he thought angrily.

Officer Dawkins walked to the north end of the stadium and saw a Wells Fargo armored car parked at the lower-level loading dock. One man was trying to sling out bags of what had to be coins.

'What's the problem?'

'The driver's beat his knee up, he's off having it fixed. Can you give me a hand?'

'Inside or outside?' Dawkins asked.

'You hand them out, okay? Be careful, they're heavy mothers.'

'Gotcha.' Dawkins hopped inside. The interior of the armored truck was lined with shelves holding innumerable bags of mainly quarters, it looked like. He lifted one, and it was as heavy as he'd been told. The police officer stuck his clipboard in his belt and went to work, handing them out to the loading dock, where the guard set them on a two-wheel hand-truck. Trust the sarge to stick him with this.

Yankevich met the lieutenant at the media entrance. Both walked over to the truck in question. The lieutenant looked inside. 'A big box with "Sony" written on it . . . wait a minute. Says it's a commercial videotape machine.'

Sergeant Yankevich filled his boss in on what Dawkins had told him. 'It's probably nothing, but –'

'Yeah – but. Let me find the ABC guy. I'm also going to call the bomb squad. Stay here and keep an eye on the thing.'

'I have a Slim Jim in my car. If you want, I can get in easy enough.' Every cop knows how to break into cars.

'I don't think so. We'll let the bomb guys think it over – besides, it's probably just what it looks like. If they came down to replace a broken tapedeck – well, maybe the broken one was fixed and they decided they didn't need it.'

'Okay, Lieutenant.' Yankevich walked inside to get another cup of coffee to keep warm, then returned to the out-of-doors he loved so much. The sun was setting behind the Rockies, and even in zero weather with a bitter wind, it was always something beautiful to watch. The police sergeant walked past the network up-link vans to watch the glowing orange ball dip through one of the blowing snow clouds. Some things were better than football. When the last edge of the sun dipped below the ridge line, he turned back, deciding to take another look at the box inside the truck. He would not make it.

CHAPTER 35

Three Shakes

The timer just outside the bomb case reached 5:00:00, and things began to happen.

First, high-voltage capacitors began to charge and small pyrotechnics adjacent to the tritium reservoirs at both ends of the bomb fired. These drove pistons, forcing the tritium down narrow metal tubes. One tube led into the Primary, the other into the Secondary. There was no hurry here, and the objective was to mix the various collections of lithium-deuteride with the fusion-friendly tritium atoms. Elapsed time was ten seconds.

At 5:00:10, the timer sent out a second signal.

Time Zero.

The capacitors discharged, sending an impulse down a wire into a divider network. The length of the first wire was 50 centimeters. This took one and two-thirds nanoseconds. The impulse entered a dividing network using kryton switches—each of them a small and exceedingly fast device using self-ionized and radioactive krypton gas to time its discharges with remarkable precision. Using pulse-compression to build their amperage, the dividing network split the impulse into seventy different wires, each of which was exactly one meter in length. The relayed impulses required three-tenths of a shake (three nanoseconds) to transit this distance. The wires all had to be of the same length, of course, because all of the seventy explosive blocks were supposed to detonate at the same instant. With the krytons and the simple expedient of cutting each wire to the same length, this was easy to achieve.

The impulses reached the detonators simultaneously.

Each explosive block had three separate detonators, and none of them failed to function. The detonators were small wire filaments, sufficiently thin that the arriving current exploded each. The impulse was transferred into the explosive blocks, and the physical detonation process began 4.4 nanoseconds after the signal was transmitted by the timer. The result was not an explosion, but an *im*plosion, since the explosive force was mainly focused inward.

The high-explosives blocks were actually very sophisticated laminates of two materials, each laced with dust from light and heavy metals. The outer layer in each case was a relatively slow explosive with a detonation speed of just over seven thousand meters per second. The explosive wave in each expanded radially from the detonator, quickly reaching the edge of the block. Since the blocks were detonated from the outside-in, the blast front traveled inward through the blocks. The border between the slow and fast explosives contained bubbles – called voids – which began to change the shock-wave from spherical-shaped to a planar, or flat wave, which was refocused again to match exactly its metallic target, called 'drivers.'

The 'driver' in each case was a piece of carefully-shaped tungsten-rhenium. These were hit by a force wave traveling at more than nine thousand eight hundred meters (six miles) per second. Inside the tungsten-rhenium was a one-centimeter layer of beryllium. Beyond that was a one-millimeter thickness of uranium 235, which though thin weighed almost as much as the far thicker beryllium. The entire metallic mass was driving across a vacuum, and since the implosion was focused on a central point, the actual closing speed of opposite segments of the bomb was 18,600 meters (or 11.5 miles) per second.

The central aiming point of the explosives and the metallic projectiles was a ten kilogram (22 pound) mass of radioactive plutonium 239. It was shaped like a glass tumbler whose top had been bent outwards and down towards the bottom, creating two parallel walls of metal.

Ordinarily denser than lead, the plutonium was compressed further by the million-atmospheres pressure of the implosion. This had to be done very quickly. The plutonium 239 mass also included a small but troublesome quantity of plutonium 240, which was even less stable and prone to pre-ignition. The outer and inner surfaces were slammed together and driven in turn towards the geometric center of the weapon.

The final external act came from a device called a 'zipper.' Operating off the third signal from the still-intact electronic timer, the zipper was a miniature particle accelerator, a very compact mini-cyclotron that looked remarkably like a hand-held hair-dryer. This fired deuterium atoms at a beryllium target. Neutrons traveling ten percent of the speed of light were generated in vast numbers and traveled down a metal tube into the center of the Primary, called the Pit. The neutrons were timed to arrive just as the plutonium reached half of its peak density.

Ordinarily, a material weighing roughly twice an equivalent mass of lead, the plutonium was already ten times denser than that and still accelerating inward. The bombardment of neutrons entered a mass of still-compressing plutonium.

Fission.

The plutonium atom has an atomic weight of 239, that being the combined number of neutrons and protons in the atomic nucleus. What began happened at literally millions of places at once, but each event was precisely the same. An invading 'slow' neutron passed close enough to a plutonium nucleus to fall under the Strong Nuclear Force that holds atomic nuclei together. The neutron was pulled into the atom's center, changing the energy state of the host nucleus and kicking it into an unstable state. The once symmetrical atomic nucleus began gyrating wildly and was torn apart by force fluctuations. In most cases a neutron or proton disappeared entirely, converted to energy in homage to Einstein's law $E = MC^2$. The energy that resulted from the disappearance of the particles was released in the form of gamma and X-radiation, or any of thirty or so other but less important routes. Finally, the atomic nucleus released two or three additional neutrons. This was the important part. The process that had required only one neutron to start released two or three more, each traveling at over 10 percent of the speed of light – 20,000 miles per second – through space occupied by a plutonium mass two hundred times the density of water. The majority of the newly-liberated atomic particles found targets to hit.

A chain-reaction merely means that the process builds on itself, that the energy released is sufficient to continue the process without outside assistance. The fission of the plutonium proceeded in steps called 'doublings.' The energy liberated by each step was double that of the preceding one, and that of each subsequent step was doubled again. What began as a trivial amount of energy and just a handful of freed particles doubled and redoubled, and the interval between steps was measured in fractions of nanoseconds. The rate of increase – that is, the acceleration of the chain reaction – is called the 'Alpha,' and is the most important variable in the fission process. An Alpha of 1,000 means that the number of doublings per microsecond is a vast number, 2^{1000} – the number 2 multiplied by itself one *thousand* times. At peak fission – between 2^{50} and 2^{53} – the bomb would be generating 10 billion billion watts of power, one hundred thousand times the electrical-generating capacity of the entire world. Fromm had designed the bomb to do just that – and that was only ten percent of the weapon's total designed output. The Secondary had yet to be affected. No part of it had yet been touched by the forces only a few inches away.

But the fission process had scarcely begun.

Some of the gamma rays, traveling at the speed of light, were outside the bomb case while the plutonium was still being compressed by the explosives. Even nuclear reactions take time. Other gamma rays started to impact on the Secondary. The majority of the gammas streaked through a gas cloud that only a few microseconds earlier had been the chemical explosive blocks, heating it far beyond the temperatures chemicals alone could achieve. Made up of very light atoms like carbon and oxygen, this cloud emitted a vast quantity of low-frequency 'soft' X-rays. To this point, the device was functioning exactly as Fromm and Ghosn had planned.

The fission process was seven nanoseconds – 0.7 shakes – old when something went wrong.

Radiation from the fissioning plutonium blazed in on the tritium-impregnated lithium-deuteride that occupied the geometric center of the Pit. The reason Manfred Fromm had left the tritium extraction to last lay in his basic engineer's conservatism. Tritium is an unstable gas, with a half-life of 12.3 years, meaning that a quantity of pure tritium will, after that time, be composed half of tritium and half of ^{3}He. Called 'helium-three,' ^{3}He is a form of that second-lightest of elements whose nucleus lacks an extra neutron, and craves another. By filtering the gas through a thin block of palladium, the ^{3}He would have been easily separated out, but Ghosn hadn't known about that. As a result, more than a fifth of the tritium was the wrong material. It could hardly have been a worse material.

The intense bombardment from the adjacent fission reaction seared the lithium compound. Normally a material half the density of salt, it was compressed to a metallic state that exceeded the density of the earth's core. What began was actually a fusion reaction, though a small one, releasing huge quantities of new neutrons, and also changing many of the lithium atoms into more tritium, which broke down – 'fused' – under the intense pressure to release yet more neutrons. The additional neutrons generated were supposed to invade the plutonium mass, boosting the Alpha and causing at least a doubling of the weapon's unboosted fission yield. This had been the first method of increasing the power of the second-generation nuclear weapons. But the presence of ^{3}He poisoned the reaction, trapping nearly a quarter of the high-energy neutrons in uselessly stable helium atoms.

For several more nanoseconds, this did not matter.

797

The plutonium was still increasing its reaction rate, still doubling, still increasing its Alpha at a rate only expressible numerically.

Energy was now flooding into the Secondary. The metallically-coated straws flashed to plasma, pressing inward on the Secondary. Radiant energy in quantities not found on the surface of the sun vaporized but also reflected off elliptical surfaces, delivering yet more energy to the Secondary assembly, called the *Holraum*. The plasma from the immolated straws pounded inward towards the second reservoir of lithium compounds. The dense uranium 238 fins just outside the Secondary pit also flashed to dense plasma, driving inward through the vacuum, then striking and compressing the tubular containment of more ^{238}U around the central container which held the largest quantity of lithium-deuteride/tritium. The forces were immense, and the structure was pounded with a degree of pressure greater than that of a healthy stellar core.

But not enough.

The Primary's reaction had already slackened. Starved of neutrons by the presence of the ^{3}He poison, the bomb's explosive force began to blow apart the reaction mass as soon as the physical forces reached their balance. The chain reaction reached a moment of stability, at last unable to sustain its geometric rate of growth; the last two chain-reaction doublings were lost entirely, and what should have been a total Primary yield of seventy thousand tons of TNT was halved, halved again, and in fact ended with a total yield of eleven thousand two hundred tons of high explosive.

Fromm's design had been as perfect as the circumstances and materials allowed. An equivalent weapon less than a quarter the size was possible, but his specifications were more than adequate. A massive safety factor in the energy budget had been planned for. Even a thirty kiloton yield would have been enough to ignite the 'sparkplug' in the Secondary to start a massive fusion 'burn,' but thirty-KT was not reached. The bomb was technically called a 'fizzle.'

But it was a fizzle equivalent to eleven thousand two hundred tons of TNT. That could be represented by a cube of high explosives seventy-five feet high, seventy-five feet long, and seventy-five feet thick, as much as could be carried by nearly four hundred trucks, or one medium-sized ship – but conventional explosives could never have detonated with anything approaching this deadly efficiency; in fact, a conventional explosion of this magnitude is a practical impossibility. For all that, it was still a fizzle.

As yet no perceptible physical effects had even left the bomb case, much less the truck. The steel case remained largely intact, though that would rapidly change. Gamma radiation had already escaped, along with X-rays, but these were invisible. Visible light had not yet emerged from the plasma cloud that had only three 'shakes' before been over a thousand pounds of exquisitely designed hardware . . . and yet, everything that was to happen had already taken place. All that remained now was the distribution of the energy already released by natural laws which neither knew nor cared about the purposes of their manipulators.

CHAPTER 36

Weapons Effects

Sergeant Ed Yankevich should have been the first to notice what was happening. His eyes were on the van, and he was walking in that direction, scarcely forty feet away, but the human nervous system works in milliseconds and no faster.

The fizzle had just ended when the first radiation reached the police officer. These were gamma rays, which are actually photons, the same stuff that light waves are made of, but far more energetic. They were already attacking the body of the truck as well, causing the sheet steel to fluoresce like neon. Immediately behind the gammas were X-rays, also composed of photons but less energetic. The difference was lost on Yankevich, who would be the first to die. The intense radiation was most readily absorbed by his bones, which rapidly heated to incandescence, while at the same time the neurons of his brain were simultaneously excited as though each had become a flashbulb. In fact, Sergeant Yankevich was unable to notice a thing. He literally disintegrated, exploded from within by the tiny fraction of energy his body was able to absorb as the rest raced through him. But the gammas and X-rays were heading in all possible directions at the speed of light, and their next effect was one no one had anticipated.

Adjacent to the van, whose body was now being reduced to molecular bits of metal, was ABC's 'A' satellite unit. Inside were several people who would have no more time to sense their fate than Sergeant Yankevich. The same was true of the elaborate and expensive electrical equipment in the van. But at the rear of this vehicle, pointing south and upward was a large parabolic-dish antenna, not unlike the kind used for radar. In the center of this, like the stamen of a flower, was the wave guide, essentially a metal tube with a square cross-section, whose inside dimensions roughly approximated the wave-length of the signal it was now broadcasting to a satellite 22,600 miles over the equator.

The wave guide of the 'A' unit, and soon thereafter each of the eleven trucks lined up west of it, was struck by the gammas and X-rays. In the process, electrons were blasted off the atoms of the metal – in some cases the guides were lined with gold plate, which accentuated the process – which gave up their energy at once in the form of photons. These photons formed waves whose frequency was roughly that of the satellite up-link transmitters. There was one difference: the up-link trucks were in no case transmitting as much as one thousand watts of radio-frequency – RF – energy, and in most cases far less than that. The energy transfer from the 'A' unit's wave guide, however, released nearly a million watts of energy in one brief, orgasmic pulse that ended in less than a microsecond as the antenna and the associated truck were also vaporized by the searing energy front. Next to go was the ABC 'B' unit, then TWI. NHK, which was send-ing the Superbowl to Japan, was the fourth van in the line. There were eight more. All were destroyed. This process took approximately fifteen 'shakes.' The satellites to which they transmitted were a long distance away. It would take the energy roughly an eighth of a second to span the distance, a relative eternity.

Next to emerge from the explosion – the truck was now part of it – was light and heat energy. The first blast of light escaped just before the expanding fireball blocked it. The second installment escaped soon there-after, radiating in all directions. This generated the two-phase pulse which is characteristic of nuclear deton-ations.

The next energy effect was blast. This was actually a secondary effect. The air absorbed much of the soft X-rays and was burned into an opaque mass which stopped further electromagnetic radiation, transforming it into mechanical energy that expanded at several times the speed of sound, but before that energy had a chance to damage anything, more distant events were already underway.

The primary ABC video link was actually by fiber-optic cable – a high-quality landline – but the cable ran through the 'A' van and was cut even before the stadium itself was damaged. The backup link was through the Telstar 301 satellite, and the Pacific Coast was serviced by Telstar 302. ABC used the Net-1 and Net-2 primary links on each bird. Also using Telstar 301 was Trans World International, which represented the NFL's world-wide rights and distributed the game to most of Europe, plus Israel and Egypt. TWI sent the same video signal to all its European clients, and also provided facilities for separate audio uplinks in the various European languages, which usually meant more than one audio link per country. Spain, for example, accounted for five dialects, each of which had its own audio sideband-channel. NHK, broadcasting to Japan, used both the JISO-F2R satellite and its regular full-time link, Westar 4, which was owned and operated by Hughes Aerospace. Italian TV used Major Path 1 of the Teleglobe satellite (owned by the Intelsat conglomerate) to feed its own viewers, plus those in Dubai and whatever Israelis didn't like the play-by-play through TWI and Telstar. Teleglobe's Major Path 2 was delegated to serve most of South America. Also present, either right at the stadium or a short distance away, were CNN, ABC's own news division, CBS Newsnet, and ESPN. Local Denver stations had their own satellite trucks on the scene, their uses mainly rented to outsiders.

There was a total of 37 active satellite up-link trucks using either microwave or Ku-band transmitters to generate a total of 48 active video, and 168 active audio signals, all feeding over a billion sports fans in seventy-one countries when the gamma and X-ray flux struck. In most cases, the impact generated a signal in the wave guides, but in six trucks, the traveling-wave tubes themselves were illuminated first and put out a gigantic pulse on exactly the proper frequencies. Even that was beside the point, however. Resonances and otherwise inconsequential irregularities within the wave guides meant that wide segments of the satellites orbiting over the Western Hemisphere were being worked by the TV crews at Denver. What happened to them is expressed simply. Their sensitive antennas were designed to receive billionths of watts. Instead, they were suddenly bombarded with between one and ten thousand times that on many separate channels. That surge overloaded an equal number of the front-end amplifiers inside the satellites. The computer software running the satellites took note of this and began to activate isolation switches to protect the sensitive equipment from the spike. Had the incident affected merely one such receiver, service would have been restored at once and nothing further would have happened, but commercial communications satellites are immensely expensive artifacts, costing hundreds of millions of dollars to build, and hundreds of millions more to launch into orbit. When more than five amplifiers recorded spikes, the software automatically began shutting circuits down, lest possibly serious damage to the entire satellite result. When twenty or more were affected, the software took the further step of deactivating all onboard circuits, and next firing off an emergency signal to its command ground station to say that something very serious had just happened. The safety software on the satellites were all customized variations of a single, very conservative program designed to safeguard billions of dollars' worth of nearly irreplaceable assets. In a brief flicker of time, a sizable fraction of the world's satellite communications dropped out of existence. Cable television and telecommunications systems all ceased, even before the technicians who managed their operations knew that something had gone disastrously wrong.

Pete Dawkins was resting for a moment. He thought of it as protecting the armored truck. The Wells Fargo guard was off delivering another few hundred pounds of quarters, and the police officer was sitting, his back against the shelves full of coin bags, listening to his radio. The Chargers were coming up to the line for a third-and-five at the Vikings' forty-seven. At that moment, the darkening sky outside turned incandescent yellow, then red – not the friendly, gentle red of a sunset, but a searing violet that was far brighter than that color could possibly have been. His mind barely had time to register that fact when it was assaulted by a million other things at once. The earth rose beneath him. The armored car was tossed up and sideways like a toy kicked by a child. The open rear door was slammed shut as if struck by a cannon. The body of the truck sheltered him from the shockwave – as did the body of the stadium, though Dawkins had not the time to realize it. Even so, he was nearly blinded by the flash that did reach him, and deafened by the over-pressure wave that swept across him like the crushing hand of a giant. Had Dawkins been less disoriented, he might have thought *earthquake*, but even that idea did not occur to him. Survival did. The noise had not stopped, nor had the shaking, when he realized that he was trapped inside a vehicle whose fuel tank contained perhaps as much as fifty gallons of gasoline. He blinked his eyes clear and started crawling out the shattered windshield towards the brightest spot he could see. He did not notice that the backs of his hands looked worse than any sunburn he'd ever had. He did not realize that he could not hear a thing. All he cared about was getting to the light.

Outside Moscow, in a bunker under sixty meters of concrete, is the national headquarters of *Voyska PVO*, the Soviet air-defense service. A new facility, it was designed much like its Western counterparts in the form of a theater, since this configuration allowed the maximum number of people to see the data displayed on the large wall that was required for the map displays which were needed for their duties. It was 03:00:13 local time, according to the digital clock over the display, 00:00:13 Zulu (Greenwich Mean) Time, 19:00:13 in Washington, D.C.

On duty was Lieutenant General Ivan Grigoriyevich

Kuropatkin, a former – he would have said 'current' – fighter pilot, now fifty-one years of age. The third-ranking man at this post, he was taking his place in the normal duty rotation. Though as a very senior officer he could have opted for more convenient hours, the new Soviet military was to be founded on professionalism, and professional officers, he thought, led by example. Arrayed around him were his usual battle staff, composed of colonels, majors, plus a leavening of captains and lieutenants for menial work.

The job of *Voyska PVO* was to defend the Soviet Union against attack. In the missile age and in the absence of an effective defense against ballistic missiles – both sides were still working on that – his duties were more to warn than defend. Kuropatkin didn't like that, but neither could he change it. In geo-synchronous orbit over the coast of Peru was a pair of satellites, called Eagle-I and -II, whose task it was to watch the United States and spot a missile launch just as soon as the missiles left their silos. The same satellites could also spot an SLBM launch from the Gulf of Alaska, though their coverage that far north was somewhat dependent on weather which, at the moment, was vile. The display from the orbiting Eagles was in the infra-red spectrum, which mainly measured heat. The display was presented as the camera perceived it, without border lines or other computer-generated data which, the Russian designers thought, simply cluttered the display unnecessarily. Kuropatkin was not looking up, but rather at a junior officer who seemed to be doing a calculation of some sort, when something caught his eye. His gaze shifted automatically, entirely without conscious thought, and it took fully a second for him to realize why.

There was a white dot in the center of the display.

'*Nichevo . . .*' He shook that off at once. 'Isolate and zoom in!' he ordered loudly. The colonel working the controls was sitting right next to him, and was already doing just that.

'Central United States, General. Double-flash thermal signature, that is a probable nuclear detonation,' the colonel said mechanically, his professional judgment overpowering his intellectual denial.

'Coordinates.'

'Working, General.' The distance from the Center to the satellite ensured a delay in getting things to happen. By the time the satellite's telescopic lens started moving in, the thermal signature from the fireball was expanding rapidly. Kuropatkin's immediate impression was that this could not possibly be a mistake, and as hot as that image was, what materialized in the pit of his stomach was a fist of ice.

'Central U.S., looks like the city of *Densva*.'

'Denver, what the hell's in Denver?' Kuropatkin demanded. 'Find out.'

'Yes, General.'

Kuropatkin was already reaching for a telephone. This line was a direct link to the Ministry of Defense and also the residence of the Soviet President. He spoke quickly but clearly.

'Attention: This is General-Lieutenant Kuropatkin at PVO Moscow Center. We have just registered a nuclear detonation in the United States. I repeat: we have just registered a nuclear detonation in the United States.'

One voice on the line swore. That would be President Narmonov's watch staff.

The other voice, that of the Defense Ministry's senior watch officer, was more reasoned. 'How sure are you of this?'

'Double-flash signature,' Kuropatkin replied, astounded at his own coolness. 'I'm watching the fireball expansion now. This *is* a nuclear event. I will call in more data as soon as I have it – what?' he asked a junior officer.

'General, Eagle-II just took one hell of an energy spike, four of the SHF links just shut down momentarily, and another is gone completely,' a major said, leaning over the General's desk.

'What happened, what was it?'

'I don't know.'

'Find out.'

The picture went blank just as San Diego were coming up for their third-and-five at the forty-seven. Fowler finished off his fourth beer of the afternoon and set the glass down in annoyance. Damned TV people. Someone probably tripped over a plug, and he'd miss a play or two in what looked like one hell of a game. He ought to have gone to this one, despite the advice of the Secret Service. He glanced over to see what Elizabeth was watching, but her screen had suddenly gone blank as well. Had one of the Marines driven over the cable with a snow-plow? Good help certainly was hard to come by, the President grumped. But no, that wasn't right. The ABC affiliate – Baltimore's Channel 13, WJZ – put up its 'Network Difficulty – Please Stand By' graphic, whereas Elizabeth's channel was just random noise now. How very odd. Like any male TV viewer, Fowler picked up the TV controller and changed channels. CNN was off the air, too, but the local Baltimore and Washington stations were not. He'd just started wondering what that meant when a phone started ringing. It had an unusually atonal, strident sound, and was one of the four kept on the lower shelf of the coffee table that sat right in front of his couch. He reached down for it before he realized which one it was, and that delayed understanding caused his skin to go cold. It was the red phone, the one from North American Aerospace Defense Command at Cheyenne Mountain, Colorado.

'This is the President,' Fowler said in a gruff, suddenly frightened voice.

'Mr President, this is Major General Joe Borstein. I am the senior NORAD watch officer. Sir, we have just registered a nuclear detonation in the Central United States.'

'What?' the President said after two or three seconds' pause.

'Sir, there's been a nuclear explosion. We're checking the exact location now, but it appears to have been in the Denver area.'

'Are you sure?' the President asked, fighting to keep calm.

'We're re-checking our instruments now, sir, but, yes,

we're pretty sure. Sir, we don't know what happened or how it got there, but there was a nuclear explosion. I urge you to get to a place of safety at once while we try and figure out what's going on.'

Fowler looked up. Neither TV picture had changed and now alarm klaxons were erupting all over the Presidential compound.

Offutt Air Force Base, just outside Omaha, Nebraska, was once known as Fort Crook. The former cavalry post had a splendid if somewhat anachronistic collection of red brick dwellings for its most senior officers, in the rear of which was stabling for the horses they no longer needed, and in front of which was a flat parade ground of sufficient size to exercise a regiment of cavalry. About a mile from that was the headquarters of the Strategic Air Command, a much more modern building with its own antique, a B-17 Flying Fortress of World War II, sitting outside. Also outside the building but below ground was the new command post, completed in 1989. A capacious room, local wags joked that it had been built because Hollywood's rendition of such rooms was better than the one SAC had originally built for itself, and the Air Force had decided to alter its reality to fit a fictional image.

Major General Chuck Timmons, Deputy Chief of Staff (Operations), had availed himself of the opportunity to stand his watch here instead of in his upstairs office, and had in fact been watching the Superbowl out of one eye on one of the eight large-screen TVs, but on two of the others had been real-time imagery from the Defense Support Program Satellites, called the DSPS birds, and he had caught the double-flash at Denver just as fast as everyone else. Timmons dropped the pencil he'd been working with. Behind his battle-staff seat were several glassed-in rooms – there were two levels of such rooms – which contained the fifty or so support personnel who kept SAC operating around the clock. Timmons lifted his phone and punched the button for the senior intelligence officer.

'I see it, sir.'

'Possible mistake?'

'Negative, sir, test circuitry says the bird's working just fine.'

'Keep me posted.' Timmons turned to his deputy. 'Get the boss in here. Beep everybody, I want a full emergency-action team and a full battle-staff – and I want it now!' To his operations officer: 'Get Looking Glass up now! I want the alert wings postured for takeoff, and I want an immediate alert flashed to everybody.'

In the glassed-in room behind the General and to his left, a sergeant pushed a few buttons. Though SAC had long since ceased keeping aircraft in the air around the clock, thirty percent of SAC's aircraft were typically kept on alert status at any time. The order out to the alert wings was sent by land-line and used a computer-generated voice, because it had been decided that a human might get excited and slur his words. The orders took perhaps twenty seconds to be transmitted, and the operations officers at the alert wings were galvanized to action.

At the moment, that meant two wings, the 416th Bomb Wing at Griffiss Air Force Base, Plattsburg, New York, which flew the B-52, and the 384th, which flew the B-1B out of nearby McConnell Air Force Base in Kansas. At the latter, crewmen in their ready rooms, nearly all of whom had also been watching the Superbowl, raced out the door to waiting vehicles which took them to their guarded aircraft. The first man from each crew of four slapped the emergency-startup button that was part of the nosewheel assembly, then ran further aft to sprint up the ladder into the aircraft. Even before the crews were strapped in, the engines were starting up. The ground crews yanked off the red-flagged safety pins. Rifle-armed sentries got out of the way of the aircraft, training their weapons outward to engage any possible threat. To this point, no one knew that this was anything more than a particularly ill-timed drill.

At McConnell, the first aircraft to move was the wing commander's personal B-1B. An athletic forty-five, the colonel also had the advantage of having his aircraft parked closest to the alert shack. As soon as all four of his engines were turning and the way cleared, he tripped his brakes and began to taxi his aircraft towards the end of the runway. That took two minutes, and on reaching the spot, he was told to wait.

At Offutt, the alert KC-135 was under no such restrictions. Called 'Looking Glass,' the converted – and twenty-five-year-old – Boeing 707 had aboard a general officer and a complete if downsized battle-staff. It was just lifting off into the falling darkness. Onboard radios and command links were just coming on line, and the officer aboard hadn't yet learned what all the hubbub was about. Behind him on the ground, three more additional and identical aircraft were being prepped for departure.

'What gives, Chuck?' CINC-SAC said as he came in. He was wearing casual clothes, and his shoes were not tied yet.

'Nuclear detonation at Denver, also some trouble on satellite communications links that we just found out about. I've postured the alert aircraft. Looking Glass just lifted off. Still don't know what the hell's going on, but Denver just blew up.'

'Get 'em off,' the Commander-in-Chief Strategic Air Command ordered. Timmons gestured to a communications officer, who relayed the order. Twenty seconds later, the first B-1B roared down the runway at McConnell.

It was not a time for niceties. A Marine captain pushed open the door into the President's cabin and tossed two white parkas at Fowler and Elliot even before the first Secret Service agent showed up.

'Right now, sir!' he urged. 'Chopper's still broke, sir.'

'Where to?' Pete Connor arrived with his overcoat unbuttoned, just in time to hear what the Marine had said.

'Command post, 'less you say different. Chopper's broke,' the captain said yet again. 'Come on, sir!' he nearly screamed at the President.

'Bob!' Elliot said in some alarm. She didn't know what the President had heard over the phone, merely that he looked pale and sick. Both donned their parkas and came outside. They saw that a full squad of Marines lay in the snow, their loaded rifles pointed outward. Six more stood around the Hummer whose engine was screaming in neutral.

At Anacostia Naval Air Station in Washington, the crew of Marine Two – it wouldn't be Marine One until the President got aboard – was just lifting off amid a worrisome cloud of snow, but in a few seconds they were above the ground effect and able to see fairly well. The pilot, a major, turned his aircraft northwest, wondering what the hell was happening. The only people who knew anything knew merely that they didn't know very much. For a few minutes, this would not matter. As with any organization, responses to a sudden emergency were planned beforehand and had been thoroughly rehearsed both to get things done and to attenuate the panic that might come from indecision mixed with danger.

'What the hell is going on in Denver that I need to know about?' General Kuropatkin asked in his hole outside Moscow.

'Nothing I know of,' his intelligence officer replied honestly.

That's a big help, the General thought. He lifted the phone to the Soviet military intelligence agency, the GRU.

'Operations/Watch Center,' a voice answered.

'This is General Kuropatkin at PVO Moscow.'

'I know the reason for your call,' the GRU colonel assured him.

'What is happening at Denver? Is there a nuclear-weapons storage facility, anything like that?'

'No, General. Rocky Mountain Arsenal is near there. That is a storage center for chemical weapons, in the process of being deactivated. It's turning into a depot for the American reserve army – they call it the National Guard – tanks and mechanized equipment. Outside

Denver is Rocky Flats. They used to fabricate weapons components there, but –'

'Where exactly?' Kuropatkin asked.

'Northwest of the city. I believe the explosion is in the southern part of Denver, General.'

'Correct. Go on.'

'Rocky Flats is also in the process of deactivation. To the best of our knowledge, there are no more weapons components to be found there.'

'Do they transport weapons through there? I *must know something*?' The General was finally getting excited.

'I have nothing more to tell you. We're as much in the dark as you. Perhaps KGB has more, but we do not.'

You couldn't shoot a man for honesty, Kuropatkin knew. He switched lines again. Like most professional soldiers, he had little use for spies, but the next call was a necessity.

'State Security, command center,' a male voice said.

'American department, the duty watch officer.'

'Stand by.' There was the usual chirping and clicking, and a female voice answered next. 'American desk.'

'This is General-Lieutenant Kuropatkin at PVO Moscow Center,' the man said yet again. 'I need to know what, if anything, is happening in the Central United States, the city of Denver.'

'Very little, I would imagine. Denver is a major city, and a large administrative center for the American government, the second-largest after Washington, in fact. It is a Sunday evening there, and very little should be happening, at the moment.' Kuropatkin heard pages riffling. 'Oh, yes.'

'Yes, what?'

'The final game in the championship-elimination series of American-rules football. It is being played in the new Denver city stadium which, I believe, is an enclosed structure.'

Kuropatkin managed not to curse the woman for that irrelevancy. 'I don't need *that*. Is there any civil unrest, any sort of disturbance or ongoing problem? A weapons-storage facility, a secret base of some sort that I don't know about?'

'General, everything we have on such subjects is available to you. What is the nature of your inquiry?'

'Woman, there has been a nuclear explosion there.'

'In Denver?'

'Yes!'

'Where, exactly?' she asked, cooler than the General was.

'Stand by.' Kuropatkin turned. 'I need coordinates on the explosion and I need them now!'

'Thirty-nine degrees forty minutes north latitude, one hundred five degrees six minutes west longitude. Those numbers are approximate,' the lieutenant on the satellite desk added. 'Our resolution isn't very good in the infra-red spectrum, General.' Kuropatkin relayed the numbers.

'Wait,' the woman's voice said. 'I need to fetch a map.'

Andrey Il'ych Narmonov was asleep. It was now three-ten in the morning in Moscow. The phone woke him, and an instant later his bedroom door opened. Narmonov nearly panicked at the second event. No one ever entered his bedroom without permission. It was KGB Major Pavel Khrulev, the assistant chief of the president's personal security detail.

'My President, there is an emergency. You must come with me at once.'

'What is the matter, Pasha?'

'There has been a nuclear explosion in America.'

'What – who?'

'That is all I know. We must go at once to the command bunker. The car is waiting. Don't bother getting dressed.' Khrulev tossed him a robe.

Ryan stubbed out his cigarette, still annoyed at the 'Technical Difficulty – Please Stand By' sign that was keeping him from watching the game. Goodley came in with a couple cans of Coke. Dinner was already ordered.

'What gives?' Goodley asked.

'Picture went out.' Ryan took his Coke and popped it open.

At SAC Headquarters, a lieutenant-colonel at the far left side of the third row of battle-staff seats consulted the TV-controller card. The room had eight TV displays, arranged in two horizontal rows of four. One could call up more than fifty individual displays, and the woman was an intelligence officer whose first instinct was to check the new channels. A quick manipulation of her controller showed that both CNN and its subsidiary CNN Headline News were off the air. She knew that they used different satellite circuits, and that piqued her curiosity, perhaps the most important aspect of intelligence work. The system also allowed access to other cable channels, and she started going through them. HBO was off the air. Showtime was off the air. ESPN was off the air. She checked her directory and concluded that at least four satellites were not functioning. At that point, the colonel got up and walked over to CINC-SAC.

'Sir, there's something very odd here,' she said.

'What's that?' CINC-SAC said without turning.

'At least four commercial satellites appear to be down. That includes a Telstar, an Intelsat, and a Hughes bird. They're all down, sir.'

That notification caused CINC-SAC to turn. 'What else can you tell me?'

'Sir, NORAD reports that the explosion was in the Denver metropolitan area, very close to the Skydome where they were playing the Superbowl. SecState and SecDef were both at the game, sir.'

'Christ, you're right,' CINC-SAC realized instantly.

At Andrews Air Force Base, the National Emergency Airborne Command Post – NEACP, pronounced 'Kneecap' – was positioned on the ramp with two of its four engines turning, waiting for someone to arrive so that the crew could take off.

*

Captain Jim Rosselli had barely been on duty for an hour when this nightmare arrived. He sat in the NMCC Crisis Management Room, wishing a flag officer was here. That was not to be. While there had once been a General or Admiral in the National Military Command Center at all times, the thaw between East and West and the downsizing of the Pentagon now meant that a senior officer was always on call, but the day-to-day administrative work was handled by captains and colonels. It could have been worse, Rosselli thought. At least he knew what it was to have lots of nuclear weapons at his disposal.

'What the *fuck* is going on?' Lieutenant-Colonel Richard Barnes asked the wall. He knew that Rosselli didn't know.

'Rocky, can we save that for another time?' Rosselli asked calmly. His voice was dead-level. One might never have known from looking at or listening to the captain that he was excited, but the former submarine commander's hands were so moist that by rubbing them on his trousers he'd already created a damp spot that their navy-blue color made invisible.

'You got it, Jim.'

'Call General Wilkes, let's get him in here.'

'Right.' Barnes punched a button on the secure phone, calling Brigadier General Paul Wilkes, a former bomber pilot who lived in official housing on Bolling Air Force Base, just across the Potomac from National Airport.

'Yeah,' Wilkes said gruffly.

'Barnes here, sir. We need you in the NMCC immediately.' That was all the colonel had to say. 'Immediately' is a word that has special meaning for an aviator.

'On the way.' Wilkes hung up and muttered further: 'Thank God for four-wheel-drive.' He struggled into an olive-drab winter parka and headed out the door without bothering with boots. His personal car was a Toyota Land Cruiser that he liked for driving the back country. It started at once, and he backed out, struggling across roads not yet plowed.

*

The Presidential Crisis Room at Camp David was an anachronistic leftover from the bad old days, or so Bob Fowler had thought on first seeing it over a year before. Constructed during the Eisenhower Administration, it had been designed to resist nuclear attack in an age when the accuracy of a missile was measured in miles rather than yards. Blasted into the living granite rock of the Catoctin Mountains of western Maryland, it had a solid sixty feet of overhead protection, and until 1975 or so had been a highly secure and survivable shelter. About thirty feet wide and forty deep, with a ten-foot ceiling, it contained a staff of twelve, mostly Navy communications types, of whom six were enlisted men. The equipment was not quite as modern as that on NEACP or certain other facilities that the President might use. He sat at a console that looked like 1960s NASA in configuration. There was even an ashtray built into the desktop. In front of him was a bank of television sets. The chair was a comfortable one, even if the situation decidedly was not. Elizabeth Elliot took the one next to his.

'Okay,' President J. Robert Fowler said, 'what the hell is going on?'

The senior briefing officer, he saw, was a Navy lieutenant-commander. That was not very promising.

'Sir, your helicopter is down with a mechanical problem. A second Marine helo is on its way here now to get you to Kneecap. We have CINC-SAC and CINC-NORAD on line. These buttons here give you direct lines to all the other CINCs.' By this, the naval officer meant the Commanders-in-Chief of major joint-service commands: CINCLANT was Commander-in-Chief Atlantic, Admiral Joshua Painter, USN; there was a corresponding CINC-PAC in charge of Pacific area forces, and both were traditionally Navy posts. CINC-SOUTH was in Panama, CINC-CENT in Bahrain, CINC-FOR — heading Forces Command — was at Fort McPherson in Atlanta, Georgia, all three of which were traditionally Army posts. There were others as well, including SACEUR, Supreme Allied Commander Europe, the chief NATO military officer, who at the moment was an Air

Force four-star general. Under the existing command system, the service chiefs actually had no command authority. Instead, they advised the Secretary of Defense, who in turn advised the President. Presidential orders were issued from the President through the SecDef directly to the CINCs.

But the SecDef . . .

Fowler looked for the button labeled NORAD and pushed it.

'This is the President. I am in my Camp David communications room.'

'Mr President, this is still Major General Borstein. CINC-NORAD is not here, sir. He was in Denver for the Superbowl. Mr President, it is my duty to advise you that our instruments put the detonation either at or very near the Skydome stadium in Denver. It would appear very likely that Secretaries Bunker and Talbot are both dead, along with CINC-NORAD.'

'Yes,' Fowler said. There was no emotion in his voice. He'd already reached that conclusion.

'The Vice-CINC is traveling at the moment. I will be the senior NORAD officer for the next few hours until someone more senior manages to get back.'

'Very well. Now: what the hell is going on?'

'Sir, we do not know. The detonation was not preceded by anything unusual. There was not – I repeat, sir, *not* – a ballistic inbound track prior to the explosion. We are trying to contact the air controllers at Stapleton International Airport to have them check their radar tapes for a possible airborne delivery vehicle. We didn't see anything coming in on any of our scopes.'

'Would you have seen an inbound aircraft?'

'Not necessarily, sir,' General Borstein replied. 'It's a good system, but there are ways to beat it, especially if you use a single aircraft. In any case, Mr President, there are some things we need to do at once. Can we talk about that for a moment?'

'Yes.'

'Sir, on my own command authority as acting-CINC-NORAD, I have placed my command on DEFCON-ONE alert. As you know, NORAD has that authority, and also nuclear-release authority for defensive purposes only.'

'You will not release any nuclear weapons without my authorization,' Fowler said forcefully.

'Sir, the only nukes we have in our inventory are in storage,' Borstein said. His voice was admirably mechanical, the other uniformed people thought. 'I propose that we next initiate a conference call with CINC-SAC.'

'Do it,' Fowler ordered. It happened instantly.

'Mr President, this is CINC-SAC,' General Peter Fremont, USAF announced. His voice was all business.

'What the hell is going on?'

'Sir, we do not know that, but there are some things we should do immediately.'

'Go on.'

'Sir, I recommend that we immediately place all of our strategic forces on a higher alert level. I recommend DEFCON-TWO. If we are dealing with a nuclear attack, we should posture our forces to maximum readiness. That will enable us to respond to an attack with the greatest possible effect. It could also have the effect of deterring whoever got this thing underway, in the event that he might have – or we could give him – second thoughts.'

'If I can add to that, sir, we should also increase our readiness across the board. If for no other reason, the availability of military units to provide assistance and to reduce possible civilian panic might be very useful. I recommend DEFCON-THREE for conventional forces.'

'Better to do that selectively, Robert,' Liz Elliot said.

'I heard that – who is it?' Borstein asked.

'This is the National Security Advisor,' Liz said, a touch too loudly. She was as pale as her white silk blouse. Fowler was still under control. Elliot was struggling to do the same.

'We have not met, Dr Elliot. Unfortunately, our command-and-control systems do not allow us to do that selectively – at least not very fast. By sending out the alert now, however, we can activate all the units we need, then select the units we need to do things while they come on line. That will save us at least an hour. That is my recommendation.'

'I concur in that,' General Fremont added at once.

'Very well, do it,' Fowler said. It sounded reasonable enough.

The communications were handled through separate channels. CINC-SAC handled the strategic forces. The first Emergency Action Message used the same robotic voice that had already scrambled the alerted SAC wings. While the SAC bomber bases already knew that they were being alerted, the DEFCON-TWO notice made it official and far more ominous. Fiber-optic land-lines carried a similar notice to the Navy's Extremely Low Frequency radio system located in Michigan's Upper Peninsula region. This signal had to be sent out by mechanical Morse. The nature of this radio system was such that it could only send out its characters very slowly, rather like the speed of a novice typist, and it acted as a cueing system, telling submarines to come to the surface for a more detailed message to be delivered by satellite radios.

At King's Bay, Georgia, Charleston, South Carolina, and Groton, Connecticut, and at three other locations in the Pacific, signals by land-line and satellite link were received by the duty staffs of the missile submarine squadrons, most of them aboard submarine tenders. Of America's thirty-six missile submarines in service at the moment, nineteen were at sea, on 'deterrence patrol,' as it was called. Two were in yard-overhaul status, and were totally unavailable for duty. The rest were tied up alongside tenders, except for USS *Ohio*, which was in the boat shed at Bangor. All had reduced crews aboard, though not one had her CO aboard this Sunday evening. That didn't really matter. The 'boomers' all had two crews, and in every case one of the two commanding officers assigned to each boat was within thirty minutes of his command. All carried beepers, which went off almost simultaneously. The duty crews aboard each submarine began preparations for immediate sortie. The

Command Duty Officer on each boomer was an officer who had passed the stringent test required before a submariner could be 'qualified for command.' Their operational orders were clear: when this sort of alert came, they had to get to sea just as fast as possible. Most thought it a drill, but drills for strategic forces were a serious business. Already, tugboats were lighting up their diesels to help the slate-gray hulls away from the tenders. Deck crews were removing safety lines and stanchions, as men who'd been aboard the tenders scrambled down the ladders to their various ships. Aboard, division officers and assistants checked their rosters to see who was aboard and who was not. The fact of the matter was that these warships, like all warships, were overmanned. They could easily sail and operate with half a crew if they had to. DEFCON-TWO meant that they had to.

Captain Rosselli and the NMCC staff handled the conventional forces. Pre-set recordings went directly to the individual units. In the Army, that meant division level. In the Air Force, it was at the wing level, and in the Navy, it was at the squadron level. The conventional forces were going to DEFCON-THREE. Captain Rosselli and Colonel Barnes handled voice lines to higher command levels. Even when talking to three-star officers with no less than twenty-five years of service each, it was necessary to tell every single one that: *no, sir, this is not repeat not a drill.*

American military units all over the world went instantly on alert. As was to be expected, those units which ordinarily maintained high alert levels responded the most quickly. One of these was the Berlin Brigade.

CHAPTER 37

Human Effects

'Captain, we have an Emergency Action Message on the ELF.'

'What?' Ricks asked, turning away from the chart table.

'Emergency Action Message, Captain.' The communications officer handed over the brief code group.

'Great time for a drill.' Ricks shook his head and said, 'Battle Stations. Alert-One.'

A petty officer immediately activated the 1-MC and made the announcement. 'General Quarters, General Quarters, all hands man your battle stations.' Next came an electronic alarm sure to end the most captivating of dreams.

'Mr Pitney,' Ricks said over the noise. 'Antenna depth.'

'Aye, Captain. Diving officer, make your depth six-zero feet.'

'Make my depth six-zero feet, aye. Helm, ten degrees up on the fairwater planes.'

'Ten degrees up on the fairwater planes, aye.' The young crewman – helm duty is typically given to very junior men – pulled back on the aircraft-like wheel. 'Sir, my planes are up ten degrees.'

'Very well.'

Barely had that been done when people flooded into the control room. The Chief of the Boat – *Maine*'s senior enlisted man – took his battle station at the air-manifold panel. He was the submarine's senior Diving Officer. Lieutenant-Commander Claggett entered the conn to back the captain up. Pitney, the boat's navigator, was already at his post, which was conning officer. Various enlisted men took their seats at weapons consoles. Aft, officers and men assumed their positions as different as the Missile Control Center – MCC – which monitored the status of *Maine*'s twenty-four Trident missiles, and the auxiliary equipment room, which was mainly concerned with the ship's backup diesel engine.

In the control room, the IC – internal communications – man of the watch called off the compartments as they reported in as manned and ready.

'What gives?' Claggett asked Ricks. The captain merely handed over the brief EAM slip.

'Drill?'

'I suppose. Why not?' Ricks asked. 'It's a Sunday, right?'

'Still bumpy up on the roof?'

As though on cue, *Maine* started taking rolls. The depth gauge showed 290 feet, and the massive submarine suddenly rocked ten degrees to starboard. Throughout the vessel, men rolled their eyes and grumbled. There was scarcely a man aboard who hadn't lost it at least once. This was the perfect environment for motion sickness. With no outside references – submarines are conspicuously short of windows and portholes – the eyes saw something that clearly was not moving while the inner ears reported that movement was definitely taking place. The same thing that had affected nearly all of the Apollo astronauts began to affect these sailors. Unconsciously, men shook their heads sharply, as though to repel a bothersome insect. They uniformly hoped that whatever the hell they were up to – no one from Ricks on down knew as yet what was happening – they'd soon be able to get back where they belonged – four hundred feet, where the ship's motion was imperceptible.

'Level at six-zero feet, sir.'

'Very well,' Pitney replied.

'Conn, sonar, contact lost on Sierra-16. Surface noise is screwing us all up.'

'What's the last position?' Ricks asked.

'Last bearing was two-seven-zero, estimated range four-nine thousand yards,' Ensign Shaw replied.

'Okay. Run up the UHF antenna. Up scope,' he also ordered the quartermaster of the watch. *Maine* was taking twenty-degree rolls now, and Ricks wanted to see why. The quartermaster rotated the red-and-white control wheel, and the oiled cylinder hissed up on hydraulic power.

'Wow,' the captain said as he put his hands on the handles. He could feel the power of the sea slapping the exposed top of the instrument. He bent down to look.

'We have a UHF signal coming in now, sir,' the communications officer reported.

'That's nice,' Ricks said. 'I'd call that thirty-foot seas, people, mostly rollers, some are breaking over. Well, we can shoot through that if we have to,' he added almost as a joke. After all, this had to be a drill.

'How's the sky?' Claggett asked.

'Overcast – no stars.' Ricks stood back and slapped the handles up. 'Down 'scope.' He turned to Claggett. 'X, we want to get back tracking our friend just as soon as we can.'

'Aye, Cap'n.'

Ricks was about to lift the phone to MCC. He wanted to tell the missile-control crew that he wanted this drill over just as fast as they could arrange it. The communications officer was in the compartment before he could push the proper button.

'Captain, this isn't a drill.'

'What do you mean?' Ricks noticed that the lieutenant didn't look very happy.

'DEFCON-TWO, sir.' He handed over the message.

'What?' Ricks scanned the message, which was brief and chillingly to the point. 'What the hell's going on?' He handed it off to Dutch Claggett.

'DEFCON-TWO? We've never been at DEFCON-TWO, not as long as I've been in . . . I remember a DEFCON-THREE once, but I was a plebe then . . .'

Around the compartment, men traded glances. The American military has five alert levels, numbered five through one. DEFCON-FIVE was denoted normal peacetime operations. FOUR was slightly higher, calling for increased manning of certain posts, keeping more people — mainly meaning pilots and soldiers — close to their airplanes or tanks, as the case might be. DEFCON-THREE was far more serious. At that point units were fully manned for operational deployment. At DEFCON-TWO units began to deploy, and this level was saved for the imminent threat of war. DEFCON-ONE was a level to which American forces had never been called. At that point, war was to be considered something more than a threat. Weapons were loaded and aimed in anticipation of orders to shoot.

But the entire DEFCON system was more haphazard than one might imagine. Submarines generally kept a higher-than-normal state of alert as a part of routine operations. Missile submarines, always ready to launch their birds in a matter of minutes, were effectively at DEFCON-TWO all the time. The notice from the FLTSATCOM merely made it official, and a lot more ominous.

'What else?' Ricks asked communications.

'That's it, sir.'

'Any news come in, any threat warning?'

'Sir, we got the usual news broadcast yesterday. I was planning to get the next one in about five hours — you know, so we'd have the Superbowl score.' The lieutenant paused. 'Sir, there was nothing in the news, and nothing official about any crisis.'

'So what the hell is going on?' Ricks asked rhetorically. 'Well, that doesn't really matter, does it?'

'Captain,' Claggett said, 'for starters, I think we need to break off from our friend at two-seven-zero.'

'Yeah. Bring her around northeast, X. He's not due for another turn soon, and that'll open the range pretty fast, then we'll head north to open further.'

Claggett looked at the chart, mainly as a matter of habit to see that the water was deep. It was. They were, in fact, astride the great-circle route from Seattle to Japan. On command, USS *Maine* turned to port. A right turn would have been just as easy, but this way they would immediately start opening the range on the Akula which they'd been tracking for several days. In a minute, this put the submarine broadside to the thirty-footers rolling just a few feet over their heads and made the submarine's sail almost exactly that, a target for the natural forces at work. The boat took a forty-degree roll. All over the submarine, men braced and grabbed for loose gear.

'Take her down a little, Captain?' Claggett asked.

'In a few minutes. Let's see if there's any followup on the satellite channel.'

Three pieces of what had once been one of the most magnificent evergreen trees in Oregon had now been in the North Pacific for several weeks. The logs had still been green and heavy when they'd fallen off the MV *George McReady*. Since becoming just another entry in the flotsam on the sea, they'd soaked in more water, and the heavy steel chain that held them together changed what should have been a slightly positive buoyancy into neutral buoyancy. They could not quite get to the surface, at least not in these weather conditions. The pounding of the seas defeated every attempt at rising to the sunlight – of which there was none at the moment – and they hovered like blimps, turning slowly as the sea struggled mightily to break their chains.

A junior sonarman aboard *Maine* heard something, something at zero-four-one, almost dead ahead. It was an odd sound, he thought, metallic, like a tinkle but deeper. Not a ship, he thought, not a biologic. It was almost lost in the surface noise, and wouldn't settle down on bearing . . .

'Shit!' He keyed his microphone. 'Conn, sonar – sonar contact close aboard!'

'What?' Ricks dashed into sonar.

'Don't know what, but it's close, sir!'

'Where?'

'Can't tell, like both sides of the bow – not a ship, I don't know what the hell it is, sir!' The petty officer checked off the pip on his screen while his ears strained to identify the sound. 'Not a point source – it's *close*, sir!'

'But –' Ricks stopped, turned, and shouted on reflex: 'Emergency dive!' He knew it was too late for that.

The entire length of USS *Maine* reverberated like a bass drum as one of the logs struck the fiberglass dome over the bow sonar array.

There were three sections of what had once been a single tree. The first hit axially just on the edge of the sonar dome, doing very little damage because the submarine was only doing a few knots, and everything about her hull was built for strength. The noise was bad enough. The first log was shunted aside, but there were two more, and the center one tapped the hull once just outside the control room.

The helmsman responded at once to the captain's command, pushing his control yoke all the way to the stops. The stern of the submarine rose at once, into the path of the logs. *Maine* had a cruciform stern. There was a rudder both above and below the propeller shaft. To the left and right were the stern planes, which operated like the stabilizers of an aircraft. On the outer surface of each was another vertical structure that looked like an auxiliary rudder, but was in fact a fitting for sonar sensors. The chain between two of the logs fouled on that. Two logs were outboard, and one inboard. The inboard one was just long enough to reach the spinning propeller. The resulting noise was the worst anyone had ever heard. *Maine*'s seven-bladed screw was made of manganese-bronze alloy that had been shaped into its nearly perfect configuration over a period of seven months. It was immensely strong, but not this strong. Its scimitar-shaped blades struck the log one after another, like a slow, inefficient saw. Each impact gouged or dented the outboard edges. The officer in the maneuvering room, aft, had already decided to stop the shaft before the order to do so arrived. Outside the hull, not a hundred feet from his post, he heard the screams of abused metal as the sonar fitting was wrenched off the starboard stern plane, along with it went the additional fitting that held the submarine's towed array sonar. At that point, the logs, one of them now badly splintered, fell off into the submarine's wake, and the worst of the noise stopped.

'What the fuck was that?' Ricks nearly screamed.

'Tail's gone, sir. We just lost the tail,' a sonarman said. 'Right side lateral array is damaged, sir.' Ricks was already out of the room. The petty officer was talking to himself.

'Conn, maneuvering room,' a speaker was saying. 'Something just pounded the hell out of our screw. I'm checking for damage to the shaft now.'

'Stern planes are damaged, sir. Very sluggish on the controls,' the helmsman said. The Chief of the Boat pulled the youngster off the seat and took his place. Slowly and carefully, the Master Chief worked the control wheel.

'Damaged hydraulics, feels like. The trim tabs – ' these were electrically powered '– look okay.' He worked the wheel left and right. 'Rudder is okay, sir.'

'Lock the stern planes in neutral. Ten degrees up on the fairwater planes.' This order came from the XO.

'Aye.'

'So, what was it?' Dubinin asked.

'Metallic – an enormous mechanical transient, bearing zero-five-one.' The officer tapped the blazing mark on his screen. 'Low frequency as you see, like a drum . . . but this noise here, much higher pitch. I heard that on my phones, sounded like a machinegun. Wait a minute . . .' Senior Lieutenant Rykov said, thinking rapidly. 'The frequency – I mean the interval of the impulses – that was a blade-rate, that was a propeller . . . only thing it could be . . .'

'And now?' the captain asked.

'Gone completely.'

'I want the entire sonar crew on duty.' Captain Dubinin returned to control. 'Come about, new course zero-four-zero. Speed ten.'

*

Getting a Soviet Army truck was simplicity itself. They'd stolen it, along with a staff car. It was just after midnight in Berlin, and since it was a Sunday night, the streets were empty. Berlin is as lively a city as any in the world, but Monday there is a workday, and work is something that Germans take seriously. What little traffic there was came from people late to leave their local *Gasthaus*, or perhaps a few workers whose jobs required round-the-clock manning. What mattered was that traffic was agreeably light, allowing them to get to their destination right on time.

There used to be a wall, Günther Bock thought. On one side was the American Berlin detachment, and on the other a Soviet detachment, each with a small but heavily used exercise area adjacent to their barracks. The wall was gone now, leaving nothing but grass between two mechanized forces. The staff car pulled up to the Soviet gate. The sentry there was a senior sergeant of twenty years with pimples on his face and an untidy uniform. His eyes went a little wide when he saw the three stars on Keitel's shoulderboards.

'Stand at attention!' Keitel roared in perfect Russian. The boy complied at once. 'I am here from Army Command to conduct an unannounced readiness inspection. You will not report our arrival to anyone. Is that clear?'

'Yes, Colonel!'

'Carry on – and clean up that filthy uniform before I come back through here or you'll find yourself on the Chinese border! Move!' Keitel ordered Bock, who was sitting at the wheel.

'*Zu Befehl, Herr Oberst,*' Bock replied after he moved off. It was funny, actually. There were a few humorous aspects to all this, Bock thought. A few. But you had to have the right sense of humor for it.

The regimental headquarters was in an old building once used by Hitler's Wehrmacht that the Russians had used more than they had maintained. It did have the usual garden outside, and in the summer one could see the flowers arranged to duplicate the unit's patch. This one was a Guards Tank Regiment, though one with a history to which its soldiers paid little attention, judging by the sentry at the gate. Bock pulled right up to the door. Keitel and the rest dismounted from their vehicles and walked into the front door like gods in a bad mood.

'Who's the duty officer of this whorehouse?' Keitel bellowed. A corporal just pointed. Corporals do not dispute the orders of staff-grade officers. The duty officer, they found, was a major, perhaps thirty years of age.

'What is this?' the young officer asked.

'I am Colonel Ivanenko of the Inspectorate. *This* is an unannounced operational-readiness inspection. Hit your alarm!' The major walked two steps and punched a button that set off sirens all over the camp area.

'Next, call your regimental commander, and get his drunken ass over here! What is your readiness state, Major?' Keitel demanded, without giving the man a chance to take a breath. The junior officer stopped in mid-reach for the phone, not knowing which order he was supposed to follow first. '*Well!*'

'Our readiness is in accordance with unit norms, Colonel Ivanenko.'

'You have a chance to prove that.' Keitel turned to one of the others. 'Take this child's name!'

Less than two thousand meters away, they could see lights going on at the American base in what had so recently been West Berlin.

'They're having a drill also,' Keitel/Ivanenko observed. 'Splendid. We'd better be faster than they are,' he added.

'What is this?' The regimental commander, also a colonel, arrived without his buttons done.

'*This* looks like a sorry spectacle!' Keitel boomed. '*This* is an unannounced readiness inspection. You have a regiment to lead, Colonel. I suggest you get to it without asking any further questions.'

'But –'

'But *what?*' Keitel demanded. '*Don't you know what a readiness inspection is?*'

There was one thing about dealing with Russians, Keitel thought. They were arrogant, overbearing, and they hated Germans, however much they protested otherwise. On the other hand, when browbeaten, they were predictable. Even though his rank insignia was no higher than this man's, he had a louder voice, and that was all he needed.

'I'll show you what my boys can do.'

'We'll be outside to watch,' Keitel assured him.

'Dr Ryan, you'd better get down here.' The line clicked off.

'Okay,' Jack said. He grabbed his cigarettes and walked down to room 7-F-27, the CIA's Operations Center. Located on the north side of the building, it was the counterpart to operations rooms in many other government agencies. In the center of the twenty-by-thirty-foot room, once you got past the cipher lock on the door, was a large circular table with a lazy-Susan bookcase in the center, and six seats around it. The seats had overhead plaques to designate their functions: Senior Duty Officer, Press, Africa – Latin America, Europe – USSR, Near-East – Terrorism, and South Asia – East Asia – Pacific. The wall clocks showed the time in Moscow, Beijing, Beirut, Tripoli, and, of course, Greenwich Mean. There was an adjacent conference room that looked down on the CIA's internal courtyard.

'What gives?' Jack asked, arriving with Goodley in his wake.

'According to NORAD, a nuclear device just went off in Denver.'

'I hope that's a fucking joke!' Jack replied. That, too, was a reflex. Before the man had a chance to respond, Ryan's stomach turned over. Nobody made jokes like that one.

'I wish it were,' the Senior Duty Officer replied.

'What do we know?'

'Not much.'

'Anything? Threat board?' Jack asked. Again it was reflexive. If there had been anything, he would have heard it by now. 'Okay – where's Marcus?'

'Coming home in the C-141, somewhere between Japan and the Aleutians. You're it, sir,' the SDO pointed out, quietly thanking a beneficent God that it wasn't himself. 'President's at Camp David. SecDef and SecState –'

'Dead?' Ryan asked.

'It would appear so, sir.'

Ryan closed his eyes. 'Holy Jesus. The Vice President?'

'At his official residence. We've only been going about three minutes. The NMCC watch officer is a Captain James Rosselli. General Wilkes is on the way in. DIA's on line. They – I mean the President just ordered DEFCON-TWO on our strategic forces.'

'Anything from the Russians?'

'Nothing unusual at all. There's a regional air-defense exercise underway in Eastern Siberia. That's all.'

'Okay, alert all the stations. Put the word out that I want to hear anything they might have – anything. They are to hit every source they can just as fast as they can.' Jack paused one more time. 'How sure are we that this really happened?'

'Sir, two DSPS satellites copied the flash. We have a KH-11 that's going to be overhead in about twenty minutes, and I've directed NPIC to put every camera they have on Denver. NORAD says it's a definite nuclear detonation, but there's no word on yield or damage. The explosion seems to be in the immediate area of the stadium – like *Black Sunday*, sir, but real. This is definitely not a drill, not if we're jacking the strategic forces to DEFCON-TWO, sir.'

'Inbound ballistic track? Aircraft delivery?'

'Negative on the first, there was no launch warning, and no ballistic radar track.'

'What about a FOBS?' Goodley asked. A weapon could be delivered by satellite. That was the purpose of a Fractional-Orbital Bombardment System.

'They would have caught that,' the SDO replied. 'I already asked. On the aircraft side, they don't know yet. They're trying to check air-traffic-control tapes.'

'So we don't know jack shit.'

'Correct.'

'President check in with us yet?' Ryan asked.

'No, but we have an open line there. He has the National Security Advisor there also.'

'Most likely scenario?'

'I'd say terrorism.'

Ryan nodded. 'So would I. I'm taking over the conference room. Okay, I want DO, DI, DS&T in here immediately. If you need choppers to fetch them in, order 'em.' Ryan walked into the room, leaving the door open.

'Christ,' Goodley said. 'You sure you want me here?'

'Yes, and when you have an idea, you say it out loud. I forgot about FOBS.' Jack lifted the phone and punched the FBI button.

'Command Center.'

'This is CIA, Deputy Director Ryan speaking. Who is this?'

'Inspector Pat O'Day. I have Deputy-Assistant Director Murray here also. You're on speaker, sir.'

'Talk to me, Dan.' Jack put his phone on speaker, also. A watch officer handed him a cup of coffee.

'We don't know anything. No heads-up at all, Jack. Thinking terrorists?'

'At the moment, it seems the most plausible alternative.'

'How sure are you of that?'

'Sure?' Ryan shook his head at the phone, Goodley saw. 'What's "sure" mean, Dan?'

'I hear you. We're still trying to figure out what happened here, too. I can't even get CNN on the TV to work.'

'What?'

'One of my communications people says the satellites are all out,' Murray explained. 'Didn't you know that?'

'No.' Jack pointed for Goodley to get back into the Ops Center and find out. 'If that's true, it could scratch the terrorism idea. Jesus, that's scary!'

'It's true, Jack. We've checked.'

'They think ten commercial commosats are nonfunctional,' Goodley said. 'All the defense birds are on line, though. Our commlinks are okay.'

'Find the most senior S&T guy you can find – or one

of our commo people – and ask him what could snuff out satellites. Move!' Jack ordered. 'Where's Shaw?'

'On his way in. Going to be a while the way the roads are.'

'Dan, I'll give you everything I get here.'

'It'll be a two-way street.' The line went dead.

The most horrible thing was that Ryan didn't know what to do next. It was his job to gather data and forward it to the President, but he had no data. What information there was would come in through military circuits. CIA had failed again, Ryan told himself. Someone had done something to his country, and he hadn't warned anyone. People were dead because his agency had failed in its mission. Ryan was Deputy Director, the man who really ran the shop for the political drone placed over his head. The failure was personal. A million people dead, maybe, and there he was, all alone in an elegant little conference room staring at a wall with nothing on it. He hunted a line to NORAD and punched it.

'NORAD,' a disembodied voice answered.

'This is the CIA Operations Center, Deputy Director Ryan speaking. I need information.'

'We do not have much, sir. We think the bomb exploded in the immediate vicinity of the Skydome. We are trying to estimate yield, but nothing yet. A helicopter has been dispatched from Lowery Air Force Base.'

'Will you keep us posted?'

'Yes, sir.'

'Thank you.' That was a big help, Ryan thought. Now he knew that someone else didn't know anything.

There was nothing magical about a mushroom cloud, Battalion Chief Mike Callaghan of the Denver City Fire Department knew. He'd seen one before, as a rookie firefighter. It had been a fire in the Burlington yards just outside the city, in 1968. A propane tank-car had let go, right next to another trainload of bombs *en route* to the Navy's munitions terminal at Oakland, California. The chief back then had had the good sense to pull his men back when the tank ruptured, and from a quarter mile away they'd watched a hundred tons of bombs go off in a hellish firecracker series. There had been a mushroom then also. A large mass of hot air rose, roiling as it went into an annular shape. It created an updraft, drawing air upward into its donut-shaped center, making the stem of the mushroom . . .

But this one was much larger.

He was behind the wheel of his red-painted command car, following the first alarm, three Seagrave pumper units, an aerial ladder truck, and two ambulances. It was a pitiful first response. Callaghan lifted his radio and ordered a general alarm. Next he ordered his men to approach from up-wind.

Christ, what had happened here?

It couldn't be that. . . . most of the city was still intact.

Chief Callaghan didn't know much, but he knew there was a fire to fight and people to rescue. As the car turned off the last side-street onto the boulevard leading to the stadium he saw the main smoke mass. The parking lot, of course. It had to be. The mushroom cloud was blowing rapidly southwest towards the mountains. The parking lot was a mass of fire and flame from burning gasoline and oil and auto parts. A powerful gust of wind cleared the smoke briefly, just enough that he could see that there had been a stadium here . . . a few sections were still . . . not intact, but you could tell what they were – had been only a few minutes before. Callaghan shut that out. He had a fire to fight. He had people to rescue. The first pump unit pulled up at a hydrant. They had good water here. The stadium was fully sprinklered, and that system fed off two thirty-six-inch high-pressure mains that gridded around the complex.

He left his car next to the first big Seagrave and climbed on top of the fire engine. Some heavy structural material – the stadium roof, he supposed – was in the parking lot to his right. More had landed a quarter mile away in the mercifully empty parking lot of a shopping center. Callaghan used his portable radio to order the next wave of rescue units to check both the shopping center and the residential area that lay beyond it. The smaller fires would have to wait. There were people in the stadium who needed help, but his firefighters would have to fight through two hundred yards of burning cars to get to them . . .

Just then he looked up to see a blue Air Force rescue helicopter. The UH-1N landed thirty yards away. Callaghan ran over towards it. The officer inside the back, he saw, was an Army major.

'Callaghan,' he said. 'Battalion chief.'

'Griggs,' the major replied. 'You need a look-around?'

'Right.'

'Kay.' The major spoke into his headset, and the helicopter lifted off. Callaghan grabbed a seatbelt, but didn't strap in.

It didn't take long. What appeared to be a wall of smoke from street level became discrete pillars of black and gray smoke from overhead. Perhaps half of the cars had ignited. He could use one of the driving lanes to get closer in, but some of the way was blocked by wrecked and burning cars. The chopper made a single circuit, bouncing through the roiled, hot air. Looking down, Callaghan could see a mass of melted asphalt, some of it still glowing red. The only spot not giving off smoke was the south end of the stadium itself, which seemed to glisten, though he didn't know why. What they could see appeared to be a crater whose dimensions were hard to judge, since they could only catch bits and pieces of it at a time. It took a long look to determine that parts of the stadium structure remained standing, perhaps four or five sections, Callaghan thought. There had to be people in there.

'Okay, I've seen enough,' Callaghan told Griggs. The officer handed him a headset so that they could speak coherently.

'What is this?'

'Just what it looks like, far as I can tell,' Griggs replied. 'What do you need?'

'Heavy-lift and rigging equipment. There are probably people in what's left of the stadium. We gotta get in to them. But what about the – what about radiation?'

The major shrugged. 'I don't know. When I leave here, I'm picking up a team from Rocky Flats. I work at the Arsenal, and I know a little about this, but the specialists are at Rocky Flats. There's a NEST team there. I need to get them down here ASAP. Okay, I'll call the guard people at the Arsenal, we can get the heavy equipment down here fast. Keep your people to windward. Keep your people at this end. Do not attempt to approach from any other direction, okay?'

'Right.'

'Set up a decontamination station right there where your engines are. When people come out, hose them down – strip them and hose them down. Understand?' the major asked as the chopper touched down. 'Then get them to the nearest hospital. Upwind – remember that everything has to go northeast into the wind so you know you're safe.'

'What about fallout?'

'I'm no expert, but I'll give you the best I got. Looks like it was a small one. Not much fallout. The suction from the fireball and the surface wind should have driven most of the radioactive shit away from here. Not all, but most. It should be okay for an hour or so – exposure, I mean. By that time, I'll have the NEST guys here and they can tell you for sure. Best I can do for now, Chief. Good luck.'

Callaghan jumped out and ran clear. The chopper lifted right off, heading northwest for Rocky Flats.

'Well?' Kuropatkin asked.

'General, we measure yield by the initial and residual heat emissions. There is something odd about this, but my best figure is between one hundred fifty and two hundred kilotons.' The major showed his commander the calculations.

'What's odd about it?'

'The energy from the initial flash was low. That might mean some clouds were in the way. The residual heat is quite high. This was a major detonation, comparable to a very large tactical warhead, or a small strategic one.'

836

'Here's the target book,' a lieutenant said. It was just that, a cloth-bound quarto-sized volume whose thick pages were actually fold-out maps. It was intended for use in strike-damage evaluation. The map of the Denver area had a plastic overlay that showed the targeting of Soviet strategic missiles. A total of eight birds were detailed on the city, five SS-18s and three SS-19s, totalling no fewer than sixty-four warheads and twenty megatons of yield. Someone, Kuropatkin reflected, thought Denver a worthy target.

'We're assuming a ground-burst?' Kuropatkin asked.

'Correct,' the major replied. He used a compass to draw a circle centered on the stadium complex. 'A two-hundred-kiloton device would have a lethal blast radius this wide . . .'

The map was color-coded. Hard-to-kill structures were colored brown. Dwellings were yellow. Green denoted commercial and other buildings deemed easy targets to destroy. The stadium, he saw, was green, as was nearly everything immediately around it. Well inside the lethal radius were hundreds of houses and low-rise apartment buildings.

'How many in the stadium?'

'I called KGB for an estimate,' the lieutenant said. 'It's an enclosed structure – with a roof. The Americans like their comforts. Total capacity is over sixty thousand.'

'My God,' General Kuropatkin breathed. 'Sixty thousand there . . . at least another hundred thousand inside this radius. The Americans must be insane by now.' *And if they think we did it . . .*

'Well?' Borstein asked.

'I ran the numbers three times. Best guess, one-fifty-KT, sir,' the captain said.

Borstein rubbed his face. 'Christ. Casualty count?'

'Two hundred-K, based on computer modeling and a quick look at the maps we have on file,' she answered. 'Sir, if somebody's thinking terrorist device, they're wrong. It's too big for that.'

Borstein activated the conference line to the President and CINC-SAC.

'We have some early numbers here.'

'Okay, I'm waiting,' the President said. He stared at the speaker as though it were a person.

'Initial yield estimates look like one hundred fifty kilotons.'

'That big?' General Fremont's voice asked.

'We checked the numbers three times.'

'Casualties?' CINC-SAC asked next.

'On the order of two hundred thousand initial dead. Add fifty more to that from delayed effects.'

President Fowler recoiled backwards as though slapped across the face. For the past five minutes, he had denied as much as he could. This most important of denials had just vanished. Two hundred thousand people dead. His citizens, the people he'd sworn to preserve, protect, and defend.

'What else?' his voice asked.

'I didn't catch that,' Borstein said.

Fowler took a deep breath and spoke again. 'What else do you have?'

'Sir, our impression here is that the yield is awfully high for a terrorist device.'

'I'd have to concur in that,' CINC-SAC said. 'An IND – an improvised nuclear device, that is, what we'd expect from unsophisticated terrorists – should not be much more than twenty-KT. This sounds like a multi-stage weapon.'

'Multi-stage?' Elliot said towards the speaker.

'A thermonuclear device,' General Borstein replied. 'An H-Bomb.'

'Ryan here, who's this?'

'Major Fox, sir, at NORAD. We have an initial feel for yield and casualties,' the major read off the bomb numbers.

'Too big for a terrorist weapon,' said an officer from the Directorate of Science and Technology.

'That's what we think, sir.'

'Casualties?' Ryan asked.

'Probable prompt-kill number is two hundred thousand or so. That includes the people at the stadium.'

I have to wake up, Ryan told himself, his eyes screwed tightly shut. *This has to be a fucking nightmare, and I'm going to wake up from it.* But he opened his eyes, and nothing had changed at all.

Robby Jackson was sitting in the cabin of the carrier's skipper, Captain Ernie Richards. They had been half-listening to the game, but mainly discussing tactics for an upcoming wargame. The *Theodore Roosevelt* battlegroup would approach Israel from the west, simulating an attacking enemy. The enemy in this case was the Russians. It seemed highly unlikely, of course, but you had to set some rules for the game. The Russians, in this case, were going to be clever. The battlegroup would be broken up to resemble a loose assembly of merchant ships instead of a tactical formation. The first attack wave would be fighters and attack-bombers squawking 'international' on their IFF boxes, and would try to approach Ben Gurion International Airport in the guise of peaceful airliners, the better to get inside Israeli airspace unannounced. Jackson's operations people had already purloined airliner schedules and were examining the time factors, the better to make their first attack seem as plausible as possible. The odds against them were long. It was not expected that *TR* could do much more than annoy the IAF and the new USAF contingent. But Jackson liked long odds.

'Turn up the radio, Rob. I forgot what the score is.'

Jackson leaned across the table and turned the dial, but got music. The carrier had her own on-board TV system, and was also radio-tuned to the U.S. Armed Forces network. 'Maybe the antenna broke,' the Air Wing Commander observed.

Richards laughed. 'At a time like this? I could have a mutiny aboard.'

'That would look good on the old fit-rep, wouldn't it?'

Someone knocked at the door. 'Come!' Richards said. It was a yeoman.

'Flash-traffic, sir.' The petty officer handed the clipboard over.

'Anything important?' Robby asked.

Richards just handed the message over. Then he lifted the growler phone and punched up the bridge. 'General quarters.'

'What the hell?' Jackson murmured. 'DEFCON-THREE – why, for Christ's sake?'

Ernie Richards, a former attack pilot, had a reputation as something of a character. He'd reinstituted the traditional Navy practice of bugle calls to announce drills. In this case, the 1-MC speaker system blared forth the opening bars of John Williams' frantic call to arms in *Star Wars*, followed by the usual electronic gonging.

'Let's go, Rob.' Both men started running down to the Combat Information Center.

'What can you tell me?' Andrey Il'ych Narmonov asked.

'The bomb had a force of nearly two hundred kilotons. That means a large device, a hydrogen bomb,' General Kuropatkin said. 'The death count will be well over one hundred thousand dead. We also have indications of a strong electromagnetic pulse that struck one of our early-warning satellites.'

'What could account for that?' The questioner here was one of Narmonov's military advisors.

'We do not know.'

'Do we have any nuclear weapons unaccounted for?' Kuropatkin heard his president ask.

'Absolutely not,' a third voice replied.

'Anything else?'

'With your permission, I would like to order *Voyska PVO* to a higher alert level. We already have a training exercise under way in Eastern Siberia.'

'Is that provocative?' Narmonov asked.

'No, it is totally defensive. Our interceptors cannot harm anyone more than a few hundred kilometers from our own borders. For the moment, I will keep all my aircraft within Soviet airspace.'

'Very well, you may proceed.'

In his underground control center, Kuropatkin merely pointed to another officer, who lifted a phone. The Soviet air-defense system had already been prepped, of course; inside a minute radio messages were being broadcast, and long-range search radars came on all over the country's periphery. Both the messages and the radar signals were immediately detected by National Security Agency assets, both on the ground and in orbit.

'Anything else I should do?' Narmonov asked his advisors.

A Foreign Ministry official spoke for all of them. 'I think doing nothing is probably best. When Fowler wishes to speak with us, he will do so. He has trouble enough without our interfering.'

The American Airlines MD-80 landed at Miami International Airport and taxied over to the terminal. Qati and Ghosn rose from their first-class seats and left the aircraft. Their bags would be transferred automatically to the connecting flight, not that either one particularly cared about that, of course. Both men were nervous, but less so than one might have expected. Death was something both had accepted as an overt possibility for this mission. If they survived, so much the better. Ghosn didn't panic until he realized that there was no unusual activity at all. There should have been some, he thought. He found a bar and looked for the usual elevated television set. It was tuned to a local station. There was no game coverage. He debated asking a question, but decided not to. It was a good decision. He had only to wait a minute before he overheard another voice asking what the score was.

'It was fourteen–seven Vikings,' another voice answered. 'Then the goddamned signal was lost.'

'When?'

'About ten minutes ago. Funny they don't have it back yet.'

'Earthquake, like the Series game in San Francisco?'

'Your guess is as good as mine, man,' the bartender replied.

Ghosn stood and left for the walk back to the departure lounge.

'What does CIA have?' Fowler asked.

'Nothing at the moment, sir. We're collecting data, but you know everything that we – wait a minute.' Ryan took the message form that the Senior Duty Officer handed him. 'Sir, I have a flash here from NSA. The Russian air-defense system just went to a higher alert level. Radars are all coming on, and there's a lot of radio chatter.'

'What does that mean?' Liz Elliot asked.

'It means that they want to increase their ability to protect themselves. PVO isn't a threat to anybody unless they're approaching or inside Soviet airspace.'

'But why would they do it?' Elliot asked again.

'Maybe they're afraid somebody will attack them.'

'God damn it, Ryan!' the President shouted.

'Mr President, excuse me. That was not a flippant remark. It is literally true. Voyska PVO is a defense system like our NORAD. Our air-defense and warning systems are now at a higher alert status. So are theirs. It's a defensive move only. They have to know that we've had this event. When there's trouble of this sort, it's natural to activate your own defenses, just as we have done.'

'It's potentially disturbing,' General Borstein said at NORAD HQ. 'Ryan, you forget we have been attacked. They have not. Now, before they've even bothered to call us, they're jacking up their alert levels. I find that a little worrisome.'

'Ryan, what about those reports that we got about missing Soviet nuclear weapons?' Fowler asked. 'Could that fit into this situation?'

'What missing nukes?' CINC-SAC demanded. 'Why the hell didn't I hear about that?'

'What kind of nukes?' Borstein asked a second later.

'That was an unconfirmed report from a penetration agent. There are no details,' Ryan answered, then realized he had to press on. 'The sum of the information received is this: we've been told that Narmonov has political problems with his military; that they are unhappy with the way he's doing things; that in the ongoing pull-back from Germany, an unspecified number of nuclear weapons – probably tactical ones – have turned up missing; that KGB is conducting an operation to determine what, if anything, is missing. Supposedly Narmonov is personally concerned that he might be the target of political blackmail, and that the blackmail could have a nuclear dimension. *But*, and I must emphasize the *but*, we have been totally unable to confirm these reports, despite repeated attempts, and we are examining the possibility that our agent is lying to us.'

'Why didn't you tell us that?' Fowler asked.

'Mr President, we're in the process of formulating our assessment now. The work is still on-going, sir, I mean, we've been doing it over the weekend.'

'Well, it sure as hell wasn't one of ours,' General Fremont said heatedly. 'And it's no goddamned terrorist bomb, it's too goddamned big for that. *Now* you tell us that the Russians may have a short inventory. That's more than disturbing, Ryan.'

'And it could explain the increased alert level at PVO,' Borstein added ominously.

'Are you two telling me,' the President asked, 'that this could have been a Soviet device?'

'There aren't all that many nuclear powers around,' Borstein replied first. 'And the yield of this device is just too damned big for amateurs.'

'Wait a minute.' Jack jumped in again. 'You have to remember that the facts we have here are very thin. There is a difference between information and speculation. You have to remember that.'

'How big are Soviet tactical nuclear weapons?' Liz Elliot wanted to know.

CINC-SAC handled that one: 'A lot like ours. They have little one-kiloton ones for artillery rounds, and they have warheads up to five hundred-KT left over from the SS-20s they did away with.'

'In other words, the yield of this explosion falls into the range of the Soviet warhead types that we have heard are missing?'

'Correct, Dr Elliot,' General Fremont replied.

At Camp David, Elizabeth Elliot leaned back in her chair and turned to the President. She spoke too softly for the speaker-phone to catch her words.

'Robert, you were supposed to be at that game, along with Brent and Dennis.'

It was strange that he hadn't had that thought enter his mind yet, Fowler told himself. He, too, leaned back. 'No,' he replied. 'I cannot believe that the Russians would attempt such a thing.'

'What was that?' a voice on the speaker asked.

'Wait a minute,' the President said too quietly.

'Mr President, I didn't catch what you said.'

'*I said, wait a minute!*' Fowler shouted. He put his hand over the speaker for a moment. 'Elizabeth, it's our job to get control of this situation and we will. Let's try to put this personal stuff aside for the moment.'

'Mr President, I want you on Kneecap just as fast as you can get there,' CINC-SAC said. 'This situation could be very serious indeed.'

'If we're going to get control, Robert, we must do it quickly.'

Fowler turned to the naval officer standing behind him. 'When's the chopper due in?'

'Twenty-five minutes, sir, then thirty more to get you to Andrews for Kneecap.'

'Almost an hour . . .' Fowler looked at the wall clock, as people do when they know what time it is, know what time it will take to do something, and look at the clock anyway. 'The radio links on the chopper aren't enough for this. Tell the chopper to take Vice President Durling to Kneecap. General Fremont?'

'Yes, Mr President.'

'You have extra Kneecaps there, don't you?'

'Yes, I do, sir.'

'I'm sending the Vice President up on the primary. You send a spare down here. You can land it at Hagerstown, can't you?'

'Yes, sir, we can use the Fairchild-Republic airfield, where they used to build the A-10s.'

'Okay, do that. It'll take me an hour to get to Andrews, and I cannot afford to waste an hour. It's my job to settle this thing down, and I need that hour.'

'That, sir, is a mistake,' Fremont said in the coldest voice he had. It would take two hours to get the aircraft to central Maryland.

'That may be, but it's what I'm going to do. This is not a time for me to run away.'

Behind the President, Pete Connor and Helen D'Agustino traded a baleful look. They had no illusions on what would happen if there were a nuclear attack on the United States. Mobility was the President's best defense, and he had just thrown that away.

The radio message from Camp David went out at once. The Presidential helicopter was just crossing the Washington Beltway when it turned and went back southeast. It landed on the grounds of the U.S. Naval Observatory. Vice President Roger Durling and his entire family jumped aboard. They didn't even bother strapping in. Secret Service agents, with their Uzi sub-machineguns out, knelt inside the aircraft. All Durling knew was what the Secret Service detail had told him. Durling told himself that he had to relax, that he had to keep his head. He looked at his youngest child, a boy only four years old. To be that age again, he'd thought only the day before, to be that age again and be able to grow up in a world where the chance of a major war no longer existed. All the horrors of his youth, the Cuban Missile Crisis that had marked his freshman year in college, his service as a platoon leader in the 82nd Airborne, a year of which had been in Vietnam. War experience made Durling a most unusual liberal politician. He hadn't run from it. He'd taken his chances and remembered having two men die in his arms. Just yesterday, he'd looked at his son and thanked God that he wouldn't have to know any of that.

And now, this. His son still didn't know anything more than that they were getting a surprise helicopter ride, and he loved to fly. His wife knew more, and there were tears streaming from her eyes as she stared back at him.

The Marine VH-3 touched down within fifty yards of the aircraft. The first Secret Service agent leaped off and saw a platoon of Air Force security police marking the way to the stairs. The Vice President was practically dragged towards them, while a burly agent picked up his young son and ran the distance. Two minutes later, before people had even strapped in, the pilot of the National Emergency Airborne Command Post – Kneecap – firewalled his engines and roared down runway Zero-One Left. He headed east for the Atlantic Ocean, where a KC-10 tanker was already orbiting to top off the Boeing's tanks.

'We have a major problem here,' Ricks said in the maneuvering room. *Maine* had just tried to move. At any speed over three knots, the propeller screeched like a banshee. The shaft was slightly bent, but they'd live with that for a while. 'All seven blades must be damaged. If we try for anything over three we make noise. Over five and we'll lose the shaft bearings in a matter of minutes. The outboard motor can give us two or three knots, but that's noisy too. Comments?' There were none. No one aboard doubted Ricks' engineering expertise. 'Options?'

'Kinda thin, aren't they?' Dutch Claggett observed.

Maine had to stay near the surface. At this alert level, she had to be ready to launch in minutes. Ordinarily they could have gone to a deeper depth, if for no other reason than to reduce the horrible motion the ship was taking right now from surface turbulence, but her reduced speed made coming up too time-consuming.

'How close is *Omaha*?' the chief engineer asked.

'Probably within a hundred miles, and there's P-3s at Kodiak – but we still have that Akula out there to worry about,' Claggett said. 'Sir, we can hang tough right here and wait it out.'

'No, we have a hurt boomer. We need some kind of support.'

'That means radiating,' the XO pointed out.

'We'll use a SLOT buoy.'

'At two knots through the water, that doesn't buy us much, sir. Captain, radiating is a mistake.'

Ricks looked at his chief engineer, who said, 'I like the idea of having a friend around.'

'So do I,' the captain said. It didn't take long. The buoy was on the surface in seconds and immediately began broadcasting a short message in UHF. It was programmed to continue broadcasting for hours.

'We're going to have a nationwide panic on our hands,' Fowler said. That was not his most penetrating observation. He had a growing panic in his own command center, and knew it. 'Is there anything coming out of Denver?'

'Nothing on any commercial TV or radio channel that I know of,' a voice at NORAD replied.

'Okay, you people stand by.' Fowler searched his panel for another button.

'FBI Command Center. Inspector O'Day speaking.'

'This is the President,' Fowler said unnecessarily. It was a direct line and the light on the FBI panel was neatly labeled. 'Who's in charge down there?'

'I am Deputy Assistant Director Murray, Mr President. I'm the senior man at the moment.'

'How are your communications?'

'They're okay, sir. We have access to the military commsats.'

'One thing we have to worry about is a nationwide panic. To prevent that, I want you to send people to all the TV network headquarters. I want your people to explain to them that they may not broadcast anything about this. If necessary, you are directed to use force to prevent it.'

Murray didn't like that. 'Mr President, that is against –'

'I know the law, okay? I used to be a prosecutor. This is necessary to preserve life and order, and it will be done, Mr Murray. That is a Presidential Order. Get to it.'

'Yes, sir.'

CHAPTER 38

First Contacts

The various communications-satellite operators were fiercely independent companies and very often ruthless competitors, but they were not enemies. Between them were agreements informally called treaties. There was always the possibility that one satellite or another could go down, whether from an internal breakdown or collision with space debris that was becoming a real worry for them. Accordingly, there were mutual-assistance agreements specifying that in the event one operator lost a bird, his associates would take up the slack, just as newspapers in the same city traditionally agreed to share printing facilities in the event of a fire or natural disaster. To back up these agreements, there were open phone lines between the various corporate headquarters. Intelsat was the first to call Telstar.

'Bert, we just had two birds go down,' Intelsat's duty engineer reported in a slightly shaken voice. 'What gives?'

'Shit, we just lost three, and Westar 4 and Teleglobe are down, too. We've had complete system failures here. Running checks now – you?'

'Same here, Bert. Any ideas?'

'None. We're talking like nine birds down, Stacy. Fuck!' The man paused. 'Ideas? Wait a minute, getting somewhere . . . okay, it's software. We're interrogating 301 now . . . they got spiked . . . Jesus! 301 got spiked on over a hundred freqs! Somebody just tried to zorch us.'

'That's how it looks here, too. But who?'

'Sure as hell wasn't a hacker . . . this would take mega-watts to do that on just one channel.'

'Bert, that's exactly what I'm getting. Phone links, everything spiked at once. You in any hurry to light them back up?'

'You kidding me? I got a billion worth of hardware up there. Till I find out what the hell clobbered them, they stay down. I've got my senior VP on the way in now. The Pres was out in Denver,' Bert added.

'Mine, too, but my chief engineer is snowed in. Damned if I'm going to put my ass on the line. I think we should cooperate on this, Bert.'

'No arguments with me, Stace. I'll whistle up Fred Kent at Hughes and see what he thinks. It'll take a while for us to review everything and do full systems checks. I'm staying down until I know – and I mean *know* – what happened here. We got an industry to protect, man.'

'Agreed. I won't light back up without talking to you.'

'Keep me posted on anything you find out?'

'You got it, Bert. I'll be back to you in an hour, one way or another.'

The Soviet Union is a vast country, by far the largest in the world both in area and in the expanse of its borders. All of those borders are guarded, since both the current country and all its precursors have been invaded many times. Border defenses include the obvious – troop concentrations, airfields, and radar posts – and the subtle, like radio reception antennas. The latter were designed to listen in on radio and other electronic emissions. The information was passed on by landline or microwave links to Moscow Center, the headquarters of the Committee for State Security, the KGB, at #2 Dzerzhinskiy Square. The KGB's Eighth Chief Directorate is tasked to communications intelligence and communications security. It has a long and distinguished history that has benefited from another traditional Russian strength, a fascination with theoretical mathematics. The relationship between ciphers and mathematics is a logical one, and the most recent manifestation of this was the work

of a bearded, thirtyish gnome of a man who was fasci-
nated with the work of Benoit Mandelbrot at Harvard
University, the man who had effectively invented fractal
geometry. Uniting this work with that of MacKenzie's
work on Chaos Theory at Cambridge University in England, the young Russian genius had invented a genuinely
new theoretical way of looking at mathematical formulae. It was generally conceded by that handful of people
who understood what he was talking about that his work
was easily worth a Planck Medal. It was an historical
accident that his father happened to be a General in the
KGB's Chief Border Guards Directorate, and that as a
result the Committee for State Security had taken
immediate note of his work. The mathematician now
had everything a grateful Motherland could offer, and
someday he'd probably have that Planck Medal also.

He'd needed two years to make his theoretical breakthrough into something practical, but fifteen months
earlier he'd made his first 'recovery' from the U.S. State
Department's most secure cipher, called STRIPE. Six
months after that he'd proven conclusively that it was
similar in structure to everything the U.S. military used.
Cross-checking with another team of cryptanalysts who
had access to the work of the Walker spy ring, and the
even more serious work done by Pelton, what had
resulted only six months earlier was a systematic penetration of American encryption systems. It was still
not perfect. Daily keying procedures occasionally proved
impossible to break. Sometimes they went as much as a
week without recovering one message, but they'd gone
as many as three days recovering over half of what they
received, and their results were improving by the month.
Indeed, the main problem seemed to be that they didn't
have the computer hardware to do all the work they
should have been able to do, and the 8th Directorate
was busily training more linguists to handle the message
traffic they were receiving.

Sergey Nikolayevich Golovko had been awakened
from a sound sleep and driven to his office to add his
name to the people all over the world shocked into

frightened sobriety. A First Chief Directorate man all of his life, his job was to examine the collective American mind and advise his President on what was going on. The decrypts flooding onto his desk were the most useful tool.

He had no less than thirty such messages which bore one of two messages. All strategic forces were being ordered to Defense Condition Two, and all conventional forces were coming to Defense Condition Three. The American President was panicking, KGB's First Deputy Chairman thought. There was no other explanation. *Was it possible that he thought the Soviet Union had committed this infamy?* That was the most frightening thought of his life.

'Another one, naval one.' The messenger dropped it on his desk.

Golovko needed only one look. 'Flash this to the navy immediately.' He had to call his President with the rest. Golovko lifted the phone.

For once the Soviet bureaucracy worked quietly. Minutes later, an extremely low-frequency signal went out, and the submarine *Admiral Lunin* went to the surface to copy the full message. Captain Dubinin read it as the printer generated it.

AMERICAN SUBMARINE USS MAINE
REPORTS LOCATION AS 50D—55M—09SN 153D
—01M—23SW. PROPELLER DISABLED BY
COLLISION OF UNKNOWN CAUSE.

Dubinin left the communications room and made for the chart table. 'Where were we when we copied that transient?'

'Here, Captain, and the bearing was here.' The navigator traced the line with his pencil.

Dubinin just shook his head. He handed the message over. 'Look at this.'

'What do you suppose he's doing?'

'He'll be close to the surface. So . . . we'll go up, just

under the layer, and we'll move quickly. Surface noise will play hell with his sonar. Fifteen knots.'

'You suppose he was following us?'

'Took you long enough to realize that, didn't it?' Dubinin measured the distance to the target. 'Very proud, this one. We'll see about that. You know how the Americans boast of taking hull photographs? Now, my young lieutenant, now it will be our turn!'

'What does this mean?' Narmonov asked the First Deputy Chairman.

'The Americans have been attacked by forces unknown, and the attack was serious, causing major loss of life. It is to be expected that they will increase their military readiness. A major consideration will be the maintenance of public order,' Golovko replied over the secure phone line.

'And?'

'And, unfortunately, all their strategic weapons happen to be aimed at the *Rodina*.'

'But we had no part in this!' the Soviet president objected.

'Correct. You see, such responses are automatic. They are planned in advance and become almost reflexive moves. Once attacked, you become highly cautious. Counter-moves are planned in advance, so that you may act rapidly while applying your intellectual capacities to an analysis of the problem without additional and unnecessary distractions.'

The Soviet President turned to his Defense Minister. 'So, what should we do?'

'I advise an increase in our alert status. Defensive-only, of course. Whoever conducted this attack might, after all, attempt to strike us also.'

'Approved,' Narmonov said bluntly. 'Highest peace-time alert.'

Golovko frowned at his telephone receiver. His choice of words had been exquisitely correct: reflexive. 'May I make a suggestion?'

'Yes,' the Defense Minister said.

'If it is possible, perhaps it would be well to tell our forces the reason for the alert. It might lessen the shock of the order.'

'It's a needless complication,' Defense thought.

'The Americans have not done this,' Golovko said urgently, 'and that was almost certainly a mistake. Please consider the state of mind of people suddenly taken from ordinary peacetime operations to an elevated state of alert. It will only require a few additional words. Those few words could be important.'

'Good idea,' Narmonov thought. 'Make it so,' he ordered Defense.

'We will soon hear from the Americans on the Hot Line,' Narmonov said. 'What will they say?'

'That is hard to guess, but whatever it is, we should have a reply ready for them, just to settle things down, to make sure they know we had nothing to do with it.'

Narmonov nodded. That made good sense. 'Start working on it.'

The Soviet defense-communications agency operators grumbled at the signal they'd been ordered to dispatch. For ease of transmission, the meat of the signal should have been contained in a single five-letter code group that could be transmitted, decrypted, and comprehended instantly by all recipients, but that was not possible now. The additional sentences had to be edited down to keep the transmission from being too long. A major did this, got it approved by his boss, a Major General, and sent it out over no less than thirty communications links. The message was further altered to apply to specific military services.

The *Admiral Lunin* had only been on her new course for five minutes when a second ELF signal arrived. The communications officer fairly ran into the control room with it.

GENERAL ALERT LEVEL TWO. THERE HAS BEEN A NUCLEAR DETONATION OF UNKNOWN ORIGIN IN THE UNITED STATES. AMERICAN

STRATEGIC AND CONVENTIONAL FORCES
HAVE BEEN ALERTED FOR POSSIBLE WAR. ALL
NAVAL FORCES WILL SORTIE AT ONCE. TAKE
ALL NECESSARY PROTECTIVE MEASURES.

'Has the world gone mad?' the captain asked the message. He got no reply. 'That's all?'

'That is all, no cueing to put the antenna up.'

'These are not proper instructions,' Dubinin objected. '"All necessary protective measures"? What do they mean by that? Protecting ourselves, protecting the Motherland – what the hell do they mean?'

'Captain,' the *Starpom* said, 'General Alert Two carries its own rules of action.'

'I know that,' Dubinin said, 'but do they apply here?'

'Why else would the signal have been sent?'

A Level Two General Alert was something unprecedented for the Soviet Military. It meant that the rules of action were not those of a war but not those of peace either. Though Dubinin, like every other Soviet ship captain, fully understood his duties, the implications of the order seemed far too frightening . . . The thought passed, however. He was a naval officer. He had his orders. Whoever had given those orders must have understood the situation better than he. The commanding officer of the *Admiral Lunin* stood erect and turned to his second-in-command.

'Increase speed to twenty-five knots. Battle stations.'

It happened just as fast as men could move. The New York FBI office, set in the Jacob Javits Federal Office Building on the southern end of Manhattan, dispatched its men north, and the light Sunday traffic made it easy. The unmarked but powerful cars screamed uptown to the various network headquarters buildings. The same thing happened in Atlanta, where agents left the Martin Luther King Building for CNN Headquarters. In each case, no fewer than three agents marched into the master control rooms and laid down the law: nothing from Denver would go out. In no case did the network employees know why this was so, they were so busy trying to reestablish contact. The same thing happened in Colorado, where, under the direction of Assistant Special-Agent-in-Charge Walter Hoskins, the local field division's agents invaded all the network affiliates, and the local phone company, where they cut all long-distance lines over the furious objections of the Bell employees. But Hoskins had made one mistake. It came from the fact that he didn't watch much television.

KOLD was an independent station that was also trying to become a superstation. Like TBS, WOR, and a few others, it had its own satellite link to cover a wide viewing area. A daring financial gamble, it had not yet paid off for the investors who were running the station on a highly leveraged shoestring out of an old and almost windowless building northeast of the city. The station used one of the Anik-series Canadian satellites and reached Alaska, Canada, and the North-Central US reasonably well with its programming, which was mainly old network shows.

The KOLD building had once been Denver's first network television station, and was constructed in the pattern originally required by the Federal Communications Commission in the 1930s: monolithic reinforced concrete, fit to survive an enemy bomb attack – the specifications pre-dated nuclear weapons. The only windows were in the executive offices on the south side of the building. It was ten minutes after the event that someone passed by the open door of the program manager. He stopped cold, turned and ran back to the newsroom. In another minute, a cameraman entered onto the freight elevator that ran all the way to the roof. The picture, hard-wired into the control room and then sent out on a Ku-Band transmitter to the Anik satellite, which was untouched by earlier events, broke into the reruns of *The Adventures of Dobie Gillis* across Alaska, Montana, North Dakota, Idaho, and three Canadian provinces. In Calgary, Alberta, a reporter for a local paper who'd never got over her crush on Dwayne Hickman was startled by the picture and the voice-over, and called her city desk.

Her breathless report went out at once on the Reuters wire. Soon thereafter, CBC uplinked the video to Europe on one of their unaffected Anik satellites.

By that time, the Denver FBI had a pair of men entering the KOLD building. They laid down the law to a news crew that protested about the First Amendment of the U.S. Constitution, which argument carried less weight than the men with guns who shut the power down to their transmitter. The FBI agents at least apologized as they did so. They needn't have bothered. What had been a fool's errand from the beginning was already an exercise in futility.

'So, what the hell is going on?' Richards asked his staff.

'We have no idea, sir. No reason was given for the alert,' the communications officer said lamely.

'Well, it leaves us between two chairs, doesn't it?' That was a rhetorical question. The *TR* battlegroup was just passing Malta, and was now in range of targets in the Soviet Union. That required 'The Stick's' A-6E Intruders to take off, climb rapidly to cruising altitude, and top off their tanks soon thereafter, but at that point they had the gas to make it all the way to their targets on or near the Kerch Peninsula. Only a year before, U.S. Navy carriers, though carrying a sizable complement of thermonuclear bombs, had not been part of the SIOP. This acronym, pronounced 'Sy-Op' stood for 'Single Integrated Operations Plan,' and was the master blueprint for dismantling the Soviet Union. The draw-down of strategic missiles – mostly land-based ones for the United States – had radically reduced the number of available warheads, and, like planners everywhere, the Joint Strategic Targeting Staff, co-located with headquarters SAC, tried to make up for the short-fall in any way they could. As a result, whenever an aircraft carrier was in range of Soviet targets, it assumed its SIOP tasking. In the case of USS *Theodore Roosevelt*, it meant that about the time the ship passed east of Malta, she became not a conventional-theater force, but a nuclear-strategic force. To fulfill this mission, *TR* carried fifty B-61-Mod-8 nuclear gravity bombs in a special, heavily-guarded magazine. The B-61 had FUFO – for 'full fusing option,' more commonly called 'dial-a-yield' – that selected an explosive power ranging from ten to five hundred kilotons. The bombs were twelve feet long, less than a foot in diameter, weighed a mere seven hundred pounds, and were nicely streamlined to cut air resistance. Each A-6E could carry two of them, with all of its other hardpoints occupied by auxiliary fuel tanks to allow a combat radius of more than a thousand miles. Ten of them were the explosive equivalent of a whole squadron of Minuteman missiles. Their assigned targets were naval, on the principle that people most often kill friends, or at least associates, rather than total strangers. One assigned SIOP mission, for example, was to reduce the Nikolayev Shipyard on the Dniepr River to a radioactive puddle. Which was, incidentally, where the Soviet carrier *Kuznetzov* had been built.

The captain's additional problem was that his battlegroup commander, an Admiral, had taken the chance to fly into Naples for a conference with the Commander of the United States Sixth Fleet. Richards was on his own.

'Where's our friend?' *Roosevelt*'s CO asked.

'About two hundred fifty miles back,' the operations officer said. 'Close.'

'Let's get the plus-fives right up, skipper,' Jackson said. 'I'll take two and orbit right about here to watch the back door.' He tapped the chart.

'Play it cool, Rob.'

'No sweat, Ernie.' Jackson walked to a phone. 'Who's up?' he asked the VF-1 ready room. 'Good.' Jackson went off to get his flight suit and helmet.

'Gentlemen,' Richards said, as Jackson left, 'since we are now east of Malta, we are now part of the SIOP, therefore a strategic and not a conventional asset, and DEFCON-TWO applies to us. If anyone here needs a refresher on the DEFCON-TWO Rules of Engagement, you'd better do it fast. Anything that might be construed as a threat to us may be engaged and destroyed on my authority as battlegroup commander. Questions?'

'Sir, we don't know what is happening,' the ops officer pointed out.

'Yeah. We'll try to think first, but, people, let's get our collective act together. Something bad is happening, and we're at DEFCON-TWO.'

It was a fine, clear night on the flight deck. Jackson briefed Commander Sanchez and their respective RIOs, then the plane captains for the two Tomcats sitting on the waist cats walked the flight crews out to them. Jackson and Walters got aboard. The plane captain helped strap both in, then disappeared downward and removed the ladder. Captain Jackson ran through the start-up sequence, watching his engine instruments come into normal idle. The F-14D was currently armed with four radar-homing Phoenix missiles and four infra-red Sidewinders.

'Ready back there, Shredder?' Jackson asked.

'Let's do it, Spade,' Walter replied.

Robby pushed his throttles to the stops, then jerked them around the detente and into afterburner, and signaled his readiness to the catapult officer, who looked down the deck to make sure it was clear. The officer fired off a salute to the aircraft.

Jackson blinked his flying lights in reply, dropping his hand to the stick and pulling his head back against the rest. A second later, the cat officer's lighted wand touched the deck. A petty officer hit the firing button, and steam jetted into the catapult machinery.

For all his years at this business, his senses never quite seemed to be fast enough. The acceleration of the catapult nearly jerked his eyeballs around inside their sockets. The dim glow lights of the deck vanished behind him. The back of the aircraft settled, and they were off. Jackson made sure he was actually flying before taking the aircraft out of burner, then he retracted his gear and flaps, and started a slow climb to altitude. He was just through a thousand feet when 'Bud' Sanchez and 'Lobo' Alexander pulled alongside.

'There go the radars,' Shredder said, taking note of his instruments. The entire *TR* battlegroup shut down every emission in a matter of seconds. Now, noone would be able to track them from their own electronic noise.

Jackson settled down. Whatever this was, he told himself, it couldn't be all that bad, could it? It was a beautifully clear night, and the higher he got, the clearer it became through the panoramic canopy of his fighter. The stars were discrete pinpricks of light, and their twinkling ceased almost entirely as they reached thirty thousand feet. He could see the distant strobes of commercial aircraft, and the coastlines of half a dozen countries. A night like this, he thought, could make a poet of a peasant. It was for moments like these that he'd become a pilot. He turned west, with Sanchez on his wing. There were some clouds that way, he realized at once. He couldn't see all that many stars.

'Okay,' Jackson ordered, 'let's get a quick picture.'

The Radar Intercept Officer activated his systems. The F-14D had just been fitted with a new Hughes-built radar called an LPI for 'low probability of intercept.' Though using less power than the AWG-9 system it had replaced, the LPI combined greater sensitivity with a far lower chance of being picked up by another aircraft's threat receiver. It also had vastly improved look-down performance.

'There they are,' Walters reported. 'Nice circular formation.'

'They have anything up?'

'Everything I see has a transponder on.'

''Kay, we'll be on station in another few minutes.'

Fifty miles behind them, an E-2C Hawkeye airborne-early-warning bird was coming off the number-two catapult. Behind it, two KA-6 tankers were firing up, along with more fighters. The tankers would soon arrive at Jackson's station to top off his fuel tanks, enabling the CAG to stay aloft for four more hours. The E-2C was the most important. It climbed out at full military power, turning south to take station fifty miles from its mother ship. As soon as it reached twenty-five thousand, its surveillance radar switched on, and the onboard crew of three operators began cataloging their contacts. Their data was sent by digital link back to the carrier and also to the group air-warfare officer aboard the Aegis cruiser, USS *Thomas Gates*, whose call-sign was Stetson.

'Nothing much, skipper.'

'Okay, we're on station. Let's orbit and searchlight around.' Jackson turned his aircraft into a shallow right turn, with Sanchez in close formation.

The Hawkeye spotted them first. They were almost directly under Jackson and his two Tomcats, and out of the detection cone of their radars for the moment.

'Stetson, this is Falcon-Two, we have four bogies on the deck, bearing two-eight-one, one hundred miles out.' The reference was for *TR*'s position.

'IFF?'

'Negative, their speed is four hundred, altitude seven hundred, course one-three-five.'

'Amplify,' the AWO said.

'They're in a loose finger-four, Stetson,' the Hawkeye controller said. 'Estimate we have tactical fighters here.'

'I got something,' Shredder reported to Jackson a moment later. 'On the deck, looks like two – no, four aircraft, heading southeast.'

'Whose?'

'Not ours.'

In *TR*'s combat information center, no one as yet had a clue what was going on, but the group intelligence staff was doing its best to find out. What they had learned to this point was that most satellite news channels seemed to be down, though all military satellite links were up and running. A further electronic sweep of the satellite spectrum showed that a lot of video circuits were unaccountably inactive, as were the satellite phone links. So addicted were the communications people to the high-tech channels, that it required the services of a third-class radioman to suggest sweeping short-wave bands.

The first they found was BBC. The newsflash was recorded and raced into CIC. The voice spoke with the quiet assurance that the British Broadcasting Corporation was known for:

'Reuters reports a nuclear detonation in the Central United States. The Denver, Color*ahdo*' – the Brits have trouble pronouncing some American state names – 'television station, KOLD, broadcast via satellite a picture of a mushroom cloud over Denver, along with a voice report of a massive explosion. Station KOLD is now off the air, and attempts to reach Denver by telephone have not yet been successful. There has as yet been no official comment whatever on this incident.'

'Holy Christ,' someone said for all of them. Captain Richards looked around the room at his staff.

'Well, now we know why we're at DEFCON-TWO. Let's get some more fighters up. F-18s forward of us, -14s aft. I want four A-6s loaded with B-61s and briefed on SIOP targets. One squadron of -18s loaded with anti-ship missiles, and start planning an Alpha Strike on the *Kuznetzov* battlegroup.'

'Captain,' a talker called. 'Falcon reports four inbound tactical aircraft.'

Richards had only to turn around to see the main tactical display, a radar scope fully three feet across. The four new contacts showed up as inverted V-shapes with course vectors. Closest point of approach was less than twenty miles, easily within range of air-to-surface missiles.

'Have Spade ID those bandits right now!'

'. . . close and identify,' was the order from the Hawkeye control aircraft.

'Roger,' Jackson acknowledged. 'Bud, go loose.'

'Roger.' Commander Sanchez eased his stick to the left to open the distance between his fighter and Jackson's. Called the 'Loose Deuce,' the formation enabled the aircraft to be mutually supporting and also impossible to attack simultaneously. As he split off, both aircraft tipped down and dove at full dry power. In a few seconds, they were through Mach-One.

'Boresighted,' Shredder told his driver. 'I'm activating the TV system.'

The Tomcat was built with a simple identification device. It was a television camera with a ten-power telescopic lens that worked equally well in daylight and darkness. Lieutenant Walters was able to slave the TV into the radar system, and in a few seconds he had four dots that grew rapidly as the Tomcats overtook them. 'Twin rudder configuration.'

'Falcon, this is Spade. Inform Stick we have visual but no ID, and we are closing.'

Major Pyotr Arabov was no tenser than usual. An instructor pilot, he was teaching three Libyans the intricacies of night over-water navigation. They'd turned over the Italian island of Pantelleria thirty minutes earlier, and were now inbound for Tripoli and home. Formation flying at night was difficult for the three Libyans, though each had over three hundred hours in type, and over-water flying was the most dangerous of all. Fortunately, they had picked a good night for it. The star-filled sky gave them a good horizon reference. Better to learn the easy way first, Arabov thought, and at this altitude. A true tactical profile, at one hundred meters and higher speed on a cloudy night could be exceedingly dangerous. He was not any more impressed with the airmanship of these Libyans than the U.S. Navy had been on several occasions, but they did seem willing to learn, and that was something. Besides, their oil-rich country, having learned its own lessons from the Iraqis, had decided that if it were to have an air force at all, it had better have a properly trained one. That meant the Soviet Union could sell a lot more of its MiG-29s, despite the fact that sales in the Israel area were now severely curtailed. It also meant that Major Arabov was being paid partly in hard currency.

The instructor pilot looked left and right to see that

the formation was — well, not exactly tight, but close enough. The aircraft were behaving sluggishly with two fuel tanks under each wing. Each fuel tank had stabilizing fins, and looked rather like bombs, actually.

'They're carrying something, skipper. MiG-29s, for sure.'

'Right.' Jackson checked the display himself, then keyed his radio. 'Stick, this is Spade, over.'

'Go ahead.' The digital radio circuit allowed Jackson to recognize Captain Richards' voice.

'Stick, we have ID on the bogies. Four MiG-two-niners. They appear to have under-wing cargo. Course, speed, and altitude unchanged.' There was a brief pause. 'Splash the bandits.'

Jackson's head snapped up. 'Say again, Stick.'

'Spade, this is Stick: splash the bandits. Acknowledge.'

He called them 'bandits', Jackson thought. *And he knows more than I do.*

'Roger, engaging now. Out.' Jackson keyed his radio again. 'Bud, follow me in.'

'Shit!' Shredder observed. 'Recommend we target two Phoenix, left pair and right pair.'

'Do it,' Jackson replied, setting the weapons switch on the top of his stick to the AIM-54 setting. Lieutenant Walters programmed the missiles to keep their radars quiet until they were merely a mile out.

'Ready. Range is sixteen-thousand. Birds are in acquisition.'

Jackson's heads-up display showed the correct symbology. A beeping tone in his headset told him that the first missile was ready to fire. He squeezed the trigger once, waited a second, then squeezed again.

'Shit!' Michael 'Lobo' Alexander observed, half a mile away.

'You know better than that!' Sanchez snarled back at him.

'Sky is clear. I don't see anything else around us.'

Jackson closed his eyes to save as much of his vision as possible from the yellow-white exhaust flames of the missiles. They rapidly pulled away, accelerating to over three thousand miles per hour, almost a mile per second. Jackson watched them home in as he positioned his aircraft for another shot if the Phoenixes failed to function properly.

Arabov made another instrument check. There was nothing unusual. His threat receivers showed only air-search radars, though one reading had disappeared a few minutes earlier. Other than that, this was an exceedingly routine training mission, proceeding straight and level on a direct course towards a fixed point. His threat receivers had not detected the LPI radar which had been tracking him and his flight of four over the past five minutes. It was able, however, to detect the powerful homing radar in a Phoenix missile.

A bright red warning light flashed on, and a screeching sound abused his hearing. Arabov looked down to check his instruments. They seemed to be functioning, but this wasn't – his next move was to turn his head. He just had time to see a half-moon of yellow light and ghostly, star-lit smoke trail, then a flash.

The Phoenix targeted on the right-hand pair exploded just a few feet from them. The one hundred thirty-five pound warhead filled their air with high-speed fragments which shredded both MiGs. The same happened to the left-hand pair. The air was filled with an incandescent cloud of exploding jet fuel and airplane parts. Three pilots were killed directly by the explosion. Arabov was rocketed out of the disintegrating fighter by his ejection seat, whose parachute opened a scant two hundred feet over the water. Already unconscious from the unexpected shock of ejection, the Russian major was saved by systems that anticipated his injuries. An inflatable collar held his head above water, a UHF radio began screaming for the nearest rescue helicopter, and a powerful blue-white strobe light started flashing in the darkness. Around him were a few thin patches of burning fuel and nothing else.

*

Jackson watched the entire process. He'd probably set an all-time one-shot record. Four aircraft on one missile salvo. But there had been no skill involved. As with his Iraqi victim, they hadn't known he was there. Any new nugget right out of the RAG could have done this. It was murder, not war – what war? he asked, was there a war? – and he didn't even know why.

'Splash four MiGs,' he said over the radio. 'Stick, this is Spade, splash four. Returning to CAP station, we need some gas.'

'Roger, Spade, tankers are overhead now. We copy you splashed four.'

'Uh, Spade, what the fuck is going on?' Lieutenant Walters asked.

'I wish I knew, Shredder.' *Did I just fire the first shot in a war? What war?*

Despite his earlier screaming, the Guards tank regiment was about as sharp a Russian unit as Keitel had ever seen. Their T-80 main battle tanks looked slightly toy-like with their reactive armor panels festooned on turret and hull, but they were also low-slung dangerous-looking vehicles whose enormously long 125mm guns left no doubt as to their identity and purpose. The supposed inspection team was moving about in groups of three. Keitel had the most dangerous mission, as he was with the regimental commander. Keitel – 'Colonel Ivanenko' – checked his watch as he walked behind the real colonel.

Just two hundred meters away, Günther Bock and two other ex-Stasi officers approached a tank crew. They were boarding their vehicle as the officers approached.

'Stop!' one ordered.

'Yes, Colonel,' the junior sergeant who commanded the tank replied.

'Step down. We are going to inspect your vehicle.'

The commander, gunner, and driver assembled in front of their vehicle while the other crews boarded theirs. Bock waited for the neighboring tanks to button up, then shot all three Russians with his silenced automatic. The three bodies were tossed under the tank. Bock took the gunner's seat, and looked around for the controls he'd been briefed on. Not twelve hundred meters away, parked at right angles to his tank, were over fifty American M1A1 tanks whose crews were also boarding their vehicles.

'Power coming on,' the driver reported over the intercom. The diesel engine roared to life along with all the others.

Bock flipped the loading switch to Armor-Piercing Fin-Stabilized Discarding-Sabot round and punched the load button. Automatically, the breech to the tank's main gun dropped open, and first the shell, then the propellant charge were rammed home, and the breech shut by itself. That, Bock thought, was easy enough. Next he depressed the gunsight and selected an American tank. It was easy to spot. The American tank park was lit up like any parking lot so that trespassers might easily be spotted. The laser gave him a range display, and Bock elevated the gun to the proper stadimeter line. The wind he estimated as zero. It was a calm night. Bock checked his watch and waited for the sweep hand to reach the twelve. Then he squeezed the triggers. Bock's T-80 rocked backwards, along with three others. Two-thirds of a second later, the shell struck the turret of the American tank. The results were impressive. He'd struck the ammo compartment in the rear of the turret. The forty rounds of ammunition ignited at once. Blow-out panels vented most of it straight up, but the protective fire-doors inside the vehicle had already been blown out by the shell, and the crew incinerated in their seats as their two-million-dollar tank turned into a mottled green-and-brown volcano, along with two others.

One hundred meters to the north, the regimental commander froze in mid-sentence, turning towards the noise in disbelief.

'What's going on?' he managed to shout, before Keitel shot him in the back of the head.

Bock had already fired his second round into the engine box of another tank, and was loading a third. Seven M1A1s were burning before the first American gunner got a round loaded. The huge turret swung around while tank commanders screamed orders at their drivers and gunners. Bock saw the operating turret and swung towards it. His round missed wide to the left, but struck another Abrams behind the first. The American shot also missed high, because the gunner was excited. His second round was instantly loaded, and the American exploded a T-80 two down from Bock's. Günther decided to leave this American alone.

'We're under attack – commence firing commence firing!' the 'Soviet' tank commanders screamed into their own command circuits.

Keitel ran to the command vehicle. 'I am Colonel Ivanenko. Your commander is dead – get moving! Take those crazy bastards out while we still have a regiment left!'

The operations officer hesitated, having not the slightest idea what was happening, only able to hear the gunfire. But the orders came from a colonel. He lifted his radio, dialed up the battalion command circuit and relayed the instruction.

There was the expected moment's hesitation. At least ten American tanks were now burning, but four were shooting back. Then the entire Soviet line opened fire, and three of the active American tanks were blown apart. Those shielded by the front row began firing off smoke and maneuvering, mainly backwards, as the Soviet tanks started to roll. Keitel watched in admiration as the Soviet T-80s moved out. Seven of them remained still, of which four were burning. Two more blew up before they crossed the line where once a wall had stood.

It was worth it, Keitel thought, just for this moment. Whatever Günther had in mind, it was worth it to see the Russians and Americans killing each other.

Admiral Joshua Painter arrived at CINCLANT headquarters just in time to catch the dispatch from *Theodore Roosevelt*.

'Who's in command there?'

'Sir, the battlegroup commander flew into Naples.

Senior officer in the group is Captain Richards,' Fleet Intelligence replied. 'He said he had four MiGs inbound and armed, and since we're at DEFCON-TWO, he splashed them as a potential threat to the group.'

'Whose MiGs?'

'Could be from the *Kuznetzov* group, sir.'

'Wait a minute – you said DEFCON-TWO?'

'*TR*'s east of Malta now, sir, SIOP applies,' Fleet Operations pointed out.

'Does anybody know what's going on?'

'I sure as hell don't,' the Fleet Intelligence Officer replied honestly.

'Get me Richards on a voice line.' Painter stopped. 'What's the fleet status?'

'Everything alongside has orders to prepare to get underway, sir. That's automatic.'

'But why are we *at* DEFCON-THREE here?'

'Sir, they haven't told us that.'

'Fabulous.' Painter pulled the sweater over his head and yelled for coffee.

'*Roosevelt* on line two, sir,' the intercom called. Painter punched the button and put the phone on speaker.

'This is CINCLANT.'

'Richards here, sir.'

'What's going on?'

'Sir, we're fifteen minutes into a DEFCON-TWO alert here. We had a flight of MiG-29s inbound, and I ordered them splashed.'

'Why?'

'They appeared to be armed, sir, and we copied a radio transmission about the explosion.'

Painter went instantly cold. 'What explosion?'

'Sir, BBC reports a nuclear detonation in Denver. The local TV station that originated the report, they say, is now off the air. With that kind of information, I took the shot. I'm senior officer present. It's my battlegroup here. Sir, unless you have some more questions, I have things to do here.'

Painter knew he had to get out of the man's way. 'Use your head, Ernie. Use your goddamned head.'

'Aye aye, sir. Out.' The line went dead.

'Nuclear explosion?' Fleet Intelligence asked.

Painter had a hot line to the National Military Command Center. He activated it. 'This is CINCLANT.'

'Captain Rosselli, sir.'

'Have we had a nuclear explosion?'

'That's affirmative, sir. In the Denver area, NORAD estimates yield in the low hundreds and high casualties. That's all we know. We haven't got the word out to everyone yet.'

'Well, here's something else for you to know: *Theodore Roosevelt* just intercepted and splashed four MiG-29s inbound. Keep me posted. Unless otherwise directed, I'm putting everything to sea.'

Bob Fowler was into his third cup of coffee already. He was cursing himself for having drunk those four, strong German beers like he was Archie Bunker or something, and one of his fears was that the people here would notice the alcohol on his breath. Intellect told him that his thought processes might be somewhat affected by the alcohol intake, but he'd had the drinks over a period of hours, and natural processes plus the coffee either already had or soon would purge it from his system entirely.

For the first time, he was grateful for the death of his wife Marion. He'd been there at the bedside, had watched his beloved wife die. He knew what grief and tragedy were, and however dreadful the deaths of all those people in Denver might be, he told himself, he had to step back from it, had to set it aside, had to concentrate on preventing the death of anyone else.

So far, Fowler told himself, things had gone well. He had moved quickly to cut off the spread of the news. A nationwide panic was something that he didn't need. His military services were at a higher level of alert that would either prevent or deter an additional attack for some indefinite period of time.

'Okay,' he said on the conference line to NORAD and SAC. 'Let's summarize what has happened to this point.'

NORAD answered: 'Sir, we've had a single nuclear detonation in the hundred-kiloton range. There has as yet been no report from the scene. Our forces are moving to a high state of alert. Satellite communications are down –'

'Why?' Elizabeth Elliot asked in a voice more brittle than Fowler's. 'What could have done that?'

'We don't know. A nuclear detonation in space might, from EMP effects – that's electromagnetic pulse. When a nuclear device explodes at high altitude, most of its energy is released in the form of electromagnetic radiation. The Russians know more about the practical effects of such explosions than we do; they have more empirical data from their tests at Novaya Zemlya back in the 1960s. But we have no evidence of such an explosion, and we should have noticed it. Therefore, a nuclear attack on satellites is most unlikely. Next possibility is a massive blast of electromagnetic energy from a ground source. Now, the Russians *have* pumped a lot of money into microwave weapons-research. They have a ship in the Eastern Pacific with lots of antennas aboard. It's the *Yuri Gagarin*. She's classed as a space-event-support ship, and she has four enormous high-gain antennas. That ship is currently three hundred miles off the coast of Peru, well within sight of the injured satellites. Supposedly, the ship is supporting operations for the *Mir* space station. Aside from that, we're out of guesses. I have an officer talking with Hughes Aerospace right now to see what their thinking is.

'Okay, we're still trying to get ATC tapes from Stapleton to see if an aircraft might have delivered the bomb, and we are awaiting word from rescue and other teams dispatched to the site of the explosion. That's all I have.'

'We have two wings fully in the air, and more coming on line as we speak,' CINC-SAC said next. 'All my missile wings are alerted. My Vice-CINC is in the air in Looking Glass Auxiliary West, and another Kneecap is about to take off for where you are, sir.'

'Anything happening in the Soviet Union?'

'Their air-defense people are increasing their alert level, as we have already discussed,' General Borstein replied. 'We're getting other radio activity, but nothing we can classify yet. There is no indication of an attack on the United States.'

'Okay.' The President let out a breath. Things were bad, but not out of control. All he had to do was get things settled down, and then he could go forward. 'I'm going to open the direct line to Moscow.'

'Very well, sir,' NORAD replied.

A Navy chief yeoman was two seats away from President Fowler. His computer terminal was already lit up. 'You want to slide down here, Mr President,' the chief said. 'I can't cross-deck my display to your screen.'

Fowler crab-walked his swivel chair the eight feet to the chief's place.

'Sir, the way this works is, I type in what you say here, and it's relayed directly through the NMCC computers in the Pentagon – all they do is encipher it – but when the Russians reply, it arrives in the Hot Line room in Russian, is translated there, and then sent here from the Pentagon. There's a backup at Fort Ritchie in case something goes wrong in D.C. We have land-line and two separate satellite links. Sir, I can type about as fast as you can speak.' The chief yeoman's nametag read ORONTIA, and Fowler couldn't decide what his ancestry was. He was a good twenty pounds overweight, but he sounded relaxed and competent. Fowler would settle for that. Chief Orontia also had a pack of cigarettes sitting next to his keyboard. The President stole one, ignoring the no-smoking signs that hung on every wall. Orontia lit it with a Zippo.

'All ready, sir.' Chief Pablo Orontia looked sideways at his Commander-in-Chief. His gaze didn't betray the fact that he'd been born in Pueblo, Colorado, and still had family there. The President would settle things down, that was his job. Orontia's job, he reasoned, was to do his best to help the man. Orontia had served his country in two wars and many other crises, mainly as an admiral's yeoman on carriers, and now he turned off his feelings as he had trained himself to do.

'Dear President Narmonov . . .'

Captain Rosselli watched the first for-real transmission on the Hot Line since his arrival in Washington. The message was put up on the IBM-PC/AT and encrypted, then the computer operator hit the return button to transmit it. He really should be back at his desk, Jim thought, but what went through here might be vital to what he was doing.

'As you have probably been told there has been a major explosion in the central part of my country. I have been told that it was a nuclear explosion and that the loss of life is severe,' President Narmonov read, with his advisors at his side.

'About what one would expect,' Narmonov said. 'Send our reply.'

'Jesus, that was fast!' the Army colonel on duty remarked and began his translation. A Marine sergeant typed the English version, which was automatically linked to Camp David, Fort Ritchie, and the State Department. The computers printed out hard copy that was sent almost as fast to SAC, NORAD, and the intelligence agencies via facsimile printer.

> AUTHENTICATOR: TIMETABLE TIMETABLE
> TIMETABLE
> REPLY FROM MOSCOW
> PRESIDENT FOWLER:
> WE HAVE NOTED THE EVENT. PLEASE
> ACCEPT OUR DEEPEST SYMPATHY AND THAT OF
> THE SOVIET PEOPLE. HOW IS SUCH AN
> ACCIDENT POSSIBLE?

'Accident?' Fowler asked.

'That was awfully fast, Robert,' Elliot observed at once. 'Too damned fast. His English isn't very good. The message had to be translated, and you take time to read

things like this. Their reply must have been canned —
made up in advance . . . what does that mean?' Liz asked,
almost talking to herself, as Fowler formulated his next
message. *What's going on here? Who is doing this, and
why . . . ?*

> PRESIDENT NARMONOV:
> I REGRET TO INFORM YOU THAT THIS WAS
> NOT AN ACCIDENT. THERE IS NO AMERICAN
> NUCLEAR DEVICE WITHIN A HUNDRED MILES,
> NOR WERE ANY US WEAPONS IN TRANSIT IN
> THE AREA. THIS WAS A DELIBERATE ACT BY
> UNKNOWN FORCES.

'Well, that's no surprise,' Narmonov said. He congratulated himself for correctly predicting the first message from America. 'Send the next reply,' he told the
communicator. To his advisers: 'Fowler is an arrogant
man, with the weaknesses of arrogance, but he is no fool.
He will be very emotional about this. We must settle
him down, calm him. If he can keep control of himself,
his intelligence will allow him to maintain control of
the matter.'

'My President,' said Golovko, who had just arrived in
the command center. 'I think this is a mistake.'

'What do you mean?' Narmonov asked in some
surprise.

'It is a mistake to tailor your words to what you think
of the man, his character, and his mental state. People
change under stress. The man at the other end of that
telephone line may not be the same man whom you met
in Rome.'

The Soviet President dismissed that idea. 'Nonsense.
People like that never change. We have enough of them
here. I've been dealing with people like Fowler all my
life.'

> PRESIDENT FOWLER:
> IF THIS IS IN FACT A DELIBERATE ACT THEN
> IT IS A CRIME WHOLLY WITHOUT
> PRECEDENT IN HUMAN HISTORY. WHAT

MADMAN WOULD DO SUCH A THING, AND TO WHAT PURPOSE? SUCH ACTION MIGHT ALL TOO EASILY LEAD TO GLOBAL CATASTROPHE. YOU MUST BELIEVE THAT THE SOVIET UNION HAD NOTHING TO DO WITH THIS INFAMOUS ACT.

'Too fast, Robert,' Elliot said. '"You must believe"? What is this guy trying to say?'

'Elizabeth, you're reading too much into this,' Fowler replied.

'These responses are *canned*, Robert! Canned. He's answering too fast. He had them prepared in advance. That means something.'

'Like what?'

'Like we were supposed to be *at the game*, Robert! It looks to me like these were tailored for somebody else – like Durling. What if the bomb was supposed to get you, too, along with Brent and Dennis?'

'I have to set that aside, I told you that!' Fowler said angrily. He paused and took a deep breath. He could not allow himself to get angry. He had to stay calm. 'Look, Elizabeth –'

'You *can't* set that aside! You have to consider that possibility, because if it was planned, that tells us something about what is going on.'

'Dr Elliot is right,' NORAD said over the open phone line. 'Mr President, you are entirely correct to distance yourself from this event in an emotional sense, but you have to consider all possible aspects of the operational concept that may be at work here.'

'I am compelled to agree with that,' CINC-SAC added.

'So, what do I do?' Fowler asked.

'Sir,' NORAD said, 'I don't like this "you must believe" stuff, either. It might be a good idea to let him know that we're ready to defend ourselves.'

'Yeah,' General Fremont agreed. 'He knows that, anyway, if his people are doing their job right.'

'But what if he takes our alert level as a threat?'

'They won't, sir,' NORAD assured him. 'It's just how

anybody would do business in a case like this. Their senior military leadership is very professional.'

Dr Elliot stirred at that remark, Fowler noted. 'Okay, I'll tell him we've alerted our forces, but that we don't have any evil intentions.'

> PRESIDENT NARMONOV:
> WE HAVE NO REASON TO SUSPECT SOVIET INVOLVEMENT IN THIS INCIDENT. HOWEVER WE MUST ACT PRUDENTLY. WE HAVE BEEN THE VICTIM OF A VICIOUS ATTACK, AND MUST TAKE ACTION TO PROTECT OURSELVES AGAINST ANOTHER. ACCORDINGLY I HAVE PLACED OUR ARMED FORCES ON A PRECAUTIONARY ALERT. THIS IS ALSO NECESSARY FOR THE MAINTENANCE OF PUBLIC ORDER, AND TO ASSIST IN RESCUE OPERATIONS. YOU HAVE MY PERSONAL ASSURANCE THAT WE WILL TAKE NO OFFENSIVE ACTION WITHOUT JUST CAUSE.

'That's reassuring,' Narmonov said dryly. 'Nice of him to let us know about the alert.'

'We know,' Golovko said, 'and he must know that we already know.'

'He does not know that we know the extent of his alert,' the Defense Minister said. 'He cannot know that we are reading their codes. The alert level of their forces is more than precautionary. The American strategic forces have not been at this readiness status since 1962.'

'Really?' Narmonov asked.

'General, this is not technically true,' Golovko said urgently. 'Their ordinary level of readiness is very high for American strategic forces, even when their military posture is Defense Condition Five. The change to which you refer is inconsequential.'

'Is this true?' Narmonov asked.

The Defense Minister shrugged. 'It depends on how you look at it. Their land-based rocket force is always at a higher level of alert than ours because of the lower maintenance requirements of their rockets. The same is true of their submarines, which spend far more time at sea than ours do. The technical difference may be small, but the psychological difference is not. The increased level of alert tells their people that something horrible is underway. I think that is significant.'

'I do not,' Golovko shot back.

Marvelous, Narmonov thought, *two of my most important advisors cannot agree on something this important* . . .

'We need to reply,' the Foreign Minister said.

> PRESIDENT FOWLER:
> WE HAVE NOTED YOUR INCREASED ALERT
> STATUS. SINCE MOST OF YOUR WEAPONS
> ARE IN FACT POINTED AT THE SOVIET UNION
> WE MUST ALSO TAKE PRECAUTIONS. I
> SUGGEST THAT IT IS VITAL THAT NEITHER OF
> OUR TWO COUNTRIES TAKE ANY ACTION THAT
> MIGHT SEEM PROVOCATIVE.

'That's the first time he didn't have it canned,' Elliot said. 'First he says "I didn't do it," now he says we better not provoke him. What's he really thinking?'

Ryan looked over the faxes of all six messages. He handed them to Goodley. 'Tell me what you think.'

'Pure vanilla. Looks like everyone is playing a very cautious game, and that's what they should be doing. We alert our forces as a precaution, and they do the same. Fowler's said that we have no reason to think they did it – that's good. Narmonov says both sides should play it cool on provoking the other side – that's good, too. So far, so good,' Ben Goodley thought.

'I agree,' the Senior Duty Officer said.

'That makes it unanimous,' Jack said. *Thank God. Bob, I didn't know you had it in you.*

Rosselli walked back to his desk. Okay, things appeared to be more or less under control.

'Where the hell have you been?' Rocky Barnes asked.

'Hot Line room, things appear to be fairly cool.'
'Not anymore, Jim.'

General Paul Wilkes was almost there. It had taken nearly twenty minutes to get from his house onto I-295 and from there to I-395, a total distance of less than five miles. Snowplows had barely touched this road, and now it was cold enough that what had been salted was freezing to ice anyway. Worst of all, those few D.C. drivers who were venturing out were showing their customary driving skill. Even those with four-wheel-drives were acting as though the additional traction made them immune to the laws of physics. Wilkes had just passed over South Capitol Street, and was now heading downhill towards the Maine Avenue exit. To his left, some maniac in a Toyota was passing him, and then came right, to head for the exit into downtown D.C. The Toyota skidded sideways on a patch of ice that front-wheel drive didn't master. There was no chance to avoid it. Wilkes broadsided the car at about fifteen miles per hour.

'The hell with it,' he said aloud. He didn't have time for this. The General backed up a few feet and started to maneuver around before the driver even got out. He didn't check his mirror. As he changed lanes, he was rear-ended by a tractor-trailer doing about twenty-five. It was enough to drive the General's car over the concrete divider and into the face of another car. Wilkes was killed instantly.

CHAPTER 39

Echoes

Elizabeth Elliot stared blankly at the far wall as she sipped her coffee. It was the only thing that made sense. All the warnings they'd had and ignored. It all fit. The Soviet military was making a power-play, and targeting Bob Fowler had to be part of it. *We should have been there*, she thought. *He wanted to go to the game, and everyone expected him to, because Dennis Bunker owned one of the teams. I would have been there, too. I could be dead now. If they wanted to kill Bob, then they also wanted to kill me . . .*

> PRESIDENT NARMONOV:
> I AM GRATIFIED THAT WE AGREE ON THE NECESSITY FOR CAUTION AND REASON. I MUST NOW CONFER WITH MY ADVISERS SO THAT WE MAY ASCERTAIN THE CAUSE OF THIS HORRIBLE EVENT, AND ALSO TO BEGIN RESCUE OPERATIONS. I WILL KEEP YOU INFORMED.

The reply that came back was almost immediate.

> PRESIDENT FOWLER:
> WE WILL STAND BY.

'That's simple enough,' the President said, looking at the screen.

'Think so?' Elliot asked.

'What do you mean?'

'Robert, we've had a nuclear explosion at a location that you were supposed to be at. That's number one. Number two: we've had reports of missing Soviet nuclear weapons. Number three: how do we really know that it's Narmonov at the other end of this computer modem?' Liz asked.

'What?'

'Our best intelligence suggests the possibility of a *coup d'état* in Russia, doesn't it? But we're acting as though such intelligence did not exist, *even though* we've had what very easily could be a tactical nuclear weapon – exactly what we think is missing – explode over here. We are not considering all of the potential dimensions here.' Dr Elliot turned to the speaker phone. 'General Borstein, how hard is it to get a nuclear device into the United States?'

'With our border controls, it's child's play,' NORAD replied. 'What are you saying, Dr Elliot?'

'I'm saying that we've had hard intel for some time now that Narmonov is in political trouble – that his military is acting up, *and* that there's a nuclear dimension. Okay, what if they stage a coup? A Sunday evening – Monday morning – is good timing, because everyone's asleep. We always assumed that the nuclear element was for domestic blackmail – but what if the operation was more clever than that? What if they figured they could decapitate our government in order to prevent our interference with their coup? Okay, the bomb goes off, and Durling is on Kneecap – just like he is right now – and they're talking to him. They can predict what we're going to think, and they pre-plan their statements over the Hot Line. We go on automatic alert, and so do they – you see? We *can't* interfere with the coup in any way.'

'Mr President, before you evaluate that possibility, I think you need some outside advice from the intelligence community,' CINC-SAC said.

Another phone lit up. The yeoman got it.

'For you, Mr President, NMCC.'

'Who is this?' Fowler asked.

'Sir, this is Captain Jim Rosselli at the National Military Command Center. We have two reports of contact between U.S. and Soviet forces. USS *Theodore Roosevelt* reports that they have splashed – that means shot down, sir – a flight of four inbound Russian MiG-29 aircraft –'

'What? Why?'

'Sir, under the Rules of Engagement, the captain of a ship has the right to take defense action to protect his command. *Theodore Roosevelt* is now at DEFCON-TWO, and as the alert level changes, you get more latitude in what you can do, and when you can take action. Sir, the second is as follows: there is an unconfirmed report of shots being exchanged between Russian and American tanks in Berlin. SACEUR says the radio message stopped – I mean, it was cut off, sir. Before that, a U.S. Army captain reported that Soviet tanks were attacking the Berlin Brigade at its base in southern Berlin, and that a tank battalion of ours was just about wiped out, sir. They were attacked in their lager by Soviet forces stationed just across from them. Those two things – the reports, I mean, were almost simultaneous. The reported times were just two minutes apart, Mr President. We're trying to reestablish contact with Berlin right now, going through SACEUR at Mons, Belgium.'

'Christ,' Fowler observed. 'Elizabeth, does this fit into your scenario?'

'It could show that they're not kidding, that they are serious about not being interfered with.'

Most of the American forces had escaped out of the lager. The senior officer on the scene had decided on the spot to turn and run for cover in the woods and residential streets around the brigade base. He was a lieutenant-colonel, the brigade executive officer. The colonel commanding the brigade was nowhere to be found, and the XO was now considering his options. The brigade had two mechanized infantry battalions, and one of tanks. From the last, only nine of fifty-two M1A1s had gotten away. He could see the glow from the rest of them, still burning in their lager.

A DEFCON-THREE alert out of nowhere, and then minutes later, this. Over forty tanks and a hundred men lost, shot down without warning. Well, he'd see about that.

The Berlin Brigade had been in place since long before

his birth, and scattered throughout its encampment were defensive positions. The colonel dispatched his remaining tanks, and ordered his Bradley fighting vehicles to volley-fire their TOW-2 missiles.

The Russian tanks had overrun the tank lager and stopped. They had no further orders. Battalion commanders were not yet in control of their formations, left behind by the mad dash of the T-80s across the line, and the regimental commander was nowhere to be found. Without orders, the tank companies stopped, sitting still, looking for targets. The regimental executive officer was also missing, and when the senior battalion commander realized this, his tank dashed off to the headquarters vehicle, since he was the next-senior officer in the regiment. It was amazing, he thought. First the readiness drill, next the flash alert from Moscow, and then the Americans had started shooting. He hadn't a clue what was going on. Even the barracks and administrative buildings were still lit up, he realized. Someone would have to get those lights off. His T-80 was back-lit as though on a target range.

'Command tank, two o'clock, skylined, moving left to right,' a sergeant told a corporal.

'Identified,' the gunner replied over the intercom.

'Fire.'

'On the way.' The corporal squeezed his trigger. The seal-cap blew off the missile tube, and the TOW-2 blasted out, trailing behind a thin control wire. The target was about twenty-five hundred meters away. The gunner kept his cross-hairs on target, guiding the anti-tank missile to its target. It took eight seconds, and the gunner had the satisfaction of seeing detonation right in the center of the turret.

'Target,' the Bradley commander said, indicating a direct hit. 'Cease fire. Now let's find another one of these fuckers ... ten o'clock, tank, coming around the PX!'

The turret came left. 'Identified!'

*

'Okay, what does CIA make of this?' Fowler asked.

'Sir, again, all we have is scattered and unconnected information,' Ryan replied.

'*Roosevelt* has a Soviet carrier battlegroup a few hundred miles behind them, and they carry MiG-29s,' Admiral Painter said.

'They're even closer to Libya, and our friend the colonel has a hundred of the same aircraft.'

'Flying over water at midnight?' Painter asked. 'When's the last time you heard of the Libyans doing that – and twenty-some miles from one of our battlegroups!'

'What about Berlin?' Liz Elliot asked.

'We don't know!' Ryan stopped and took a deep breath. 'Remember that we just don't know much.'

'Ryan, what if SPINNAKER was right?' Elliot asked.

'What do you mean?'

'What if there is a military coup going on right now over there, and they set a bomb off over here to keep us from interfering, to decapitate us?'

'That's totally crazy,' Jack answered. 'Risk a war? Why do it? What would we do if there were a coup? Attack at once?'

'Their military might expect us to,' Elliot pointed out.

'Disagree. I think SPINNAKER might have been lying to us from the beginning on this issue.'

'Are you making this up?' Fowler asked. It was coming home to the President now that he might actually have been the real target of the bomb, that Elizabeth's theoretical model for the Russian plan was the only thing that made sense.

'No, sir!' Ryan snapped back indignantly. 'I'm the *hawk* here, remember? The Russian military is too smart to pull something like this. It's too big a gamble.'

'Then explain the attacks on our forces!' Elliot said.

'We don't know for sure that there have been attacks on our forces.'

'So, now you think our people are lying?' Fowler asked.

'Mr President, you are not thinking this through. Okay, let's assume that there is an on-going coup in the Soviet Union – I don't accept that hypothesis, but let's assume it, okay? The purpose, you say, for exploding the bomb over here is to keep us from interfering. Fine. Then why attack our military forces if they want us to sit on our hands?'

'To show that they're serious,' Elliot fired back.

'That's crazy! It's tantamount to telling us they *did* explode the bomb here. Do you think they would expect us not to respond to a nuclear attack?' Ryan demanded, then answered his own question: '*It does not make sense!*'

'Then give me something that does,' Fowler said.

'Mr President, we are in the very earliest stages of a crisis. The information we have coming in now is scattered and confused. Until we know more, trying to put a spin on it is dangerous.'

Fowler's face bore down on the speaker phone. 'Your job is to tell me what's going on, not to give me lessons in crisis-management. When you have something I can use, get back to me!'

'What in the hell are they thinking?' Ryan asked.

'Is there something I don't know here?' Goodley asked. The young academic looked as alarmed as Ryan felt.

'Why should you be any different from the rest of us?' Jack snapped back, and regretted it. 'Welcome to crisis-management. Nobody knows crap, and you're expected to make good decisions anyway. Except it's not possible, it just isn't.'

'The thing with the carrier scares me,' the S&T man observed.

'Wrong. If we only splashed four aircraft, it's only a handful of people,' Ryan pointed out. 'Land combat is something else. If we really have a battle going on in Berlin, that's the scary one, almost as bad as an attack on some of our strategic assets. Let's see if we can get hold of SACEUR.'

The nine surviving M1A1 tanks were racing north along a Berlin avenue, along with a platoon of Bradley fighting vehicles. Street lights were on, heads sticking out windows and it was instantly apparent to the few onlookers that whatever was happening wasn't a drill. All the tanks had the speed governors removed from their engines, and they could all have been arrested in America for violating the national interstate highway limit. One mile north of their camp, they turned east. Leading the formation was a senior NCO who knew Berlin well – this was his third tour in the once-divided city – well enough that he had a perfect spot in mind, if the Russians hadn't got there first. There was a construction site. A memorial to the Wall and its victims was going up after a long competition. It overlooked the Russian and American compounds which were soon to be vacated, and bulldozers had pushed up a high berm of dirt for the sculpture that would sit atop it. But it wasn't there yet, just a thick dirt ramp. The Soviet tanks were milling about on their objective, probably waiting for their infantry to show up or something. They were taking TOW hits from the Bradleys, and returning fire into the woods.

'Christ, they're going to kill those Bradley guys,' the unit commander – a captain whose tank was the last survivor of his company – said. 'Okay, find your spots.' That took another minute. Then the tanks were hull-down, just their guns and the tops of turrets showing. 'Straight down the line! Commence firing, fire at will.'

All nine tanks fired at once. The range was just over two thousand meters, and now the element of surprise was with someone else. Five Russian tanks died with the first volley, and six more in the second, as the Abrams tanks went into rapid fire.

In the trees with the Bradleys, the brigade XO watched the north end of the Russian line crumple. That was the only word for it, he thought. The tank crews were all combat vets, and now they had the edge. The northernmost Russian battalion tried to reorient itself, but one of his Bradleys had evidently scored on its commander, and there was confusion there. Why the Russians hadn't pressed home the attack was one question that floated about the rear of his brain, but that was something to save for the after-action report. Right now he saw that they had screwed up, and that was a good thing for him and his men.

'Sir, I've got Seventh Army.' A sergeant handed him a microphone.

'What's happening over there?'

'General, this is Lieutenant Colonel Ed Long, we just got our ass attacked by the regiment across town from us. No warning at all, they just came into our kazerne like Jeb Stuart. We've got 'em stopped, but I've lost most of my tanks. We need some help here.'

'Losses?'

'Sir, I've lost over forty tanks, eight Bradleys, and at least two hundred men.'

'Opposition?'

'One regiment of tanks. Nothing else yet, but they have lots of friends, sir. I could sure use some myself.'

'I'll see what I can do.'

General Kuropatkin checked his status board. Every radar system that was not down for repair was now operating. Satellite information told him that two SAC bases were empty. That meant their aircraft were now airborne and flying towards the Soviet Union along with KC-135 tankers. Their missile fields would also be at full alert. His Eagle satellites would give launch-warning, announcing that his country had thirty minutes left to live. Thirty minutes, the General thought. Thirty minutes and the reason of the American president were all that stood between life and death for his country.

'Air activity picking up over Germany,' a colonel said. 'We show some American fighters coming out from Ramstein and Bitberg, heading east. Total of eight aircraft.'

'What do we have on the American Stealth fighters?'

'There is a squadron – eighteen of them – at Ramstein. Supposedly, the Americans are demonstrating them for possible sale to their NATO allies.'

'They could be all in the air right now,' Kuropatkin noted, 'carrying nuclear weapons, for that matter.'

'Correct, they can easily carry two B-61-type weapons each. With high-altitude cruise, they could be over Moscow before we knew it . . .'

'And with their bombsights . . . they could lay their weapons exactly on any target they wish . . . two and a half hours from the time they lift off . . . my God.' In the weapon's earth-penetration mode, it could be placed close enough to eliminate the president's shelter. Kuropatkin lifted his phone. 'I need to talk to the President.'

'Yes, General, what is it?' Narmonov asked.

'We have indications of American air activity over Germany.'

'There's more than that. A Guards regiment in Berlin reports being under attack by American troops.'

'That's mad.'

And the report came in not five minutes after my friend Fowler promised not to do anything provocative. 'Speak quickly, I have enough business here already.'

'President Narmonov. Two weeks ago, a squadron of American F-117A Stealth fighters arrived at their Ramstein air base, ostensibly for demonstration to their NATO allies. The Americans said they want to sell them. Each of those aircraft can carry two half-megaton weapons.'

'Yes?'

'I cannot detect them. They are virtually invisible to everything we have.'

'What are you telling me?'

'From the time they leave their bases, then refuel, they can be over Moscow in less than three hours. We would have no more warning than Iraq had.'

'Are they truly that effective?'

'One reason we left so many people in Iraq was to observe closely what the Americans are capable of. Our people never saw that American plane on a radar scope, neither ours nor the French scopes Saddam had. Yes, they are that good.'

'But why should they wish to do such a thing?' Narmonov demanded.

887

'Why would they attack our regiment in Berlin?' the Defense Minister asked in reply.

'I thought this place was proof against anything in their arsenal.'

'Not against a nuclear gravity bomb delivered with high accuracy. We are only one hundred meters down here,' Defense said. *In the old battle between warhead and armor, warhead always wins . . .*

'Back to Berlin,' Narmonov said. 'Do we know what's happening there?'

'No, what we have has come from junior officers only.'

'Get someone in there to find out. Tell our people to fall back if they can do so safely – and take defensive action only. Do you object to that?'

'No, that is prudent.'

The National Photographic Intelligence Center, NPIC, is located at the Washington Navy Yard, in one of several windowless buildings housing highly sensitive government activities. At the moment, they had a total of three KH-11 photographic and two KH-12 'Lacrosse' radar-imaging satellites in orbit. At 00:26:46 Zulu Time, one of the -11s came within optical range of Denver. All of its cameras zoomed in on the city, especially its southern suburbs. The images were down-linked in real time to Fort Belvoir, Virginia, and sent from there to NPIC by fiber-optic cable. At NPIC, they were recorded in two-inch videotape. Analysis started immediately.

This aircraft was a DC-10. Qati and Ghosn again availed themselves of first-class seating, pleased and amazed at their good luck. The word had gotten out only minutes before the flight was called. As soon as the report had gone out on the Reuters wire, it had been inevitable. AP and UPI had instantly picked it up, and all television stations subscribed to the wire services. Surprised that the networks had not yet put out their own special bulletins, the local affiliates ran with it anyway. The one thing about it that had surprised Qati was the silence. As the word spread like a wave through the terminal building, what lay behind it was not shouting and panic, but an eerie silence that allowed one to hear the flight calls and other background noises normally submerged by the cacophony of voices in such public areas. So the Americans faced tragedy and death, the Commander thought. The lack of passion surprised him.

It was soon behind him in any case. The DC-10 accelerated down the runway and lifted off. A few minutes later, it was over international waters, heading towards a neutral country and safety. One more connection, both men thought in a silence of their own. One more connection, and they would disappear completely. Who would have expected such luck?

'The infra-red emissions are remarkable,' the photo-analyst thought aloud. It was his first nuclear detonation. 'I have damage and secondary fires up to a mile from the stadium. Not much of the stadium itself. Too much smoke and IR interference. Next pass, if we're lucky, we ought to have some visible-light imagery.'

'What can you tell us about casualty count?' Ryan asked.

'What I have is inconclusive. Mainly the visible-light shots show smoke that's obscuring everything. Infra-red levels are very impressive. Lots of fires immediately around the stadium itself. Cars, I guess, gas tanks cooking off.'

Jack turned to the senior Science and Technology officer. 'Who do we have up in the photo section?'

'Nobody,' S&T replied. 'Weekend, remember? We let NPIC handle weekend work unless we expect something hot.'

'Who's the best guy?'

'Andy Davis, but he lives in Manassas. He'll never make it in.'

'God damn it.' Ryan picked up the phone again. 'Send us the best ten photos you have,' he told NPIC.

'You'll have them in two or three minutes.'

'How about someone to evaluate the bomb effects?'

'I can do that,' S&T said. 'Ex-Air Force. I used to work intel for SAC.'

'Run with it.'

The nine Abrams tanks had by now accounted for nearly thirty of the Russian T-80s. The Soviets had pulled south to find cover of their own. Their return fire had killed three more of the M1A1s, but now the odds were a lot more even. The captain commanding the tank detachment sent his Bradleys east to conduct reconnaissance. As with their first dash, there were people watching them, but for the most part they did this from windows now unlit. The street lights worried one Bradley commander, who took a rifle and began shooting them out, to the horror of Berliners who had the courage to watch.

'*Was nun?*' Keitel asked. What now?

'Now we get the devil away from here and disappear. Our work is done,' Bock replied, turning the wheel to the left. A northerly escape route seemed best. They'd dump the car and truck, change their clothes, and vanish. They might even survive all this, Bock thought. Wouldn't that be something? But his main thought was that he'd avenged his Petra. It had been the Americans and Russians who'd brought her death about. Germans had only been the pawns of the great players, and the great players were paying now, Bock told himself, were paying now and would pay more. Revenge wasn't so cold a dish after all, was it?

'Russian staff car,' the gunner said, 'and a GAZ truck.'

'Chain gun.' The track commander took his time identifying the inbound targets. 'Wait.'

'I *love* killin' officers . . .' The gunner centered the sight for his 25mm cannon. 'On target, sarge.'

For all his experience as a terrorist, Bock was not a soldier. He took the dark, square shape two blocks away for a large truck. His plan had worked. The American alert, so perfectly timed, could only mean that Qati and

890

Ghosn had done their job exactly as he'd envisioned five months earlier. His eyes shifted as he saw what looked like a flashbulb and a streak of light that went over his head.

'Fire, hose 'em!'

The gunner had his selector switch on rapid fire. The 25-millimeter chain gun was wonderfully accurate, and the tracers allowed you to walk fire right into the target. The first long burst hit the truck. There might be armed soldiers in the truck, he reasoned. The initial rounds went into the engine block, shattering it into fragments, then, as the vehicle surged forward, the next burst swept through the cab and cargo area. The truck collapsed on two flattened front tires and ground to a halt, the wheel rims digging grooves in the asphalt. By that time, the gunner had shifted fire and put a short burst through the staff car. This target merely lost control and slammed into a parked BMW. Just to make sure, the gunner hit the car again, and then the truck. Someone actually got out of the truck, probably wounded already from the way he moved. Two more 25mm rounds fixed that.

The track commander moved immediately. One does not linger where one has killed. Two minutes later, they found another surveillance spot. Police cars were racing down the streets, their blue lights flashing. One of them stopped a few hundred meters from the Bradley, backed up and raced off, the track commander saw. Well, he'd always known German cops were smart.

Five minutes after the Bradley departed for another block, the first Berliner, an exceedingly courageous physician, came out his front door and went to the staff car. Both men were dead, each torso ripped to shreds by the cannon shells, though both faces were intact except for the splashed blood. The truck was an even greater mess. One of the men there might have survived for a few minutes, but by the time the doctor got there, it was far too late. He found it odd that they all wore Russian officers' uniforms. Not knowing what else to do, he called the police. Only later did he realize how disproportionate his understanding of the events outside his home had been.

'They weren't kidding about the infra-red signature. This must have been some bomb,' the S&T guy observed. 'Damage is a little funny, though . . . hmph.'

'What do you mean, Ted?' Ryan asked.

'I mean the ground damage ought to be worse than this . . . must be shadows and reflections.' He looked up. 'Sorry. Shock waves don't go through things – like a hill, I mean. There must have been reflections and shadows here, that's all. These houses here ought not to be there anymore.'

'I still don't know what you mean,' Ryan said.

'There are always anomalies in cases like this. I'll get back to you when I have this figured out, okay?' Ted Ayres asked.

Walter Hoskins sat in his office because he didn't know what else to do, and as most senior man present, he had to answer the phones. All he needed to do was turn to see what the stadium was. The pall of smoke was only five miles away through his windows, one of which was cracked. Part of him wondered if he should send a team down there, but he had no such orders. He turned his chair to look that way again, amazed that the window was almost intact. After all, it was supposed to have been a nuclear bomb, and it was only five miles. The remains of the cloud were now over the front range of the Rockies, still intact enough that you could tell what it had been, and behind it like a wake was another black plume of fires from the bomb area. The destruction must be . . .

. . . not enough. Not enough? What a crazy thought. With nothing else to do, Hoskins lifted the phone and dialed up Washington. 'Give me Murray.'

'Yeah, Walt.'

'How busy are you?'

'Not very, as a matter of fact. How is it at your end?'

'We have the TV stations and phones shut down. I

hope the President will be there when I have to explain that one to the judge.'

'Walt, this isn't the time –'

'Not why I called.'

'Well, then you want to tell me?'

'I can see it from here, Dan,' Hoskins said, in a voice that was almost dreamy.

'How bad is it?'

'All I see is the smoke, really. The mushroom cloud is over the mountains now, all orange, like. Sunset, it's high enough to catch the sunset, I guess. I can see lots of little fires. They're lighting up the smoke from the stadium area. Dan?'

'Yeah, Walt?' Dan responded. The man seemed to be in shock, Murray thought.

'Something odd.'

'What's that?'

'My windows aren't broken. I'm only five miles from there, and only one of my windows is cracked, even. Odd, isn't it?' Hoskins paused. 'I have some stuff here that you said you wanted, pictures and stuff.' Hoskins leafed through the documents that had been set in his IN basket. 'Marvin Russell sure picked a busy day to die. Anyway, I have the passport stuff you wanted. Important?'

'It can wait.'

'Okay.' Hoskins hung up.

'Walt's losing it, Pat,' Murray observed.

'You blame him?' O'Day asked.

Dan shook his head. 'No.'

'If this gets worse . . .' Pat observed.

'How far out is your family?'

'Not far enough.'

'Five miles,' Murray said quietly.

'What?'

'Walt said that his office is just five miles away, he can see it from there. His windows aren't broken, even.'

'Bullshit,' O'Day replied. 'He must really be out of it. Five miles, that's less than nine thousand yards.'

'What do you mean?'

'NORAD said the bomb was a hundred-kiloton range. That'll break windows over a hell of a long distance. Only takes half a pound or so of overpressure to do a window.'

'How do you know?'

'Used to be in the Navy – intelligence, remember? I had to evaluate the damage distances for Russian tactical nukes once. A hundred-kiloton bomb at nine thousand yards won't sink you, but it'll wreck everything topside, scorch paint, start small fires. Bad news, man.'

'Curtains, like?'

'Ought to,' O'Day thought aloud. 'Yeah, regular curtains would light up, especially if they're dark ones.'

'Walt's not so far out of it that he'd miss a fire in his office . . .' Murray lifted his phone to Langley.

'Yeah, what is it, Dan?' Jack said into the speaker.

'What number do you have on the size of the explosion?'

'According to NORAD, one-fifty, maybe two hundred kilotons, size of a big tactical weapon or a small strategic one,' Ryan said. 'Why?' On the other side of the table, the S&T officer looked up from the photos.

'I just talked to my ASAC Denver. He can see the stadium area from his office – five miles, Jack. He's only got one cracked window.'

'Bull,' S&T noted.

'What do you mean?' Ryan asked.

'Five miles, that's eight thousand meters,' Ted Ayres pointed out. 'The thermal pulse alone should fry the place, and the shock wave would sure as hell blow a plate-glass window out.'

Murray heard that. 'Yeah, that's what a guy here just said. Hey, my guy might be a little out of it – shock, I mean – but he'd notice a fire next to his desk, don't you think?'

'Do we have anything from people on the scene yet?' Jack asked Ayres.

'No, the NEST team is on the way, but the imagery tells us a lot, Jack.'

'Dan, how quick can you get somebody to the scene?' Ryan asked.

'I'll find out.'

'Hoskins.'

'Dan Murray, Walt. Get some people down there fast as you can. You stay put to coordinate.'

'Okay.'

Hoskins gave the proper orders, wondering just how badly he might be endangering his people. Then, with nothing else to do, he looked over the file on his desk. Marvin Russell, he thought, yet another criminal who died of dumb. Drug dealers. Didn't they ever learn?

Roger Durling was grateful when the Kneecap aircraft disengaged from the tanker. The converted 747 had the usual pussycat ride, but not when in close proximity to a KC-10 tanker. It was something only his son enjoyed. Aboard in the conference room were an Air Force brigadier, a Navy captain, a Marine major, and four other field- and staff-grade officers. All the data the President got came to Kneecap automatically, including the Hot Line transcripts.

'You know, what they're saying is okay, but it sure as hell would be nice to know what everyone's thinking.'

'What if this really is a Russian attack?' the General asked.

'Why would they do it?'

'You've heard the chatter between the President and CIA, sir.'

'Yeah, but that Ryan guy's right,' Durling said. 'None of this makes any sense.'

'So, who ever said the world had to make sense? What about the contact in the Med and Berlin?'

'Forward-deployed forces. We go on alert, and they go on alert, and they're close to each other, and someone goofs. You know, like Gavrilio Prinzip shooting the

Archduke. An accident happens and then things just slide down the chute.'

'That's why we have the Hot Line, Mr Vice President.'

'True,' Durling conceded. 'And so far it seems to be working.'

They made the first fifty yards easily, but then it got harder, and soon it went from hard to impossible. Callaghan had a total of fifty firefighters trying to fight their way on, with a hundred more in support. On reflection, he had a continuous water spray over every man and woman. If nothing else, he reasoned, he would wash whatever fallout or dust or whatever the hell was out here off his people and into the sewer drains – that which didn't freeze first, that is. The men in front were coated with ice that made a translucent layer on their turn-out coats.

The biggest problem was the cars. They'd been tossed about like toys, laying on their sides or tops, leaking gasoline that collected into burning puddles that were being supplied faster than they burned off. Callaghan ordered a truck in. One at a time, his men ran cables to the frames of the wrecked cars, and the truck dragged them clear, but this was horribly time-consuming. It would take forever to get in to the stadium. And there were people in there. He was sure of it. There had to be. Callaghan just stood there, out of the water spray, guilty that he was warmer than his people. He turned when he heard the roar of a large diesel engine.

'Hello.' It was a man wearing the uniform of a U.S. Army colonel. The nametag on his parka read LYLE. 'I hear you need heavy equipment.'

'What you got?'

'I have three engineer tanks, M728s, just rolling in now. Got something else, too.'

'What's that?'

'A hundred MOPP suits, you know, chemical warfare gear. It ain't perfect, but it's better than what your people got on. Warmer, too. Why don't you pull your people off and get them outfitted. Truck's over there.' The colonel pointed.

Callaghan hesitated for a moment, but decided that he couldn't turn this offer down. He called his people off and pulled them back to don the military gear. Colonel Lyle tossed him an outfit.

'The water fog's a good idea, ought to keep dust and stuff down. So, what do you want us to do?'

'You can't tell from here, but there's still some structure in there. I think there might be survivors. I have to find out. Can you help us get through these cars?'

'Sure.' The colonel lifted his own radio and ordered the first vehicle in. The M728, Callaghan saw, was essentially a tank with a dozer blade on the front, and a big A-frame and winch on the back of the turret. There was even an odd-looking short-barrelled gun.

'This isn't going to be very neat. Can you live with that?'

'Screw neat – get in there!'

'Okay.' Lyle picked up the interphone at the left rear of the vehicle. 'Make a hole,' he ordered.

The driver revved up the diesel just as the first firemen returned. He made a sincere effort to avoid the fire hoses – even so he split eight two-and-a-half-inch lines. The blade dropped, and the tank crashed into the mass of burning cars at twenty miles per hour. It made a hole, all right, about thirty feet deep. Then the tank backed off and started widening it.

'Jesus,' Callaghan observed. 'What do you know about radiation stuff?'

'Not much. I checked with the NEST guys before I drove down. They ought to be here any time. Until then . . .' Lyle shrugged. 'You really think there's live ones in there?'

'Part of the structure is still there. I saw it from the chopper.'

'No shit?'

'Yeah, I saw it.'

'But that's crazy. The NORAD guys say it was a big one.'

897

'What?' Callaghan shouted over the noise of the tank.

'The bomb, it was supposed to be a big one. There shouldn't even be a parking lot here.'

'You mean this was a *little* one?' Callaghan looked at the man as though he were crazy.

'Hell, yes!' Lyle stopped for a moment. 'If there's people in there . . .' He ran to the back of the tank and grabbed the phone. A moment later, the M728 stopped.

'What's the matter?'

'If there are survivors, hell, we might squash one this way. I just told him to take it easier. God damn, you're right. And I thought you were crazy.'

'What do you mean?' Callaghan shouted again, waving his firefighters to put their spray on the tank also.

'There may be survivors in there. This bomb was a hell of a lot smaller than they told me on the phone.'

'*Maine*, this is Sea Devil One-Three,' the P-3C Orion called. 'We're about forty minutes out from your position. What seems to be the problem?'

'We have screw and shaft damage, and we have an Akula in the neighborhood, last fix five-zero thousand yards southwest,' Ricks answered.

'Roger that. We'll see if we can drive him off for you. We'll report when we get on station. Out.'

'Captain, we can do three knots, let's do that, north, open as much as we can,' Claggett said.

Ricks shook his head. 'No, we'll stay quiet.'

'Sir, our friend out there must have copied the collision transient. He will be coming this way. We've lost our best sonar. Smart move is to evade as best we can.'

'No, the smart move is to stay covert.'

'Then at least launch a MOSS.'

'That makes sense, sir,' the weapons officer thought.

'Okay, program it to sound like we are now, and give it a southerly course.'

'Right.' *Maine*'s number-three torpedo tube was loaded with a MOSS, a Mobile Submarine Simulator. Essentially a modified torpedo itself, the MOSS contained a sonar transducer connected to a noise generator, instead of a warhead. It would radiate the sound of an Ohio-class submarine, and was designed to simulate a damaged one. Since shaft damage was one of the few reasons that an Ohio might make noise, that option was already programmed in. The weapons officer selected the proper noise track, and launched the weapon a few minutes later. The MOSS sped off to the south, and two thousand yards away, it began radiating.

The skies had cleared over Charleston, South Carolina. What had fallen as snow in Virginia and Maryland had been mainly sleet here. The afternoon sun had removed most of that, returning the antebellum city to its normally pristine state. As the Admiral commanding Submarine Group Six watched from the tender, two of his ballistic-missile submarines started down the Cooper River for the sea and safety. He wasn't the only one to watch. One hundred ninety miles over his head, a Soviet reconnaissance satellite made its pass, continuing up the coast to Norfolk, where the sky was also clearing. The satellite down-linked its pictures to the Russian intelligence center on Cuba's western tip. From there it was immediately relayed by communications satellite. Most of the Russian satellites used high-polar orbits, and had not been affected by the EMP. The imagery was in Moscow in a matter of seconds.

'Yes?' the Defense Minister asked.

'We have imagery of three American naval bases. Missile submarines at Charleston and King's Bay are putting to sea.'

'Thank you.' The Defense Minister replaced the phone. Another threat. He relayed it at once to President Narmonov.

'What does that mean?'

'It means that the military action taken by the Americans is not merely defensive. Some of the submarines in question carry the Trident D-5 missile, which has first-strike capability. You'll recall how interested the Americans were in forcing us to eliminate our SS-18s?'

'Yes, and they are removing a large number of their Minutemen,' Narmonov said. 'So?'

'So, they don't *need* land-based missiles to make a first-strike. They can do it from submarines. We cannot. We depend on our land-based ICBMs for that.'

'And what of our SS-18s?'

'We're removing the warheads from some of them even as we speak, and if they ever get that damned deactivation facility working, we'll be in full compliance with the treaty – we are now, in fact, just the damned Americans don't admit it.' The Defense Minister paused. Narmonov wasn't getting it. 'In other words, while we have eliminated some of our most accurate missiles, the Americans still have theirs. We are at a strategic disadvantage.'

'I have not had much sleep, and my thinking is not at its best,' Narmonov said testily. 'You *agreed* to this treaty document only a year ago, and now you're telling me that we are threatened by it?'

They're all the same, the Defense Minister thought. *They never listen, they never really pay attention. Tell them something a hundred times and they just don't hear you!*

'The elimination of so many missiles and warheads changes the correlation of forces –'

'Rubbish! We're still equal in every way!' President Narmonov objected.

'That is not the question. The important factor is the relationship between the number of launchers – and their relative vulnerability – and the number of warheads available to both sides. We can still strike first and eliminate the American land-based missile force with our land-based missiles. That is why they were so willing to remove half of theirs. But the majority of their warheads are at sea, and now, for the first time, such sea-based missiles are totally adequate for a disarming first strike.'

'Kuropatkin,' Narmonov said. 'Are you hearing this?'

'Yes, I am. The Defense Minister is correct. The additional dimension, if I may say it, is that the reduction in the number of launchers has changed the overall ratio of launchers-to-warheads. For the first time in a generation, a truly disarming first-strike is possible, especially if the Americans are able to decapitate our government with their first strike.'

'And they could do that with the Stealth fighters they put in Germany,' Defense concluded the statement.

'Wait a minute. Are you telling me that Fowler blew up his own city as an excuse to attack us? What madness is this?' Now the Soviet president began to understand fear.

The Defense Minister spoke slowly and clearly. 'Whoever detonated that weapon is beside the point. If Fowler begins to think that it was our doing, he has the ability to act against us. Comrade President, you must understand this: technically speaking, our country is on the edge of annihilation. Less than thirty minutes separate their land-based missiles from us. Twenty minutes for their sea-based ones, and as little as two hours from those goddamned invisible tactical bombers, which would be the most advantageous opening move. All that separates us from destruction is the mental state of President Fowler.'

'I understand.' The Soviet president was quiet for half a minute. He stared off at the status board on the far wall. When he spoke, his voice showed the anger that comes from fright. 'What do you propose we should do – attack the Americans? I will not do such a thing.'

'Of course not, but we would be well-advised to place our strategic forces on full alert. The Americans will take note of this, and realize that a disarming attack is not possible, and we can settle this affair down long enough for reason to take hold.'

'Golovko?'

The First Deputy Chairman of the KGB shrank from the inquiry. 'We know that they are at full alert status. It is possible that our doing the same will provoke them.'

'If we do not, we present ourselves as a much more inviting target.' The Defense Minister was inhumanly calm, perhaps the only man in the room who was fully in control of himself. 'We know that the American president is under great stress, that he has lost many thousands of his citizens. He might lash out without thinking. He is much less likely to do so if he knows that we are in a position to respond in kind. We do not dare to show weakness at a time like this. Weakness always invites attack.'

Narmonov looked around the room for a dissenting opinion. There was none. 'Make it so,' he told Defense.

'We still haven't heard anything from Denver,' Fowler said, rubbing his eyes.

'I wouldn't expect much,' General Borstein replied.

NORAD's command post is literally inside of a mountain. The entrance tunnel had a series of steel blast-doors. The structures inside were designed to survive anything that could be aimed at them. Shock-absorbing springs and bags of compressed air isolated the people and machines from the granite floors. Overhead were steel roofs to stop any rock fragments that might be blasted free by a near-miss. Borstein didn't expect to survive an attack. There was a whole regiment of Soviet SS-18 Mod 4s tasked to the destruction of this post and a few others. Instead of ten or more MIRVs, they carried a single *twenty-five-*megaton warhead whose only plausible military mission was to turn Cheyenne Mountain into Cheyenne Lake. That was a pleasant thought. Borstein was a fighter pilot by trade. He'd started off in the F-100, called the 'Hun,' by its drivers, graduated from there to F-4 Phantoms, and commanded an F-15 squadron in Europe. He'd always been a tactical guy, stick and rudder, scarf and goggles: kick the tires, light the fires, first one up's the leader. Borstein frowned at the thought. Even he wasn't old enough to remember those days. His job was continental air defense, to keep people from blowing his country up. He'd failed. A nearby piece of America was blown up, along with his boss, and he didn't know why or how or who. Borstein was not a man accustomed to failure, but failure was what he saw on his map display.

'General!' a major called to him.

'What is it?'

'Picking up some radio and microwave chatter. First

guess is that Ivan's alerting his missile regiments. Ditto in some naval bases. Flash traffic outbound from Moscow.'

'Christ!' Borstein lifted his phone again.

'Never done it?' Elliot asked.

'Strange but true,' Borstein said. 'Even during the Cuban Missile Crisis, the Russians never put their ICBMs on alert.'

'I don't believe it,' Fowler snorted. 'Never?'

'The General's right,' Ryan said. 'The reason is that their telephone system historically has been in pretty bad shape. I guess they've finally gotten it fixed enough –'

'What do you mean?'

'Mr President, God is in the details. You send alert messages by voice – we do it that way, and so do the Soviets. The Russian phone system stinks, and you don't want to use a flukey system for orders of that importance. That's why they've been investing so much money in fixing it up, just as we have invested a lot in our command-and-control-systems. They use a lot of fiber-optic cable now, just like we do, plus a whole new set of microwave relays. That's how we're catching it,' Jack explained. 'Scatter off the microwave repeaters.'

'Another couple of years, they'll be fully fiber-optic, and we wouldn't have known,' General Fremont added. 'I don't like this.'

'Neither do I,' Ryan said, 'but we're at DEFCON-TWO also, aren't we?'

'They don't know that. We didn't tell them that,' Liz Elliot said.

'Unless they're reading our mail. I've told you we have reports that they've penetrated our cipher systems.'

'NSA says you're crazy.'

'Maybe I am, but NSA's been wrong before, too.'

'What do you think Narmonov's mental state is?'

As scared as I am! Ryan wondered. 'Sir, there's no telling that.'

'And we don't even know if it's really him,' Elliot put in.

'Liz, I reject your hypothesis,' Jack snapped over the conference line. 'The only thing you have to support it comes from my agency, and we have our doubts about it.' *Christ, I'm sorry I ever took that report in*, he told himself.

'Cut that out, Ryan!' Fowler snarled back. 'I need facts, not arguments now, okay?'

'Sir, as I keep pointing out, we do not as yet have sufficient information on which to base any decision.'

'Balls,' the colonel next to General Fremont said.

'What do you mean?' CINC-SAC turned away from the speaker-phone.

'Dr Elliot is right, sir. What she said earlier makes sense.'

'Mr President,' they heard a voice say. 'We have a Hot Line transmission coming in.'

> PRESIDENT FOWLER:
> WE HAVE JUST RECEIVED A REPORT THAT A
> US ARMY UNIT IN BERLIN HAS ATTACKED A
> SOVIET UNIT WITHOUT WARNING.
> CASUALTIES ARE REPORTED SEVERE. PLEASE
> EXPLAIN WHAT IS HAPPENING.

'Oh, shit,' Ryan said, looking at the fax.

'I need opinions, people,' Fowler said over the conference line.

'The best thing is to say that we have no knowledge of this incident,' Elliot said. 'If we admit knowledge, we have to assume some responsibility.'

'This is a singularly bad time to lie,' Ryan said forcefully. Even he thought he was overdoing it. *They won't listen to you if you shout, Jack, boy . . .*

'Tell that to Narmonov,' Elliot shot back. 'They attacked us, remember?'

'So the reports say, but –'

'Ryan, are you saying our people lied?' Borstein snarled from Cheyenne Mountain.

'No, General, but at times like this the news is chancy, and you know that as well as I do!'

'If we deny knowledge, we can avoid taking a stand that we might have to back down from, and we avoid challenging them for the moment,' the National Security Advisor insisted. 'Why are they bringing this up now?' she asked.

'Mr President, you used to be a prosecutor,' Ryan said. 'You know how unreliable eyewitness accounts can be. Narmonov could be asking that question in good faith. My advice is to answer it honestly.' Jack turned to Goodley, who gave him a thumbs-up.

'Robert, we're not dealing with civilians, we're dealing with professional soldiers, and they ought to be good observers. Narmonov is accusing us of something we didn't do,' Elliot countered. 'Soviet troops do not initiate combat operations without orders. Therefore, he must know that his accusation is false. If we admit knowledge, we will appear to admit his charge is true. I don't know what game he's playing — whoever that is at the other end of the line — but if we simply say we don't know what he's talking about, we buy ourselves time.'

'I strongly disagree with that,' Jack said, as calmly as he could manage.

> PRESIDENT NARMONOV:
> AS YOU KNOW, I AM MAINLY CONCERNED
> WITH EVENTS WITHIN OUR OWN BORDERS.
> I HAVE AS YET NO INFORMATION FROM
> BERLIN. THANK YOU FOR YOUR INQUIRY. I
> JUST ORDERED MY PEOPLE TO CHECK INTO
> IT.

'Opinions?'

'The bastard's lying through his teeth,' the Defense Minister said. 'Their communications system is too good for that.'

'Robert, Robert, why do you lie when I know you are lying . . . ?' Narmonov said, his head down. The Soviet president now had his own questions to ask. Over the past two or three months, his contacts with America had grown slightly cold. When he asked for some additional credits, he was put off. The Americans were insisting on full compliance with the arms-reduction agreement, even though they knew what the problem was, and even though he'd given Fowler his word face-to-face that everything would be done. What had changed? Why had Fowler retreated from his promises? What the hell was he doing now?

'It's more than just a lie, more than just this lie,' the Defense Minister observed, after a moment.

'What do you mean?'

'He has emphasized again that his interest is in rescue of casualties in the Denver area, but we know he has placed his strategic forces on full alert. Why has he not told us of this?'

'Because he is afraid of provoking us . . . ?' Narmonov asked. His words seemed rather hollow even to himself.

'Possibly,' Defense admitted. 'But they do not know the success we've had reading their codes. Perhaps they think they have concealed this from us.'

'No,' Kuropatkin said in his command center. 'I must disagree with that. We could hardly fail to see some of these indicators. They should know that we are aware of some aspects of their strategic alert.'

'But not all.' The Defense Minister turned to stare at Narmonov. 'We must face the possibility that the American president is no longer rational.'

'The first time?' Fowler asked.

Elizabeth Elliot nodded. She was quite pale now. 'It's not widely known, Robert, but it is true. The Russians have never placed their Strategic Rocket Forces on alert. Until now.'

'Why now?' the President asked.

'Robert, the only thing that makes sense is that it isn't Narmonov over there.'

'But how can we be sure?'

'We can't. All we have is this computer link. There's no voice link, no visual link.'

'Dear God.'

CHAPTER 40

Collisions

'Ryan, how do we know it's really Narmonov over there?'

'Mr President, who else would it be?'

'God damn it, Ryan! You're the one who brought me the reports!'

'Mr President, you have to settle down,' Jack said, in a voice that wasn't particularly calm. 'Yes, I brought you that information, and I also told you it was unconfirmed, and I just told you a few minutes ago that we have reason to believe that it may not ever have been true at all.'

'Can't you see your own data? You're the one who warned us that there might be some missing nukes!' Elliot pointed out. 'Well, they turned up – they turned up here, right where we were supposed to be!'

Christ, she's even more rattled than he is, Helen D'Agustino told herself. She traded a look with Pete Connor, who was pasty-white. *This is going too fast.*

'Look, Liz, I keep telling you that our information is too damned thin. We don't have enough to make any kind of informed judgment here.'

'But why have they gone on nuclear alert?'

'For the same reason that we have!' Ryan shouted back. 'Maybe if both sides would back off –'

'Ryan, don't tell me what to do,' Fowler said quietly. 'What I want from you is information. We make the decisions here.'

Jack turned away from the speaker-phone. Now he was losing it, Goodley thought, now Ryan was pale and sick-looking. The Deputy Director of Central Intelligence stared out the windows at the CIA courtyard and the largely empty building beyond. He took a few deep breaths and turned back.

'Mr President,' Jack said under taut control, 'our opinion is that President Narmonov is in control of the Soviet government. We do not know the origin of the explosion in Denver, but there is no information in our possession that would lead us to believe that it was a Soviet weapon. Our opinion is that for the Soviets to undertake such an operation would be lunacy, and even if their military were in control – after a coup about which we have no information at all, sir – such a miscalculation is unlikely to the point of – the likelihood is so low as to approach zero, sir. That is CIA's position.'

'And Kadishev?' Fowler asked.

'Sir, we have evidence just developed yesterday and today to suggest that his reports may be false. We cannot confirm one of the meetings that should –'

'*One!* You can't confirm *one* meeting?' Elliot asked.

'Will you let me talk?' Jack snarled, losing it again. 'Damn it, it was Goodley who did this work, not me!' He paused for a breath. 'Dr Goodley noted some subtle differences in the nature of the reports and decided to check up on them. All of Kadishev's reports supposedly came from face-to-face meetings with Narmonov. In one case we cannot reconcile the schedules of both men. We cannot be sure they met in that case at all. If they didn't meet, then Kadishev is a liar.'

'I suppose you've considered the possibility that they met in secret?' Elliot inquired acidly. 'Or do you think that a subject like this would be handled as a routine business matter! Do you think he'd be discussing a possible coup in a routine scheduled meeting!'

'I keep telling you that his information has never been confirmed, not by us, not by the Brits, not by anybody.'

'Ryan, would you expect that a conspiracy leading to a military coup, especially in a country like the Soviet Union, would be handled in the utmost secrecy?' Fowler asked.

'Of course.'

'Then would you necessarily expect to have it confirmed by other sources?' Fowler asked, talking like a lawyer in a courtroom.

'No, sir,' Ryan admitted.

'Then this is the best information we have, isn't it?'

'Yes, Mr President, if it's true.'

'You say that you have no firm evidence to confirm it?'

'Correct, Mr President.'

'But you have no hard information to contradict it, either, do you?'

'Sir, we have reasons —'

'Answer my question!'

Ryan's right hand compressed into a tight, white fist. 'No, Mr President, nothing hard.'

'And for the past few years he's given us good, reliable information?'

'Yes, sir.'

'So, based on the record of Mr Kadishev, this is the best available information?'

'Yes, sir.'

'Thank you. I suggest, Dr Ryan, that you try to develop additional information. When you get it, I'll listen to it.' The line clicked off.

Jack stood slowly. His legs were stiff and sore from the stress of the moment. He took one step to the window and lit a cigarette. 'I blew it,' he told the world. 'Oh, Christ, I've blown it . . .'

'Not your fault, Jack,' Goodley offered.

Jack spun around. 'That'll look real good on my fucking tombstone, won't it? "It wasn't his fault" the fucking world blew up!'

'Come on, Jack, it's not that bad.'

'Think so? Did you hear their voices?'

The Soviet carrier *Kuznetzov* didn't launch aircraft in the manner of U.S. carriers. Rather, it had a ski-jump bow configuration. The first MiG-29 raced forward from its starting point and went up the angled ramp and into the air. This manner of takeoff was hard on pilots and aircraft, but it worked. Another aircraft followed, and both turned to head east. They'd barely gotten to altitude when the flight leader noted a buzz in his headphones.

'Sounds like an emergency beeper on the guard frequency,' he said to his wingman. 'Sounds like one of ours.'

'*Da*, east-south-east. It is one of ours. Who do you suppose it is?'

'I have no idea.' The flight leader passed this information on to *Kuznetzov*, and received instructions to investigate.

'This is Falcon-Two,' the Hawkeye reported. 'We have two inbounds from the Russkie carrier, fast movers, bearing three-one-five and two-five-zero miles from Stick.'

Captain Richards looked at the tactical display. 'Spade, this is Stick. Close and warn them off.'

'Roger,' Jackson replied. He'd just topped his fuel tanks off. Jackson could stay up for another three hours or so, and he still carried six missiles.

'"Warn them off?"' Lieutenant Walter asked.

'Shredder, I don't know what's going on, either.' Jackson brought the stick around. Sanchez did the same, again splitting out to a wide interval.

The two pairs of aircraft flew on reciprocal courses at a closing speed of just under a thousand miles an hour. Four minutes later, both Tomcats went active on their radars. Ordinarily that would have alerted the Russians to the fact that American fighters were in the area, and that the area might not be totally healthy. But the new American radars were stealthy, and were not picked up.

It turned out that this didn't matter. A few seconds later, the Russians activated their own radar systems.

'Two fighters coming in towards us!'

The Russian flight leader checked his own radar display and frowned. The two MiGs were only supposed to be guarding their own task force. The alert had come in, and the fighters went up. Now he was on what might be a rescue mission, and had no particular desire to play foolish games with American aircraft, especially at night. He knew that the Americans knew he was about. His threat receiver did detect the emanations from their airborne early-warning aircraft.

'Come right,' he ordered. 'Down to one thousand meters to look for that beeper.' He'd leave his radar on, however, to show that he didn't wish to be trifled with.

'They're evading to the left, going down.'

'Bud, you have the lead,' Jackson said. Sanchez had the most missiles. Robby would cover his tail.

'Stick, this is Falcon-Two, both inbounds are breaking south and diving for the deck.'

As Richards watched, the course vectors changed on both inbound aircraft. Their course tracks were not actually converging with the *Roosevelt* group at the moment, though they would be coming fairly close.

'What are they up to?'

'Well, they don't know where we are, do they?' the Operations Officer pointed out. 'Their radars are on, though.'

'Looking for us, then?'

'That would be my guess.'

'Well, now we know where the other four came from.' Captain Richards picked up the mike to talk to Jackson and Sanchez.

'Splash 'em,' was the order. Robby took high cover. Sanchez went down, pulling behind and below both MiGs.

'I've lost the Americans.'

'Forget them! We're looking for a rescue beeper, remember?' The flight leader craned his neck. 'Is that a strobe light? On the surface at two o'clock . . . ?'

'I have it.'

'Follow me down!'

'Evading, down and right!' Bud called. 'Engaging now.'

He was a bare two thousand yards aft of the MiGs. Sanchez selected a Sidewinder and lined his aircraft up on the 'south guy,' the trailing wingman. As the Tomcat continued to close, the pilot got the warbling tone in his earphones, and triggered off his missile. The AIM-9M Sidewinder leaped off its launch rail, straight into the starboard engine of the MiG-29, which exploded. Barely had that happened when Sanchez triggered off a second 'Winder.

'Splash one.'

'What the hell!' The flight leader caught the flash out the corner of his eye and turned to see his wingman's aircraft heading down before a trail of yellow. He wrenched his stick left, his throttle hand punching the flare/chaff-release button, as his eyes searched the darkness for his attacker.

Sanchez's second missile missed right. It didn't matter. He was still tracking, and the MiG's turn brought the target right into the path of his 20mm cannon. One quick burst detached part of the MiG's wing. The pilot barely ejected in time. Sanchez watched the chute deploy. A minute later, as he orbited overhead, he saw that both Russians seemed to have survived the incident. That was fine with Bud.

'Splash two. Stick, we have two good chutes on the splashes . . . wait a minute, there's three strobes down there,' Jackson called. He gave the position, and almost instantly a helicopter lifted off from *Theodore Roosevelt*.

'Spade, is it supposed to be this easy?' Walters asked.

'I thought the Russians were smarter than this myself,' the captain admitted. 'This is like first day of duck season.'

Ten minutes later, *Kuznetzov* made a radio call for its two MiGs, and got no reply.

The Air Force helicopter returned from Rocky Flats. Major Griggs alighted with five men, all of them dressed in protective gear. Two of them ran to find Chief Callaghan close to the M728 engineer tanks.

'Ten more minutes, if we're lucky,' Colonel Lyle shouted from atop the lead tank.

'Who's in charge here?' one of the NEST team asked.

'Who are you?'

'Parsons, team leader.' Laurence Parsons was the head of the on-duty Nuclear Emergency Search Team, yet another failure for this day. Their job was to locate nuclear devices before they went off. Three such teams were kept on duty around the clock, one just outside Washington, another in Nevada, and the third, recently activated at Rocky Flats to help make up for the retirement of the Energy Department's weapons-fabrication facility outside Denver. It had been anticipated, of course, that they wouldn't always be able to get there in time. He held a radiation counter in his hand, and didn't like what he saw. 'How long have your people been here?'

'About half an hour, maybe forty minutes.'

'Ten more minutes, I want everybody away from here. You're taking Rems here, Chief.'

'What do you mean? The major said the fallout is all —'

'What you're getting is from neutron activation. It's hot here!'

Callaghan cringed at the thought. His life was being attacked by something he couldn't see or feel. 'There may be people inside. We're almost there.'

'Then do it fast! I mean *fast!*' Parsons and his team started moving back to the helicopter. They had their own work to do. At the chopper, they met a man in civilian clothes.

'Who the fuck are you?' Parsons demanded.

'FBI! What happened here?'

'Take a guess!'

'Washington needs information!'

'Larry, it's hotter here than it is at the stadium!' another NEST team member reported.

'Makes sense,' Parsons said. 'Ground burst.' He pointed. 'Far side, down-wind side. In-close was shielded some.'

'What can you tell me?' the FBI agent asked.

'Not much,' Parsons said, over the sound of the turn-

913

ing rotor. 'Ground burst, yield under twenty KT, all I got.'

'It's dangerous here?'

'Hell, yes! Set up – where, where?'

'How about at the Aurora Presbyterian Hospital, two miles up-wind?' a NESTer suggested. 'Across from Aurora Mall. Ought to be okay there.'

'You know where that is?' Parsons asked.

'Yes!'

'Then move out! Ken, you tell these people to get the hell out of here, it's twenty percent hotter here than in close. We have to get samples. Ken, you make sure they clear the area in ten minutes – fifteen max. Drag them out if you have to. Start here!'

'Right.'

The FBI agent ducked as the helicopter lifted off. The NEST team member began running down the line of fire trucks, waving for them to get away. The agent decided to do the same. After a few minutes, he got in his car and headed northeast.

'Shit, I forgot about the neutrons,' Major Griggs said.

'Thanks a lot!' Callaghan screamed over the sound of the tank.

'It's okay, they cut it off at a hundred. A hundred won't really hurt anybody.'

Callaghan heard the sound of the engines pulling away. 'What about the people inside?' The chief found the interphone at the back of the tank. 'Listen up, we have ten minutes and we gotta get the hell out of here. Lean on it!'

'You got it, man,' the tank commander replied. 'Better get clear. I'll give you a ten count.'

Callaghan ran to the side. Colonel Lyle jumped off and did the same. Inside the vehicle, the driver backed off ten yards, took the engine to the red line, and slipped the brake. The M728 crushed five vehicles, slamming them aside. The tank was moving at perhaps a mile per hour, but it didn't stop. Its treads ripped up the asphalt, then it was through.

The area immediately next to the stadium structure

was amazingly intact. Most of the wreckage from the roof and upper wall had been thrown hundreds of yards, but here there were only small piles of brick and concrete fragments. Too much for a wheeled vehicle, but clear enough that men could walk. Firefighters advanced and sprayed everything. The asphalt was still very hot, and the water steamed off it. Callaghan ran in front of the tank, waving for his men to go left and right.

'You know what this looks like?' a NEST team member said, as the helicopter circled the ruined stadium.

'Yeah, Chernobyl. They had firemen there, too.' Parsons turned away from that thought. 'Head downwind,' he told the pilot. 'Andy, what do you make of this?'

'Ground burst, and this wasn't any hundred-KT weapon, Larry, not even twenty-five.'

'What screwed up NORAD's estimate, do you think?'

'The parking lot. Asphalt, plus all those burning cars – it's the perfect black-body material – it's even *black*, for God's sake! I'm surprised the thermal pulse didn't look bigger than that – and everything around here is white from the snow 'n' ice, right? They got a mega-reflection, plus a huge energy contrast.'

'Makes sense, Andy,' Parsons agreed. 'Terrorists?'

'That's my bet for now, Larry. But we gotta get some residue to be sure.'

The sounds of battle had died down. The Bradley commander heard scattered firing and guessed that the Russians had pulled back part way, maybe all the way to their own kazerne. It made sense, both side's tanks had been badly mauled, and it was now a battle for infantrymen and their fighting vehicles. Foot soldiers, he knew, were smarter than tankers. It came from wearing a shirt instead of a foot of iron. Vulnerability made you think. He changed position yet again. It was odd how this worked, though he'd practiced the maneuver often enough. The vehicle ran close to a corner, and a man would dismount to peer around it.

'Nothin', sarge. It's all – wait! Something moving, 'bout two miles down the street . . .' The soldier raised a pair of glasses. 'BDRM! The missile kind.'

Okay, the sergeant thought, *that'll be the reconnaissance element for the next wave.* His job was entirely straightforward. Reconnaissance was a two-part job. His job was both to find the enemy, and to prevent the enemy from finding things.

'Another one!'

'Get ready to move. Traverse right, targets to the right,' he added for the gunner.

'Ready, sarge.'

'Go!' The Bradley's armored body rocked backwards as a vehicle leaped into the intersection. The gunner brought his turret around. It looked like a small-bore shooting gallery. There were two BDRM armored scout cars heading straight towards them. The gunner engaged the leader, exploding the anti-tank missile launcher on top. The BDRM veered to the left and rammed some parked cars. Already, the gunner shifted fire to the second, which jerked right to evade, but the street was too narrow for that. The chain gun was a nice compromise between a machinegun and a cannon. The gunner was able to walk his tracers into the target, and had the satisfaction of watching it explode. But –

'Back fast – now!' the sergeant screamed into the intercom. There had been a third BDRM back there. The Bradley retreated the way it had come. Barely had it gotten behind the buildings when a missile streaked down the street it had crossed, trailing a thin wire behind it. The missile exploded a few hundred meters away.

'Time to leave, turn us around,' the track commander said. Then he activated his radio. 'This is Delta Three-Three. We have contact with reconnaissance vehicles. Two destroyed, but the third one spotted us. We got more friends coming in, sir.'

'General, we've pushed them back across the line, I can hold out against what's here, but if more gets in to us, we're screwed,' Colonel Lang said. 'Sir, we need help here!'

'Okay, I'll have some air to you in ten minutes. Fast-movers on the way now.'

'That's a start, but I need more than that, sir.'

SACEUR turned to his operations officer. 'What's ready?'

'Second of the Eleventh Cav, sir. They're moving out of their kazerne right now.'

'What's between them and Berlin?'

'Russians? Not much. If they move fast . . .'

'Move 'em out.' SACEUR walked back to his desk and lifted the phone for Washington.

'Yes, what is it?' Fowler asked.

'Sir, it appears that the Russians are bringing reinforcements into Berlin. I have just ordered the 2nd Squadron, 11th Armored Cav to move towards Berlin to reinforce. I also have aircraft heading in now to assess the situation.'

'Do you have any idea what they're up to?'

'None, sir, it makes no damned sense at all, but we still have people being killed. What are the Russians telling you, Mr President?'

'They're asking why we attacked them, General.'

'Are they nuts?' *Or is it something else?* SACEUR wondered. *Something really frightening?*

'General,' it was a woman's voice, probably that Elliot woman, SACEUR thought. 'I want to be very clear on this. Are you sure that the Soviets initiated the attack?'

'Yes, ma'am!' SACEUR replied heatedly. 'The commander of the Berlin Brigade is probably dead. The XO is Lieutenant-Colonel Edward Long. I know the kid, he's good. He says the Russians opened fire on the brigade without warning while they were responding to the alert you sent out from D.C. They didn't even have their tubes loaded. I repeat, ma'am, the Russians are the ones who started shooting, and that's definite. Now, do I have your permission to reinforce?'

'What happens if you don't?' Fowler asked.

917

'In that case, Mr President, you have about five thousand letters to write.'

'Look, okay, send in the reinforcements. Tell Berlin to take no offensive action. We're trying to get things settled down.'

'I wish you luck, Mr President, but right now I have a command to run.'

> PRESIDENT NARMONOV:
> WE HAVE RECEIVED WORD FROM EUROPE THAT A SOVIET TANK REGIMENT LAUNCHED AN ATTACK ON OUR BERLIN BRIGADE WITHOUT WARNING. I JUST TALKED TO OUR COMMANDER, AND HE CONFIRMS THAT THIS IS TRUE. WHAT IS HAPPENING? WHY DID YOUR TROOPS ATTACK OUR TROOPS?

'Have we heard anything from Berlin yet?' Narmonov asked.

The Defense Minister shook his head. 'No, the lead reconnaissance elements should be getting in now. Radio communications are a disaster. Our VHF radios work poorly in cities because they are line-of-sight only. What we're getting is fragmented, mainly tactical communications between sub-unit commanders. We have not established contact with the regimental commander. He may be dead. After all,' Defense pointed out, 'the Americans like to go after commanders first.'

'So, we really do not know what is going on?'

'No, but I am *certain* that no Soviet commander would open fire on Americans without just cause!'

Golovko closed his eyes and swore under his breath. Now the Defense Minister was showing the strain.

'Sergey Nikolay'ch?' Narmonov asked.

'We have nothing more to report from KGB. You may expect that all of the American land-based missiles are fully on alert, as are all their submarine missiles at sea. We estimate that the American missile submarines in port will all have sortied in a matter of hours.'

'And our missile submarines?'

'One is leaving the dock now. The rest are preparing to do so. It will take most of the day to get them all out.'

'Why are we so slow?' Narmonov demanded.

'The Americans have two complete crews for their boats. We have only one. It's simply easier for them to surge them out this way.'

'So, you are telling me that their strategic forces are totally ready, or nearly so, and ours are not?'

'All of our land-based rockets are fully prepared.'

'President Narmonov, your reply to the Americans . . . ?'

'What do I say now?' Andrey Il'ych asked.

A colonel entered the room. 'Report from Berlin.' He handed it to the Defense Minister.

'The Americans are in the eastern part of the city. The first wave of scout cars was taken under fire. Four vehicles, the officer commanding was killed in one of them. We've returned fire and gotten two American vehicles . . . no contact as yet with our regiment.' The Defense Minister looked at the other one. 'Carrier *Kuznetzov* reports that he launched a two-plane patrol. They detected a rescue radio signal and went to investigate. Contact was then lost. They have an American carrier battlegroup four hundred kilometers away, and request instructions.'

'What does that mean?'

The Defense Minister checked the times on the second dispatch. 'If our planes are not back by now, they are nearly out of fuel. We must assume they were lost, cause unknown, but the close proximity of the American carrier is troubling . . . What the *hell* are they doing?'

PRESIDENT FOWLER:

I AM CERTAIN THAT NO SOVIET COMMANDER WOULD ATTACK AMERICAN TROOPS WITHOUT ORDERS, AND THERE WERE NO SUCH ORDERS. WE HAVE SENT ADDITIONAL TROOPS INTO BERLIN TO INVESTIGATE, AND THEY WERE ATTACKED BY YOUR FORCES IN THE EASTERN PART OF THE CITY, WELL AWAY FROM YOUR ENCAMPMENT. WHAT ARE YOU DOING?

'What the hell is he talking about? What am *I* doing?

What the hell is he doing!' Fowler growled. A light came on. It was the CIA. The President pushed the button, adding a new line to his conference call.

'That depends on who ''he'' is,' Elliot warned.

'Yes, what is it?'

'Mr President, what we have here is simple confusion.'

'Ryan! We don't want analysis, we want information. Do you have any?' Liz shouted.

'The Soviets are sortieing their ships out of the Northern Fleet ports. One missile submarine is supposed to be heading out.'

'So, their land-based missiles are fully alerted?'

'Correct.'

'And they're adding to their submarine missile force also?'

'Yes, Mr President.'

'Do you have any good news?'

'Sir, the news is that there is no real news right now, and you're –'

'Listen, Ryan. One last time: I want information from you and nothing else. You brought me that Kadishev stuff and now you're saying it was all wrong. So, why should I believe you now?'

'Sir, when I gave it to you I told you it was not confirmed!'

'I think we may have confirmation now,' Liz pointed out. 'General Borstein, if they're fully on line, what exactly is the threat?'

'The fastest thing they can get to us is an ICBM. Figure one regiment of SS-18s targeted on the Washington area, and most of the others targeted on our missile fields in the Dakotas, plus the sub bases at Charleston, King's Bay, Bangor, and the rest. Warning time will be twenty-five minutes.'

'And we will be targets here?' Liz asked.

'That is a reasonable assumption, Dr Elliot.'

'So, they will try to use SS-18s to finish what the first weapon missed?'

'If that was their work, yes.'

'General Fremont, how far out is the backup Kneecap?'

'Dr Elliot, it took off about ten minutes ago. It'll be at Hagerstown in ninety-five minutes. They have some good tail winds.' CINC-SAC regretted that addition almost at once.

'So, if they are thinking about an attack, and they launch it within the next hour and a half, we're dead here?'

'Yes.'

'Elizabeth, it's our job to prevent that, remember?' Fowler said quietly.

The National Security Advisor looked over at the President. Her face might have been made of glass, it looked so brittle. It wasn't supposed to be like this. She was the chief advisor to the most powerful man in the world, in a place of ultimate safety, guarded by dedicated servants, but less than thirty minutes from the time some faceless, nameless Russian made a decision, perhaps one made already, she'd be dead. Dead, a few ashes in the wind, certainly no more than that. Everything she'd worked for, all the books and classes and seminars would have ended in a blinding, annihilating flash.

'Robert, we don't even know who we're talking to,' she said in an uneven voice.

'Back to their message, Mr President,' General Fremont said. '"Additional troops to investigate." Sir, that sounds like reinforcements.'

A rookie fireman found the first survivor, crawling up the concrete ramp from the basement loading dock. It was amazing he'd made it. His hands had second-degree burns, and the crawl had ground bits of glass and concrete and Lord knew what into his injuries. The firefighter lifted the man – it was a cop – and carried him off to the evacuation point. The two remaining fire engines sprayed both men with water, then they were ordered to strip, and they were hosed again. The police officer was semi-conscious, but tore a sheet of paper off the clipboard he'd been holding, and all during the ambulance ride he was trying to tell the fireman something, but the firefighter was too cold, too tired, and much too scared to pay attention. He'd done his job, and might have lost his life in the process. It was altogether too much for a twenty-year-old who simply stared at the wet floor of the ambulance and shivered inside his blanket.

The entranceway had been topped with a pre-stressed concrete lintel. That had been shattered by the blast, with one piece blocking the way in. A soldier from the tank snaked a cable from the turret-mounted winch around the largest of the remaining blocks. As he did this, Chief Callaghan kept staring at his watch. It was too late to stop now in any case. He had to see this through if he died in the process.

The cable went taut, pulling the concrete fragment clear. Miraculously, the remainder of the entranceway did not collapse. Callaghan led the way through the rubbled opening, with Colonel Lyle behind him.

The emergency lights were on, and it seemed that every sprinkler head had gone off. This part of the stadium was where the main came into the structure, Callaghan remembered, and that explained the falling water. There were other sounds, the kind that came from people. Callaghan went into a men's room and found two women, both sitting in the water, both of their coats sprinkled with their own vomit.

'Get 'em out of here!' he shouted to his men. 'Go both ways, give it a quick check, and get back here fast as you can!' Callaghan checked all the toilet stalls. They were unoccupied. Another look at the room showed nothing else. They'd come all this way for two women in the wrong bathroom. Just two. The chief looked at Colonel Lyle, but there really wasn't anything to say. Both men walked out into the concourse.

It took Callaghan a moment to realize it, even though it was right there, an entrance to the stadium's lower level. Whereas only a short time before the view would have been of the stadium south side, and the roof, what he now saw was the mountains, still outlined in orange by a distant setting sun. The opening called to him, and as though in a trance, he walked up the ramp.

It was a scene from hell. Somehow this section had

been shielded one way or another from the blast. But not the thermal pulse. There were perhaps three hundred seats, still largely intact, still with people in them. What had once been people. They were burned black, charcoaled like overdone meat, worse than any fire victim he'd ever seen in nearly thirty years of fighting fires. At least three hundred, still sitting there, looking at where the field had been.

'Come on, Chief,' Major Lyle said, pulling him away. The man collapsed, and Lyle saw him vomiting inside his gas mask. The colonel got it off him, and pulled him clear. 'Time to leave. It's all over here. You've done your job.' It turned out that four more people were still alive. The firemen loaded them on the engine deck of the tank, which drove off at once to the evacuation point. The remaining firefighters there washed everything off, and departed, too.

Perhaps the only good luck of the day, Larry Parsons thought, was the snow cover. It had attenuated the thermal damage to the adjacent buildings. Instead of hundreds of house fires, there were only a few. Better, the afternoon sun of the previous day had been just intense enough to form a crust on the yards and roofs around the stadium. Parsons was looking for material on that crust. He and his men searched with scintillometers. The almost incredible fact of the matter was that while a nuclear bomb converted much of its mass into energy, the total mass lost in the process was minuscule. Aside from that, matter is very hard to destroy, and he was searching for residue from the device. This was easier than one might have thought. The material was dark, on a flat white surface, and it was also highly radioactive. He had a choice of six very hot spots, two miles downrange of the stadium. Parsons had taken the hottest. Dressed in his lead-coated protective suit, he was trudging across a snow-covered lawn. Probably an elderly couple, he thought. No kids had built a snowman or lain down to make angels. The rippling sound of the counter grew larger . . . there.

The residue was hardly larger in size than dust particles, but there were many of them, probably pulverized gravel and paving material from the parking lot, Parsons thought. If he were very lucky, it had been sucked up through the center of the fireball, and bomb residue had affixed itself to it. If he were lucky. Parsons scooped up a trowel's worth and slid it into a plastic bag. This he tossed to his teammate, who dropped the bag into a lead bucket.

'Very hot stuff, Larry!'

'I know. Let me get one more.' He scooped up another sample and bagged it as well. Then he lifted his radio.

'Parsons here. You got anything?'

'Yeah, three nice ones, Larry. Enough, I think, for an assay.'

'Meet me at the chopper.'

'On the way.'

Parsons and his partner walked off, ignoring the wide eyes watching from behind windows. Those people were not his concern for the moment. Thank God, he thought, that they hadn't bothered him with questions. The helicopter sat in the middle of a street, its rotor still turning.

'Where to?' Andy Bowler asked.

'We're going to the command center – shopping center. Should be nice and cold there. You take the samples back and run them through the spectrometer.'

'You should come along.'

'Can't,' Parsons said with a shake of the head. 'I have to call into D.C. This isn't what they told us. Somebody goofed, and I gotta tell them. Have to use a landline for that.'

The conference room had at least forty phone lines routed into it, one of which was Ryan's direct line. The electronic warble caught his attention. Jack pushed the flashing button and lifted the receiver.

'Ryan.'

'Jack, what's going on?' Cathy Ryan asked her husband. There was alarm but not panic in her voice.

'What do you mean?'

'The local TV station says an atomic bomb went off in Denver. Is there a war, Jack?'

'Cathy, I can't – no, honey, there's no war going on, okay?'

'Jack, they showed a picture. Is there anything I need to know?'

'You know almost everything I know. Something happened. We don't know what, exactly, and we're trying to find out. The President's at Camp David with the National Security Advisor and –'

'Elliot?'

'Yes. They're talking to the Russians right now. Honey, I have work to do.'

'Should I take the children somewhere?'

The proper thing, and the honorable and dramatic thing, Jack told himself, was to tell his wife to stay home, that they had to share the risks with everyone else, but the fact was there was no place of safety that he knew. Ryan looked out the window, wondering what the hell he should say.

'No.'

'Liz Elliot is advising the President?'

'That's right.'

'Jack, she's a small, weak person. Maybe she's smart, but inside she's weak.'

'I know. Cathy, I really have things to do here.'

'Love you.'

'And I love you, too, babe. Bye.' Jack replaced the receiver. 'The word's out,' he announced, 'pictures and all.'

'Jack!' It was the Senior Duty Officer. 'AP just sent out a flash: shooting in Berlin between U.S. and Soviet forces. Reuters is reporting the explosion in Denver.'

Ryan got on the phone to Murray. 'You have the wire services?'

'Jack, I knew this wouldn't work.'

'What do you mean?'

'The President told us to shut the networks down. I guess we goofed somewhere.'

'Super. You should have refused that one, Dan.'

'I tried, okay?'

There were just too many redundancies, too many nodes. Two satellites serving the United States were still up and operating, and so were nearly all of the microwave-repeater systems that had preceded them. The networks didn't merely run out of New York and Atlanta. NBC's Los Angeles bureau, after a surreptitious call from Rockefeller Center, took over for that network. CBS and ABC accomplished the same out of Washington and Chicago, respectively. The irate reporters also let the public know that FBI agents were 'holding hostage' the network news headquarters people in the most heinous abuse yet of the First Amendment. ABC was outraged that its crew had been killed, but that was a small thing compared to the scope of the story. The proverbial cat was out of the bag, and phone lines at the White House press office lit up. Many reporters had the direct number to Camp David as well. There was no statement from the President. That only made things worse. The CBS affiliate in Omaha, Nebraska, had only to drive past SAC headquarters to note the beefed-up guard force and the empty flight line. Those pictures would be on nation-wide in a matter of minutes, but it was the local news teams who did the best and the worst work. There is scarcely a city or town in America that lacks a National Guard armory, or a base for reservists. Concealing the activity at all of them was tantamount to concealing a sunrise, and the wire-service printers reported activity everywhere. All that was needed to punctuate those reports was the few minutes of tape from KOLD in Denver, running almost continuously now, to explain what was going on, and why.

The phones at the Aurora Presbyterian were all being used. Parsons knew that he could have forced his way onto one, but it was easier to run across the street to a largely deserted shopping center. He found an FBI agent there, wearing a blue 'raid' jacket that proclaimed his identity in large block letters.

'You the guy from the stadium?' Parsons' head gear was gone, but he still wore the metallic coat and pants.

'Yeah.'

'I need a phone.'

'Save your quarters.' They were standing outside a men's clothing store. The door had alarm tape on it, but looked cheap. The agent pulled out his service pistol and fired five rounds, shattering the glass. 'After you, pal.'

Parsons ran to the counter and lifted the store phone, dialing his headquarters in Washington. Nothing happened.

'Where are you calling?'

'D.C.'

'The long-distance lines are down.'

'What do you mean? The phone company shouldn't be hurt from this.'

'We did it. Orders from Washington,' the agent explained.

'What fucking idiot ordered that?'

'The President.'

'Outstanding. I gotta get a call out.'

'Wait.' The agent took the phone and called his own office.

'Hoskins.'

'This is Larry Parsons, NEST team leader, can you relay something to Washington?'

'Sure.'

'The bomb was a ground-burst, less than fifteen kilotons. We have samples of the residue, and it's on the way to Rocky Flats for spectroscopy. You know how to get that out?'

'Yes, I can do that.'

'Okay.' Parsons hung up.

'You have pieces from the bomb?' the FBI agent asked incredulously.

'Sounds crazy, doesn't it? That's what fallout is, bomb residue that gets attached to dirt particles.'

'So what?'

'So, we can figure out a lot from that. Come on,' he told the agent. Both men ran back across the street towards the hospital. An FBI agent, Parsons decided, was a useful fellow to have around.

'Jack, got something from Denver, came in through Walt Hoskins. The bomb was a ground burst, fifty or so kilotons. The NEST guys have residue, and they're going to test it.'

Ryan took his notes. 'Casualty count?'

'Didn't say.'

'Fifty kilotons,' the S&T man observed. 'Low for what the satellites said, but possible. Still, too goddamned big for an IND.'

The F-16C wasn't exactly ideal for this mission, but it was fast. Four had left Ramstein only twenty minutes earlier. Put aloft by the initial DEFCON-THREE alert, they'd come east to what they still referred to as the inter-German border. They'd not even arrived there when new orders had sent them towards the southern end of Berlin to get a look at what was happening at the Berlin Brigade's kazerne. Four F-15s from Bitburg joined for top-cover. All eight USAF fighters were loaded for air-to-air missions only, with two extra fuel tanks each in the place of bombs for the F-16s, and conformal fuel cells for the Eagles. From ten thousand feet, they could see the flashes and explosions on the ground. The flight of four broke into two elements of two each, and went down for a closer look, while the Eagles orbited overhead. The problem, it was later decided, was two-fold. First, the pilots were simply too surprised at the turn of events to consider all the possibilities; adding to this was the fact that American aircraft losses over Iraq had been so minor as to make the pilots forget that this was a different place.

The Russian tank regiment had both SA-8 and SA-11 missiles, plus the normal complement of Shilka 23mm flak vehicles. The anti-air company commander had waited for this moment, not illuminating his radars, playing it smart, as the Iraqis had singularly failed to do. He waited until the American aircraft were under a thousand meters before giving his order.

Barely had their threat receivers come on when a swarm of missiles rose from the eastern edge of the Russian encampment. The Eagles, high up, had a much better chance at evasion. The F-16 Fighting Falcons, descending right into the SAM trap, had almost none. Two were blotted out in a matter of seconds. The second pair dodged the first wave of SAMs, but one was caught in the frag pattern of second-wave SA-11 it almost but not quite evaded. That pilot ejected successfully, but died when he landed too hard on the roof of an apartment building. The fourth F-16 escaped by skimming the roof-tops and screaming west on full burner. Two of the Eagles joined him. A total of five American aircraft crashed into the city. Only one of the pilots lived. The escaping aircraft radioed the news to Commander U.S. Air Forces Europe at Ramstein. Already, he had twelve F-16s arming up with heavy ordnance. The next wave would be different.

> PRESIDENT NARMONOV:
> WE SENT SOME AIRCRAFT INTO BERLIN TO INVESTIGATE THE SITUATION THERE. THEY WERE SHOT DOWN WITHOUT WARNING BY SOVIET MISSILES. WHY WAS THIS DONE?

'What does this mean?'

'"Shot down without warning"? There's a *battle* under way, and that's why the aircraft were sent there! The regiment has anti-aircraft troops,' the Defense Minister explained. 'They only have short-range, low-altitude rockets. If the Americans were just looking from a safe height – ten thousand meters – we couldn't even have touched them. They must have been lower, probably trying to support their troops with an air attack. That's the only way we could have gotten them.'

'But we have no information?'

'No, we have not established contact yet.'

'We will not answer this one.'

'That is a mistake,' Golovko said.

'This situation is dangerous enough already,' Narmonov said angrily. 'We do not know what is going on there. How can I respond when he claims to have information which I do not?'

'If you do not respond, you appear to admit the incident.'

'We admit nothing!' the Defense Minister shouted. 'We could not even have done this unless they were attacking us, and we don't know whether it really happened or not.'

'So, tell them that,' Golovko suggested. 'Perhaps if they understand that we are as confused as they, they will also understand that –'

'But they won't understand, and they won't believe. They've already accused us of launching this attack, and they won't believe that we have no control over the area.'

Narmonov retreated to a corner table and poured himself a cup of tea, while the intelligence and defense advisors traded – arguments? Was that the right word? The Soviet President looked up at the ceiling. This command center dated back to Stalin. A spur off one of the Moscow subway lines built by Lazar Kaganovich, Stalin's pet Jewish anti-semite and his most trusted henchman, it was fully a hundred meters down, but now his people told him that it was not truly a place of safety after all.

What was Fowler thinking? Narmonov asked himself. The man was undoubtedly shaken by the murder of so many American citizens, but how could it be possible that he was thinking that the Soviets were responsible? And what was actually happening? A battle in Berlin, a possible clash between naval forces in the Mediterranean, all unrelated – or were they?

Did it matter? Narmonov stared at a picture on the wall and realized that, no, it did not matter. He and Fowler were both politicians for whom appearances had more weight than reality, and perceptions more importance than facts. The American had lied to him in Rome over a trivial matter. Was he lying now? If he were, then none of the past ten years of progress mattered at all, did they? It had all been for nothing.

'How do wars begin?' Narmonov asked himself quietly in the corner. In history, wars of conquest were started by strong men who wished to grow stronger still. But the time for men of imperial ambition had passed. The last such criminal had died not so long before. All that had changed in the twentieth century. The First World War had been started – how? A tubercular assassin had killed a buffoon so unloved that his own family had ignored the funeral. An overbearing diplomatic note had prompted Czar Nikolay II to leap to the defense of people he hadn't loved, and then the timetables had begun. Nikolay had the last chance, Narmonov remembered. The last of the Czars had held in his hand the chance to stop it all, but hadn't. If only he'd known what his decision for war would mean he might have found the strength to stop it, but in his fear and his weakness he'd signed the mobilization order that had ended one age and begun another. That war had begun because small, frightened men feared war less than showing weakness.

Fowler is such a man, Narmonov told himself. *Proud, arrogant, a man who lied in a small thing lest I think less of him. He will be angered by the deaths. He will fear additional deaths, but he will fear displaying weakness even more. My country is at the mercy of such a man.*

It was an elegant trap Narmonov was in. The irony of it might have evoked a tight, bitter smile, but instead the Soviet President set down his tea, for his stomach would take no more hot, bitter liquid. He could not afford to show weakness either, could he? That would only encourage Fowler to yet more irrationality. Part of Andrey Il'ych Narmonov asked if what he thought of Jonathan Robert Fowler might also apply to himself . . . But he had no reply. To do nothing would display weakness, wouldn't it?

*

'No answer?' Fowler asked the chief yeoman.

'No, sir, nothing yet.' Orontia's eyes were locked on the computer screen.

'My God,' the President muttered. 'All those people dead.'

And I could have been one of them, Liz Elliot thought, the idea coming back to her like waves on a beach, crashing in, ebbing away only to crash back again. *Someone wanted to kill us, and I am part of that 'us'. And we don't know who or why . . .*

'We can't let this go any farther.'

We don't even know what we are trying to stop. Who is doing this? Why are they doing it? Liz looked over at the clock and calculated the time to the arrival of the Kneecap aircraft. *We should have gone out on the first one. Why didn't we think to have it fly to Hagerstown to pick us up! We're stuck here in a perfect target, and if they want to kill us, this time, they'll get us, won't they?*

'How can we stop it?' Liz asked. 'He's not even answering us.'

Sea Devil One-Three, a P-3C Orion anti-submarine aircraft out of Kodiak Naval Air Station, was buffeting through the winds at low altitude, about five hundred feet. It laid the first line of ten DIFAR sonobuoys ten miles southwest of *Maine*'s position. In the back, the sonar operators were strapped tightly into their high-backed seats, most with a vomit bag close by as they tried to make sense of their displays. It took several minutes for things to firm up.

'Christ, that's my boat,' Jim Rosselli said. He dialed Bangor and asked for Commodore Mancuso.

'Bart, what gives?'

'*Maine* reported a collision, shaft and screw damage. There's a P-3 riding shotgun on her right now, and we have *Omaha* heading towards her flat-out. That's the good news. The bad news is that *Maine* was tracking an Akula at the time.'

'She was *what?*'

'Harry sold me and OP-02 on the idea, Jim. Too late

to worry about it now. It should be okay. The Akula was way off. You heard what Harry did to *Omaha* last year, right?'

'Yeah, I thought he stripped a gear.'

'Look, it should be okay. I'm surging my boats right now, Jim. Unless you need me for something else, I'm kinda busy.'

'Right.' Rosselli hung up.

'What gives?' Rocky Barnes asked.

Rosselli handed over the message. 'My old sub, disabled in the Gulf of Alaska, and there's a Russian prowling around.'

'Hey, they're quiet, right? You told me that. The Russians don't even know where they are.'

'Yeah.'

'Cheer up, Jim. I probably knew some of those F-16 drivers who got snuffed over Berlin.'

'Where the hell is Wilkes? He should have been here by now,' Rosselli said. 'He's got a good car.'

'No tellin', man. What the fuck is going on?'

'I don't know, Rocky.'

'We've got a long one coming in,' Chief Orontia said. 'Here it comes.'

PRESIDENT FOWLER:
WE HAVE NO INFORMATION FROM BERLIN ON THE MATTER TO WHICH YOU REFER. COMMUNICATIONS HAVE BROKEN DOWN. MY ORDERS HAVE GONE OUT TO OUR TROOPS, AND IF THEY HAVE GOTTEN THEM THEN THEY WILL TAKE NO ACTION EXCEPT IN SELF-DEFENSE. PERHAPS THEY FELT THEMSELVES TO BE UNDER ATTACK BY YOUR AIRCRAFT AND ACTED TO DEFEND THEMSELVES. IN ANY CASE WE ARE TRYING EVEN NOW TO REESTABLISH CONTACT WITH THE TROOPS, BUT OUR FIRST ATTEMPT TO REACH THEM WAS STOPPED BY AMERICAN TROOPS WHO WERE WELL OUTSIDE THEIR CAMP. YOU ACCUSE US OF HAVING OPENED FIRE, YET I HAVE TOLD YOU THAT OUR FORCES HAVE NO SUCH ORDERS, AND THE ONLY

DEFINITE WORD WE HAVE TELLS US THAT YOUR
FORCES WERE WELL INTO OUR ZONE OF THE CITY WHEN
THEY STRUCK.

MR PRESIDENT, I CANNOT RECONCILE YOUR WORDS
WITH THE FACTS WE HAVE. I MAKE NO ACCUSATION,
BUT I KNOW OF NOTHING MORE THAT I CAN SAY TO
ASSURE YOU THAT SOVIET FORCES HAVE TAKEN NO
ACTION WHATEVER AGAINST AMERICAN FORCES.

YOU HAVE TOLD US THAT YOUR ALERTING OF YOUR
FORCES IS DEFENSIVE ONLY, BUT WE HAVE INDICATIONS
THAT YOUR STRATEGIC FORCES ARE ON A VERY HIGH
STATE OF ALERT. YOU SAY YOU HAVE NO REASON
TO BELIEVE THAT WE ARE TO BLAME FOR THIS
INFAMY, YET YOUR MOST ALERT FORCES ARE THOSE
ARRAYED AGAINST MY COUNTRY. WHAT DO YOU
WISH ME TO THINK? YOU ASK FOR PROOF OF MY
GOOD INTENTIONS, BUT ALL OF YOUR ACTIONS
APPEAR TO LACK THEM.

'He's blustering,' Liz Elliot observed at once. 'Whoever
it is over there is rattled. Good, we may get the upper
hand yet.'

'Good?' CINC-SAC asked. 'You realize that this frightened person you're talking about has a whole lot of
missiles pointing at us. I don't read it that way, Dr Elliot.
I think we have an angry man here. He's thrown our
inquiries right back in our face.'

'What do you mean, General?'

'He says he knows we're alerted. Okay, that's no surprise, but he also says that those weapons are pointed at
him. He's accusing us of threatening him now – with
nukes, Mr President. That matters a hell of a lot more
than the piss-ant business in Berlin.'

'I agree,' General Borstein added. 'He's trying to bluster us, sir. We asked about a couple of lost airplanes, and
we get all this tossed back at us.'

Fowler punched up CIA again. 'Ryan, you got the latest
one?'

'Yes, sir.'

'What do you make of Narmonov's mental state?'

'Sir, he's a little angry right now, and also very concerned about our defensive posture. He's trying to find a way out of this.'

'I don't read it that way. He's rattled.'

'Well, who the hell isn't?' Jack asked. 'Of *course* he's rattled, the same as everyone else.'

'Look, Ryan, we are in control up here.'

'I never said otherwise, Liz,' Jack replied, biting off what he really thought. 'This is a grave situation, and he's as concerned as we are. He's trying to figure out what's happening the same as everyone else. The problem is nobody really knows anything.'

'Well, whose fault is that? That is your job, isn't it?' Fowler asked testily.

'Yes, Mr President, and we're working on it. A lot of people are.'

'Robert, does this sound like Narmonov? You've met the man, you've spent time with him.'

'Elizabeth, I just don't know.'

'It's the only thing that makes sense . . .'

'Liz, who says that any of this has to make sense?' Ryan asked.

'This weapon was a big one, right, General Borstein?'

'That's what our instruments tell us, yes.'

'Who has bombs that large?'

'Us, the Russians, the Brits, the French. Maybe the Chinese have weapons like this, but we don't think so; theirs are big and clunky. Israel has warheads in this range. That's it. India, Pakistan, South Africa all probably have fission weapons, but not large enough for this.'

'Ryan, is that correct information?' Elliot asked.

'Yes, it is.'

'So, if it wasn't Britain, France or Israel, then who the hell was it?'

'God damn it, Liz! *We don't know*, okay? We do not know, and this isn't a fucking Sherlock Holmes mystery. Eliminating who it wasn't doesn't tell us who it was! You can't convert the absence of information into a conclusion.'

935

'Does CIA know everybody who has weapons of this type?' Fowler asked.

'Yes, sir, we think we do.'

'How confident are you in that?'

'Until today, I would have bet my life on it.'

'So, again, you are not telling me the truth, are you?' Fowler observed coldly.

Jack stood from his chair. 'Sir, you may be the President of the United States, but don't you ever accuse me of lying again! My wife just called here to ask if she should take the kids somewhere, and if you think I'd be so goddamned dumb as to play games at a time like this, you, sir, are the one who needs help!'

'Thank you, Ryan, that will be all.' The line clicked off.

'Jesus!' the Senior Duty Officer observed.

Jack looked around the room for a waste basket. He just made it in time. Ryan fell to his knees and vomited into it. He reached for a can of Coke and washed his mouth out, spitting back into the basket. No one spoke until he rose.

'They just don't understand,' Jack said quietly. He stretched, then lit a cigarette. 'They just don't understand.

'You see, this is all very simple. There is a difference between not knowing anything and understanding that you don't know. We have a crisis, and all the players are reverting to type. The President is thinking like a lawyer, trying to be cool, doing what he knows how to do, running down the evidence and trying to make a case, interrogating the witnesses, trying to reduce everything, playing that game. Liz is fixed on the fact that she might have been blown up, can't set that aside. Well.' Ryan shrugged. 'I guess I can understand that. I've been there, too. She's a political scientist, looking for a theoretical model. She's feeding that to the president. She has a real elegant model, but it's based on crap, isn't it, Ben?'

'You left out something, Jack,' Goodley pointed out.

Ryan shook his head. 'No, Ben, I just haven't gotten

there yet. Because I can't control my *fucking* temper, they won't listen to me now. I should have known, I had my warning – I even saw it coming – but I let my temper get the best of me again. And you know the funny part? If it wasn't for me, Fowler would still be in Columbus, Ohio, and Elliot would be teaching shiny young faces at Bennington.' Jack walked to the window again. It was dark outside, and the lighted room made it into a mirror.

'What are you talking about?'

'That, gentlemen, is a secret. Maybe that's what they'll put on the stone: "Here lies John Patrick Ryan. He tried to do the right thing – and look what happened." I wonder if Cathy and the kids will make it . . .'

'Come on, it's not that bad,' the Senior Duty Officer observed, but all the others in the room felt the chill.

Jack turned. 'Isn't it? Don't you see where this is heading? They're not listening to anybody. They're not listening. They might listen to Dennis Bunker or Brent Talbot, but they're both air pollution, little bits of fallout somewhere over Colorado. I'm the closest thing in town to an advisor right now, and I got myself tossed out.'

CHAPTER 41

The Field of Camlan

The *Admiral Lunin* was going too fast for safety. Captain Dubinin knew that, but chances like this did not come along often. This was, in fact, the first, and the captain wondered if it might also be the last. Why were the Americans on a full-blown nuclear alert – yes, of course, a possible nuclear explosion in their country was a grave matter, but could they be so mad as to assume that a Soviet had done such a thing?

'Get me a polar projection chart,' he said to a quarter-master. Dubinin knew what he would see, but it wasn't a time for remembrance, it was a time for hard facts. The meter-square sheet of hard paper was on the table a moment later. Dubinin took a pair of dividers and walked them from *Maine*'s estimated position to Moscow, and to the strategic rocket fields in the central part of his country.

'Yes.' It could hardly be more clear, could it?

'What is it, Captain?' the *Starpom* asked.

'USS *Maine*, according to our intelligence estimates, is in the northernmost patrol sector of the missile submarines based at Bangor. That makes good sense, doesn't it?'

'Yes, Captain, based on what little we know of their patrol patterns.'

'She carries the D-5 rocket, twenty-four of them, eight or so warheads per rocket . . .' He paused. There had been a time when he'd been able to do such calculations in his head instantly.

'One hundred ninety-two, Captain,' the executive officer said for him.

'Correct, thank you. That includes nearly all of our SS-18s, less those being deactivated by treaty, and the CEP accuracy of the D-5 makes it likely that those one hundred ninety-two warheads will destroy roughly one hundred sixty of their targets, which, in turn, accounts for more than a fifth of our total warhead count, and our most accurate warheads at that. Remarkable, isn't it?' Dubinin asked quietly.

'You really think they're that good?'

'The Americans demonstrated their marksmanship ability over Iraq, didn't they? I for one have never doubted the quality of their weapons.'

'Captain, we know that the American D-5 submarine rockets are the most likely first-strike tool . . .'

'Continue the thought.'

The *Starpom* looked at the chart. 'Of course. This is the closest one.'

'Indeed. USS *Maine* is the point of the lance aimed at our country.' Dubinin tapped the chart with his dividers. 'If the Americans launch an attack, the first rockets will fly from this point, and nineteen minutes after that, they will hit. I wonder if our comrades in the Strategic Rocket Forces can respond that quickly . . . ?'

'But, Captain, what can we do about this?' the executive officer asked dubiously.

Dubinin pulled the chart off the table and slid it back into its open drawer. 'Nothing. Not a thing. We cannot attack preemptively without orders or grave provocation, can we? According to our best intelligence, he can launch his rockets at intervals of fifteen seconds, probably less, really. The manual becomes less important in war, doesn't it? Say four minutes from the first to the last. You have to do a ladder-north strike pattern to avoid warhead fratricide. That doesn't matter, if you examine the physics of the event. I looked at that while I was at Frunze, you know. Since our rockets are liquid-fueled, they cannot launch while the attack is under way. Even if their electronic components can withstand the electromagnetic effects, they are too fragile structurally to tolerate the physical forces. So, unless we can launch with confidence before the enemy warheads fall, our tactics are to ride it out and launch a few minutes later. For our part here, if he can launch in four minutes, that means we have to be within six thousand meters, hear the first launch transient, and fire our own torpedo immediately to have any hope of stopping him from firing his last rocket, don't we?'

'A difficult task.'

The captain shook his head. 'An impossible task. The only thing that makes sense is for us to eliminate him before he receives his launch order, but we cannot do that without orders, and we have no such orders.'

'So what do we do?'

'Not very much we can do.' Dubinin leaned over the chart table. 'Let's assume that he's truly disabled, and that we have an accurate position fix. We still have to detect him. If his engine plant is down at minimums, hearing him will be nearly impossible, especially if he's up against the surface noise. If we go active, what's to stop him from launching a torpedo against us? If he does that, we can fire back – and hope to survive, ourselves. Our weapon might even hit him, but then again it might not. If he does not shoot as soon as he hears our active sonar . . . maybe we can close enough that we can intimidate him, force him down. We'll lose him again when he goes under the layer . . . but if we can force him down . . . and then stay atop the layer, blasting away with our active sonar . . . perhaps we can keep him from going to missile-firing depth.' Dubinin frowned mightily. 'Not an especially brilliant plan, is it? If one of them suggested it – ' he waved to the junior officers conning the ship '– I'd tear a strip off their young backs. But I don't see anything better. Do you?'

'Captain, that makes us exceedingly vulnerable to attack.' The idea was more accurately described as suicidal, the Starpom thought, though he was sure Dubinin knew that.

'Yes, it does, but if that is what is required to prevent this bastard from getting to firing depth, it is exactly what I propose to do. I see no alternative.'

PRESIDENT NARMONOV:

PLEASE UNDERSTAND THE POSITION WE ARE IN. THE WEAPON WHICH DESTROYED DENVER WAS OF SUCH A SIZE AND TYPE AS TO MAKE IT VERY UNLIKELY THAT THIS CRIME WAS COMMITTED BY TERRORISTS, YET WE HAVE TAKEN NO ACTION WHATEVER TO RETALIATE AGAINST ANYONE. WERE YOUR COUNTRY ATTACKED, YOU TOO WOULD ALERT YOUR STRATEGIC FORCES. WE HAVE SIMILARLY ALERTED OURS, ALONG WITH OUR CONVENTIONAL FORCES. FOR TECHNICAL REASONS IT WAS NECESSARY TO INITIATE A GLOBAL ALERT INSTEAD OF A MORE SELECTIVE ONE. BUT AT NO TIME HAVE I ISSUED ANY INSTRUCTIONS TO COMMENCE OFFENSIVE OPERATIONS. OUR ACTIONS TO THIS POINT HAVE BEEN DEFENSIVE ONLY, AND HAVE SHOWN CONSIDERABLE RESTRAINT.

WE HAVE NO EVIDENCE TO SUGGEST THAT YOUR COUNTRY HAS INITIATED ACTION AGAINST OUR HOMELAND, BUT WE HAVE BEEN INFORMED THAT YOUR TROOPS IN BERLIN HAVE ATTACKED OURS, AND HAVE ALSO ATTACKED AIRCRAFT ATTEMPTING TO INSPECT THE AREA. WE ARE SIMILARLY INFORMED THAT SOVIET AIRCRAFT HAVE APPROACHED AN AMERICAN CARRIER GROUP IN THE MEDITERRANEAN.

PRESIDENT NARMONOV, I URGE YOU TO RESTRAIN YOUR FORCES. IF WE CAN END THE PROVOCATIONS, WE CAN END THIS CRISIS, BUT I CANNOT TELL MY PEOPLE NOT TO DEFEND THEMSELVES.

'"Restrain your forces"? God damn it,' the Defense Minister swore. 'We haven't *done* anything! He's accusing *us* of provoking *him*! *His* tanks have invaded east Berlin, *his* fighter-bombers have attacked our forces there, and he just confirmed the fact that his carrier aircraft have attacked ours! And this arrogant madman now says that we must not provoke him! What does he expect us to do – run away everywhere we see an American?'

'That might be the most prudent thing we can do,' Golovko observed.

'Run like a thief from a policeman?' Defense asked sarcastically. 'You ask that we should do that?'

'I suggest it as a possibility to be considered.' The First Deputy Chairman of KGB stood his ground bravely, Narmonov thought.

'The important part of this message is the second sentence,' the Foreign Minister pointed out. His analysis was all the more chilling for its matter-of-fact tone. 'They say that they do not believe this was a terrorist attack. Who is left as a likely attacker, then? He goes on to say that America has not retaliated against anyone *yet*. The subsequent statement that they have no evidence to suggest that we perpetrated this infamy is, I think, rather hollow when juxtaposed with the first paragraph.'

'And running away will only make it more clear to him that we are the ones who started this,' Defense added.

'More clear?' Golovko asked.

'I must agree with that,' Narmonov said, looking up from his chair. 'I must assume now that Fowler is not rational. This communique is not well-reasoned. He is accusing us, quite explicitly.'

'What is the nature of the explosion?' Golovko asked the Defense Minister.

'A weapon of that size is indeed too large for terrorists. Our studies indicate that a first- or even second-generation fission device might be achievable, but the maximum yield for such a device is certainly less than a hundred – probably less than forty kilotons. Our instruments tell us that this device was well over a hundred. That means a third-generation fission weapon, or more likely, a multi-stage fusion device. To do that is not the work of amateurs.'

'So, then, who could have done it?' Narmonov asked.

Golovko looked over to his president. 'I have no idea. We did uncover a possible DDR bomb project. They were producing plutonium, as you all know, but we have good reason to believe that the project never truly got underway. We've looked at ongoing projects in South America. They are not to this point, either. Israel has such capabilities, but what reason would they have to do this? Attack their own guardian? If China were to do something like this, they would more likely attack us. We have the land and resources they need, and America has much more value to them as a trading partner than as an enemy. No, for this to be a project of a nation-state means that only one of a handful has the ability to do it, and the problems of operational security are virtually insurmountable. Andrey Il'ych, if you *directed* KGB to do this, we probably could not. The type of individual necessary for such a mission – by that I mean the skill, intelligence, dedication – are not qualities which you find in a psychotic; murder on this scale, likely to bring about such a crisis as this, would require a diseased personality. KGB has no such people, for the obvious reason.'

'So, you are telling me that you have no information, and that you can find no sensible hypothesis to explain the events of this morning?'

'That is the case, Comrade President. I wish I could report something else, but I cannot.'

'What sort of advice is Fowler getting?'

'I don't know,' Golovko admitted. 'Secretaries Talbot and Bunker are both dead. Both were watching the football match – Defense Secretary Bunker was the owner of one of the teams, in fact. The Director of CIA is either still in Japan or on his way back from there.'

'The Deputy Director is Ryan, correct?'

'That is true.'

'I know him. He is not a fool.'

'No, he is not, but he is also being dismissed. Fowler dislikes him, and we have learned that Ryan has been asked to resign. Therefore, I cannot say who is advising President Fowler, except for Elizabeth Elliot, the National Security Advisor, with whom our ambassador is not impressed.'

'You tell me, then, that this weak, vain man is probably not getting good advice from anyone?'

'Yes.'

'That explains much.' Narmonov leaned back and closed his eyes. 'So, I am the only one who can give him good advice, but he probably thinks I am the one who killed his city. Splendid.' It was perhaps the most penetrating analysis of the night, but wrong.

> PRESIDENT FOWLER:
>
> FIRST OF ALL, I HAVE DISCUSSED THIS MATTER WITH MY MILITARY COMMANDERS AND HAVE BEEN ASSURED THAT NO SOVIET ATOMIC WARHEAD IS MISSING.
>
> SECOND, WE HAVE MET, YOU AND I, AND I HOPE YOU KNOW THAT I WOULD NEVER HAVE GIVEN SUCH A CRIMINAL ORDER AS THIS.
>
> THIRD, ALL OF OUR ORDERS TO OUR MILITARY FORCES HAVE BEEN OF A DEFENSIVE NATURE. I HAVE AUTHORIZED NO OFFENSIVE ACTION WHATEVER.
>
> FOURTH, I HAVE ALSO MADE INQUIRIES WITH OUR INTELLIGENCE SERVICES, AND I REGRET TO INFORM YOU THAT WE TOO HAVE NO IDEA WHO COULD HAVE COMMITTED THIS INHUMAN ACT. WE WILL WORK TO CHANGE THAT, AND ANY INFORMATION WE DEVELOP WILL BE SENT TO YOU AT ONCE.
>
> MR PRESIDENT, I WILL GIVE NO FURTHER ORDERS TO MY FORCES OF ANY KIND UNLESS PROVOKED. THE SOVIET MILITARY IS IN A DEFENSIVE POSTURE AND WILL REMAIN SO.

'Oh, God,' Elliot rasped. 'How many lies do we have here?' Her finger traced down the computer screen.

'One, we know that they have missing warheads. That is a lie.

'Two, why is he stressing the fact that it's really him, that you two met in Rome? Why bother doing that unless he thinks that we suspect it's *not* Narmonov at all? The real guy wouldn't do that, he wouldn't have to, would he? Probably a lie.

'Three, we know that they've attacked us in Berlin. That's a lie.

'Four, he brings up the KGB for the first time. I wonder why. What if they actually have a cover plan ... after intimidating us – beautiful, after intimidating us, they offer us their cover plan, and we have to buy it.

'Five, now he's warning us not to provoke him. They're in a "defensive posture," eh? Some posture.' Liz paused. 'Robert, this is spin-control pure and simple. He's trying to take us out.'

'That's the way I read it, too. Comments, anyone?'

'The non-provocation statement is troubling,' CINC-SAC replied. General Fremont was watching his status boards. He now had ninety-six bombers in the air, and over a hundred tankers. His missile fields were on line. The Defense Support Program satellites had their Cassegrain-focus telescopic cameras zoomed in on the Soviet missile fields instead of on wide-field scanning mode. 'Mr President, there is something we need to discuss right about now.'

'What is that, General?'

Fremont spoke in his best calm-professional voice. 'Sir, the build-down of the respective strategic-missile forces on both sides has affected the calculus of a nuclear strike. Before, when we had over a thousand ICBMs, neither we nor the Soviets ever expected that a disarming first-strike was a real strategic possibility. It just demanded too much. Things are different now. Improvements in missile technology plus the reduction in the number of fixed high-value targets now means that such a strike is a theoretical possibility. Add to that Soviet delays in deactivating their older SS-18s to comply with the strategic-arms treaty, and we have what may well be a strategic posture on their part in which such a strike may be an attractive option. Remember that we've been reducing our missile stocks faster than they. Now, I know that Narmonov gave you a personal assurance that he'd be fully in compliance with the treaty in four more weeks, but those missile regiments are still active as far as we can tell.

'Now,' Fremont went on, 'if that intelligence you have that Narmonov was being threatened by his military is correct – well, sir, the situation is pretty clear, isn't it?'

'Make it clearer, General,' Fowler said, so quietly that CINC-SAC barely heard him.

'Sir, what if Dr Elliot is right, what if they really expected you to be at the game? Along with Secretary Bunker, I mean. The way our command-and-control works, that would have severely crippled us. I'm not saying they would have attacked, but certainly they would have been in a position, while denying responsibility for the Denver explosion, to – well, to announce their change in government in such a way as to prevent us, by simple intimidation, from acting against them. That's bad enough. But they've missed their target, so to speak, haven't they? Okay, now what are they thinking? They may be thinking that you suspect that they've done this thing, and that you're angry enough to retaliate in one way or another. If they're thinking that, sir, they might also be thinking that their best way of protecting themselves is to disarm us quickly. Mr President, I'm not saying that they are thinking that way, but that they might be.' And a cold evening grew colder still.

'And how do we stop them from launching, General?' Fowler asked.

'Sir, the only thing that will keep them from launching is the certainty that the strike will not work. That's particularly true if we're dealing with their military. They're good. They're smart. They're rational. They think before they act, like all good soldiers. If they know we're ready to shoot at the first hint of an attack, then that attack becomes militarily futile, and it will not be initiated.'

'That's good advice, Robert,' Elliot said.

'What's NORAD think?' Fowler asked. The President didn't think to consider that he was asking a two-star general to evaluate the opinion of a four-star.

'Mr President, if we are to get some rationality back into this situation, that would appear to be the way to do it.'

'Very well. General Fremont, what do you propose?'

'Sir, at this point, we can advance our strategic-forces readiness to DEFCON-ONE. The codeword for that is SNAPCOUNT. At that point we are at maximum readiness.'

'Won't that provoke them?'

'Mr President, no, it should not. Two reasons. First, we are already at a high state of alert, they know it, and while they are clearly concerned, they have not objected in any way. That's the one sign of rationality we've seen to this point. Second, they won't know until we tell them that we've upped things a notch. We don't have to tell them until they do something provocative.'

Fowler sipped at his newest cup of coffee. He'd have to visit the bathroom soon, he realized.

'General, I'm going to hold off on that. Let me think that one over for a few minutes.'

'Very well, sir.' Fremont's voice did not reveal any overt disappointment, but a thousand miles from Camp David, CINC-SAC turned to look at his Deputy Chief of Staff (Operations).

'What is it?' Parsons asked. There was nothing more for him to do at the moment. Having made his urgent phone call, and having decided to let his fellow NEST team members handle the lab work, he'd decided to assist the doctors. He'd brought instruments to evaluate the radiation exposure to the firefighters and handful of survivors, something in which the average physician has little expertise. The situation was not especially cheerful. Of the seven people who had survived the explosion at the stadium, five already showed signs of extreme radiation sickness. Parsons evaluated their exposures at anywhere from four hundred to over a thousand Rems. Six hundred was the maximum exposure normally compatible with survival, though, with heroic treatment, higher exposures had been survived. If one called living another year or two with three or four varieties of cancer breaking out in one's body 'survival.' The last one, fortunately, seemed to have the least. He was still cold, though his hands and face were badly burned, but he hadn't vomited yet. He was also quite deaf.

It was a young man, Parsons saw. The clothing in the bag next to his bed included a handgun and a badge – a cop. He also held something in his hand, and when the boy looked up, he saw the FBI agent standing next to the NEST leader.

Officer Pete Dawkins was deep in shock, nearly insensate. His shaking came both from being cold and wet, and from the aftermath of more terror than any man had ever faced and survived. His mind had divided itself into three or four separate areas, all of which were operating along different paths and at different speeds, and none of them were particularly sane or coherent. What held part of one such area together was training. While Parsons ran some sort of instrument over the clothing he'd worn only a short time before, Dawkins' damaged eyes saw standing next to him another man in a blue plastic windbreaker. On the sleeves and over the chest were printed 'FBI.' The young officer sprang upwards, disconnecting himself from the IV line. That caused both a doctor and a nurse to push him back down, but Dawkins fought them with the strength of madness, holding out his hand to the agent.

Special Agent Bill Clinton was also badly shaken. Only the vagaries of scheduling had saved his life. He, too, had had a ticket for the game, but he'd had to give it to another member of his squad. From that misfortune, which had enraged the young agent only four days earlier, his life had been spared. What he'd seen at the stadium had stunned him. His exposure to radiation – only forty Rems, according to Parsons – terrified him, but Clinton, too, was a cop, and he took the paper from Dawkins' hand.

It was, he saw, a list of cars. One was circled and had a question-mark scribbled next to the license plate.

'What's this mean?' Clinton asked, leaning past a nurse who was trying to restart Dawkins' IV line.

'Van,' the man gasped, not hearing, but knowing the question. 'Got in . . . asked sarge to check it out, but — south side, by the TV trucks. ABC van, little one, two guys, I let them in. Not on my list.'

'South side, does that mean anything?' Clinton asked Parsons.

'That's where it was.' Parsons leaned down. 'What did they look like, the two men?' He gestured at the paper, then pointed at himself and Clinton.

'White, both thirties, ordinary . . . said they came from Omaha . . . with a tape machine. Thought it was funny they came from Omaha . . . told Sergeant Yankevich . . . went to check it out right before.'

'Look,' a doctor said, 'this man is in very bad shape, and I have to —'

'Back off,' Clinton said.

'Did you look in the truck?'

Dawkins only stared. Parsons grabbed a piece of paper and drew a truck on it, stabbing at the picture with his pencil.

Dawkins nodded, on the edge of consciousness. 'Big box, three feet "SONY" printed on it — they said it was a tape deck. Truck from Omaha . . . but —' he pointed at the list.

Clinton looked. 'Colorado tags!'

'I let it in,' Dawkins said just before he collapsed.

'Three-foot box . . .' Parsons said quietly.

'Come on.' Clinton ran out of the emergency room. The nearest phone was at the admitting desk. All four were being used. Clinton took one right out of the hand of an admitting clerk, hung up and cleared the line.

'What are you doing!'

'Shut up!' the agent commanded. 'I need Hoskins . . . Walt, this is Clinton at the hospital. I need you to run a tag number. Colorado E-R-P-five-two-zero. Suspicious van at the stadium. Two men were driving it, white, thirties, ordinary-looking. The witness is a cop, but now he's passed out.'

'Okay. Who's with you?'

'Parsons, the NEST guy.'

'Get down here – no, stay put, but keep this line open.' Hoskins put that line on hold, then dialed another from memory. It was for the Colorado Department of Motor Vehicles. 'This is the FBI, I need a quick tag check. Your computer up?'

'Yes, sir,' a female voice assured him.

'Edward Robert Paul Five Two Zero.' Hoskins looked down at his desk. Why did that sound familiar?

'Very well.' Hoskins heard the tapping. 'Here we go, that's a brand-new van registered to Mr Robert Friend of Roggen. You need the license number for Mr Friend?'

'Christ,' Hoskins said.

'Excuse me, sir?' He read off the number. 'That's correct.'

'Can you check two other license numbers?'

'Surely.' He read them off. 'First one's an incorrect number ... so's the second – wait a minute, these numbers are just like –'

'I know. Thank you.' Hoskins set the phone down. 'Okay, Walt, think fast ...' First he needed more information from Clinton.

'Murray.'

'Dan, this is Walt Hoskins. Something just came in you need to know.'

'Shoot.'

'Our friend Marvin Russell parked a van at the stadium. The NEST guy says that the place where he parked it is pretty close to where the bomb went off. There was at least one – no, wait a minute – okay. There was one other guy in there with him, and the other one must have been driving the rental car. Okay. Inside the van was a large box. The van was painted up like an ABC vehicle, but Russell was found dead a couple miles away. So, he must have dropped off the van and left. Dan, this looks like how the bomb might have gotten there.'

'What else do you have, Walt?'

'I have passport photos and other ID for two other people.'

'Fax 'em.'

'On the way.' Hoskins left for the communications room. On the way he grabbed another agent. 'Get the Denver homicide guys who're working the Russell case – wherever they are, get 'em on the phone real fast.'

'Thinking terrorism again?' Pat O'Day asked. 'I thought the bomb was too big for that.'

'Russell was a suspected terrorist, and we think he might – shit!' Murray exclaimed.

'What's that, Dan?'

'Tell Records I want the photos from Athens that're in the Russell file.' The deputy assistant director waited for the call to be made. 'We had an inquiry from the Greeks, one of their officers got murdered and they sent us some photos. I thought at the time it might be Marvin, but . . . there was somebody else in there, a car, I think. We had him in profile, I think . . .'

'Fax coming in from Denver,' a woman announced.

'Bring it over,' Murray commanded.

'Here's page one.' The rest arrived rapidly.

'Airline ticket . . . connecting ticket. Pat –'

O'Day took it. 'I'll run it down.'

'Shit, look at this!'

'Familiar face?'

'It looks like . . . Ismael Qati, maybe? I don't know the other one.'

'Mustache and hair are wrong, Dan,' O'Day thought, turning away from his phone. 'A little thin, too. Better call Records to see what they have current on the mutt. You don't want to jump too fast, man.'

'Right.' Murray lifted his phone.

'Good news, Mr President,' Borstein said from inside Cheyenne Mountain. 'We have a KH-11 pass coming up through the Central Soviet Union. It's almost dawn there now, clear weather for a change, and we'll get a look at some missile fields. The bird's already programmed. NPIC is real-timing it into here and Offutt also.'

'But not here,' Fowler groused. Camp David had never been set up for that, a remarkable oversight, Fowler thought. It did go into Kneecap, which was where he should have gone when he'd had the chance. 'Well, tell me what you see.'

'Will do, sir, this ought to be very useful for us,' Borstein promised.

'Coming up now, sir,' a new voice said. 'Sir, this is Major Costello, NORAD intel. We couldn't have timed this much better. The bird is going to sweep very close to four regiments, south to north, at Zhangiz Tobe, Alyesk, Uzhur, and Gladkaya, all but the last are SS-18 bases. Gladkaya is SS-11s, old birds. Sir, Aleysk is one of the places they're supposed to be deactivating, but haven't yet . . .'

The morning sky was clear at Alyesk. First light was beginning to brighten the northeastern horizon, but none of the soldiers of the Strategic Rocket Forces bothered to look. They were weeks behind schedule and their current orders were to correct that deficiency. That such orders were nearly impossible was beside the point. At each of the forty launch silos was a heavy articulated truck. The SS-18s – the Russians actually called them RS-20s, for Rocket, Strategic, Number 20 – were old ones, more than eleven years, in fact, which was why the Soviets had agreed to eliminate them. Powered by liquid-fueled motors, the fuels and oxidizers in question were dangerous, corrosive chemicals – unsymmetrical dimethyl hydrazine and nitrogen tetroxide – and the fact that they were called 'storable' liquids was a relative statement. They were more stable than cryogenic fuels, insofar as they did not require refrigeration, but they were toxic to the point of nearly instant lethality to human contact, and they were necessarily highly reactive. One safeguard was the encapsulation of the missiles in steel capsules which were loaded like immense rifle cartridges into the silos, a Soviet design innovation that protected the delicate silo instrumentation from the chemicals. That the Soviets bothered with such systems at all was not – as American intelligence officers carped – to take advantage of their higher energy impulse, but rather a result of the fact that the Soviets had lagged in developing a reliable and powerful solid fuel for its missiles, a situation only recently remedied with the new SS-25. Though undeniably large and powerful, the SS-18 – given the ominous NATO codename of 'SATAN' – was an ill-tempered, pitiless bitch to maintain, and the crews were delighted to be rid of them. More than one Strategic Rocket Forces soldier had been killed in maintenance and training accidents, just as Americans had lost men with its counterpart U.S. missile, the Titan-II. All of the Alyesk birds were tagged for elimination, and that was the reason for the presence of the men and the transporter trucks. But first, the warheads had to be removed. The Americans could watch the missiles in the destruction process, but the warheads were still the most secret of artifacts. Under the watchful eyes of a colonel, the nose shroud was removed from Rocket Number 31 by a small crane, exposing the MIRVs. Each of the conically shaped multiple independently-targetable re-entry vehicles was about forty centimeters in width at the bottom, tapering to a needle point one hundred fifty centimeters above its base. Each also represented about half a megaton of three-stage thermonuclear device. The soldiers treated the MIRVs with all the respect they so clearly deserved.

'Okay, getting some pictures now,' Fowler heard Major Costello say. 'Not much activity . . . sir, we're isolating on just a few of the silos, the ones that we can see the best – there's woods all over there, Mr President, but because of the angle of the satellite we know which ones we can see clearly . . . okay, there's one, Tobe Silo Zero-Five . . . nothing unusual . . . the command bunker is right there . . . I can see guards patrolling around . . . more than usual . . . I see five – seven people – we can get them real good in infra-red, it's cold there, sir.

Nothing else. Nothing else unusual, sir . . . good. Okay, coming up on Alyesk now – Jeez!'

'What is it?'

'Sir, we're looking at four silos on four different cameras . . .'

'Those are service trucks,' General Fremont said, from the SAC command center. 'Service trucks at all four. Silo doors are open, Mr President.'

'What does that mean?'

Costello took the question: 'Mr President, these are all -18 Mod 2s, fairly old ones. They were supposed to be deactivated by now, but they haven't been. We now have five silos in sight, sir, and all five have service trucks there. I can see two with people standing around, doing something to the missiles.'

'What's a service truck?' Liz Elliot asked.

'Those are the trucks they use to transport the missiles. They also have all the tools you use to work on them. There's one truck per bird – actually more than one. It's a big semi-truck, like a hook 'n' ladder truck, actually, with storage bins built in for all the tools and stuff – Jim, they look like they pulled the shroud – yeah! There are the warheads, it's lit up, and they're doing something to the RVs . . . I wonder what?'

Fowler nearly exploded. It was like listening to a football game on the radio, and – 'What does all this mean!'

'Sir, we can't tell . . . coming up to Uzhur now. Not much activity, Uzhur has the new mark of the -18, the Mod 5 . . . no trucks, I can see sentries again. Mr President, I would estimate that we have more than the usual number of sentries around. Gladkaya next . . . that'll take a couple of minutes . . .'

'Why are the trucks there?' Fowler asked.

'Sir, all I can say is that they appear to be working on the birds.'

'*God damn it! Doing* what*!*' Fowler screamed into the speaker phone.

The reply was very different from the cool voice of a few minutes earlier. 'Sir, there's no way we can tell that.'

'Then tell me what you *do* know!'

'Mr President, as I already said, these missiles are old ones, they're maintenance-intensive, and they were scheduled for destruction, but they're overdue for that. We observed increased site security at all three SS-18 regiments, but at Alyesk every bird we saw had a truck and a maintenance crew there, and the silos were all open. That's all we can tell from these pictures, sir.'

'Mr President,' General Borstein said, 'Major Costello has told you everything he can.'

'General, you told me that we'd get something useful from this. *What* did we get?'

'Sir, it may be significant that there's all that work going on at Alyesk.'

'But you don't know what the work is!'

'No, sir, we don't,' Borstein admitted rather sheepishly.

'Could they be readying those missiles for launch?'

'Yes, sir, that is a possibility.'

'My God.'

'Robert,' the National Security Advisor said, 'I am getting very frightened.'

'Elizabeth, we don't have time for this.' Fowler collected himself. 'We must maintain control of ourselves, and control the situation. We must. We must convince Narmonov –'

'Robert, don't you *see!* It's *not him!* That's the only thing that makes *sense*. We don't know who we're dealing with!'

'What can we do about it?'

'I don't know!'

'Well, whoever it is, they don't want a nuclear war. Nobody would. It's too crazy,' the President assured her, sounding almost like a parent.

'Are you sure of that? Robert, are you really sure? They tried to kill *us!*'

'Even if that's true, we have to set it aside.'

'But we *can't*. If they were willing to try once, they will be willing to try again! Don't you see?'

Just a few feet behind him, Helen D'Agustino realized that she'd read Liz Elliot correctly the previous summer.

She was as much a coward as a bully. And now whom did the President have to advise him? Fowler rose from his chair and headed for the bathroom. Pete Connor trailed along as far as the door, because even Presidents are not allowed to make that trip alone. 'Daga' looked down on Dr Elliot. Her face was – what? the Secret Service agent asked herself. It was beyond fear. Agent D'Agustino was every bit as frightened herself, but she didn't – that was unfair, wasn't it? Nobody was asking her for advice, nobody was asking her to make sense of this mess. Clearly, none of it made sense at all. It simply didn't. At least no one was asking her about it, but that wasn't her job. It was Liz Elliot's job.

'I got a contact here,' one of the sonar operators said aboard Sea Devil One-Three. 'Buoy three, bearing two-one-five . . . blade count now . . . single screw – nuclear submarine contact! Not American, screw's not American.'

'Got him on four,' another sonarman said. 'This dude's hauling ass, blade count shows over twenty, maybe twenty-five knots, bearing my buoy is three-zero-zero.'

'Okay,' the Tacco said, 'I have a posit. Can you give me drift?'

'Bearing now two-one-zero!' the first one responded. 'This guy is moving!'

Two minutes later, it was clear, the contact was heading straight for USS *Maine.*

'Is this possible?' Jim Rosselli asked. The radio message had gone from Kodiak straight to the NMCC. The commander of the patrol squadron didn't know what to do and was screaming for instructions. The report came in the form of a RED ROCKET, copied off also to CINCPAC, who would also be requesting direction from above.

'What do you mean?' Barnes asked.

'He's heading straight for where *Maine* is. How the hell could he know where she is?'

'How'd we find out?'

'SLOT buoy, radio – oh, no, that asshole hasn't maneuvered clear?'

'Kick this to the President?' Colonel Barnes asked.

'I guess.' Rosselli lifted the phone.

'This is the President.'

'Sir, this is Captain Jim Rosselli at the National Military Command Center. We have a disabled submarine in the Gulf of Alaska, USS *Maine*, an Ohio-class missile boat. Sir, she has prop damage and cannot maneuver. There is a Soviet attack submarine heading straight towards her, about ten miles out. We have a P-3C Orion ASW aircraft that is now tracking the Russian. Sir, he requests instructions.'

'I thought they can't track our missile submarines.'

'Sir, nobody can, but in this case they must have DF – I mean used direction-finders to locate the sub when she radioed for help. *Maine* is a missile submarine, part of SIOP, and is under DEFCON-TWO Rules of Engagement. Therefore, so is the Orion that's riding shotgun for her. Sir, they want to know what to do.'

'How important is *Maine*?' Fowler asked.

General Fremont took that. 'Sir, that sub is part of the SIOP, a big part, over two hundred warheads, very accurate ones. If the Russians can take her out, they've hurt us badly.'

'How badly?'

'Sir, it makes one hell of a hole in our war plan. *Maine* carries the D-5 missile, and they are tasked counterforce. They're supposed to attack missile fields and selected command-and-control assets. If something happens to her, it would take literally hours to patch up that hole in the plan.'

'Captain Rosselli, you're Navy, right?'

'Yes, Mr President – sir, I have to tell you that I was CO of *Maine*'s Gold Crew until a few months ago.'

'How soon before we have to make a decision?'

'Sir, the Akula is inbound at twenty-five knots, currently about twenty thousand yards from our boat. Technically speaking, they're within torpedo range right now.'

'What are my options?'

'You can order an attack or not order an attack,' Rosselli replied.

'General Fremont?'

'Mr President – no, Captain Rosselli?'

'Yes, General?'

'How sure are you that the Russians are boring straight in on our boat?'

'The signal is quite positive on that, sir.'

'Mr President, I think we have to protect our assets. The Russians won't be real pleased with an attack on one of their boats, but it's an attack boat, not a strategic asset. If they challenge us on this, we can explain it. What I want to know is why they ordered the boat in this way. They must know that it would alarm us.'

'Captain Rosselli, you have my authorization for the aircraft to engage and destroy the submarine.'

'Aye aye, sir.' Rosselli lifted the other phone. 'GRAY BEAR, this is MARBLEHEAD –' the current codename for the NMCC '– National Command Authority approves I repeat *approves* your request. Acknowledge.'

'MARBLEHEAD, this is GRAY BEAR, we copy request to engage is approved.'

'That's affirmative.'

'Roger. Out.'

The Orion turned in. Even the pilots were feeling the effects of the weather now. Technically, it was still light, but the low ceiling and heavy seas made it seem that they were flying down an immense and bumpy corridor. That was the bad news. The good news was that their contact was acting dumb, running very fast, below the layer, and almost impossible to miss. The Tacco in back coached him in along the Akula's course. Sticking out the tail of the converted Lockheed Electra airliner was a sensitive device called a magnetic anomaly detector. It reported on variations in the earth's magnetic field, such as those caused by the metallic mass of a submarine.

'Madman madman madman, smoke away!' the system operator called. He pushed a button to release a smoke float. In front, the pilot immediately turned left to set up another run. This he did, then a third, turning left each time.

'Okay, how's this look back there?' the pilot asked.

'Solid contact, nuclear-powered sub, positive Russian. I say let's do it this time.'

'Fair enough,' the pilot observed.

'Jesus!' the co-pilot muttered.

'Open the doors.'

'Coming open now. Safeties off, release is armed, weapon is hot.'

'Okay, I have it set,' the Tacco said. 'Clear to drop.'

It was too easy. The pilot lined up on the smoke floats, which were almost perfectly in a row. He passed over the first, then the second, then the third . . .

'Dropping now-now-now! Torp away!' The pilot added power and climbed a few hundred feet.

The Mark 50 ASW torpedo dropped clear, retarded by a small parachute that automatically released when the fish hit the water. The new and very sophisticated weapon was powered by an almost noiseless propulsor instead of a propeller, and had been programmed to stay covert until it reached the target depth of five hundred feet.

It was just about time to slow down, Dubinin thought, another few thousand meters. His gamble, he felt, had been a good one. It seemed a wholly reasonable supposition that the American missile submarine would stay near the surface. If he'd guessed right, then by racing in just below the layer – he was running on one hundred ten meters – then surface noise would keep the Americans from hearing him, and he could conduct the remainder of the search more covertly. He was about to congratulate himself for a good tactical decision.

'Torpedo sonar on the starboard bow!' Lieutenant Rykov screamed from sonar.

'Rudder left! Ahead flank! Where is the torpedo?'

Rykov: 'Depression angle fifteen! Below us!'

'Emergency surface! Full rise on the planes! New course three-zero-zero!' Dubinin dashed into sonar.

'What the hell?'

Rykov was pale. 'I can't hear screws . . . just that damned sonar . . . looking away – no, it's in acquisition now!'

Dubinin turned: 'Countermeasures – three – now!'

'Cans away!'

Admiral Lunin's countermeasures operators rapidly fired off three fifteen-centimeter cans of gas-generating material. These filled the water with bubbles, making a target for the torpedo, but one that didn't move. The Mark 50 had already sensed the submarine's presence and was turning in.

'Coming through one hundred meters,' the *Starpom* called. 'Speed twenty-eight knots.'

'Level off at fifteen, but don't be afraid of broaching.'

'Understood! Twenty-nine knots.'

'Lost it, the curve in the towed array just ruined our reception.' Rykov's hands went up in frustration.

'Then we must be patient,' Dubinin said. It wasn't much of a joke, but the sonar crew loved him for it.

'The Orion just engaged the inbound, sir, just picked up an ultrasonic sonar, very faint, bearing two-four-zero. It's one of ours, it's a Mark 50, sir.'

'That ought to take care of him,' Ricks observed. 'Thank God.'

'Passing through fifty meters, leveling out, ten degrees on the planes. Speed thirty-one.'

'Countermeasures didn't work . . .' Rykov said. The towed array was straightening out, and the torpedo was still back there.

'No propeller noises?'

'None . . . I should be able to hear them even at this speed.'

'Must be one of their new ones . . .'

'The Mark 50? It's supposed to be a very clever little fish.'

'We will see about that. Yevgeniy, remember the surface action?' Dubinin smiled.

The *Starpom* did a superb job of maintaining control, but the thirty-foot seas guaranteed that the submarine would broach – break the surface – as the waves and troughs swept overhead. The torpedo was a scant three hundred meters behind when the Akula leveled out. The American Mark 50 anti-submarine torpedo was not a smart weapon, but a 'brilliant' one. It had identified and ignored the countermeasures Dubinin had ordered only minutes before, and, using a powerful ultrasonic sonar, was now looking for the sub in order to conclude its mission. But here physical laws intervened in favor of the Russians. It is widely believed that sonar reflects off the metal hull of a ship, but this is not true. Rather, sonar reflects off the air inside a submarine, or more precisely off the border of water and air through which the sound energy cannot pass. The Mark 50 was programmed to identify these air-water boundaries as ships. As the torpedo rocketed after its prey, it began to see immense ship-shapes stretching as far as its sonar could reach. Those were waves. Though the weapon had been programmed to ignore a flat surface and thus avoid a problem called 'surface capture,' its designers had not addressed the problem of a heavy, rolling sea. The Mark 50 selected the nearest such shape, raced towards it –

– and sprang into clear air like a leaping salmon. It crashed into the back of the next wave, reacquired the same immense target shape –

– and leaped again. This time the torpedo hit at a slight angle. Dynamic forces caused it to turn and race north inside the body of a wave, sensing huge ships both left and right. It turned left, springing into the air yet again, but this time it hit the next wave hard enough to detonate its contact fuse.

'That was close!' Rykov said.

'No, not close, perhaps a thousand meters, but probably more.' The captain leaned into the control room. 'Slow to five knots, down to thirty meters.'

'We hit it?'

'I don't know, sir,' the operator said. 'He went shallow in a hurry, and the fish went charging up after him, circled around some – ' the sonarman traced his finger on the display. 'Then it exploded here, close to where the Akula disappeared into the surface noise. Can't say – no break-up noises, sir, I have to call it a miss.'

'Bearing and distance to the target?' Dubinin asked.

'Roughly nine thousand meters, bearing zero-five-zero,' the *Starpom* replied. 'What is the plan now, Captain?'

'We will locate and destroy the target,' said Captain First Rank Valentin Borissovich Dubinin.

'But – '

'We have been attacked. Those bastards tried to kill us!'

'That was an aerial weapon,' the executive officer pointed out.

'I heard no airplane. We have been attacked. We will defend ourselves.'

'Well?'

Inspector Pat O'Day was making furious notes. American Airlines, like all the major carriers, had its ticket information on computer. With a ticket number and flight numbers, he could track anyone down. 'Okay,' he told the woman on the other end. 'Wait a minute.' O'Day turned. 'Dan, there were only six first-class tickets on that flight from Denver to Dallas–Fort Worth, the flight was nearly empty – but it hasn't taken off yet because of ice and snow in Dallas. We have the names for two other first-class passengers who changed to a Miami flight. Now, the Dallas connection was for Mexico City. The two who changed through Miami were also booked on a DC-10 out of Miami into Mexico City. That plane's off, one hour out of Mexico.'

'Turn it around?'

'They say they can't because of fuel.'

'One hour – Christ!' Murray swore.

O'Day ran a large hand over his face. As scared as everyone else in America – more so, since everyone in the command center had informed reason to be frightened – Inspector Patrick Sean O'Day was trying mightily to set everything aside and concentrate on whatever he had at hand. It was too slim and too circumstantial to be considered hard evidence as yet. He'd seen too many coincidences in his twenty years with the Bureau. He'd also seen major cases break on thinner stuff than this. You ran with what you had, and they had this.

'Dan, I –'

A messenger came in from the Records Division. She handed over two files to Murray. The deputy assistant director opened the Russell file first, rummaging for the Athens photo. Next he took out the most recent photo of Ismael Qati. He set both next to the passport photos just faxed in from Denver.

'What do you think, Pat?'

'The passport one of this guy still looks thin for Mr Qati . . . cheekbones and eyes are right, mustache isn't. He's losing hair, too, if this is him . . .'

'Go with the eyes?'

'The eyes are right, Dan, the nose – yeah, it's him. Who's this other mutt?'

'No names, just these frames from Athens. Fair skin, dark hair, well-groomed. Haircut's right, hairline is right.' He checked the descriptive data on the license and passport. 'Height, little guy, build – it fits, Pat.'

'I agree, I agree about eighty percent worth, man. Who's the Legal Attaché in Mexico City?'

'Bernie Montgomery – shit! he's in town to meet with Bill.'

'Try Langley?'

'Yeah.' Murray lifted his CIA line. 'Where's Ryan?'

'Right here, Dan. What gives?'

'We have something. First, a guy named Marvin

Russell, Sioux Indian, member of the Warrior Society, he dropped out of sight last year, somewhere in Europe, we thought. He turned up with his throat cut in Denver today. There were two people with him, they flew out. One, we have a picture but no name. The other may be Ismael Qati.'

That bastard! 'Where are they?'

'We think they're aboard an American Airlines flight from Miami to Mexico City, first-class tickets, about an hour out from the terminal.'

'And you think there's a connection?'

'A vehicle registered to Marvin Russell, a/k/a Robert Friend of Roggen, Colorado, was on the stadium grounds. We have fake IDs from two people, probably Qati and the unknown subject, recovered from the murder scene. There's plenty enough to arrest on suspicion of murder.'

Yeah, Jack thought. Had the situation not been so horrible, Ryan would have laughed at that. 'Murder, eh? You going to try and make the arrest?'

'Unless you have a better idea.'

Ryan was quiet for a moment. 'Maybe I do. Hold on for a minute.' He lifted another phone and dialed the United States Embassy in Mexico City. 'This is Ryan calling for the Station Chief. Tony? Jack Ryan here. Is Clark still there? Good, put him on.'

'Jesus, Jack, what the hell is – ' Ryan cut him off.

'Shut up, John. I have something for you to do. We have two people coming in to the airport there on an American flight from Miami, due in about an hour. We'll fax you the photos in a few minutes. We think they might be involved in this.'

'So, it's a terrorist gig?'

'Best thing we have, John. We want those two, and we want them fast.'

'Might be a problem from the local cops, Jack,' Clark warned. 'I can't exactly have a shoot-out down here.'

'Is the ambassador in?'

'I think so.'

'Transfer me over and stand by.'

'Right.'

'Ambassador's office,' a female voice said.

'This is CIA Headquarters, and I need the ambassador right now!'

'Surely.' The secretary was a cool one, Ryan thought.

'Yeah, what is it?'

'Mr Ambassador, this is Jack Ryan, Deputy Director of CIA –'

'This is an open phone line.'

'I know that! Shut up and listen. There are two people coming into Mexico City airport in an American Airlines flight from Miami. We need to pick them up and get them back here just as fast as we can.'

'Our people?'

'No, we think they're terrorists.'

'That means arresting them, clearing it through the local legal system and –'

'*We don't have time for that!*'

'Ryan, we can't strong-arm these people, they won't stand for it.'

'Mr Ambassador, I want you to call the President of Mexico right now, and I want you to tell him that we need his cooperation – it's life-and-death, okay? If he doesn't agree immediately, I want you to tell him this, and I need you to write it down. Tell him that we know about his retirement plan. Okay? Use those exact words, *we know about his retirement plan.*'

'What does that mean?'

'It means that you say exactly that, do you understand?'

'Look, I don't like playing games and –'

'Mr Ambassador, if you do not do exactly what I'm telling you, I will have one of my people render you unconscious and then have the DCM make the call.'

'You can't threaten me like that!'

'I just did, pal, and if you think I'm kidding, you just fucking try me!'

'Temper, Jack,' Ben Goodley cautioned.

Ryan looked away from the phone. 'Sir, excuse me. It's very tense here, okay, we've had a nuclear device go off in Denver, and this may be the best lead we have.

965

Look, there isn't time for niceties. Please. Play along with me. Please.'

'Very well.'

Ryan let out a breath. 'Okay. Tell him also that one of our people, a Mr Clark, will be at the airport security office in a few minutes. Mr Ambassador, I cannot emphasize enough how important this is. Please do it now.'

'I'll do it. You'd better calm down up there,' the career foreign-service officer advised.

'We're trying very hard, sir. Please have your secretary transfer me back to the Station Chief. Thank you.' Ryan looked over to Goodley. 'Just hit me over the fucking head if you feel the need, Ben.'

'Clark.'

'We're faxing some photos down, along with their names and seat assignments. Okay, you are to check in with the airport security boss before you grab 'em. You still have the airplane down there?'

'Right.'

'When you have 'em, get 'em aboard, and get 'em the hell up here.'

'Okay, Jack. We're on it.'

Ryan killed the line and picked up on Murray. 'Fax the data you have to our Station Chief Mexico. I have two field officers on the scene, good ones, Clark and Chavez.'

'Clark?' Murray asked, as he handed the fax information to Pat O'Day. 'The same one who —'

'That's the man.'

'I wish him luck.'

The tactical problem was complex. Dubinin had an anti-submarine aircraft overhead and could not afford to make a single mistake. Somewhere ahead was an American missile submarine that he fully intended to destroy. He had ordered it to protect himself, the captain reasoned. He had been fired upon with a live weapon. That changed matters greatly. He really should radio fleet command for instructions, or at least to announce his intentions, but with an aircraft overhead that was

966

suicide, and he'd brushed close enough to death for one day. The attack on *Admiral Lunin* could only mean that the Americans were planning an attack on his country. They'd violated their favorite international hobbyhorse – the seas were free for the passage of all. They'd attacked him in international waters before he was close enough to commit a hostile act. Someone, therefore, thought there was a state of war. Fine, Dubinin thought. So be it.

The submarine's towed-array sonar was drooping well below the level of the boat, and the sonar crewmen were now concentrating as they never had.

'Contact,' Lieutenant Rykov called. 'Sonar contact, bearing one-one-three, single screw . . . noisy, sounds like a damaged submarine . . .'

'You're certain it's not a surface contact?'

'Positive . . . surface traffic is well south of this track because of the storms. The sound is definitely character-istic of a submarine power plant . . . noisy, as though from some damage . . . southerly drift . . . bearing one-one-five now.'

Valentin Borissovich turned to shout into the control room: 'Estimated distance to target's reported position?'

'Seven thousand meters!'

'Long, long shot . . . southerly drift . . . speed?'

'Difficult to tell . . . less than six knots, certainly . . . there's a blade-rate there, but it's faint, and I can't read it.'

'We may not get more than one shot . . .' Dubinin whispered to himself. He went back to control. 'Weapons! Set up a torpedo on a course of one-one-five, initial search depth seventy meters, activation point . . . four thousand meters.'

'Very well.' The lieutenant made the proper adjust-ment to his board. 'Set for tube one . . . weapon is hot, ready! Outer door is closed, Captain.'

Dubinin turned to look at the executive officer. Ordi-narily a very sober man – he scarcely drank even at cer-emonial dinners – the *Starpom* nodded approval. The captain didn't need it, but was grateful for it even so.

'Open outer door.'

967

'Outer door is open.' The weapons officer flipped the plastic cover off the firing switch.

'Fire.'

The lieutenant stabbed the button home. 'Weapon is free.'

'Conn, sonar! Transient, transient, bearing one-seven-five — *torpedo in the water bearing one-nine-five!*'

'All ahead full!' Ricks shouted to the helm.

'Captain!' Claggett screamed. 'Belay that order!'

'What?' The youngster at the helm was all of nineteen, and had never heard a captain's order countermanded. 'What do I do, sir?'

'Captain, if you goose the engines like that, we lose the shaft in about fifteen seconds!'

'Shit, you're right.' Ricks was pink beneath the red battle lights in the control room. 'Tell the engine room, best safe speed, helm, right ten degrees rudder, come north, new course zero-zero-zero.'

'Right ten degrees rudder, aye.' The boy's voice quavered as he turned the wheel. Fear is as contagious as plague. 'Sir, my rudder is right ten degrees, coming to new course zero-zero-zero.'

Ricks swallowed and nodded. 'Very well.'

'Conn, sonar, bearing to torpedo is now bearing one-nine-zero, torpedo going left to right, torpedo is not pinging at this time.'

'Thank you,' Claggett replied.

'Without our tail, we're going to lose track of it real quick.'

'That's true, sir. Captain, how about we let the Orion know what's going on?'

'Good idea, run up the antenna.'

'Sea Devil One-Three, this is *Maine*.'

'*Maine*, this is One-Three, we are still evaluating that torpedo we dropped and —'

'One-Three, we have a torpedo in the water one-eight-zero. You missed the guy. Start another search pattern south of us. I think this bird is engaging our MOSS.'

'Roger, on the way.' The Tacco informed Kodiak that there was a for-real battle going on now.

'Mr President,' Ryan said, 'we may have some useful information here, sir.' Jack was sitting down in front of the speaker phone, his hands flat on the table and wet enough to leave marks on the Formica top, Goodley saw. For all that, he envied Ryan's ability to control himself.

'What might that be?' Fowler asked harshly.

Ryan's head dropped at the tone of the reply. 'Sir, the FBI has just informed us that they have information on two, possibly three, confirmed terrorist suspects in Denver today. Two of them are believed to be on an airliner inbound to Mexico. I have people in the area, and we're going to try and pick them up, sir.'

'Wait a minute,' Fowler said. 'We *know* that this wasn't a terrorist act.'

'Ryan, this is General Fremont. How was this information developed?'

'I don't know all the details, but they have information on an automobile – a truck, I think, a van, that was at the site. They've checked the tag number and the owner – the owner turned up dead, and we ran the other two down by their airline tickets and –'

'Hold it!' CINC-SAC cut Ryan off. 'How the *hell* can anyone know that – a survivor from the bomb site? For Christ's sake, man, this was a hundred kiloton weapon –'

'Uh, General, the best number we have now – it came from the FBI – is fifty-KT, and –'

'The FBI?' Borstein said from NORAD. 'What the hell do they know about this? Anyway, a fifty-kiloton weapon wouldn't leave any survivors for over a mile around. Mr President, that cannot be good information.'

'Mr President, this is the NMCC,' Ryan heard on the same line. 'We just received a message from Kodiak. That Soviet submarine is attacking USS *Maine*. There is a torpedo in the water, *Maine* is attempting to evade.'

969

Jack heard something, he wasn't sure what, over the speakerphone.

'Sir,' Fremont said at once, 'this is a very ominous development.'

'I understand that, General,' the President said just loudly enough to hear. 'General – SNAPCOUNT.'

'What the hell's that?' Goodley asked quietly.

'Mr President, that is a mistake. We have a solid piece of information here. You wanted information from us, and now we have it!' Ryan barked rapidly, almost losing it again. His hands went from flat to fists. Jack struggled with himself again, and regained control. 'Sir, this is a real indicator.'

'Ryan, it looks to me like you've been lying and misleading me all day,' Fowler said, in a voice that hardly sounded human at all. The line went dead for the last time.

The final alert signal was sent out simultaneously over dozens of circuits. The duplication of channels, their known function, the brevity of the message, and the identical encipherment pattern told the Soviets much, even before the receipted signal was input into their computers. When the single word came out, it was reprinted in the Kremlin command center only seconds later. Golovko took the dispatch off the machine.

'SNAPCOUNT,' he said simply.

'What is that?' President Narmonov asked.

'A code-word.' Golovko's mouth went white for a moment. 'It's a term from American football, I think. It means the set of numbers used before the – the quarterback takes the ball to begin a play.'

'I don't understand,' Narmonov said.

'Once the Americans had the code-word COCKED-PISTOL to denote complete strategic readiness. The meaning is unambiguous to anyone, yes?' The KGB's Deputy Chairman went on, as though in a dream: 'This word, to an American, would mean much the same thing. I can only conclude that –'

'Yes.'

CHAPTER 42

Asp and Sword

PRESIDENT NARMONOV:

I SEND THIS TO YOU, OR YOUR SUCCESSOR, AS A
WARNING.

WE HAVE JUST RECEIVED A REPORT THAT A SOVIET
SUBMARINE IS EVEN NOW ATTACKING AN
AMERICAN MISSILE SUBMARINE. AN ATTACK ON OUR
STRATEGIC ASSETS WILL NOT BE TOLERATED, AND WILL
BE INTERPRETED AS THE PRECURSOR TO AN ATTACK
AGAINST THE UNITED STATES.

I MUST FURTHER ADVISE YOU THAT OUR
STRATEGIC FORCES ARE AT THEIR MAXIMUM STATE
OF READINESS. WE ARE PREPARED TO DEFEND
OURSELVES.

IF YOU ARE SERIOUS IN YOUR PROTESTATIONS OF
INNOCENCE, I URGE YOU TO CEASE ALL AGGRESSIVE
ACTS WHILE THERE IS STILL TIME.

'"Successor"? What the hell does *that* mean?' Narmonov turned away for a moment, then looked at Golovko. 'What is happening here? Is Fowler ill? Is he mad,
what goes on here? What's this submarine business?'
When he finished talking, his mouth remained open like
that of a hooked fish. The Soviet President was gulping
his breaths now.

'We had a report of a disabled American missile submarine in the Eastern Pacific, and sent a submarine to
investigate, but that submarine has no authorization to
attack,' the Defense Minister said.

'Are there any circumstances under which our men
might do this?'

'None. Without authorization from Moscow, they

may act only in self-defense.' The Defense Minister looked away, unable to bear the gaze of his President. He had no wish to speak again, but neither did he have a choice. 'I no longer think this is a controllable situation.'

'Mr President.' It was an Army warrant officer. He opened his briefcase – 'the football' – and removed a ring binder. The first divider was bordered in red. Fowler flipped to it. The page read:

SIOP
Major Attack Option
Skyfall

'So, what the hell is Snapcount?' Goodley asked.

'That's as high as alerts go, Ben. That means the pistol is cocked and pointed, and you can feel the pressure on the trigger.'

'How the hell did we –'

'Drop it, Ben! However the fuck we got here, we *are* here.' Ryan stood and started walking around. 'We better start thinking very fast, people.'

The Senior Duty officer started: 'We have to make Fowler understand –'

'He can't understand,' Goodley said harshly. 'He can't understand if he isn't listening.'

'State and Defense are out – they're both dead,' Ryan pointed out.

'Vice President – Kneecap.'

'Very good, Ben ... do we have a button for that ... yes!' Ryan pushed it.

'Kneecap.'

'This is CIA, DDCI Ryan speaking. I need to talk to the Vice President.'

'Wait one, sir.' It turned out to be a short 'one.'

'This is Roger Durling. Hello, Ryan.'

'Hello, Mr Vice President. We have a problem here,' Jack announced.

'What went wrong? We've been copying the Hot Line messages. They were kinda tense but okay until about twenty minutes ago. What the hell went wrong?'

'Sir, the President is convinced that there has been a *coup d'état* in the Soviet Union.'

'What? Whose fault is that?'

'Mine, sir,' Ryan admitted. 'I'm the jerk who delivered the information. Please set that aside. The President isn't listening to me.'

Jack was amazed to hear a brief, bitter laugh. 'Yeah, Bob doesn't listen to me very much either.'

'Sir, we have to get to him. We now have information that this may have been a terrorist incident.'

'What information is that?' Jack ran it down in about a minute. 'That's thin,' Durling observed.

'It may be thin, sir, but it's all we got, and it's a god-damned sight better than anything else we've got in.'

'Okay, stop for a minute. Right now I want your evaluation of the situation.'

'Sir, my best read is that the President is wrong, it *is* Andrey Il'ych Narmonov over there. It's approaching dawn in Moscow. President Narmonov is suffering from sleep-deprivation, he's just as scared as we are – and from that last message he's wondering if President Fowler is crazy or not. That is a bad combination. We have reports of isolated contact between Soviet and American forces. Christ knows what really happened, but both sides are reading it as aggressive acts. What's really happening is simple chaos – forward-deployed forces bumping, but they're shooting because of alert levels on both sides. It's cascading on itself.'

'Agreed, I agree with all of that. Go on.'

'Somebody has to back down and do it very fast. Sir, you have to talk to the President. He won't even take my calls now. Talbot and Bunker are both dead, and there's nobody else he'll listen to.'

'What about Arnie van Damm?'

'Fuck!' Ryan snarled. How had he forgotten Arnie? 'Where is he?'

'I don't know. I can have the Secret Service find out real fast. What about Liz?'

'She's the one who came up with the brilliant idea that Narmonov isn't there.'

'Bitch,' Durling observed. He'd worked so hard and wasted so much political capital to get Charlie Alden into that job. 'Okay, I'll try to get through to him. Stand by.'

'Right.'

'The Vice President is calling, sir. Line Six.'

Fowler punched the button. 'Make it fast, Roger.'

'Bob, you need to get this thing back under control.'

'What do you think I've been trying to do!'

Durling was sitting in a high-backed leather chair. He closed his eyes. The tone of the answer said it all. 'Bob, you have made things worse instead of better. You have to step back from this for a moment. Take a deep breath, walk around the room – think! There is no reason to expect that the Russians did this. Now, I just talked to CIA, and they said –'

'Ryan, you mean?'

'Yes, he just filled me in and –'

'Ryan's been lying to me.'

'Bullshit, Bob.' Durling kept his voice level and reasonable. He called it his country-doctor voice. 'He's too much of a pro for that.'

'Roger, I know you mean well, but I don't have time for psychoanalysis. We have what may be a nuclear strike about to be launched on us. The good news, I suppose, is that you'll survive. I wish you luck, Roger. Wait – there's a Hot Line message coming in.'

> PRESIDENT FOWLER:
>
> THIS IS ANDREY IL'YCH NARMONOV COMMUNICATING TO YOU.
>
> THE SOVIET UNION HAS TAKEN NO AGGRESSIVE ACTS AGAINST THE UNITED STATES. NONE AT ALL. WE HAVE NO INTEREST IN HARMING YOUR COUNTRY. WE WISH TO BE LEFT ALONE, AND TO LIVE IN PEACE.
>
> I HAVE AUTHORIZED NO ACTION WHATEVER AGAINST ANY AMERICAN FORCES OR CITIZENS, YET YOU THREATEN US. IF YOU ATTACK US, WE MUST

THEN ATTACK YOU ALSO, AND MILLIONS WILL DIE.
WILL IT ALL BE AN ACCIDENT?

THE CHOICE IS YOURS. I CANNOT STOP YOU FROM
ACTING IRRATIONALLY. I HOPE THAT YOU WILL REGAIN
CONTROL OF YOURSELF. TOO MANY LIVES ARE AT RISK
FOR EITHER OF US TO ACT IRRATIONALLY.

'At least we're still getting these,' Goodley noted.

'Yeah, it just makes things so much better. It's going
to set him off,' Ryan announced. 'This one's really going
to do it. You can't tell an irrational person that he's
losing it . . .'

'Ryan, this is Durling.' Ryan fairly leaped at the
button.

'Yes, Mr Vice President.'

'He didn't – he didn't listen, and then this new one
came in, and he reacted rather badly to it.'

'Sir, can you open a channel to SAC?'

'No, I'm afraid not. They're on a conference call with
NORAD and Camp David. Part of the problem, Jack, the
President knows he's vulnerable there and he's afraid –
well . . .'

'Yeah, everyone's afraid, aren't we?'

There was silence for a moment, and Ryan wondered
if Durling felt guilty for being in a place of relative safety.

At Rocky Flats, the residue samples were loaded into a
gamma-ray spectrometer. It had taken longer than
expected, due to a minor equipment problem. The operators stood behind a shield and used lead-lined rubber
gloves and yard-long tongs to move the samples out of
the lead bucket, then waited for the technician to activate the machine.

'Okay – this is a hot one, all right.'

The machine had two displays, one on a cathode-ray
tube, with a back-up paper print-out. It measured the
energy of the photo-electrons generated by the gamma
radiation within the instrument. The precise energy
state of these electrons identified both the element and
the isotope of the source. These showed as lines or spikes

on the graphic display. The relative intensity of the various energy lines – shown as the height of the spike – determined the proportions. A more precise measurement would require insertion of the sample in a small reactor for re-activation, but this system was good enough for the moment.

The technician flipped to the Beta Channel. 'Whoa, look at that tritium line! What did you say the yield on this thing was?'

'Under fifteen.'

'Well, it had a shitload of tritium, doc, look at all that!' The technician – he was a masters candidate – made a notation on his pad, and switched back to the Gamma Channel. 'Okay, plutonium we've got some 239, 240; neptunium, americium, gadolinium, curium, promethium, uranium some U235, some 238 . . . this was a sophisticated beast, guys.'

'Fizzle,' one of the NESTers said, reading the numbers. 'We're looking at the remains of a fizzle. This was not an IND. All that tritium . . . Christ, this was supposed to be a two-stager, that's too much for a boosted fission weapon – it's a fucking H-Bomb!'

The technician adjusted his dials to fine-tune the display. 'Look at the 239/240 mix . . .'

'Get the book!'

Sitting on the shelf opposite the spectrometer was a three-inch binder of red vinyl.

'Savannah River,' the technician said. 'They've always had that gadolinium problem . . . Hanford does it another way . . . they always seem to generate too much promethium . . .'

'Are you crazy?'

'Trust me,' the technician said. 'My thesis is on contamination problems at the plutonium plants. Here's the numbers!' He read them off.

A NESTer flipped to the index, then back to a page. 'It's close! Close! Say the gadolinium again!'

'Zero point zero five eight times ten to the minus seven, plus or minus point zero zero two.'

'Holy Mary Mother of God!' The man turned the book around.

'Savannah River . . . That's not possible . . .'

'1968, it was a vintage year. It's our stuff. It's our fucking plutonium.'

The senior NESTer blinked his disbelief away. 'Okay, let me call D.C.'

'Can't,' the technician said as he refined his readings. 'The long-distance lines are all down.'

'Where's Larry?'

'Aurora Presbyterian, working with the FBI guys. I put the number on a post-it over the phone in the corner. I think he's working D.C. through them.'

'Murray.'

'Hoskins, I just heard from Rocky Flats. Dan, this sounds nuts: the NEST team says the weapon used American plutonium. I asked him to confirm it, and he did – said he asked the same thing. The plutonium came from the DOE plant at Savannah River, turned out in February 1968, K Reactor. They have chapter and verse, he says they can even tell you what part of K Reactor – sounds like bullshit to me, too, but he's the friggin' expert.'

'Walt, how the hell am I going to get anybody to believe that?'

'Dan, that's what the man told me.'

'I need to talk to him.'

'The phone lines are down, remember. I can get him in here in a few minutes.'

'Do that, and do it fast.'

'Yeah, Dan?'

'Jack, the NEST team just reported into our Denver office. The material in the bomb was American.'

'What?'

'Listen, Jack, we've all said that, okay? The NEST team got fallout samples and analyzed them, and they say the uranium – no, plutonium – came from Savannah River, 1968. I have the NESTer team leader coming in to the Denver Field Division now. The long-distance lines are down, but I can patch through our system and you can talk to him directly.'

Ryan looked at the Science and Technology officer. 'Tell me what you think.'

'Savannah River, they've had problems there, like a thousand pound MUF.'

'Muff?'

'M-U-F, acronym: material unaccounted for. Lost material.'

'Terrorists,' Ryan said positively.

'Starting to make sense,' S&T agreed.

'Oh, God, and he won't listen to me now!' Well, there was still Durling.

'That's hard to believe,' the Vice President said.

'Sir, it's hard data, checked by the NEST team at Rocky Flats, it's hard, scientific data. It may sound nuts, but it's objective fact.' *I hope, oh God, I hope.* Durling could hear Ryan thinking it. 'Sir, this was definitely not a Russian weapon – that's the important thing. We are *certain* it was not a Soviet weapon. Tell the President right now!'

'Will do.' Durling nodded to the Air Force communications sergeant.

'Yes, Roger,' the President said.

'Sir, we've just received some important information.'

'What now?' the President sounded tired unto death.

'It came to me from CIA, but they got it from the FBI. The NEST team has identified the bomb material as definitely not Russian. They think the bomb material is American.'

'That is crazy!' Borstein announced. 'We do not have any missing weapons. We take damned good care of those things!'

'Roger, you got that from Ryan, didn't you?'

'Yes, Bob, I did.'

Durling heard a long sigh over the line. 'Thank you.'

The Vice President's hand trembled as he lifted the other phone. 'He didn't buy it.'

'He's *got* to buy it, sir, it's *true!*'

'I'm out of ideas here. You were right, Jack, he's not listening to anyone now.'

'New Hot Line message, sir.'

> PRESIDENT NARMONOV:
> YOU ACCUSE ME OF IRRATIONALITY. WE HAVE TWO
> HUNDRED THOUSAND DEAD, AN ATTACK ON OUR
> FORCES IN BERLIN, AN ATTACK ON OUR NAVY BOTH
> IN THE MEDITERRANEAN AND THE PACIFIC . . .

'He's close to doing it. God damn it! We've got the information he needs to stop this thing in its tracks and –'

'I'm out of ideas,' Durling said over the speaker-phone. 'These damned messages over the Hot Line are making things worse instead of better, and –'

'That seems to be the key problem, doesn't it?' Ryan looked up. 'Ben, you good driving in snow?'

'Yeah, but –'

'*Come on!*' Ryan raced out of the room. They caught an elevator to the first floor, Jack ran into the security room. 'Keys to the car!'

'Here, sir!' A very frightened young man tossed them over. The CIA's security force kept its vehicles just off the VIP lot. The blue GMC Jimmy four-wheel-drive was unlocked.

'Where are we going?' Goodley asked as he got into the driver's-side door.

'Pentagon, River entrance, and get us there fast.'

'What was it?' The torpedo had circled something, but not exploded, and finally ran out of fuel.

'Not enough mass to set off the magnetic exploder – too small to hit directly . . . must have been a decoy,' Dubinin said. 'Where's that original intercept?' A sailor handed it over. '"*Propeller disabled by collision,*" God damn it! We were tracking a bad power plant, not a damaged screw.' The captain smashed his fist down on the chart table hard enough to draw blood. 'Come north, go active!'

'Oh, shit, conn, sonar, we have an active low-frequency sonar bearing one-nine-zero.'

'Warm up the weapons!'

'Sir, if we deploy the outboard, we'll get another two or three knots,' Claggett said.

'Too noisy!' Ricks snapped back.

'Sir, we're up in the surface noise. The high-freqs from the outboard motor won't matter much up here. His active sonar is low-freq, and that active stuff's liable to detect us whether we're noisy or not. What we need now is distance, sir, if he gets too close, the Orion can't engage to support us.'

'We have to take him out.'

'Bad move, sir. We're on SNAPCOUNT status now, if we have to shoot, that takes priority. Putting a unit in the water will tell us just where to look. Captain, we need distance to keep out of his active sonar, and we can't risk a shot.'

'No! Weapons officer, set it up!'

'Aye, sir.'

'Communications, tell the Orion to get us some help!'

'Here's the last one, Colonel.'

'Well, that was fast enough,' the regimental commander said.

'The boys are getting lots of practice,' the major standing next to him observed, as the tenth and final RV was lifted off the SS-18 at Alyesk. 'Be careful there, sergeant.'

It was ice that did it. A few minutes earlier, some snow had blown into the missile capsule. The shuffling of boots had crushed and melted it, but then the sub-zero temperatures had refrozen it into an invisible, paper-thin skim of ice. The sergeant was in the process of stepping back off the fold-down catwalk when he slipped, and his wrench went flying. It bounced off the railing, twirling like a baton for a moment. The sergeant grabbed for it, but missed, and it went down.

'*RUN!*' the colonel screamed. The sergeant needed no encouragement. The corporal on the crane swung the warhead clear and himself jumped from the vehicle. They all knew to go upwind.

The wrench nearly made it all the way down, but it struck an interior fitting and went sideways, gouging the skin of the first stage in two places. The missile skin was also the missile tankage, and both the fuel and oxidizer were released. The two chemicals formed small clouds – only a few grams of each were leaking – but the chemicals were hypergolic. They ignited on contact. That happened two minutes after the wrench began its fall.

The explosion was a powerful one. It knocked the colonel down, over two hundred meters from the silo. He instinctively rolled behind a thick pine-tree as the crushing overpressure wave swept by. He looked a moment later to see the silo topped by a pillar of flame. His men had all made it – a miracle, he thought. His next thought reflected the humor that so often accompanies an escape from death: *Well, that's one less missile for the Americans to bother us about!*

The Defense Support Program Satellite already had its sensor focused on the Russian missile fields. The energy bloom was unmistakable. The signal was down-linked to Alice Springs in Australia, and from there back up to a USAF communications satellite, which relayed it to North America. It took just over half a second.

'Possible launch – possible launch at Alyesk!'

In that moment, everything changed for Major General Joe Borstein. His eyes focused on the real-time display and his first thought was that it had happened, despite everything, all the changes, all the progress, all the treaties, somehow it had happened, and he was watching it and he would be there to watch it all happen until the SS-18 with his name on it landed on Cheyenne Mountain ... This wasn't dropping bombs on the Paul Doumer

Bridge, or hassling fighters over Germany. This was the end of life.

Borstein's voice was the sound of sandpaper. 'I only see one . . . where's the bird?'

'No bird no bird no bird,' a female captain announced. 'The boom is too big, more like an explosion. No bird, no bird. This is not a launch, I repeat this is *not* a launch.'

Borstein saw that his hands were shaking. They hadn't done that the time he'd been shot down, nor the time he'd crashed at Edwards, nor the times he'd driven airplanes through weather too foul for hailstones. He looked around at his people and saw in their faces the same thing he'd just felt in the pit of his stomach. Somehow it had been like watching a dreadfully scary movie to this point, but it was not a movie now. He lifted the phone to SAC and switched off the input to the Gold Phone line to Camp David.

'Pete, did you copy that?'

'I sure did, Joe.'

'We, uh, we better settle this thing down, Pete. The President's losing it.'

CINC-SAC paused for a beat before responding. 'I almost lost it, but I just got it back.'

'Yeah, I hear you, Pete.'

'What the hell was that?'

Borstein flipped the switch back on. 'Mr President, that was an explosion, we think, in the Alyesk missile fields. We, uh, sure had a scare there for a moment, but there is no bird in the air – say again, Mr President, there are no birds flying now. That was a definite false alarm.'

'What does it mean?'

'Sir, I do not know that. Perhaps – they were servicing the missiles, sir, and maybe they had an accident. It's happened before – we had the same problem with the Titan-II.'

'General Borstein is correct,' CINC-SAC confirmed soberly. 'That's why we got rid of the Titan-II . . . Mr President?'

'Yes, General?'

'Sir, I recommend we try to cool things down some more, sir.'

'And just how do we do that?' Fowler wanted to know. 'What if that was related to their alert activity?'

The ride down the George Washington Parkway was uneventful. Though covered with snow, Goodley had maintained a steady forty miles per hour in four-wheel-drive, and not lost control once, getting around abandoned cars like a race-car driver at Daytona. He pulled into the River/Mall entrance to the Pentagon. The civilian guard there was backed up by a soldier now, whose M-16 rifle was undoubtedly loaded.

'CIA!' Goodley said.

'Wait.' Ryan handed over his badge. 'In the slot. I think it'll work here.'

Goodley did as he was told. Ryan's high-level badge had the right electronic code for this security device. The gate went up, and the road barrier went down, clearing the way. The soldier nodded. If the pass worked, everything had to be okay, right?

'Right up to the first set of doors.'

'Park it?'

'Leave it! You come in with me.'

Security inside the River Entrance was also beefed up. Jack tried to pass through the metal detector, but was stopped by pocket change that he then threw on the floor in a rage. 'NMCC?'

'Come with me, sir.'

The entrance to the National Military Command Center was barred by a wall of bullet-resistant glass, behind which was a black female sergeant armed with a revolver.

'CIA, I have to get in.' Ryan held his badge against the black pad, and again it worked.

'Who are you, sir?' a Navy petty officer asked.

'DDCI. You take me to whoever's running this.'

'Follow me, sir. The man you want to see is Captain Rosselli.'

'*Captain!* No flag officer?'

'General Wilkes got lost, sir, we don't know where the hell he is.' The enlisted man turned through a door.

Ryan saw a Navy captain and an Air Force lieutenant-colonel, a status board, and a gang of multiple-line phones. 'You Rosselli?'

'That's right, and you?'

'Jack Ryan, DDCI.'

'You picked a bad place to come to, pal,' Colonel Barnes observed.

'Anything changed?'

'Well, we just had what looked like a missile launch in Russia –'

'Jesus!'

'No bird came up, maybe an explosion in the hole. You have anything we need to know?'

'I need a line into the FBI command center, and I need to talk to both of you.'

'That's crazy,' Rosselli said, two minutes later.

'Maybe so.' Ryan lifted the line. 'Dan, Jack here.'

'Where the hell are you, Jack? I just called Langley.'

'Pentagon. What do you have on the bomb?'

'Stand by, I have a patch through to Dr Larry Parsons. He's the NEST boss. He's on now.'

'Okay, this is Ryan, Deputy Director of CIA. Talk to me.'

'The bomb was made of American plutonium. That's definite. They've rechecked the sample four times. Savannah River Plant, February 1968, K Reactor.'

'You're sure?' Jack asked, wishing very hard that the answer would be affirmative.

'Positive, crazy as it sounds, it was our stuff.'

'What else?'

'Murray tells me you have had problems with the yield estimate. Okay, I've been there, okay? This was a small device, less than fifteen – that's *one-five* – kiloton yield. There are survivors from the scene – not many, but I've seen them myself, okay? I'm not sure what screwed up the initial estimate, but I have *been* there and I'm telling you it was a little one. It also seems to have been a fizzle. We're trying to ascertain more about that now – but this is the important part, okay? The bomb material was definitely American in origin. One hundred percent sure.'

Rosselli leaned over to make sure that this phone line was a secure one into FBI headquarters. 'Wait a minute. Sir, this is Captain Jim Rosselli, U.S. Navy. I have a masters in nuclear physics. Just to make sure this is what I'm hearing, I want you to give me the 239/240 proportions, okay?'

'Wait a minute and I will . . . Okay, 239 was nine eight point nine three; 240 is zero point four five. You want the trace elements also?'

'No, that'll do it. Thank you, sir.' Rosselli looked up and spoke quietly. 'Either he's telling the truth or he's one smart fuckin' liar.'

'Captain, I'm glad you agree. I need you to do something.'

'What's that?'

'I need to get on the Hot Line.'

'I can't allow that.'

'Captain, have you been keeping track of the messages?'

'No, Rocky and I haven't had time. We've got three separate battles going on and –'

'Let's go look.'

Ryan hadn't been in there before, which struck him as odd. The printed copies of the messages were being kept on a clipboard. There were six people in the room, and they all looked ashen.

'Christ, Ernie –' Rosselli observed.

'Anything lately?' Jack asked.

'Nothing since the President sent one out twenty minutes ago.'

'It was going fine when I was here right after – oh, my God . . .' Rosselli observed as he got to the bottom.

'The President has lost it,' Jack said. 'He refuses to take information from me, and he refuses to listen to Vice President Durling. Now, this is real simple, okay? I know President Narmonov. He knows me. With what the FBI just gave us, what you just heard, Captain, I think

985

I might be able to accomplish something. If not –'

'Sir, that is not possible,' Rosselli replied.

'Why?' Jack asked. Though his heart was racing, he forced himself to control his breathing. He had to be cool be cool be cool now.

'Sir, the whole point of this link is that the only two people on it are –'

'One of them, maybe both now, is not playing with a full deck. Captain, you can see where we are. I can't force you to do this. I'm asking you to think. You just used your head a moment ago. Use it again,' Ryan said calmly.

'Sir, they'll lock us up for doing this,' the Link supervisor said.

'You have to be alive to be locked up,' Jack said. 'We are at SNAPCOUNT right now. You people know how serious this is. Captain Rosselli, you are the senior officer present, and you make the call.'

'I see everything you put on that machine before it's transmitted.'

'Fair enough. Can I type it myself?'

'Yes. You type, and it's crossloaded and encrypted before it goes out.'

A Marine sergeant made room for him. Jack sat down and lit a cigarette, ignoring the signs prohibiting the vice. ANDREY IL'YCH, Ryan tapped in slowly, THIS IS JACK RYAN. DO YOU STILL MAKE YOUR OWN FIRES IN THE DACHA?

'Okay?'

Rosselli nodded to the NCO sitting next to Ryan. 'Transmit.'

'What is this?' the Defense Minister asked. Four men hovered over the terminal. A Soviet Army major translated.

'Something's wrong here,' the communications officer said. 'This is –'

'Send back, "Do you remember who it was who bandaged your knee?"'

'What?'

'Send it!' Narmonov said.

They waited for two minutes.

986

YOUR BODYGUARD ANATOLIY ASSISTED ME, BUT MY
TROUSERS WERE RUINED.

'It's Ryan.'

'Make sure,' Golovko said.

The translator looked at his screen. 'It says, "*And our
friend is doing well?*"'

Ryan typed: HE RECEIVED AN HONORABLE BURIAL AT
CAMP DAVID.

'What the hell?' Rosselli asked.

'There aren't twenty people in the world who know
this. He's making sure it's really me,' Jack said. His
fingers were poised over the keys.

'That looks like bullshit.'

'Okay, fine, it's bullshit, but does it *hurt* anything?'
Ryan demanded.

'Send it.'

'What the hell is this?' Fowler shouted. 'Who's doing
this –'

'Sir, we have an incoming from the President. He's
ordering us to –'

'Ignore it,' Jack said coldly.

'God damn it, I can't!'

'Captain, the President has lost control. If you allow
him to shut me off, your family, my family, a whole lot
of people are going to die. Captain, your oath is to the
Constitution, not to the President. Now, you look over
those messages again and tell me that I'm wrong!'

'From Moscow,' the translator said. '"*Ryan, what is
happening?*"'

> PRESIDENT NARMONOV:
> WE HAVE BEEN THE VICTIMS OF A TERRORIST ACT.
> THERE WAS MUCH CONFUSION HERE, BUT WE NOW
> HAVE POSITIVE EVIDENCE AS TO THE ORIGIN OF THE
> WEAPON.
> WE ARE CERTAIN THAT THE WEAPON WAS NOT

SOVIET. I REPEAT WE ARE CERTAIN THE WEAPON
WAS NOT SOVIET.

WE ARE NOW ATTEMPTING TO APPREHEND THE
TERRORISTS. WE MAY HAVE THEM WITHIN THE NEXT
FEW MINUTES.

'Send back, "Why has your president accused us of
this?"'

There was another pause of two minutes.

PRESIDENT NARMONOV:
WE HAVE BEEN THE VICTIMS OF GREAT CONFUSION
HERE. WE HAVE HAD SOME INTELLIGENCE REPORTS OF
POLITICAL TURMOIL IN THE SOVIET UNION. THESE
REPORTS WERE FALSE, BUT THEY CONFUSED US
GREATLY. IN ADDITION, THE OTHER INCIDENTS HAVE
HAD AN INCENDIARY EFFECT ON BOTH SIDES.

'That's true enough.'

'Pete, you get people in there just as fast as you can and
arrest this man!'

Connor couldn't say no to that, despite the look he
received from Helen D'Agustino. He called Secret Service headquarters and relayed the message.

'He asks, "*what you – what* do *you suggest!*"'

I ASK THAT YOU TRUST US, AND ALLOW US TO TRUST
YOU. WE BOTH MUST BACK AWAY FROM THIS. I
SUGGEST THAT BOTH YOU AND WE REDUCE THE
ALERT LEVELS OF STRATEGIC FORCES AND GIVE
ORDERS TO ALL TROOPS TO EITHER HOLD IN PLACE
OR WITHDRAW AWAY FROM ANY SOVIET OR AMERICAN
UNIT IN CLOSE PROXIMITY, AND IF POSSIBLE THAT
ALL SHOOTING BE STOPPED IMMEDIATELY.

'Well?' Ryan asked.
'Send it.'

'Can it be a trick?' the Defense Minister asked. 'Can it
not be a trick?'

'Golovko?'

'I believe that it is Ryan, and I believe he is sincere – but can he persuade his President?'

President Narmonov walked away for a moment, thinking of history, thinking of Nikolay II. 'If we stand our forces down . . . ?'

'Then they can strike us, and our ability to retaliate is cut in half!'

'Is half enough?' Narmonov asked, seeing the escape hatch, leaning towards it, praying for the opening to be real. 'Is half enough to destroy them?'

'Well . . .' Defense nodded. 'Certainly, we have more than double the amount we need to destroy them. We call it over-kill.'

'Sir, the Soviet reply reads: *"Ryan:*

'"On my order, being sent out as you read this, Soviet strategic forces are standing down. We will maintain our defensive alert for the moment, but we will stand down our offensive forces to a lower alert level which is still higher than peacetime standards. If you match our move, I propose a phased mutual stand-down over the next five hours."'

Jack's head went down on the keyboard, actually placing some characters on the screen.

'Could I have a glass of water? My throat's a little dry.'

'Mr President?' Fremont said.

'Yes, General.'

'Sir, however this happened, I think it's a good idea.'

Part of Bob Fowler wanted to hurl his coffee cup into the wall, but he stopped himself. It didn't matter, did it? It did, but not that way.

'What do you recommend?'

'Sir, just to make sure, we wait until we see evidence of a stand-down. When we do, we can back off ourselves. For starters – right now – we can rescind SNAPCOUNT without any real degradation of our readiness.'

'General Borstein?'

'Sir, I concur in that,' said the voice from NORAD.

'General Fremont: Approved.'

'Thank you, Mr President. We'll get right on it.' General Peter Fremont, United States Air Force, Commander-in-Chief Strategic Air Command turned to his Deputy Chief of Staff (Operations). 'Keep the alert going, posture the birds, but keep them on the ground. Let's get those missiles uncocked.'

'Contact ... bearing three-five-two ... range seven thousand six hundred meters.' They'd been waiting several minutes for that.

'Set it up. No wires, activation point four thousand meters out.' Dubinin looked up. He didn't know why the aircraft overhead hadn't already executed another attack.

'Set!' the weapons officer called a moment later.

'Fire!' Dubinin ordered.

'Captain, message coming in on the ELF,' the communications officer said over the squawk box.

'That's the message that announces the end of the world,' the captain sighed. 'Well, we fired our shots, didn't we?' It would have been nice to think that their action would save lives, but he knew better. It would enable the Soviet forces to kill more Americans, which wasn't quite the same thing. Everything about nuclear weapons was evil, wasn't it?

'Go deep?'

Dubinin shook his head. 'No, they seem to have more trouble with the surface turbulence than I expected. We may actually be safer here. Come right to zero-nine-zero. Suspend pinging. Increase speed to ten knots.'

Another squawk: 'We have the message – five-letter group: "Cease all hostilities!"'

'Antenna depth, quickly!'

The Mexican police proved to be extremely cooperative, and the literate Spanish of Clark and Chavez hadn't hurt very much. Four plainclothes detectives from the Federal

Police waited with the CIA officers in the lounge while four more uniformed officers with light automatic weapons took unobtrusive positions nearby.

'We don't have enough people to do this properly,' the senior *Federale* worried.

'Better to do it off the airplane,' Clark said.

'*Muy bueno, Señor.* You think they may be armed?'

'Actually, no, I don't. Guns can be dangerous when you're traveling.'

'Has this something to do with – Denver?'

Clark turned and nodded. 'We think so.'

'It will be interesting to see what such men look like.' The detective meant the eyes, of course. He'd seen the photographs.

The DC-10 pulled up to the gate and cut power to its three engines. The jetway moved a few feet to mate with the forward door.

'They travel first class,' John said unnecessarily.

'*Si.* The airline says there are fifteen first-class passengers, and they've been told to hold the rest. You will see, Señor Clark, we know our business.'

'I have no doubt of that. Forgive me if I gave that impression, *Teniente.*'

'You are CIA, no?'

'I am not permitted to say.'

'Then of course you are. What will you do with them?'

'We will speak,' Clark said simply.

The gate attendant opened the door to the jetway. Two Federal Police officers took their places left and right of the door, their jackets open. Clark prayed there would be no gunplay. The people started walking out, and the usual greetings were called from the waiting area.

'Bingo,' Clark said quietly. The police lieutenant straightened his tie to signal the men at the door. They made it easy, the last two first-class passengers to come out. Qati looked sick and pale, Clark noticed. Maybe it had been a bad flight. He stepped over the rope barrier. Chavez did the same, smiling and calling to a passenger who looked at them in open puzzlement.

'Ernesto!' John said, running up to him.

'I'm afraid I'm the wrong –'

Clark went right past the man from Miami.

Ghosn was slow to react, dulled by the flight from America, relaxed by the thought that they had escaped. By the time he started to move, he was tackled from behind. Another policeman placed a gun against the back of his head, and he was handcuffed before they hauled him to his feet.

'Well, I'll be a son-of-a-bitch,' Chavez said. 'You're the guy with the books! We've met before, sweetheart.'

'Qati,' John said to the other one. They'd already been patted down. Neither was armed. 'I've wanted to meet you for years.'

Clark took out their tickets. The police would collect their luggage. The police moved them out very quickly. The business and tourist passengers would not know that anything untoward had happened until they were told by family members in a few minutes.

'Very smooth, Lieutenant,' John said to the senior officer.

'As I said, we know our business.'

'Could you have your people phone the embassy and tell them that we got 'em both alive.'

'Of course.'

The eight men waited in a small room while the bags were collected. There could be evidence in them, and there wasn't that much of a hurry. The Mexican police lieutenant examined their faces closely, but saw nothing more or less human than what he'd seen in the faces of a hundred murderers. It was vaguely disappointing, even though he was a good-enough cop to know better. The luggage was searched, but aside from some prescription drugs – they were checked and determined not to be narcotics – there was nothing unusual. The police borrowed a courtesy van for the drive to the Gulfstream.

'I hope you have enjoyed your stay in Mexico,' the lieutenant said in parting.

'What the hell is going on?' the pilot asked. Though in civilian clothes, she was an Air Force major.

'Let me explain it like this,' Clark said. 'You Air

Scouts are going to drive the airplane to Andrews. Mr Chavez and I are going to interview these two gentlemen in back. You will not look, not hear, not think about anything that's going on in back.'

'What –'

'That was a *thought*, Major. I do not want you to have any *thoughts* about this. Do I have to explain myself again?'

'No, sir.'

'Then let's get the hell out of here.'

The pilot and co-pilot went forward. The two communications technicians sat at their consoles and drew the curtain between themselves and the main cabin.

Clark turned to see his two guests exchanging looks. That was no good. He removed Qati's tie and wrapped it around his eyes. Chavez did the same to his charge. Next both were gagged, and Clark went forward to find some earplugs. Finally, they set both men in seats as far apart as the airplane's cabin allowed. John let the plane take off before he did anything else. The fact was that he despised torture, but he needed information now, and he was prepared to do anything to get it.

'Torpedo in the water!'

'Christ, he's dead aft of us!' Ricks turned. 'Best possible speed, come left to two-seven-zero. XO, take the return shot!'

'Aye! Snapshot,' Claggett said. 'One-eight-zero, activation point three thousand, initial search depth two hundred.'

'Ready!'

'Match and shoot!'

'Three fired, sir.' It was a standard tactic. The torpedo fired on the reciprocal heading would at least force the other guy to cut the control wires to his weapon. Ricks was already in sonar.

'Missed the launch transient, sir, and didn't catch the fish very soon either. Surface noise . . .'

'Take her deep?' Ricks asked Claggett.

'This surface noise may be our best friend.'

'Okay, Dutch . . . you were right before, I should have dropped the outboard.'

'ELF message, sir – SNAPCOUNT is cancelled, sir.'

'Cancelled?' Ricks asked incredulously.

'Cancelled, yes, sir.'

'Well, isn't that good news,' Claggett said.

'Now what?' the Tacco asked himself. The message in his hand made no sense at all.

'Sir, we finally got the bastard.'

'Run your track.'

'Sir, he fired at *Maine*!'

'I know, but I can't engage.'

'That's crazy, sir.'

'Sure as hell is,' the tactical officer agreed.

'Speed?'

'Six knots, sir – maneuvering says the shaft bearings are pretty bad, sir.'

'If we try any more . . .' Ricks frowned.

Claggett nodded. '. . . the whole thing comes apart. I think it's about time for some counter-measures.'

'Do it.'

'Five-inch room, launch a spread.' Claggett turned back. 'We're not going fast enough to make a turn very useful.'

'I figure it's about even money.'

'Could be worse. Why the hell do you think they cancelled SNAPCOUNT?' the XO asked, staring at the sonar scope.

'X, I guess the danger of war is over . . . I haven't handled this well, have I?'

'Shit, skipper, who would have known?'

Ricks turned. 'Thanks, X.'

'The torpedo is now active, ping-and-listen mode, bearing one-six zero.'

'Torpedo, American Mark 48, bearing three-four-five, just went active!'

'Ahead full, maintain course,' Dubinin ordered.

'Countermeasures?' the *Starpom* asked.

The captain shook his head. 'No, no, we're at the edge of its acquisition range . . . and that would just give it a reason to turn this way. The surface conditions will help. We're not supposed to have battles in heavy weather,' Dubinin pointed out. 'It's hard on the instruments.'

'Captain, I have the satellite signal – it's an all-forces message, "Disengage and withdraw from any hostile forces, take action only for self-defense."'

'I'm going to be court-martialed,' Valentin Borissovich Dubinin observed quietly.

'You did nothing wrong, you reacted correctly at every –'

'Thank you. I hope you will testify to that effect.'

'Change in signal – change in aspect, torpedo just turned west away from us,' Lieutenant Rykov said. 'The first programmed turn must have been to the right.'

'Thank God it wasn't to the left. I think we've survived. Now, if only our weapon can miss . . .'

'Sir, it's continuing to close. The torpedo is probably in acquisition – continuous pinging now.'

'Less than two thousand yards,' Ricks said.

'Yeah,' Claggett agreed.

'Try some more countermeasures – hell, go continuous on them.' The tactical situation was getting worse. *Maine* was not moving quickly enough to make an evasive course worthwhile. The countermeasures filled the sea with bubbles, and while they might draw the Russian torpedo into a turn – their only real hope – the sad fact of the matter was that as the fish penetrated the bubbles it would find *Maine* with its sonar again. Perhaps a continuous set of such false targets would saturate the seeker. That was their best shot right now.

'Let's keep her near the surface,' Ricks added. Claggett looked at him and nodded in understanding.

'Not working, sir . . . sir, I've lost the fish aft, in the baffles now.'

'Surface the ship,' Ricks called. 'Emergency blow!'

'Surface capture?'

'And now I'm out of ideas, X.'

'Come left, parallel to the seas?'

'Okay, you do it.'

Claggett went into control. 'Up 'scope!' He took a quick look, and checked the submarine's course. 'Come right to new course zero-five-five!'

USS *Maine* surfaced for the last time into thirty-five foot seas and nearly total darkness. Her circular hull wallowed in the rolling waves, and she was slow to turn.

The countermeasures were a mistake. Though the Russian torpedo was pinging, it was mainly a wake-follower. Its seeker head tracked bubbles, and the string of countermeasures made for a perfect trail, which suddenly stopped. When *Maine* surfaced, the submarine left the bubble stream. Again, the factors involved were technical. The surface turbulence confused the wake-following software and the torpedo began its programmed circular search pattern, just under the surface. On its third circuit, it found an unusually hard echo amid the confusing shapes over its head. The torpedo turned to close, now activating its magnetic-influence fusing system. The Russian weapon was less sophisticated than the American Mark 50. It could not go higher than twenty meters of depth and so was not drawn up to the surface. The active magnetic field it generated was cast out like an invisible spider web, and when that net was disturbed by the presence of a metallic mass –

The thousand-kilo warhead exploded fifty feet from *Maine*'s already crippled stern. The twenty-thousand-ton warship shook as though rammed.

An alarm sounded instantly: '*Flooding flooding flooding in the engine room!*'

Ricks lifted the phone. 'How bad?'

'Get everybody off, sir!'

'Abandon ship! Break out the survival gear! Send out message: damaged and sinking, give our position!'

'Captain Rosselli! Flash traffic coming in.'

Ryan looked up. He'd had his drink, followed by something colder and carbonated. Whatever the message was, the naval officer could handle it.

'You Mr Ryan?' a man in a suit asked. Two more were behind him.

'Dr Ryan, yeah.'

'Secret Service, sir, the President ordered us to come here and arrest you.'

Jack laughed at that. 'What for?'

The agent looked instantly uncomfortable. 'He didn't say, sir.'

'I'm not a cop, but my dad was. I don't think you can arrest me without a charge. The law, you know? The Constitution. "Preserve, protect, and defend."'

The agent was in an instant quandary. He had orders from someone he had to obey, but he was too professional to violate the law. 'Sir, the President said . . .'

'Well, tell you what. I'll just sit right here, and you can talk to the President on that phone and find out. I'm not going anywhere.' Jack lit another cigarette and lifted another phone.

'Hello?'

'Hey, babe.'

'Jack! What's going on?'

'It's okay. It got a little tense, but we have it under control now, Cath. I'm afraid I'm going to be stuck here for a while, but it's okay, Cathy, honest.'

'Sure?'

'You worry about that new baby, not about anything else. That's an order.'

'I'm late, Jack. Just a day, but –'

'Good.' Ryan leaned back in his chair, closed his eyes, and smiled blissfully. 'You want it to be a girl, eh?'

'Yes.'

'Then I guess I do, too. Honey, I'm still busy here, but, honest, you can relax. Have to run. Bye.' He replaced the phone. 'Glad I remembered to do that.'

'Sir, the President wants to talk to you.' The senior agent handed the phone towards Ryan.

What makes you think I want to talk to him? Jack

997

nearly asked. But that would have been unprofessional. He took the phone. 'Ryan here, sir.'

'Tell me what you know,' Fowler said curtly.

'Mr President, if you give me about fifteen minutes, I can do a better job. Dan Murray at FBI knows everything I do, and I have to make contact with two officers. Is that okay, sir?'

'Very well.'

'Thank you, Mr President.' Ryan handed the phone back and placed a call to the CIA Operations Center. 'This is Ryan. Did Clark make the pickup?'

'Sir, this is an unsecure line.'

'I don't care – answer the question.'

'Yes, sir, they're flying back now. We don't have a comm link to the aircraft. It's Air Force, sir.'

'Who's the best guy to evaluate the explosion?'

'Wait.' The Senior Duty Officer passed that along to the Science and Technology man. 'He says Dr Lowell at Lawrence-Livermore.'

'Get him moving. The nearest air base is probably Travis. Get him something fast.' Ryan hung that line up and turned to the senior Hot Line officer.

'There's a VC-20 just took off from Mexico City inbound for Andrews. I have two officers and two – two other people aboard. I need to establish a comm link to the aircraft. Get someone to set that up, please.'

'Can't do it here, sir, but you can in the conference room on the other side.'

Ryan stood. 'Come with me?' he said to the Secret Service agents.

It could hardly have been more bitter, Qati thought, but a moment later he realized that this wasn't true. He had faced death for a year now, and death by any cause was still death. Had he escaped – but he had not escaped.

'Okay, let's talk.'

'I do not understand,' Qati said in Arabic.

'I have a little trouble with that accent,' Clark replied, feeling very clever. 'I learned the language from a Saudi. Please speak slowly.'

Qati allowed himself to be shaken momentarily by the use of his native tongue. He decided to reply in English to show his own cleverness. 'I will never tell you a thing.'

'Sure you will.'

Qati knew that he had to resist as long as he could. It would be worth the price.

CHAPTER 43

The Revenge of Moedred

Dubinin had little choice in the matter. As soon as he was certain that the American torpedo was dead, he ran up his satellite antenna and broadcast his report. The American Orion dropped active sonobuoys all around him but did not attack, confirming his impression that he had committed a crime little different from murder. As soon as the signal was receipted, he turned about and headed for the direction of the explosion. A seaman could do nothing else.

> PRESIDENT FOWLER:
> I REGRET TO INFORM YOU THAT A SOVIET
> SUBMARINE, AFTER BEING ATTACKED,
> COUNTERATTACKED AN AMERICAN SUBMARINE,
> POSSIBLY DAMAGING IT. IT WOULD APPEAR THAT THIS
> HAPPENED SHORTLY BEFORE I BROADCAST MY
> DISENGAGEMENT ORDER. I OFFER NO EXCUSE FOR THIS
> MISTAKE. THE INCIDENT WILL BE INVESTIGATED, AND
> IF THE FACTS WARRANT, THE CAPTAIN OF OUR
> SUBMARINE WILL BE PUNISHED SEVERELY.

'Well?'

'Mr President, I think we acknowledge, thank the man, and let this one slide, sir,' Jack replied.

'I agree. Thank you.' The line went dead again.

'That was my boat!' Rosselli snarled.

'Yeah,' Ryan said. 'Sorry to hear it. I've spent time aboard subs, with Bart Mancuso, as a matter of fact. Know him?'

'He's the squadron commander out at Bangor.'

Ryan turned. 'Oh? I didn't know. I'm sorry, Captain, but what else can we do?'

'I know,' Rosselli said quietly. 'With luck, maybe they can get the crew off . . .'

Jackson was nearly out of fuel and ready to turn back. *Theodore Roosevelt* had an Alpha Strike spotted and ready to take off when the new orders came in. The battlegroup immediately increased speed to open the distance between the American and Russian formations. It didn't seem to Jackson like running away. The Hawkeye called a warning that the Russian ships had turned west – perhaps into the wind to launch aircraft. But though four fighters were aloft, they orbited the battlegroup, which continued west. Their search radars were up, but their missile radars went down. That, he knew, was a hopeful sign.

And so, Robby told himself, *so ends my second war, if that's what it was* . . . He brought his Tomcat around, with Sanchez on his wing. Four more F-14s would orbit here, just to keep an eye on things for the next few hours.

Jackson trapped just in time to see a rescue helicopter landing forward. By the time he dismounted the aircraft, three people were in the ship's hospital. He headed down to see who they were and what had been going on. A few minutes later, he knew that he wouldn't be painting any more victory flags on his aircraft. Not for something like this.

Berlin settled down much more quickly than anyone imagined. The relief column of the 11th Armored Cavalry Regiment had only gone thirty kilometers when the halt order arrived, and it pulled off the autobahn to wait. Inside Berlin itself, the American brigade got the word first, and pulled back into the western portion of the kazerne. Russians probed forward with dismounted infantry to see what was happening, but without orders to renew the attack, they remained tensely in place. Soon the area was flooded with police cars, much to the bemusement of the soldiers. Twenty minutes after the

Americans began moving, communications were reestablished with Moscow, and the Russians pulled farther back into their defensive positions. A number of unexplained bodies were found, including the regimental commander and his executive officer, plus three tank crews, all of whom had been killed with small-arms fire. But the most important discovery was made by a Berlin policeman, who was the first to examine the truck and staff car ripped apart by 25 mm cannon slugs from a Bradley. The 'Russians' were all dead, but none had identity disks. The policeman immediately called for assistance, which was dispatched at once. Two of the faces looked familiar to the cop, though he couldn't remember why.

'Jack.'

'Hi, Arnie, grab a seat.'

'What happened, Jack?'

Ryan shook his head. His mental state was one of giddiness. His reason told him that sixty thousand people had died, but despite that, the relief at having stopped something a hundred times worse had left him in a slightly drunken condition. 'Not really sure yet, Arnie. You know the important part.'

'The President sounds like hell.'

A grunt. 'You ought to have heard him a couple hours ago. He lost it, Arnie.'

'That bad?'

Jack nodded. 'That bad.' A pause. 'Maybe anybody would have, maybe you just can't expect a guy to deal with this, but — but that's his job, man.'

'You know, he once told me that he was most grateful for Reagan and the others because of the changes, the fact that something like this wasn't really possible anymore.'

'Listen, man, as long as those goddamned things exist, it's possible.'

'You advocating disarmament?' van Damm asked.

Ryan looked up again. The giddiness was gone now. 'I got the stars out of my eyes a long time ago. What I'm saying is, if it's possible, you damned well think about it. He didn't. He didn't even look at the wargames we ran. He was just so sure it would never happen. Well, it did, didn't it?'

'How did Liz do?'

'Don't ask. The Boss needed good advice, and he didn't get any from her.'

'And you?'

'He didn't listen to me, and that's partly my fault, I guess.'

'Hey, it's over.'

Jack nodded again. 'Yeah.'

'Ryan, call for you.'

Jack took the phone. 'Ryan here. Yeah, okay. Go slower.' He listened for several minutes, making notes. 'Thanks, John.'

'What was that?'

'A confession. Is the helicopter ready?'

'At the pad. On the other side,' one of the Secret Service men said.

The helicopter was a VH-60. Ryan climbed aboard and strapped in, along with van Damm and three agents. The chopper lifted off at once. The sky was clearing. The wind was still lively, but there were stars to be seen in the west.

'Where's the Vice President?' van Damm asked.

'Kneecap,' an agent replied. 'He stays up six more hours till we're sure this is over.'

Jack didn't even hear. He had his ear-protectors in, and took the chance to lean back and stare into space. The helicopter even had a bar, he saw. What a nice way to travel.

'They wanted to start a nuclear war?' Chavez asked.

'That's what they said.' Clark washed his hands. It wasn't that bad. He'd only broken four of Qati's fingers. It was the way you worked the broken bones that really mattered. Ghosn – they now knew his name – had taken a little more, but both stories were almost identical.

'I heard it, too, man, but –'

'Yeah. Ambitious fuckers, weren't they?' Clark put some ice cubes into a bag and walked back to rest it on

Qati's hand. He had his information now, and he was not a sadist. The sensible thing, he thought, was to toss their asses out of the airplane here and now, but that wasn't his job either. Both terrorists were manacled to their seats. Clark took a chair in the back so that he could keep an eye on both. Their luggage was there also. He decided to rummage through it now that he had the time.

'Hello, Ryan,' the President said from his chair. 'Hi, Arnie.'

'Bad day, Bob,' van Damm offered.

'Very.' The man had aged. It seemed a cliché, but it was true. His skin was sallow, the eyes sitting at the bottom of dark-rimmed wells. Though he was normally a carefully groomed man, Fowler's hair was askew. 'Ryan, you have them?'

'Yes, sir, two of our field officers grabbed them in Mexico City. Their names are Ismael Qati and Ibrahim Ghosn. You know who Qati is. We've been after that guy for a long time. He had a piece of the Beirut bombing, two aircraft incidents, lots of other things, mainly to do with Israel. Ghosn is one of his people, evidently an engineer by profession. They were somehow able to fabricate the weapon.'

'Whose sponsorship?' the President asked.

'We – our man, that is – had to sweat that out of them. Sir, that's a technical violation –'

Fowler's eyes flared into life. 'I forgive them! Get on with it.'

'Sir, they say the, uh, operation was bankrolled and supported by the Ayatolla Mahmoud Haji Daryaei.'

'Iran.' Not a question, a statement. Fowler's eyes became more animated.

'Correct. As you know, Iran isn't exactly pleased with how our actions in the Gulf worked out, and – sir, according to our people, this is what they said:

'It was a two-part plan. Part one was the bomb in Denver. Part two was an incident in Berlin. They had another guy working with them, Günther Bock, former

Red Army Faction guy, his wife was arrested by the Germans last year and she later hanged herself. The objective, Mr President, was to drive us and the Russians into a nuclear exchange – or at the least to so screw up our relations that the situation in the Gulf would revert to chaos. That would serve Iranian interests – or so Daryaei supposedly thinks.'

'How did they get the weapon?'

'They say it's Israeli – was Israeli,' Ryan corrected himself. 'Evidently it got lost in 1973. We have to check that with the Israelis, but it makes sense. The plutonium came from Savannah River, and it's probably part of the big MUF they had some years back. We've long suspected that the first generation of Israeli nukes was fabricated from material obtained over here.'

Fowler stood. 'You're telling me that this fucking *mullah* did this – and killing a hundred thousand Americans wasn't *enough? He wanted to start a nuclear war, too!*'

'That is the information, sir.'

'Where is he?'

'As a matter of fact, Mr President, we know quite a lot about him. He has supported several terrorist groups as you know. He was the loudest Islamic voice against the Vatican Treaty, but he lost a lot of prestige when it started working, and that did not improve his disposition very much. Daryaei lives in Qum in Iran. His political faction is losing some of its power, and there's already been an attempt on his life.'

'Is their story plausible?'

'Yes, Mr President, it is.'

'You think Daryaei capable of such a thing?'

'On the record, sir, I would have to say that he is. Yes.'

'He lives in Qum?'

'Correct. It's a city with a religious history, very important to the Shi'a branch of Islam. I don't know the exact population, certainly more than a hundred thousand.'

'Where in Qum does he live?'

'That's the problem. He moves around a lot. He was

nearly killed last year, and he learned from that. Never sleeps in the same place twice, so we hear. He stays in the same part of the city, but I can't give you a location better than plus or minus a mile or so.'

'He did this?'

'So it would seem, Mr President. That's our best data.'

'But you can't localize him better than a mile.'

'Yes, sir.'

Fowler contemplated that for a few seconds before speaking, but when he did, Ryan's blood turned to ice.

'That's close enough.'

> PRESIDENT NARMONOV:
>
> WE HAVE APPREHENDED THE TERRORISTS AND DETERMINED THE EXTENT OF THE OPERATION . . .

'Is this possible?'

'Yes, I would say so,' Golovko replied. 'Daryaei is a fanatic. He loathes the Americans.'

'Those *barbarians* tried to bait us into —'

'Let them handle it,' Golovko advised. 'It is they who suffered the worst losses.'

'You know what he will wish to do?'

'Yes, Comrade President, as do you.'

> PRESIDENT FOWLER:
>
> PENDING EXAMINATION OF THE EVIDENCE I WILL ACCEPT YOUR LAST COMMUNICATION AS FACT. WE WASH OUR HANDS OF THIS. WHATEVER ACTION YOU FEEL IS NECESSARY. WE WILL NOT OBJECT NOW OR IN THE FUTURE. THESE MADMEN WERE WILLING TO DESTROY US BOTH. TO HELL WITH THEM.

'Christ, Andruska,' Ryan murmured. *That's a clear statement!* The President read the message off the screen without a word.

Ryan had been under the impression that Narmonov had kept control of his emotions, but now the reverse seemed to be true. Fowler sat rock-steady in his chair, surveying the room with calm eyes.

'The world will learn a lesson from this,' Fowler said. 'I'll make sure that nobody ever does this again.'

Another phone line went off. 'Mr President, FBI, sir.'

'Yes?'

'Mr President, this is Murray, we've just had a flash from the *Bundeskriminalamt* – that's the German Federal Criminal Police – that they've found the body of one Günther Bock in eastern Berlin, dressed in the uniform of a Russian army colonel. There were nine others similarly dressed, one of whom is believed to be a former colonel in the Stasi. The data we got from Qati and the other one is confirmed on that side, sir.'

'Murray, I want an opinion. Are you confident in the confessions?'

'Sir, generally speaking, when we bag these guys they sing like canaries. It's not the Mafia, there's no law of *omertà*.'

'Thank you, Mr Murray.' Fowler looked up at Ryan. 'Well?'

'Sounds like we got good stuff from them.'

'So, we agree for once.' Fowler punched his SAC button. 'General Fremont?'

'Yes, Mr President?'

'How quickly can you re-target a missile? I want to attack a city in Iran.'

'What?'

'I'll let Deputy Director Ryan explain.'

'Those sons-of-bitches.' Fremont spoke for everyone in the room.

'Yes, General, and I intend to get the man who did this, and get him in a way that will send a message that nobody will ever forget. The leader of Iran has committed an act of war against the United States of America. I intend to reply exactly in proportion to his act. I want a missile targeted on Qum. How long will that take?'

'Ten minutes at least, sir, let me, uh, check with my operations people.' CINC-SAC flipped off his microphone switch. 'Christ.'

'Pete,' the Deputy Chief of Staff (Operations) said, 'the

1007

man is right. That fucker almost killed us all – us and the Russians! For *profit*, for political *profit!*'

'I don't like it.'

'You have to retarget the bird. I suggest a Minuteman-III out of Minot. The three RVs'll flatten the place. I'll need ten minutes.'

Fremont nodded.

'Mr President, you can wait.'

'No, I'm not going to wait. Ryan, you know what they did, you know why they did it. It was an act of war –'

'An act of terrorism, sir.'

'State-sponsored terrorism is war – your own position paper from six years ago said that!'

Jack had not known that Fowler'd read it, and being hoist on his own petard came as a surprise. 'Well, yes, sir, I did say that, but –'

'That *holy man* tried to kill – *did* kill thousands of Americans, and tried to trick us and the Russians into killing two *hundred million* more! He almost succeeded.'

'Yes, sir, that is also true, but –' Fowler cut him off with a raised hand and continued to speak in the placid voice of a man whose decision had been made.

'It was an act of war. I will reply in kind. That's decided. I'm the President. I'm the Commander-in-Chief. I am the one who evaluates and acts upon the safety and security of the United States. I decide what the military of this country does. This man slaughtered thousands of our citizens, and used a nuclear weapon to do it. I have decided that I will reply in kind. Under the Constitution, that is my right, and my duty.'

'Mr President,' van Damm spoke. 'The American people –'

Fowler's anger appeared, but only briefly. '*The American people will* demand *that I act!* But that's not the only reason. I must act. I must reply to this – just to make sure it never happens again!'

'Please think it through, sir.'

'Arnold, I have.'

Ryan looked over at Pete Connors and Helen D'Agustino. Both concealed their feelings with marvelous skill. The rest of the room approved of Fowler's purpose, and Jack already knew that he was not the one to reason with the man. He looked at the clock and wondered what would come next.

'Mr President, this is General Fremont.'

'I'm here, General.'

'Sir, we have re-targeted a Minuteman-III missile in North Dakota for the target specified. I – sir, have you thought this through?'

'General, I am your commander-in-chief. Is the missile readied for launch?'

'Sir, the launch sequence will take about a minute from the time you give the order.'

'The order is given.'

'Sir, it's not that simple. I need an ID check. You've been briefed on the procedure, sir.'

Fowler reached for his wallet and removed a plastic card, much like a credit card. On it were ten different eight-number groups. Only Fowler knew which one he was supposed to read.

'Three-Three-Six-Zero-Four-Two-Zero-Nine.'

'Sir, I confirm your identification code. Next, Mr President, the order must be confirmed.'

'What?'

'Sir, the two-man rule applies. In the event of an overt attack, I can be the second man, but since that is not the case, someone on my list must confirm the order.'

'I have my chief of staff right here.'

'Sir, negative on that, the rule is that to be on the list you must be an elected official or one approved by Congress – the Senate, that is – like a cabinet secretary.'

'I'm on the list,' Jack said.

'Is that Dr Ryan, DDCI?'

'Correct, General.'

'Deputy Director Ryan, this is CINC-SAC,' Fremont said in a voice that oddly mimicked the robotic one used to issue SAC orders. 'Sir, I have received a nuclear-launch order. I need you to confirm that order, but first

I also need to verify your identity, sir. Could you please read your identification code?'

Jack reached for his own ID card and read off his code group. Ryan could hear Fremont or one of his people flipping through the pages of a book.

'Sir, I confirm your identification as Dr John Patrick Ryan, Deputy Director of Central Intelligence.'

Jack looked at Fowler. If he didn't do it, the President would just get someone else. It really was that simple, wasn't it? And was Fowler wrong – was he really wrong?

'It's my responsibility, Jack,' Fowler said, standing at Ryan's side, resting his hand on Jack's shoulder. 'You're just confirming it.'

'Dr Ryan, CINC-SAC here, I repeat, sir, I have a nuclear-launch order from the President, and I require confirmation, sir.'

Ryan looked at his President, then leaned down to the microphone. He struggled for the breath to speak. 'CINC-SAC, this is John Patrick Ryan. I am DDCI.' Jack paused, then went on quickly:

'Sir, I do *not* confirm this order. I repeat, General, this is *NOT* a valid launch order. Acknowledge at once!'

'Sir, I copy negative approval of the order.'

'That is correct,' Jack said, his voice growing stronger. 'General, it is my duty to inform you that in my opinion the President is not, I repeat *NOT* in command of his faculties. I urge you to consider that if another launch order is attempted.' Jack rested his hands on the desk, took a deep breath, and snapped back erect.

Fowler was slow to react, but when he did, he pressed his face against Jack's. 'Ryan, I order you –'

Jack's emotions exploded one last time: 'To do what? To kill a hundred thousand people – and why?'

'What they tried to do –'

'What you damned near *let* them do!' Ryan jabbed a finger into the President's chest. 'You're the one who fucked up! You're the one who took us to the edge – and now the real reason you're willing to slaughter a whole city is because you're mad, because your pride is hurt, and you want to get even. You want to show them that nobody can push *you* around! *That's the reason, isn't it!* *ISN'T IT?'* Fowler went white. Ryan lowered his voice. 'You need a better reason than that to kill people. I know. I've had to do that. I *have* killed people. You want this man killed, we can do it, but I'm not going to help you kill a hundred thousand others just to take out the one man you want.'

Ryan stepped back. He dropped his ID card on the desk and walked from the room.

'Jesus!' Chuck Timmons observed. They'd heard the entire exchange over the hot mike. Everyone in SAC headquarters had.

'Yeah,' Fremont said. 'Thank Him. But first deactivate that missile!' The Commander-in-Chief Strategic Air Command had to think for a moment. He couldn't remember if Congress was in session or not, but that was beside the point. He ordered his communications officer to place a call to the chairmen and ranking minority members of the Senate and House armed-services committees. When all four were on line, they'd stage a conference call with the Vice President, who was still aboard Kneecap.

'Jack?' Ryan turned.

'Yeah, Arnie?'

'Why?'

'That's why they have a two-man rule. There are a hundred thousand people in that city – probably more. I can't recall how big it is.' Jack looked into the cold clear sky. 'Not on my conscience. If we needed Daryaei dead, there are other ways.' Ryan blew smoke into the wind. 'And that fucker'll be just as dead.'

'I think you were right. I want you to know that.'

Jack turned. 'Thank you, sir.' A long pause. 'Where's Liz, by the way?'

'Back in the cabin, under sedation. She didn't cut the mustard, did she?'

'Arnie, today nobody did. Mainly we were lucky. You can tell the President that I'm resigning effective – oh,

Friday, I guess. Good a day as any. Someone else'll have to decide on the replacement.'

The President's Chief of Staff was quiet for a moment, then brought things back to the main issue. 'You know what you've just started here, don't you?'

'Constitutional crisis, Arnie?' Jack flipped the butt into the snow. 'Not my first, Arnie, not my first. I need to ride that chopper back to Andrews.'

'I'll take care of it.'

They'd just crossed into U.S. territory when a thought struck John Clark. Qati's bags had those medications. One was Prednizone, and another was Comazine. Prednizone was a steroid . . . often used to mitigate the adverse effects of – he got up from his seat and looked at Qati. Though still blindfolded, the man was different from the most recent photos he'd seen of the man, thinner, his hair was – the man had cancer, Clark thought. What did that mean? He got on the radio and called that information ahead.

The Gulfstream was a few minutes later getting in. Ryan was awakened on the couch in the VIP lounge on the south side of the Andrews complex. Murray was next to him, still awake. Three FBI vehicles were there. Clark, Chavez, Qati and Ghosn were loaded into them, and the convoy of four-wheel-drives headed into D.C.

'What are we going to do with them?' Murray asked.

'I have an idea, but we need to do something first.'

'What, exactly?'

'You have an interrogation room at the Hoover Building?'

'No, Buzzard's Point, the Washington Field Office,' Murray said. 'Did your guy Mirandize them?'

'Yeah, I told him he had to do that, right before he started cutting their balls off.' Ryan turned as he heard a loud noise. Kneecap was landing on the same Runway Zero-One it had left ten or so hours before. They must have shut down the strategic systems quicker than expected, Jack thought.

The *Admiral Lunin* surfaced amid the flares and smoke floats dropped by the P-3. It was much too far for a rescue aircraft to come out, at least in this weather. The seas hadn't moderated, and the light was bad, but Dubinin's was the only ship in the area, and he did the best he could to start rescue operations.

The interrogation room was ten by ten, with a cheap table and five equally cheap chairs. There was no two-way mirror. That trick had been around far too long. Instead, two fiber-optic cables ran out of the room and into cameras, one from a light switch, and the other from what looked like a nail hole in the door frame.

Both terrorists were set in place, looking somewhat the worse for wear. The broken fingers both sported offended the professional ethic of the FBI, but Murray decided to pass on that. Clark and Chavez went off for coffee.

'As you see,' Ryan told them, 'you failed. Washington is still here.'

'And Denver?' Ghosn asked. 'I know about Denver.'

'Yes, you did manage to do something there, but the guilty parties have already paid.'

'What do you mean?' Qati asked.

'I mean that Qum isn't there anymore. Your friend Daryaei is now explaining his misdeeds to Allah.'

They were just too tired, Ryan thought. Fatigue was the worst enemy of men, even worse than the dull pain in his hand. Qati didn't show horror at all. His next error was worse.

'You have made an enemy of all Islam. All that you have done to make peace in the region will be *as nothing!* because of this.'

'Was that your objective?' Ryan asked in considerable surprise, drawing on the two hours of sleep he'd had. 'Was *that* what you wanted to do? Oh, my God!'

'Your god?' Qati spat.

'What of Marvin Russell?' Murray asked.

'We killed him. He was merely an infidel,' Qati said.

Murray looked at Ghosn. 'This is true? Wasn't he a guest in your camp?'

'He was with us for some months, yes. The fool's help was indispensable.'

'And you murdered him.'

'Yes, along with two hundred thousand others.'

'Tell me,' Jack said. 'Isn't there a line in the Koran that goes something like, "if a man shall enter your tent and eat your salt, even though he be an infidel, you will protect him"?'

'You quote poorly – and what do you care of the Koran?'

'You might be surprised.'

CHAPTER 44

The Breeze of Evening

Ryan's next call was to Arnie van Damm. He explained what he had learned.

'My God! They were willing to –'

'Yeah, and it almost worked,' Ryan said huskily. 'Clever, weren't they?'

'I'll tell him.'

'I have to report this, Arnie. I have to tell the Vice President.'

'I understand.'

'One more thing.'

'What's that?'

The request he made was approved, largely because no one had a better idea. After the two terrorists had had their hands treated, they were bedded down separately in FBI holding cells.

'What do you think, Dan?'

'It's – Christ, Jack, where are the words for something like this?'

'The man's got cancer,' Clark said. 'He figures that if he has to die – why not a bunch of others? Dedicated son-of-a-bitch, isn't he?'

'What are you going to do?' Murray asked.

'We don't have a federal death-penalty statute, do we?'

'No, neither does Colorado as a matter of fact.' Murray took a moment to understand where Ryan was heading. 'Oh.'

Golovko had considerable trouble tracking Ryan down with his phone call. The report on his desk from Dr Moiseyev, sitting there amid all the other things, had dumbfounded him, but on learning Jack's plans, it was easy to set the rendezvous.

Perhaps the only good news of the week was the rescue. The *Admiral Lunin* pulled into Kodiak harbor at dawn. Alongside the pier, she offloaded her guests. Of the *Maine*'s crew of one hundred fifty-seven, perhaps a hundred had gotten off before the submarine was claimed by the sea. Dubinin and his crew had rescued eighty-one of them, and recovered eleven bodies, one of which was Captain Harry Ricks. Professionals regarded it as an incredible feat of seamanship, though the news media failed to cover the story until the Soviet submarine had put back to sea. Among the first to call home was Ensign Ken Shaw.

Joining them on the trip out of Andrews was Dr Woodrow Lowell of the Lawrence-Livermore Laboratory, a bearded, bearish man, known to his friends as Red because of his hair. He'd spent six hours in Denver reviewing the damage patterns.

'I have a question,' Jack said to him. 'How was it the yield estimates were so far off? That almost made us think the Russians did it.'

'It was a parking lot,' Lowell replied. 'It was made of macadam, a mixture of gravel and asphalt. The energy from the bomb liberated various complex hydrocarbons from the upper layer of the pavement and ignited it – like a great big fuel-air explosive bomb. The water vapor there – from the snow that flashed away – caused another reaction that released more energy. What resulted was a flame-front double the diameter of the nuclear fireball. Add to that the fact that snow cover reflected a lot of the energy, and you got a huge augmentation of the apparent energy released. It would have fooled anybody. Then afterwards, the pavement had another effect. It radiated residual heat very rapidly. The short version is, the energy signature was much larger than the actual yield justified. Now, you want the real bad news?' Lowell asked.

'Okay.'

'The bomb was a fizzle.'

'What do you mean?'

'I mean it should have been much larger, and we don't know why. The bomb residue was lousy with tritium. The design yield was at least ten times what it actually delivered.'

'You mean?'

'Yeah, if this thing had worked . . .'

'We *were* lucky, weren't we?'

'If you want to call that luck, yeah.'

Somehow Jack slept for most of the flight.

The aircraft landed the next morning at Beersheba. Israeli military personnel met the aircraft and convoyed everyone to Jerusalem. The press had found out some of what was happening, but not enough to be a bother, not on a secure Israeli Air Force Base. That would come later. Prince Ali bin Sheik was waiting outside the VIP building.

'Your Highness.' Jack nodded to him. 'Thank you for coming.'

'How could I not?' Ali handed over a newspaper.

Jack scanned the headline. 'I didn't think that would stay secret very long.'

'It's true, then?'

'Yes, sir.'

'And you stopped it?'

'Stopped it?' Ryan shrugged. 'I just wouldn't – it was a lie, Ali. I was lucky I guessed – no, that's not true. I didn't know that until later. It's just that I couldn't put my name to it, that's all. Your Highness, that's not important now. There are some things I have to do. Sir, will you help us?'

'With anything, my friend.'

'Ivan Emmettovich!' Golovko called. And to Ali, 'Your Royal Highness.'

'Sergey Nikolay'ch. Avi.' The Russian walked up with Avi Ben Jakob at his side.

'Jack,' John Clark said. 'You guys want to get to a

better spot? One mortar round sure would waste a lot of top spooks, y'know?'

'Come with me,' Avi said, who led them inside. Golovko briefed them on what he had.

'The man is still alive?' Ben Jakob asked.

'Suffering all the pains of hell, but yes, for another few days.'

'I cannot go to Damascus,' Avi said.

'You never told us you lost a nuke,' Ryan said.

'What do you mean?'

'You know what I mean. The press doesn't have that yet, but they will in another day or two. Avi, you never told us there was something lost out there! Do you know what that might have meant to us?' Ryan asked.

'We assumed that it had broken up. We tried to search for it, but –'

'Geology,' Dr Lowell said. 'The Golan Heights are volcanic, lots of basaltic rock, makes for a high background count, and that means it's hard to track in on a hot spot – but you still should have told us. We have some tricks at Livermore we might have used, stuff not too many people know about.'

'I am sorry, but it is done,' General Ben Jakob said. 'You fly to Damascus, then?'

They used Prince Ali's plane for that, a personal Boeing 727 whose flight crew, Jack learned, was exclusively composed of former drivers from the President's Wing. It was nice to travel first class. The mission was covert, and the Syrians cooperated. Representatives from the U.S., Soviet, and Saudi embassies attended a brief meeting at the Syrian Foreign Ministry, and then they went off to the hospital.

He'd been a powerful man, Jack could see, but he was wasting away like dead, rotting meat. Despite the oxygen line under his nose, his skin was almost blue. All his visitors had to wear protective gear, and Ryan was careful to keep back. Ali handled the interrogation.

'You know why I am here?'

The man nodded.

'As you hope to see Allah, you will tell me what you know.'

The armored column of the 10th Armored Cavalry Regiment ran from the Negev to the border of Lebanon. Overhead was a full squadron of F-16s, and another of Tomcats from the USS *Theodore Roosevelt*. The Syrian army was also deployed in force, though its air force was staying out of the way. The Middle East had taken its lesson on American air power. The display of force was massive and unequivocal. The word was out: nobody would get in the way. The vehicles drove deep into the small, abused country, and finally onto a valley road. The spot had been marked on the map by a dying man anxious to save what remained of his soul, and only an hour's work was needed to determine the exact location. Army engineers found the entrance and checked for booby-traps, then waved the others in.

'God Almighty,' Dr Lowell said, swinging a powerful light around the darkened room. More engineers swept the room, checking for wires on the machines, and carefully checking every drawer of every table before the rest were allowed farther than the door. Then Lowell went to work. There was a set of plans that he took outside to read in the light.

'You know,' he said after fifteen minutes of total silence, 'I never really appreciated how easy this was. We've had this illusion that you really needed to –' He stopped. 'Illusion, that's the right word.'

'What are you telling me?'

'It was supposed to be a five-hundred-kiloton device.'

'If it had gone off right, we would have known it had to be the Russians,' Jack said. 'No one could have stopped it. We wouldn't be here now.'

'Yeah, I think we have to adjust our threat estimate some.'

'Doc, we think we found something,' an Army officer said. Dr Lowell went inside, then returned to don protective clothing.

'So large as that?' Golovko asked, staring at the plans.

'Clever people. Do you know how hard it was for me to persuade the President that – excuse me. I didn't, did I? If this had been a big one, I would have believed the report.'

'And what report is that?' Golovko asked.

'Can we conduct a little business?'

'If you wish.'

'You're holding someone we want,' Jack said.

'Lyalin?'

'Yes.'

'He betrayed his country. He will suffer for it.'

'Sergey, first, he gave us nothing that we could use against you. That was his deal. We only got the take from THISTLE, his Japanese network. Second, except for him and what he gave us, we might not be here now. Turn him loose.'

'In return for what?'

'We have an agent who told us that Narmonov was being blackmailed by your military, and that your military was using some missing tactical nuclear weapons to make it stick. That's why we suspected that the weapon might have been yours.'

'But that's a lie!'

'He was very convincing,' Ryan replied. 'I almost believed it myself. The President and Dr Elliot did believe it, and that's why things got so bad on us. I'll gladly hang this bastard out to dry, but it's betraying a confidence . . . remember our conversation in my office, Sergey? If you want that name, you have to pay.'

'That man we will shoot,' Golovko promised.

'No, you can't.'

'What do you mean?'

'We've cut him off, and all I said was that he lied to us. He gave us stuff that wasn't true, even in your country it does not constitute espionage, does it? Better not to kill him. You'll understand, if we can make this deal.'

The First Deputy Chairman considered that for a moment. 'You can have Lyalin – three days. You have my word, Jack.'

'Our man has the codename of SPINNAKER. Oleg Kirilovich – '

'Kadishev? *Kadishev!*'

'You think you're disappointed? You ought to see it from my side.'

'This is the truth – no games now, Ryan?'

'On that, sir, you have my word of honor. I wouldn't mind seeing him shot, but he's a politician, and in this case he really didn't commit espionage, did he? Do something creative with him. Make him dogcatcher somewhere,' Jack suggested.

Golovko nodded. 'It will be done.'

'A pleasure doing business with you, Sergey. A shame about Lyalin.'

'What do you mean?' Golovko asked.

'The stuff he was giving us – both of us – it's really too valuable to lose . . .'

'We do not do business to that degree, Ryan, but I admire your sense of humor.'

Dr Lowell emerged from the structure just then, carrying a lead bucket.

'What's in there?'

'I think it's some plutonium. Want to take a closer look? You could end up like our friend in Damascus.' Lowell handed the bucket to a soldier, and to the engineer-commander he said, 'Move everything out, box it, ship it. I want to examine everything. Make sure you move everything out.'

'Yes, sir,' the colonel said. 'And the sample?'

Four hours later, they were in Dimona, the Israeli nuclear 'research' facility, where there was another gamma-ray spectrometer. While technicians ran the test, Lowell went over the plans again, shaking his head. To Ryan, the drawings looked like the diagram of a computer chip or something similarly incomprehensible.

'It's big, clunky. Ours are less than a quarter this size . . . but you know how long it took us to build something of this size and yield?' Lowell looked up. 'Ten years.

They did it in a cave in five months. How's that for progress, Dr Ryan?'

'I didn't know. We always figured a terrorist's device – but what went wrong?'

'Probably something with the tritium. We had two fizzles back in the fifties, helium contamination. Not too many people know about that. That's my best guess. The design needs some further looking at – we'll computer-model it – but on gross examination, it looks like a fairly competent – oh, thank you.' Lowell took the spectrometry print-out from the Israeli technician. He shook his head and spoke very softly:

'Savannah River, K Reactor, 1968 – it was a *very* good year.'

'This is the one? You're sure?'

'Yeah, this is the one. The Israelis told me the type of weapon they lost, the mass of plutonium – except for the scraps, it's all here.' Lowell tapped the design sheets. 'That's it, that's all of it,' he said.

'Until the next time,' Lowell added.

Always a student of the law and its administration, Deputy Assistant Director Daniel E. Murray observed the proceedings with interest. Rather odd that they used priests instead of lawyers, of course, but damn if it didn't work. The trial took just a day. It was scrupulously fair and admirably swift. The sentence didn't bother Murray, either.

They flew to Riyadh aboard Prince Ali's aircraft, leaving the USAF transport at Beersheba. There would be no indecent haste in the administration of sentence. There had to be time for prayer and reconciliation, and no one wanted to treat this any differently from a more pedestrian case. It also gave time for people to sit and reflect, and in Ryan's case to meet with another surprise. Prince Ali brought him in to Ryan's accommodations.

'I am Mahmoud Haji Daryaei,' the man said, unnecessarily. Jack knew his face well enough from the CIA file. He also knew that the last time Daryaei had spoken with an American, the ruler of Iran had been Mohammed Reza Pahlavi.

'What can I do for you?' Ryan asked. Ali handled the translation for both of them.

'Is it true? What I have been told, I wish to know that it is true.'

'Yes, sir, it is true.'

'Why should I believe you?' The man was approaching seventy years of age, with a deeply-lined face and black, angry eyes.

'Then why did you ask the question?'

'Insolence does not please me.'

'Attacks against American citizens do not please me,' Ryan answered.

'I had nothing to do with this, you know that.'

'I do now, yes. Will you answer a question? If they had asked for your help, would you have given it?'

'No,' Daryaei said.

'Why should I believe that?'

'To slaughter so many people, even unbelievers, is a crime before God.'

'Besides,' Ryan added, 'you know how we would react to such a thing.'

'You accuse me of the ability to do such a thing?'

'You accuse us of such things regularly. But in this case, you were mistaken.'

'You hate me.'

'I have no love for you,' Jack admitted readily. 'You are the enemy of my country. You have supported those who kill my fellow citizens. You have taken pleasure in the deaths of people whom you have never met.'

'And yet you refused to allow your President to kill me.'

'That is incorrect. I refused to allow my President to destroy the city.'

'Why?'

'If you truly think yourself a man of God, how can you ask such a question?'

'You are an unbeliever!'

'Wrong. I believe, just as you do, but in a different way.

1023

Are we so different? Prince Ali doesn't think so. Does peace between us frighten you so much as that? Or do you fear gratitude more than hate? In any case, you asked why, and I will answer. I was asked to assist in the deaths of innocent people. I could not live with that on my conscience. It was as simple as that. Even the deaths of those I should perhaps consider unbelievers. Is that so hard for you to understand?'

Prince Ali said something that he didn't bother to translate, perhaps a quote from the Koran. It sounded stylized and poetic. Whatever it was, Daryaei nodded and spoke one last time to Ryan.

'I will consider this. Goodbye.'

Durling settled into the chair for the first time. Arnold van Damm sat across the room.

'You handled matters well.'

'Was there anything else we could have done?'

'I suppose not. It's today, then?'

'Right.'

'Ryan's handling it?' Durling asked, looking through the summary sheets.

'Yes, it seemed the best thing to do.'

'I want to see him when he gets back.'

'Didn't you know? He resigned. As of today, he's out,' van Damm said.

'The hell you say!'

'He's out,' Arnie reiterated.

Durling shook his finger at the man. 'Before you leave, you tell him that I want him in my office.'

'Yes, Mr President.'

The executions were at noon on Saturday, six days after the bomb exploded. The people gathered, Ghosn and Qati were led out into the market square. They were given time to pray. It was a first for Jack, being a spectator at something like this. Murray just stood, his face set. Clark and Chavez, along with a gaggle of security personnel, were mainly watching the crowd.

'It just seems so inconsequential,' Ryan said as the event got underway.

'It is not! The world will learn from this,' Prince Ali said solemnly. 'Many will learn. This is justice happening. That is the lesson.'

'Some lesson.' Ryan turned to look at his companions atop the building. He'd had time to reflect, and all he saw was – what? Ryan didn't know. He'd done his job, but what had it all meant? 'The deaths of sixty thousand people who never should have died put an end to wars that need never have been? Is that how history is made, Ali?'

'All men die, Jack. *Insh-Allah*, never again in numbers so great. You stopped it, you prevented something worse. What you did, my friend . . . the blessings of God go with you.'

'I would have confirmed the launch order,' Avi said, his voice uncomfortable in its frankness. 'And then? I would have blown my brains out, perhaps? Who can say? Of this I am certain: I would not have had the courage to say no.'

'Nor I,' Golovko said.

Ryan said nothing as he looked back down at the square. He'd missed the first one, but that was all right.

Even though Qati knew it was coming, it didn't matter. As with so many things in life, it was all controlled by reflex. A soldier prodded his side with a sword, barely enough to break the skin. Instantly, Qati's back arched, his neck extended itself in an involuntary flinch. The captain of the Saudi Special Forces already had his sword moving. He must have practiced, Jack realized a moment later, because the head was removed with a single stroke as deceptively powerful as a ballet master's. Qati's head landed a meter or so away, and then the body flopped down, blood spraying from the severed vessels. He could see the arms and legs tightening against the restraints, but that, too, was mere reflex. The blood pumped out in a steady rhythm as Qati's heart continued to work, striving to preserve a life already departed. Finally, that, too, stopped, and all that was left of Qati were separated parts and a dark stain on the ground. The Saudi captain wiped the sword clean on what looked like a bolt of silk, replaced it in the golden scabbard, and walked into a path the crowd made for him.

The crowd did not exult. In fact, there was no noise at all. Perhaps a collective intake of breath, a few murmured prayers from the more devout among those present; for whose souls the prayers were offered only they and their God could say. At once, those in the front row began to depart. A few from inside the crowd who'd been denied a view came to the fence line, but they stayed there for only a moment before going about their business. After the prescribed interval, the body parts would be collected and given a proper burial in accordance with the religion that each of them had defiled.

Jack didn't know what emotion he was supposed to feel. He'd seen enough death. He knew that much. But these deaths did not touch his heart at all, and now he wondered and worried a little about that.

'You asked me how history is made, Jack,' Ali said. 'You have just seen it.'

'What do you mean?'

'You do not need us to tell you,' Golovko said.

The men who started a war, or tried to, executed like criminals in the market square, Jack thought. *Not a bad precedent.*

'Maybe you're right, maybe it will make people think twice before the next time.' *That's an idea whose time has come.*

'In all our countries,' Ali said, 'the sword is the symbol of justice ... an anachronism, perhaps, from a time when men acted as men. But a sword still has a use.'

'Certainly it is precise,' Golovko observed.

'So, Jack, you have fully left government service?' Ali asked, after a moment. Ryan turned away from the scene, just as everyone else had done.

'Yes, Your Highness.'

'And those foolish "ethics" laws no longer apply. Good.' Ali turned. The Special Forces officer appeared as though by magic. The salute he gave Prince Ali was the sort to impress Kipling. The sword came next. The scabbard was wrought gold encrusted with jewels. The hilt was gold and ivory, and you could see where parts of it had been worn down by generations of strong hands. Manifestly the weapon of a king.

'This is three hundred years old,' Ali said, turning to Ryan. 'It has been carried in peace and war by my ancestors. It even has a name – *Breeze of Evening* is the best I can do in English. It means more than that, of course. We wish you to have it, Dr Ryan, as a reminder of those who died – and those who did not, because of you. It has killed many times. His Majesty believes that the sword has killed enough.'

Ryan took the scimitar from the Prince's hand. The gold scabbard was nicked and abraded by generations of sandstorms and battles, but Ryan saw that his reflection was not so terribly distorted as he might have feared. The blade, he saw, on drawing it partway, was mirror-bright, still rippled from the Damascus smith who'd shaped the steel into its fearful and effective purpose. Such a dichotomy, Ryan thought, smiling without knowing it, that something so beautiful could have so terrible a purpose. Such irony. And yet –

He'd keep the sword, hang it in a place of honor, look at it from time to time to remind himself of what it and he had done. And just maybe –

'Killed enough?' Ryan slid the sword back into its sheath and let it fall to his side. 'Yes, Your Highness. I think we all have.'

AFTERWORD

Now that the tale is told, a few things need to be made clear. All of the material in this novel relating to weapons technology and fabrication is readily available in any one of dozens of books. For reasons which I hope will be obvious to the reader, certain technical details have been altered, sacrificing plausibility in the interests of obscurity. This was done to salve my conscience, *not* in any reasonable expectation that it matters a damn.

The Manhattan Project of World War II still represents the most remarkable congregation of scientific talent in human history, never equalled, and perhaps never to be exceeded. The vastly expensive project broke new scientific ground and produced many additional discoveries. Modern computer theory, for example, largely grew from bomb-related research, and the first huge main-frame computers were mainly used for bomb-design.

I was first bemused, then stunned, as my research revealed just how easy such a project might be today. It is generally known that nuclear secrets are not as secure as we would like – in fact the situation is worse than even well-informed people appreciate. What required billions of dollars in the 1940s is much less expensive today. A modern personal computer has far more power and reliability than the first Eniac, and the 'hydrocodes' which enable a computer to test and validate a weapon's design are easily duplicated. The exquisite machine tools used to fabricate parts can be had for the asking. When I asked explicitly for specifications for the very machines used at Oak Ridge and elsewhere, they arrived Federal Express the next day. Some highly-specialized items designed specifically for bomb manufacture may now be found in stereo speakers. The fact of the matter is that a sufficiently wealthy individual could, over a period of from five to ten years, produce a multi-stage thermonuclear device. Science is all in the public domain, and allows few secrets.

Delivery of such a device is child's play. I could base that statement on 'extensive conversations' with various police and security agencies, but it doesn't take long for a person to say, 'Are you kidding?' I heard that phrase more than once. Probably no country – certainly no liberal democracy – can secure its borders against such a threat.

So, that's the problem. What might be the solution? For starters, international controls over the traffic in nuclear materials and technology ought to be made something more than the joke they currently are. Nuclear weapons cannot be un-invented, and I personally think that nuclear power is a safe and environmentally benign alternative to the use of fossil fuels, but any tool must be used with care, and this tool admits of abuses too fearful for us to ignore.

PEREGRINE CLIFF, February 1991